THE BRIDE OF LAMMERMOOR

WALTER SCOTT (1771–1832) was born in Edinburgh of a Border family. After attending the High School and University of Edinburgh he followed his father into the profession of the law, becoming an advocate (barrister) in 1792. In 1799 he was appointed Sheriff-Depute for the county of Selkirk, and in 1806 a Clerk of the Court of Session—appointments which he retained until the end of his life. His first major publication was a collection of ballads entitled *The Minstrelsy of the Scottish Border* (1802–3). He became famous as a poet with *The Lay of the Last Minstrel* (1805), *Marmion* (1808), and *The Lady of the Lake* (1810). In 1814 he published his first novel, *Waverley*, set during the Jacobite rising of 1745. Its success encouraged him to produce more historical novels, set in different countries and periods. Those set in Scotland, like *The Bride of Lammermoor*, have usually been regarded as his best. Scott's work was widely acclaimed in Europe and America. He spent the income from his writings on establishing a house and estate at Abbotsford, near Melrose. He was awarded a baronetcy by the Prince Regent in 1818. Partnership in the printing firm of James Ballantyne and Co. involved him in a financial crash in 1826. His last years were darkened by illness and the need to continue his output of writing to pay off the debts incurred. His *Journal* of those years is the most moving of his works. He died at Abbotsford in 1832; his biography was written by his son-in-law, John Gibson Lockhart.

FIONA ROBERTSON is a Lecturer in English Literature at the University of Durham, and a former Research Fellow of Hertford College, Oxford.

THE WORLD'S CLASSICS

SIR WALTER SCOTT

The Bride of Lammermoor

Edited with an Introduction by
FIONA ROBERTSON

Oxford   New York

OXFORD UNIVERSITY PRESS

1991

Oxford University Press, Walton Street, Oxford OX2 6DP

Oxford New York Toronto
Delhi Bombay Calcutta Madras Karachi
Petaling Jaya Singapore Hong Kong Tokyo
Nairobi Dar es Salaam Cape Town
Melbourne Auckland

and associated companies in
Berlin Ibadan

Oxford is a trade mark of Oxford University Press

British Library Cataloguing in Publication Data

Scott. Sir, Walter, 1771–1832
The Bride of Lammermoor.
I.Title II. Robertson, Fiona
823.7

ISBN 0–19–281791–4

Library of Congress Cataloging in Publication Data

Scott, Walter, Sir, 1771–1832
The Bride of Lammermoor/ Sir Walter Scott; edited with an introduction by Fiona Robertson
p. cm.—(The World's Classics)
Includes bibliographical references.

I. Robertson, Fiona. II. Title. III. Series.
PR5317.B7 1991
823.7 dc20

ISBN 0–19–281791–4

Typeset by Pentacor PLC
Printed in Great Britain by
BPCC Hazell Books
Aylesbury, Bucks

CONTENTS

CONTENTS

INTRODUCTION

The story is a dismal one, and I doubt sometimes whether it will bear working out to much length after all. Query, if I shall make it so effective in two volumes as my mother does in her quarter of an hour's crack by the fireside? But *nil desperandum*.[1]

The 'dismal' story on which Scott based his eighth novel, *The Bride of Lammermoor*, told of the ill-fated marriage of Janet Dalrymple (the daughter of the great Scottish lawyer James Dalrymple, 1st Viscount Stair) to David Dunbar of Baldoon in 1669. According to popular tradition, Janet Dalrymple had secretly become engaged to a man of her own choice, Lord Rutherford, but, under pressure from her family, she renounced this engagement and married Baldoon, who was Rutherford's nephew. She died a month after her wedding.

Scott had heard the story of Janet Dalrymple many times, especially from his mother, Anne Rutherford, and from his great-aunt, Margaret Swinton, whose tales of mystery and horror haunted his imagination long after her death in 1780.[2] He always spoke of *The Bride of Lammermoor* as a story he could have told no other way, privileging tradition over personal creativity, the narrative sequences laid down by previous story-tellers over the new pace and emphasis of his own novel. Near the end of his life, when he was travelling in Italy in a vain attempt to restore his failing health, he was questioned about the fate of Clara

[1] Letter to James Ballantyne, in *The Letters of Sir Walter Scott*, ed. H. J. C. Grierson, *et al.*, 12 vols., 1932–7, v. 186 (subsequently *Letters*). Writing to Lady Louisa Stuart in January 1820, a month after his mother's death, he told the story of a visit paid by Mr and Mrs Scott of Harden the day before her final collapse: 'She had told them with great accuracy the real story of the Bride of Lammermuir, and pointed out wherein it differed from the novel. She had all the names of the parties, and detailed (for she was a great genealogist) their connexion with existing families.' (*Letters*, vi. 119.)

[2] Scott describes Margaret Swinton in a short story based on another of her tales, 'My Aunt Margaret's Mirror' (written in 1827 and published in *The Keepsake for 1829*, 1828). For details of Scott's additions to his source-tale, see Claire Lamont, 'Scott as Story-teller: *The Bride of Lammermoor*', *Scottish Literary Journal*, vii (1980), 113–26.

Mowbray, the heroine of his novel *St. Ronan's Well* (1823), who dies in a fit of insanity brought on by romantic melancholia. Scott replied that he could not save her, adding that 'of all the murders that I have committed in that way, and few men have been guilty of more, there is none that went so much to my heart as the poor Bride of Lammermoor; but it could not be helped—it is all true'.[3] Towards the end of *The Bride of Lammermoor* itself, the narrator states:

By many readers this may be deemed overstrained, romantic, and composed by the wild imagination of an author, desirous of gratifying the popular appetite for the horrible; but those who are read in the private family history of Scotland during the period in which the scene is laid, will readily discover, through the disguise of borrowed names and added incidents, the leading particulars of AN OWER TRUE TALE.[4]

This reminder, however, is interestingly placed. It ends the chapter in which Scott's heroine, Lucy Ashton, driven to desperate insanity by her family's persecution and by her lover's haughty lack of faith, stabs her husband on their wedding night. By drawing attention to the 'OWER TRUE TALE', the narrator limits his responsibility for the disturbing implications of his story and explicitly distances himself from the 'public appetite' for gratuitous horror. The factual basis of the novel may have served a comparable function for Scott. There is a note of relief as well as of sadness, after all, in Scott's later explanation of his literary 'murder': 'it could not be helped—it is all true'.

The novel which Scott produced from his traditional sources is complex and rewarding. Thomas Hardy considered it an exception for Scott, 'an almost perfect specimen of form':[5] its structure, based on an interlinked series of betrothals and burials, is tight, even oppressive. Although Scott had told many stories of love before, in previous novels and poems, *The Bride of Lammermoor* was his first romantic tragedy. It is a tale of love and family feud set in a socially and politically unstable period of Scottish history, a reflection on the problems of telling stories

---

[3] John Gibson Lockhart, *Memoirs of the Life of Sir Walter Scott, Bart.*, 2nd edn., 10 vols., 1839, x. 191 (subsequently *Life of Scott*).

[4] p. 340.

[5] *Thomas Hardy's Personal Writings*, ed. Harold Otel, 1967, p. 121.

about the past, and a tale of psychological terror which conveys some of Scott's most disturbing insights into emotional and sexual politics.

The Bride of Lammermoor was published with A Legend of Montrose as the Third Series of Tales of My Landlord in June 1819. When the two tales appeared, Scott's reputation as a novelist was unrivalled. He had begun his literary career as a poet and collector of old Scottish ballads, turning to prose fiction with his first novel, Waverley, in 1814. His novels appeared anonymously, allowing him to engage in a game of mystery and bluff with his readers which was to become more complex as his career progressed, and he did not formally acknowledge authorship of them until 1827, five years before his death. Like the novels which had gone before, The Bride of Lammermoor and A Legend of Montrose were greeted with enthusiasm and curiosity. Blackwood's Edinburgh Magazine delayed its literary notices to make sure of including some discussion of the two new tales, and commented: 'It is truly a most epicurean custom which we have all got into of expecting three or four volumes of this kind every year.'[6] From early in its history, however, The Bride of Lammermoor has been marked out as an exception among Scott's works, even regarded as an aberration which has to be explained by careful reference to his life and personality. It quickly acquired a reputation as the most passionate and tragic of the Waverley Novels. As the review in Blackwood's declared: 'It is the only true romance of the whole set;—in purpose, tenor, and conclusion—it is a pure and magnificent tragical romance.'[7] Scott's son-in-law and biographer, John Gibson Lockhart, thought The Bride of Lammermoor 'the most pure and powerful of all the tragedies that Scott ever penned',[8] and it is still the novel to which most critics would turn in order to counter E. M. Forster's influential complaint against Scott: 'think how all Scott's laborious mountains and scooped-out glens and carefully ruined abbeys call out for passion, passion, and how it is never there!'[9] This reputation rests partly on

---

[6] Blackwood's Edinburgh Magazine, v (June 1819), 340–53, quoted from p. 340.
[7] Blackwood's Edinburgh Magazine, v. 342.
[8] Life of Scott, vi. 88.
[9] Aspects of the Novel, and Related Writings (1927), ed. Oliver Stallybrass, 1974, p. 21.

circumstances beyond Scott's control, for many readers come to
The Bride of Lammermoor with Donizetti's operatic interpretation, *Lucia di Lammermoor* (1835), in mind, and conscious of later
works which use *Lucia di Lammermoor* as a byword for emotional
liberation (including Flaubert's *Madame Bovary* and Forster's
Where Angels Fear to Tread).[10] Even more importantly, *The Bride
of Lammermoor* has been thought to draw passion from key events
in Scott's own emotional experience. In Lucy Ashton's incon-
stancy and Ravenswood's bitter taunts, biographers have found
the scars of Scott's failed love-affair with Williamina Belsches
twenty years earlier. Scott had hoped to marry Williamina,
although she came from a family markedly more aristocratic and
wealthy than his own, and he was distraught when she married
his friend William Forbes, the son of a rich banker, early in 1797.
He met and married Charlotte Charpentier later the same year,
but still thought in middle age that the wound of his youthful
romance would never heal.[11]

Adding to the weight of biographical expectation, Lockhart's
vivid and influential account of the way in which Scott worked
on *The Bride of Lammermoor* has encouraged interpretations which
make it seem the product of Scott's deepest desires and fears,
released by the delirium of illness ('primitive tremors from
primordial deeps', as one biographer has described them).[12]
During the months in which he worked on the Third Series of
Tales of My Landlord, Scott became so seriously ill that when the
novels appeared they were expected to be his last, and were even
taken as proof that he could not after all be the mysterious 'Author
of *Waverley*'. Lockhart tells how Scott dictated the bulk of *The
Bride of Lammermoor* to two amanuenses, John Ballantyne and
William Laidlaw, while dazed with pain:

John Ballantyne told me, that after the first day he always took care to
have a dozen of pens made before he seated himself opposite to the sofa
on which Scott lay, and that though he often turned himself on his pillow

[10] Gustave Flaubert, *Madame Bovary*, 1856, Part 2, ch. 15; E. M. Forster, *Where
Angels Fear to Tread*, 1905, ch. 6.

[11] 'Broken-hearted for two years—My heart handsomely pieced again—but
the crack will remain till my dying day', as he wrote in 1825: see *The Journal of
Sir Walter Scott,* ed. W. E. K. Anderson, 1972, p. 43 (subsequently *Journal*).

[12] Edgar Johnson, *Sir Walter Scott: The Great Unknown*, 2 vols., 1970, p. 670.

with a groan of torment, he usually continued the sentence in the same breath. But when dialogue of peculiar animation was in progress, spirit seemed to triumph altogether over matter—he arose from his couch and walked up and down the room, raising and lowering his voice, and as it were acting the parts. It was in this fashion that Scott produced the far greater portion of The Bride of Lammermoor—the whole of the Legend of Montrose—and almost the whole of Ivanhoe.[13]

When he read the published version of *The Bride of Lammermoor*, according to James Ballantyne, 'he did not recollect one single incident, character, or conversation it contained!'[14] Yet although there is no reason to doubt either Scott's pain of mind and body towards the end of his work on the novel or his imperfect memory of it when published, the extant manuscript shows that only the last fifth of the novel could have been dictated in the way Lockhart describes.[15] The notion that Scott composed *The Bride of Lammermoor* in a semi-conscious state in which his repressed emotions broke free is misleading, but it has had a lasting impact on the way in which the novel is read. Readers and critics are often more willing to accept—even to look for—evidence of emotional and psychological discord in *The Bride of Lammermoor* than in most other works by Scott, while, at the same time, they effectively marginalize the novel, reducing its questions and doubts to temporary and personal bad dreams. It is particularly ironic that Scott, who has lost so many readers through his supposed reluctance to consider serious psychological and emotional problems in his work, should have this, his most intricate and searching love-story, explained away as a relic of personal distress.

When *The Bride of Lammermoor* first appeared, the account of its genesis and composition offered to the reading public differed radically from both the 'quarter of an hour's crack by the fireside' and the miracle of inspired perseverance described by Lockhart. To protect his rather precarious anonymity, Scott developed increasingly complex frame-stories for his novels, publishing them as the work of a series of reclusive scholars, learned editors,

---

[13] *Life of Scott*, vi. 67–8.
[14] Ibid. 89.
[15] See Note on the Text.

and enthusiasts for local legend.[16] He liked to personalize stories, giving them the trappings of authenticity but at the same time pointing out their necessary limitations as records of history and character. This process is essential to the effect of *The Bride of Lammermoor*. Like many of his novels, *The Bride of Lammermoor* properly has two frame-narratives. The first, the story of Peter Pattieson and Dick Tinto, which occupies its opening chapter, was the only introductory preamble when the novel was published in 1819. The second, Scott's own introduction, was written just over ten years later for the revised edition of his works, known as the 'Magnum Opus'. The original frame-story is typically both evasive and illuminating. Like the previous *Tales of My Landlord,* the novel is presented as the work of Peter Pattieson, schoolmaster of the imaginary village of Gandercleugh in the Scottish Borders and an enthusiastic collector of old tales and legends, which he claims to narrate with careful attention to probability and historical fact. After his death, his manuscripts are prepared for publication by his pompous and opinionated executor, Jedediah Cleishbotham, who further deflects authority for the tales away from Scott, or indeed from any other answerable source. In his introduction to the First Series (*The Black Dwarf* and *Old Mortality*, 1816), Cleishbotham declares, defensively: 'I am NOT the writer, redacter, or compiler, of the Tales of my Landlord; nor am I, in one single iota, answerable for their contents, more or less.'[17] The frame-story of Pattieson and Cleishbotham reminds readers that story-tellers may be unreliable, prejudiced, and obtuse, and that the stories they tell can give only brief and perhaps misleading insights into past times.

In the first chapter, Pattieson tells the life story of his friend Dick Tinto, another dead provincial artist doomed to obscurity. In Scott's characteristically unassuming and whimsical way, this chapter provides both general aesthetic comment and a specific orientation for the novel which it introduces. Pattieson reflects

---

[16] In the frame-narrative of *Quentin Durward* (1823), the 'Author' explicitly denies that he is Walter Scott, and discusses with a French aristocrat the merits and demerits of a previous work, humorously mistitled 'The Bridle of Lammermore'.

[17] *The Waverley Novels*, 48 vols., 1829–33, ix, p. vi (subsequently *Magnum*).

upon the proper style of prose fiction, arguing with Tinto over the proportion of dialogue which a novel ought to contain. He muses on the quality of artistic fame, on the relationship of art to the demands of its consumers, and on the injustices of its parasitical critics and patrons, with their 'dinners and hints'. The story of Dick Tinto is also a morality tale for the artist, a practical demonstration of Scott's interest in popular art and his reservations about his own celebrity. Tinto disdains to paint inn-signs, which earns him money, and aspires to fame as a portraitist and painter of 'history-pieces', which leads him to London and bankruptcy. Some readers and critics have objected to this leisurely start, condemning it as 'extraordinarily irrelevant' to the story which follows.[18] Yet it serves a vital function in preparing the reader for the novel's provisional, arbitrary, and morally ambiguous presentation of history.

According to Pattieson, Tinto has heard the story of an unspecified domestic drama by chance from the gossip of an old peasant woman, and is inspired to produce a preparatory sketch for a painting based on this story. Confident that the subject speaks for itself, he shows this sketch to Pattieson in an attempt to prove his point that pictures are more communicative than written words. Pattieson fails to deduce the story from the picture, and is referred back to Tinto's manuscript notes, on which he decides to base a novel, *The Bride of Lammermoor*. In deference to Tinto's arguments, it is to be an experiment in descriptive prose rather than dialogue. Tinto's painterly prejudices influence the novel in several important ways. Even the description of the physical appearance of his notebook repeats the interdependence of narrative and picture in which the tale originates: '["] Here are my notes of the tale," said poor Dick, handing a parcel of loose scraps, partly scratched over with his pencil, partly with his pen, where outlines of caricatures, sketches of turrets, mills, old gables, and dovecots, disputed the ground with his written memoranda.'[19] No other novel by Scott refers to quite so many paintings or shows such an interest in the artists' efforts to fix

[18] See George Levine, *The Realistic Imagination: English Fiction from Frankenstein to Lady Chatterley*, 1981, p. 90.
[19] p. 25.

characters on canvas for future interpretation. The portrait of Sir William and Lady Ashton subversively captures Sir William's 'domestic thraldom', just as the paintings of his parents expose his lowly origins to Ravenswood's scorn. The portrait of the down-to-earth cooper, Gibbie Girder, to which the artist has added an incongruous 'French grace', both marks and mocks his wealth and ambition. The spirit of the Ravenswoods lives on in their former home through the painting of their ancestor, Malisius. In one scene, young Henry Ashton is frightened of Ravenswood because of his uncanny resemblance to the portrait of Malisius, and thinks he has walked out of the canvas to avenge his family's wrongs. From the perspective of the opening chapter, all the novel's characters may be seen as similarly reanimated figures from a painting.

Tinto's desire to capture human character and situation in visually striking scenes also prepares for the narrative technique of the novel, in which landscape, architecture, and the physical positioning of the characters are unusually expressive. In his description of the funeral of Ravenswood's father, for example, which is said to be 'worthy of an artist's pencil', Pattieson presents the mourners as indistinct, muffled figures with drawn swords, a background group throwing into relief the only personalized figure, Ravenswood himself, as he struggles to express individual emotion in a set piece of public grief. Later, as the attraction between Ravenswood and Lucy Ashton develops, Sir William Ashton sees them for one moment illuminated against the ominous background of Wolf's Crag by a sudden flash of lightning:

Every object might have been for an instant seen distinctly. The slight and half-sinking form of Lucy Ashton, the well-proportioned and stately figure of Ravenswood, his dark features, and the fiery, yet irresolute expression of his eyes,—the old arms and scutcheons which hung on the walls of the apartment, were for an instant distinctly visible to the Keeper by a strong red brilliant glare of light.[20]

Tinto's visual art influences the way in which Pattieson represents relationships, and, through them, history. The implicit parallel between the novel and Tinto's incomplete, mannered history-piece, which signally fails to convey any understanding of the human relationships it depicts, continually undermines the apparent coherence and objectivity of Pattieson's verbal history. This first chapter alerts readers to the possibilities and the shortcomings of a highly self-conscious piece of historical reconstruction.

Within the main body of the novel, readers are reminded both of its provisionality and of the attempts of the narrator to anchor it in acceptable public history. According to the narrator, the 'OWER TRUE TALE' may be found in family records, in ballads, and in public histories. Characters comment that Wolf's Crag has been mentioned many times in the records of the nation. Pattieson tells of his researches into records of witchcraft trials to discover the eventual fate of Ailsie Gourlay. Many other stories are referred to, including Caleb Balderstone's tale of 'Auld Micklestob', Craigengelt's recollection of Lord Castle-Cuddy, and Sir William Ashton's reference to the legal case of Sir Coolie Condiddle. Johnnie Mortsheugh, the sexton, tells his own story of the conduct of the Ravenswoods at the battle of Bothwell Bridge. Everything works to remind the reader that the story told in the novel is itself a culmination of many others. When the three village hags discuss the catastrophe of Lucy's wedding night, the contradictory reports of what happened, which Scott was later to make the subject of his introduction for the Magnum Opus, can already be seen weaving themselves into the tale:

'And is it true, then,' mumbled the paralytic wretch, 'that the bride was trailed out of her bed and up the chimley by evil spirits, and that the bridegroom's face was wrung round ahint him?'

'Ye needna care wha did it, or how it was done,' said Ailsie Gourlay; 'but I'll uphaud it for nae stickit job, and that the lairds and leddies ken weel this day.'

'And was it true,' said Annie Winnie, 'sin ye ken sae mickle about it, that the picture of Auld Sir Malise Ravenswood came down on the ha' floor, and led out the brawl before them a'?'[21]

The ease with which stories are distorted becomes especially sinister when, towards the end of the novel, Ailsie Gourlay dominates Lucy's imagination by telling her stories, poisoned versions of the old romances which she once loved to read.

[21] p. 342.

Among these is the story of Ravenswood's encounter with the wraith of blind Alice, slenderly based on his 'hasty enquiries' at her cottage. Peter Pattieson's rational narrative is continually threatened by the undermining, discordant stories which it struggles to keep in check.

The historical introduction and notes written for the Magnum Opus edition of the novel present the reader with a different kind of researcher and local historian: Scott himself. He is the most convincingly personalized of all the narrators of the Waverley Novels, but in many ways he is also the most partial and interested. This new introduction cites folk legends and satirical verses about the Dalrymple history, emphasizing that they constitute opinion and point of view rather than verifiable fact. Instead of fixing the novel by declaring its historical sources, Scott adds to the reader's sense that the story must always remain open and incomplete. His new introduction grants no absolute authority to historical records. Indeed, it shows again that one story generates another, and that there is no such thing as a disinterested historian. Similarly, the long notes which Scott inserted at the end of chapters are whimsical and arbitrary as well as informative. The note which tells the story of the servant John, for example, is far from being an adequate justification for the account of Caleb's depredations on the Girders' kitchen, which it is introduced to support. The note on the 'Poor-Man-of-Mutton' is an excuse to tell an amusing story about the barriers of custom and rumour between the English and the Scots. These notes are stories in themselves, subject to the same play of internal verification and the same inconclusiveness as the main text, and they continue rather than replace the suggestions about the conditions and limitations of narrative which Scott first conveyed through the frame-narrative of Pattieson and Tinto.

The representation of the past given in *The Bride of Lammermoor* is, then, carefully framed and consciously artistic. Like Dick Tinto's sketch for a history-piece, the novel achieves a temporary stasis and coherence which is contrasted to the inclusiveness and flexibility of oral tradition. Pattieson sets the story of Lucy and Ravenswood not in the vaguely evoked late seventeenth century of Tinto's historical sketch, but in the social and political uphea-

vals of the period of the Act of Union (1707), which brought
Scotland into formal legislative and administrative union with
England. The novel contrasts two families, one ancient and
declining, the other newly rich and thriving. The legal expertise
and political sharpness of Sir William Ashton have won him the
estate of the ancient aristocratic family of Ravenswood. New
cunning has triumphed over old aristocratic carelessness. Ashton
is a man of the Revolution of 1688–9, Lord Ravenswood an
adherent of the old order and the Stewart inheritance. Ravenswood's son Edgar, Master of Ravenswood, however, is torn
between an emotional tie to the old system of feud and vengeance
and an intellectual acceptance of the new, which suggests reconciliation and progress as the proper responses to the loss of his
ancestral inheritance.[22] Aware that there are no true representatives of 'old' and 'new' forces in society, Scott locates the
conflict of the times within the psychology of his hero. In an
early conversation with Bucklaw, Ravenswood clearly states his
reluctance to relive the past in the shape of outdated allegiance
to the Stewart line and looks forward to a time when 'Whig' and
'Tory' will be mere idle nicknames. He is educated, rational, and
open-minded, not at all the gloomy avenger he first wishes to
be. Emotionally, however, he is governed by aristocratic pride
and consciousness of rank, 'that spirit of which he perhaps had
too much',[23] and eventually he allies himself to the political
faction of the Marquis of A—— entirely on grounds of kinship.

With equal shrewdness, the novel shows that Sir William
Ashton, who seems at first glance to be securely on the side of
the new, is an outdated politician, in danger of losing the
Ravenswood estate through Ravenswood's appeal to the House
of Lords against the decision of the Scottish Court of Session.
Ashton's social and domestic situation is just as insecure as his

[22] Some of the situations and ideas developed in *The Bride of Lammermoor* had
appeared in Scott's work before. An aristocratic family tricked out of its estate is
the main subject of *Guy Mannering* (1815). *The Black Dwarf* (1816) tells of a
heroine persecuted by her family because she loves her father's enemy. An
impoverished and resentful hero torn between proud gestures and enlightened
reason is the central figure in Scott's play *The Doom of Devorgoil* (written 1817–18
and published in 1830).

[23] p. 244.

place in politics. He is unfamiliar with his own estate and awkward with his tenants. When he tries to befriend blind Alice by allowing her to remain on his land rent-free for the rest of her life, she calmly replies that this provision had been one of the conditions of his purchasing the Ravenswood estate. He misjudges the reward to be given to his gamekeeper Norman, and harries his servants with instructions for the proper reception of his important guest, the Marquis of A——. Details such as this glance disdainfully at the idea of social and personal progress. They are balanced, however, by the complex presentation of the relationship between Ravenswood and his former tenants at Wolf's-hope. Scott vividly conveys the remnants of the old inbred loyalty, the emotional ties between traditional groups in a community redefining itself economically and politically. Against the fanatical loyalty of Caleb Balderstone, a remnant of a dying feudal society,[24] he sets the collected professionalism of Ashton's personal servant Lockhard. Against old retainers like blind Alice and Norman the gamekeeper, who glory in their memories of the Ravenswood past, he sets the devastatingly articulate indictments of Mortsheugh the sexton, whose tale of the battle of Bothwell Bridge is the novel's most assured handling of the complex unspoken bargains between leaders and followers. *The Bride of Lammermoor* considers the responsibilities of different classes and groups within society towards each other, showing how these are fulfilled in practice through a haphazard mixture of self-interest and sentiment. In Wolf's-hope, men strive to win preferment and social advantage through personal favour and patronage, imitating the methods of the politicians who govern them. In the world of national politics, the Marquis of A——, a natural supporter of the exiled Stewart family, wins power in the court of Queen Anne. Sir William Ashton, who starts the novel as the Marquis's political opponent, ends it by protesting that their political principles are not, after all, incompatible. Despite the personal tragedies which they cause, political loyalties

---

[24] Reviewers felt that the characterization of Caleb was a little overstretched, and Scott himself came to agree that 'he might have sprinkled rather too much parsley over his chicken' (*Life of Scott*, vi. 88). Modern critics regard him as an essential component in the novel's presentation of declining feudal values.

in *The Bride of Lammermoor* are a matter of opportunity and expediency, not principle.

If *The Bride of Lammermoor* defines itself in relation to a story which Dick Tinto's history-piece has already told, it also, and even more persistently, defines itself in relation to other literary works. Its intrusive literary references (in chapter epigraphs, narratorial analogy, and the characters' own words) continually threaten to absorb all the characters into other stories and roles. The relationship between Sir William and Lady Ashton, for example, is explicitly likened to that between Macbeth and his wife. Ravenswood's inheritance of revenge recalls *Hamlet*, the lovers caught between feuding families recall *Romeo and Juliet*, and the three village hags are compared to the witches of *Macbeth*. The characters themselves seem at times to find established role-playing easier than independent thought and action. Many of them slide with suspicious ease into an indirect language of proverb, quotation, Latin maxim, and jocular colloquialism. Even the sportsman Bucklaw is an enthusiast for the stage, more comfortable when quoting from his favourite melodramatic speeches and the sayings of his favourite dramatist, Dryden, than when making up love-speeches of his own. The struggle against literary stereotypes in an effort to maintain identity and autonomy is particularly intense for the hero and heroine, who enter into a fantasy romance which increasingly typecasts their behaviour. For the reader, Ravenswood is marked out as a romantic avenger by his gloomy appearance, his haughtiness, and his fatalism. For Ravenswood himself, however, self-expression is a continual battle against these roles, a struggle to personalize the rhetoric of revenge tragedy. Ironically, he has a marked tendency to think in terms of roles, sharing the narrator's fascination with their glamour, and he also has more than a little of his ancestor Malisius's instinct and taste for the melodramatic. His betrothal to Lucy is precipitated by his romantic fantasy of himself, and his inability to resist conveying this to her: 'Forget that so stern a vision has crossed your path of life—and let me pursue mine, sure that I can meet with no worse misfortune after the moment it divides me from your side.'[25] As an effective way of saying

[25] p. 207.

farewell to her for ever, and encouraging her to forget him, his
words on this occasion are hopelessly misjudged. He is less sure
of his own motives and feelings here than he realizes, of course,
but there is a certain bitter truth in Lucy's response to his
Darcy-like explanations of the love which has overcome pride:
'If such are your sentiments . . . you have played a cruel game
with me.'[26] Ravenswood's romantic role-playing, however, has
an ironic end. As the novel reaches its climax, he finds himself
increasingly determined by the role he plays in relation to the
Ashtons, a fitting parallel to his fears of becoming absorbed into
their political and social group. When he asks Lucy whether she
recognizes him during the contract-signing scene, Lady Ashton
breaks in: 'My daughter . . . has no occasion to dispute the identity
of your person; the venom of your present language is sufficient
to remind her, that she speaks with the mortal enemy of her
father.'[27] By the time he follows the Ashton procession, an
ominous thirteenth, to Lucy's interment, his sense of personal
identity has been eroded by his consciousness of responsibility
for her death. The loss of distinctive personality is registered in
his brief, charged, exchange with Sholto:

'I cannot doubt that I speak to the Master of Ravenswood?' No answer
was returned. 'I cannot doubt,' resumed the Colonel, trembling with
rising passion, 'that I speak to the murderer of my sister?'
    'You have named me but too truly,' said Ravenswood, in a hollow and
tremulous voice.[28]

Within the restrictions already imposed by the double frame
and the intrusive reminders of other literary works, the independent development of the plot is further impeded by an
oppressive use of omen, symbolic prefiguration, and prophecy.
Lucy Ashton has no sooner been introduced to the reader than
the narrator comments: 'Her life had hitherto flowed on in a
uniform and gentle tenor, and happy for her had not its present

---

[26] p. 208. 'Also read again and for the third time at least Miss Austen's very
finely written novel of *Pride and Prejudice*', Scott noted in March 1826 (*Journal*,
p. 114).
[27] p. 325.
[28] p. 343.

smoothness of current resembled that of the stream as it glides downwards to the waterfall!'[29] Omens and symbols abound. The description of Wolf's Crag, perilously perched on the edge of a huge cliff at the farthest point of the former Ravenswood lands, corresponds to the state of the family. So do the disorderly burial-ground tended by the resentful Mortsheugh, and the broken-down Mermaiden's Fountain. Early in the novel, in a scene heavy with sexual symbolism, Ravenswood kills a wild bull, one of the ancient heraldic symbols of his family, to save Lucy and her father. The narrator explains that the cattle had in the past been protected on the lands of the Scottish nobility, and were supposed to be much declined from the 'formidable re-mains' of their ancestors: even the bull itself, therefore, is a kind of symbol of a declining aristocratic order, enraged by the usurpation of its ancient territories. Later, when Ravenswood and Lucy have completed their secret engagement, a raven, which is said to have been sitting unnaturally close to them as they exchange vows, falls dead at their feet, its blood spattering Lucy's white gown. Direct prophecies are fulfilled, the most notable being the prophecy of Thomas the Rhymer, told by Caleb Balderstone, and the predictions of the spaewife who was present at Ravenswood's birth, recounted by Ailsie Gourlay. These give the story an air of inevitability which may seem to reduce the impact of the characters', and the author's, responsi-bility for what happens. Yet the novel is very critical of fatalism as an attitude of mind. Many characters, particularly Ravens-wood, regard fate as an irresistible force limiting their actions, and hence their responsibilities. Largely through Ravenswood's influence and through the baleful presence of the village hags, fatalism spreads throughout the novel and, most tragically, infects Lucy, who comes to declare in resigned despair that her love for Ravenswood was doomed from the start. She gives herself up to fatalism as a final gesture of her powerlessness and passivity. Underlying *The Bride of Lammermoor* is a frustrated activity, an impulse towards decisive actions and words, which criticizes the central characters' declining faith and strength.

[29] p. 42.

As the omens and prophecies suggest, characters in *The Bride of Lammermoor* engage in a losing struggle against the evil, inescapable, past, and a predetermined future. Its young people are dominated and supplanted by their parents, or forced to re-enact past feuds and guilts. Lady Ashton even takes Lucy's place as Bucklaw's partner to open the dancing at the wedding celebrations.[30] At several points in the novel's development, the action of the present is literally interrupted by stories about the past. The reader first encounters Sir William Ashton, for example, as he ponders how best to exploit the riot which has broken out at the Ravenswood funeral. Instead of reaching a decision, Sir William allows his thoughts to wander to the legend of Malisius de Ravenswood, which the narrator promptly relates. Similarly, the first meeting of Lucy and Ravenswood is interrupted as the narrator recounts the legend of the Mermaiden's Fountain, a spot rumoured to be fatal to the Ravenswood family. Anticipating the romance of Ravenswood and Lucy, the story of Raymond of Ravenswood and the nymph of the fountain tells of a secret love which is destroyed by the man's lack of faith, leading to the death of both lovers. The narrative veers off to encapsulate the present in the legendary past, and the new lovers give place to the old. In the novel as a whole, the young inheritors are denied independence and autonomy, trapped in distorted forms of childishness and inactivity. The mysterious appearance of the portrait of Malisius de Ravenswood in the castle hall during the wedding celebrations is a particularly clear example of how evil and disruptive forces threaten to take over the characters of the hero and heroine. Ravenswood's resemblance to the portrait of his ancestor has already been noticed, and the identification is true to one side of his psychology: even when he is betrothed to Lucy, his repressed desire for vengeance distorts his attempts at love and friendship, making him cruel and demanding, unable to resist disparaging comments on Lucy's fidelity, family, and religious faith. At Lucy's wedding, the celebrations suddenly cease as the guests notice the painting of Malisius, and realize that they are

---

[30] There are comic variations of this, as in the scene of the Marquis's arrival at Ravenswood Castle, when Sir William introduces Lucy as 'his wife, Lady Ashton' (p. 235).

being watched over, figuratively, by the old spirit of vengeance. Lady Ashton calms them by explaining that the picture of Malisius must have been placed there by a 'crazy wench' employed at the castle, whose imagination is steeped in the history of the Ravenswood family. As the reader later learns, Ailsie Gourlay has moved the painting into the hall, but Lady Ashton's hasty explanation applies prophetically, and ironically, to Lucy herself. For a moment, the characters of Ravenswood and Malisius, Lucy and Ailsie Gourlay, are merged.

The 'crazy wench', who is at once Lucy, Ailsie, and a figment of Lady Ashton's misogynistic imagination, disrupts the novel as well as the bridal ceremonial. Critics have recently drawn attention to the important and disturbing connections which *The Bride of Lammermoor* makes between insanity and gender, pointing out Lucy's place in a cult of beautiful, vicitimized madwomen (sentimentalized Ophelias, in particular) which reinforces the association of femininity with emotionalism and irrationality.[31] Philip Martin has shown that Lucy's madness may be read as a celebratory escape as well as a punitive sacrifice, and has argued that this possibility disrupts the novel's sexual ideology. Scott's presentation of the gender issue becomes far more pressing, however, when Lucy's madness is considered as part of a pattern of female behaviour in the novel as a whole. *The Bride of Lammermoor* is profoundly troubled by images of female rule and female violence, which culminate in Lucy's desperate rebellion, but which are a steady source of uneasy humour and disparaging comment throughout.[32] Lady Ashton, condemned as a false mother and an overbearing wife, is the most obvious image of female insubordination and the misrule to which it leads. In character, she is said to resemble Sarah, Duchess of Marlborough, the embodiment of female domination over a fond queen. In

---

[31] Elaine Showalter, *The Female Malady: Women, Madness, and English Culture, 1830–1980*, 1987, pp. 14–17; Philip W. Martin, *Mad Women in Romantic Writing*, 1987, pp. 99–107.

[32] Nancy Moore Goslee discusses problems of gender in Scott's poetry in 'Witch or Pawn: Women in Scott's Narrative Poetry', in *Romanticism and Feminism*, ed. Anne K. Mellor, 1988, pp. 115–36. Judith Wilt considers femininity in *The Heart of Midlothian*, *The Pirate*, and *Redgauntlet* in *Secret Leaves*, 1985, ch. 4.

traditional versions of the Dalrymple story, Lady Stair, the
original of Lady Ashton, was rumoured to have been a witch,
whose evil actions could be understood as the result of her pact
with the devil. Scott dismisses such rumours, but replaces them
by creating for Lady Ashton a female psychology which is deeply
indebted to the idea of evil forces and unnatural power. Of the
novel's other female characters, blind Alice has survived her
husband and children and is regarded as a witch by the common
people. The three village hags gloat over Ravenswood's body
('broad in the shouthers, and narrow around the lungies—he wad
mak a bonny corpse—I wad like to hae the streaking and winding
o' him'), sounding a disturbing note of female sexual rapacious-
ness.[33] Even the Girder household is a *petit-bourgeois* parody of
female government, with Dame Loup-the-Dike, a low-life version of Lady Ashton, having subjugated her dead husband and
now threatening the domestic rule of her son-in-law. In a
confrontation which anticipates the angry encounter between
Ravenswood and Lady Ashton at Lucy's betrothal, Dame Loup-
the-Dike with her iron ladle and Girder with his whip challenge
each other over Caleb's theft of the wild ducks, the issue at stake
being the punishment Girder intends to inflict on his wife. Girder,
the reader is told, is 'not of that class of lords and masters whose
wives are viceroys over them'.[34] The implied contrast with 'the
Lord Keeper's Lady Keeper'[35] is important, and helps to clarify
the sexual roles being worked out in the novel. In the sub-plot,
however, male rule triumphs, temporarily at least. The reader last
glimpses Girder as he declares that he will hear no more female
chatter about the visit of the Marquis and Ravenswood. This
maintains the sub-plot's comfortable comedy, and leaves the
more troubling implications about female power to be worked
out through the complex tragedy of Lucy's madness.

Lucy is the archetypal heroine of her society: beautiful, pale,
dependent, and disposed by character and upbringing to promote
harmony and reconciliation. Her subordination to Ravenswood
repeats her existing relationship within her own family, as the

[33] p. 251.
[34] p. 148.
[35] p. 223, echoing *Othello* II.i. 74.

daughter who puts the wishes of everyone else before her own. Her song, 'Look not thou on beauty's charming', suggests an extreme of renunciation and unworldliness akin to death. Yet there are hints from the first that this passive creature has strong emotions and a susceptible imagination. Introducing her, the narrator notes that she appears passive only because nothing has yet happened to arouse her. Later, he gives subtle indications that in Lucy's romantic fantasies her beauty and grace bring her power as well as protection. When she meets Ravenswood, she imagines for herself the romantic influence which will win him from his determined enmity towards her family:

Would he have equally shunned their acknowledgments and avoided their intimacy, had her father's request been urged more mildly, less abruptly, and softened with the grace which women so well know how to throw into their manner, when they mean to mediate betwixt the headlong passions of the ruder sex? This was a perilous question to ask her own mind—perilous both in the idea and in its consequences.[36]

Lucy's frustrated and unacknowledged expectation of control through love culminates in the violence she enacts towards Bucklaw. In this violence there are tantalizing links back to the woman who first told Scott the story of Janet Dalrymple: his great-aunt, Margaret Swinton. Margaret Swinton was murdered by a trusted female servant when Scott was a young boy, and her death seemed to Scott to have been the trigger of his earliest sense of horror. He recalls it in his 1831 introduction to 'My Aunt Margaret's Mirror':

She was a kind relation of my own, and met her death in a manner so shocking, being killed in a fit of insanity by a female attendant who had been attached to her person for half a lifetime, that I cannot now recall her memory, child as I was when the catastrophe occurred, without a painful re-awakening of perhaps the first images of horror that the scenes of real life stamped on my mind.[37]

The Bride of Lammermoor complicates this 'image of horror' by combining the figures of victim and murderer into one character.

---

[36] p. 64.
[37] Magnum, xli. 292–3.

As the perfection of feminine charm and gentleness, with her 'somewhat childish' beauty and slender form, Lucy is a focus for the novel's sentimentality and also for its fears.

Throughout the novel, she and Ravenswood represent enduring fantasies of feminine passivity and masculine activity in their looks, manners, interests, and passions. Ravenswood, 'perhaps the best *lover* the author ever yet drew', according to Scott's friend Lady Louisa Stuart,[38] seems designed to complete and support Lucy. As Sir William Ashton reflects: 'Then his daughter—his favourite child—his constant playmate—seemed formed to live happy in a union with such a commanding spirit as Ravenswood; and even the fine, delicate, fragile form of Lucy Ashton seemed to require the support of the Master's muscular strength and masculine character.'[39] Ravenswood himself is entangled in the same fantasy of power and passivity: 'he felt that the softness of a mind, amounting almost to feebleness, rendered her even dearer to him, as a being who had voluntarily clung to him for protection, and made him the arbiter of her fate for weal or woe.'[40] This fantasy of dependence, however, conceals destructive differences of disposition, education, and spirit, which Scott develops at some length in the chapter following the betrothal. *The Bride of Lammermoor* appears to endorse an ideal of sexual relationship by which Lucy is made complete by Ravenswood, but it also shows that this is a construction of the romantic imagination which deals in fantasies of passivity and forces lovers into emotionally destructive roles of support and dependence. The novel's narrator has difficulty in accommodating this negative view of the ideal, and Ravenswood's share of responsibility for Lucy's insanity and death, which he clearly recognizes ('You have named me but too truly'), becomes one of the problems of the closing chapters of the novel. The narrator wavers between indignation at female betrayal, by which Lucy can be described somewhat melodramatically as Lady Ashton's 'victim', and anxious prevarication about male culpability. He is at pains to emphasize Bucklaw's innocence, presenting him as a rough but

---

[38] Quoted in *Letters*, v. 473 n.
[39] p. 181.
[40] p. 216.

right-thinking young man whose social unease makes him unable
to interpret Lucy's behaviour. The narrator's anger and anxiety
at the sexual exploitation of Lucy is displaced on to the figure of
her power-usurping, 'unnatural' mother, avoiding the responsibility of her weak father, her tyrannical lover, and her careless
husband. The closing statements of the novel ring with the
narrator's indignation at Lady Ashton's actions, but considerably
simplify the broader social complicities which the tale has exposed.

  The link between powerlessness and voicelessness is a particularly interesting aspect of Lucy's plight. Lucy's single act of
violence against Bucklaw takes place offstage, unaccompanied by
eloquence or even expostulation. Her silence is painful, but her
right to express her feelings and thoughts has in any case been
limited by the manners of the time. She is first seen singing
someone else's words, disclaiming their relevance to her own
situation. Asked to explain her anxiety after the first interview
between her father and blind Alice, she feels obliged to attribute
her fears to the presence of the wild cattle rather than show that
she has heard and understood Alice's remarks. Her language is
taken from her when her mother dictates her final letter of appeal
to Ravenswood: even when she secretly forwards another, she
repeats the words her mother has prescribed. Faced with Ravenswood's angry demands during the contract-signing scene, she
cannot speak. It is fitting that she should finally enact rather than
voice her feelings. She is finally found crouching like a wild
animal in her wedding-chamber, reduced to gibbering and the
gestures of 'an exulting demoniac', a description which neatly
marks her identity with the witch-figures who have so twisted
her. Lucy's decline into incoherence and silence are important
registers of her social helplessness and, at the same time, the only
way that the novel can contain the spectacle of female violence
to which it is inevitably drawn. She dies 'without her being able
to utter a word explanatory of the fatal scene';[41] unlike Bucklaw,
whose decision not to speak on the subject is a matter of
chivalrous choice, declared with a measured dignity new to him.
It is no accident that Lucy's only recorded response to her

[41] p. 339.

attempted murder of her new husband ('So, you have ta'en up your bonny bridegroom?') sounds very unlike any of her previous speeches.[42] Like most of Scott's characters of higher rank, Lucy does not use dialect terms. The words are, in fact, taken from the reports of Janet Dalrymple's marriage, signalling both Lucy's loss of personal identity in madness, and her re-assimilation to the source tale. She slips back into the reported history in which she originated.

Yet Lucy's violence leaves the world of male rivalries and ambitions curiously empty. The political and social interests which had dominated earlier sections of the novel are suddenly deflated. Ravenswood never reaches the spot where he is to fight a duel with Sholto Ashton. As Sholto impatiently awaits him, the figure of the horseman crossing the sands suddenly becomes 'invisible, as if it had melted into the air'.[43] He does not so much die as disappear. Sir William's ambitions to give his family an estate, an aristocratic status, are thwarted when his sons die without heirs. The surviving figure of the novel is evil and female.

It is not surprising that *The Bride of Lammermoor* itself has been explained away as a form of temporary creative insanity, placed reassuringly outside Scott's usual creative methods and interests. The traditions of criticism which present it as a novel about historical change, about the responsibilities of the present towards the dead past, continue Scott's own tactics, moving his tales away from psychological problems towards public, social, ones. Yet the technical assurance of the novel, its insistence on history as something to be transformed, and misrepresented, by art, had always made these protective critical manoeuvres unnecessary. The ending of *The Bride of Lammermoor* may seem abrupt, even evasive, in a way which goes beyond the simple expediency of ending a story briskly, but this only throws the reader back on its beginning, which had emphasized the partiality and mystery of story-telling. Even the characters seem to merge back into the narrative traditions which formed them, to fade into legend and hearsay. The memorial to Lady Ashton ironically replaces the

[42] p. 338.
[43] p. 347.

statues which symbolized repentance and reconciliation at the end of *Romeo and Juliet*, and the lovers themselves survive only in the manuscript of a dead schoolmaster, based on a preparatory sketch by an artist who never achieved more than temporary fame.

NOTE ON THE TEXT

SCOTT wrote to Archibald Constable and James Ballantyne in September 1818 that he had begun work on a Third Series of *Tales of My Landlord*. The later stages of his work (from March 1819) were seriously interrupted by illness and by the distress caused by news of the death of the Duke of Buccleuch, and only the help of two amanuenses, William Laidlaw and John Ballantyne, enabled him to complete it.[1] When the Third Series appeared, Scott replied to a letter of praise from Lady Louisa Stuart:

I am very glad your Ladyship found the tales in some degree worth your notice. It cost me a terrible effort to finish them for between distress of mind and body I was very unfit for literary composition. But in justice to my booksellers I was obliged to dictate while I was scarce able to speak for pain.[2]

However, the manuscript (in the Signet Library, Edinburgh)[3] shows that only the last fifth of the novel could have been dictated to Laidlaw and Ballantyne in the way described by Lockhart in his *Life of Scott*, and there is no justification for interpretations of the novel based on the assumption that it was composed throughout in imaginatively liberating delirium.[4]

The Bride of Lammermoor was published with *A Legend of Montrose* in June 1819 by Constable in Edinburgh and the firms of Longman and Hurst Robinson in London. Later in 1819, it made up volumes xi and xii and of the 12-volume 8vo *Novels and Tales of the Author of Waverley*, the first of several collections of Scott's works to appear throughout the 1820s. Two other formats of *Novels and Tales* appeared in 1821 (16-volume 12mo) and 1823 (12-volume 18mo), and there were new editions of the 1819 8vo in 1822, and of the 1821 12mo in 1825. The most

[1] For details of Scott's illness, see Edgar Johnson, *Sir Walter Scott: The Great Unknown*, pp. 643–54. His letters of April and May 1819 testify to his physical and mental distress: *Letters*, v. 343, 379, 392.

[2] *Letters*, v. 472–4.

[3] I am grateful to the Librarian of the Signet Library for permission to consult and to quote from the manuscript.

[4] Jane Millgate discusses the inaccuracies of Lockhart's account in *Walter Scott: The Making of the Novelist*, 1984, ch. 9.

important changes made after the first edition, however, were those made for the Magnum Opus, the new collected edition published by Robert Cadell between 1829 and 1833, for which Scott revised, corrected, and wrote new introductions and notes. He planned to amend his work without introducing intrusive changes, but in the case of *The Bride of Lammermoor* (which appeared in 1830) the changes in the political and legal framework were important and intended to be systematic. He entered his revisions in volumes of the novels specially bound with blank interleaves (the 'interleaved set' acquired by the National Library of Scotland in 1986). The interleaved volumes used for *The Bride of Lammermoor* were made up from the second (1822) edition of the 1819 8vo *Novels and Tales*. The only important subsequent editions of Scott's work were the Centenary edition of 1870–1 (including a few notes by D. Laing), and the Dryburgh edition of 1892–4, both prepared using the interleaved set, which was then in the possession of their publishers, A. & C. Black. The Border edition of 1892–4, with its unrevised text, was introduced and lightly annotated by Andrew Lang.

The present edition is based on the Magnum Opus, with corrections as listed below. Given the current interest in returning to early states of the texts of Scott's novels, some discussion of the grounds for this choice is appropriate. Scott used all stages of his texts—manuscript, proof, and print—as opportunities for revision. No single state possesses final authority, and the stages of work which can be regarded as creative, rather than as simply editorial and corrective, differ from novel to novel. In the case of *The Bride of Lammermoor*, the stages of creative work lasted longer than usual. The revisions made for the Magnum Opus produced a text which differed substantially from the first edition, and each text has its virtues. I have chosen the Magnum Opus here because Scott added some inspired passages during this last stage of work on the text, and because I believe that the apparatus of notes and introduction, and the revised historical scheme, add to the qualities of the novel rather than detract from them.[5] The

---

[5] The case for preferring the first edition state of the text is given by Jane Millgate (as cited above). Her arguments are too detailed to be entered into here, but they centre on the claim that in the Magnum Opus Ravenswood's downfall

following survey summarizes my analysis of the extent and nature of the revisions made at different stages in the publication history of *The Bride of Lammermoor*, paying particular attention to the new directions and emphases observable in the Magnum Opus.

The extant manuscript ends at a point corresponding to p. 276 of this edition (reading 'Speak out you old fool and let me know . . .'), with some passages missing. Revisions on the verso of the last page show that the manuscript was originally longer. It is written throughout in Scott's usual regular, difficult, hand, with relatively few deletions but with many corrections and additions. Several significant passages were added as afterthoughts, including the analysis of Lucy's romantic reading and pliancy, important details of Sir William Ashton's reports to the Privy Council, and Ravenswood's reaction to the Ashton family portraits. Readings which have been lost between manuscript and first edition include: Ravenswood's 'shooting dress of dark green richly laced with gold' (which becomes the more sober 'shooting-dress of dark cloth', p. 60); Bucklaw's unwillingness 'to skeleter [or skelder, i.e. 'scamper'] or shift about like' Craigengelt (which becomes 'to shelter or shift about like', p. 70); Craigengelt's hope of 'worming' himself into Bucklaw's confidence (which becomes 'working', p. 221); Bucklaw's dry comment that if Craigengelt had survived the honeymoon period in his married friends' households 'you might have made good your position' (which becomes 'you might have made a good year's pension', p. 222); and the Marquis's belittling colloquial reference to Ashton 'brattling' at the bar (which becomes 'battling', p. 264).

To preserve his anonymity, Scott's manuscripts, and the corrections he later made on proof sheets, were transcribed before they reached the compositor. First proofs were checked in-house, and second and third proofs, with James Ballantyne's questions and suggestions, were sent to Scott. Scott knew that the speed

seems gratuitous because it occurs in a changed political and legal situation in which he can obtain effective redress. I believe that neither state of the text conveys the satisfying integration of personal and public resonances which Millgate claims for the first edition, and that to seek such integration is to make questionable assumptions about the kind of artistic effects Scott achieves. Towards the end of the novel, moreover, personal desires and frustrations take over from cultural and legal ones, and this holds for both first edition and Magnum Opus.

with which he composed could cause problems for his publishers. In a note to James Ballantyne written on one of the packages enclosing a chapter of *The Bride of Lammermoor*, he acknowledged: 'These matters will need more than your usual carefulness. Look sharp—double sharp—my trust is constant in thee.'[6] Many minor corrections were made for the first edition, inserting missing words (especially prepositions), and transforming spellings like 'Wolfshope' and 'Wolfscrag' into more acceptable form. Most importantly, his publishers had the task of organizing Scott's minimal manuscript punctuation and paragraphing into conventional printed form. An incomplete set of proof sheets for *The Bride of Lammermoor* (corresponding to pp. 312–49 in this edition), with corrections by Scott and Ballantyne, is in the National Library of Scotland (MS 3401 (ii)).[7] This set of proofs appears to deal with material which Scott had dictated, for on one sheet Ballantyne, battling with an epigraph from Crabbe, laments that 'when not aided by the context, we can do nothing with Mr. Laidlaw's hand'. For this reason, the number of corrections Scott had to make may be unrepresentative, but the proofs provide interesting evidence of mistakes averted, new thoughts added at a late stage, and the influence of Ballantyne's opinions. Only in proof, for example, did Scott add Lucy's words 'When the diamonds are gone, what signifies the casket?' (p. 314) and 'It was the link that bound me to life.' (p. 330.) Ballantyne's comments of praise, enquiry, and sympathy testify to his engagement with the text, and one indignant outburst led to a significant revision. In the final paragraph of the novel, Scott had originally written that 'Lady Ashton lived to the verge of extreme old age, the only survivor of the group of unhappy persons, whose misfortunes were *in a great degree* owing to her implacability.'[8] Ballantyne objected to the qualification, exclaiming in the margin 'Old jade! They were *altogether* owing to her implacability.' Scott followed his suggestion, producing the unequivocal judgement given in the printed text.

---

[6] *Letters*, v. 373.
[7] I am grateful for permission to quote from the proofs.
[8] Here, as afterwards where appropriate, I have italicized the words added.

In addition to straightforward misprints and mistakes in chapter-numbers, the first edition contained several inconsistencies, particularly in the naming of characters and places (such as 'Norman', instead of 'Edgar', Ravenswood, and 'Bittlebrain'). Some of the more glaring errors were corrected for the first edition of *Novels and Tales* later in 1819, but many survived, to await correction either in later issues of *Novels and Tales* or, in many instances, in the Magnum Opus. One reading of 'Norman' Ravenswood survived until 1821. Until the Magnum Opus, Bucklaw was said to come 'already' instead of 'at length' into his inheritance (p. 217), and Lucy was described as 'petrified to stone' (p. 321). Adjustments to grammar and punctuation, which became more systematic over the various stages of *Novels and Tales*, were probably the work of compositors and house readers, but some revisions show signs of Scott's active involvement. The significant alteration of Lucy's being 'devoutly' rather than just 'devotedly' attached to Ravenswood (p. 215), the extra 'ha! ha!'s added to Caleb's triumph over Dingwall (p. 273), and the spirited addition 'clean and clear wud' to Mysie's speech (formerly just 'wud', p. 128), suggest that he approached new editions of his novels as opportunities for new thinking rather than just as exercises in correction. This impulse became marked and systematic during work on the Magnum Opus.

The major revision made for the Magnum Opus was a change in the dating of the action from before to after the Act of Union in 1707. This necessitated many alterations and additions to passages describing the legal processes of Ravenswood's appeal for restoration of his lands. My notes give details of the most significant previous readings at the relevant points. Scott (himself a lawyer, and for many years a Clerk to the Court of Session) seems to have been uncertain about the exact status of appeals to the Scottish Parliament against decisions of the Court of Session in the years between the Claim of Right in 1689 and the Act of Union in 1707, and removed this doubt by having Ravenswood appeal to the House of Lords instead. Scott added several passages expanding on this procedure, as well as a note (21 in this edition) which misleadingly implies that a post-Union dating had always been intended. However, he did not revise the many comments which still suggest a pre-Union dating, and the historical scheme of the novel is correspondingly inconsistent. This is no reason to reject the revised text. *The Bride of Lammermoor* had always contained inconsistent historical references, although the Magnum Opus arguably exacerbated the problem by encouraging readers to think that a precise dating had been intended. In *all* states of the text, references to the Scottish Privy Council (abolished in 1708), to the murder of Sir George Lockhart in 1689 (which is described as a 'recent' event), and to 'the king' suggest a pre-Union dating; while references to English customs and excise officials (who extended their jurisdiction to Scotland after the Union) and to Law's scheme of 1717 (which is said to be 'recently broached'), indicate a post-Union dating.

Many of the improvements made for the Magnum Opus were matters of presentation. Punctuation marks, especially exclamation marks, question marks, and commas around sub-clauses, were added more liberally than before. Many hyphens were removed to provide more modern readings, and spelling was more consistently modernized. Accents on foreign language words were added, and Scott's unreliable Latin was rather patchily corrected. However, some errors appeared for the first time, and others, including the variant spellings of 'Mortsheugh' and 'Bide-the-bent', were never caught. These have been corrected for the present edition. I have not, however, attempted to remove the inconsistencies in naming Lady Ashton ('Eleanor' and 'Margaret') and Girder ('Gibbie' and 'John'). Many revisions were made, as at earlier stages of the text, to avoid repetition. Indicators of speaker and subject (such as 'continued the reverend monitor' and 'replied the younger man') were added, many of them needlessly fussy. Scott clarified confusing sentences, usually making small adjustments rather than radical changes, but occasionally seizing the opportuntity to add new detail, nearly always for the better. He added 'under escort of the generous lion' to the reference to Spenser's Una in Lucy Ashton's romantic fantasies (p. 40), and expanded Ravenswood's explosion of contempt for the Ashton family portraits ('such scarecrows as these' replacing 'such as these', p. 191). He revised Lady Ashton's determination that Lucy's marriage should bring her 'fortune, and a gentleman' to the more precise and more patronizing 'easy fortune, and a respectable country gentleman' (p. 228). He clarified the puzzling sentence describing the end of the visit paid by Ravenswood and the Marquis to the Girders (which had read 'The two landladies, old and young, in all kindly greeting, stood simpering at the door . . .'), revising it to read 'The two landladies, old and young, having received in all kindly greeting, a kiss from each of their noble guests, stood simpering at the door . . .' (p. 283).

Several revisions, although slight in themselves, significantly adjusted the tone and implications of the narrator's comments. Scott revised the sentence describing Alice's dress as 'remarkably clean, forming in that particular a strong contrast to those of her rank', so that it read 'uncommonly clean, forming in that particular a strong contrast to most of her rank' (p. 48). He toned down the criticism of female education and manners, revising the comment on p. 55 which had originally read: 'it was not then, as now, a necessary part of a young lady's education, to indulge in causeless tremors of the nerves.' He modified the criticism of Scottish peasants to read 'when pressed to admit a claim which his conscience owns, *or perhaps his feelings,* and his interest inclines him to deny' (p. 137), and the description of Bucklaw as 'detached *in some degree* from the best society' (p. 303). He removed even the possibility of seeming to endorse popular superstitions about Lady Ashton's supernatural powers by describing her conduct not as 'truly diabolical', as in earlier editions, but as 'truly detestable and diabolical' (p. 309). These are signs of a more cautious Scott, and in one instance his moderation undeniably weakens the reading. Until the Magnum Opus, the conduct of the Ashton family at Lucy's funeral had been roundly but ungrammatically condemned, as they attended the service with 'as little attendance and ceremony as could possibly be dispensed with'. Scott obscured the criticism by revising this to 'such moderate attendance and ceremony as could not possibly be dispensed with' (p. 341).

Revisions to descriptions of Sir William Ashton illustrate how the Magnum Opus adjusted judgement of character. In previous editions, politicians reward him 'without trusting or respecting him', whereas they do so in the Magnum Opus 'without absolutely trusting or greatly re[s]pecting him' (p. 161). Ravenswood is brought to admit that he might have misjudged not just Ashton's 'character' in general, but more precisely his 'personal character' (p. 171). Revisions were made to convey more convincingly his subtlety of speech, so that he refers to 'another person, *whom some call* one of your worst and most interested enemies', p. 182), and writes 'something more explicitly, *which seemed to intimate*' a willingness to compromise with Ravenswood before appeal proceedings begin (p. 290).

In keeping with this, a series of important interpolations enlivened speeches, particularly speeches by minor characters. Lord Turntippet's speech was enhanced by the addition of a final 'Eh?' (p. 67). Ravenswood's reply to Caleb's news of the hunt was given an extra dryness with the addition of 'pray?' (p. 105). Mr Dingwall's speech was greatly improved by being delivered 'with a grin' (p. 139). Girder's flat enquiry 'And what was his name, I pray ye?' became 'And what might *his* name be, I pray ye?' (p. 149). Bucklaw was made to address Craigengelt as 'Craigie' throughout, rather than the less affectionate 'Craig'. Lady Ashton's injunction to her husband to attend to 'the dignity of your family also' became more waspish with the addition of the clause 'as far as it requires any looking after' (p. 238). Her description of the alliance with Bucklaw as 'an event so desirable' became the more flattering 'so extremely desirable' (p. 297). The Marquis's temporizing speech after Ravenswood's summary dismissal was enhanced by the small but telling addition that he 'would not *otherwise* have suffered my kinsman to depart alone' (p. 242). These small touches add significantly to the spiritedness and appropriateness of the novel's dialogues. On the other hand, many changes were made in favour of more polished speech, such as the substitution of 'said he internally' for 'thought he to himself' (p. 173), and 'draw conclusions from' for 'judge of' (p. 198). Henry's childish question about the competing coaches, 'will they both belong to the Marquis of A——?', had been much more natural than the more formally correct revision, '*can* they both belong to the Marquis of A——?' (p. 231).

Certain scenes received special attention. The scenes in the Girders' kitchen were greatly embellished, Scott adding such striking details as 'with arms disposed as if they were about to be a-kimbo at the next reply', 'much encouraged by the turn of the debate', and 'and whiles a dirk into the bargain'. Girder's condemnation of Caleb for having fought against 'Argyle' was changed: in the Magnum Opus he has fought against 'the saints at Bothwell Brigg' (p. 150). Scott also subtly revised Ravenswood's encounter with Alice's wraith, having him wonder at finding her '*alone and* at a distance from her habitation', and see her rise '*slowly* from her seat' (p. 246). He rewrote Ravenswood's later demand, 'Is *that*, madam, your hand?', replacing it with the more forceful 'Is *that* your handwriting, madam?' (p. 323), and clarified the speech in which Bucklaw forbids future discussion of his wedding night, 'If a lady shall question me henceforward upon the incidents of that unhappy night, I shall remain silent, and in future consider her as *one who has shown herself* desirous to break off her friendship with me; *in a word, I will never speak to her again.*' (p. 339.)

The Magnum Opus, therefore, changed the historical setting of the novel by a few, significant, years, but failed to refer consistently to this new dating. It clarified speakers, subjects, and confusing sentences, embellished punctuation, modernized spelling, and avoided repetition. It added and adjusted details, and modified implied judgements of certain characters and issues. The new historical introduction gave details of the source-story (previously, the only frame for the tale had been the story of Pattieson and Tinto). On the whole, the Magnum Opus presents a more considered text with some inspired revisions and additions which it would be a pity to lose. As I have argued in my introduction, it also adds to the novel's range of stories and story-tellers. Scott's expansive antiquarian comments do not supersede, and need not stifle, the novel's other types of narrative authority.

The Present Edition

The following changes have been made to the text of the Magnum Opus, most representing a return to first edition or other earlier readings to replace inaccuracies which entered the text during revision. There are oddities in the spellings which remain, but some (such as 'canvass', 'story', 'loath') are acceptable alternatives to the usual forms: the first edition usually had 'canvas' and 'story', but not consistently. Scott or his compositors changed the standard spelling of 'confidant' to 'confident' during revisions, and I have allowed this to stand. Only in changing 'waves' to 'waives' have I altered a spelling positively chosen during revisions to the text. In resetting, double quotation marks for a first quotation have been replaced by single ones.

p. 21	unfilled cann/unfilled can (MS and 1823 reading)
p. 24	Elibabeth–chamber/Elizabeth–chamber (1st edn. reading)
p. 28	Abon Hassan/Abou Hassan
p. 37	hair-brained/hare-brained (1st edn. reading, and in keeping with the spelling elsewhere)
pp. 49, 292 (twice)	dependent(s)/dependant(s) (as elsewhere)
p. 80	abit/a bit (1823 reading)
p. 84	timorous courteous glance/timorous cautious glance (MS reading)
pp. 88, 89, 149	Balderston/Balderstone
p. 115	waving/waiving (1st edn. reading)
p. 139	done by the Lord of Ravenswood/done by the Lords of Ravenswood (1st edn. reading)
p. 142	find it's way/find its way
p. 143	its shamefu' epicurism/it's shamefu' epicurism (1st edn. reading)
pp. 144–52 (six times)	Bide-the-Bent/Bide-the-bent (as in his later appearance: MS has 'Bidethebent')
p. 155	auld een, that has/auld een, that hae (1st edn. reading)
p. 161	repecting him/respecting him

p. 189	Bittlebrains' House/Bittlebrains House (1st edn. reading, preferable because Scott retains the capital 'H', indicating that this is the name of the house: it is also called this on p. 126)
p. 223	acting a/acting as (1st edn. reading)
p. 230	'Middleton's Mad World my Masters'/Middleton's 'Mad World my Masters' (MS has no inverted commas, suggesting that the earlier reading is a compositor's error not intended, but never caught, by Scott)
p. 235	wave ceremony/waive ceremony (1st edn. reading)
p. 263	veiw/view (1st edn. reading)
p. 299	waves insisting/waives insisting (1st edn. reading)
pp. 332–4 (four times)	Mortheuch/Mortsheugh (as in earlier scene: MS shows that this was the original spelling)
p. 344	Wolf's-Crag/Wolf's Crag (1st edn. reading)
p. 347	Wolf's hope/Wolf's-hope (1st edn. reading)

Originally, all the notes written for the first edition, as well as the shorter notes added for the Magnum Opus, were printed at the foot of the page. The longer notes written for the Magnum Opus were printed at the end of the relevant chapter. In this edition, all Scott's notes are printed together at the end of the novel, and indicated in the text by a superscript numeral. My own explanatory notes are indicated in the text with an asterisk, and printed after Scott's notes.

SELECT BIBLIOGRAPHY

SIR WALTER SCOTT: PERSONAL WRITINGS, BIOGRAPHIES, REFERENCE

The Letters of Sir Walter Scott, ed. H. J. C. Grierson, *et al.*, 12 vols., 1932–7.

The Journal of Sir Walter Scott, ed. W. E. K. Anderson, 1972.

Lockhart, John Gibson, *Memoirs of the Life of Sir Walter Scott, Bart.*, 2nd edn., 10 vols., 1839.

Johnson, Edgar, *Sir Walter Scott: The Great Unknown*, 2 vols. paginated as 1, 1970.

Corson, James C., *A Bibliography of Sir Walter Scott, 1797–1940*, 1943.

—— *Notes and Index to Sir Herbert Grierson's Edition of the Letters of Sir Walter Scott*, 1979.

Rubenstein, Jill, *Sir Walter Scott: A Reference Guide*, 1978.

EARLY CRITICISM

Bagehot, Walter, Review of 'The Waverley Novels', *National Review*, vi (Apr. 1858), 444–72.

Carlyle, Thomas, 'Sir Walter Scott' (1838), in *The Works of Thomas Carlyle*, ed. H. D. Traill, 30 vols., 1896–9, xxix. 22–87.

Hayden, John O., *Scott: The Critical Heritage*, 1970.

Hazlitt, William, 'Sir Walter Scott' (1824), in *The Spirit of the Age*, 1825.

Hillhouse, James T., *The Waverley Novels and their Critics*, 1936.

Review of *Tales of My Landlord*, Third Series, *Blackwood's Edinburgh Magazine*, v (June 1819), 340–53.

—— *Edinburgh Magazine*, iv (June 1819), 547–54.

—— *Edinburgh Monthly Review*, ii (Aug. 1819), 160–84.

Senior, Nassau, Review of *Rob Roy, The Heart of Midlothian, The Bride of Lammermoor, A Legend of Montrose, Ivanhoe, The Monastery, The Abbot,* and *Kenilworth*, *Quarterly Review*, xxvi (Oct. 1821), 109–48.

Stephen, Leslie, 'Hours in a Library No. III—Some Words About Sir Walter Scott', *Cornhill Magazine*, xxiv (Sept. 1871), 278–93.

RECENT CRITICISM: GENERAL

Brown, David, *Walter Scott and the Historical Imagination*, 1979.

Cockshut, A. O. J., *The Achievement of Walter Scott*, 1969.

Cooney, Seamus, 'Scott's Anonymity—Its Motives and Consequences', *Studies in Scottish Literature*, x (1973), 207–19.

Cottom, Daniel, *The Civilized Imagination: A Study of Ann Radcliffe, Jane Austen, and Sir Walter Scott*, 1985.

Craig, David, *Scottish Literature and the Scottish People 1680–1830*, 1961.

Crawford, Thomas, *Scott*, Writers and Critics Series, 1965.

Daiches, David, 'Scott's Achievement as a Novelist', *Nineteenth-Century Fiction*, vi (1952), 80–95, 153–73.

Edwards, Simon, 'Producing Voices: The Discursive Art of Walter Scott', in Kathleen Parker and Martin Priestman (eds.), *Peasants and Countrymen in Literature*, 1982, pp. 123–52.

Farrell, John P., *Revolution as Tragedy: The Dilemma of the Moderate from Scott to Arnold*, 1980.

Fleishman, Avrom, *The English Historical Novel*, 1971.

Gordon, Robert C., *Under Which King? A Study of the Scottish Waverley Novels*, 1969.

Goslee, Nancy Moore, 'Witch or Pawn: Women in Scott's Narrative Poetry', in Anne K. Mellor (ed.), *Romanticism and Feminism*, 1988, pp. 115–36.

Hart, Francis R., *Scott's Novels: The Plotting of Historic Survival*, 1966.

—— 'Scottish Gothic', *The Scottish Novel: A Critical Survey*, 1978, ch. 1.

—— 'Scott's Endings: The Fictions of Authority', *Nineteenth-Century Fiction*, xxxiii (1978), 48–68.

Hartveit, Lars, *Dream Within a Dream: A Thematic Approach to Scott's Vision of Fictional Reality*, Norwegian Studies in English, xviii, 1974.

Kerr, James, *Fiction Against History: Scott as Storyteller*, 1989.

Lascelles, Mary, *The Story-Teller Retrieves the Past*, 1980.

Levine, George, *The Realistic Imagination: English Fiction from Frankenstein to Lady Chatterley*, 1981, chs. 4 and 5.

Lukács, Georg, *The Historical Novel*, 1937, trans. Hannah and Stanley Mitchell, 1962.

McMaster, Graham, *Scott and Society*, 1981.

Millgate, Jane, *Walter Scott: The Making of the Novelist*, 1984.

—— *Scott's Last Edition: A Study in Publishing History*, 1987.

Morse, David, *Romanticism: A Structural Analysis*, 1982.

Muir, Edwin, *Scott and Scotland: The Predicament of the Scottish Writer*, 1936.

Parsons, Coleman O., *Witchcraft and Demonology in Scott's Fiction: With Chapters on the Supernatural in Scottish Literature*, 1964.

Punter, David, *The Literature of Terror: A History of Gothic Fictions from 1765 to the Present Day*, 1980.

Shaw, Harry E., *The Forms of Historical Fiction: Sir Walter Scott and His Successors*, 1983.

Waswo, Richard, 'Story as Historiography in the Waverley Novels', *English Literary History*, xlvii (1980), 304–30.

Welsh, Alexander, *The Hero of the Waverley Novels*, 1963.

Wilson, A. N., *The Laird of Abbotsford: A View of Sir Walter Scott*, 1980.

Wilt, Judith, *Secret Leaves: The Novels of Walter Scott*, 1985.

RECENT CRITICISM: *THE BRIDE OF LAMMERMOOR*

Farrell, John P., '*The Bride of Lammermoor* as Oracular Text in Emily Brontë, Tennyson, and Hardy', *South Central Review*, i (1984), 53–63.

Franklin, Caroline, 'Feud and Faction in *The Bride of Lammermoor*', *Scottish Literary Journal*, xiv (1987), 18–31.

Garside, Peter D., 'Union and *The Bride of Lammermoor*', *Studies in Scottish Literature*, xix (1984), 72–93.

Gordon, Robert C., '*The Bride of Lammermoor*: A Novel of Tory Pessimism', *Nineteenth-Century Fiction*, xii (1957), 110–24.

—— 'The Marksman of Ravenswood: Power and Legitimacy in *The Bride of Lammermoor*', *Nineteenth Century Literature*, xli (1986), 49–71.

Hartveit, Lars, *Scott's 'The Bride of Lammermoor': An Assessment of Attitude*, 1962.

Hollingworth, Brian, 'The Tragedy of Lucy Ashton, the Bride of Lammermoor', *Studies in Scottish Literature*, xix (1984), 94–105.

Hook, Andrew D., '*The Bride of Lammermoor*: A Reexamination', *Nineteenth-Century Fiction*, xxii (1967), 111–26.

Kerr, James, 'Scott's Dreams of the Past: *The Bride of Lammermoor* as Political Fantasy', *Studies in the Novel*, xviii (1986), 125–42.

Lamont, Claire, 'Scott as Story-teller: *The Bride of Lammermoor*', *Scottish Literary Journal*, vii (1980), 113–26.

Martin, Philip W., *Mad Women in Romantic Writing*, 1987, ch. 4.

Millgate, Jane, 'Text and Context: Dating the Events of *The Bride of Lammermoor*', *The Bibliotheck*, ix (1979), 200–13.

Parsons, Coleman O., 'The Dalrymple Legend in *The Bride of Lammermoor*', *Review of English Studies*, xix (1943), 51–8.

Politi, Jina, 'Narrative and Historical Transformations in *The Bride of Lammermoor*', *Scottish Literary Journal*, xv (1988), 70–81.

Showalter, Elaine, *The Female Malady: Women, Madness, and English Culture, 1830–1980*, 1987.

A CHRONOLOGY OF SIR WALTER SCOTT

1771   Born in Edinburgh, son of Walter Scott, W. S., and Anne Rutherford.

1772–3   Suffered from poliomyelitis which left him lame.

1779–83   Attended the High School, Edinburgh.

1783–6   Attended classes at Edinburgh University; 1786, apprenticed to his father.

1792   Admitted to Faculty of Advocates.

1796   *The Chase*, and *William and Helen*, translated from Bürger, issued anonymously.

1797   Married Charlotte Charpentier.

1799   *Goetz of Berlichingen*, translated from Goethe; *Tales of Terror*; appointed Sheriff-Depute of Selkirkshire.

1801   Contributed to M. G. Lewis's *Tales of Wonder*.

1802–3   *The Minstrelsy of the Scottish Border*.

1804   Moved to Ashestiel.

1805   *The Lay of the Last Minstrel*; entered into partnership with James Ballantyne & Co., printers; started *Waverley*.

1806   Appointed a Principal Clerk of Session.

1808   *Marmion*; edition of *The Works of John Dryden*; completed Joseph Strutt's *Queen-Hoo Hall*.

1810   *The Lady of the Lake*; resumed *Waverley*, but laid it aside again.

1812   Moved to Abbotsford.

1813   *Rokeby*; declined offer of Poet Laureateship.

1814   *Waverley*; edition of *The Works of Jonathan Swift*.

1815   *The Lord of the Isles*; *Guy Mannering*.

1816   *The Antiquary; The Black Dwarf* and *Old Mortality* (*Tales of My Landlord*, 1st series).

1817   *Rob Roy*.

1818   *The Heart of Midlothian* (*Tales of My Landlord*, 2nd series); accepted Baronetcy (gazetted 1820).

1819   *The Bride of Lammermoor* and *A Legend of Montrose* (*Tales of My Landlord*, 3rd series); *Ivanhoe*.

1820   *The Monastery*; *The Abbot*; his daughter, Sophia, married J. G. Lockhart.

1821   *Kenilworth*.

1822   *The Pirate*; *The Fortunes of Nigel*; *Peveril of the Peak*.

1823   *Quentin Durward*.

1824   *St. Ronan's Well*; *Redgauntlet*.

1825   *The Betrothed* and *The Talisman* (*Tales of the Crusaders*); began *Journal*.

1826   Financial collapse, caused by the bankruptcy of Archibald Constable & Co., and James Ballantyne & Co.; *Woodstock*.

1827   Acknowledged authorship of Waverley novels; *Life of Napoleon*.

1827–8 *Chronicles of the Canongate* (two series).

1828–31 *Tales of a Grandfather* (four series).

1829   *Anne of Geierstein*; Magnum series of Waverley Novels starts to appear.

1830   *Letters on Demonology and Witchcraft*; Magnum *Bride of Lammermoor*.

1831   Voyage to Mediterranean in search of health.

1832   *Count Robert of Paris* and *Castle Dangerous* (*Tales of My Landlord*, 4th series).

        Died at Abbotsford, 21 September.

TALES OF MY LANDLORD

THIRD SERIES

*

Hear, Land o' Cakes and brither Scots,
Frae Maidenkirk to Jonny Groats',
If there's a hole in a' your coats,
     I rede ye tent it;
A chiel's amang you takin' notes,
      An' faith he'll prent it!

         (Burns)

Ahora bien, dixo il Cura, traedme, senor huésped, aquesos libros, que los quiero ver. Que me place, respondió el, y entrando, en su aposento, sacó dél una maletilla vieja cerrada con una cadenilla, y abriéndola, halló en ella tres libros grandes y unos papeles de muy buena letra escritos de mano.

(Don Quixote, Parte I. Capitulo 32)

It is mighty well, said the priest; pray, landlord, bring me those books, for I have a mind to see them. With all my heart, answered the host; and, going to his chamber, he brought out a little old cloke-bag, with a padlock and chain to it, and, opening it, he took out three large volumes, and some manuscript papers written in a fine character.

(Jarvis's *Translation*)*

INTRODUCTION

TO THE

BRIDE OF LAMMERMOOR

THE author, on a former occasion,[1] declined giving the real source from which he drew the tragic subject of this history, because, though occurring at a distant period, it might possibly be unpleasing to the feelings of the descendants of the parties.* But as he finds an account of the circumstances given in the Notes to Law's Memorials,[2] by his ingenious friend Charles Kirkpatrick Sharpe, Esq.,* and also indicated in his reprint of the Rev. Mr Symson's poems, appended to the Description of Galloway,* as the original of the Bride of Lammermoor, the author feels himself now at liberty to tell the tale as he had it from connexions of his own, who lived very near the period, and were closely related to the family of the Bride.*

It is well known that the family of Dalrymple, which has produced, within the space of two centuries, as many men of talent, civil and military, and of literary, political, and professional eminence, as any house in Scotland, first rose into distinction in the person of James Dalrymple, one of the most eminent lawyers that ever lived, though the labours of his powerful mind were unhappily exercised on a subject so limited as Scottish Jurisprudence, on which he has composed an admirable work.*

He married Margaret, daughter to Ross of Balniel, with whom he obtained a considerable estate. She was an able, politic, and high-minded woman, so successful in what she undertook, that the vulgar, no way partial to her husband or her family, imputed her success to necromancy. According to the popular belief, this Dame Margaret purchased the temporal prosperity of her family from the Master whom she served, under a singular condition, which is thus narrated by the historian of her grandson, the great Earl of Stair.* 'She lived to a great age, and at her death desired that she might not be put under ground, but that her coffin should be placed upright on one end of it, promising, that while she remained in that situation, the Dalrymples should continue in prosperity. What was the old lady's motive for such a request, or whether she really made such a promise, I cannot take upon me to determine; but it is certain her coffin stands upright in the aisle of the church of Kirkliston, the burial place of the family.'[3] The talents of this accomplished race were sufficient to have accounted for the dignities which many members of the family attained, without any supernatural assistance. But their extraordinary prosperity was attended by some equally singular family misfortunes, of which that which befell their eldest daughter was at once unaccountable and melancholy.

Miss Janet Dalrymple, daughter of the first Lord Stair, and Dame Margaret Ross, had engaged herself without the knowledge of her parents to the Lord Rutherford, who was not acceptable to them either on account of his political principles, or his want of fortune. The young couple broke a piece of gold together, and pledged their troth in the most solemn manner; and it is said the young lady imprecated dreadful evils on herself should she break her plighted faith. Shortly after, a suitor who was favoured by Lord Stair, and still more so by his lady, paid his addresses to Miss Dalrymple. The young lady refused the proposal, and being pressed on the subject, confessed her secret engagement. Lady Stair, a woman accustomed to universal submission, (for even her husband did not dare to contradict her,) treated this objection as a trifle, and insisted upon her daughter yielding her consent to marry the new suitor, David Dunbar, son and heir to David Dunbar of Baldoon, in Wigtonshire. The first lover, a man of very high spirit, then interfered by letter, and insisted on the right he had acquired by his troth plighted with the young lady. Lady Stair sent him for answer, that her daughter, sensible of her undutiful behaviour in entering into a contract unsanctioned by her parents, had retracted her unlawful vow, and now refused to fulfil her engagement with him.

The lover, in return, declined positively to receive such an answer from any one but his mistress in person; and as she had to deal with a man who was both of a most determined character,

and of too high condition to be trifled with, Lady Stair was obliged
to consent to an interview between Lord Rutherford and her
daughter. But she took care to be present in person, and argued
the point with the disappointed and incensed lover with pertinacity equal to his own. She particularly insisted on the Levitical law,
which declares, that a woman shall be free of a vow which her
parents dissent from. This is the passage of Scripture she founded
on:—

'If a man vow a vow unto the Lord, or swear an oath to bind
his soul with a bond; he shall not break his word, he shall do
according to all that proceedeth out of his mouth.

'If a woman also vow a vow unto the Lord, and bind herself by
a bond, being in her father's house in her youth;

'And her father hear her vow, and her bond wherewith she hath
bound her soul, and her father shall hold his peace at her: then all
her vows shall stand, and every bond wherewith she hath bound
her soul shall stand.

'But if her father disallow her in the day that he heareth; not
any of her vows, or of her bonds wherewith she hath bound her
soul, shall stand: and the Lord shall forgive her, because her father
disallowed her.'—Numbers, xxx. 2, 3, 4, 5.

While the mother insisted on these topics, the lover in vain
conjured the daughter to declare her own opinion and feelings.
She remained totally overwhelmed, as it seemed,—mute, pale,
and motionless as a statue. Only at her mother's command, sternly
uttered, she summoned strength enough to restore to her plighted
suitor the piece of broken gold, which was the emblem of her
troth. On this he burst forth into a tremendous passion, took leave
of the mother with maledictions, and as he left the apartment,
turned back to say to his weak, if not fickle mistress, 'For you,
madam, you will be a world's wonder;' a phrase by which some
remarkable degree of calamity is usually implied. He went abroad,
and returned not again. If the last Lord Rutherford was the
unfortunate party, he must have been the third who bore that title,
and who died in 1685.*

The marriage betwixt Janet Dalrymple and David Dunbar of
Baldoon now went forward, the bride showing no repugnance,

but being absolutely passive in every thing her mother commanded or advised. On the day of the marriage, which, as was then usual, was celebrated by a great assemblage of friends and relations, she was the same—sad, silent, and resigned, as it seemed, to her destiny. A lady, very nearly connected with the family,* told the author that she had conversed on the subject with one of the brothers of the bride, a mere lad at the time, who had ridden before his sister to church. He said her hand, which lay on his as she held her arm round his waist, was as cold and damp as marble. But, full of his new dress, and the part he acted in the procession, the circumstance, which he long afterwards remembered with bitter sorrow and compunction, made no impression on him at the time.

The bridal feast was followed by dancing; the bride and bridegroom retired as usual, when of a sudden the most wild and piercing cries were heard from the nuptial chamber. It was then the custom, to prevent any coarse pleasantry which old times perhaps admitted, that the key of the nuptial chamber should be intrusted to the brideman.* He was called upon, but refused at first to give it up, till the shrieks became so hideous that he was compelled to hasten with others to learn the cause. On opening the door, they found the bridegroom lying across the threshold, dreadfully wounded, and streaming with blood. The bride was then sought for: She was found in the corner of the large chimney, having no covering save her shift, and that dabbled in gore. There she sat grinning at them, mopping and mowing, as I heard the expression used; in a word, absolutely insane. The only words she spoke were, 'Tak up your bonny bridegroom.' She survived this horrible scene little more than a fortnight, having been married on the 24th of August, and dying on the 12th of September 1669.*

The unfortunate Baldoon recovered from his wounds, but sternly prohibited all enquiries respecting the manner in which he had received them. If a lady, he said, asked him any question upon the subject, he would neither answer her nor speak to her again while he lived; if a gentleman, he would consider it as a mortal affront, and demand satisfaction as having received such. He did not very long survive the dreadful catastrophe, having met with a fatal injury by a fall from his horse, as he rode between Leith and Holyrood-house, of which he died the next day, 28th March 1682.* Thus a few years removed all the principal actors in this frightful tragedy.

Various reports went abroad on this mysterious affair, many of them very inaccurate, though they could hardly be said to be exaggerated. It was difficult at that time to become acquainted with the history of a Scottish family above the lower rank; and strange things sometimes took place there, into which even the law did not scrupulously enquire.

The credulous Mr Law says, generally, that the Lord President Stair had a daughter, who 'being married, the night she was *bride in*, [that is, bedded bride,] was taken from her bridegroom and *harled* [dragged] through the house, (by spirits, we are given to understand,) and soon afterwards died. Another daughter,' he says, 'was possessed by an evil spirit.'*

My friend, Mr Sharpe, gives another edition of the tale. According to his information, it was the bridegroom who wounded the bride. The marriage, according to this account, had been against her mother's inclination, who had given her consent in these ominous words: 'You may marry him, but soon shall you repent it.'*

I find still another account darkly insinuated in some highly scurrilous and abusive verses, of which I have an original copy.* They are docketed as being written 'Upon the late Viscount Stair and his family, by Sir William Hamilton of Whitelaw. The marginals by William Dunlop, writer in Edinburgh, a son of the Laird of Househill, and nephew to the said Sir William Hamilton.' There was a bitter and personal quarrel and rivalry betwixt the author of this libel, a name which it richly deserves, and Lord President Stair;* and the lampoon, which is written with much more malice than art, bears the following motto:—

'Stair's neck, mind, wife, sons, grandson, and the rest,
Are wry, false, witch, pests, parricide, possessed.'*

This malignant satirist, who calls up all the misfortunes of the family, does not forget the fatal bridal of Baldoon. He seems, though his verses are as obscure as unpoetical, to intimate, that the

violence done to the bridegroom was by the intervention of the
foul fiend to whom the young lady had resigned herself, in case
she should break her contract with her first lover. His hypothesis
is inconsistent with the account given in the note upon Law's
Memorials, but easily reconcilable to the family tradition.

> 'In al Stair's offspring we no difference know,
> They doe the females as the males bestow;
> So he of's daughter's marriage gave the ward,
> Like a true vassal, to Glenluce's Laird;
> He knew what she did to her suitor plight,
> If she her faith to Rutherfurd should slight,
> Which, like his own, for greed he broke outright.
> Nick did Baldoon's posterior right deride,
> And, as first substitute, did seize the bride;
> Whate'er he to his mistress did or said,
> He threw the bridegroom from the nuptial bed,
> Into the chimney did so his rival maul,
> His bruised bones ne'er were cured but by the fall.'[4]*

One of the marginal notes ascribed to William Dunlop, applies
to the above lines. 'She had betrothed herself to Lord Rutherfoord
under horrid imprecations, and afterwards married Baldoon, his
nevoy, and her mother was the cause of her breach of faith.'

The same tragedy is alluded to in the following couplet and
note:—

> 'What train of curses that base brood pursues,
> When the young nephew weds old uncle's spouse.'*

The note on the word *uncle* explains it as meaning 'Rutherfoord, who should have married the Lady Baldoon, was Baldoon's
uncle.' The poetry of this satire on Lord Stair and his family was,
as already noticed, written by Sir William Hamilton of Whitelaw,
a rival of Lord Stair for the situation of President of the Court of
Session; a person much inferior to that great lawyer in talents, and
equally ill-treated by the calumny or just satire of his contemporaries, as an unjust and partial judge.* Some of the notes are by
that curious and laborious antiquary Robert Milne, who, as a
virulent Jacobite, willingly lent a hand to blacken the family of
Stair.[5]*

Another poet of the period, with a very different purpose, has left an elegy, in which he darkly hints at and bemoans the fate of the ill-starred young person, whose very uncommon calamity Whitelaw, Dunlop, and Milne, thought a fitting subject for buffoonery and ribaldry. This bard of milder mood was Andrew Symson, before the Revolution minister of Kirkinner, in Galloway, and after his expulsion as an Episcopalian, following the humble occupation of a printer in Edinburgh. He furnished the family of Baldoon, with which he appears to have been intimate, with an elegy on the tragic event in their family. In this piece he treats the mournful occasion of the bride's death with mysterious solemnity.

The verses bear this title—'On the unexpected death of the virtuous Lady Mrs Janet Dalrymple, Lady Baldoon, younger,' and afford us the precise dates of the catastrophe, which could not otherwise have been easily ascertained. 'Nupta August 12. Domum Ducta August 24. Obiit September 12. Sepult. September 30, 1669.'* The form of the elegy is a dialogue betwixt a passenger and a domestic servant. The first, recollecting that he had passed that way lately, and seen all around enlivened by the appearances of mirth and festivity, is desirous to know what had changed so gay a scene into mourning. We preserve the reply of the servant as a specimen of Mr Symson's verses, which are not of the first quality:—

> ———'Sir, 'tis truth you've told,
> We did enjoy great mirth; but now, ah me!
> Our joyful song's turn'd to an elegie.
> A virtuous lady, not long since a bride,
> Was to a hopeful plant by marriage tied,
> And brought home hither. We did all rejoice,
> Even for her sake. But presently our voice
> Was turn'd to mourning for that little time
> That she'd enjoy: She waned in her prime,
> For Atropos,* with her impartial knife,
> Soon cut her thread, and therewithal her life;
> And for the time we may it well remember,
> It being in unfortunate September;

Where we must leave her till the resurrection,
'Tis then the Saints enjoy their full perfection.'[6]*

Mr Symson also poured forth his elegiac strains upon the fate of the widowed bridegroom, on which subject, after a long and querulous effusion, the poet arrives at the sound conclusion, that if Baldoon had walked on foot, which it seems was his general custom, he would have escaped perishing by a fall from horseback. As the work in which it occurs is so scarce as almost to be unique,* and as it gives us the most full account of one of the actors in this tragic tale which we have rehearsed, we will, at the risk of being tedious, insert some short specimens of Mr Symson's composition. It is entitled,—

'A Funeral Elegie, occasioned by the sad and much lamented death of that worthily respected, and very much accomplished gentleman, David Dunbar, younger of Baldoon, only son and apparent heir to the right worshipful Sir David Dunbar of Baldoon, Knight Baronet. He departed this life on March 28, 1682, having received a bruise by a fall, as he was riding the day preceding betwixt Leith and Holy-Rood-House; and was honourably interred in the Abbey church of Holy-Rood-House, on April 4, 1682.'

'Men might, and very justly too, conclude
Me guilty of the worst ingratitude,
Should I be silent, or should I forbear
At this sad accident to shed a tear;
A tear! said I? ah! that's a petit thing,
A very lean, slight, slender offering,
Too mean, I'me sure, for me, wherewith t'attend
The unexpected funeral of my friend—
A glass of briny tears charged up to th' brim,
Would be too few for me to shed for him.'

The poet proceeds to state his intimacy with the deceased, and the constancy of the young man's attendance on public worship, which was regular, and had such effect upon two or three others that were influenced by his example,

'So that my Muse 'gainst Priscian* avers,

He, only he, *were* my parishioners;
Yea, and my only hearers.'

He then describes the deceased in person and manners, from which it appears that more accomplishments were expected in the composition of a fine gentleman in ancient than modern times:

'His body, though not very large or tall,
Was sprightly, active, yea and strong withal.
His constitution was, if right I've guess'd,
Blood mixt with choler, said to be the best.
In's gesture, converse, speech, discourse, attire,
He practis'd that which wise men still admire,
Commend, and recommend. What's that? you'l say;
'Tis this: He ever choos'd the middle way
'Twixt both th' extremes. Amost in ev'ry thing
He did the like, 'tis worth our noticing:
Sparing, yet not a niggard; liberal,
And yet not lavish or a prodigal,
As knowing when to spend and when to spare;
And that's a lesson which not many are
Acquainted with. He bashful was, yet daring
When he saw cause, and yet therein but sparing;
Familiar, yet not common, for he knew
To condescend, and keep his distance too.
He us'd, and that most commonly, to go
On foot; I wish that he had still done so.
Th' affairs of court were unto him well known:
And yet mean while he slighted not his own.
He knew full well how to behave at court,
And yet but seldome did thereto resort;
But lov'd the country life, choos'd to inure
Himself to past'rage and agriculture;
Proving, improving, ditching, trenching, draining,
Viewing, reviewing, and by those means gaining;
Planting, transplanting, levelling, erecting
Walls, chambers, houses, terraces; projecting
Now this, now that device, this draught, that measure,
That might advance his profit with his pleasure.
Quick in his bargains, honest in commerce,
Just in his dealings, being much averse
From quirks of law, still ready to refer

His cause t' an honest country arbiter.
He was acquainted with cosmography,
Arithmetic, and modern history;
With architecture and such arts as these,
Which I may call specifick sciences
Fit for a gentleman; and surely he
That knows them not, at least in some degree,
May brook the title, but he wants the thing,
Is but a shadow scarce worth noticing.
He learned the French, be 't spoken to his praise,
In very little more than fourty days.'

Then comes the full burst of woe, in which, instead of saying much himself, the poet informs us what the ancients would have said on such an occasion:

'A heathen poet, at the news, no doubt,
Would have exclaimed, and furiously cry'd out
Against the fates, the destinies and starrs,
What! this the effect of planetarie warrs!
We might have seen him rage and rave, yea worse,
'Tis very like we might have heard him curse
The year, the month, the day, the hour, the place,
The company, the wager, and the race;
Decry all recreations, with the names
Of Isthmian, Pythian, and Olympick games;
Exclaim against them all both old and new,
Both the Nemæan and the Lethæan too:*
Adjudge all persons under highest pain,
Always to walk on foot, and then again
Order all horses to be hough'd, that we
Might never more the like adventure see.'

Supposing our readers have had enough of Mr Sympson's verses, and finding nothing more in his poem worthy of transcription, we return to the tragic story.

It is needless to point out to the intelligent reader, that the witchcraft of the mother consisted only in the ascendency of a powerful mind over a weak and melancholy one, and that the harshness with which she exercised her superiority in a case of delicacy, had driven her daughter first to despair, then to frenzy. Accordingly, the author has endeavoured to explain the tragic tale on this principle.* Whatever resemblance Lady Ashton may be supposed to possess to the celebrated Dame Margaret Ross, the reader must not suppose that there was any idea of tracing the portrait of the first Lord Viscount Stair in the tricky and mean-spirited Sir William Ashton. Lord Stair, whatever might be his moral qualities, was certainly one of the first statesmen and lawyers of his age.*

The imaginary castle of Wolf's Crag has been identified by some lover of locality with that of Fast Castle.* The author is not competent to judge of the resemblance betwixt the real and imaginary scene, having never seen Fast Castle except from the sea. But fortalices of this description are found occupying, like ospreys' nests, projecting rocks, or promontories, in many parts of the eastern coast of Scotland, and the position of Fast Castle seems certainly to resemble that of Wolf's Crag as much as any other, while its vicinity to the mountain ridge of Lammermoor,* renders the assimilation a probable one.

We have only to add, that the death of the unfortunate bride-groom by a fall from horseback, has been in the novel transferred to the no less unfortunate lover.

THE

BRIDE OF LAMMERMOOR

*

CHAPTER I

By cauk and keel to win your bread,
Wi' whigmaleeries for them wha need,
Whilk is a gentle trade indeed
      To carry the gaberlunzie on.

                  (*Old Song*) *

FEW have been in my secret while I was compiling these narratives, nor is it probable that they will ever become public during the life of their author. Even were that event to happen, I am not ambitious of the honoured distinction, *digito monstrarier.* * I confess, that, were it safe to cherish such dreams at all, I should more enjoy the thought of remaining behind the curtain unseen, like the ingenious manager of Punch and his wife Joan, and enjoying the astonishment and conjectures of my audience. Then might I, perchance, hear the productions of the obscure Peter Pattieson praised by the judicious, and admired by the feeling, engrossing the young, and attracting even the old; * while the critic traced their fame up to some name of literary celebrity, and the question when, and by whom, these tales were written, filled up the pause of conversation in a hundred circles and coteries. * This I may never enjoy during my lifetime; but farther than this, I am certain, my vanity should never induce me to aspire.

I am too stubborn in habits, and too little polished in manners, to envy or aspire to the honours assigned to my literary contemporaries. I could not think a whit more highly of myself, were I even found worthy to 'come in place as a lion,' for a winter in the great metropolis. * I could not rise, turn round, and show all my honours, from the shaggy mane to the tufted tail, roar you an 'twere any nightingale,* and so lie down again like a well-behaved beast of show, and all at the cheap and easy rate of a cup of coffee, and a slice of bread and butter as thin as a wafer. And I could ill stomach the fulsome flattery with which the lady of the evening indulges her show-monsters on such occasions, as she crams her parrots with sugar-plums, in order to make them talk before company. I cannot be tempted to 'come aloft' for these marks of distinction, and, like imprisoned Sampson, I would rather remain—if such must be the alternative—all my life in the mill-house, grinding for my very bread, than be brought forth to make sport for the Philistine lords and ladies.* This proceeds from no dislike, real or affected, to the aristocracy of these realms. But they have their place, and I have mine; and, like the iron and earthen vessels in the old fable,* we can scarce come into collision without my being the sufferer in every sense. It may be otherwise with the sheets which I am now writing. These may be opened and laid aside at pleasure; by amusing themselves with the perusal, the great will excite no false hopes; by neglecting or condemning them, they will inflict no pain; and how seldom can they converse with those whose minds have toiled for their delight, without doing either the one or the other.

In the better and wiser tone of feeling, which Ovid only expresses in one line to retract in that which follows, I can address these quires—

*Parve, nec invideo, sine me, liber, ibis in urbem.**

Nor do I join the regret of the illustrious exile, that he himself could not in person accompany the volume, which he sent forth to the mart of literature, pleasure, and luxury. Were there not a hundred similar instances on record, the fate of my poor friend and school-fellow, Dick Tinto,* would be sufficient to warn me against seeking happiness, in the celebrity which attaches itself to a successful cultivator of the fine arts.

Dick Tinto, when he wrote himself artist, was wont to derive his origin from the ancient family of Tinto, of that ilk, in Lanarkshire, and occasionally hinted that he had somewhat derogated from his gentle blood, in using the pencil for his principal means of support. But if Dick's pedigree was correct, some of his ancestors must have suffered a more heavy declension, since the good man his father executed the necessary, and, I trust, the honest, but certainly not very distinguished employment, of tailor in ordinary to the village of Langdirdum in the west.* Under his humble roof was Richard born, and to his father's humble trade was Richard, greatly contrary to his inclination, early indentured. Old Mr Tinto had, however, no reason to congratulate himself upon having compelled the youthful genius of his son to forsake its natural bent. He fared like the schoolboy, who attempts to stop with his finger the spout of a water cistern, while the stream, exasperated at this compression, escapes by a thousand uncalculated spirts, and wets him all over for his pains. Even so fared the senior Tinto, when his hopeful apprentice not only exhausted all the chalk in making sketches upon the shopboard, but even executed several caricatures of his father's best customers, who began loudly to murmur, that it was too hard to have their persons deformed by the vestments of the father, and to be at the same time turned into ridicule by the pencil of the son. This led to discredit and loss of practice, until the old tailor, yielding to destiny, and to the entreaties of his son, permitted him to attempt his fortune in a line for which he was better qualified.

There was about this time, in the village of Langdirdum, a peripatetic brother of the brush, who exercised his vocation *sub Jove frigido*,* the object of admiration to all the boys of the village, but especially to Dick Tinto. The age had not yet adopted, amongst other unworthy retrenchments, that illiberal measure of economy, which, supplying by written characters the lack of symbolical representation, closes one open and easily accessible avenue of instruction and emolument against the students of the fine arts. It was not yet permitted to write upon the plastered door-way of an alehouse, or the suspended sign of an inn, 'The Old Magpie,' or 'The Saracen's Head,' substituting that cold description for the lively effigies of the plumed chatterer, or the turban'd frown of the terrific soldan. That early and more simple age considered alike the necessities of all ranks, and depicted the symbols of good cheer so as to be obvious to all capacities; well judging, that a man, who could not read a syllable, might nevertheless love a pot of good ale as well as his better-educated neighbours, or even as the parson himself. Acting upon this liberal principle, publicans as yet hung forth the painted emblems of their calling, and sign-painters, if they seldom feasted, did not at least absolutely starve.

To a worthy of this decayed profession, as we have already intimated, Dick Tinto became an assistant; and thus, as is not unusual among heaven-born geniuses in this department of the fine arts, began to paint before he had any notion of drawing.

His talent for observing nature soon induced him to rectify the errors, and soar above the instructions, of his teacher. He particularly shone in painting horses, that being a favourite sign in the Scottish villages; and, in tracing his progress, it is beautiful to observe, how by degrees he learned to shorten the backs, and prolong the legs, of these noble animals, until they came to look less like crocodiles, and more like nags. Detraction, which always pursues merit with strides proportioned to its advancement, has indeed alleged, that Dick once upon a time painted a horse with five legs, instead of four. I might have rested his defence upon the license allowed to that branch of his profession, which, as it permits all sorts of singular and irregular combinations, may be allowed to extend itself so far as to bestow a limb supernumerary on a favourite subject. But the cause of a deceased friend is sacred; and I disdain to bottom it so superficially. I have visited the sign in question, which yet swings exalted in the village of Langdirdum; and I am ready to depone upon oath, that what has been idly mistaken or misrepresented as being the fifth leg of the horse, is, in fact, the tail of that quadruped, and, considered with reference to the posture in which he is delineated, forms a circumstance, introduced and managed with great and successful, though daring art. The nag being represented in a rampant or rearing posture, the tail, which is prolonged till it touches the ground, appears to form a *point d'appui*, and gives the firmness of a tripod to the figure, without which it would be difficult to conceive, placed as the feet are, how the courser could maintain his ground without tumbling backwards. This bold conception has fortunately fallen into the custody of one by whom it is duly valued; for, when Dick, in his more advanced state of proficiency, became dubious of the propriety of so daring a deviation from the established rules of art, and was desirous to execute a picture of the publican himself in exchange for this juvenile production, the courteous offer was declined by his judicious employer, who had observed, it seems, that when his ale failed to do its duty in conciliating his guests, one glance at his sign was sure to put them in good humour.

It would be foreign to my present purpose to trace the steps by which Dick Tinto improved his touch, and corrected, by the rules of art, the luxuriance of a fervid imagination. The scales fell from his eyes on viewing the sketches of a contemporary, the Scottish Teniers, as Wilkie has been deservedly styled.* He threw down the brush, took up the crayons, and, amid hunger and toil, and suspense and uncertainty, pursued the path of his profession under better auspices than those of his original master. Still the first rude emanations of his genius (like the nursery rhymes of Pope, could these be recovered)* will be dear to the companions of Dick Tinto's youth. There is a tankard and gridiron painted over the door of an obscure change-house in the Back-wynd of Gander-cleugh—But I feel I must tear myself from the subject, or dwell on it too long.

Amid his wants and struggles, Dick Tinto had recourse, like his brethren, to levying that tax upon the vanity of mankind which he could not extract from their taste and liberality—in a word, he painted portraits. It was in this more advanced state of proficiency, when Dick had soared above his original line of business, and highly disdained any allusion to it, that, after having been es-tranged for several years, we again met in the village of Gander-cleugh, I holding my present situation, and Dick painting copies of the human face divine* at a guinea per head. This was a small premium, yet, in the first burst of business, it more than sufficed for all Dick's moderate wants; so that he occupied an apartment at the Wallace Inn, cracked his jest with impunity even upon mine host himself, and lived in respect and observance with the chambermaid, hostler, and waiter.

Those halcyon days were too serene to last long.* When his honour the Laird of Gandercleugh, with his wife and three daughters, the minister, the gauger, mine esteemed patron Mr Jedediah Cleishbotham, and some round dozen of the feuars and farmers, had been consigned to immortality by Tinto's brush, custom began to slacken, and it was impossible to wring more than crowns and half-crowns from the hard hands of the peasants, whose ambition led them to Dick's painting-room.

Still, though the horizon was overclouded, no storm for some time ensued. Mine host had Christian faith with a lodger, who had been a good paymaster as long as he had the means. And from a portrait of our landlord himself, grouped with his wife and daughters, in the style of Rubens,* which suddenly appeared in the best parlour, it was evident that Dick had found some mode of bartering art for the necessaries of life.

Nothing, however, is more precarious than resources of this nature. It was observed, that Dick became in his turn the whetstone of mine host's wit,* without venturing either at defence or retaliation; that his easel was transferred to a garret-room, in which there was scarce space for it to stand upright; and that he no longer ventured to join the weekly club, of which he had been once the life and soul. In short, Dick Tinto's friends feared that he had acted like the animal called the sloth, which, having eaten up the last green leaf upon the tree where it has established itself, ends by tumbling down from the top, and dying of inanition.* I ventured to hint this to Dick, recommended his transferring the exercise of his inestimable talent to some other sphere, and forsaking the common which he might be said to have eaten bare.

'There is an obstacle to my change of residence,' said my friend, grasping my hand with a look of solemnity.

'A bill due to my landlord, I am afraid'? replied I, with heartfelt sympathy; 'if any part of my slender means can assist in this emergence'——

'No, by the soul of Sir Joshua!'* answered the generous youth, 'I will never involve a friend in the consequences of my own misfortune. There is a mode by which I can regain my liberty; and to creep even through a common sewer, is better than to remain in prison.'

I did not perfectly understand what my friend meant. The muse of painting appeared to have failed him, and what other goddess he could invoke in his distress, was a mystery to me. We parted, however, without further explanation, and I did not again see him until three days after, when he summoned me to partake of the *foy* with which his landlord proposed to regale him ere his departure for Edinburgh.

I found Dick in high spirits, whistling while he buckled the small knapsack, which contained his colours, brushes, pallets, and clean shirt. That he parted on the best terms with mine host, was obvious from the cold beef set forth in the low parlour, flanked by two mugs of admirable brown stout; and I own my curiosity was excited concerning the means through which the face of my friend's affairs had been so suddenly improved. I did not suspect Dick of dealing with the devil, and by what earthly means he had extricated himself thus happily, I was at a total loss to conjecture.

He perceived my curiosity, and took me by the hand. 'My friend,' he said, 'fain would I conceal, even from you, the degradation to which it has been necessary to submit, in order to accomplish an honourable retreat from Gandercleugh. But what avails attempting to conceal that, which must needs betray itself even by its superior excellence? All the village—all the parish—all the world—will soon discover to what poverty has reduced Richard Tinto.'

A sudden thought here struck me—I had observed that our landlord wore, on that memorable morning, a pair of bran new velveteens, instead of his ancient thicksets.

'What,' said I, drawing my right hand, with the fore-finger and thumb pressed together, nimbly from my right haunch to my left shoulder, 'you have condescended to resume the paternal arts to which you were first bred—long stitches, ha, Dick?'

He repelled this unlucky conjecture with a frown and a pshaw, indicative of indignant contempt, and leading me into another room, showed me, resting against the wall, the majestic head of Sir William Wallace, grim as when severed from the trunk by the orders of the felon Edward.*

The painting was executed on boards of a substantial thickness, and the top decorated with irons, for suspending the honoured effigy upon a sign-post.

'There,' he said, 'my friend, stands the honour of Scotland, and my shame—yet not so—rather the shame of those, who, instead of encouraging art in its proper sphere, reduce it to these unbecoming and unworthy extremities.'

I endeavoured to smooth the ruffled feelings of my misused and indignant friend. I reminded him, that he ought not, like the stag in the fable, to despise the quality which had extricated him from difficulties, in which his talents, as a portrait or landscape painter, had been found unavailing.* Above all, I praised the execution, as well as conception, of his painting, and reminded him, that far from feeling dishonoured by so superb a specimen of his talents being exposed to the general view of the public, he ought rather to congratulate himself upon the augmentation of his celebrity, to which its public exhibition must necessarily give rise.

'You are right, my friend—you are right,' replied poor Dick, his eye kindling with enthusiasm; 'why should I shun the name of an—an'—(he hesitated for a phrase)—'an out-of-doors artist? Hogarth has introduced himself in that character in one of his best engravings—Domenichino, or somebody else, in ancient times—Moreland in our own, have exercised their talents in this manner.* And wherefore limit to the rich and higher classes alone the delight which the exhibition of works of art is calculated to inspire into all classes? Statues are placed in the open air, why should Painting be more niggardly in displaying her master-pieces than her sister Sculpture? And yet, my friend, we must part suddenly; the carpenter is coming in an hour to put up the—the emblem; and truly, with all my philosophy, and your consolatory encouragement to boot, I would rather wish to leave Gandercleugh before that operation commences.'

We partook of our genial host's parting banquet, and I escorted Dick on his walk to Edinburgh. We parted about a mile from the village, just as we heard the distant cheer of the boys which accompanied the mounting of the new symbol of the Wallace-Head. Dick Tinto mended his pace to get out of hearing—so little had either early practice or recent philosophy reconciled him to the character of a sign-painter.

In Edinburgh, Dick's talents were discovered and appreciated, and he received dinners and hints from several distinguished judges of the fine arts. But these gentlemen dispensed their criticism more willingly than their cash, and Dick thought he needed cash more than criticism. He therefore sought London, the universal mart of talent, and where, as is usual in general marts of most descriptions, much more of each commodity is exposed to sale than can ever find purchasers.

Dick, who, in serious earnest, was supposed to have considerable natural talents for his profession, and whose vain and sanguine disposition never permitted him to doubt for a moment of ultimate success, threw himself headlong into the crowd which jostled and struggled for notice and preferment. He elbowed others, and was elbowed himself; and finally, by dint of intrepidity, fought his way into some notice, painted for the prize at the Institution, had pictures at the exhibition at Somerset-house, and damned the hanging committee. *But poor Dick was doomed to lose the field he fought so gallantly. In the fine arts, there is scarce an alternative betwixt distinguished success and absolute failure; and as Dick's zeal and industry were unable to ensure the first, he fell into the distresses which, in his condition, were the natural consequences of the latter alternative. He was for a time patronised by one or two of those judicious persons who make a virtue of being singular, and of pitching their own opinions against those of the world in matters of taste and criticism. But they soon tired of poor Tinto, and laid him down as a load, upon the principle on which a spoilt child throws away its plaything. Misery, I fear, took him up, and accompanied him to a premature grave, to which he was carried from an obscure lodging in Swallow-street, where he had been dunned by his landlady within doors, and watched by bailiffs without, until death came to his relief.* A corner of the Morning Post noticed his death,* generously adding, that his manner displayed considerable genius, though his style was rather sketchy; and referred to an advertisement, which announced that Mr Varnish, a well-known printseller, had still on hand a very few drawings and paintings by Richard Tinto, Esquire, which those of the nobility and gentry, who might wish to complete their collections of modern art, were invited to visit without delay. So ended Dick Tinto! a lamentable proof of the great truth, that in the fine arts mediocrity is not permitted, and that he who cannot ascend to the very top of the ladder, will do well not to put his foot upon it at all.

The memory of Tinto is dear to me, from the recollection of the many conversations which we have had together, most of them turning upon my present task. He was delighted with my progress, and talked of an ornamented and illustrated edition, with heads, vignettes, and *culs de lampe*, all to be designed by his own patriotic and friendly pencil. He prevailed upon an old sergeant of invalids to sit to him in the character of Bothwell, the life-guard's-man of Charles the Second, and the bell-man of Gander-cleugh in that of David Deans.* But while he thus proposed to unite his own powers with mine for the illustration of these narratives, he mixed many a dose of salutary criticism with the panegyrics which my composition was at times so fortunate as to call forth.

'Your characters,' he said, 'my dear Pattieson, make too much use of the *gob box*; they *patter* too much—(an elegant phraseology, which Dick had learned while painting the scenes of an itinerant company of players)—there is nothing in whole pages but mere chat and dialogue.'

'The ancient philosopher,' said I in reply, 'was wont to say, "Speak, that I may know thee;"* and how is it possible for an author to introduce his *personæ dramatis* to his readers in a more interesting and effectual manner, than by the dialogue in which each is represented as supporting his own appropriate character?'

'It is a false conclusion,' said Tinto; 'I hate it, Peter, as I hate an unfilled can.* I will grant you, indeed, that speech is a faculty of some value in the intercourse of human affairs, and I will not even insist on the doctrine of that Pythagorean toper, who was of opinion, that over a bottle speaking spoiled conversation.* But I will not allow that a professor of the fine arts has occasion to embody the idea of his scene in language, in order to impress upon the reader its reality and its effect. On the contrary, I will be judged by most of your readers, Peter, should these tales ever become public, whether you have not given us a page of talk for every single idea which two words might have communicated, while the posture, and manner, and incident, accurately drawn, and brought out by appropriate colouring, would have preserved all that was worthy of preservation, and saved these everlasting said he's and said she's, with which it has been your pleasure to encumber your pages.'

I replied, 'that he confounded the operations of the pencil and the pen; that the serene and silent art, as painting has been called by one of our first living poets,* necessarily appealed to the eye, because it had not the organs for addressing the ear; whereas poetry, or that species of composition which approached to it, lay under the necessity of doing absolutely the reverse, and addressed itself to the ear, for the purpose of exciting that interest which it could not attain through the medium of the eye.'

Dick was not a whit staggered by my argument, which he contended was founded on misrepresentation. 'Description,' he said, 'was to the author of a romance exactly what drawing and tinting were to a painter; words were his colours, and, if properly employed, they could not fail to place the scene, which he wished to conjure up, as effectually before the mind's eye,* as the tablet or canvass presents it to the bodily organ. The same rules,' he contended, 'applied to both, and an exuberance of dialogue, in the former case, was a verbose and laborious mode of composition which went to confound the proper art of fictitious narrative with that of the drama, a widely different species of composition, of which dialogue was the very essence, because all, excepting the language to be made use of, was presented to the eye by the dresses, and persons, and actions of the performers upon the stage. But as nothing,' said Dick, 'can be more dull than a long narrative written upon the plan of a drama, so where you have approached most near to that species of composition, by indulging in prolonged scenes of mere conversation, the course of your story has become chill and constrained, and you have lost the power of arresting the attention and exciting the imagination, in which upon other occasions you may be considered as having succeeded tolerably well.'

I made my bow in requital of the compliment, which was probably thrown in by way of *placebo*, and expressed myself willing at least to make one trial of a more straight-forward style of composition, in which my actors should do more, and say less, than in my former attempts of this kind. Dick gave me a patronizing and approving nod, and observed, that, finding me so docile, he would communicate, for the benefit of my muse, a subject which he had studied with a view to his own art.

'The story,' he said, 'was, by tradition, affirmed to be truth, although, as upwards of a hundred years had passed away since the events took place, some doubts upon the accuracy of all the particulars might be reasonably entertained.'

When Dick Tinto had thus spoken, he rummaged his portfolio for the sketch from which he proposed one day to execute a picture of fourteen feet by eight. The sketch, which was cleverly executed, to use the appropriate phrase, represented an ancient hall, fitted up and furnished in what we now call the taste of Queen Elizabeth's age. The light, admitted from the upper part of a high casement, fell upon a female figure of exquisite beauty, who, in an attitude of speechless terror, appeared to watch the issue of a debate betwixt two other persons. The one was a young man, in the Vandyke dress common to the time of Charles I.,* who, with an air of indignant pride, testified by the manner in which he raised his head and extended his arm, seemed to be urging a claim of right, rather than of favour, to a lady, whose age, and some resemblance in their features, pointed her out as the mother of the younger female, and who appeared to listen with a mixture of displeasure and impatience.

Tinto produced his sketch with an air of mysterious triumph, and gazed on it as a fond parent looks upon a hopeful child, while he anticipates the future figure he is to make in the world, and the height to which he will raise the honour of his family. He held it at arms' length from me,—he held it closer,—he placed it upon the top of a chest of drawers, closed the lower shutters of the casement, to adjust a downward and favourable light,—fell back to the due distance, dragging me after him,—shaded his face with his hand, as if to exclude all but the favourite object,—and ended by spoiling a child's copy book, which he rolled up so as to serve for the darkened tube of an amateur.* I fancy my expressions of enthusiasm had not been in proportion to his own, for he presently exclaimed with vehemence, 'Mr Pattieson, I used to think you had an eye in your head.'

I vindicated my claim to the usual allowance of visual organs.

'Yet, on my honour,' said Dick, 'I would swear you had been born blind, since you have failed at the first glance to discover the subject and meaning of that sketch. I do not mean to praise my own performance, I leave these arts to others; I am sensible of my deficiencies, conscious that my drawing and colouring may be improved by the time I intend to dedicate to the art. But the conception—the expression—the positions—these tell the story to every one who looks at the sketch; and if I can finish the picture without diminution of the original conception, the name of Tinto shall no more be smothered by the mists of envy and intrigue.'

I replied, 'That I admired the sketch exceedingly; but that to understand its full merit, I felt it absolutely necessary to be informed of the subject.'

'That is the very thing I complain of,' answered Tinto; 'you have accustomed yourself so much to these creeping twilight details of yours, that you are become incapable of receiving that instant and vivid flash of conviction, which darts on the mind from seeing the happy and expressive combinations of a single scene, and which gathers from the position, attitude, and countenance of the moment, not only the history of the past lives of the personages represented, and the nature of the business on which they are immediately engaged, but lifts even the veil of futurity, and affords a shrewd guess at their future fortunes.'

'In that case,' replied I, 'Painting excels the Ape of the renowned Gines de Passamont, which only meddled with the past and the present;* nay, she excels that very Nature who affords her subjects; for I protest to you, Dick, that were I permitted to peep into that Elizabeth-chamber, and see the persons you have sketched conversing in flesh and blood, I should not be a jot nearer guessing the nature of their business, than I am at this moment while looking at your sketch. Only generally, from the languishing look of the young lady, and the care you have taken to present a very handsome leg on the part of the gentleman, I presume there is some reference to a love affair between them.'

'Do you really presume to form such a bold conjecture?' said Tinto. 'And the indignant earnestness with which you see the man urge his suit—the unresisting and passive despair of the younger female—the stern air of inflexible determination in the elder woman, whose looks express at once consciousness that she is acting wrong, and a firm determination to persist in the course she has adopted'——

'If her looks express all this, my dear Tinto,' replied I, interrupting him, 'your pencil rivals the dramatic art of Mr Puff in the Critic, who crammed a whole complicated sentence into the expressive shake of Lord Burleigh's head.'*

'My good friend, Peter,' replied Tinto, 'I observe you are perfectly incorrigible; however, I have compassion on your dulness, and am unwilling you should be deprived of the pleasure of understanding my picture, and of gaining, at the same time, a subject for your own pen. You must know then, last summer, while I was taking sketches on the coast of East Lothian and Berwickshire, I was seduced into the mountains of Lammermoor by the account I received of some remains of antiquity in that district. Those with which I was most struck, were the ruins of an ancient castle in which that Elizabeth-chamber, as you call it, once existed. I resided for two or three days at a farm-house in the neighbourhood, where the aged goodwife was well acquainted with the history of the castle, and the events which had taken place in it. One of these was of a nature so interesting and singular, that my attention was divided between my wish to draw the old ruins in landscape, and to represent, in a history-piece, the singular events which have taken place in it. Here are my notes of the tale,' said poor Dick, handing a parcel of loose scraps, partly scratched over with his pencil, partly with his pen, where outlines of caricatures, sketches of turrets, mills, old gables, and dovecots, disputed the ground with his written memoranda.

I proceeded, however, to decipher the substance of the manuscript as well as I could, and wove it into the following Tale, in which, following in part, though not entirely, my friend Tinto's advice, I endeavoured to render my narrative rather descriptive than dramatic. My favourite propensity, however, has at times overcome me, and my persons, like many others in this talking world, speak now and then a great deal more than they act.

CHAPTER II

Well, lords, we have not got that which we have;
'Tis not enough our foes are this time fled,
Being opposites of such repairing nature.

(*Second Part of Henry VI*) *

IN the gorge of a pass or mountain glen, ascending from the fertile
plains of East Lothian, there stood in former times an extensive
castle, of which only the ruins are now visible. Its ancient proprietors were a race of powerful and warlike barons, who bore the
same name with the castle itself, which was Ravenswood.* Their
line extended to a remote period of antiquity, and they had
intermarried with the Douglasses, Humes, Swintons, Hays, and
other families of power and distinction in the same country.*
Their history was frequently involved in that of Scotland itself, in
whose annals their feats are recorded. The Castle of Ravenswood,
occupying, and in some measure commanding, a pass betwixt
Berwickshire or the Merse, as the south-eastern province of
Scotland is termed, and the Lothians, was of importance both in
times of foreign war and domestic discord. It was frequently
besieged with ardour, and defended with obstinacy, and, of
course, its owners played a conspicuous part in story. But their
house had its revolutions, like all sublunary things; it became
greatly declined from its splendour about the middle of the 17th
century; and towards the period of the Revolution,* the last
proprietor of Ravenswood Castle saw himself compelled to part
with the ancient family seat, and to remove himself to a lonely
and sea-beaten tower, which, situated on the bleak shores between Saint Abb's Head and the village of Eyemouth, looked out
on the lonely and boisterous German Ocean.* A black domain of
wild pasture-land surrounded their new residence, and formed the
remains of their property.

Lord Ravenswood, the heir of this ruined family, was far from
bending his mind to his new condition of life. In the civil war of

1689, he had espoused the sinking side, and although he had escaped without the forfeiture of life or land, his blood had been attainted, and his title abolished.* He was now called Lord Ravenswood only in courtesy.

This forfeited nobleman inherited the pride and turbulence, though not the fortune of his house, and, as he imputed the final declension of his family to a particular individual, he honoured that person with his full portion of hatred. This was the very man who had now become, by purchase, proprietor of Ravenswood, and the domains of which the heir of the house now stood dispossessed. He was descended of a family much less ancient than that of Lord Ravenswood, and which had only risen to wealth and political importance during the great civil wars.* He himself had been bred to the bar, and had held high offices in the state, maintaining through life the character of a skilful fisher in the troubled waters of a state divided by factions, and governed by delegated authority;* and of one who contrived to amass considerable sums of money in a country where there was but little to be gathered, and who equally knew the value of wealth, and the various means of augmenting it, and using it as an engine of increasing his power and influence.

Thus qualified and gifted, he was a dangerous antagonist to the fierce and imprudent Ravenswood. Whether he had given him good cause for the enmity with which the Baron regarded him, was a point on which men spoke differently. Some said the quarrel arose merely from the vindictive spirit and envy of Lord Ravenswood, who could not patiently behold another, though by just and fair purchase, become the proprietor of the estate and castle of his forefathers. But the greater part of the public, prone to slander the wealthy in their absence, as to flatter them in their presence, held a less charitable opinion. They said, that the Lord Keeper (for to this height Sir William Ashton had ascended)* had, previous to the final purchase of the estate of Ravenswood, been concerned in extensive pecuniary transactions with the former proprietor; and, rather intimating what was probable, than affirming any thing positively, they asked which party was likely to have the advantage in stating and enforcing the claims arising out of these complicated affairs, and more than hinted the advantages which the cool lawyer and able politician must necessarily possess over the hot, fiery, and imprudent character, whom he had involved in legal toils and pecuniary snares.

The character of the times aggravated these suspicions. 'In those days there was no king in Israel.'* Since the departure of James VI. to assume the richer and more powerful crown of England, there had existed in Scotland contending parties, formed among the aristocracy, by whom, as their intrigues at the court of St James's chanced to prevail, the delegated powers of sovereignty were alternately swayed.* The evils attending upon this system of government, resemble those which afflict the tenants of an Irish estate, the property of an absentee.* There was no supreme power, claiming and possessing a general interest with the community at large, to whom the oppressed might appeal from subordinate tyranny, either for justice or for mercy. Let a monarch be as indolent, as selfish, as much disposed to arbitrary power as he will, still, in a free country, his own interests are so clearly connected with those of the public at large, and the evil consequences to his own authority are so obvious and imminent when a different course is pursued, that common policy, as well as common feeling, point to the equal distribution of justice, and to the establishment of the throne in righteousness. Thus, even sovereigns, remarkable for usurpation and tyranny, have been found rigorous in the administration of justice among their subjects, in cases where their own power and passions were not compromised.

It is very different when the powers of sovereignty are delegated to the head of an aristocratic faction, rivalled and pressed closely in the race of ambition by an adverse leader. His brief and precarious enjoyment of power must be employed in rewarding his partisans, in extending his influence, in oppressing and crushing his adversaries. Even Abou Hassan, the most disinterested of all viceroys, forgot not, during his caliphate of one day, to send a *douceur* of one thousand pieces of gold to his own household;*and the Scottish vicegerents, raised to power by the strength of their faction, failed not to embrace the same means of rewarding them.

The administration of justice, in particular, was infected by the most gross partiality. A case of importance scarcely occurred, in which there was not some ground for bias or partiality on the part of the judges, who were so little able to withstand the temptation, that the adage, 'Show me the man, and I will show you the law,'* became as prevalent as it was scandalous. One corruption led the way to others still more gross and profligate. The judge who lent his sacred authority in one case to support a friend, and in another to crush an enemy, and whose decisions were founded on family connexions, or political relations, could not be supposed inaccessible to direct personal motives; and the purse of the wealthy was too often believed to be thrown into the scale to weigh down the cause of the poor litigant. The subordinate officers of the law affected little scruple concerning bribery. Pieces of plate, and bags of money, were sent in presents to the king's counsel, to influence their conduct, and poured forth, says a contemporary writer, like billets of wood upon their floors, without even the decency of concealment.*

In such times, it was not over uncharitable to suppose, that the statesman, practised in courts of law, and a powerful member of a triumphant cabal, might find and use means of advantage over his less skilful and less favoured adversary; and if it had been supposed that Sir William Ashton's conscience had been too delicate to profit by these advantages, it was believed that his ambition and desire of extending his wealth and consequence, found as strong a stimulus in the exhortations of his lady, as the daring aim of Macbeth in the days of yore.*

Lady Ashton was of a family more distinguished than that of her lord, an advantage which she did not fail to use to the uttermost, in maintaining and extending her husband's influence over others, and, unless she was greatly belied, her own over him. She had been beautiful, and was stately and majestic in her appearance. Endowed by nature with strong powers and violent passions, experience had taught her to employ the one, and to conceal, if not to moderate, the other. She was a severe and strict observer of the external forms, at least, of devotion;* her hospitality was splendid, even to ostentation; her address and manners, agreeable to the pattern most valued in Scotland at the period, were grave, dignified, and severely regulated by the rules of etiquette. Her character had always been beyond the breath of slander. And yet, with all these qualities to excite respect, Lady Ashton was seldom mentioned in the terms of love or affection. Interest,—the interest of her family, if not her own,—seemed too obviously the motive of her actions; and where this is the case, the sharp-judging and malignant public are not easily imposed upon by outward show. It was seen and ascertained, that, in her most graceful courtesies and compliments, Lady Ashton no more lost sight of her object than the falcon in his airy wheel turns his quick eyes from his destined quarry; and hence, something of doubt and suspicion qualified the feelings with which her equals received her attentions. With her inferiors these feelings were mingled with fear; an impression useful to her purposes, so far as it enforced ready compliance with her requests, and implicit obedience to her commands, but detrimental, because it cannot exist with affection or regard.

Even her husband, it is said, upon whose fortunes her talents and address had produced such emphatic influence, regarded her with respectful awe rather than confiding attachment; and report said, there were times when he considered his grandeur as dearly purchased at the expense of domestic thraldom. Of this, however, much might be suspected, but little could be accurately known; Lady Ashton regarded the honour of her husband as her own, and was well aware how much that would suffer in the public eye should he appear a vassal to his wife. In all her arguments, his opinion was quoted as infallible; his taste was appealed to, and his sentiments received, with the air of deference which a dutiful wife might seem to owe to a husband of Sir William Ashton's rank and character. But there was something under all this which rung false and hollow; and to those who watched this couple with close, and perhaps malicious scrutiny, it seemed evident, that, in the haughtiness of a firmer character, higher birth, and more decided views of aggrandizement, the lady looked with some contempt on her husband, and that he regarded her with jealous fear, rather than with love or admiration.

Still, however, the leading and favourite interests of Sir William Ashton and his lady were the same, and they failed not to work in concert, although without cordiality, and to testify, in all exterior circumstances, that respect for each other, which they were aware was necessary to secure that of the public.

Their union was crowned with several children, of whom three survived. One, the eldest son, was absent on his travels; the second, a girl of seventeen, and the third, a boy about three years younger, resided with their parents in Edinburgh, during the sessions of the Scottish Parliament and Privy-council, at other times in the old Gothic castle of Ravenswood, to which the Lord Keeper had made large additions in the style of the seventeenth century.*

Allan Lord Ravenswood, the late proprietor of that ancient mansion and the large estate annexed to it, continued for some time to wage ineffectual war with his successor concerning various points to which their former transactions had given rise, and which were successively determined in favour of the wealthy and power-ful competitor, until death closed the litigation, by summoning Ravenswood to a higher bar. The thread of life, which had been long wasting, gave way during a fit of violent and impotent fury, with which he was assailed on receiving the news of the loss of a cause, founded, perhaps, rather in equity than in law,* the last which he had maintained against his powerful antagonist. His son witnessed his dying agonies, and heard the curses which he breathed against his adversary, as if they had conveyed to him a legacy of vengeance. Other circumstances happened to exasperate a passion, which was, and had long been, a prevalent vice in the Scottish disposition.

It was a November morning, and the cliffs which overlooked the ocean were hung with thick and heavy mist, when the portals of the ancient and half-ruinous tower, in which Lord Ravenswood had spent the last and troubled years of his life, opened, that his mortal remains might pass forward to an abode yet more dreary and lonely. The pomp of attendance, to which the deceased had, in his latter years, been a stranger, was revived as he was about to be consigned to the realms of forgetfulness.

Banner after banner, with the various devices and coats of this ancient family and its connexions, followed each other in mourn-ful procession from under the low-browed archway of the court-yard. The principal gentry of the country attended in the deepest mourning, and tempered the pace of their long train of horses to the solemn march befitting the occasion. Trumpets, with banners of crape attached to them, sent forth their long and melancholy notes to regulate the movements of the procession. An immense train of inferior mourners and menials closed the rear, which had not yet issued from the castle-gate, when the van had reached the chapel where the body was to be deposited.

Contrary to the custom, and even to the law of the time, the body was met by a priest of the Scottish Episcopal communion, arrayed in his surplice, and prepared to read over the coffin of the deceased the funeral service of the church.* Such had been the desire of Lord Ravenswood in his last illness, and it was readily complied with by the tory gentlemen, or cavaliers, as they affected to style themselves, in which faction most of his kinsmen were enrolled.* The presbyterian church-judicatory of the bounds, considering the ceremony as a bravading insult upon their authority, had applied to the Lord Keeper, as the nearest privy-councillor, for a warrant to prevent its being carried into effect;* so that, when the clergyman had opened his prayer-book, an officer of the law, supported by some armed men, commanded him to be silent. An insult, which fired the whole assembly with indignation, was particularly and instantly resented by the only son of the deceased, Edgar, popularly called the Master of Ravenswood,* a youth of about twenty years of age. He clapped his hand on his sword, and, bidding the official person to desist at his peril from farther interruption, commanded the clergyman to proceed. The man attempted to enforce his commission, but as an hundred swords at once glittered in the air, he contented himself with protesting against the violence which had been offered to him in the execution of his duty, and stood aloof, a sullen and moody spectator of the ceremonial, muttering as one who should say, 'You'll rue the day that clogs me with this answer.'*

The scene was worthy of an artist's pencil. Under the very arch of the house of death, the clergyman, affrighted at the scene, and trembling for his own safety, hastily and unwillingly rehearsed the solemn service of the church, and spoke dust to dust, and ashes to ashes, over ruined pride and decayed prosperity. Around stood the relations of the deceased, their countenances more in anger than in sorrow,* and the drawn swords which they brandished forming a violent contrast with their deep mourning habits. In the countenance of the young man alone, resentment seemed for the moment overpowered by the deep agony with which he beheld his nearest, and almost his only friend, consigned to the tomb of his ancestry. A relative observed him turn deadly pale, when, all rites being now duly observed, it became the duty of the chief mourner to lower down into the charnel vault, where mouldering coffins showed their tattered velvet and decayed plating, the head of the corpse which was to be their partner in corruption. He stept to the youth and offered his assistance, which, by a mute motion, Edgar Ravenswood rejected. Firmly, and without a tear, he performed that last duty. The stone was laid on the sepulchre, the door of the aisle was locked, and the youth took possession of its massive key.

As the crowd left the chapel, he paused on the steps which led to its Gothic chancel. 'Gentlemen and friends,' he said, 'you have this day done no common duty to the body of your deceased kinsman. The rites of due observance, which, in other countries, are allowed as the due of the meanest Christian, would this day have been denied to the body of your relative—not certainly sprung of the meanest house in Scotland—had it not been assured to him by your courage. Others bury their dead in sorrow and tears, in silence and in reverence; our funeral rites are marred by the intrusion of bailiffs and ruffians, and our grief—the grief due to our departed friend—is chased from our cheeks by the glow of just indignation. But it is well that I know from what quiver this arrow has come forth. It was only he that dug the grave who could have the mean cruelty to disturb the obsequies; and Heaven do as much to me and more, if I requite not to this man and his house the ruin and disgrace he has brought on me and mine!'

A numerous part of the assembly applauded this speech, as the spirited expression of just resentment; but the more cool and judicious regretted that it had been uttered. The fortunes of the heir of Ravenswood were too low to brave the farther hostility which they imagined these open expressions of resentment must necessarily provoke. Their apprehensions, however, proved groundless, at least in the immediate consequences of this affair.

The mourners returned to the tower, there, according to a custom but recently abolished in Scotland, to carouse deep healths to the memory of the deceased, to make the house of sorrow ring with sounds of jovialty and debauch, and to diminish, by the expense of a large and profuse entertainment, the limited revenues of the heir of him whose funeral they thus strangely honoured.* It was the custom, however, and on the present occasion it was fully observed. The tables swam in wine, the populace feasted in the court-yard, the yeomen in the kitchen and buttery; and two years' rent of Ravenswood's remaining property hardly defrayed the charge of the funeral revel. The wine did its office on all but the Master of Ravenswood, a title which he still retained, though forfeiture had attached to that of his father.* He, while passing around the cup which he himself did not taste, soon listened to a thousand exclamations against the Lord Keeper, and passionate protestations of attachment to himself, and to the honour of his house. He listened with dark and sullen brow to ebullitions which he considered justly as equally evanescent with the crimson bubbles on the brink of the goblet, or at least with the vapours which its contents excited in the brains of the revellers around him.

When the last flask was emptied, they took their leave, with deep protestations—to be forgotten on the morrow, if, indeed, those who made them should not think it necessary for their safety to make a more solemn retractation.

Accepting their adieus with an air of contempt which he could scarce conceal, Ravenswood at length beheld his ruinous habitation cleared of this confluence of riotous guests, and returned to the deserted hall, which now appeared doubly lonely from the cessation of that clamour to which it had so lately echoed. But its space was peopled by phantoms, which the imagination of the young heir conjured up before him—the tarnished honour and degraded fortunes of his house, the destruction of his own hopes, and the triumph of that family by whom they had been ruined. To a mind naturally of a gloomy cast, here was ample room for meditation, and the musings of young Ravenswood were deep and unwitnessed.

The peasant, who shows the ruins of the tower, which still crown the beetling cliff and behold the war of the waves, though no more tenanted save by the sea-mew and cormorant, even yet affirms, that on this fatal night the Master of Ravenswood, by the bitter exclamations of his despair, evoked some evil fiend, under whose malignant influence the future tissue of incidents was woven. Alas! what fiend can suggest more desperate counsels, than those adopted under the guidance of our own violent and unresisted passions?

CHAPTER III

Over Gods forebode, then said the King,
That thou shouldst shoot at me.

(*William Bell, Clim o' the Cleugh*, &c.) *

ON the morning after the funeral, the legal officer, whose authority had been found insufficient to effect an interruption of the funeral solemnities of the late Lord Ravenswood, hastened to state before the Keeper the resistance which he had met with in the execution of his office.

The statesman was seated in a spacious library, once a banqueting-room in the old Castle of Ravenswood, as was evident from the armorial insignia still displayed on the carved roof, which was vaulted with Spanish chestnut, and on the stained glass of the casement, through which gleamed a dim yet rich light, on the long rows of shelves, bending under the weight of legal commentators and monkish historians, whose ponderous volumes formed the chief and most valued contents of a Scottish historian of the period. * On the massive oaken table and reading-desk, lay a confused mass of letters, petitions, and parchments; to toil amongst which was the pleasure at once and the plague of Sir William Ashton's life. His appearance was grave and even noble, well becoming one who held an high office in the state; and it was not, save after long and intimate conversation with him upon topics of pressing and personal interest, that a stranger could have discovered something vacillating and uncertain in his resolutions; an infirmity of purpose, arising from a cautious and timid disposition, which, as he was conscious of its internal influence on his mind, he was, from pride as well as policy, most anxious to conceal from others.

He listened with great apparent composure to an exaggerated account of the tumult which had taken place at the funeral, of the contempt thrown on his own authority, and that of the church and state; nor did he seem moved even by the faithful report of the insulting and threatening language which had been uttered by young Ravenswood and others, and obviously directed against himself. He heard, also, what the man had been able to collect, in a very distorted and aggravated shape, of the toasts which had been drunk, and the menaces uttered, at the subsequent entertainment. In fine, he made careful notes of all these particulars, and of the names of the persons by whom, in case of need, an accusation, founded upon these violent proceedings, could be witnessed and made good, and dismissed his informer, secure that he was now master of the remaining fortune, and even of the personal liberty, of young Ravenswood.

When the door had closed upon the officer of the law, the Lord Keeper remained for a moment in deep meditation; then, starting from his seat, paced the apartment as one about to take a sudden and energetic resolution. 'Young Ravenswood,' he muttered, 'is now mine—he is my own—he has placed himself in my hand, and he shall bend or break. I have not forgot the determined and dogged obstinacy with which his father fought every point to the last, resisted every effort at compromise, embroiled me in lawsuits, and attempted to assail my character when he could not otherwise impugn my rights. This boy he has left behind him—this Edgar—this hot-headed, hare-brained fool, has wrecked his vessel before she has cleared the harbour. I must see that he gains no advantage of some turning tide which may again float him off. These memoranda, properly stated to the Privy Council, cannot but be construed into an aggravated riot, in which the dignity both of the civil and ecclesiastical authorities stand committed. * A heavy fine might be imposed; an order for committing him to Edinburgh or Blackness Castle seems not improper; even a charge of treason might be laid on many of these words and expressions, though God forbid I should prosecute the matter to that extent. * No, I will not;—I will not touch his life, even if it should be in my power;—and yet, if he lives till a change of times, what follows?— Restitution—perhaps revenge. I know Athole promised his interest to old Ravenswood, and here is his son already bandying and making a faction by his own contemptible influence. * What a ready tool he would be for the use of those who are watching the downfall of our administration!'

While these thoughts were agitating the mind of the wily statesman, and while he was persuading himself that his own interest and safety, as well as those of his friends and party, depended on using the present advantage to the uttermost against young Ravenswood, the Lord Keeper sate down to his desk, and proceeded to draw up, for the information of the Privy Council, an account of the disorderly proceedings which, in contempt of his warrant, had taken place at the funeral of Lord Ravenswood. The names of most of the parties concerned, as well as the fact itself, would, he was well aware, sound odiously in the ears of his colleagues in administration, and most likely instigate them to make an example of young Ravenswood, at least, *in terrorem.* *

It was a point of delicacy, however, to select such expressions as might infer the young man's culpability, without seeming directly to urge it, which, on the part of Sir William Ashton, his father's ancient antagonist, could not but appear odious and invidious. While he was in the act of composition, labouring to find words which might indicate Edgar Ravenswood to be the cause of the uproar, without specifically making such a charge, Sir William, in a pause of his task, chanced, in looking upward, to see the crest of the family, (for whose heir he was whetting the arrows, and disposing the toils of the law,) carved upon one of the corbeilles from which the vaulted roof of the apartment sprung. It was a black bull's head, with the legend, 'I bide my time;' * and the occasion upon which it was adopted mingled itself singularly and impressively with the subject of his present reflections.

It was said by a constant tradition, that a Malisius de Ravenswood had, in the thirteenth century, been deprived of his castle and lands by a powerful usurper, who had for a while enjoyed his spoils in quiet. At length, on the eve of a costly banquet, Ravenswood, who had watched his opportunity, introduced himself into the castle with a small band of faithful retainers. The serving of the expected feast was impatiently looked for by the guests, and clamorously demanded by the temporary master of the castle. Ravenswood, who had assumed the disguise of a sewer upon the occasion, answered, in a stern voice, 'I bide my time;' and at the same moment a bull's head, the ancient symbol of death, was placed upon the table.* The explosion of the conspiracy took place upon the signal, and the usurper and his followers were put to death. Perhaps there was something in this still known and often repeated story, which came immediately home to the breast and conscience of the Lord Keeper; for, putting from him the paper on which he had begun his report, and carefully locking the memoranda which he had prepared, into a cabinet which stood beside him, he proceeded to walk abroad, as if for the purpose of collecting his ideas, and reflecting farther on the consequences of the step which he was about to take, ere yet they became inevitable.

In passing through a large Gothic anteroom, Sir William Ashton heard the sound of his daughter's lute. Music, when the performers are concealed, affects us with a pleasure mingled with surprise, and reminds us of the natural concert of birds among the leafy bowers. The statesman, though little accustomed to give way to emotions of this natural and simple class, was still a man and a father. He stopped, therefore, and listened, while the silver tones of Lucy Ashton's voice mingled with the accompaniment in an ancient air, to which some one had adapted the following words:—

> 'Look not thou on beauty's charming,—
> Sit thou still when kings are arming,—
> Taste not when the wine-cup glistens,—
> Speak not when the people listens,—
> Stop thine ear against the singer,—
> From the red gold keep thy finger,—
> Vacant heart, and hand, and eye,—
> Easy live and quiet die.'

The sounds ceased, and the Keeper entered his daughter's apartment.

The words she had chosen seemed particularly adapted to her character; for Lucy Ashton's exquisitely beautiful, yet somewhat girlish features, were formed to express peace of mind, serenity, and indifference to the tinsel of worldly pleasure. Her locks, which were of shadowy gold, divided on a brow of exquisite whiteness, like a gleam of broken and pallid sunshine upon a hill of snow. The expression of the countenance was in the last degree gentle, soft, timid, and feminine, and seemed rather to shrink from the most casual look of a stranger, than to court his admiration. Something there was of a Madonna cast, perhaps the result of delicate health, and of residence in a family, where the dispositions of the inmates were fiercer, more active, and energetic, than her own.

Yet her passiveness of disposition was by no means owing to an indifferent or unfeeling mind. Left to the impulse of her own taste and feelings, Lucy Ashton was peculiarly accessible to those of a romantic cast. Her secret delight was in the old legendary tales of ardent devotion and unalterable affection, chequered as they so often are with strange adventures and supernatural horrors. This was her favoured fairy realm, and here she erected her aerial palaces. But it was only in secret that she laboured at this delusive, though delightful architecture. In her retired chamber, or in the woodland bower which she had chosen for her own, and called after her name, she was in fancy distributing the prizes at the tournament, or raining down influence from her eyes on the valiant combatants; or she was wandering in the wilderness with Una, under escort of the generous lion; or she was identifying herself with the simple, yet noble-minded Miranda, in the isle of wonder and enchantment. *

But in her exterior relations to things of this world, Lucy willingly received the ruling impulse from those around her. The alternative was, in general, too indifferent to her to render resistance desirable, and she willingly found a motive for decision in the opinion of her friends, which perhaps she might have sought for in vain in her own choice. Every reader must have observed in some family of his acquaintance, some individual of a temper soft and yielding, who, mixed with stronger and more ardent minds, is borne along by the will of others, with as little power of opposition as the flower which is flung into a running stream. It usually happens that such a compliant and easy disposition, which resigns itself without murmur to the guidance of others, becomes the darling of those to whose inclinations its own seem to be offered, in ungrudging and ready sacrifice.

This was eminently the case with Lucy Ashton. Her politic, wary, and worldly father, felt for her an affection, the strength of which sometimes surprised him into an unusual emotion. Her elder brother, who trode the path of ambition with a haughtier step than his father, had also more of human affection. A soldier, and in a dissolute age, he preferred his sister Lucy even to pleasure, and to military preferment and distinction. Her younger brother, at an age when trifles chiefly occupied his mind, made her the confident of all his pleasures and anxieties, his success in field-sports, and his quarrels with his tutor and instructors. To these details, however trivial, Lucy lent patient and not indifferent attention. They moved and interested Henry, and that was enough to secure her ear.

Her mother alone did not feel that distinguished and predominating affection, with which the rest of the family cherished Lucy. She regarded what she termed her daughter's want of spirit, as a decided mark, that the more plebeian blood of her father predominated in Lucy's veins, and used to call her in derision her Lammermoor Shepherdess. To dislike so gentle and inoffensive a being was impossible; but Lady Ashton preferred her eldest son, on whom had descended a large portion of her own ambitious and undaunted disposition, to a daughter whose softness of temper seemed allied to feebleness of mind. Her eldest son was the more partially beloved by his mother, because, contrary to the usual custom of Scottish families of distinction, he had been named after the head of the house.*

'My Sholto,' she said, 'will support the untarnished honour of his maternal house, and elevate and support that of his father. Poor Lucy is unfit for courts, or crowded halls. Some country laird must be her husband, rich enough to supply her with every comfort, without an effort on her own part, so that she may have nothing to shed a tear for but the tender apprehension lest he may break his neck in a fox-chase. It was not so, however, that our house was raised, nor is it so that it can be fortified and augmented. The Lord Keeper's dignity is yet new; it must be borne as if we were used to its weight, worthy of it, and prompt to assert and maintain it. Before ancient authorities, men bend, from customary and hereditary deference; in our presence, they will stand erect, unless they are compelled to prostrate themselves. A daughter fit for the sheep-fold or the cloister, is ill qualified to exact respect where it is yielded with reluctance; and since Heaven refused us a third boy, Lucy should have held a character fit to supply his place. The hour will be a happy one which disposes her hand in marriage to some one whose energy is greater than her own, or whose ambition is of as low an order.'

So meditated a mother, to whom the qualities of her children's hearts, as well as the prospect of their domestic happiness, seemed light in comparison to their rank and temporal greatness. But, like many a parent of hot and impatient character, she was mistaken in estimating the feelings of her daughter, who, under a semblance of extreme indifference, nourished the germ of those passions which sometimes spring up in one night, like the gourd of the prophet,* and astonish the observer by their unexpected ardour and intensity. In fact, Lucy's sentiments seemed chill, because nothing had occurred to interest or awaken them. Her life had hitherto flowed on in a uniform and gentle tenor, and happy for her had not its present smoothness of current resembled that of the stream as it glides downwards to the waterfall!

'So, Lucy,' said her father, entering as her song was ended, 'does your musical philosopher teach you to contemn the world before you know it?—that is surely something premature. Or did you but speak according to the fashion of fair maidens, who are always to hold the pleasures of life in contempt till they are pressed upon them by the address of some gentle knight?'

Lucy blushed, disclaimed any inference respecting her own choice being drawn from her selection of a song, and readily laid aside her instrument at her father's request that she would attend him in his walk.

A large and well-wooded park, or rather chase, stretched along the hill behind the castle, which occupying, as we have noticed, a pass ascending from the plain, seemed built in its very gorge to defend the forest ground which arose behind it in shaggy majesty. Into this romantic region the father and daughter proceeded, arm in arm, by a noble avenue overarched by embowering elms, beneath which groups of the fallow-deer were seen to stray in distant perspective. As they paced slowly on, admiring the differ-

ent points of view, for which Sir William Ashton, notwithstanding the nature of his usual avocations, had considerable taste and
feeling, they were overtaken by the forester, or park-keeper, who,
intent on silvan sport, was proceeding with his cross-bow over his
arm, and a hound led in leash by his boy, into the interior of the
wood.

'Going to shoot us a piece of venison, Norman?' said his master,
as he returned the woodman's salutation.

'Saul, your honour, and that I am. Will it please you to see the
sport?'

'O no,' said his lordship, after looking at his daughter, whose
colour fled at the idea of seeing the deer shot, although had her
father expressed his wish that they should accompany Norman, it
was probable she would not even have hinted her reluctance.

The forester shrugged his shoulders. 'It was a disheartening
thing,' he said, 'when none of the gentles came down to see the
sport. He hoped Captain Sholto would be soon hame, or he might
shut up his shop entirely; for Mr Harry was kept sae close wi' his
Latin nonsense, that, though his will was very gude to be in the
wood from morning till night, there would be a hopeful lad lost,
and no making a man of him. It was not so, he had heard, in Lord
Ravenswood's time—when a buck was to be killed, man and
mother's son ran to see; and when the deer fell, the knife was
always presented to the knight, and he never gave less than a dollar
for the compliment. And there was Edgar Ravenswood—Master
of Ravenswood that is now—when he goes up to the wood—
there hasna been a better hunter since Tristrem's time—when Sir
Edgar hauds out,[7] down goes the deer, faith.* But we hae lost a'
sense of wood-craft on this side of the hill.'

There was much in this harangue highly displeasing to the Lord
Keeper's feelings; he could not help observing that his menial
despised him almost avowedly for not possessing that taste for
sport, which in those times was deemed the natural and indispensable attribute of a real gentleman. But the master of the game is,
in all country houses, a man of great importance, and entitled to
use considerable freedom of speech. Sir William, therefore, only
smiled and replied, he had something else to think upon to-day
than killing deer; meantime, taking out his purse, he gave the

ranger a dollar for his encouragement. The fellow received it as the waiter of a fashionable hotel receives double his proper fee from the hands of a country gentleman,—that is, with a smile, in which pleasure at the gift is mingled with contempt for the ignorance of the donor. 'Your honour is the bad paymaster,' he said, 'who pays before it is done.* What would you do were I to miss the buck after you have paid me my wood-fee?'

'I suppose,' said the Keeper, smiling, 'you would hardly guess what I mean were I to tell you of a *conditio indebiti?*' *

'Not I, on my saul—I guess it is some law phrase—but sue a beggar, and—your honour knows what follows.*—Well, but I will be just with you, and if bow and brach fail not, you shall have a piece of game two fingers fat on the brisket.'

As he was about to go off, his master again called him, and asked, as if by accident, whether the Master of Ravenswood was actually so brave a man and so good a shooter as the world spoke him?

'Brave!—brave enough, I warrant you,' answered Norman; 'I was in the wood at Tyninghame,* when there was a sort of gallants hunting with my lord; on my saul, there was a buck turned to bay made us all stand back; a stout old Trojan of the first head, ten-tyned branches, and a brow as broad as e'er a bullock's. Egad, he dashed at the old lord, and there would have been inlake among the peerage, if the Master had not whipt roundly in, and ham-strung him with his cutlass. He was but sixteen then, bless his heart!'

'And is he as ready with the gun as with the couteau?' said Sir William.

'He'll strike this silver dollar out from between my finger and thumb at fourscore yards, and I'll hold it out for a gold merk; what more would ye have of eye, hand, lead, and gunpowder?'

'O no more to be wished, certainly,' said the Lord Keeper; 'but we keep you from your sport, Norman. Good morrow, good Norman.'

And humming his rustic roundelay, the yeoman went on his road, the sound of his rough voice gradually dying away as the distance betwixt them increased:—

The monk must arise when the matins ring,
  The abbot may sleep to their chime;
But the yeoman must start when the bugles sing,
  'Tis time, my hearts, 'tis time.

There's bucks and raes on Bilhope braes,
  There's a herd on Shortwood Shaw;
But a lily-white doe in the garden goes,
  She's fairly worth them a'.*

'Has this fellow,' said the Lord Keeper, when the yeoman's song had died on the wind, 'ever served the Ravenswood people, that he seems so much interested in them? I suppose you know, Lucy, for you make it a point of conscience to record the special history of every boor about the castle.'

'I am not quite so faithful a chronicler, my dear father; but I believe that Norman once served here while a boy, and before he went to Ledington, whence you hired him. But if you want to know any thing of the former family, Old Alice is the best authority.'

'And what should I have to do with them, pray, Lucy,' said her father, 'or with their history or accomplishments?'

'Nay, I do not know, sir; only that you were asking questions of Norman about young Ravenswood.'

'Pshaw, child!' replied her father, yet immediately added, 'And who is old Alice? I think you know all the old women in the country.'

'To be sure I do, or how could I help the old creatures when they are in hard times? And as to old Alice, she is the very empress of old women, and queen of gossips, so far as legendary lore is concerned. She is blind, poor old soul, but when she speaks to you, you would think she has some way of looking into your very heart. I am sure I often cover my face, or turn it away, for it seems as if she saw one change colour, though she has been blind these twenty years. She is worth visiting, were it but to say you have seen a blind and paralytic old woman have so much acuteness of perception, and dignity of manners. I assure you, she might be a countess from her language and behaviour.—Come, you must go to see Alice; we are not a quarter of a mile from her cottage.'

'All this, my dear,' said the Lord Keeper, 'is no answer to my question, who this woman is, and what is her connexion with the former proprietor's family?'

'O, it was something of a nourice-ship, I believe; and she remained here, because her two grandsons were engaged in your service. But it was against her will, I fancy; for the poor old creature is always regretting the change of times and of property.'

'I am much obliged to her,' answered the Lord Keeper. 'She and her folk eat my bread and drink my cup, and are lamenting all the while that they are not still under a family which never could do good, either to themselves or any one else!'

'Indeed,' replied Lucy, 'I am certain you do old Alice injustice. She has nothing mercenary about her, and would not accept a penny in charity, if it were to save her from being starved. She is only talkative, like all old folk, when you put them upon stories of their youth; and she speaks about the Ravenswood people, because she lived under them so many years. But I am sure she is grateful to you, sir, for your protection, and that she would rather speak to you, than to any other person in the whole world beside. Do, sir, come and see old Alice.'

And with the freedom of an indulged daughter, she dragged the Lord Keeper in the direction she desired.

CHAPTER IV

Through tops of the high trees she did descry
A little smoke, whose vapour, thin, and light,
Reeking aloft, uprolled to the sky,
Which cheerful sign did send unto her sight,
That in the same did wonne some living wight.

(Spenser)*

LUCY acted as her father's guide, for he was too much engrossed
with his political labours, or with society, to be perfectly acquainted with his own extensive domains, and, moreover, was
generally an inhabitant of the city of Edinburgh; and she, on the
other hand, had, with her mother, resided the whole summer in
Ravenswood, and, partly from taste, partly from want of any other
amusement, had, by her frequent rambles, learned to know each
lane, alley, dingle, or bushy dell,

'And every bosky bourne from side to side.'*

We have said that the Lord Keeper was not indifferent to the
beauties of nature; and we add, in justice to him, that he felt them
doubly, when pointed out by the beautiful, simple, and interesting
girl, who, hanging on his arm with filial kindness, now called him
to admire the size of some ancient oak, and now the unexpected
turn, where the path developing its maze from glen or dingle,
suddenly reached an eminence commanding an extensive view of
the plains beneath them, and then gradually glided away from the
prospect to lose itself among rocks and thickets, and guide to
scenes of deeper seclusion.

It was when pausing on one of those points of extensive and
commanding view, that Lucy told her father they were close by
the cottage of her blind protégée; and on turning from the little
hill, a path which led around it, worn by the daily steps of the
infirm inmate, brought them in sight of the hut, which, embo-
somed in a deep and obscure dell, seemed to have been so situated

purposely to bear a correspondence with the darkened state of its inhabitant.

The cottage was situated immediately under a tall rock, which in some measure beetled over it, as if threatening to drop some detached fragment from its brow on the frail tenement beneath. The hut itself was constructed of turf and stones, and rudely roofed over with thatch, much of which was in a dilapidated condition. The thin blue smoke rose from it in a light column, and curled upward along the white face of the incumbent rock, giving the scene a tint of exquisite softness. In a small and rude garden, surrounded by straggling elder-bushes, which formed a sort of imperfect hedge, sat near to the bee-hives, by the produce of which she lived, that 'woman old,'* whom Lucy had brought her father hither to visit.

Whatever there had been which was disastrous in her fortune— whatever there was miserable in her dwelling, it was easy to judge, by the first glance, that neither years, poverty, misfortune, nor infirmity, had broken the spirit of this remarkable woman.

She occupied a turf-seat, placed under a weeping birch of unusual magnitude and age, as Judah is represented sitting under her palm-tree,* with an air at once of majesty and of dejection. Her figure was tall, commanding, and but little bent by the infirmities of old age. Her dress, though that of a peasant, was uncommonly clean, forming in that particular a strong contrast to most of her rank, and was disposed with an attention to neatness, and even to taste, equally unusual. But it was her expression of countenance which chiefly struck the spectator, and induced most persons to address her with a degree of deference and civility very inconsistent with the miserable state of her dwelling, and which, nevertheless, she received with that easy composure which showed she felt it to be her due. She had once been beautiful, but her beauty had been of a bold and masculine cast, such as does not survive the bloom of youth; yet her features continued to express strong sense, deep reflection, and a character of sober pride, which, as we have already said of her dress, appeared to argue a conscious superiority to those of her own rank. It scarce seemed possible that a face, deprived of the advantage of sight, could have expressed character so strongly; but her eyes, which were almost totally closed, did not, by the display of their sightless orbs, mar the countenance to which they could add nothing. She seemed in a ruminating posture, soothed, perhaps, by the murmurs of the busy tribe around her, to abstraction, though not to slumber.

Lucy undid the latch of the little garden gate, and solicited the old woman's attention. 'My father, Alice, is come to see you.'

'He is welcome, Miss Ashton, and so are you,' said the old woman, turning and inclining her head towards her visitors.

'This is a fine morning for your bee-hives, mother,' said the Lord Keeper, who, struck with the outward appearance of Alice, was somewhat curious to know if her conversation would correspond with it.

'I believe so, my lord,' she replied; 'I feel the air breathe milder than of late.'

'You do not,' resumed the statesman, 'take charge of these bees yourself, mother?—How do you manage them?'

'By delegates, as kings do their subjects,' resumed Alice; 'and I am fortunate in a prime minister—Here, Babie.'

She whistled on a small silver call which hung around her neck, and which at that time was sometimes used to summon domestics, and Babie, a girl of fifteen, made her appearance from the hut, not altogether so cleanly arrayed as she would probably have been had Alice had the use of her eyes, but with a greater air of neatness than was upon the whole to have been expected.

'Babie,' said her mistress, 'offer some bread and honey to the Lord Keeper and Miss Ashton—they will excuse your awkwardness, if you use cleanliness and dispatch.'

Babie performed her mistress's command with the grace which was naturally to have been expected, moving to and fro with a lobster-like gesture, her feet and legs tending one way, while her head, turned in a different direction, was fixed in wonder upon the laird, who was more frequently heard of than seen by his tenants and dependants. The bread and honey, however, deposited on a plantain leaf, was offered and accepted in all due courtesy. The Lord Keeper, still retaining the place which he had occupied on the decayed trunk of a fallen tree, looked as if he wished to prolong the interview, but was at a loss how to introduce a suitable subject.

'You have been long a resident on this property?' he said, after a pause.

'It is now nearly sixty years since I first knew Ravenswood,' answered the old dame, whose conversation, though perfectly civil and respectful, seemed cautiously limited to the unavoidable and necessary task of replying to Sir William.

'You are not, I should judge by your accent, of this country originally?' said the Lord Keeper, in continuation.

'No; I am by birth an Englishwoman.'

'Yet you seem attached to this country as if it were your own.'

'It is here,' replied the blind woman, 'that I have drank the cup of joy and of sorrow which Heaven destined for me.* I was here the wife of an upright and affectionate husband for more than twenty years—I was here the mother of six promising children— it was here that God deprived me of all these blessings—it was here they died, and yonder, by yon ruined chapel, they lie all buried—I had no country but theirs while they lived—I have none but theirs now they are no more.'

'But your house,' said the Lord Keeper, looking at it, 'is miserably ruinous?'

'Do, my dear father,' said Lucy, eagerly, yet bashfully, catching at the hint, 'give orders to make it better,—that is, if you think it proper.'

'It will last my time, my dear Miss Lucy,' said the blind woman; 'I would not have my lord give himself the least trouble about it.'

'But,' said Lucy, 'you once had a much better house, and were rich, and now in your old age to live in this hovel!'

'It is as good as I deserve, Miss Lucy; if my heart has not broke with what I have suffered, and seen others suffer, it must have been strong enough, and the rest of this old frame has no right to call itself weaker.'

'You have probably witnessed many changes,' said the Lord Keeper; 'but your experience must have taught you to expect them.'

'It has taught me to endure them, my lord,' was the reply.

'Yet you knew that they must needs arrive in the course of years?' said the statesman.

'Ay; as I know that the stump, on or beside which you sit, once a tall and lofty tree, must needs one day fall by decay, or by the axe; yet I hoped my eyes might not witness the downfall of the tree which overshadowed my dwelling.'*

'Do not suppose,' said the Lord Keeper, 'that you will lose any interest with me, for looking back with regret to the days when another family possessed my estates. You had reason, doubtless, to love them, and I respect your gratitude. I will order some repairs in your cottage, and I hope we shall live to be friends when we know each other better.'

'Those of my age,' returned the dame, 'make no new friends. I thank you for your bounty—it is well intended undoubtedly; but I have all I want, and I cannot accept more at your lordship's hands.'

'Well, then,' continued the Lord Keeper, 'at least allow me to say, that I look upon you as a woman of sense and education beyond your appearance, and that I hope you will continue to reside on this property of mine rent-free for your life.'

'I hope I shall,' said the old dame, composedly; 'I believe that was made an article in the sale of Ravenswood to your lordship, though such a trifling circumstance may have escaped your recollection.'

'I remember—I recollect,' said his lordship, somewhat confused. 'I perceive you are too much attached to your old friends to accept any benefit from their successor.'

'Far from it, my lord; I am grateful for the benefits which I decline, and I wish I could pay you for offering them, better than what I am now about to say.' The Lord Keeper looked at her in some surprise, but said not a word. 'My lord,' she continued, in an impressive and solemn tone, 'take care what you do; you are on the brink of a precipice.'

'Indeed?' said the Lord Keeper, his mind reverting to the political circumstances of the country. 'Has any thing come to your knowledge—any plot or conspiracy?'

'No, my lord; those who traffic in such commodities do not call into their councils the old, blind, and infirm. My warning is of another kind. You have driven matters hard with the house of

Ravenswood. Believe a true tale—they are a fierce house, and there is danger in dealing with men when they become desperate.'

'Tush,' answered the Keeper; 'what has been between us has been the work of the law, not my doing; and to the law they must look, if they would impugn my proceedings.'

'Ay, but they may think otherwise, and take the law into their own hand, when they fail of other means of redress.'

'What mean you?' said the Lord Keeper. 'Young Ravenswood would not have recourse to personal violence?'

'God forbid I should say so! I know nothing of the youth but what is honourable and open—honourable and open, said I?—I should have added, free, generous, noble. But he is still a Ravenswood, and may bide his time. Remember the fate of Sir George Lockhart.'[8]*

The Lord Keeper started as she called to his recollection a tragedy so deep and so recent. The old woman proceeded: 'Chiesley, who did the deed, was a relative of Lord Ravenswood. In the hall of Ravenswood, in my presence, and in that of others, he avowed publicly his determination to do the cruelty which he afterwards committed. I could not keep silence, though to speak it ill became my station. "You are devising a dreadful crime," I said, "for which you must reckon before the judgement-seat." Never shall I forget his look, as he replied, "I must reckon then for many things, and will reckon for this also." Therefore I may well say, beware of pressing a desperate man with the hand of authority. There is blood of Chiesley in the veins of Ravenswood, and one drop of it were enough to fire him in the circumstances in which he is placed—I say, beware of him.'

The old dame had, either intentionally or by accident, harped aright the fear of the Lord Keeper. The desperate and dark resource of private assassination, so familiar to a Scottish baron in former times, had even in the present age been too frequently resorted to under the pressure of unusual temptation, or where the mind of the actor was prepared for such a crime. Sir William Ashton was aware of this; as also that young Ravenswood had received injuries sufficient to prompt him to that sort of revenge, which becomes a frequent though fearful consequence of the partial administration of justice. He endeavoured to disguise from

Alice the nature of the apprehensions which he entertained; but so ineffectually, that a person even of less penetration than nature had endowed her with must necessarily have been aware that the subject lay near his bosom. His voice was changed in its accent as he replied to her, that the Master of Ravenswood was a man of honour; and, were it otherwise, that the fate of Chiesley of Dalry was a sufficient warning to any one who should dare to assume the office of avenger of his own imaginary wrongs. And having hastily uttered these expressions, he rose and left the place without waiting for a reply.

CHAPTER V

——Is she a Capulet?
O dear account! my life is my foe's debt.

(Shakespeare)*

THE Lord Keeper walked for nearly a quarter of a mile in profound silence. His daughter, naturally timid, and bred up in those ideas of filial awe and implicit obedience which were inculcated upon the youth of that period, did not venture to interrupt his meditations.

'Why do you look so pale, Lucy?' said her father, turning suddenly round and breaking silence.

According to the ideas of the time, which did not permit a young woman to offer her sentiments on any subject of importance unless especially required to do so, Lucy was bound to appear ignorant of the meaning of all that had passed betwixt Alice and her father, and imputed the emotion he had observed to the fear of the wild cattle which grazed in that part of the extensive chase through which they were now walking.

Of these animals, the descendants of the savage herds which anciently roamed free in the Caledonian forests, it was formerly a point of state to preserve a few in the parks of the Scottish nobility. Specimens continued within the memory of man to be kept at least at three houses of distinction, Hamilton namely, Drumlanrick, and Cumbernauld.* They had degenerated from the ancient race in size and strength, if we are to judge from the accounts of old chronicles, and from the formidable remains frequently discovered in bogs and morasses when drained and laid open. The bull had lost the shaggy honours of his mane, and the race was small and light made, in colour a dingy white, or rather a pale yellow, with black horns and hoofs.* They retained, however, in some measure, the ferocity of their ancestry, could not be domesticated on account of their antipathy to the human race, and were often dangerous if approached unguardedly, or wantonly disturbed. It was this last reason which has occasioned their being extirpated at the places we have mentioned, where probably they would otherwise have been retained as appropriate inhabitants of a Scottish woodland, and fit tenants for a baronial forest. A few, if I mistake not, are still preserved at Chillingham Castle, in Northumberland, the seat of the Earl of Tankerville.*

It was to her finding herself in the vicinity of a group of three or four of these animals, that Lucy thought proper to impute those signs of fear, which had arisen in her countenance for a different reason. For she had been familiarized with the appearance of the wild cattle, during her walks in the chase; and it was not then, as it may be now, a necessary part of a young lady's demeanour, to indulge in causeless tremors of the nerves. On the present occasion, however, she speedily found cause for real terror.

Lucy had scarcely replied to her father in the words we have mentioned, and he was just about to rebuke her supposed timidity, when a bull, stimulated either by the scarlet colour of Miss Ashton's mantle, or by one of those fits of capricious ferocity to which their dispositions are liable, detached himself suddenly from the group which was feeding at the upper extremity of a grassy glade, that seemed to lose itself among the crossing and entangled boughs. The animal approached the intruders on his pasture ground, at first slowly, pawing the ground with his hoof, bellowing from time to time, and tearing up the sand with his horns, as if to lash himself up to rage and violence.

The Lord Keeper, who observed the animal's demeanour, was aware that he was about to become mischievous, and, drawing his daughter's arm under his own, began to walk fast along the avenue, in hopes to get out of his sight and his reach. This was the most injudicious course he could have adopted, for, encouraged by the appearance of flight, the bull began to pursue them at full speed. Assailed by a danger so imminent, firmer courage than that of the Lord Keeper might have given way. But paternal tenderness, 'love strong as death,' sustained him.* He continued to support and drag onward his daughter, until, her fears altogether depriving her of the power of flight, she sunk down by his side; and when he could no longer assist her to escape, he turned round and placed himself betwixt her and the raging animal, which advancing in full career, its brutal fury enhanced by the rapidity of the pursuit, was now within a few yards of them. The Lord Keeper had no weapons; his age and gravity dispensed even with the usual appendage of a walking sword,—could such appendage have availed him any thing.

It seemed inevitable that the father or daughter, or both, should have fallen victims to the impending danger, when a shot from the neighbouring thicket arrested the progress of the animal. He was so truly struck between the junction of the spine with the skull, that the wound, which in any other part of his body might scarce have impeded his career, proved instantly fatal. Stumbling forward with a hideous bellow, the progressive force of his previous motion, rather than any operation of his limbs, carried him up to within three yards of the astonished Lord Keeper, where he rolled on the ground, his limbs darkened with the black death-sweat, and quivering with the last convulsions of muscular motion.

Lucy lay senseless on the ground, insensible of the wonderful deliverance which she had experienced. Her father was almost equally stupified, so rapid and unexpected had been the transition from the horrid death which seemed inevitable, to perfect security. He gazed on the animal, terrible even in death, with a species of mute and confused astonishment, which did not permit him distinctly to understand what had taken place; and so inaccurate was his consciousness of what had passed, that he might have supposed the bull had been arrested in its career by a thunderbolt, had he not observed among the branches of the thicket the figure of a man, with a short gun or musquetoon in his hand.

This instantly recalled him to a sense of their situation—a glance at his daughter reminded him of the necessity of procuring her assistance. He called to the man, whom he concluded to be one of his foresters, to give immediate attention to Miss Ashton, while he himself hastened to call assistance. The huntsman approached them accordingly, and the Lord Keeper saw he was a stranger, but was too much agitated to make any farther remarks. In a few hurried words, he directed the shooter, as stronger and more active than himself, to carry the young lady to a neighbouring fountain, while he went back to Alice's hut to procure more aid.

The man to whose timely interference they had been so much indebted, did not seem inclined to leave his good work half finished. He raised Lucy from the ground in his arms, and conveying her through the glades of the forest by paths with which he seemed well acquainted, stopped not until he laid her in safety by the side of a plentiful and pellucid fountain, which had been once covered in, screened and decorated with architectural ornaments of a Gothic character. But now the vault which had covered it being broken down and riven, and the Gothic font ruined and demolished, the stream burst forth from the recess of the earth in open day, and winded its way among the broken sculpture and moss-grown stones which lay in confusion around its source.

Tradition, always busy, at least in Scotland, to grace with a legendary tale a spot in itself interesting, had ascribed a cause of peculiar veneration to this fountain. A beautiful young lady met one of the Lords of Ravenswood while hunting near this spot, and, like a second Egeria, had captivated the affections of the feudal Numa.* They met frequently afterwards, and always at sunset, the charms of the nymph's mind completing the conquest which her beauty had begun, and the mystery of the intrigue adding zest to both. She always appeared and disappeared close by the fountain, with which, therefore, her lover judged she had some inexplicable connexion. She placed certain restrictions on their intercourse, which also savoured of mystery. They met only once a-week—Friday was the appointed day—and she explained to the Lord of Ravenswood, that they were under the necessity of separating so soon as the bell of a chapel, belonging to a hermitage in the adjoining wood, now long ruinous, should toll the hour of vespers. In the course of his confession, the Baron of Ravenswood intrusted the hermit with the secret of this singular amour, and Father Zachary drew the necessary and obvious consequence, that his patron was enveloped in the toils of Satan, and in danger of destruction, both to body and soul. He urged these perils to the Baron with all the force of monkish rhetoric, and described, in the most frightful colours, the real character and person of the apparently lovely Naiad, whom he hesitated not to denounce as a limb of the kingdom of darkness. The lover listened with obstinate incredulity; and it was not until worn out by the obstinacy of the anchoret, that he consented to put the state and condition of his mistress to a certain trial, and for that purpose acquiesced in Zachary's proposal, that on their next interview the vespers bell should be rung half an hour later than usual. The hermit maintained and bucklered his opinion, by quotations from *Malleus Maleficarum*, *Sprengerus*, *Remigius*, and other learned demonologists, that the Evil One, thus seduced to remain behind the appointed hour, would assume her true shape, and, having appeared to her terrified lover as a fiend of hell, would vanish from him in a flash of sulphurous lightning.* Raymond of Ravenswood acquiesced in the experiment, not incurious concerning the issue, though confident it would disappoint the expectations of the hermit.

At the appointed hour the lovers met, and their interview was protracted beyond that at which they usually parted, by the delay of the priest to ring his usual curfew. No change took place upon the nymph's outward form; but as soon as the lengthening shadows made her aware that the usual hour of the vespers chime was passed, she tore herself from her lover's arms with a shriek of despair, bid him adieu for ever, and, plunging into the fountain, disappeared from his eyes. The bubbles occasioned by her descent were crimsoned with blood as they arose, leading the distracted Baron to infer, that his ill-judged curiosity had occasioned the death of this interesting and mysterious being. The remorse which he felt, as well as the recollection of her charms, proved the penance of his future life, which he lost in the battle of Flodden not many months after.* But, in memory of his Naiad, he had previously ornamented the fountain in which she appeared to reside, and secured its waters from profanation or pollution, by the small vaulted building of which the fragments still remained scattered around it. From this period the house of Ravenswood was supposed to have dated its decay.

Such was the generally received legend, which some, who would seem wiser than the vulgar, explained, as obscurely intimating the fate of a beautiful maid of plebeian rank, the mistress of this Raymond, whom he slew in a fit of jealousy, and whose blood was mingled with the waters of the locked fountain, as it was commonly called. Others imagined that the tale had a more remote origin in the ancient heathen mythology. All however agreed, that the spot was fatal to the Ravenswood family; and that to drink of the waters of the well, or even approach its brink, was as ominous to a descendant of that house, as for a Grahame to wear green, a Bruce to kill a spider, or a St Clair to cross the Ord on a Monday. *

It was on this ominous spot that Lucy Ashton first drew breath after her long and almost deadly swoon. Beautiful and pale as the fabulous Naiad in the last agony of separation from her lover, she was seated so as to rest with her back against a part of the ruined wall, while her mantle, dripping with the water which her protector had used profusely to recall her senses, clung to her slender and beautifully proportioned form.

The first moment of recollection brought to her mind the danger which had overpowered her senses—the next called to remembrance that of her father. She looked around—he was nowhere to be seen—'My father—my father!' was all that she could ejaculate.

'Sir William is safe,' answered the voice of a stranger—'perfectly safe, and will be with you instantly.'

'Are you sure of that?' exclaimed Lucy—'the bull was close by us—do not stop me—I must go to seek my father!'

And she arose with that purpose; but her strength was so much exhausted, that, far from possessing the power to execute her purpose, she must have fallen against the stone on which she had leant, probably not without sustaining serious injury.

The stranger was so near to her, that, without actually suffering her to fall, he could not avoid catching her in his arms, which, however, he did with a momentary reluctance, very unusual when youth interposes to prevent beauty from danger. It seemed as if her weight, slight as it was, proved too heavy for her young and athletic assistant, for, without feeling the temptation of detaining her in his arms even for a single instant, he again placed her on the stone from which she had risen, and retreating a few steps, repeated hastily, 'Sir William Ashton is perfectly safe, and will be here instantly. Do not make yourself anxious on his account—

Fate has singularly preserved him. You, madam, are exhausted, and must not think of rising until you have some assistance more suitable than mine.'

Lucy, whose senses were by this time more effectually collected, was naturally led to look at the stranger with attention. There was nothing in his appearance which should have rendered him unwilling to offer his arm to a young lady who required support, or which could have induced her to refuse his assistance; and she could not help thinking, even in that moment, that he seemed cold and reluctant to offer it. A shooting-dress of dark cloth intimated the rank of the wearer, though concealed in part by a large and loose cloak of a dark brown colour. A Montero cap and a black feather drooped over the wearer's brow, and partly concealed his features, which, so far as seen, were dark, regular, and full of majestic, though somewhat sullen, expression.* Some secret sorrow, or the brooding spirit of some moody passion, had quenched the light and ingenuous vivacity of youth in a countenance singularly fitted to display both, and it was not easy to gaze on the stranger without a secret impression either of pity or awe, or at least of doubt and curiosity allied to both.

The impression which we have necessarily been long in describing, Lucy felt in the glance of a moment, and had no sooner encountered the keen black eyes of the stranger, than her own were bent on the ground with a mixture of bashful embarrassment and fear. Yet there was a necessity to speak, or at least she thought so, and in a fluttered accent she began to mention her wonderful escape, in which she was sure that the stranger must, under Heaven, have been her father's protector, and her own.

He seemed to shrink from her expressions of gratitude, while he replied abruptly, 'I leave you, madam,'—the deep melody of his voice rendered powerful, but not harsh, by something like a severity of tone—'I leave you to the protection of those to whom it is possible you may have this day been a guardian angel.'

Lucy was surprised at the ambiguity of his language, and, with a feeling of artless and unaffected gratitude, began to deprecate the idea of having intended to give her deliverer any offence, as if such a thing had been possible. 'I have been unfortunate,' she said, 'in endeavouring to express my thanks—I am sure it must be so, though I cannot recollect what I said—but would you but stay till my father—till the Lord Keeper comes—would you only permit him to pay you his thanks, and to enquire your name?'

'My name is unnecessary,' answered the stranger; 'your father— I would rather say Sir William Ashton—will learn it soon enough, for all the pleasure it is likely to afford him.'

'You mistake him,' said Lucy earnestly; 'he will be grateful for my sake and for his own. You do not know my father, or you are deceiving me with a story of his safety, when he has already fallen a victim to the fury of that animal.'

When she had caught this idea, she started from the ground, and endeavoured to press towards the avenue in which the accident had taken place, while the stranger, though he seemed to hesitate between the desire to assist and the wish to leave her, was obliged, in common humanity, to oppose her both by entreaty and action.

'On the word of a gentleman, madam, I tell you the truth; your father is in perfect safety; you will expose yourself to injury if you venture back where the herd of wild cattle grazed.—If you will go'—for, having once adopted the idea that her father was still in danger, she pressed forward in spite of him—'If you *will* go, accept my arm, though I am not perhaps the person who can with most propriety offer you support.'

But, without heeding this intimation, Lucy took him at his word. 'O if you be a man,' she said,—'if you be a gentleman, assist me to find my father! You shall not leave me—you must go with me—he is dying perhaps while we are talking here!'

Then, without listening to excuse or apology, and holding fast by the stranger's arm, though unconscious of any thing save the support which it gave, and without which she could not have moved, mixed with a vague feeling of preventing his escape from her, she was urging, and almost dragging him forward, when Sir William Ashton came up, followed by the female attendant of blind Alice, and by two wood-cutters, whom he had summoned from their occupation to his assistance. His joy at seeing his daughter safe, overcame the surprise with which he would at another time have beheld her hanging as familiarly on the arm of a stranger, as she might have done upon his own.

'Lucy, my dear Lucy, are you safe?—are you well?' were the only words that broke from him as he embraced her in ecstasy.

'I am well, sir, thank God! and still more that I see you so;—but this gentleman,' she said, quitting his arm, and shrinking from him, 'what must he think of me?' and her eloquent blood,* flushing over neck and brow, spoke how much she was ashamed of the freedom with which she had craved, and even compelled his assistance.

'This gentleman,' said Sir William Ashton, 'will, I trust, not regret the trouble we have given him, when I assure him of the gratitude of the Lord Keeper for the greatest service which one man ever rendered to another—for the life of my child—for my own life, which he has saved by his bravery and presence of mind. He will, I am sure, permit us to request'——

'Request nothing of ME, my lord,' said the stranger, in a stern and peremptory tone; 'I am the Master of Ravenswood.'

There was a dead pause of surprise, not unmixed with less pleasant feelings. The Master wrapt himself in his cloak, made a haughty inclination towards Lucy, muttering a few words of courtesy, as indistinctly heard as they seemed to be reluctantly uttered, and, turning from them, was immediately lost in the thicket.

'The Master of Ravenswood!' said the Lord Keeper, when he had recovered his momentary astonishment—'Hasten after him—stop him—beg him to speak to me for a single moment.'

The two foresters accordingly set off in pursuit of the stranger. They speedily reappeared, and, in an embarrassed and awkward manner, said the gentleman would not return. The Lord Keeper took one of the fellows aside, and questioned him more closely what the Master of Ravenswood had said.

'He just said he wadna come back,' said the man, with the caution of a prudent Scotchman, who cared not to be the bearer of an unpleasant errand.

'He said something more, sir,' said the Lord Keeper, 'and I insist on knowing what it was.'

'Why, then, my lord,' said the man, looking down, 'he said— But it wad be nae pleasure to your lordship to hear it, for I daresay the Master meant nae ill.'

'That's none of your concern, sir; I desire to hear the very words.'

'Weel, then,' replied the man, 'he said, Tell Sir William Ashton, that the next time he and I forgather, he will not be half sae blithe of our meeting as of our parting.'

'Very well, sir,' said the Lord Keeper, 'I believe he alludes to a wager we have on our hawks—it is a matter of no consequence.'

He turned to his daughter, who was by this time so much recovered as to be able to walk home. But the effect which the various recollections, connected with a scene so terrific, made upon a mind which was susceptible in an extreme degree, was more permanent than the injury which her nerves had sustained. Visions of terror, both in sleep and in waking reveries, recalled to her the form of the furious animal, and the dreadful bellow with which he accompanied his career; and it was always the image of the Master of Ravenswood, with his native nobleness of countenance and form, that seemed to interpose betwixt her and assured death. It is, perhaps, at all times dangerous for a young person to suffer recollection to dwell repeatedly, and with too much complacency, on the same individual; but in Lucy's situation it was almost unavoidable. She had never happened to see a young man of mien and features so romantic and so striking as young Ravenswood; but had she seen an hundred his equals or his superiors in those particulars, no one else could have been linked to her heart by the strong associations of remembered danger and escape, of gratitude, wonder, and curiosity. I say curiosity, for it is likely that the singularly restrained and unaccommodating manners of the Master of Ravenswood, so much at variance with the natural expression of his features and grace of his deportment, as they excited wonder by the contrast, had their effect in riveting her attention to the recollection. She knew little of Ravenswood, or the disputes which had existed betwixt her father and his, and perhaps could in her gentleness of mind hardly have comprehended the angry and bitter passions which they had engendered. But she knew that he was come of noble stem; was poor, though descended from the noble and the wealthy; and she felt that she could sympathise with the feelings of a proud mind, which urged him to recoil from the proffered gratitude of the new proprietors of his father's house and domains. Would he have equally shunned their acknowledgments and avoided their intimacy, had her father's request been urged more mildly, less abruptly, and softened with the grace which women so well know how to throw into their manner, when they mean to mediate betwixt the headlong passions of the ruder sex? This was a perilous question to ask her own mind—perilous both in the idea and in its consequences.

Lucy Ashton, in short, was involved in those mazes of the imagination which are most dangerous to the young and the sensitive. Time, it is true, absence, change of scene and new faces, might probably have destroyed the illusion in her instance as it has done in many others; but her residence remained solitary, and her mind without those means of dissipating her pleasing visions. This solitude was chiefly owing to the absence of Lady Ashton, who was at this time in Edinburgh, watching the progress of some state-intrigue; the Lord Keeper only received society out of policy or ostentation, and was by nature rather reserved and unsociable; and thus no cavalier appeared to rival or to obscure the ideal picture of chivalrous excellence which Lucy had pictured to herself in the Master of Ravenswood.

While Lucy indulged in these dreams, she made frequent visits to old blind Alice, hoping it would be easy to lead her to talk on the subject, which at present she had so imprudently admitted to occupy so large a portion of her thoughts. But Alice did not in this particular gratify her wishes and expectations. She spoke readily, and with pathetic feeling, concerning the family in general, but seemed to observe an especial and cautious silence on the subject of the present representative. The little she said of him was not altogether so favourable as Lucy had anticipated. She hinted that he was of a stern and unforgiving character, more ready to resent than to pardon injuries; and Lucy combined with great alarm the hints which she now dropped of these dangerous qualities, with Alice's advice to her father, so emphatically given, 'to beware of Ravenswood.'

But that very Ravenswood, of whom such unjust suspicions had been entertained, had, almost immediately after they had been uttered, confuted them, by saving at once her father's life and her own. Had he nourished such black revenge as Alice's dark hints seemed to indicate, no deed of active guilt was necessary to the full gratification of that evil passion. He needed but to have withheld for an instant his indispensable and effective assistance, and the object of his resentment must have perished, without any direct aggression on his part, by a death equally fearful and certain. She conceived, therefore, that some secret prejudice, or the suspicions incident to age and misfortune, had led Alice to form conclusions injurious to the character, and irreconcilable both with the generous conduct and noble features of the Master of Ravenswood. And in this belief Lucy reposed her hope, and went on weaving her enchanted web of fairy tissue, as beautiful and transient as the film of the gossamer, when it is pearled with the morning dew, and glimmering to the sun.

Her father, in the meanwhile, as well as the Master of Ravenswood, were making reflections, as frequent though more solid than those of Lucy, upon the singular event which had taken place. The Lord Keeper's first task, when he returned home, was to ascertain by medical advice that his daughter had sustained no injury from the dangerous and alarming situation in which she had been placed. Satisfied on this topic, he proceeded to revise the memoranda which he had taken down from the mouth of the person employed to interrupt the funeral service of the late Lord Ravenswood. Bred to casuistry, and well accustomed to practise the ambidexter ingenuity of the bar, it cost him little trouble to soften the features of the tumult which he had been at first so anxious to exaggerate. He preached to his colleagues of the Privy Council the necessity of using conciliatory measures with young men, whose blood and temper were hot, and their experience of life limited. He did not hesitate to attribute some censure to the conduct of the officer, as having been unnecessarily irritating.

These were the contents of his public dispatches. The letters which he wrote to those private friends into whose management the matter was likely to fall, were of a yet more favourable tenor. He represented that lenity in this case would be equally politic and popular, whereas, considering the high respect with which the rites of interment are regarded in Scotland, any severity exercised against the Master of Ravenswood for protecting those of his father from interruption, would be on all sides most unfavourably construed. And, finally, assuming the language of a generous and high-spirited man, he made it his particular request that this affair should be passed over without severe notice. He alluded with delicacy to the predicament in which he himself stood with young Ravenswood, as having succeeded in the long train of litigation by which the fortunes of that noble house had been so much reduced, and confessed it would be most peculiarly acceptable to his own feelings, could he find means in some sort to counterbalance the disadvantages which he had occasioned the family, though only in the prosecution of his just and lawful rights. He therefore made it his particular and personal request that the matter should have no farther consequences, and insinuated a desire that he himself should have the merit of having put a stop to it by his favourable report and intercession. It was particularly remarkable, that, contrary to his uniform practice, he made no special communication to Lady Ashton upon the subject of the tumult; and although he mentioned the alarm which Lucy had received from one of the wild cattle, yet he gave no detailed account of an incident so interesting and terrible.

There was much surprise among Sir William Ashton's political friends and colleagues on receiving letters of a tenor so unexpected. On comparing notes together, one smiled, one put up his eyebrows, a third nodded acquiescence in the general wonder, and a fourth asked, if they were sure these were *all* the letters the Lord Keeper had written on the subject. 'It runs strangely in my mind, my lords, that none of these advices contain the root of the matter.'

But no secret letters of a contrary nature had been received, although the question seemed to imply the possibility of their existence.

'Well,' said an old grey-headed statesman, who had contrived, by shifting and trimming, to maintain his post at the steerage through all the changes of course which the vessel had held for thirty years, 'I thought Sir William would hae verified the auld Scottish saying, "as soon comes the lamb's skin to market as the auld tup's." '*

'We must please him after his own fashion,' said another, 'though it be an unlooked-for one.'

'A wilful man maun hae his way,'*answered the old counsellor.

'The Keeper will rue this before year and day are out,' said a third; 'the Master of Ravenswood is the lad to wind him a pirn.'⁹

'Why,what would you do, my lords, with the poor young fellow?' said a noble Marquis present; 'the Lord Keeper has got all his estates—he has not a cross to bless himself with.'

On which the ancient Lord Turntippet replied,

> ' "If he hasna gear to fine,
> He has shins to pine"—

And that was our way before the Revolution—* *Luitur cum persona, qui luere non potest cum crumena.*¹⁰—Hegh, my lords, that's gude law Latin.'*

'I can see no motive,' replied the Marquis, 'that any noble lord can have for urging this matter farther; let the Lord Keeper have the power to deal in it as he pleases.'

'Agree, agree—remit to the Lord Keeper, with any other person for fashion's sake—Lord Hirplehooly, who is bed-ridden—one to be a quorum—Make your entry in the minutes, Mr Clerk—And now, my lords, there is that young scattergood, the Laird of Bucklaw's fine to be disponed upon—I suppose it goes to my Lord Treasurer?'*

'Shame be in my meal-poke, then,' exclaimed Lord Turntippet, 'and your hand aye in the nook of it!* I had set that down for a by bit between meals for mysell.'

'To use one of your favourite saws, my lord,' replied the Marquis, 'you are like the miller's dog, that licks his lips before the bag is untied—the man is not fined yet.'*

'But that costs but twa skarts of a pen,' said Lord Turntippet; 'and surely there is nae noble lord that will presume to say, that I, wha hae complied wi' a' compliances, tane all manner of tests, abjured all that was to be abjured, and sworn a' that was to be sworn, for these thirty years bypast,* sticking fast by my duty to the state through good report and bad report, shouldna hae something now and then to synd my mouth wi' after sic drouthy wark? Eh?'

'It would be very unreasonable indeed, my lord,' replied the Marquis, 'had we either thought that your lordship's drought was quenchable, or observed any thing stick in your throat that required washing down.'

And so we close the scene on the Privy Council of that period.

CHAPTER VI

For this are all these warriors come,
    To hear an idle tale;
And o'er our death-accustom'd arms
    Shall silly tears prevail?

          (Henry Mackenzie)*

On the evening of the day when the Lord Keeper and his daughter were saved from such imminent peril, two strangers were seated in the most private apartment of a small obscure inn, or rather alehouse, called the Tod's Den, about three or four miles from the Castle of Ravenswood, and as far from the ruinous tower of Wolf's Crag, betwixt which two places it was situated.

One of these strangers was about forty years of age, tall, and thin in the flanks, with an aquiline nose, dark penetrating eyes, and a shrewd but sinister cast of countenance. The other was about fifteen years younger, short, stout, ruddy-faced, and red-haired, with an open, resolute, and cheerful eye, to which careless and fearless freedom, and inward daring, gave fire and expression, notwithstanding its light grey colour.* A stoup of wine, (for in those days it was served out from the cask in pewter flagons,) was placed on the table, and each had his quaigh or bicker" before him. But there was little appearance of conviviality. With folded arms, and looks of anxious expectation, they eyed each other in silence, each wrapt in his own thoughts, and holding no communication with his neighbour.

At length the younger broke silence by exlcaiming, 'What the foul fiend can detain the Master so long? he must have miscarried in his enterprise.—Why did you dissuade me from going with him?'

'One man is enough to right his own wrong,' said the taller and older personage; 'we venture our lives for him in coming thus far on such an errand.'

'You are but a craven after all, Craigengelt,' answered the younger, 'and that's what many folk have thought you before now.'

'But what none has dared to tell me,' said Craigengelt, laying his hand on the hilt of his sword; 'and, but that I hold a hasty man no better than a fool,* I would'—he paused for his companion's answer.

'*Would* you?' said the other coolly; 'and why do you not then?'

Craigengelt drew his cutlass an inch or two, and then returned it with violence into the scabbard—'Because there is a deeper stake to be played for, than the lives of twenty harebrained gowks like you.'

'You are right there,' said his companion, 'for if it were not that these forfeitures, and that last fine that the old driveller Turntippet is gaping for, and which, I daresay, is laid on by this time, have fairly driven me out of house and home, I were a coxcomb and a cuckoo to boot, to trust your fair promises of getting me a commission in the Irish brigade,—what have I to do with the Irish brigade?* I am a plain Scotchman, as my father was before me; and my grand-aunt, Lady Girnington, cannot live for ever.'

'Ay, Bucklaw,' observed Craigengelt, 'but she may live for many a long day; and for your father, he had land and living, kept himself close from wadsetters and money-lenders, paid each man his due, and lived on his own.'

'And whose fault is it that I have not done so too?' said Bucklaw—'whose but the devil's and yours, and such like as you, that have led me to the far end of a fair estate? and now I shall be obliged, I suppose, to shelter and shift about like yourself—live one week upon a line of secret intelligence from Saint Germains—another upon a report of a rising in the Highlands—get my breakfast and morning-draught of sack from old Jacobite ladies, and give them locks of my old wig for the Chevalier's hair—second my friend in his quarrel till he comes to the field, and then flinch from him lest so important a political agent should perish from the way.* All this I must do for bread, besides calling myself a captain!'

'You think you are making a fine speech now,' said Craigengelt, 'and showing much wit at my expense. Is starving or hanging better than the life I am obliged to lead, because the present fortunes of the king cannot sufficiently support his envoys?'

'Starving is honester, Craigengelt, and hanging is like to be the end on't—But what you mean to make of this poor fellow Ravenswood, I know not—he has no money left, any more than I—his lands are all pawned and pledged, and the interest eats up the rents, and is not satisfied, and what do you hope to make by meddling in his affairs?'

'Content yourself, Bucklaw; I know my business,' replied Craigengelt. 'Besides that his name, and his father's services in 1689, will make such an acquisition sound well both at Versailles and Saint Germains—you will also please be informed, that the Master of Ravenswood is a very different kind of a young fellow from you. He has parts and address, as well as courage and talents, and will present himself abroad like a young man of head as well as heart, who knows something more than the speed of a horse or the flight of a hawk. I have lost credit of late, by bringing over no one that had sense to know more than how to unharbour a stag, or take and reclaim an eyess. The Master has education, sense, and penetration.'

'And yet is not wise enough to escape the tricks of a kidnapper, Craigengelt?' replied the younger man. 'But don't be angry; you know you will not fight, and so it is as well to leave your hilt in peace and quiet, and tell me in sober guise how you drew the Master into your confidence?'

'By flattering his love of vengeance, Bucklaw,' answered Craigengelt. 'He has always distrusted me, but I watched my time, and struck while his temper was red-hot with the sense of insult and of wrong. He goes now to expostulate, as he says, and perhaps thinks, with Sir William Ashton. I say, that if they meet, and the lawyer puts him to his defence, the Master will kill him; for he had that sparkle in his eye which never deceives you when you would read a man's purpose. At any rate, he will give him such a bullying as will be construed into an assault on a privy-councillor; so there will be a total breach betwixt him and government; Scotland will be too hot for him, France will gain him, and we will all set sail together in the French brig L'Espoir,* which is hovering for us off Eyemouth.'

'Content am I,' said Bucklaw; 'Scotland has little left that I care about; and if carrying the Master with us will get us a better reception in France, why, so be it, a God's name. I doubt our own merits will procure us slender preferment; and I trust he will send a ball through the Keeper's head before he joins us. One or two of these scoundrel statesmen should be shot once a-year, just to keep the others on their good behaviour.'

'That is very true,' replied Cragengelt; 'and it reminds me that I must go and see that our horses have been fed, and are in readiness; for, should such deed be done, it will be no time for grass to grow beneath their heels.'* He proceeded as far as the door, then turned back with a look of earnestness, and said to Bucklaw, 'Whatever should come of this business, I am sure you will do me the justice to remember, that I said nothing to the Master which could imply my accession to any act of violence which he may take it into his head to commit.'

'No, no, not a single word like accession,' replied Bucklaw; 'you know too well the risk belonging to these two terrible words, art and part.'* Then, as if to himself, he recited the following lines:

'The dial spoke not, but it made shrewd signs,
And pointed full upon the stroke of murder.'*

'What is that you are talking to yourself?' said Craigengelt, turning back with some anxiety.

'Nothing—only two lines I have heard upon the stage,' replied his companion.

'Bucklaw,' said Craigengelt, 'I sometimes think you should have been a stage-player yourself; all is fancy and frolic with you.'

'I have often thought so myself,' said Bucklaw. 'I believe it would be safer than acting with you in the Fatal Conspiracy.*— But away, play your own part, and look after the horses like a groom as you are.—A play-actor—a stage-player!' he repeated to himself; 'that would have deserved a stab, but that Craigengelt's a coward—And yet I should like the profession well enough— Stay—let me see—ay—I would come out in Alexander—

"Thus from the grave I rise to save my love,
Draw all your swords, and quick as lightning move;

When I rush on, sure none will dare to stay,
'Tis love commands, and glory leads the way." '*

As with a voice of thunder, and his hand upon his sword, Bucklaw repeated the ranting couplets of poor Lee, Craigengelt re-entered with a face of alarm.

'We are undone, Bucklaw! the Master's led horse has cast himself over his halter in the stable, and is dead lame—his hackney will be set up with the day's work, and now he has no fresh horse; he will never get off.'

'Egad, there will be no moving with the speed of lightning this bout,' said Bucklaw, drily. 'But stay, you can give him yours.'

'What! and be taken myself? I thank you for the proposal,' said Craigengelt.

'Why,' replied Bucklaw, 'if the Lord Keeper should have met with a mischance, which for my part I cannot suppose, for the Master is not the lad to shoot an old and unarmed man—but *if* there should have been a fray at the Castle, you are neither art nor part in it, you know, so have nothing to fear.'

'True, true,' answered the other, with embarrassment; 'but consider my commission from Saint Germains.'

'Which many men think is a commission of your own making, noble captain.—Well, if you will not give him your horse, why, d—n it, he must have mine.'

'Yours?' said Craigengelt.

'Ay, mine,' repeated Bucklaw; 'it shall never be said that I agreed to back a gentleman in a little affair of honour, and neither helped him on with it nor off from it.'

'You will give him your horse? and have you considered the loss?'

'Loss! why, Grey Gilbert cost me twenty Jacobuses,* that's true; but then his hackney is worth something, and his Black Moor is worth twice as much were he sound, and I know how to handle him. Take a fat sucking mastiff whelp, flay and bowel him, stuff the body full of black and grey snails, roast a reasonable time, and baste with oil of spikenard, saffron, cinnamon and honey, anoint with the dripping, working it in'——

'Yes, Bucklaw; but in the meanwhile, before the sprain is cured, nay, before the whelp is roasted, you will be caught and hung. Depend on it, the chase will be hard after Ravenswood. I wish we had made our place of rendezvous nearer to the coast.'

'On my faith, then,' said Bucklaw, 'I had best go off just now, and leave my horse for him—Stay, stay, he comes, I hear a horse's feet.'

'Are you sure there is only one?' said Craigengelt; 'I fear there is a chase; I think I hear three or four galloping together—I am sure I hear more horses than one.'

'Pooh, pooh, it is the wench of the house clattering to the well in her pattens. By my faith, Captain, you should give up both your captainship and your secret service, for you are as easily scared as a wild-goose. But here comes the Master alone, and looking as gloomy as a night in November.'

The Master of Ravenswood entered the room accordingly, his cloak muffled around him, his arms folded, his looks stern, and at the same time dejected. He flung his cloak from him as he entered, threw himself upon a chair, and appeared sunk in a profound reverie.

'What has happened? What have you done?' was hastily demanded by Craigengelt and Bucklaw in the same moment.

'Nothing,' was the short and sullen answer.

'Nothing? and left us, determined to call the old villain to account for all the injuries that you, we, and the country, have received at his hand? Have you seen him?'

'I have,' replied the Master of Ravenswood.

'Seen him? and come away without settling scores which have been so long due?' said Bucklaw; 'I would not have expected that at the hand of the Master of Ravenswood.'

'No matter what you expected,' replied Ravenswood; 'it is not to you, sir, that I shall be disposed to render any reason for my conduct.'

'Patience, Bucklaw,' said Craigengelt, interrupting his companion, who seemed about to make an angry reply. 'The Master has been interrupted in his purpose by some accident; but he must excuse the anxious curiosity of friends, who are devoted to his cause like you and me.'

'Friends, Captain Craigengelt!' retorted Ravenswood, haught-ily; 'I am ignorant what familiarity has passed betwixt us to entitle you to use that expression. I think our friendship amounts to this, that we agreed to leave Scotland together so soon as I should have visited the alienated mansion of my fathers, and had an interview with its present possessor, I will not call him proprietor.'

'Very true, Master,' answered Bucklaw; 'and as we thought you had a mind to do something to put your neck in jeopardy, Craigie and I very courteously agreed to tarry for you, although ours might run some risk in consequence. As to Craigie, indeed, it does not very much signify, he had gallows written on his brow in the hour of his birth;* but I should not like to discredit my parentage by coming to such an end in another man's cause.'

'Gentlemen,' said the Master of Ravenswood, 'I am sorry if I have occasioned you any inconvenience, but I must claim the right of judging what is best for my own affairs, without rendering explanations to any one. I have altered my mind, and do not design to leave the country this season.'

'Not to leave the country, Master!' exclaimed Craigengelt. 'Not to go over, after all the trouble and expense I have incurred—after all the risk of discovery, and the expense of freight and demur-rage!'*

'Sir,' replied the Master of Ravenswood, 'when I designed to leave this country in this haste, I made use of your obliging offer to procure me means of conveyance; but I do not recollect that I pledged myself to go off, if I found occasion to alter my mind. For your trouble on my account, I am sorry, and I thank you; your expense,' he added, putting his hand into his pocket, 'admits a more solid compensation—freight and demurrage are matters with which I am unacquainted, Captain Craigengelt, but take my purse and pay yourself according to your own conscience.' And accordingly he tendered a purse with some gold in it to the soi-disant captain.

But here Bucklaw interposed in his turn. 'Your fingers, Craigie, seem to itch for that same piece of green net-work,' said he; 'but I make my vow to God, that if they offer to close upon it, I will chop them off with my whinger. Since the Master has changed his mind, I suppose we need stay here no longer; but in the first place I beg leave to tell him'——

'Tell him any thing you will,' said Craigengelt, 'if you will first allow me to state the inconveniences to which he will expose himself by quitting our society, to remind him of the obstacles to his remaining here, and of the difficulties attending his proper introduction at Versailles and Saint Germains, without the countenance of those who have established useful connexions.'

'Besides forfeiting the friendship,' said Bucklaw, 'of at least one man of spirit and honour.'

'Gentlemen,' said Ravenswood, 'permit me once more to assure you, that you have been pleased to attach to our temporary connexion more importance than I ever meant that it should have. When I repair to foreign courts, I shall not need the introduction of an intriguing adventurer, nor is it necessary for me to set value on the friendship of a hot-headed bully.' With these words, and without waiting for an answer, he left the apartment, remounted his horse, and was heard to ride off.

'Mortbleu!' said Captain Craigengelt, 'my recruit is lost!'

'Ay, Captain,' said Bucklaw, 'the salmon is off with hook and all. But I will after him, for I have had more of his insolence than I can well digest.'

Craigengelt offered to accompany him; but Bucklaw replied, 'No, no, Captain, keep you the cheek of the chimney-nook till I come back; it's good sleeping in a haill skin.*

> "Little kens the auld wife that sits by the fire,
> How cauld the wind blaws in hurle-burle swire." ' *

And singing as he went, he left the apartment.

CHAPTER VII

Now, Billy Bewick, keep good heart,
  And of thy talking let me be;
But if thou art a man, as I am sure thou art,
  Come over the dike and fight with me.

(Old Ballad) *

THE Master of Ravenswood had mounted the ambling hackney
which he before rode, on finding the accident which had happened to his led horse, and, for the animal's ease, was proceeding
at a slow pace from the Tod's Den towards his old tower of Wolf's
Crag, when he heard the galloping of a horse behind him, and,
looking back, perceived that he was pursued by young Bucklaw,
who had been delayed a few minutes in the pursuit by the
irresistible temptation of giving the hostler at the Tod's Den some
recipe for treating the lame horse. This brief delay he had made
up by hard galloping, and now overtook the Master where the
road traversed a waste moor. 'Halt, sir,' cried Bucklaw; 'I am no
political agent—no Captain Craigengelt, whose life is too important to be hazarded in defence of his honour. I am Frank Hayston
of Bucklaw, and no man injures me by word, deed, sign, or look,
but he must render me an account of it.'

'This is all very well, Mr Hayston of Bucklaw,' replied the
Master of Ravenswood, in a tone the most calm and indifferent;
'but I have no quarrel with you, and desire to have none. Our
roads homeward, as well as our roads through life, lie in different
directions; there is no occasion for us crossing each other.'

'Is there not?' said Bucklaw, impetuously. 'By Heaven! but I say
that there is, though—you called us intriguing adventurers.'

'Be correct in your recollection, Mr Hayston; it was to your
companion only I applied that epithet, and you know him to be
no better.'

'And what then? He was my companion for the time, and no man shall insult my companion, right or wrong, while he is in my company.'

'Then, Mr Hayston,' replied Ravenswood, with the same composure, 'you should choose your society better, or you are like to have much work in your capacity of their champion. Go home, sir, sleep, and have more reason in your wrath to-morrow.'*

'Not so, Master, you have mistaken your man; high airs and wise saws shall not carry it off thus. Besides, you termed me bully, and you shall retract the word before we part.'

'Faith, scarcely,' said Ravenswood, 'unless you show me better reason for thinking myself mistaken than you are now producing.'

'Then, Master,' said Bucklaw, 'though I should be sorry to offer it to a man of your quality, if you will not justify your incivility, or retract it, or name a place of meeting, you must here undergo the hard word and the hard blow.'

'Neither will be necessary,' said Ravenswood; 'I am satisfied with what I have done to avoid an affair with you. If you are serious, this place will serve as well as another.'

'Dismount then, and draw,' said Bucklaw, setting him an example. 'I always thought and said you were a pretty man; I should be sorry to report you otherwise.'

'You shall have no reason, sir,' said Ravenswood, alighting, and putting himself into a posture of defence.

Their swords crossed, and the combat commenced with great spirit on the part of Bucklaw, who was well accustomed to affairs of the kind, and distinguished by address and dexterity at his weapon. In the present case, however, he did not use his skill to advantage; for, having lost temper at the cool and contemptuous manner in which the Master of Ravenswood had long refused, and at length granted him satisfaction, and urged by his impatience, he adopted the part of an assailant with inconsiderate eagerness. The Master, with equal skill, and much greater composure, remained chiefly on the defensive, and even declined to avail himself of one or two advantages afforded him by the eagerness of his adversary. At length, in a desperate lunge, which he followed with an attempt to close, Bucklaw's foot slipped, and he fell on the short grassy turf on which they were fighting. 'Take your life, sir,' said the Master of Ravenswood, 'and mend it, if you can.'

'It would be but a cobbled piece of work, I fear,' said Bucklaw, rising slowly and gathering up his sword, much less disconcerted with the issue of the combat than could have been expected from the impetuosity of his temper. 'I thank you for my life, Master,' he pursued. 'There is my hand, I bear no ill-will to you, either for my bad luck or your better swordmanship.'

The Master looked steadily at him for an instant, then extended his hand to him.—'Bucklaw,' he said, 'you are a generous fellow, and I have done you wrong. I heartily ask your pardon for the expression which offended you; it was hastily and incautiously uttered, and I am convinced it is totally misapplied.'

'Are you indeed, Master?' said Bucklaw, his face resuming at once its natural expression of light-hearted carelessness and audacity; 'that is more than I expected of you; for, Master, men say you are not ready to retract your opinions and your language.'

'Not when I have well considered them,' said the Master.

'Then you are a little wiser than I am, for I always give my friend satisfaction first, and explanation afterwards. If one of us falls, all accounts are settled; if not, men are never so ready for peace as after war.—But what does that bawling brat of a boy want?' said Bucklaw. 'I wish to Heaven he had come a few minutes sooner! and yet it must have been ended some time, and perhaps this way is as well as any other.'

As he spoke, the boy he mentioned came up, cudgelling an ass, on which he was mounted, to the top of its speed, and sending, like one of Ossian's heroes, his voice before him,—— 'Gentlemen,—gentlemen, save yourselves! for the gudewife bade us tell ye there were folk in her house had taen Captain Craigengelt, and were seeking for Bucklaw, and that ye behoved to ride for it.'

'By my faith, and that's very true, my man,' said Bucklaw; 'and there's a silver sixpence for your news, and I would give any man twice as much would tell me which way I should ride.'

'That will I, Bucklaw,' said Ravenswood; 'ride home to Wolf's Crag with me. There are places in the old tower where you might lie hid, were a thousand men to seek you.'

'But that will bring you into trouble yourself, Master; and unless you be in the Jacobite scrape already, it is quite needless for me to drag you in.'

'Not a whit; I have nothing to fear.'

'Then I will ride with you blithely, for, to say the truth, I do not know the rendezvous that Craigie was to guide us to this night; and I am sure that, if he is taken, he will tell all the truth of me, and twenty lies of you, in order to save himself from the withie.'

They mounted, and rode off in company accordingly, striking off the ordinary road, and holding their way by wild moorish unfrequented paths, with which the gentlemen were well acquainted from the exercise of the chase, but through which others would have had much difficulty in tracing their course. They rode for some time in silence, making such haste as the condition of Ravenswood's horse permitted, until night having gradually closed around them, they discontinued their speed, both from the difficulty of discovering their path, and from the hope that they were beyond the reach of pursuit or observation.

'And now that we have drawn bridle a bit,' said Bucklaw, 'I would fain ask you a question, Master.'

'Ask, and welcome,' said Ravenswood, 'but forgive my not answering it, unless I think proper.'

'Well, it is simply this,' answered his late antagonist,—'What, in the name of old Sathan, could make you, who stand so highly on your reputation, think for a moment of drawing up with such a rogue as Craigengelt, and such a scape-grace as folk call Bucklaw?'

'Simply, because I was desperate, and sought desperate associates.'

'And what made you break off from us at the nearest?' again demanded Bucklaw.

'Because I had changed my mind,' said the Master, 'and renounced my enterprise, at least for the present. And now that I have answered your questions fairly and frankly, tell me what makes you associate with Craigengelt, so much beneath you both in birth and in spirit?'

'In plain terms,' answered Bucklaw, 'because I am a fool, who have gambled away my land in these times. My grand-aunt, Lady

Girnington, has taen a new tack of life, I think, and I could only hope to get something by a change of government. Craigie was a sort of gambling acquaintance; he saw my condition; and, as the devil is always at one's elbow, told me fifty lies about his credentials from Versailles, and his interest at Saint Germains, promised me a captain's commission at Paris, and I have been ass enough to put my thumb under his belt. I daresay, by this time, he has told a dozen pretty stories of me to the government. And this is what I have got by wine, women, and dice, cocks, dogs, and horses.'

'Yes, Bucklaw,' said the Master, 'you have indeed nourished in your bosom the snakes that are now stinging you.'*

'That's home as well as true, Master,' replied his companion; 'but, by your leave, you have nursed in your bosom one great goodly snake that has swallowed all the rest, and is as sure to devour you as my half dozen are to make a meal on all that's left of Bucklaw, which is but what lies between bonnet and boot-heel.'

'I must not,' answered the Master of Ravenswood, 'challenge the freedom of speech in which I have set example. What, to speak without a metaphor, do you call this monstrous passion, which you charge me with fostering?'

'Revenge; my good sir, revenge; which, if it be as gentleman-like a sin as wine and wassail, with their *et cæteras*, is equally unchristian, and not so bloodless. It is better breaking a park-pale to watch a doe or damsel, than to shoot an old man.'

'I deny the purpose,' said the Master of Ravenswood. 'On my soul, I had no such intention; I meant but to confront the oppressor ere I left my native land, and upbraid him with his tyranny and its consequences. I would have stated my wrongs so that they would have shaken his soul within him.'

'Yes,' answered Bucklaw, 'and he would have collared you, and cried help, and then you would have shaken the soul *out* of him, I suppose. Your very look and manner would have frightened the old man to death.'

'Consider the provocation,' answered Ravenswood—'consider the ruin and death procured and caused by his hard-hearted cruelty—an ancient house destroyed, an affectionate father murdered!* Why, in our old Scottish days, he that sat quiet under such wrongs, would have been held neither fit to back a friend nor face a foe.'

'Well, Master, I am glad to see that the devil deals as cunningly with other folk as he deals with me; for whenever I am about to commit any folly, he persuades me it is the most necessary, gallant, gentlemanlike thing on earth, and I am up to saddlegirths in the bog before I see that the ground is soft. And you, Master, might have turned out a murd——a homicide, just out of pure respect for your father's memory.'

'There is more sense in your language, Bucklaw,' replied the Master, 'than might have been expected from your conduct. It is too true, our vices steal upon us in forms outwardly as fair as those of the demons whom the superstitious represent as intriguing with the human race, and are not discovered in their native hideousness until we have clasped them in our arms.'

'But we may throw them from us, though,' said Bucklaw, 'and that is what I shall think of doing one of these days,—that is, when old Lady Girnington dies.'

'Did you ever hear the expression of the English divine?' said Ravenswood—' "Hell is paved with good intentions"*—as much as to say, they are more often formed than executed.'

'Well,' replied Bucklaw, 'but I will begin this blessed night, and have determined not to drink above one quart of wine, unless your claret be of extraordinary quality.'

'You will find little to tempt you at Wolf's Crag,' said the Master. 'I know not that I can promise you more than the shelter of my roof; all, and more than all, our stock of wine and provisions was exhausted at the late occasion.'

'Long may it be ere provision is needed for the like purpose,' answered Bucklaw; 'but you should not drink up the last flask at a dirge; there is ill luck in that.'

'There is ill luck, I think, in whatever belongs to me,' said Ravenswood. 'But yonder is Wolf's Crag, and whatever it still contains is at your service.'

The roar of the sea had long announced their approach to the cliffs, on the summit of which, like the nest of some sea-eagle, the founder of the fortalice had perched his eyry. The pale moon, which had hitherto been contending with flitting clouds, now shone out, and gave them a view of the solitary and naked tower, situated on a projecting cliff that beetled on the German Ocean. On three sides the rock was precipitous; on the fourth, which was that towards the land, it had been originally fenced by an artificial ditch and drawbridge, but the latter was broken down and ruinous, and the former had been in part filled up, so as to allow passage for a horseman into the narrow court-yard, encircled on two sides with low offices and stables, partly ruinous, and closed on the landward front by a low embattled wall, while the remaining side of the quadrangle was occupied by the tower itself, which, tall and narrow, and built of a greyish stone, stood glimmering in the moonlight, like the sheeted spectre of some huge giant. A wilder, or more disconsolate dwelling, it was perhaps difficult to conceive.* The sombrous and heavy sound of the billows, successively dashing against the rocky beach at a profound distance beneath, was to the ear what the landscape was to the eye—a symbol of unvaried and monotonous melancholy, not unmingled with horror.

Although the night was not far advanced, there was no sign of living inhabitant about this forlorn abode, excepting that one, and only one, of the narrow and stanchelled windows which appeared at irregular heights and distances in the walls of the building, showed a small glimmer of light.

'There,' said Ravenswood, 'sits the only male domestic that remains to the house of Ravenswood; and it is well that he does remain there, since otherwise, we had little hope to find either light or fire. But follow me cautiously; the road is narrow, and admits only one horse in front.'

In effect, the path led along a kind of isthmus, at the peninsular extremity of which the tower was situated, with that exclusive attention to strength and security, in preference to every circumstance of convenience, which dictated to the Scottish barons the choice of their situations, as well as their style of building.

By adopting the cautious mode of approach recommended by the proprietor of this wild hold, they entered the court-yard in safety. But it was long ere the efforts of Ravenswood, though loudly exerted by knocking at the low-browed entrance, and repeated shouts to Caleb to open the gate and admit them, received any answer.

'The old man must be departed,' he began to say, 'or fallen into some fit; for the noise I have made would have waked the seven sleepers.'*

At length a timid and hesitating voice replied,—'Master—Master of Ravenswood, is it you?'

'Yes, it is I, Caleb; open the door quickly.'

'But is it you in very blood and body? For I would sooner face fifty deevils as my master's ghaist, or even his wraith,*—wherefore, aroint ye, if ye were ten times my master, unless ye come in bodily shape, lith and limb.'

'It is I, you old fool,' answered Ravenswood, 'in bodily shape, and alive, save that I am half dead with cold.'

The light at the upper window disappeared, and glancing from loop-hole to loop-hole in slow succession, gave intimation that the bearer was in the act of descending, with great deliberation, a winding staircase occupying one of the turrets which graced the angles of the old tower. The tardiness of his descent extracted some exclamations of impatience from Ravenswood, and several oaths from his less patient and more mercurial companion. Caleb again paused ere he unbolted the door, and once more asked, if they were men of mould* that demanded entrance at this time of night?

'Were I near you, you old fool,' said Bucklaw, 'I would give you sufficient proofs of *my* bodily condition.'

'Open the gate, Caleb,' said his master, in a more soothing tone, partly from his regard to the ancient and faithful seneschal, partly perhaps because he thought that angry words would be thrown away, so long as Caleb had a stout iron-clenched oaken door betwixt his person and the speakers.

At length Caleb, with a trembling hand, undid the bars, opened the heavy door, and stood before them, exhibiting his thin grey hairs, bald forehead, and sharp high features, illuminated by a quivering lamp which he held in one hand, while he shaded and protected its flame with the other. The timorous cautious glance which he threw around him—the effect of the partial light upon his white hair and illumined features, might have made a good painting; but our travellers were too impatient for security against the rising storm, to permit them to indulge themselves in studying the picturesque. 'Is it you, my dear master? is it you yourself, indeed?' exclaimed the old domestic. 'I am wae ye suld hae stude waiting at your ain gate; but wha wad hae thought o' seeing ye sae sune, and a strange gentleman with a—(Here he exclaimed apart, as it were, and to some inmate of the tower, in a voice not meant to be heard by those in the court)—Mysie—Mysie woman! stir for dear life, and get the fire mended; take the auld three-legged stool, or ony thing that's readiest that will make a lowe.—I doubt we are but puirly provided, no expecting ye this some months, when doubtless ye wad hae been received conform till your rank, as gude right is; but natheless'——

'Natheless, Caleb,' said the Master, 'we must have our horses put up, and ourselves too, the best way we can. I hope you are not sorry to see me sooner than you expected?'

'Sorry, my lord!—I am sure ye sall aye be my lord wi' honest folk, as your noble ancestors hae been these three hundred years, and never asked a whig's leave.* Sorry to see the Lord of Ravenswood at ane o' his ain castles!—(Then again apart to his unseen associate behind the screen)—Mysie, kill the brood-hen without thinking twice on it; let them care that come ahint.*—No to say it's our best dwelling,' he added, turning to Bucklaw; 'but just a strength for the Lord of Ravenswood to flee until,—that is, no to *flee*, but to retreat until in troublous times, like the present, when it was ill convenient for him to live farther in the country in ony of his better and mair principal manors; but, for its antiquity, maist folk think that the outside of Wolf's Crag is worthy of a large perusal.'

'And you are determined we shall have time to make it,' said Ravenswood, somewhat amused with the shifts the old man used to detain them without doors, until his confederate Mysie had made her preparations within.

'O, never mind the outside of the house, my good friend,' said Bucklaw; 'let's see the inside, and let our horses see the stable, that's all.'

'O yes, sir—ay, sir,—unquestionably, sir—my lord and ony of his honourable companions'——

'But our horses, my old friend—our horses; they will be dead-foundered by standing here in the cold after riding hard, and mine is too good to be spoiled; therefore, once more, our horses,' exclaimed Bucklaw.

'True—ay—your horses—yes—I will call the grooms;' and sturdily did Caleb roar till the old tower rang again,—'John—William—Saunders!— The lads are gane out, or sleeping,' he observed, after pausing for an answer, which he knew that he had no human chance of receiving. 'A' gaes wrang when the Master's out by; but I'll take care o' your cattle mysell.'

'I think you had better,' said Ravenswood, 'otherwise I see little chance of their being attended to at all.'

'Whisht, my lord,—whisht, for God's sake,' said Caleb, in an imploring tone, and apart to his master; 'if ye dinna regard your ain credit, think on mine; we'll hae hard eneugh wark to mak a decent night o't, wi' a' the lees I can tell.'

'Well, well, never mind,' said his master; 'go to the stable. There is hay and corn, I trust?'

'Ou ay, plenty of hay and corn;' this was uttered boldly and aloud, and, in a lower tone, 'there was some half fous o' aits, and some taits o' meadow-hay, left after the burial.'

'Very well,' said Ravenswood, taking the lamp from his domestic's unwilling hand, 'I will show the stranger up stairs myself.'

'I canna think o' that, my lord;—if ye wad but have five minutes, or ten minutes, or, at maist, a quarter of an hour's patience, and look at the fine moonlight prospect of the Bass and North-Berwick Law* till I sort the horses, I would marshal ye up, as reason is ye suld be marshalled, your lordship and your honourable visitor. And I hae lockit up the siller candlesticks, and the lamp is not fit'——

'It will do very well in the meantime,' said Ravenswood, 'and you will have no difficulty for want of light in the stable, for, if I recollect, half the roof is off.'

'Very true, my lord,' replied the trusty adherent, and with ready wit instantly added, ' and the lazy sclater loons have never come to put it on a' this while, your lordship.'

'If I were disposed to jest at the calamities of my house,' said Ravenswood, as he led the way up stairs, 'poor old Caleb would furnish me with ample means. His passion consists in representing things about our miserable *menage*, not as they are, but as, in his opinion, they ought to be; and, to say the truth, I have been often diverted with the poor wretch's expedients to supply what he thought was essential for the credit of the family, and his still more generous apologies for the want of those articles for which his ingenuity could discover no substitute. But though the tower is none of the largest, I shall have some trouble without him to find the apartment in which there is a fire.'

As he spoke thus, he opened the door of the hall. 'Here, at least,' he said, 'there is neither hearth nor harbour.'

It was indeed a scene of desolation. A large vaulted room, the beams of which, combined like those of Westminster-Hall,*were rudely carved at the extremities, remained nearly in the situation in which it had been left after the entertainment at Allan Lord Ravenswood's funeral. Overturned pitchers, and black jacks, and pewter stoups, and flagons, still cumbered the large oaken table; glasses, those more perishable implements of conviviality, many of which had been voluntarily sacrificed by the guests in their enthusiastic pledges to favourite toasts, strewed the stone floor with their fragments. As for the articles of plate, lent for the purpose by friends and kinsfolk, those had been carefully withdrawn so soon as the ostentatious display of festivity, equally unnecessary and strangely timed, had been made and ended. Nothing, in short, remained that indicated wealth; all the signs were those of recent wastefulness, and present desolation. The black cloth hangings, which, on the late mournful occasion, replaced the tattered moth-eaten tapestries, had been partly pulled down, and, dangling from the wall in irregular festoons, disclosed the rough stone-work of the building, unsmoothed either by plaster or the chisel. The seats thrown down, or left in disorder, intimated the careless confusion which had concluded the mournful revel. 'This room,' said Ravenswood, holding up the lamp—'this room, Mr Hayston, was riotous when it should have been sad; it is a just retribution that it should now be sad when it ought to be cheerful.'

They left this disconsolate apartment, and went up stairs, where, after opening one or two doors in vain, Ravenswood led the way into a little matted anteroom, in which, to their great joy, they found a tolerably good fire, which Mysie, by some such expedient as Caleb had suggested, had supplied with a reasonable quantity of fuel. Glad at the heart to see more of comfort than the castle had yet seemed to offer, Bucklaw rubbed his hands heartily over the fire, and now listened with more complacency to the apologies which the Master of Ravenswood offered. 'Comfort,' he said, 'I cannot provide for you, for I have it not for myself; it is long since these walls have known it, if, indeed, they were ever acquainted with it. Shelter and safety, I think, I can promise you.'

'Excellent matters, Master,' replied Bucklaw, 'and, with a mouthful of food and wine, positively all I can require to-night.'

'I fear,' said the Master, 'your supper will be a poor one; I hear the matter in discussion betwixt Caleb and Mysie. Poor Balderstone is something deaf, amongst his other accomplishments, so that much of what he means should be spoken aside is overheard by the whole audience, and especially by those from whom he is most anxious to conceal his private manœuvres—Hark!'

They listened, and heard the old domestic's voice in conversation with Mysie to the following effect. 'Just mak the best o't, mak the best o't, woman; it's easy to put a fair face on ony thing.'

'But the auld brood-hen?—she'll be as teugh as bow-strings and bend-leather!'

'Say ye made a mistake—say ye made a mistake, Mysie,' replied the faithful seneschal, in a soothing and undertoned voice; 'tak it a' on yoursell; never let the credit o' the house suffer.'

'But the brood-hen,' remonstrated Mysie,—'ou, she's sitting some gate aneath the dais in the hall, and I am feared to gae in in the dark for the bogle;* and if I didna see the bogle, I could as ill see the hen, for it's pit-mirk, and there's no another light in the house, save that very blessed lamp whilk the Master has in his ain hand. And if I had the hen, she's to pu', and to draw, and to dress; how can I do that, and them sitting by the only fire we have?'

'Weel, weel, Mysie,' said the butler, 'bide ye there a wee, and I'll try to get the lamp wiled away frae them.'

Accordingly, Caleb Balderstone entered the apartment, little aware that so much of his by-play had been audible there. 'Well, Caleb, my old friend, is there any chance of supper?' said the Master of Ravenswood.

'*Chance* of supper, your lordship?' said Caleb, with an emphasis of strong scorn at the implied doubt,—'How should there be ony question of that, and us in your lordship's house?—Chance of supper, indeed!—But ye'll no be for butcher-meat? There's walth o' fat poultry, ready either for spit or brander—The fat capon, Mysie!' he added, calling out as boldly as if such a thing had been in existence.

'Quite unnecessary,' said Bucklaw, who deemed himself bound in courtesy to relieve some part of the anxious butler's perplexity, 'if you have any thing cold, or a morsel of bread.'

'The best of bannocks!' exclaimed Caleb, much relieved; 'and, for cauld meat, a' that we hae is cauld eneugh,—howbeit maist of the cauld meat and pastry was gien to the poor folk after the ceremony of interment, as gude reason was; nevertheless'——

'Come, Caleb,' said the Master of Ravenswood, 'I must cut this matter short. This is the young laird of Bucklaw; he is under hiding, and therefore, you know'——

'He'll be nae nicer than your lordship's honour, I'se warrant,' answered Caleb, cheerfully, with a nod of intelligence; 'I am sorry that the gentleman is under distress, but I am blithe that he canna say muckle agane our house-keeping, for I believe his ain pinches may match ours;—no that we are pinched, thank God,' he added, retracting the admission which he had made in his first burst of joy, 'but nae doubt we are waur aff than we hae been, or suld be. And for eating,—what signifies telling a lee? there's just the hinder end of the mutton-ham that has been but three times on the table, and the nearer the bane the sweeter, as your honours weel ken; and—there's the heel of the ewe-milk kebbuck, wi' a bit of nice butter, and—and—that's a' that's to trust to.' And with great alacrity he produced his slender stock of provisions, and placed them with much formality upon a small round table betwixt the two gentlemen, who were not deterred either by the homely quality or limited quantity of the repast from doing it full justice. Caleb in the meanwhile waited on them with grave officiousness, as if anxious to make up, by his own respectful assiduity, for the want of all other attendance.

But alas! how little on such occasions can form, however anxiously and scrupulously observed, supply the lack of substantial fare! Bucklaw, who had eagerly eaten a considerable portion of the thrice-sacked mutton-ham, now began to demand ale.

'I wadna just presume to recommend our ale,' said Caleb; 'the maut was ill made, and there was awfu' thunner last week; but siccan water as the Tower well has ye'll seldom see, Bucklaw, and that I'se engage for.'

'But if your ale is bad, you can let us have some wine,' said Bucklaw, making a grimace at the mention of the pure element which Caleb so earnestly recommended.

'Wine?' answered Caleb, undauntedly, 'eneugh of wine; it was but twa days syne—wae's me for the cause—there was as much wine drunk in this house as would have floated a pinnace. There never was lack of wine at Wolf's Crag.'

'Do fetch us some then,' said his master, 'instead of talking about it.' And Caleb boldly departed.

Every expended butt in the old cellar did he set a-tilt, and shake with the desperate expectation of collecting enough of the grounds of claret to fill the large pewter measure which he carried in his hand. Alas! each had been too devoutly drained; and, with all the squeezing and manœuvring which his craft as a butler suggested, he could only collect about half a quart that seemed presentable. Still, however, Caleb was too good a general to renounce the field without a stratagem to cover his retreat. He undauntedly threw down an empty flagon, as if he had stumbled at the entrance of the apartment; called upon Mysie to wipe up the wine that had never been spilt, and placing the other vessel on the table, hoped there was still enough left for their honours. There was indeed; for even Bucklaw, a sworn friend to the grape, found no encouragement to renew his first attack upon the vintage of Wolf's Crag, but contented himself, however reluctantly, with a draught of fair water. Arrangements were now made for his repose; and as the secret chamber was assigned for this purpose, it furnished Caleb with a first-rate and most plausible apology for all deficiencies of furniture, bedding, &c.

'For wha,' said he, 'would have thought of the secret chaumer being needed? it has not been used since the time of the Gowrie Conspiracy,* and I durst never let a woman ken of the entrance to it, or your honour will allow that it wad not hae been a secret chaumer lang.'

CHAPTER VIII

The hearth in hall was black and dead,
  No board was dight in bower within,
Nor merry bowl nor welcome bed;
  'Here's sorry cheer,' quoth the Heir of Linne.

(*Old Ballad*) *

THE feelings of the prodigal Heir of Linne, as expressed in that excellent old song, when, after dissipating his whole fortune, he found himself the deserted inhabitant of 'the lonely lodge,' might perhaps have some resemblance to those of the Master of Ravenswood in his deserted mansion of Wolf's Crag. The Master, however, had this advantage over the spendthrift in the legend, that if he was in similar distress, he could not impute it to his own imprudence. His misery had been bequeathed to him by his father, and, joined to his high blood, and to a title which the courteous might give, or the churlish withhold, at their pleasure, it was the whole inheritance he had derived from his ancestry.

Perhaps this melancholy, yet consolatory reflection, crossed the mind of the unfortunate young nobleman with a breathing of comfort. Favourable to calm reflection, as well as to the Muses, the morning, while it dispelled the shades of night, had a composing and sedative effect upon the stormy passions by which the Master of Ravenswood had been agitated on the preceding day.* He now felt himself able to analyse the different feelings by which he was agitated, and much resolved to combat and to subdue them. The morning, which had arisen calm and bright, gave a pleasant effect even to the waste moorland view which was seen from the castle on looking to the landward; and the glorious ocean, crisped with a thousand rippling waves of silver, extended on the other side, in awful yet complacent majesty, to the verge of the horizon. With such scenes of calm sublimity the human heart sympathizes even in its most disturbed moods, and deeds of honour and virtue are inspired by their majestic influence.

To seek out Bucklaw in the retreat which he had afforded him was the first occupation of the Master, after he had performed, with a scrutiny unusually severe, the important task of self-examination.* 'How now, Bucklaw?' was his morning's salutation—'how like you the couch in which the exiled Earl of Angus once slept in security, when he was pursued by the full energy of a king's resentment?'*

'Umph!' returned the sleeper awakened;* 'I have little to complain of where so great a man was quartered before me, only the mattress was of the hardest, the vault somewhat damp, the rats rather more mutinous than I would have expected from the state of Caleb's larder; and if there had been shutters to that grated window, or a curtain to the bed, I should think it, upon the whole, an improvement in your accommodations.'

'It is, to be sure, forlorn enough,' said the Master, looking around the small vault; 'but if you will rise and leave it, Caleb will endeavour to find you a better breakfast than your supper of last night.'

'Pray, let it be no better,' said Bucklaw, getting up, and endeavouring to dress himself as well as the obscurity of the place would permit,—'let it, I say, be no better, if you mean me to persevere in my proposed reformation. The very recollection of Caleb's beverage has done more to suppress my longing to open the day with a morning-draught than twenty sermons would have done. And you, Master, have you been able to give battle valiantly to your bosom-snake? You see I am in the way of smothering my vipers one by one.'

'I have commenced the battle, at least, Bucklaw, and I have had a fair vision of an angel who descended to my assistance,' replied the Master.

'Woe's me!' said his guest, 'no vision can I expect, unless my aunt, Lady Girnington, should betake herself to the tomb; and then it would be the substance of her heritage rather than the appearance of her phantom that I should consider as the support of my good resolutions.—But this same breakfast, Master,—does the deer that is to make the pasty run yet on foot, as the ballad has it?'*

'I will enquire into that matter,' said his entertainer; and, leaving the apartment, he went in search of Caleb, whom, after some difficulty, he found in an obscure sort of dungeon, which had been in former times the buttery of the castle. Here the old man was employed busily in the doubtful task of burnishing a pewter flagon until it should take the hue and semblance of silver-plate. 'I think it may do—I think it might pass, if they winna bring it ower muckle in the light o' the window!' were the ejaculations which he muttered from time to time, as if to encourage himself in his undertaking, when he was interrupted by the voice of his master. 'Take this,' said the Master of Ravenswood, 'and get what is necessary for the family.' And with these words he gave to the old butler the purse which had on the preceding evening so narrowly escaped the fangs of Craigengelt. The old man shook his silvery and thin locks, and looked with an expression of the most heartfelt anguish at his master as he weighed in his hand the slender treasure, and said in a sorrowful voice, 'And is this a' that's left?'

'All that is left at present,' said the Master, affecting more cheerfulness than perhaps he really felt, 'is just the green purse and the wee pickle gowd, as the old song says;* but we shall do better one day, Caleb.'

'Before that day comes,' said Caleb, 'I doubt there will be an end of an auld sang, and an auld serving-man to boot.*But it disna become me to speak that gate to your honour, and you looking sae pale. Tak back the purse, and keep it to be making a show before company; for if your honour would just tak a bidding, and be whiles taking it out afore folk and putting it up again, there's naebody would refuse us trust, for a' that's come and gane yet.'

'But, Caleb,' said the Master, 'I still intend to leave this country very soon, and desire to do so with the reputation of an honest man, leaving no debt behind me, at least of my own contracting.'

'And gude right ye suld gang away as a true man, and so ye shall; for auld Caleb can tak the wyte of whatever is taen on for the house, and then it will be a' just ae man's burden; and I will live just as weel in the tolbooth as out of it, and the credit of the family will be a' safe and sound.'

The Master endeavoured, in vain, to make Caleb comprehend, that the butler's incurring the responsibility of debts in his own person, would rather add to than remove the objections which he had to their being contracted. He spoke to a premier, too busy in devising ways and means to puzzle himself with refuting the arguments offered against their justice or expediency.

'There's Eppie Sma'trash will trust us for ale,' said Caleb to himself; 'she has lived a' her life under the family—and maybe wi' a soup brandy—I canna say for wine—she is but a lone woman, and gets her claret by a runlet at a time—but I'll work a wee drap out o' her by fair means or foul. For doos, there's the doocot—there will be poultry amang the tenants, though Luckie Chirnside says she has paid the kain twice ower. We'll mak shift, an it like your honour—we'll mak shift—keep your heart abune, for the house sall haud its credit as lang as auld Caleb is to the fore.'

The entertainment which the old man's exertions of various kinds enabled him to present to the young gentlemen for three or four days, was certainly of no splendid description, but it may readily be believed it was set before no critical guests; and even the distresses, excuses, evasions, and shifts of Caleb, afforded amusement to the young men, and added a sort of interest to the scrambling and irregular style of their table. They had indeed occasion to seize on every circumstance that might serve to diversify or enliven time, which otherwise passed away so heavily.

Bucklaw, shut out from his usual field-sports and joyous carouses by the necessity of remaining concealed within the walls of the castle, became a joyless and uninteresting companion. When the Master of Ravenswood would no longer fence or play at shovel-board—when he himself had polished to the extremity the coat of his palfrey with brush, currycomb, and hair-cloth—when he had seen him eat his provender, and gently lie down in his stall, he could hardly help envying the animal's apparent acquiescence in a life so monotonous. 'The stupid brute,' he said, 'thinks neither of the race-ground or the hunting-field, or his green paddock at Bucklaw, but enjoys himself as comfortably when haltered to the rack in this ruinous vault, as if he had been foaled in it, and I, who have the freedom of a prisoner at large, to range through the dungeons of this wretched old tower, can hardly, betwixt whistling and sleeping, contrive to pass away the hour till dinner-time.'

And with this disconsolate reflection, he wended his way to the bartizan or battlements of the tower, to watch what objects might appear on the distant moor, or to pelt, with pebbles and pieces of lime, the sea-mews and cormorants which established themselves incautiously within the reach of an idle young man.

Ravenswood, with a mind incalculably deeper and more powerful than that of his companion, had his own anxious subjects of reflection, which wrought for him the same unhappiness that sheer ennui and want of occupation inflicted on his companion. The first sight of Lucy Ashton had been less impressive than her image proved to be upon reflection. As the depth and violence of that revengeful passion, by which he had been actuated in seeking an interview with the father, began to abate by degrees, he looked back on his conduct towards the daughter as harsh and unworthy towards a female of rank and beauty. Her looks of grateful acknowledgment, her words of affectionate courtesy, had been repelled with something which approached to disdain; and if the Master of Ravenswood had sustained wrongs at the hand of Sir William Ashton, his conscience told him they had been unhandsomely resented towards his daughter. When his thoughts took this turn of self-reproach, the recollection of Lucy Ashton's beautiful features, rendered yet more interesting by the circumstances in which their meeting had taken place, made an impression upon his mind at once soothing and painful. The sweetness of her voice, the delicacy of her expressions, the vivid glow of her filial affection, embittered his regret at having repulsed her gratitude with rudeness, while, at the same time, they placed before his imagination a picture of the most seducing sweetness.

Even young Ravenswood's strength of moral feeling and rectitude of purpose at once increased the danger of cherishing these recollections, and the propensity to entertain them. Firmly resolved as he was to subdue, if possible, the predominating vice in his character, he admitted with willingness—nay, he summoned up in his imagination, the ideas by which it could be most powerfully counteracted; and, while he did so, a sense of his own harsh conduct towards the daughter of his enemy naturally induced him, as if by way of recompense, to invest her with more of grace and beauty than perhaps she could actually claim.

Had any one at this period told the Master of Ravenswood that he had so lately vowed vengeance against the whole lineage of him whom he considered, not unjustly, as author of his father's ruin and death, he might at first have repelled the charge as a foul calumny; yet, upon serious self-examination, he would have been compelled to admit, that it had, at one period, some foundation in truth, though, according to the present tone of his sentiments, it was difficult to believe that this had really been the case.

There already existed in his bosom two contradictory passions,—a desire to revenge the death of his father, strangely qualified by admiration of his enemy's daughter. Against the former feeling he had struggled, until it seemed to him upon the wane; against the latter he used no means of resistance, for he did not suspect its existence. That this was actually the case, was chiefly evinced by his resuming his resolution to leave Scotland. Yet, though such was his purpose, he remained day after day at Wolf's Crag, without taking measures for carrying it into execution. It is true, that he had written to one or two kinsmen, who resided in a distant quarter of Scotland, and particularly to the Marquis of A——,* intimating his purpose; and when pressed upon the subject by Bucklaw, he was wont to allege the necessity of waiting for their reply, especially that of the Marquis, before taking so decisive a measure.

The Marquis was rich and powerful; and although he was suspected to entertain sentiments unfavourable to the government established at the Revolution, he had nevertheless address enough to head a party in the Scottish Privy Council, connected with the high church faction in England, and powerful enough to menace those to whom the Lord Keeper adhered, with a probable subversion of their power.* The consulting with a personage of such importance was a plausible excuse, which Ravenswood used to Bucklaw, and probably to himself, for continuing his residence at Wolf's Crag; and it was rendered yet more so by a general report which began to be current, of a probable change of ministers and measures in the Scottish administration.* These rumours, strongly asserted by some, and as resolutely denied by others, as their wishes or interest dictated, found their way even to the ruinous Tower of Wolf's Crag, chiefly through the medium of Caleb the butler, who, among his other excellences, was an ardent politician, and seldom made an excursion from the old fortress to the neighbouring village of Wolf's-hope, without bringing back what tidings were current in the vicinity.

But if Bucklaw could not offer any satisfactory objections to the delay of the Master in leaving Scotland, he did not the less suffer with impatience the state of inaction to which it confined him; and it was only the ascendency which his new companion had acquired over him, that induced him to submit to a course of life so alien to his habits and inclinations.

'You were wont to be thought a stirring active young fellow, Master,' was his frequent remonstrance; 'yet here you seem determined to live on and on like a rat in a hole, with this trifling difference, that the wiser vermin chooses a hermitage where he can find food at least; but as for us, Caleb's excuses become longer as his diet turns more spare, and I fear we shall realize the stories they tell of the sloth,—we have almost eat up the last green leaf on the plant, and have nothing left for it but to drop from the tree and break our necks.'*

'Do not fear it,' said Ravenswood; 'there is a fate watches for us, and we too have a stake in the revolution that is now impending, and which already has alarmed many a bosom.'

'What fate—what revolution?' enquired his companion. 'We have had one revolution too much already, I think.'*

Ravenswood interrupted him by putting into his hands a letter.

'O,' answered Bucklaw, 'my dream's out—I thought I heard Caleb this morning pressing some unfortunate fellow to a drink of cold water, and assuring him it was better for his stomach in the morning than ale or brandy.'

'It was my Lord of A——'s courier,' said Ravenswood, 'who was doomed to experience his ostentatious hospitality, which I believe ended in sour beer and herrings—Read, and you will see the news he has brought us.'

'I will as fast as I can,' said Bucklaw; 'but I am no great clerk, nor does his lordship seem to be the first of scribes.'

The reader will peruse, in a few seconds, by the aid of our friend Ballantyne's types,* what took Bucklaw a good half hour in perusal, though assisted by the Master of Ravenswood. The tenor was as follows:—

'*Right Honourable our Cousin,*

'Our hearty commendations premised, these come to assure you of the interest which we take in your welfare, and in your purposes towards its augmentation. If we have been less active in showing forth our effective good-will towards you than, as a loving kinsman and blood-relative, we would willingly have desired, we request that you will impute it to lack of opportunity to show our good-liking, not to any coldness of our will. Touching your resolution to travel in foreign parts, as at this time we hold the same little advisable, in respect that your ill-willers may, according to the custom of such persons, impute motives for your journey, whereof, although we know and believe you to be as clear as ourselves, yet natheless their words may find credence in places where the belief in them may much prejudice you, and which we should see with more unwillingness and displeasure than with means of remedy.

'Having thus, as becometh our kindred, given you our poor mind on the subject of your journeying forth of Scotland, we would willingly add reasons of weight, which might materially advantage you and your father's house, thereby to determine you to abide at Wolf's Crag, until this harvest season shall be passed over. But what sayeth the proverb, *verbum sapienti,*—a word is more to him that hath wisdom than a sermon to a fool.* And albeit we have written this poor scroll with our own hand, and are well assured of the fidelity of our messenger, as him that is many ways bounden to us, yet so it is, that sliddery ways crave wary walking,* and that we may not peril upon paper matters which we would gladly impart to you by word of mouth. Wherefore, it was our purpose to have prayed you heartily to come to this our barren Highland country to kill a stag, and to treat of the matters which we are now more painfully inditing to you anent.* But commodity does not serve at present for such our meeting, which, therefore, shall be deferred intil sic time as we may in all mirth rehearse those things whereof we now keep silence. Meantime, we pray you to think that we are, and will still be, your good kinsman and well-wisher, waiting but for times of whilk we do, as it were, entertain a twilight prospect, and appear and hope to be also your effectual well-doer. And in which hope we heartily write ourself,

> 'Right Honourable,
>   'Your loving cousin,
>   'A——.

'Given from our poor
house of B——,*&c.'

Superscribed—'For the right honourable, and our honoured kinsman, the Master of Ravenswood—These, with haste, haste, post haste—ride and run until these be delivered.'*

'What think you of this epistle, Bucklaw?' said the Master, when his companion had hammered out all the sense, and almost all the words of which it consisted.

'Truly, that the Marquis's meaning is as great a riddle as his manuscript. He is really in much need of Wit's Interpreter, or the Complete Letter-Writer,* and were I you, I would send him a copy by the bearer. He writes you very kindly to remain wasting your time and your money in this vile, stupid, oppressed country, without so much as offering you the countenance and shelter of his house. In my opinion, he has some scheme in view in which he supposes you can be useful, and he wishes to keep you at hand, to make use of you when it ripens, reserving the power of turning you adrift, should his plot fail in the concoction.'

'His plot?—then you suppose it is a treasonable business,' answered Ravenswood.

'What else can it be?' replied Bucklaw; 'the Marquis has been long suspected to have an eye to Saint Germains.'

'He should not engage me rashly in such an adventure,' said Ravenswood; 'when I recollect the times of the first and second Charles, and of the last James, truly I see little reason, that, as a man or a patriot, I should draw my sword for their descendants.'*

'Humph!' replied Bucklaw; 'so you have set yourself down to mourn over the crop-eared dogs, whom honest Claver'se treated as they deserved?'*

'They first gave the dogs an ill name, and then hanged them,'*
replied Ravenswood. 'I hope to see the day when justice shall be
open to Whig and Tory, and when these nick-names shall only
be used among coffee-house politicians, as slut and jade are among
apple-women, as cant terms of idle spite and rancour.'*

'That will not be in our days, Master—the iron has entered too
deeply into our sides and our souls.'*

'It will be, however, one day,' replied the Master; 'men will not
always start at these nick-names as at a trumpet-sound. As social
life is better protected, its comforts will become too dear to be
hazarded without some better reason than speculative politics.'

'It is fine talking,' answered Bucklaw; 'but my heart is with the
old song,—

> "To see good corn upon the rigs,
> And a gallows built to hang the Whigs,
> And the right restored where the right should be,
> O, that is the thing that would wanton me." '*

'You may sing as loudly as you will, *cantabit vacuus,*'*—answered
the Master; 'but I believe the Marquis is too wise, at least too
wary, to join you in such a burden. I suspect he alludes to a
revolution in the Scottish Privy Council, rather than in the British
kingdoms.'

'O, confusion to your state-tricks!' exclaimed Bucklaw, 'your
cold calculating manœuvres, which old gentlemen in wrought
nightcaps and furred gowns execute like so many games at chess,
and displace a treasurer or lord commissioner as they would take
a rook or a pawn. Tennis for my sport, and battle for my earnest!
My racket and my sword for my plaything and bread-winner! And
you, Master, so deep and considerate as you would seem, you have
that within you makes the blood boil faster than suits your present
humour of moralizing on political truths. You are one of those
wise men who see every thing with great composure till their
blood is up, and then—woe to any one who should put them in
mind of their own prudential maxims!'

'Perhaps,' said Ravenswood, 'you read me more rightly than I
can myself. But to think justly will certainly go some length in

helping me to act so. But hark! I hear Caleb tolling the dinner-bell.'

'Which he always does with the more sonorous grace, in proportion to the meagreness of the cheer which he has provided,' said Bucklaw; 'as if that infernal clang and jangle, which will one day bring the belfry down the cliff, could convert a starved hen into a fat capon, and a blade-bone of mutton into a haunch of vension.'

'I wish we may be so well off as your worst conjectures surmise, Bucklaw, from the extreme solemnity and ceremony with which Caleb seems to place on the table that solitary covered dish.'

'Uncover, Caleb! uncover, for Heaven's sake!' said Bucklaw; 'let us have what you can give us without preface—Why, it stands well enough, man,' he continued, addressing impatiently the ancient butler, who, without reply, kept shifting the dish, until he had at length placed it with mathematical precision in the very midst of the table.

'What have we got here, Caleb?' enquired the Master in his turn.

'Ahem! sir, ye suld have known before; but his honour the Laird of Bucklaw is so impatient,' answered Caleb, still holding the dish with one hand, and the cover with the other, with evident reluctance to disclose the contents.

'But what is it, a God's name—not a pair of clean spurs, I hope, in the Border fashion of old times?'*

'Ahem! ahem!' reiterated Caleb, 'your honour is pleased to be facetious—natheless, I might presume to say it was a convenient fashion, and used, as I have heard, in an honourable and thriving family. But touching your present dinner, I judged that this being Saint Magdalen's Eve, who was a worthy queen of Scotland in her day,* your honours might judge it decorous, if not altogether to fast, yet only to sustain nature with some slight refection, as ane saulted herring or the like.' And, uncovering the dish, he displayed four of the savoury fishes which he mentioned, adding, in a subdued tone, 'that they were no just common herring neither, being every ane melters, and sauted with uncommon care by the housekeeper (poor Mysie) for his honour's especial use.'

'Out upon all apologies!' said the Master, 'let us eat the herrings, since there is nothing better to be had—but I begin to think with you, Bucklaw, that we are consuming the last green leaf, and that, in spite of the Marquis's political machinations, we must positively shift camp for want of forage, without waiting the issue of them.'

CHAPTER IX

Ay, and when huntsmen wind the merry horn,
And from its covert starts the fearful prey,
Who, warm'd with youth's blood in his swelling veins,
Would, like a lifeless clod, outstretched lie,
Shut out from all the fair creation offers?

(Ethwald, Act I. Scene I) *

LIGHT meals procure light slumbers;* and therefore it is not surprising, that, considering the fare which Caleb's conscience, or his necessity, assuming, as will sometimes happen, that disguise, had assigned to the guests of Wolf's Crag, their slumbers should have been short.

In the morning Bucklaw rushed into his host's apartment with a loud halloo, which might have awaked the dead.

'Up! up! in the name of Heaven—the hunters are out, the only piece of sport I have seen this month; and you lie here, Master, on a bed that has little to recommend it, except that it may be something softer than the stone floor of your ancestor's vault.'

'I wish,' said Ravenswood, raising his head peevishly, 'you had forborne so early a jest, Mr Hayston—it is really no pleasure to lose the very short repose which I had just begun to enjoy, after a night spent in thoughts upon fortune far harder than my couch, Bucklaw.'

'Pshaw, pshaw!' replied his guest; 'get up—get up—the hounds are abroad—I have saddled the horses myself, for old Caleb was calling for grooms and lackeys, and would never have proceeded without two hours' apology, for the absence of men that were a hundred miles off.—Get up, Master—I say the hounds are out—get up, I say—the hunt is up.' And off ran Bucklaw.

'And I say,' said the Master, rising slowly, 'that nothing can concern me less. Whose hounds come so near to us?'

'The Honourable Lord Bittlebrains',' answered Caleb, who had followed the impatient Laird of Bucklaw into his master's bedroom, 'and truly I ken nae title they have to be yowling and howling within the freedoms and immunities of your lordship's right of free forestry.'*

'Nor I, Caleb,' replied Ravenswood, 'excepting that they have bought both the lands and the right of forestry, and may think themselves entitled to exercise the rights they have paid their money for.'

'It may be sae, my lord,' replied Caleb; 'but it's no gentleman's deed of them to come here and exercise such like right, and your lordship living at your ain castle of Wolf's Crag. Lord Bittlebrains would do weel to remember what his folk have been.'

'And we what we now are,' said the Master, with suppressed bitterness of feeling. 'But reach me my cloak, Caleb, and I will indulge Bucklaw with a sight of this chase. It is selfish to sacrifice my guest's pleasure to my own.'

'Sacrifice!' echoed Caleb, in a tone which seemed to imply the total absurdity of his master making the least concession in deference to any one—'Sacrifice, indeed!—but I crave your honour's pardon—and whilk doublet is it your pleasure to wear?'

'Any one you will, Caleb—my wardrobe, I suppose, is not very extensive.'

'Not extensive!' echoed his assistant; 'when there is the grey and silver that your lordship bestowed on Hew Hildebrand, your outrider—and the French velvet that went with my lord your father—(be gracious to him!)—my lord your father's auld wardrobe to the puir friends of the family, and the drap-de-berry'—

'Which I gave to you, Caleb, and which, I suppose, is the only dress we have any chance to come at, except that I wore yesterday—pray, hand me that, and say no more about it.'

'If your honour has a fancy,' replied Caleb, 'and doubtless it's a sad-coloured suit, and you are in mourning—nevertheless, I have never tried on the drap-de-berry—ill wad it become me—and your honour having no change of claiths at this present—and it's weel brushed, and as there are leddies down yonder'—

'Ladies!' said Ravenswood; 'and what ladies, pray?'

'What do I ken, your lordship?—looking down at them from the Warden's Tower, I could but see them glent by wi' their bridles ringing, and their feathers fluttering, like the court of Elfland.'

'Well, well, Caleb,' replied the Master, 'help me on with my cloak, and hand me my sword-belt.—What clatter is that in the court-yard?'

'Just Bucklaw bringing out the horses,' said Caleb, after a glance through the window, 'as if there werena men eneugh in the castle, or as if I couldna serve the turn of ony o' them that are out o' the gate.'

'Alas! Caleb, we should want little, if your ability were equal to your will,' replied his master.

'And I hope your lordship disna want that muckle,' said Caleb; 'for, considering a' things, I trust we support the credit of the family as weel as things will permit of,—only Bucklaw is aye sae frank and sae forward.—And there he has brought out your lordship's palfrey, without the saddle being decored wi' the broidered sumpter-cloth! and I could have brushed it in a minute.'

'It is all very well,' said his master, escaping from him, and descending the narrow and steep winding staircase, which led to the court-yard.

'It *may* be a' very weel,' said Caleb, somewhat peevishly; 'but if your lordship wad tarry a bit, I will tell you what will *not* be very weel.'

'And what is that?' said Ravenswood, impatiently, but stopping at the same time.

'Why, just that ye suld speer ony gentleman hame to dinner; for I canna mak anither fast on a feast day, as when I cam ower Bucklaw wi' Queen Margaret—and, to speak truth, if your lordship wad but please to cast yoursell in the way of dining wi' Lord Bittlebrains, I'se warrand I wad cast about brawly for the morn; or if, stead o' that, ye wad but dine wi' them at the change-house, ye might mak your shift for the lawing; ye might say ye had forgot your purse—or that the carline awed ye rent, and that ye wad allow it in the settlement.'

'Or any other lie that came uppermost, I suppose?' said his master. 'Good by, Caleb; I commend your care for the honour of the family.' And, throwing himself on his horse, he followed Bucklaw, who, at the manifest risk of his neck, had begun to gallop down the steep path which led from the Tower, as soon as he saw Ravenswood have his foot in the stirrup.

Caleb Balderstone looked anxiously after them, and shook his thin grey locks—'And I trust they will come to no evil—but they have reached the plain, and folk cannot say but that the horse are hearty and in spirits.'

Animated by the natural impetuosity and fire of his temper, young Bucklaw rushed on with the careless speed of a whirlwind. Ravenswood was scarce more moderate in his pace, for his was a mind unwillingly roused from contemplative inactivity, but which, when once put into motion, acquired a spirit of forcible and violent progression. Neither was his eagerness proportioned in all cases to the motive of impulse, but might be compared to the speed of a stone, which rushes with like fury down the hill, whether it was first put in motion by the arm of a giant or the hand of a boy. He felt, therefore, in no ordinary degree, the headlong impulse of the chase, a pastime so natural to youth of all ranks, that it seems rather to be an inherent passion in our animal nature, which levels all differences of rank and education, than an acquired habit of rapid exercise.

The repeated bursts of the French horn, which was then always used for the encouragement and direction of the hounds—the deep, though distant baying of the pack—the half-heard cries of the huntsmen—the half-seen forms which were discovered, now emerging from glens which crossed the moor, now sweeping over its surface, now picking their way where it was impeded by morasses; and, above all, the feeling of his own rapid motion, animated the Master of Ravenswood, at least for the moment, above the recollections of a more painful nature by which he was surrounded. The first thing which recalled him to those unpleasing circumstances, was feeling that his horse, notwithstanding all the advantages which he received from his rider's knowledge of the country, was unable to keep up with the chase. As he drew his bridle up with the bitter feeling, that his poverty excluded him from the favourite recreation of his forefathers, and indeed their sole employment when not engaged in military pursuits, he was accosted by a well-mounted stranger, who, unobserved, had kept near him during the earlier part of his career.

'Your horse is blown,' said the man, with a complaisance seldom used in a hunting-field. 'Might I crave your honour to make use of mine?'

'Sir,' said Ravenswood, more surprised than pleased at such a proposal, 'I really do not know how I have merited such a favour at a stranger's hands.'

'Never ask a question about it, Master,' said Bucklaw, who, with great unwillingness, had hitherto reined in his own gallant steed, not to outride his host and entertainer. 'Take the goods the gods provide you, as the great John Dryden says*—or stay—here, my friend, lend me that horse; I see you have been puzzled to rein him up this half hour. I'll take the devil out of him for you. Now, Master, do you ride mine, which will carry you like an eagle.'

And throwing the rein of his own horse to the Master of Ravenswood, he sprung upon that which the stranger resigned to him, and continued his career at full speed.

'Was ever so thoughtless a being!' said the Master; 'and you, my friend, how could you trust him with your horse?'

'The horse,' said the man, 'belongs to a person who will make your honour, or any of your honourable friends, most welcome to him, flesh and fell.'

'And the owner's name is——?' asked Ravenswood.

'Your honour must excuse me, you will learn that from himself.—If you please to take your friend's horse, and leave me your galloway, I will meet you after the fall of the stag, for I hear they are blowing him at bay.'

'I believe, my friend, it will be the best way to recover your good horse for you,' answered Ravenswood; and mounting the nag of his friend Bucklaw, he made all the haste in his power to the spot where the blast of the horn announced that the stag's career was nearly terminated.

These jovial sounds were intermixed with the huntsmen's shouts of 'Hyke a Talbot! Hyke a Teviot! now, boys, now!' and similar cheering halloos of the olden hunting-field, to which the impatient yelling of the hounds, now close on the object of their pursuit, gave a lively and unremitting chorus.* The straggling riders began now to rally towards the scene of action, collecting from different points as to a common centre.

Bucklaw kept the start which he had gotten, and arrived first at the spot, where the stag, incapable of sustaining a more prolonged flight, had turned upon the hounds, and, in the hunter's phrase, was at bay. With his stately head bent down, his sides white with foam, his eyes strained betwixt rage and terror, the hunted animal had now in his turn become an object of intimidation to his pursuers.* The hunters came up one by one, and watched an opportunity to assail him with some advantage, which, in such circumstances, can only be done with caution. The dogs stood aloof and bayed loudly, intimating at once eagerness and fear, and each of the sportsmen seemed to expect that his comrade would take upon him the perilous task of assaulting and disabling the animal. The ground, which was a hollow in the common or moor, afforded little advantage for approaching the stag unobserved; and general was the shout of triumph when Bucklaw, with the dexterity proper to an accomplished cavalier of the day, sprang from his horse, and dashing suddenly and swiftly at the stag, brought him to the ground by a cut on the hind leg with his short hunting sword. The pack, rushing in upon their disabled enemy, soon ended his painful struggles, and solemnized his fall with their clamour—the hunters, with their horns and voices, whooping and blowing a *mort*, or death-note, which resounded far over the billows of the adjacent ocean.

The huntsman then withdrew the hounds from the throttled stag, and on his knee presented his knife to a fair female form, on a white palfrey, whose terror, or perhaps her compassion, had till then kept her at some distance. She wore a black silk riding-mask, which was then a common fashion, as well for preserving the complexion from sun and rain, as from an idea of decorum, which did not permit a lady to appear barefaced while engaged in a boisterous sport, and attended by a promiscuous company. The richness of her dress, however, as well as the mettle and form of her palfrey, together with the silvan compliment paid to her by the huntsman, pointed her out to Bucklaw as the principal person in the field. It was not without a feeling of pity, approaching even to contempt, that this enthusiastic hunter observed her refuse the huntsman's knife, presented to her for the purpose of making the first incision in the stag's breast, and thereby discovering the quality of the venison. He felt more than half inclined to pay his compliments to her; but it had been Bucklaw's misfortune, that his habits of life had not rendered him familiarly acquainted with the higher and better classes of female society, so that, with all his natural audacity, he felt sheepish and bashful when it became necessary to address a lady of distinction.

Taking unto himself heart of grace, (to use his own phrase,) he did at length summon up resolution enough to give the fair huntress good time of the day, and trust that her sport had answered her expectation. Her answer was very courteously and modestly expressed, and testified some gratitude to the gallant cavalier, whose exploit had terminated the chase so adroitly, when the hounds and huntsmen seemed somewhat at a stand.

'Uds daggers and scabbard, madam,' said Bucklaw, whom this observation brought at once upon his own ground, 'there is no difficulty or merit in that matter at all, so that a fellow is not too much afraid of having a pair of antlers in his guts. I have hunted at force five hundred times, madam; and I never yet saw the stag at bay, by land or water, but I durst have gone roundly in on him. It is all use and wont, madam; and I'll tell you, madam, for all that, it must be done with good heed and caution; and you will do well, madam, to have your hunting-sword both right sharp and double-edged, that you may strike either fore-handed or back-handed, as you see reason, for a hurt with a buck's horn is a perilous and somewhat venomous matter.'

'I am afraid, sir,' said the young lady, and her smile was scarce concealed by her vizard, 'I shall have little use for such careful preparation.'

'But the gentleman says very right for all that, my lady,' said an old huntsman, who had listened to Bucklaw's harangue with no small edification; 'and I have heard my father say, who was a forester at the Cabrach,* that a wild boar's gaunch is more easily healed than a hurt from the deer's horn, for so says the old woodman's rhyme,—

> "If thou be hurt with horn of hart, it brings thee to thy bier;
> But tusk of boar shall leeches heal—thereof have lesser fear." '*

'An I might advise,' continued Bucklaw, who was now in his element, and desirous of assuming the whole management, 'as the hounds are surbated and weary, the head of the stag should be cabaged in order to reward them; and if I may presume to speak, the huntsman, who is to break up the stag,* ought to drink to your good ladyship's health a good lusty bicker of ale, or a tass of brandy; for if he breaks him up without drinking, the venison will not keep well.'

This very agreeable prescription received, as will be readily believed, all acceptation from the huntsman, who, in requital, offered to Bucklaw the compliment of his knife, which the young lady had declined. This polite proffer was seconded by his mistress.

'I believe, sir,' she said, withdrawing herself from the circle, 'that my father, for whose amusement Lord Bittlebrains' hounds have been out to-day, will readily surrender all care of these matters to a gentleman of your experience.'

Then, bending gracefully from her horse, she wished him good morning, and, attended by one or two domestics, who seemed immediately attached to her service, retired from the scene of action, to which Bucklaw, too much delighted with an opportunity of displaying his wood-craft to care about man or woman either,* paid little attention; but was soon stript to his doublet, with tucked-up sleeves, and naked arms up to the elbows in blood and grease, slashing, cutting, hacking, and hewing, with the precision of Sir Tristrem himself, and wrangling and disputing with all around him concerning nombles, briskets, flankards, and raven-bones, then usual terms of the art of hunting, or of butchery, whichever the reader chooses to call it, which are now probably antiquated.*

When Ravenswood, who followed a short space behind his friend, saw that the stag had fallen, his temporary ardour for the chase gave way to that feeling of reluctance which he endured, at encountering in his fallen fortunes the gaze whether of equals or inferiors. He reined up his horse on the top of a gentle eminence, from which he observed the busy and gay scene beneath him, and heard the whoops of the huntsmen gaily mingled with the cry of the dogs, and the neighing and trampling of the horses. But these jovial sounds fell sadly on the ear of the ruined nobleman. The chase, with all its train of excitations, has ever since feudal times been accounted the almost exclusive privilege of the aristocracy, and was anciently their chief employment in times of peace. The sense that he was excluded by his situation from enjoying the silvan sport, which his rank assigned to him as a special prerogative, and the feeling that new men were now exercising it over the downs, which had been jealously reserved by his ancestors for their own amusement, while he, the heir of the domain, was fain to hold himself at a distance from their party, awakened reflections calculated to depress deeply a mind like Ravenswood's, which was naturally contemplative and melancholy. His pride, however, soon shook off this feeling of dejection, and it gave way to impatience upon finding that his volatile friend Bucklaw seemed in no hurry to return with his borrowed steed, which Ravenswood, before leaving the field, wished to see restored to the obliging owner. As he was about to move towards the group of assembled huntsmen, he was joined by a horseman, who like himself had kept aloof during the fall of the deer.

This personage seemed stricken in years. He wore a scarlet cloak, buttoning high upon his face, and his hat was unlooped and slouched, probably by way of defence against the weather. His horse, a strong and steady palfrey, was calculated for a rider who proposed to witness the sport of the day, rather than to share it. An attendant waited at some distance, and the whole equipment was that of an elderly gentleman of rank and fashion. He accosted Ravenswood very politely, but not without some embarrassment.

'You seem a gallant young gentleman, sir,' he said, 'and yet appear as indifferent to this brave sport as if you had my load of years on your shoulders.'

'I have followed the sport with more spirit on other occasions,' replied the Master; 'at present, late events in my family must be my apology—and besides,' he added, 'I was but indifferently mounted at the beginning of the sport.'

'I think,' said the stranger, 'one of my attendants had the sense to accommodate your friend with a horse.'

'I was much indebted to his politeness and yours,' replied Ravenswood. 'My friend is Mr Hayston of Bucklaw, whom I daresay you will be sure to find in the thick of the keenest

THE BRIDE OF LAMMERMOOR

sportsmen. He will return your servant's horse, and take my pony in exchange—and will add,' he concluded, turning his horse's head from the stranger, 'his best acknowledgments to mine for the accommodation.'

The Master of Ravenswood having thus expressed himself, began to move homeward, with the manner of one who has taken leave of his company. But the stranger was not so to be shaken off. He turned his horse at the same time, and rode in the same direction so near to the Master, that, without outriding him, which the formal civility of the time, and the respect due to the stranger's age and recent civility, would have rendered improper, he could not easily escape from his company.

The stranger did not long remain silent. 'This, then,' he said, 'is the ancient Castle of Wolf's Crag, often mentioned in the Scottish records,' looking to the old tower, then darkening under the influence of a stormy cloud, that formed its background; for at the distance of a short mile, the chase, having been circuitous, had brought the hunters nearly back to the point which they had attained, when Ravenswood and Bucklaw had set forward to join them.

Ravenswood answered this observation with a cold and distant assent.

'It was, as I have heard,' continued the stranger, unabashed by his coldness, 'one of the most early possessions of the honourable family of Ravenswood.'

'Their earliest possession,' answered the Master, 'and probably their latest.'

'I—I—I should hope not, sir,' answered the stranger, clearing his voice with more than one cough, and making an effort to overcome a certain degree of hesitation,—'Scotland knows what she owes to this ancient family, and remembers their frequent and honourable achievements. I have little doubt, that, were it properly represented to her majesty that so ancient and noble a family were subjected to dilapidation—I mean to decay—means might be found, *ad re-ædificandum antiquam domum*'—*

'I will save you the trouble, sir, of discussing this point farther,' interrupted the Master, haughtily. 'I am the heir of that unfortunate House—I am the Master of Ravenswood. And you, sir, who seem to be a gentleman of fashion and education, must be sensible, that the next mortification after being unhappy, is the being loaded with undesired commiseration.'

'I beg your pardon, sir,' said the elder horseman—'I did not know—I am sensible I ought not to have mentioned—nothing could be farther from my thoughts than to suppose'——

'There are no apologies necessary, sir,' answered Ravenswood, 'for here, I suppose, our roads separate, and I assure you that we part in perfect equanimity on my side.'

As speaking these words, he directed his horse's head towards a narrow causeway, the ancient approach to Wolf's Crag, of which it might be truly said, in the words of the Bard of Hope, that

> 'Frequented by few was the grass-cover'd road,
> Where the hunter of deer and the warrior trode,
> To his hills that encircle the sea.'*

But, ere he could disengage himself from his companion, the young lady we have already mentioned came up to join the stranger, followed by her servants.

'Daughter,' said the stranger to the masked damsel, 'this is the Master of Ravenswood.'

It would have been natural that the gentleman should have replied to this introduction; but there was something in the graceful form and retiring modesty of the female to whom he was thus presented, which not only prevented him from enquiring to whom, and by whom, the annunciation had been made, but which even for the time struck him absolutely mute. At this moment the cloud which had long lowered above the height on which Wolf's Crag is situated, and which now, as it advanced, spread itself in darker and denser folds both over land and sea, hiding the distant objects and obscuring those which were nearer, turning the sea to a leaden complexion, and the heath to a darker brown, began now, by one or two distant peals, to announce the thunders with which it was fraught; while two flashes of lightning, following each other very closely, showed in the distance the grey turrets of Wolf's Crag, and, more nearly, the rolling billows of the ocean, crested suddenly with red and dazzling light.

The horse of the fair huntress showed symptoms of impatience and restiveness, and it became impossible for Ravenswood, as a man or a gentleman, to leave her abruptly to the care of an aged father or her menial attendants. He was, or believed himself, obliged in courtesy to take hold of her bridle, and assist her in managing the unruly animal. While he was thus engaged, the old gentleman observed that the storm seemed to increase—that they were far from Lord Bittlebrains', whose guests they were for the present—and that he would be obliged to the Master of Ravenswood to point him the way to the nearest place of refuge from the storm. At the same time he cast a wistful and embarrassed look towards the Tower of Wolf's Crag, which seemed to render it almost impossible for the owner to avoid offering an old man and a lady, in such an emergency, the temporary use of his house. Indeed, the condition of the young huntress made this courtesy indispensable; for, in the course of the services which he rendered, he could not but perceive that she trembled much, and was extremely agitated, from her apprehensions, doubtless, of the coming storm.

I know not if the Master of Ravenswood shared her terrors, but he was not entirely free from something like a similar disorder of nerves, as he observed, 'The Tower of Wolf's Crag has nothing to offer beyond the shelter of its roof, but if that can be acceptable at such a moment'—he paused, as if the rest of the invitation stuck in his throat. But the old gentleman, his self-constituted companion, did not allow him to recede from the invitation, which he had rather suffered to be implied than directly expressed.

'The storm,' said the stranger, 'must be an apology for waiving ceremony—his daughter's health was weak—she had suffered much from a recent alarm—he trusted their intrusion on the Master of Ravenswood's hospitality would not be altogether unpardonable in the circumstances of the case—his child's safety must be dearer to him than ceremony.'

There was no room to retreat. The Master of Ravenswood led the way, continuing to keep hold of the lady's bridle to prevent her horse from starting at some unexpected explosion of thunder. He was not so bewildered in his own hurried reflections, but that he remarked, that the deadly paleness which had occupied her neck and temples, and such of her features as the riding-mask left exposed, gave place to a deep and rosy suffusion; and he felt with embarrassment that a flush was by tacit sympathy excited in his own cheeks. The stranger, with watchfulness which he disguised under apprehensions for the safety of his daughter, continued to observe the expression of the Master's countenance as they ascended the hill to Wolf's Crag. When they stood in front of that ancient fortress, Ravenswood's emotions were of a very complicated description; and as he led the way into the rude court-yard, and halloo'd to Caleb to give attendance, there was a tone of sternness, almost of fierceness, which seemed somewhat alien from the courtesies of one who is receiving honoured guests.

Caleb came; and not the paleness of the fair stranger at the first approach of the thunder, nor the paleness of any other person, in any other circumstances whatever, equalled that which overcame the thin cheeks of the disconsolate seneschal, when he beheld this accession of guests to the castle, and reflected that the dinner hour was fast approaching. 'Is he daft?' he muttered to himself,—'is he clean daft a'thegither, to bring lords and leddies, and a host of folk behint them, and twal-o'-clock chappit?' Then approaching the Master, he craved pardon for having permitted the rest of his people to go out to see the hunt, observing, that 'they wad never think of his lordship coming back till mirk night, and that he dreaded they might play the truant.'

'Silence, Balderstone!' said Ravenswood, sternly; 'your folly is unseasonable.—Sir and madam,' he said, turning to his guests, 'this old man, and a yet older and more imbecile female domestic, form my whole retinue. Our means of refreshing you are more scanty than even so miserable a retinue, and a dwelling so dilapidated, might seem to promise you; but, such as they may chance to be, you may command them.'

The elder stranger, struck with the ruined and even savage appearance of the Tower, rendered still more disconsolate by the lowering and gloomy sky, and perhaps not altogether unmoved by the grave and determined voice in which their host addressed them, looked round him anxiously, as if he half repented the readiness with which he had accepted the offered hospitality. But there was now no opportunity of receding from the situation in which he had placed himself.

As for Caleb, he was so utterly stunned by his master's public and unqualified acknowledgment of the nakedness of the land,* that for two minutes he could only mutter within his hebdomadal beard, which had not felt the razor for six days, 'He's daft—clean daft—red wud, and awa wi't! But deil hae Caleb Balderstone,' said he, collecting his powers of invention and resource, 'if the family shall lose credit, if he were as mad as the seven wise masters!'* He then boldly advanced, and in spite of his master's frowns and impatience, gravely asked, 'if he should not serve up some slight refection for the young leddy, and a glass of tokay, or old sack—or'——

'Truce to this ill-timed foolery,' said the Master, sternly,—'put the horses into the stable, and interrupt us no more with your absurdities.'

'Your honour's pleasure is to be obeyed aboon a' things,' said Caleb; 'nevertheless, as for the sack and tokay which it is not your noble guests' pleasure to accept'——

But here the voice of Bucklaw, heard even above the clattering of hoofs and braying of horns with which it mingled, announced that he was scaling the pathway to the Tower at the head of the greater part of the gallant hunting train.

'The deil be in me,' said Caleb, taking heart in spite of this new invasion of Philistines,* 'if they shall beat me yet! The hellicat ne'er-do-weel!—to bring such a crew here, that will expect to find brandy as plenty as ditch-water, and he kenning sae absolutely the case in whilk we stand for the present! But I trow, could I get rid of thae gaping gowks of flunkies that hae won into the court-yard at the back of their betters, as mony a man gets preferment, I could make a' right yet.'

The measures which he took to execute this dauntless resolution, the reader shall learn in the next chapter.

CHAPTER X

With throat unslaked, with black lips baked,
    Agape they heard him call;
Gramercy they for joy did grin,
And all at once their breath drew in,
    As they had been drinking all!

(Coleridge's *Rime of the Ancient Mariner*)*

HAYSTON of Bucklaw was one of the thoughtless class who never hesitate between their friend and their jest. When it was announced that the principal persons of the chase had taken their route towards Wolf's Crag, the huntsmen, as a point of civility, offered to transfer the venison to that mansion; a proffer which was readily accepted by Bucklaw, who thought much of the astonishment which their arrival in full body would occasion poor old Caleb Balderstone, and very little of the dilemma to which he was about to expose his friend the Master, so ill circumstanced to receive such a party. But in old Caleb he had to do with a crafty and alert antagonist, prompt at supplying, upon all emergencies, evasions and excuses suitable, as he thought, to the dignity of the family.

'Praise be blest!' said Caleb to himself, 'ae leaf of the muckle gate has been swung to wi' yestreen's wind, and I think I can manage to shut the ither.'

But he was desirous, like a prudent governor, at the same time to get rid, if possible, of the internal enemy, in which light he considered almost every one who eat and drank, ere he took measures to exclude those whom their jocund noise now pronounced to be near at hand. He waited, therefore, with impatience until his master had shown his two principal guests into the Tower, and then commenced his operations.

'I think,' he said to the stranger menials, 'that as they are bringing the stag's head to the castle in all honour, we, who are in-dwellers, should receive them at the gate.'

The unwary grooms had no sooner hurried out, in compliance with this insidious hint, than, one folding-door of the ancient gate being already closed by the wind, as has been already intimated, honest Caleb lost no time in shutting the other with a clang, which resounded from donjon-vault to battlement. Having thus secured the pass, he forthwith indulged the excluded huntsmen in brief parley, from a small projecting window, or shot-hole, through which, in former days, the warders were wont to reconnoitre those who presented themselves before the gates. He gave them to understand, in a short and pithy speech, that the gate of the castle was never on any account opened during meal-times*—that his honour, the Master of Ravenswood, and some guests of quality, had just sat down to dinner—that there was excellent brandy at the hostler-wife's at Wolf's-hope down below—and he held out some obscure hint that the reckoning would be discharged by the Master; but this was uttered in a very dubious and oracular strain, for, like Louis XIV., Caleb Balderstone hesitated to carry finesse so far as direct falsehood, and was content to deceive, if possible, without directly lying.*

This annunciation was received with surprise by some, with laughter by others, and with dismay by the expelled lackeys, who endeavoured to demonstrate that their right of re-admission, for the purpose of waiting upon their master and mistress, was at least indisputable. But Caleb was not in a humour to understand or admit any distinctions. He stuck to his original proposition with that dogged, but convenient pertinacity, which is armed against all conviction, and deaf to all reasoning. Bucklaw now came from the rear of the party, and demanded admittance in a very angry tone. But the resolution of Caleb was immovable.

'If the king on the throne were at the gate,'* he declared, 'his ten fingers should never open it contrair to the established use and wont of the family of Ravenswood, and his duty as their head-servant.'

Bucklaw was now extremely incensed, and with more oaths and curses than we care to repeat, declared himself most unworthily treated, and demanded peremptorily to speak with the Master of Ravenswood himself. But to this, also, Caleb turned a deaf ear.

'He's as soon a-bleeze as a tap of tow the lad Bucklaw,' he said; 'but the deil of ony master's face he shall see till he has sleepit and waken'd on't. He'll ken himsell better the morn's morning. It sets the like o'him, to be bringing a crew of drunken hunters here, when he kens there is but little preparation to sloken his ain drought.' And he disappeared from the window, leaving them all to digest their exclusion as they best might.

But another person, of whose presence Caleb, in the animation of the debate, was not aware, had listened in silence to its progress. This was the principal domestic of the stranger—a man of trust and consequence—the same, who, in the hunting-field, had accommodated Bucklaw with the use of his horse. He was in the stable when Caleb had contrived the expulsion of his fellow-servants, and thus avoided sharing the same fate from which his personal importance would certainly not have otherwise saved him.

This personage perceived the manœuvre of Caleb, easily appreciated the motive of his conduct, and knowing his master's intentions towards the family of Ravenswood, had no difficulty as to the line of conduct he ought to adopt. He took the place of Caleb (unperceived by the latter) at the post of audience which he had just left, and announced to the assembled domestics, 'that it was his master's pleasure that Lord Bittlebrains' retinue and his own should go down to the adjacent change-house, and call for what refreshments they might have occasion for, and he should take care to discharge the lawing.'

The jolly troop of huntsmen retired from the inhospitable gate of Wolf's Crag, execrating, as they descended the steep path-way, the niggard and unworthy disposition of the proprietor, and damning, with more than silvan license, both the castle and its inhabitants. Bucklaw, with many qualities which would have made him a man of worth and judgment in more favourable circumstances, had been so utterly neglected in point of education, that he was apt to think and feel according to the ideas of the companions of his pleasures. The praises which had recently been heaped upon himself he contrasted with the general abuse now levelled against Ravenswood—he recalled to his mind the dull and monotonous days he had spent in the

Tower of Wolf's Crag, compared with the joviality of his usual life—he felt, with great indignation, his exclusion from the castle, which he considered as a gross affront, and every mingled feeling led him to break off the union which he had formed with the Master of Ravenswood.

On arriving at the change-house of the village of Wolf's-hope, he unexpectedly met with an old acquaintance just alighting from his horse. This was no other than the very respectable Captain Craigengelt, who immediately came up to him, and, without appearing to retain any recollection of the indifferent terms on which they had parted, shook him by the hand in the warmest manner possible. A warm grasp of the hand was what Bucklaw could never help returning with cordiality, and no sooner had Craigengelt felt the pressure of his fingers than he knew the terms on which he stood with him.

'Long life to you, Bucklaw!' he exclaimed; 'there's life for honest folk in this bad world yet!'

The Jacobites at this period, with what propriety I know not, used, it must be noticed, the term of *honest men* as peculiarly descriptive of their own party.

'Ay, and for others besides, it seems,' answered Bucklaw; 'otherways, how came you to venture hither, noble Captain?'

'Who—I?—I am as free as the wind at Martinmas, that pays neither land-rent nor annual;* all is explained—all settled with the honest old drivellers yonder of Auld Reekie—Pooh! pooh! they dared not keep me a week of days in durance. A certain person has better friends among them than you wot of, and can serve a friend when it is least likely.'

'Pshaw!' answered Hayston, who perfectly knew and thoroughly despised the character of this man, 'none of your cogging gibberish—tell me truly, are you at liberty and in safety?'

'Free and safe as a whig bailie on the causeway of his own borough, or a canting presbyterian minister in his own pulpit—and I came to tell you that you need not remain in hiding any longer.'

Then I suppose you call yourself my friend, Captain Craigengelt?' said Bucklaw.

'Friend!' replied Craigengelt, 'my cock of the pit? why, I am thy very Achates, man, as I have heard scholars say—hand and glove—bark and tree—thine to life and death!' *

'I'll try that in a moment,' answered Bucklaw. 'Thou art never without money, however thou comest by it. Lend me two pieces to wash the dust out of these honest fellows' throats in the first place, and then'——

'Two pieces? twenty are at thy service, my lad—and twenty to back them.'

'Ay—say you so?' said Bucklaw, pausing, for his natural penetration led him to suspect some extraordinary motive lay couched under such an excess of generosity. 'Craigengelt, you are either an honest fellow in right good earnest, and I scarce know how to believe that—or you are cleverer than I took you for, and I scarce know how to believe that either.'

'*L'un n'empeche pas l'autre,*' * said Craigengelt, 'touch and try—the gold is good as ever was weighed.'

He put a quantity of gold pieces into Bucklaw's hand, which he thrust into his pocket without either counting or looking at them, only observing, 'that he was so circumstanced that he must enlist, though the devil offered the press-money;' and then turning to the huntsmen, he called out, 'Come along, my lads—all is at my cost.'

'Long life to Bucklaw!' shouted the men of the chase.

'And confusion to him that takes his share of the sport, and leaves the hunters as dry as a drum-head,' added another, by way of corollary.

'The house of Ravenswood was ance a gude and an honourable house in this land,' said an old man, 'but it's lost its credit this day, and the Master has shown himself no better than a greedy cullion.'

And with this conclusion, which was unanimously agreed to by all who heard it, they rushed tumultuously into the house of entertainment, where they revelled till a late hour. The jovial temper of Bucklaw seldom permitted him to be nice in the choice of his associates; and on the present occasion, when his joyous debauch received additional zest from the intervention of an unusual space of sobriety, and almost abstinence, he was as happy in leading the revels, as if his comrades had been sons of princes.

Craigengelt had his own purposes, in fooling him up to the top of his bent;* and having some low humour, much impudence, and the power of singing a good song, understanding besides thoroughly the disposition of his regained associate, he readily succeeded in involving him bumper-deep in the festivity of the meeting.

A very different scene was in the meantime passing in the Tower of Wolf's Crag. When the Master of Ravenswood left the courtyard, too much busied with his own perplexed reflections to pay attention to the manœuvre of Caleb, he ushered his guests into the great hall of the castle.

The indefatigable Balderstone, who, from choice or habit, worked on from morning to night, had, by degrees, cleared this desolate apartment of the confused relics of the funeral banquet, and restored it to some order. But not all his skill and labour, in disposing to advantage the little furniture which remained, could remove the dark and disconsolate appearance of those ancient and disfurnished walls. The narrow windows, flanked by deep indentures into the wall, seemed formed rather to exclude than to admit the cheerful light; and the heavy and gloomy appearance of the thunder-sky added still farther to the obscurity.

As Ravenswood, with the grace of a gallant of that period, but not without a certain stiffness and embarrassment of manner, handed the young lady to the upper end of the apartment, her father remained standing more near to the door, as if about to disengage himself from his hat and cloak. At this moment the clang of the portal was heard, a sound at which the stranger started, stepped hastily to the window, and looked with an air of alarm at Ravenswood, when he saw that the gate of the court was shut, and his domestics excluded.

'You have nothing to fear, sir,' said Ravenswood, gravely; 'this roof retains the means of giving protection, though not welcome. Methinks,' he added, 'it is time that I should know who they are that have thus highly honoured my ruined dwelling?'

The young lady remained silent and motionless, and the father, to whom the question was more directly addressed, seemed in the situation of a performer who has ventured to take upon himself a part which he finds himself unable to present, and who comes to a pause when it is most to be expected that he should speak. While he endeavoured to cover his embarrassment with the exterior ceremonials of a well-bred demeanour, it was obvious, that in making his bow, one foot shuffled forward, as if to advance—the other backward, as if with the purpose of escape—and as he undid the cape of his coat, and raised his beaver from his face, his fingers fumbled as if the one had been linked with rusted iron, or the other had weighed equal with a stone of lead. The darkness of the sky seemed to increase, as if to supply the want of those mufflings which he laid aside with such evident reluctance. The impatience of Ravenswood increased also in proportion to the delay of the stranger, and he appeared to struggle under agitation, though probably from a very different cause. He laboured to restrain his desire to speak, while the stranger, to all appearance, was at a loss for words to express what he felt it necessary to say. At length Ravenswood's impatience broke the bounds he had imposed upon it.

'I perceive,' he said, 'that Sir William Ashton is unwilling to announce himself in the Castle of Wolf's Crag.'

'I had hoped it was unnecessary,' said the Lord Keeper, relieved from his silence, as a spectre by the voice of the exorcist; 'and I am obliged to you, Master of Ravenswood, for breaking the ice at once, where circumstances—unhappy circumstances, let me call them—rendered self-introduction peculiarly awkward.'

'And I am not then,' said the Master of Ravenswood, gravely, 'to consider the honour of this visit as purely accidental?'

'Let us distinguish a little,' said the Keeper, assuming an appearance of ease which perhaps his heart was a stranger to; 'this is an honour which I have eagerly desired for some time, but which I might never have obtained, save for the accident of the storm. My daughter and I are alike grateful for this opportunity of thanking the brave man, to whom she owes her life and I mine.'

The hatred which divided the great families in the feudal times had lost little of its bitterness, though it no longer expressed itself in deeds of open violence. Not the feelings which Ravenswood had begun to entertain towards Lucy Ashton, not the hospitality due to his guests, were able entirely to subdue, though they warmly combated, the deep passions which arose within him, at beholding his father's foe standing in the hall of the family of which he had in a great measure accelerated the ruin. His looks glanced from the father to the daughter with an irresolution, of which Sir William Ashton did not think it proper to await the conclusion. He had now disembarrassed himself of his riding-dress, and walking up to his daughter, he undid the fastening of her mask.

'Lucy, my love,' he said, raising her and leading her towards Ravenswood, 'lay aside your mask, and let us express our gratitude to the Master openly and barefaced.'

'If he will condescend to accept it,' was all that Lucy uttered; but in a tone so sweetly modulated, and which seemed to imply at once a feeling and a forgiving of the cold reception to which they were exposed, that, coming from a creature so innocent and so beautiful, her words cut Ravenswood to the very heart for his harshness. He muttered something of surprise, something of confusion, and, ending with a warm and eager expression of his happiness at being able to afford her shelter under his roof, he saluted her, as the ceremonial of the time enjoined upon such occasions. Their cheeks had touched and were withdrawn from each other—Ravenswood had not quitted the hand which he had taken in kindly courtesy—a blush, which attached more consequence by far than was usual to such ceremony, still mantled on Lucy Ashton's beautiful cheek, when the apartment was suddenly illuminated by a flash of lightning, which seemed absolutely to swallow the darkness of the hall. Every object might have been for an instant seen distinctly. The slight and half-sinking form of Lucy Ashton, the well-proportioned and stately figure of Ravenswood, his dark features, and the fiery, yet irresolute expression of his eyes,—the old arms and scutcheons which hung on the walls of the apartment, were for an instant distinctly visible to the Keeper by a strong red brilliant glare of light. Its disappearance was almost instantly followed by a burst of thunder, for the storm-cloud was very near the castle; and the peal was so sudden and dreadful, that the old tower rocked to its foundation, and every inmate concluded it was falling upon them. The soot, which had not been disturbed for centuries, showered down the huge tunnelled chimneys—lime and dust flew in clouds from the wall; and, whether the lightning had actually struck the castle, or whether through the violent concussion of the air, several heavy stones were hurled from the mouldering battlements into the roaring sea beneath. It might seem as if the ancient founder of the castle were bestriding the thunder-storm, and proclaiming his displeasure at the reconciliation of his descendant with the enemy of his house. *

The consternation was general, and it required the efforts of both the Lord Keeper and Ravenswood to keep Lucy from fainting. Thus was the Master a second time engaged in the most delicate and dangerous of all tasks, that of affording support and assistance to a beautiful and helpless being, who, as seen before in a similar situation, had already become a favourite of his imagination, both when awake and when slumbering. If the Genius of the House really condemned a union betwixt the Master and his fair guest, the means by which he expressed his sentiments were as unhappily chosen as if he had been a mere mortal. The train of little attentions, absolutely necessary to soothe the young lady's mind, and aid her in composing her spirits, necessarily threw the Master of Ravenswood into such an intercourse with her father, as was calculated, for the moment at least, to break down the barrier of feudal enmity which divided them. To express himself churlishly, or even coldly, towards an old man, whose daughter (and *such* a daughter) lay before them, overpowered with natural terror—and all this under his own roof—the thing was impossible; and by the time that Lucy, extending a hand to each, was able to thank them for their kindness, the Master felt that his sentiments of hostility towards the Lord Keeper were by no means those most predominant in his bosom.

The weather, her state of health, the absence of her attendants, all prevented the possibility of Lucy Ashton renewing her journey to Bittlebrains-House, which was full five miles distant; and the Master of Ravenswood could not but, in common courtesy, offer the shelter of his roof for the rest of the day and for the night. But a flush of less soft expression, a look much more habitual to his features, resumed predominance when he mentioned how meanly he was provided for the entertainment of his guests.

'Do not mention deficiencies,' said the Lord Keeper, eager to interrupt him and prevent his resuming an alarming topic; 'you are preparing to set out for the Continent, and your house is probably for the present unfurnished. All this we understand; but if you mention inconvenience, you will oblige us to seek accommodations in the hamlet.'

As the Master of Ravenswood was about to reply, the door of the hall opened, and Caleb Balderstone rushed in.

CHAPTER XI

Let them have meat enough, woman—half a hen;
There be old rotten pilchards—put them off too;
'Tis but a little new anointing of them,
And a strong onion, that confounds the savour.

(Love's Pilgrimage) *

THE thunderbolt, which had stunned all who were within hearing of it, had only served to awaken the bold and inventive genius of the flower of Majors-Domo. Almost before the clatter had ceased, and while there was yet scarce an assurance whether the castle was standing or falling, Caleb exclaimed, 'Heavens be praised!—this comes to hand like the boul of a pint stoup.' He then barred the kitchen door in the face of the Lord Keeper's servant, whom he perceived returning from the party at the gate, and muttering, 'How the deil cam he in?—but deil may care—Mysie, what are ye sitting shaking and greeting in the chimney-neuk for? Come here—or stay where ye are, and skirl as loud as ye can—it's a' ye're gude for—I say, ye auld deevil, skirl—skirl—louder—louder, woman—gar the gentles hear ye in the ha'—I have heard ye as far off as the Bass for a less matter. And stay—down wi' that crockery'—

And with a sweeping blow, he threw down from a shelf some articles of pewter and earthenware. He exalted his voice amid the clatter, shouting and roaring in a manner which changed Mysie's hysterical terrors of the thunder into fears that her old fellow-servant was gone distracted. 'He has dung down a' the bits o' pigs, too—the only thing we had left to haud a soup milk—and he has spilt the hatted kitt that was for the Master's dinner. Mercy save us, the auld man's gaen clean and clear wud wi' the thunner!'

'Haud your tongue, ye b——!' said Caleb, in the impetuous and overbearing triumph of successful invention, 'a's provided now—dinner and a' thing—the thunner's done a' in a clap of a hand!'

'Puir man, he's muckle astray,' said Mysie, looking at him with a mixture of pity and alarm; 'I wish he may ever come hame to himsell again.'

'Here, ye auld doited deevil,' said Caleb, still exulting in his extrication from a dilemma which had seemed insurmountable; 'keep the strange man out of the kitchen—swear the thunner came down the chimney, and spoiled the best dinner ye ever dressed—beef—bacon—kid—lark—leveret—wild fowl—venison, and what not. Lay it on thick, and never mind expenses. I'll awa up to the ha'—make a' the confusion ye can—but be sure ye keep out the strange servant.'

With these charges to his ally, Caleb posted up to the hall, but stopping to reconnoitre through an aperture, which time, for the convenience of many a domestic in succession, had made in the door, and perceiving the situation of Miss Ashton, he had prudence enough to make a pause, both to avoid adding to her alarm, and in order to secure attention to his account of the disastrous effects of the thunder.

But when he perceived that the lady was recovered, and heard the conversation turn upon the accommodation and refreshment which the castle afforded, he thought it time to burst into the room in the manner announced in the last chapter.

'Wull a wins!—wull a wins!—such a misfortune to befa' the House of Ravenswood, and I to live to see it!'

'What is the matter, Caleb?' said his master, somewhat alarmed in his turn; 'has any part of the castle fallen?'

'Castle fa'an?—na, but the sute's fa'an, and the thunner's come right down the kitchen-lumm, and the things are a' lying here awa, there awa, like the Laird o'Hotchpotch's lands—and wi' brave guests of honour and quality to entertain'—a low bow here to Sir William Ashton and his daughter—'and naething left in the house fit to present for dinner—or for supper either, for aught that I can see!'

'I verily believe you, Caleb,' said Ravenswood, drily.

Balderstone here turned to his master a half-upbraiding, half-imploring countenance, and edged towards him as he repeated, 'It was nae great matter of preparation; but just something added to your honour's ordinary course of fare—*petty cover*, as they say at the Louvre*—three courses and the fruit.'

'Keep your intolerable nonsense to yourself, you old fool!' said Ravenswood, mortified at his officiousness, yet not knowing how to contradict him, without the risk of giving rise to scenes yet more ridiculous.

Caleb saw his advantage, and resolved to improve it. But first, observing that the Lord Keeper's servant entered the apartment, and spoke apart with his master, he took the same opportunity to whisper a few words into Ravenswood's ear—'Haud your tongue, for heaven's sake, sir—if it's my pleasure to hazard my soul in telling lees for the honour of the family, it's nae business o' yours—and if ye let me gang on quietly, I'se be moderate in my banquet; but if ye contradict me, deil but I dress ye a dinner fit for a duke!'

Ravenswood, in fact, thought it would be best to let his officious butler run on, who proceeded to enumerate upon his fingers,—'No muckle provision—might hae served four persons of honour,—first course, capons in white broth—roast kid— bacon with reverence,—second course, roasted leveret—butter crabs—a veal florentine,—third course, black-cock—it's black eneugh now wi' the sute—plumdamas—a tart—a flam—and some nonsense sweet things, and comfits—and that's a',' he said, seeing the impatience of his master; 'that's just a' was o't—forby the apples and pears.'

Miss Ashton had by degrees gathered her spirits, so far as to pay some attention to what was going on; and observing the restrained impatience of Ravenswood, contrasted with the peculiar determination of manner with which Caleb detailed his imaginary banquet, the whole struck her as so ridiculous, that, despite every effort to the contrary, she burst into a fit of incontrollable laughter, in which she was joined by her father, though with more moderation, and finally by the Master of Ravenswood himself, though conscious that the jest was at his own expense. Their mirth—for a scene which we read with little emotion often appears extremely ludicrous to the spectators—made the old vault ring again. They ceased—they renewed—they ceased—they renewed again their shouts of laughter! Caleb, in the meantime, stood his ground with a grave, angry, and scornful dignity, which greatly enhanced the ridicule of the scene, and the mirth of the spectators.

At length, when the voices, and nearly the strength of the laughers, were exhausted, he exclaimed, with very little ceremony, 'The deil's in the gentles! they breakfast sae lordly, that the loss of the best dinner ever cook pat fingers to, makes them as merry as if it were the best jeest in a' George Buchanan.* If there was as little in your honours' wames, as there is in Caleb Balderstone's, less caickling wad serve ye on sic a gravaminous subject.'

Caleb's blunt expression of resentment again awakened the mirth of the company, which, by the way, he regarded not only as an aggression upon the dignity of the family, but a special contempt of the eloquence with which he himself had summed up the extent of their supposed losses;—'a description of a dinner,' as he said afterwards to Mysie, 'that wad hae made a fu' man hungry, and them to sit there laughing at it!'

'But,' said Miss Ashton, composing her countenance as well as she could, 'are all these delicacies so totally destroyed, that no scrap can be collected?'

'Collected, my leddy! what wad ye collect out of the sute and the ass? Ye may gang down yoursell, and look into our kitchen— the cookmaid in the trembling exies—the gude vivers lying a' about—beef—capons, and white broth—florentine and flams— bacon, wi' reverence, and a' the sweet confections and whim-whams; ye'll see them a', my leddy—that is,' said he, correcting himself, 'ye'll no see ony of them now, for the cook has soopit them up, as was weel her part; but ye'll see the white broth where it was spilt. I pat my fingers in it, and it tastes as like sour-milk as ony thing else; if that isna the effect of thunner, I kenna what is.—This gentleman here couldna but hear the clash of our haill dishes, china and silver thegither?'

The Lord Keeper's domestic, though a statesman's attendant, and of course trained to command his countenance upon all occasions, was somewhat discomposed by this appeal, to which he only answered by a bow.

'I think, Mr Butler,' said the Lord Keeper, who began to be afraid lest the prolongation of this scene should at length displease Ravenswood,—'I think, that were you to retire with my servant

Lockhard—he has travelled, and is quite accustomed to accidents and contigencies of every kind, and I hope betwixt you, you may find out some mode of supply at this emergency.'

'His honour kens,'—said Caleb, who, however hopeless of himself of accomplishing what was desirable, would, like the high-spirited elephant, rather have died in the effort, than brooked the aid of a brother in commission,*—'his honour kens weel I need nae counsellor, when the honour of the house is concerned.'

'I should be unjust if I denied it, Caleb,' said his master; 'but your art lies chiefly in making apologies, upon which we can no more dine, than upon the bill of fare of our thunder-blasted dinner. Now, possibly, Mr Lockhard's talent may consist in finding some substitute for that, which certainly is not, and has in all probability never been.'

'Your honour is pleased to be facetious,' said Caleb, 'but I am sure, that for the warst, for a walk as far as Wolf's-hope, I could dine forty men,—no that the folk there deserve your honour's custom. They hae been ill advised in the matter of the duty-eggs and butter, I winna deny that.'*

'Do go consult together,' said the Master, 'go down to the village, and do the best you can. We must not let our guests remain without refreshment, to save the honour of a ruined family. And here, Caleb—take my purse; I believe that will prove your best ally.'

'Purse? purse, indeed?' quoth Caleb, indignantly flinging out of the room,—'what suld I do wi' your honour's purse, on your ain grund? I trust we are no to pay for our ain?'

The servants left the hall; and the door was no sooner shut, than the Lord Keeper began to apologize for the rudeness of his mirth; and Lucy to hope she had given no pain or offence to the kind-hearted faithful old man.

'Caleb and I must both learn, madam, to undergo with good humour, or at least with patience, the ridicule which everywhere attaches itself to poverty.'

'You do yourself injustice, Master of Ravenswood, on my word of honour,' answered his elder guest. 'I believe I know more of your affairs than you do yourself, and I hope to show you, that I am interested in them; and that—in short, that your prospects are better than you apprehend. In the meantime, I can conceive nothing so respectable, as the spirit which rises above misfortune, and prefers honourable privations to debt or dependence.'

Whether from fear of offending the delicacy, or awakening the pride of the Master, the Lord Keeper made these allusions with an appearance of fearful and hesitating reserve, and seemed to be afraid that he was intruding too far, in venturing to touch, however lightly, upon such a topic, even when the Master had led to it. In short, he appeared at once pushed on by his desire of appearing friendly, and held back by the fear of intrusion. It was no wonder that the Master of Ravenswood, little acquainted as he then was with life, should have given this consummate courtier credit for more sincerity than was probably to be found in a score of his cast. He answered, however, with reserve, that he was indebted to all who might think well of him; and, apologizing to his guests, he left the hall, in order to make such arrangements for their entertainment as circumstances admitted.

Upon consulting with old Mysie, the accommodations for the night were easily completed, as indeed they admitted of little choice. The Master surrendered his apartment for the use of Miss Ashton, and Mysie, (once a person of consequence,) dressed in a black satin gown which had belonged of yore to the Master's grandmother, and had figured in the court-balls of Henrietta Maria,* went to attend her as lady's maid. He next enquired after Bucklaw, and understanding he was at the change-house with the huntsmen and some companions, he desired Caleb to call there, and acquaint him how he was circumstanced at Wolf's Crag—to intimate to him that it would be most convenient if he could find a bed in the hamlet, as the elder guest must necessarily be quartered in the secret chamber, the only spare bedroom which could be made fit to receive him. The Master saw no hardship in passing the night by the hall-fire, wrapt in his campaign-cloak; and to Scottish domestics of the day, even of the highest rank, nay, to young men of family or fashion, on any pinch, clean straw, or a dry hayloft, was always held good night-quarters.

For the rest, Lockhard had his master's orders to bring some venison from the inn, and Caleb was to trust to his wits for the honour of his family. The Master, indeed, a second time held out his purse; but, as it was in sight of the strange servant, the butler thought himself obliged to decline what his fingers itched to clutch. 'Couldna he hae slippit it gently into my hand?' said Caleb—'but his honour will never learn how to bear himsell in siccan cases.'

Mysie, in the meantime, according to a uniform custom in remote places in Scotland, offered the strangers the produce of her little dairy, 'while better meat was getting ready.' And according to another custom, not yet wholly in desuetude, as the storm was now drifting off to leeward, the Master carried the Keeper to the top of his highest tower to admire a wide and waste extent of view, and to 'weary for his dinner.' *

CHAPTER XII

'Now dame,' quoth he, 'Je vous dis sans doute,
Had I nought of a capon but the liver,
And of your white bread nought but a shiver,
And after that a roasted pigge's head,
(But I ne wold for me no beast were dead,)
Then had I with you homely sufferaunce.'

(Chaucer, *Sumner's Tale*)*

IT was not without some secret misgivings that Caleb set out upon his exploratory expedition. In fact, it was attended with a treble difficulty. He dared not tell his master the offence which he had that morning given to Bucklaw (just for the honour of the family)—he dared not acknowledge he had been too hasty in refusing the purse—and, thirdly, he was somewhat apprehensive of unpleasant consequences upon his meeting Hayston under the impression of an affront, and probably by this time under the influence also of no small quantity of brandy.

Caleb, to do him justice, was as bold as any lion where the honour of the family of Ravenswood was concerned; but his was that considerate valour which does not delight in unnecessary risks. This, however, was a secondary consideration; the main point was to veil the indigence of the house-keeping at the castle, and to make good his vaunt of the cheer which his resources could procure, without Lockhard's assistance, and without supplies from his master. This was as prime a point of honour with him, as with the generous elephant with whom we have already compared him, who, being over-tasked, broke his skull through the desperate exertions which he made to discharge his duty, when he perceived they were bringing up another to his assistance.

The village which they now approached had frequently afforded the distressed butler resources upon similar emergencies; but his relations with it had been of late much altered.

It was a little hamlet which straggled along the side of a creek formed by the discharge of a small brook into the sea, and was hidden from the castle, to which it had been in former times an appendage, by the intervention of the shoulder of a hill forming a projecting headland. It was called Wolf's-hope, (*i.e.* Wolf's Haven,) and the few inhabitants gained a precarious subsistence by manning two or three fishing-boats in the herring season, and smuggling gin and brandy during the winter months. They paid a kind of hereditary respect to the Lords of Ravenswood; but, in the difficulties of the family, most of the inhabitants of Wolf's-hope had contrived to get feu-rights[12] to their little possessions, their huts, kail-yards, and rights of commonty, so that they were emancipated from the chains of feudal dependence, and free from the various exactions with which, under every possible pretext, or without any pretext at all, the Scottish landlords of the period, themselves in great poverty, were wont to harass their still poorer tenants at will.* They might be, on the whole, termed independent, a circumstance peculiarly galling to Caleb, who had been wont to exercise over them the same sweeping authority in levying contributions which was exercised in former times in England, when 'the royal purveyors, sallying forth from under the Gothic portcullis to purchase provisions with power and prerogative, instead of money, brought home the plunder of an hundred markets, and all that could be seized from a flying and hiding country, and deposited their spoil in an hundred caverns.'[13]*

Caleb loved the memory and resented the downfall of that authority, which mimicked, on a petty scale, the grand contributions exacted by the feudal sovereigns. And as he fondly flattered himself that the awful rule and right supremacy* which assigned to the Barons of Ravenswood the first and most effective interest in all productions of nature within five miles of their castle, only slumbered, and was not departed for ever, he used every now and then to give the recollection of the inhabitants a little jog by some petty exaction. These were at first submitted to, with more or less readiness, by the inhabitants of the hamlet; for they had been so long used to consider the wants of the Baron and his family as having a title to be preferred to their own, that their actual independence did not convey to them an immediate sense of freedom. They resembled a man that has been long fettered, who, even at liberty, feels, in imagination, the grasp of the handcuffs still binding his wrists. But the exercise of freedom is quickly followed with the natural consciousness of its immunities, as the enlarged prisoner, by the free use of his limbs, soon dispels the cramped feeling they had acquired when bound.

The inhabitants of Wolf's-hope began to grumble, to resist, and at length positively to refuse compliance with the exactions of Caleb Balderstone. It was in vain he reminded them, that when the eleventh Lord Ravenswood, called the Skipper, from his delight in naval matters, had encouraged the trade of their port by building the pier, (a bulwark of stones rudely piled together,) which protected the fishing-boats from the weather, it had been matter of understanding, that he was to have the first stone of butter after the calving of every cow within the barony, and the first egg, thence called the Monday's egg, laid by every hen on every Monday in the year.

The feuars heard and scratched their heads, coughed, sneezed, and being pressed for answer, rejoined with one voice, 'They could not say;'—the universal refuge of a Scottish peasant, when pressed to admit a claim which his conscience owns, or perhaps his feelings, and his interest inclines him to deny.

Caleb, however, furnished the notables of Wolf's-hope with a note of the requisition of butter and eggs, which he claimed as arrears of the aforesaid subsidy, or kindly aid, payable as above mentioned; and having intimated that he would not be averse to compound the same for goods or money, if it was inconvenient to them to pay in kind, left them, as he hoped, to debate the mode of assessing themselves for that purpose. On the contrary, they met with a determined purpose of resisting the exaction, and were only undecided as to the mode of grounding their opposition, when the cooper, a very important person on a fishing station, and one of the Conscript Fathers of the village,* observed, 'That their hens had caickled mony a day for the Lords of Ravenswood, and it was time they suld caickle for those that gave them roosts and barley.' An unanimous grin intimated the assent of the assembly. 'And,' continued the orator, 'if it's your wull, I'll just tak a step as far as

Dunse for Davie Dingwall the writer,* that's come frae the North to settle amang us, and he'll pit this job to rights, I'se warrant him.'

A day was accordingly fixed for holding a grand *palaver* at Wolf's-hope on the subject of Caleb's requisitions, and he was invited to attend at the hamlet for that purpose.

He went with open hands and empty stomach, trusting to fill the one on his master's account, and the other on his own score, at the expense of the feuars of Wolf's-hope. But, death to his hopes! as he entered the eastern end of the straggling village, the awful form of Davie Dingwall, a sly, dry, hard-fisted, shrewd country attorney, who had already acted against the family of Ravenswood, and was a principal agent of Sir William Ashton, trotted in at the western extremity, bestriding a leathern portmanteau stuffed with the feu-charters of the hamlet,* and hoping he had not kept Mr Balderstone waiting, 'as he was instructed and fully empowered to pay or receive, compound or compensate, and, in fine, to *agé*[14] as accords, respecting all mutual and unsettled claims whatsoever, belonging or competent to the Honourable Edgar Ravenswood, commonly called the Master of Ravenswood'——

'The *Right* Honourable Edgar *Lord Ravenswood*,' said Caleb, with great emphasis; for, though conscious he had little chance of advantage in the conflict to ensue, he was resolved not to sacrifice one jot of honour.

'Lord Ravenswood, then,' said the man of business; 'we shall not quarrel with you about titles of courtesy—commonly called Lord Ravenswood, or Master of Ravenswood, heritable proprietor of the lands and barony of Wolf's Crag, on the one part, and to John Whitefish and others, feuars in the town of Wolf's-hope, within the barony aforesaid, on the other part.'

Caleb was conscious, from sad experience, that he would wage a very different strife with this mercenary champion, than with the individual feuars themselves, upon whose old recollections, predilections, and habits of thinking, he might have wrought by an hundred indirect arguments, to which their deputy-representative was totally insensible. The issue of the debate proved the reality of his apprehensions. It was in vain he strained his eloquence and ingenuity, and collected into one mass all arguments arising from antique custom and hereditary respect, from the good deeds done by the Lords of Ravenswood to the community of Wolf's-hope in former days, and from what might be expected from them in future. The writer stuck to the contents of his feu-charters—he could not see it—'twas not in the bond.* And when Caleb, determined to try what a little spirit would do, deprecated the consequences of Lord Ravenswood's withdrawing his protection from the burgh, and even hinted at his using active measures of resentment, the man of law sneered in his face.

'His clients,' he said, 'had determined to do the best they could for their own town, and he thought Lord Ravenswood, since he was a lord, might have enough to do to look after his own castle. As to any threats of stouthrief oppression, by rule of thumb, or *via facti*, as the law termed it,* he would have Mr Balderstone recollect, that new times were not as old times—that they lived on the south of the Forth, and far from the Highlands—that his clients thought they were able to protect themselves; but should they find themselves mistaken, they would apply to the government for the protection of a corporal and four red-coats, who,' said Mr Dingwall, with a grin, 'would be perfectly able to secure them against Lord Ravenswood, and all that he or his followers could do by the strong hand.'*

If Caleb could have concentrated all the lightnings of aristocracy in his eye, to have struck dead this contemner of allegiance and privilege, he would have launched them at his head, without respect to the consequences. As it was, he was compelled to turn his course backward to the castle; and there he remained for full half a day invisible and inaccessible even to Mysie, sequestered in his own peculiar dungeon, where he sat burnishing a single pewter-plate, and whistling Maggy Lauder six hours without intermission.*

The issue of this unfortunate requisition had shut against Caleb all resources which could be derived from Wolf's-hope and its purlieus, the El Dorado, or Peru,* from which, in all former cases of exigence, he had been able to extract some assistance. He had, indeed, in a manner vowed that the deil should have him, if ever he put the print of his foot within its causeway again. He had hitherto kept his word; and, strange to tell, this secession had, as he intended, in some degree, the effect of a punishment upon the refractory feuars. Mr Balderstone had been a person in their eyes connected with a superior order of beings, whose presence used to grace their little festivities, whose advice they found useful on many occasions, and whose communications gave a sort of credit to their village. The place, they acknowledged, 'didna look as it used to do, and should do, since Mr Caleb keepit the castle sae closely—but doubtless, touching the eggs and butter, it was a most unreasonable demand, as Mr Dingwall had justly made manifest.'

Thus stood matters betwixt the parties, when the old butler, though it was gall and wormwood to him,* found himself obliged either to acknowledge before a strange man of quality, and, what was much worse, before that stranger's servant, the total inability of Wolf's Crag to produce a dinner, or he must trust to the compassion of the feuars of Wolf's-hope. It was a dreadful degradation, but necessity was equally imperious and lawless.* With these feelings he entered the street of the village.

Willing to shake himself from his companion as soon as possible, he directed Mr Lockhard to Luckie Sma'trash's change-house, where a din, proceeding from the revels of Bucklaw, Craigengelt, and their party, sounded half-way down the street, while the red glare from the window overpowered the grey twilight which was now settling down, and glimmered against a parcel of old tubs, kegs, and barrels, piled up in the cooper's yard, on the other side of the way.

'If you, Mr Lockhard,' said the old butler to his companion, 'will be pleased to step to the change-house where that light comes from, and where, as I judge, they are now singing "Cauld Kail in Aberdeen,"* ye may do your master's errand about the venison, and I will do mine about Bucklaw's bed, as I return frae getting the rest of the vivers.—It's no that the venison is actually needfu',' he added, detaining his colleague by the button, 'to make up the dinner; but, as a compliment to the hunters, ye ken—and, Mr Lockhard—if they offer ye a drink o' yill, or a cup o' wine, or a glass o' brandy, ye'll be a wise man to take it, in case the thunner should hae soured ours at the castle,—whilk is ower muckle to be dreaded.'

He then permitted Lockhard to depart; and with foot heavy as lead, and yet far lighter than his heart, stepped on through the unequal street of the straggling village, meditating on whom he ought to make his first attack. It was necessary he should find some one, with whom old acknowledged greatness should weigh more than recent independence, and to whom his application might appear an act of high dignity, relenting at once and soothing. But he could not recollect an inhabitant of a mind so constructed. 'Our kail is like to be cauld eneugh too,' he reflected, as the chorus of Cauld Kail in Aberdeen again reached his ears. The minister—he had got his presentation from the late lord, but they had quarrelled about tiends;—the brewster's wife—she had trusted long—and the bill was aye scored up—and unless the dignity of the family should actually require it, it would be a sin to distress a widow woman. None was so able—but, on the other hand, none was likely to be less willing, to stand his friend upon the present occasion, than Gibbie Girder, the man of tubs and barrels already mentioned, who had headed the insurrection in the matter of the egg and butter subsidy.—'But a' comes o' taking folk on the right side, I trow,' quoth Caleb to himself; 'and I had ance the ill hap to say he was but a Johnny Newcome in our town, and the carle bore the family an ill-will ever since. But he married a bonny young quean, Jean Lightbody, auld Lightbody's daughter, him that was in the steading of Loup-the-Dyke,—and auld Lightbody was married himsell to Marion, that was about my lady in the family forty years syne—I hae had mony a day's daffing wi' Jean's mither, and they say she bides on wi' them—the carle has Jacobuses and Georgiuses baith,* an ane could get at them—and sure I am, it's doing him an honour him or his never deserved at our hand, the ungracious sumph; and if he loses by us a'thegither, he is e'en cheap o't, he can spare it brawly.'

Shaking off irresolution, therefore, and turning at once upon his heel, Caleb walked hastily back to the cooper's house, lifted the latch without ceremony, and, in a moment, found himself behind the *hallan*, or partition, from which position he could, himself unseen, reconnoitre the interior of the *but*, or kitchen apartment, of the mansion.

Reverse of the sad menage at the Castle of Wolf's Crag, a bickering fire roared up the cooper's chimney. His wife on the one side, in her pearlings and pudding sleeves, put the last finishing touch to her holiday's apparel, while she contemplated a very handsome and good-humoured face in a broken mirror, raised upon the *bink* (the shelves on which the plates are disposed) for her special accommodation. Her mother, old Luckie Loup-the-Dyke, 'a canty carline'* as was within twenty miles of her, according to the unanimous report of the *cummers*, or gossips, sat by the fire in the full glory of a grogram gown, lammer beads, and a clean cockernony, whiffing a snug pipe of tobacco, and superintending the affairs of the kitchen. For—sight more interesting to the anxious heart and craving entrails of the desponding Seneschal, than either buxom dame or canty cummer—there bubbled on the aforesaid bickering fire, a huge pot, or rather cauldron, steaming with beef and brewis; while before it revolved two spits, turned each by one of the cooper's apprentices, seated in the opposite corners of the chimney; the one loaded with a quarter of mutton, while the other was graced with a fat goose and a brace of wild ducks. The sight and scent of such a land of plenty almost wholly overcame the drooping spirits of Caleb. He turned, for a moment's space, to reconnoitre the *ben*, or parlour end of the house, and there saw a sight scarce less affecting to his feelings;—a large round table, covered for ten or twelve persons, *decored* (according to his own favourite term) with *napery* as white as snow; grand flagons of pewter, intermixed with one or two silver cups, containing, as was probable, something worthy the brilliancy of their outward appearance; clean trenchers, cutty spoons, knives and forks, sharp, burnished, and prompt for action, which lay all displayed as for an especial festival.

'The devil's in the pedling tub-coopering carle!' muttered Caleb, in all the envy of astonishment; 'it's a shame to see the like o' them gusting their gabs at sic a rate. But if some o' that gude cheer does not find its way to Wolf's Crag this night, my name is not Caleb Balderstone.'

So resolving, he entered the apartment, and, in all courteous greeting, saluted both the mother and the daughter. Wolf's Crag was the court of the barony, Caleb prime minister at Wolf's Crag;

and it has ever been remarked, that though the masculine subject who pays the taxes, sometimes growls at the courtiers by whom they are imposed, the said courtiers continue, nevertheless, welcome to the fair sex, to whom they furnish the newest small-talk and the earliest fashions. Both the dames were, therefore, at once about old Caleb's neck, setting up their throats together by way of welcome.

'Ay, sirs, Mr Balderstone, and is this you?—A sight of you is gude for sair een—sit down—sit down—the gudeman will be blithe to see you—ye nar saw him sae cadgy in your life; but we are to christen our bit wean the night, as ye will hae heard, and doubtless ye will stay and see the ordinance.—We hae killed a wether, and ane o' our lads has been out wi' his gun at the moss—ye used to like wild-fowl.'

'Na—na—gudewife,' said Caleb, 'I just keekit in to wish ye joy, and I wad be glad to hae spoken wi' the gudeman, but——' moving, as if to go away.

'The ne'er a fit ye's gang,' said the elder dame, laughing and holding him fast, with a freedom which belonged to their old acquaintance; 'wha kens what ill it may bring to the bairn, if ye owerlook it in that gate?'

'But I'm in a preceese hurry, gudewife,' said the butler, suffering himself to be dragged to a seat without much resistance; 'and as to eating'—for he observed the mistress of the dwellling bustling about to place a trencher for him—'as for eating—lack-a-day, we are just killed up yonder wi' eating frae morning to night*—it's shamefu' epicurism; but that's what we hae gotten frae the English pock-puddings.'

'Hout—never mind the English pock-puddings,' said Luckie Lightbody; 'try our puddings, Mr Balderstone—there is black pudding and white-hass—try whilk ye like best.'

'Baith gude—baith excellent— canna be better; but the very smell is eneugh for me that hae dined sae lately (the faithful wretch had fasted since daybreak.) But I wadna affront your housewifes-kep, gudewife; and, with your permission, I'se e'en pit them in my napkin, and eat them to my supper at e'en, for I am wearied of Mysie's pastry and nonsense—ye ken landward dainties aye pleased me best, Marion—and landward lasses too—(looking at the cooper's wife)—Ne'er a bit but she looks far better than when she married Gilbert, and then she was the bonniest lass in our parochine and the neest till't—But gawsie cow, goodly calf.'

The women smiled at the compliment each to herself, and they smiled again to each other as Caleb wrapt up the puddings in a towel which he had brought with him, as a dragoon carries his foraging bag to receive what may fall in his way.

'And what news at the castle?' quo' the gudewife.

'News?—the bravest news ye ever heard—the Lord Keeper's up yonder wi' his fair daughter, just ready to fling her at my lord's head, if he winna tak her out o' his arms; and I'se warrant he'll stitch our auld lands of Ravenswood to her petticoat tail.'

'Eh! sirs—ay!—and will he hae her?—and is she weel-favoured?—and what's the colour o' her hair?—and does she wear a habit or a railly?'* were the questions which the females showered upon the butler.

'Hout tout!—it wad tak a man a day to answer a' your questions, and I hae hardly a minute. Where's the gudeman?'

'Awa to fetch the minister,' said Mrs Girder, 'precious Mr Peter Bide-the-bent, frae the Moss-head—the honest man has the rheumatism wi' lying in the hills in the persecution.'*

'Ay!—a whig and a mountain-man—nae less?' said Caleb, with a peevishness he could not suppress; 'I hae seen the day, Luckie, when worthy Mr Cuffcushion and the service-book would hae served your turn, (to the elder dame,) or ony honest woman in like circumstances.'*

'And that's true too,' said Mrs Lightbody, 'but what can a body do?—Jean maun baith sing her psalms and busk her cockernony the gate the gudeman likes, and nae ither gate; for he's maister and mair at hame, I can tell ye, Mr Balderstone.'

'Ay, ay, and does he guide the gear too?' said Caleb, to whose projects masculine rule boded little good.

'Ilka penny on't—but he'll dress her as dink as a daisy, as ye see—sae she has little reason to complain—where there's ane better aff there's ten waur.'

'Aweel, gudewife,' said Caleb, crest-fallen, but not beaten off, 'that wasna the way ye guided your gudeman; but ilka land has its ain lauch.* I maun be ganging—I just wanted to round in the gudeman's lug, that I heard them say up by yonder, that Peter Puncheon that was cooper to the Queen's stores at the Timmer Burse at Leith,* is dead—sae I thought that maybe a word frae my lord to the Lord Keeper might hae served Gilbert; but since he's frae hame'——

'O but ye maun stay his hame-coming,'said the dame, 'I aye telled the gudeman ye meant weel to him; but he taks the tout at every bit lippening word.'

'Aweel, I'll stay the last minute I can.'

'And so,' said the handsome young spouse of Mr Girder, 'ye think this Miss Ashton is weel-favoured?—troth, and sae should she, to set up for our young lord, with a face, and a hand, and a seat on his horse, that might become a king's son—d'ye ken that he aye glowers up at my window, Mr Balderstone, when he chaunces to ride thro' the town, sae I hae a right to ken what like he is, as weel as ony body.'

'I ken that brawly,' said Caleb, 'for I hae heard his lordship say the cooper's wife had the blackest ee in the barony; and I said, Weel may that be, my lord, for it was her mither's afore her, as I ken to my cost—Eh, Marion? Ha, ha, ha!—Ah! these were merry days!'

'Hout awa, auld carle,' said the old dame, 'to speak sic daffing to young folk. But, Jean—fie, woman, dinna ye hear the bairn greet? I'se warrant it's that dreary weid[15] has come ower't again.'

Up got mother and grandmother, and scoured away, jostling each other as they ran, into some remote corner of the tenement, where the young hero of the evening was deposited. When Caleb saw the coast fairly clear, he took an invigorating pinch of snuff, to sharpen and confirm his resolution.

Cauld be my cast, thought he, if either Bide-the-bent or Girder taste that broche of wild-fowl this evening; and then addressing the eldest turnspit, a boy of about eleven years old, and putting a penny into his hand, he said, 'Here is twal pennies,[16] my man; carry that ower to Mrs Sma'trash, and bid her fill my mill wi' snishing, and I'll turn the broche for ye in the meantime—and she will gie ye a ginge-bread snap for your pains.'

No sooner was the elder boy departed on this mission, than Caleb, looking the remaining turnspit gravely and steadily in the face, removed from the fire the spit bearing the wild-fowl of which he had undertaken the charge, clapped his hat on his head, and fairly marched off with it. He stopped at the door of the change-house only to say, in a few brief words, that Mr Hayston of Bucklaw was not to expect a bed that evening in the castle.

If this message was too briefly delivered by Caleb, it became absolute rudeness when conveyed through the medium of a suburb landlady; and Bucklaw was, as a more calm and temperate man might have been, highly incensed. Captain Craigengelt proposed, with the unanimous applause of all present, that they should course the old fox (meaning Caleb) ere he got to cover, and toss him in a blanket. *But Lockhard intimated to his master's servants, and those of Lord Bittlebrains, in a tone of authority, that the slightest impertinence to the Master of Ravenswood's domestic, would give Sir William Ashton the highest offence. And having so said, in a manner sufficient to prevent any aggression on their part, he left the public-house, taking along with him two servants loaded with such provisions as he had been able to procure, and overtook Caleb just when he had cleared the village.

CHAPTER XIII

Should I take aught of you?—'tis true I begged now;
And what is worse than that, I stole a kindness;
And, what is worst of all, I lost my way in't.

(*Wit without Money*)*

THE face of the little boy, sole witness of Caleb's infringement upon the laws at once of property and hospitality, would have made a good picture. He sat motionless, as if he had witnessed some of the spectral appearances which he had heard told of in a winter's evening; and as he forgot his own duty, and allowed his spit to stand still, he added to the misfortunes of the evening, by suffering the mutton to burn as black as a coal. He was first recalled from his trance of astonishment by a hearty cuff, administered by Dame Lightbody, who (in whatever other respects she might conform to her name) was a woman strong of person, and expert in the use of her hands, as some say her deceased husband had known to his cost.

'What gar'd ye let the roast burn, ye ill-cleckit gude-for-nought?'

'I dinna ken,' said the boy.

'And where's that ill-deedy gett, Giles?'

'I dinna ken,' blubbered the astonished declarant.

'And where's Mr Balderstone?—and abune a', and in the name of council and kirk-session,* that I suld say sae, where's the broche wi' the wild-fowl?'

As Mrs Girder here entered, and joined her mother's exclamations, screaming into one ear while the old lady deafened the other, they succeeded in so utterly confounding the unhappy urchin, that he could not for some time tell his story at all, and it was only when the elder boy returned, that the truth began to dawn on their minds.

'Weel, sirs!' said Mrs Lightbody, 'wha wad hae thought o' Caleb Balderstone playing an auld acquaintance sic a pliskie!'

'O, weary on him!' said the spouse of Mr Girder; 'and what am I to say to the gudeman?—he'll brain me, if there wasna anither woman in a' Wolf's-hope.'

'Hout tout, silly quean,' said the mother; 'na, na—it's come to muckle, but it's no come to that neither;* for an he brain you he maun brain me, and I have gar'd his betters stand back—hands aff is fair play—we maunna heed a bit flyting.'

The tramp of horses now announced the arrival of the cooper, with the minister. They had no sooner dismounted than they made for the kitchen fire, for the evening was cool after the thunder storm, and the woods wet and dirty. The young gude-wife, strong in the charms of her Sunday gown and biggonets, threw herself in the way of receiving the first attack, while her mother, like the veteran division of the Roman legion, remained in the rear, ready to support her in case of necessity. Both hoped to protract the discovery of what had happened—the mother, by interposing her bustling person betwixt Mr Girder and the fire, and the daughter, by the extreme cordiality with which she received the minister and her husband, and the anxious fears which she expressed lest they should have 'gotten cauld.'

'Cauld?' quoth the husband surlily—for he was not of that class of lords and masters whose wives are viceroys over them—'we'll be cauld eneugh, I think, if ye dinna let us in to the fire.'

And so saying, he burst his way through both lines of defence; and, as he had a careful eye over his property of every kind, he perceived at one glance the absence of the spit with its savoury burden. 'What the deil, woman'——

'Fie for shame!' exclaimed both the women; 'and before Mr Bide-the-bent!'

'I stand reproved,' said the cooper; 'but'——

'The taking in our mouths the name of the great enemy of our souls,' said Mr Bide-the-bent——

'I stand reproved,' said the cooper.

'Is an exposing ourselves to his temptations,' continued the reverend monitor, 'and an inviting, or, in some sort, a compelling, of him to lay aside his other trafficking with unhappy persons, and wait upon those in whose speech his name is frequent.'

'Weel, weel, Mr Bide-the-bent, can a man do mair than stand reproved?' said the cooper; 'but just let me ask the women what for they hae dished the wild-fowl before we came.'

'They arena dished, Gilbert,' said his wife; 'but—but an accident'——

'What accident?' said Girder, with flashing eyes—'Nae ill come ower them, I trust? Uh?'

His wife, who stood much in awe of him, durst not reply, but her mother bustled up to her support, with arms disposed as if they were about to be a-kimbo at the next reply.—'I gied them to an acquaintance of mine, Gibbie Girder; and what about it now?'

Her excess of assurance struck Girder mute for an instant.—'And *ye* gied the wild-fowl, the best end of our christening dinner, to a friend of yours, ye auld rudas! And what might *his* name be, I pray ye?'

'Just worthy Mr Caleb Balderstone, frae Wolf's Crag,' answered Marion, prompt and prepared for battle.

Girder's wrath foamed over all restraint. If there was a circumstance which could have added to the resentment he felt, it was, that this extravagant donation had been made in favour of our friend Caleb, towards whom, for reasons to which the reader is no stranger, he nourished a decided resentment. He raised his riding-wand against the elder matron, but she stood firm, collected in herself, and undauntedly brandished the iron ladle with which she had just been *flambing* (*Anglicè,* basting) the roast of mutton. Her weapon was certainly the better, and her arm not the weakest of the two; so that Gilbert thought it safest to turn short off upon his wife, who had by this time hatched a sort of hysterical whine, which greatly moved the minister, who was in fact as simple and kind-hearted a creature as ever breathed.—'And you, ye thowless jadd, to sit still and see my substance disponed upon* to an idle, drunken, reprobate, worm-eaten, serving man, just because he kittles the lugs o' a silly auld wife wi' useless clavers, and every twa words a lee?—I'll gar you as gude'——

Here the minister interposed, both by voice and action, while Dame Lightbody threw herself in front of her daughter, and flourished her ladle.

'Am I no to chastise my ain wife?' exclaimed the cooper, very indignantly.

'Ye may chastise your ain wife if ye like,' answered Dame Lightbody; 'but ye shall never lay finger on my daughter, and that ye may found upon.'

'For shame, Mr Girder!' said the clergyman; 'this is what I little expected to have seen of you, that ye suld give rein to your sinful passions against your nearest and your dearest; and this night too, when ye are called to the most solemn duty of a Christian parent—and a' for what? for a redundancy of creature-comforts, as worthless as they are unneedful.'

'Worthless!' exclaimed the cooper; 'a better guse never walkit on stubble; twa finer dentier wild-ducks never wat a feather.'

'Be it sae, neighbour,' rejoined the minster; 'but see what superfluities are yet revolving before your fire. I have seen the day when ten of the bannocks which stand upon that board would have been an acceptable dainty to as many men, that were starving on hills and bogs, and in caves of the earth, for the Gospel's sake.'

'And that's what vexes me maist of a',' said the cooper, anxious to get some one to sympathize with his not altogether causeless anger; 'an the quean had gien it to ony suffering sant, or to ony body ava but that reaving, lying, oppressing tory villian, that rade in the wicked troop of militia when it was commanded out against the sants at Bothwell Brigg by the auld tyrant Allan Ravenswood, that is gane to his place, I wad the less hae minded it. * But to gie the principal part o' the feast to the like o' him!'——

'Aweel, Gilbert,' said the minister, 'and dinna ye see a high judgment in this?—The seed of the righteous are not seen begging their bread—think of the son of a powerful oppressor being brought to the pass of supporting his household from your fulness.'

'And, besides,' said the wife, 'it wasna for Lord Ravenswood neither, an he wad hear but a body speak—it was to help to entertain the Lord Keeper, as they ca' him, that's up yonder at Wolf's Crag.'

'Sir William Ashton at Wolf's Crag!' ejaculated the astonished man of hoops and staves.

'And hand and glove wi' Lord Ravenswood,' added Dame Lightbody.

'Doited idiot!—that auld clavering sneck-drawer wad gar ye trow the moon is made of green cheese. The Lord Keeper and Ravenswood! they are cat and dog, hare and hound.'

'I tell ye they are man and wife, and gree better than some others that are sae,' retorted the mother-in-law; 'forby, Peter Puncheon, that's cooper to the Queen's stores, is dead, and the place is to fill, and'——

'Od guide us, wull ye haud your skirling tongues!' said Girder,—for we are to remark, that this explanation was given like a catch for two voices, the younger dame, much encouraged by the turn of the debate, taking up, and repeating in a higher tone, the words as fast as they were uttered by her mother.

'The gudewife says naething but what's true, maister,' said Girder's foreman, who had come in during the fray. 'I saw the Lord Keeper's servants drinking and driving ower at Luckie Sma'trash's, ower by yonder.'

'And is their maister up at Wolf's Crag?' said Girder.

'Ay, troth is he,' replied his man of confidence.

'And friends wi' Ravenswood?'

'It's like sae,' answered the foreman, 'since he is putting up[17] wi' him.'

'And Peter Puncheon's dead?'

'Ay, ay—Puncheon has leaked out at last, the auld carle,' said the foreman; 'mony a dribble o' brandy has gaen through him in his day.—But as for the broche and the wild-fowl, the saddle's no aff your mare yet, maister, and I could follow and bring it back, for Mr Balderstone's no far aff the town yet.'

'Do sae, Will—and come here—I'll tell ye what to do when ye owertake him.'

He relieved the females of his presence, and gave Will his private instructions.

'A bonny-like thing,' said the mother-in-law, as the cooper re-entered the apartment, 'to send the innocent lad after an armed man, when ye ken Mr Balderstone aye wears a rapier, and whiles a dirk into the bargain.'

'I trust,' said the minister, 'ye have reflected weel on what ye have done, lest you should minister cause of strife, of which it is my duty to say, he who affordeth matter, albeit he himself striketh not, is in no manner guiltless.'

'Never fash your beard, Mr Bide-the-bent,' replied Girder; 'ane canna get their breath out here between wives and ministers—I ken best how to turn my ain cake.—Jean, serve up the dinner, and nae mair about it.'

Nor did he again allude to the deficiency in the course of the evening.

Meantime, the foreman, mounted on his master's steed, and charged with his special orders, pricked swiftly forth in pursuit of the marauder Caleb. That personage, it may be imagined, did not linger by the way. He intermitted even his dearly-beloved chatter, for the purpose of making more haste—only assuring Mr Lockhard that he had made the purveyor's wife give the wild-fowl a few turns before the fire, in case that Mysie, who had been so much alarmed by the thunder, should not have her kitchen-grate in full splendour. Meanwhile, alleging the necessity of being at Wolf's Crag as soon as possible, he pushed on so fast that his companions could scarce keep up with him. He began already to think he was safe from pursuit, having gained the summit of the swelling eminence which divides Wolf's Crag from the village, when he heard the distant tread of a horse, and a voice which shouted at intervals, 'Mr Caleb—Mr Balderstone—Mr Caleb Balderstone—hollo—bide a wee!'

Caleb, it may be well believed, was in no hurry to acknowledge the summons. First, he would not hear it, and faced his companions down, that it was the echo of the wind; then he said it was not worth stopping for; and, at length, halting reluctantly, as the figure of the horseman appeared through the shades of the evening, he bent up his whole soul to the task of defending his prey, threw himself into an attitude of dignity, advanced the spit, which in his grasp might with its burden seem both spear and shield,* and firmly resolved to die rather than surrender it.

What was his astonishment, when the cooper's foreman, riding up and addressing him with respect, told him, 'his master was very sorry he was absent when he came to his dwelling, and grieved that he could not tarry the christening dinner; and that he had taen the freedom to send a sma' rundlet of sack, and ane anker of brandy, as he understood there were guests at the castle, and that they were short of preparation.'

I have heard somewhere a story of an elderly gentleman, who was pursued by a bear that had gotten loose from its muzzle, until completely exhausted. In a fit of desperation, he faced round upon Bruin and lifted his cane; at the sight of which the instinct of discipline prevailed, and the animal, instead of tearing him to pieces, rose up upon his hind-legs, and instantly began to shuffle a saraband.* Not less than the joyful surprise of the senior, who had supposed himself in the extremity of peril from which he was thus unexpectedly relieved, was that of our excellent friend Caleb, when he found the pursuer intended to add to his prize, instead of bereaving him of it. He recovered his latitude, however, instantly, so soon as the foreman, stooping from his nag, where he sate perched betwixt the two barrels, whispered in his ear,—'If ony thing about Peter Puncheon's place could be airted their way, John Girder wad mak it better to the Master of Ravenswood than a pair of new gloves; and that he wad be blithe to speak wi' Maister Balderstone on that head, and he wad find him as pliant as a hoop-willow in a' that he could wish of him.'

Caleb heard all this without rendering any answer, except that of all great men from Louis XIV. downwards, namely, 'we will see about it;'* and then added aloud, for the edification of Mr Lockhard,—'Your master has acted with becoming civility and attention in forwarding the liquors, and I will not fail to represent it properly to my Lord Ravenswood. And, my lad,' he said, 'you may ride on to the castle, and if none of the servants are returned, whilk is to be dreaded, as they make day and night of it when they are out of sight, ye may put them into the porter's lodge, whilk is on the right hand of the great entry—the porter has got leave to go to see his friends, sae ye will meet no ane to steer ye.'

The foreman, having received his orders, rode on; and having deposited the casks in the deserted and ruinous porter's lodge, he returned unquestioned by any one. Having thus executed his master's commission, and doffed his bonnet to Caleb and his company as he repassed them in his way to the village, he returned to have his share of the christening festivity.[18]*

CHAPTER XIV

As, to the Autumn breeze's bugle sound,
Various and vague the dry leaves dance their round;
Or, from the garner-door, on ether borne,
The chaff flies devious from the winnow'd corn;
So vague, so devious, at the breath of heaven,
From their fix'd aim are mortal counsels driv'n.

(Anonymous) *

WE left Caleb Balderstone in the extremity of triumph at the success of his various achievements for the honour of the house of Ravenswood. When he had mustered and marshalled his dishes of divers kinds, a more royal provision had not been seen in Wolf's Crag, since the funeral feast of its deceased lord. Great was the glory of the serving-man, as he *decored* the old oaken table with a clean cloth, and arranged upon it carbonaded venison and roasted wild-fowl, with a glance, every now and then, as if to upbraid the incredulity of his master and his guests; and with many a story, more or less true, was Lockhard that evening regaled concerning the ancient grandeur of Wolf's Crag, and the sway of its Barons over the country in their neighbourhood.

'A vassal scarce held a calf or a lamb his ain, till he had first asked if the Lord of Ravenswood was pleased to accept it; and they were obliged to ask the lord's consent before they married in these days, and mony a merry tale they tell about that right as weel as others. And although,' said Caleb, 'these times are not like the gude auld times, when authority had its right, yet true it is, Mr Lockhard, and you yoursell may partly have remarked, that we of the House of Ravenswood do our endeavour in keeping up, by all just and lawful exertion of our baronial authority, that due and fitting connexion betwixt superior and vassal, whilk is in some danger of falling into desuetude, owing to the general license and misrule of these present unhappy times.'

'Umph!' said Mr Lockhard; 'and if I may enquire, Mr Balder-stone, pray do you find your people at the village yonder amenable? for I must needs say, that at Ravenswood Castle, now pertaining to my master, the Lord Keeper, ye have not left behind ye the most compliant set of tenantry.'

'Ah! but Mr Lockhard,' replied Caleb, 'ye must consider there has been a change of hands, and the auld lord might expect twa turns frae them, when the new comer canna get ane. A dour and fractious set they were, thae tenants of Ravenswood, and ill to live wi' when they dinna ken their master—and if your master put them mad ance, the whole country will not put them down.'

'Troth,' said Mr Lockhard, 'an such be the case, I think the wisest thing for us a' wad be to hammer up a match between your young lord and our winsome young leddy up by there; and Sir William might just stitch your auld barony to her gown-sleeve, and he wad sune cuitle[19] another out o' somebody else, sic a lang head as he has.'

Caleb shook his head.—'I wish,' he said, 'I wish that may answer, Mr Lockhard. There are auld prophecies about this house I wad like ill to see fulfilled wi' my auld een, that hae seen evil eneugh already.'

'Pshaw! never mind freits,' said his brother butler; 'if the young folk liked ane anither, they wad make a winsome couple. But, to say truth, there is a leddy sits in our hall-neuk, maun have her hand in that as weel as in every other job. But there's no harm in drinking to their healths, and I will fill Mrs Mysie a cup of Mr Girder's canary.'

While they thus enjoyed themselves in the kitchen, the company in the hall were not less pleasantly engaged. So soon as Ravenswood had determined upon giving the Lord Keeper such hospitality as he had to offer, he deemed it incumbent on him to assume the open and courteous brow of a well-pleased host. It has been often remarked, that when a man commences by acting a character, he frequently ends by adopting it in good earnest. In the course of an hour or two, Ravenswood, to his own surprise, found himself in the situation of one who frankly does his best to entertain welcome and honoured guests. How much of this change in his disposition was to be ascribed to the beauty and simplicity of Miss Ashton, to the readiness with which she accommodated herself to the inconveniences of her situation—how much to the smooth and plausible conversation of the Lord Keeper, remarkably gifted with those words which win the ear, must be left to the reader's ingenuity to conjecture. But Ravenswood was insensible to neither.

The Lord Keeper was a veteran statesman, well acquainted with courts and cabinets, and intimate with all the various turns of public affairs during the last eventful years of the seventeenth century. He could talk, from his own knowledge, of men and events, in a way which failed not to win attention, and had the peculiar art, while he never said a word which committed himself, at the same time to persuade the hearer that he was speaking without the least shadow of scrupulous caution or reserve. Ravenswood, in spite of his prejudices and real grounds of resentment, felt himself at once amused and instructed in listening to him, while the statesman, whose inward feelings had at first so much impeded his efforts to make himself known, had now regained all the ease and fluency of a silver-tongued lawyer of the very highest order.

His daughter did not speak much, but she smiled; and what she did say argued a submissive gentleness, and a desire to give pleasure, which, to a proud man like Ravenswood, was more fascinating than the most brilliant wit. Above all, he could not but observe, that, whether from gratitude, or from some other motive, he himself, in his deserted and unprovided hall, was as much the object of respectful attention to his guests, as he would have been when surrounded by all the appliances and means of hospitality proper to his high birth. All deficiencies passed unobserved, or, if they did not escape notice, it was to praise the substitutes which Caleb had contrived to supply the want of the usual accommodations. Where a smile was unavoidable, it was a very good-humoured one, and often coupled with some well-turned compliment, to show how much the guests esteemed the merits of their noble host, how little they thought of the inconveniences with which they were surrounded. I am not sure whether the pride of being found to outbalance, in virtue of his own personal merit, all the disadvantages of fortune, did not make as favourable an impression upon the haughty heart of the Master of Ravenswood, as the conversation of the father and the beauty of Lucy Ashton.

The hour of repose arrived. The Keeper and his daughter retired to their apartments, which were 'decored' more properly than could have been anticipated. In making the necessary arrangements, Mysie had indeed enjoyed the assistance of a gossip who had arrived from the village upon an exploratory expedition, but had been arrested by Caleb, and impressed into the domestic drudgery of the evening. So that, instead of returning home to describe the dress and person of the grand young lady, she found herself compelled to be active in the domestic economy of Wolf's Crag.

According to the custom of the time, the Master of Ravenswood attended the Lord Keeper to his apartment, followed by Caleb, who placed on the table, with all the ceremonials due to torches of wax, two rudely-framed tallow-candles, such as in those days were only used by the peasantry, hooped in paltry clasps of wire, which served for candlesticks. He then disappeared, and presently entered with two earthen flagons, (the china, he said, had been little used since my lady's time,) one filled with canary wine, the other with brandy.[20]* The canary sack, unheeding all probabilities of detection, he declared had been twenty years in the cellars of Wolf's Crag, 'though it was not for him to speak before their honours; the brandy—it was weel-kend liquor, as mild as mead, and as strong as Sampson—it had been in the house ever since the memorable revel, in which auld Micklestob* had been slain at the head of the stair by Jamie of Jenklebrae, on account of the honour of the worshipful Lady Muirend, wha was in some sort an ally of the family; natheless'——

'But to cut that matter short, Mr Caleb,' said the Keeper, 'perhaps you will favour me with a ewer of water.'

'God forbid your lordship should drink water in this family,' replied Caleb, 'to the disgrace of so honourable an house!'

'Nevertheless, if his lordship have a fancy,' said the Master, smiling, 'I think you might indulge him; for, if I mistake not, there has been water drank here at no distant date, and with good relish too.'

'To be sure, if his lordship has a fancy,' said Caleb; and re-entering with a jug of pure element—' He will scarce find such water onywhere as is drawn frae the well at Wolf's Crag—nevertheless'——

'Nevertheless, we must leave the Lord Keeper to his repose in this poor chamber of ours,' said the Master of Ravenswood, interrupting his talkative domestic, who immediately turning to the doorway, with a profound reverence, prepared to usher his master from the secret chamber.

But the Lord Keeper prevented his host's departure.—'I have but one word to say to the Master of Ravenswood, Mr Caleb, and I fancy he will excuse your waiting.'

With a second reverence, lower than the former, Caleb withdrew—and his master stood motionless, expecting, with considerable embarrassment, what was to close the events of a day fraught with unexpected incidents.

'Master of Ravenswood,' said Sir William Ashton, with some embarrassment, 'I hope you understand the Christian law too well to suffer the sun to set upon your anger.'*

The Master blushed and replied, 'He had no occasion that evening to exercise the duty enjoined upon him by his Christian faith.'

'I should have thought otherwise,' said his guest, 'considering the various subjects of dispute and litigation which have unhappily occurred more frequently than was desirable or necessary betwixt the late honourable lord, your father, and myself.'

'I could wish, my lord,' said Ravenswood, agitated by suppressed emotion, 'that reference to these circumstances should be made anywhere rather than under my father's roof.'

'I should have felt the delicacy of this appeal at another time,' said Sir William Ashton, 'but now I must proceed with what I mean to say.—I have suffered too much in my own mind, from the false delicacy which prevented my soliciting with earnestness, what indeed I frequently requested, a personal communing with your father—much distress of mind to him and to me might have been prevented.'

'It is true,' said Ravenswood, after a moment's reflection; 'I have heard my father say your lordship had proposed a personal interview.'

'Proposed, my dear Master? I did indeed propose it, but I ought to have begged, entreated, beseeched it. I ought to have torn away the veil which interested persons had stretched betwixt us, and shown myself as I was, willing to sacrifice a considerable part even of my legal rights, in order to conciliate feelings so natural as his must be allowed to have been. Let me say for myself, my young friend, for so I will call you, that had your father and I spent the same time together which my good fortune has allowed me to-day to pass in your company, it is possible the land might yet have enjoyed one of the most respectable of its ancient nobility, and I should have been spared the pain of parting in enmity from a person whose general character I so much admired and hon-oured.'

He put his handkerchief to his eyes. Ravenswood also was moved, but awaited in silence the progress of this extraordinary communication.

'It is necessary,' continued the Lord Keeper, 'and proper that you should understand, that there have been many points betwixt us, in which, although I judged it proper that there should be an exact ascertainment of my legal rights by the decree of a court of justice, yet it was never my intention to press them beyond the verge of equity.'

'My lord,' said the Master of Ravenswood, 'it is unnecessary to pursue this topic farther. What the law will give you, or has given you, you enjoy—or you shall enjoy; neither my father, nor I myself, would have received any thing on the footing of favour.'

'Favour?—no—you misunderstand me,' resumed the Keeper; 'or rather you are no lawyer. A right may be good in law, and ascertained to be so, which yet a man of honour may not in every case care to avail himself of.'

'I am sorry for it, my lord,' said the Master.

'Nay, nay,' retorted his guest, 'you speak like a young counsel-lor; your spirit goes before your wit. There are many things still open for decision betwixt us. Can you blame me, an old man desirous of peace, and in the castle of a young nobleman who has saved my daughter's life and my own, that I am desirous, anxiously desirous, that these should be settled on the most liberal principles?'

The old man kept fast hold of the Master's passive hand as he spoke, and made it impossible for him, be his predetermination what it would, to return any other than an acquiescent reply; and wishing his guest good-night, he postponed farther conference until the next morning.

Ravenswood hurried into the hall, where he was to spend the night, and for a time traversed its pavement with a disordered and rapid pace. His mortal foe was under his roof, yet his sentiments towards him were neither those of a feudal enemy nor of a true Christian. He felt as if he could neither forgive him in the one character, nor follow forth his vengeance in the other, but that he was making a base and dishonourable composition betwixt his resentment against the father and his affection for his daughter. He cursed himself, as he hurried to and fro in the pale moonlight, and more ruddy gleams of the expiring wood-fire. He threw open and shut the latticed windows with violence, as if alike impatient of the admission and exclusion of free air. At length, however, the torrent of passion foamed off its madness, and he flung himself into the chair, which he proposed as his place of repose for the night.

If, in reality,—such were the calmer thoughts that followed the first tempest of his passion,—If, in reality, this man desires no more than the law allows him—if he is willing to ⸝adjust even his acknowledged rights upon an equitable footing, what could be my father's cause of complaint?—what is mine?—Those from whom we won our ancient possessions fell under the sword of my ancestors, and left lands and livings to the conquerors; we sink under the force of the law, now too powerful for the Scottish chivalry. Let us parley with the victors of the day, as if we had been besieged in our fortress, and without hope of relief. This man may be other than I have thought him; and his daughter—but I have resolved not to think of her.

He wrapt his cloak around him, fell asleep, and dreamed of Lucy Ashton till daylight gleamed through the lattices.

CHAPTER XV

We worldly men, when we see friends and kinsmen
Past hope sunk in their fortunes, lend no hand
To lift them up, but rather set our feet
Upon their heads to press them to the bottom,
As I must yield with you I practised it;
But now I see you in a way to rise,
I can and will assist you.

(New Way to Pay Old Debts) *

THE Lord Keeper carried with him to a couch harder than he was
accustomed to stretch himself upon, the same ambitious thoughts
and political perplexities, which drive sleep from the softest down
that ever spread a bed of state. He had sailed long enough amid
the contending tides and currents of the time to be sensible of their
peril, and of the necessity of trimming his vessel to the prevailing
wind, if he would have her escape shipwreck in the storm. The
nature of his talents, and the timorousness of disposition connected
with them, had made him assume the pliability of the versatile old
Earl of Northampton, who explained the art by which he kept his
ground during all the changes of state, from the reign of Henry
VIII. to that of Elizabeth, by the frank avowal, that he was born
of the willow, not of the oak. * It had accordingly been Sir William
Ashton's policy, on all occasions, to watch the changes in the
political horizon, and, ere yet the conflict was decided, to nego-
tiate some interest for himself with the party most likely to prove
victorious. His time-serving disposition was well known, and
excited the contempt of the more daring leaders of both factions
in the state. But his talents were of a useful and practical kind, and
his legal knowledge held in high estimation; and they so far
counterbalanced other deficiencies, that those in power were glad
to use and to reward, though without absolutely trusting or greatly
respecting him.

The Marquis of A—— had used his utmost influence to effect a change in the Scottish cabinet, and his schemes had been of late so well laid and so ably supported, that there appeared a very great chance of his proving ultimately successful. * He did not, however, feel so strong or so confident as to neglect any means of drawing recruits to his standard. The acquisition of the Lord Keeper was deemed of some importance, and a friend, perfectly acquainted with his circumstances and character, became responsible for his political conversion.

When this gentleman arrived at Ravenswood Castle upon a visit, the real purpose of which was disguised under general courtesy, he found the prevailing fear, which at present beset the Lord Keeper, was that of danger to his own person from the Master of Ravenswood. The language which the blind sibyl, old Alice, had used; the sudden appearance of the Master, armed, and within his precincts, immediately after he had been warned against danger from him; the cold and haughty return received in exchange for the acknowledgments with which he loaded him for his timely protection, had all made a strong impression on his imagination.

So soon as the Marquis's political agent found how the wind sate, he began to insinuate fears and doubts of another kind, scarce less calculated to affect the Lord Keeper. He enquired with seeming interest, whether the proceedings in Sir William's complicated litigation with the Ravenswood family was out of court, and settled without the possibility of appeal? The Lord Keeper answered in the affirmative; but his interrogator was too well informed to be imposed upon. He pointed out to him, by unanswerable arguments, that some of the most important points which had been decided in his favour against the house of Ravenswood, were liable, under the Treaty of Union, to be reviewed by the British House of Peers, a court of equity of which the Lord Keeper felt an instinctive dread. This course came instead of an appeal to the old Scottish Parliament, or, as it was technically termed, 'a protestation for remeid in law.' *

The Lord Keeper, after he had for some time disputed the legality of such a proceeding, was compelled, at length, to comfort himself with the improbability of the young Master of Ravenswood's finding friends in parliament, capable of stirring in so weighty an affair.

'Do not comfort yourself with that false hope,' said his wily friend; 'it is possible that, in the next session of Parliament, young Ravenswood may find more friends and favour even than your lordship.'

'That would be a sight worth seeing,' said the Keeper, scornfully.

'And yet,' said his friend, 'such things have been seen ere now, and in our own time. There are many at the head of affairs even now, that a few years ago were under hiding for their lives; and many a man now dines on plate of silver, that was fain to eat his crowdy without a bicker; and many a high head has been brought full low among us in as short a space. Scott of Scotstarvet's "Staggering State of Scots Statesmen," of which curious memoir you showed me a manuscript, has been outstaggered in our time.'*

The Lord Keeper answered with a deep sigh, 'that these mutations were no new sights in Scotland, and had been witnessed long before the time of the satirical author he had quoted. It was many a long year,' he said, 'since Fordun had quoted as an ancient proverb, "*Neque dives, neque fortis, sed nec sapiens Scotus, prædominante invidia, diu durabit in terra.*" '*

'And be assured, my esteemed friend,' was the answer, 'that even your long services to the state, or deep legal knowledge, will not save you, or render your estate stable, if the Marquis of A—— comes in with a party in the British Parliament.* You know that the deceased Lord Ravenswood was his near ally, his lady being fifth in descent from the Knight of Tillibardine;* and I am well assured that he will take young Ravenswood by the hand, and be his very good lord and kinsman. Why should he not?—The Master is an active and stirring young fellow, able to help himself with tongue and hands; and it is such as he that finds friends among their kindred, and not those unarmed and unable Mephibosheths,* that are sure to be a burden to every one that takes them up. And so, if these Ravenswood cases be called over the coals in the House of Peers,* you will find that the Marquis will have a crow to pluck with you.'

'That would be an evil requital,' said the Lord Keeper, 'for my long services to the state, and the ancient respect in which I have held his lordship's honourable family and person.'

'Ay, but,' rejoined the agent of the Marquis, 'it is in vain to look back on past service and auld respect, my lord—it will be present service and immediate proofs of regard, which, in these sliddery times, will be expected by a man like the Marquis.'

The Lord Keeper now saw the full drift of his friend's argument, but he was too cautious to return any positive answer.

'He knew not,' he said, 'the service which the Lord Marquis could expect from one of his limited abilities, that had not always stood at his command, still saving and reserving his duty to his king and country.' *

Having thus said nothing, while he seemed to say every thing, for the exception was calculated to cover whatever he might afterwards think proper to bring under it, Sir William Ashton changed the conversation, nor did he again permit the same topic to be introduced. His guest departed, without having brought the wily old statesman the length of committing himself, or of pledging himself to any future line of conduct, but with the certainty that he had alarmed his fears in a most sensible point, and laid a foundation for future and farther treaty.

When he rendered an account of his negotiation to the Marquis, they both agreed that the Keeper ought not to be permitted to relapse into security, and that he should be plied with new subjects of alarm, especially during the absence of his lady. They were well aware that her proud, vindictive, and predominating spirit, would be likely to supply him with the courage in which he was deficient—that she was immovably attached to the party now in power, with whom she maintained a close correspondence and alliance, and that she hated, without fearing, the Ravenswood family, (whose more ancient dignity threw discredit on the newly acquired grandeur of her husband,) to such a degree, that she would have periled the interest of her own house, to have the prospect of altogether crushing that of her enemy.

But Lady Ashton was now absent. The business which had long detained her in Edinburgh, had afterwards induced her to travel to London, not without the hope that she might contribute her share to disconcert the intrigues of the Marquis at court; for she stood high in favour with the celebrated Sarah, Duchess of Marlborough, to whom, in point of character, she bore considerable resemblance.* It was necessary to press her husband hard before her return; and, as a preparatory step, the Marquis wrote to the Master of Ravenswood the letter which we rehearsed in a former chapter. It was cautiously worded, so as to leave it in the power of the writer hereafter to take as deep, or as slight an interest in the fortunes of his kinsman, as the progress of his own schemes might require. But however unwilling, as a statesman, the Marquis might be to commit himself, or assume the character of a patron, while he had nothing to give away, it must be said to his honour, that he felt a strong inclination effectually to befriend the Master of Ravenswood, as well as to use his name as a means of alarming the terrors of the Lord Keeper.

As the messenger who carried this letter was to pass near the house of the Lord Keeper, he had it in direction, that in the village adjoining to the park-gate of the castle, his horse should lose a shoe, and that, while it was replaced by the smith of the place, he should express the utmost regret for the necessary loss of time, and in the vehemence of his impatience, give it to be understood, that he was bearing a message from the Marquis of A—— to the Master of Ravenswood, upon a matter of life and death.

This news, with exaggerations, was speedily carried from various quarters to the ears of the Lord Keeper, and each reporter dwelt upon the extreme impatience of the courier, and the surprising short time in which he had executed his journey. The anxious statesman heard in silence; but in private Lockhard received orders to watch the courier on his return, to waylay him in the village, to ply him with liquor if possible, and to use all means, fair or foul, to learn the contents of the letter of which he was the bearer. But as this plot had been foreseen, the messenger returned by a different and distant road, and thus escaped the snare that was laid for him.

After he had been in vain expected for some time, Mr Dingwall had orders to make especial enquiry among his clients of Wolf's-hope, whether such a domestic belonging to the Marquis of A—— had actually arrived at the neighbouring castle. This was easily ascertained; for Caleb had been in the village one morning by five o'clock, to borrow 'twa chappins of ale and a kipper' for the messenger's refreshment, and the poor fellow had been ill for twenty-four hours at Luckie Sma'trash's, in consequence of dining upon 'saut saumon and sour drink.' So that the existence of a correspondence betwixt the Marquis and his distressed kinsman, which Sir William Ashton had sometimes treated as a bugbear, was proved beyond the possibility of further doubt.

The alarm of the Lord Keeper became very serious. Since the Claim of Right, the power of appealing from the decisions of the civil court to the Estates of Parliament, which had formerly been held incompetent, had in many instances been claimed, and in some allowed, and he had no small reason to apprehend the issue, if the English House of Lords should be disposed to act upon an appeal from the Master of Ravenswood 'for remeid in law.'* It would resolve into an equitable claim, and be decided, perhaps, upon the broad principles of justice, which were not quite so favourable to the Lord Keeper as those of strict law. Besides, judging, though most inaccurately, from courts which he had himself known in the unhappy times preceding the Scottish Union, the Keeper might have too much right to think, that in the House to which his lawsuits were to be transferred, the old maxim might prevail in Scotland which was too well recognized in former times,—'Show me the man, and I'll show you the law.' The high and unbiassed character of English judicial proceedings was then little known in Scotland; and the extension of them to that country was one of the most valuable advantages which it gained by the Union. But this was a blessing which the Lord Keeper, who had lived under another system, could not have the means of foreseeing. In the loss of his political consequence, he anticipated the loss of his lawsuit.*Meanwhile, every report which reached him served to render the success of the Marquis's intrigues the more probable, and the Lord Keeper began to think it indispensable, that he should look round for some kind of protection against the coming storm. The timidity of his temper induced him to adopt measures of compromise and conciliation. The affair of the wild bull, properly managed, might, he thought, be made to facilitate a personal communication and reconciliation betwixt the

Master and himself. He would then learn, if possible, what his own ideas were of the extent of his rights, and the means of enforcing them; and perhaps matters might be brought to a compromise, where one party was wealthy, and the other so very poor. A reconciliation with Ravenswood was likely to give him an opportunity to play his own game with the Marquis of A——. 'And besides,' said he to himself, 'it will be an act of generosity to raise up the heir of this distressed family; and if he is to be warmly and effectually befriended by the new government, who knows but my virtue may prove its own reward?'

Thus thought Sir William Ashton, covering with no unusual self-delusion his interested views with a hue of virtue; and having attained this point, his fancy strayed still farther. He began to bethink himself, 'that if Ravenswood was to have a distinguished place of power and trust—and if such a union would sopite the heavier part of his unadjusted claims—there might be worse matches for his daughter Lucy—the Master might be reponed against the attainder*—Lord Ravenswood was an ancient title, and the alliance would, in some measure, legitimate his own possession of the greater part of the Master's spoils, and make the surrender of the rest a subject of less bitter regret.'

With these mingled and multifarious plans occupying his head, the Lord Keeper availed himself of my Lord Bittlebrains's repeated invitation to his residence, and thus came within a very few miles of Wolf's Crag. Here he found the lord of the mansion absent, but was courteously received by the lady, who expected her husband's immediate return. She expressed her particular delight at seeing Miss Ashton, and appointed the hounds to be taken out for the Lord Keeper's special amusement. He readily entered into the proposal, as giving him an opportunity to reconnoitre Wolf's Crag, and perhaps to make some acquaintance with the owner, if he should be tempted from his desolate mansion by the chase. Lockhard had his orders to endeavour on his part to make some acquaintance with the inmates of the castle, and we have seen how he played his part.

The accidental storm did more to further the Lord Keeper's plan of forming a personal acquaintance with young Ravenswood, than his most sanguine expectations could have anticipated. His fear of the young nobleman's personal resentment had greatly decreased, since he considered him as formidable from his legal claims, and the means he might have of enforcing them. But although he thought, not unreasonably, that only desperate circumstances drove men on desperate measures, it was not without a secret terror, which shook his heart within him, that he first felt himself enclosed within the desolate Tower of Wolf's Crag; a place so well fitted, from solitude and strength, to be a scene of violence and vengeance. The stern reception at first given to them by the Master of Ravenswood, and the difficulty he felt in explaining to that injured nobleman what guests were under the shelter of his roof, did not soothe these alarms; so that when Sir William Ashton heard the door of the court-yard shut behind him with violence, the words of Alice rung in his ears, 'that he had drawn on matters too hardly with so fierce a race as those of Ravenswood, and that they would bide their time to be avenged.'

The subsequent frankness of the Master's hospitality, as their acquaintance increased, abated the apprehensions these recollections were calculated to excite; and it did not escape Sir William Ashton, that it was to Lucy's grace and beauty he owed the change in their host's behaviour.

All these thoughts thronged upon him when he took possession of the secret chamber. The iron lamp, the unfurnished apartment, more resembling a prison than a place of ordinary repose, the hoarse and ceaseless sound of the waves rushing against the base of the rock on which the castle was founded, saddened and perplexed his mind. To his own successful machinations, the ruin of the family had been in a great measure owing, but his disposition was crafty and not cruel; so that actually to witness the desolation and distress he had himself occasioned, was as painful to him as it would be to the humane mistress of a family to superintend in person the execution of the lambs and poultry which are killed by her own directions. At the same time, when he thought of the alternative, of restoring to Ravenswood a large proportion of his spoils, or of adopting, as an ally and member of his own family, the heir of this impoverished house, he felt as the spider may be supposed to do, when his whole web, the intricacies of which had been planned with so much art, is destroyed by the chance sweep of a broom. And then, if he should commit himself too far in this matter, it gave rise to a perilous question, which many a good husband, when under temptation to act as a free agent, has asked himself without being able to return a satisfactory answer; 'What will my wife—what will Lady Ashton say?' On the whole, he came at length to the resolution in which minds of a weaker cast so often take refuge. He resolved to watch events, to take advantage of circumstances as they occurred, and regulate his conduct accordingly. In this spirit of temporizing policy, he at length composed his mind to rest.

CHAPTER XVI

'A slight note I have about me for you, for
the delivery of which you must excuse me. It
is an offer that friendship calls upon me to do,
and no way offensive to you, since I desire
nothing but right upon both sides.'

(*King and no King*)*

WHEN Ravenswood and his guest met in the morning, the
gloom of the Master's spirit had in part returned. He, also, had
passed a night rather of reflection than of slumber; and the feelings
which he could not but entertain towards Lucy Ashton, had to
support a severe conflict against those which he had so long
nourished against her father. To clasp in friendship the hand of the
enemy of his house, to entertain him under his roof, to exchange
with him the courtesies and the kindness of domestic familiarity,
was a degradation which his proud spirit could not be bent to
without a struggle.

But the ice being once broken, the Lord Keeper was resolved
it should not have time again to freeze. It had been part of his plan
to stun and confuse Ravenswood's ideas, by a complicated and
technical statement of the matters which had been in debate
betwixt their families, justly thinking that it would be difficult for
a youth of his age to follow the expositions of a practical lawyer,
concerning actions of compt and reckoning, and of multiple-
poindings, and adjudications and wadsets, proper and improper,
and poindings of the ground, and declarations of the expiry of the
legal.* Thus, thought Sir William, I shall have all the grace of
appearing perfectly communicative, while my party will derive
very little advantage from any thing I may tell him. He therefore
took Ravenswood aside into the deep recess of a window in the
hall, and resuming the discourse of the preceding evening, expressed a hope that his young friend would assume some patience,
in order to hear him enter into a minute and explanatory detail of

those unfortunate circumstances, in which his late honourable father had stood at variance with the Lord Keeper. The Master of Ravenswood coloured highly, but was silent; and the Lord Keeper, though not greatly approving the sudden heightening of his auditor's complexion, commenced the history of a bond for twenty thousand marks, advanced by his father to the father of Allan Lord Ravenswood, and was proceeding to detail the executorial proceedings by which this large sum had been rendered a *debitum fundi*,* when he was interrupted by the Master.

'It is not in this place,' he said, 'that I can hear Sir William Ashton's explanation of the matters in question between us. It is not here, where my father died of a broken heart, that I can with decency or temper investigate the cause of his distress. I might remember that I was a son, and forget the duties of a host. A time, however, there must come, when these things shall be discussed in a place and in a presence where both of us will have equal freedom to speak and to hear.'

'Any time,' the Lord Keeper said, 'any place, was alike to those who sought nothing but justice. Yet it would seem he was, in fairness, entitled to some premonition respecting the grounds upon which the Master proposed to impugn the whole train of legal proceedings, which had been so well and ripely advised in the only courts competent.'*

'Sir William Ashton,' answered the Master, with warmth, 'the lands which you now occupy were granted to my remote ancestor for services done with his sword against the English invaders. How they have glided from us by a train of proceedings that seem to be neither sale, nor mortgage, nor adjudication for debt, but a nondescript and entangled mixture of all these rights—how annualrent has been accumulated upon principal, and no nook or coign of legal advantage left unoccupied, until our interest in our hereditary property seems to have melted away like an icicle in thaw—all this you understand better than I do. I am willing, however, to suppose, from the frankness of your conduct towards me, that I may in a great measure have mistaken your personal character, and that things may have appeared right and fitting to you, a skilful and practised lawyer, which to my ignorant understanding seem very little short of injustice and gross oppression.'

'And you, my dear Master,' answered Sir William, 'you, permit me to say, have been equally misrepresented to me. I was taught to believe you a fierce, imperious, hot-headed youth, ready, at the slightest provocation, to throw your sword into the scales of justice, and to appeal to those rude and forcible measures from which civil polity has long protected the people of Scotland. Then, since we were mutually mistaken in each other, why should not the young nobleman be willing to listen to the old lawyer, while, at least, he explains the points of difference betwixt them?'

'No, my lord,' answered Ravenswood; 'it is in the House of British Peers,[21] whose honour must be equal to their rank—it is in the court of last resort that we must parley together. The belted lords of Britain, her ancient peers, must decide, if it is their will that a house, not the least noble of their members, shall be stripped of their possessions, the reward of the patriotism of generations, as the pawn of a wretched mechanic becomes forfeit to the usurer the instant the hour of redemption has passed away. * If they yield to the grasping severity of the creditor, and to the gnawing usury that eats into our lands as moths into a raiment, it will be of more evil consequence to them and their posterity than to Edgar Ravenswood—I shall still have my sword and my cloak, and can follow the profession of arms wherever a trumpet shall sound.'

As he pronounced these words, in a firm yet melancholy tone, he raised his eyes, and suddenly encountered those of Lucy Ashton, who had stolen unawares on their interview, and observed her looks fastened on them with an expression of enthusiastic interest and admiration, which had wrapt her for the moment beyond the fear of discovery. The noble form and fine features of Ravenswood, fired with the pride of birth and sense of internal dignity—the mellow and expressive tones of his voice, the desolate state of his fortunes, and the indifference with which he seemed to endure and to dare the worst that might befall, rendered him a dangerous object of contemplation for a maiden already too much disposed to dwell upon recollections connected with him. When their eyes encountered each other, both blushed deeply, conscious of some strong internal emotion, and shunned again to meet each other's look.

Sir William Ashton had, of course, closely watched the expression of their countenances. 'I need fear,' said he internally, 'neither Parliament nor protestation; I have an effectual mode of reconciling myself with this hot-tempered young fellow, in case he shall become formidable. The present object is, at all events, to avoid committing ourselves. The hook is fixed; we will not strain the line too soon—it is as well to reserve the privilege of slipping it loose, if we do not find the fish worth landing.'

In this selfish and cruel calculation upon the supposed attachment of Ravenswood to Lucy, he was so far from considering the pain he might give to the former, by thus dallying with his affections, that he even did not think upon the risk of involving his own daughter in the perils of an unfortunate passion; as if her predilection, which could not escape his attention, were like the flame of a taper, which might be lighted or extinguished at pleasure. But Providence had prepared a dreadful requital for this keen observer of human passions, who had spent his life in securing advantages to himself by artfully working upon the passions of others.

Caleb Balderstone now came to announce that breakfast was prepared; for in those days of substantial feeding, the relics of the supper amply furnished forth the morning meal.* Neither did he forget to present to the Lord Keeper, with great reverence, a morning-draught in a large pewter cup, garnished with leaves of parsley and scurvy-grass. He craved pardon, of course, for having omitted to serve it in the great silver standing cup as behoved, being that it was at present in a silversmith's in Edinburgh, for the purpose of being overlaid with gilt.

'In Edinburgh like enough,' said Ravenswood; 'but in what place, or for what purpose, I am afraid neither you nor I know.'

'Aweel!' said Caleb, peevishly, 'there's a man standing at the gate already this morning—that's ae thing that I ken—Does your honour ken whether ye will speak wi' him or no?'

'Does he wish to speak with me, Caleb?'

'Less will no serve him,' said Caleb; 'but ye had best take a visie of him through the wicket before opening the gate—it's no every ane we suld let into this castle.'

'What! do you suppose him to be a messenger come to arrest me for debt?' said Ravenswood.

'A messenger arrest your honour for debt, and in your Castle of Wolf's Crag!—Your honour is jesting wi' auld Caleb this morning.' However, he whispered in his ear as he followed him out, 'I would be loath to do ony decent man a prejudice in your honour's gude opinion; but I would tak twa looks o' that chield before I let him within these walls.'

He was not an officer of the law, however; being no less a person than Captain Craigengelt, with his nose as red as a comfortable cup of brandy could make it, his laced cocked-hat set a little aside upon the top of his black riding periwig, a sword by his side, and pistols at his holsters, and his person arrayed in a riding suit, laid over with tarnished lace,—the very moral of one who would say, Stand, to a true man.*

When the Master had recognised him, he ordered the gates to be opened. 'I suppose,' he said, 'Captain Craigengelt, there are no such weighty matters betwixt you and me, but may be discussed in this place. I have company in the castle at present, and the terms upon which we last parted must excuse my asking you to make part of them.'

Craigengelt, although possessing the very perfection of impudence, was somewhat abashed by this unfavourable reception. 'He had no intention,' he said, 'to force himself upon the Master of Ravenswood's hospitality—he was in the honourable service of bearing a message to him from a friend, otherwise the Master of Ravenswood should not have had reason to complain of this intrusion.'

'Let it be short, sir,' said the Master, 'for that will be the best apology. Who is the gentleman who is so fortunate as to have your services as a messenger?'

'My friend Mr Hayston of Bucklaw,' answered Craigengelt, with conscious importance, and that confidence which the acknowledged courage of his principal inspired, 'who conceives himself to have been treated by you with something much short of the respect which he had reason to demand, and therefore is resolved to exact satisfaction. I bring with me,' said he, taking a piece of paper out of his pocket, 'the precise length of his sword;

and he requests you will meet him, accompanied by a friend, and equally armed, at any place within a mile of the castle, when I shall give attendance as umpire, or second, on his behoof.'

'Satisfaction—and equal arms!' repeated Ravenswood, who, the reader will recollect, had no reason to suppose he had given the slightest offence to his late inmate—'upon my word, Captain Craigengelt, either you have invented the most improbable false-hood that ever came into the mind of such a person, or your morning-draught has been somewhat of the strongest. What could persuade Bucklaw to send me such a message?'

'For that, sir,' replied Craigengelt, 'I am desired to refer you to what, in duty to my friend, I am to term your inhospitality in excluding him from your house, without reasons assigned.'

'It is impossible,' replied the Master; 'he cannot be such a fool as to interpret actual necessity as an insult. Nor do I believe, that, knowing my opinion of you, Captain, he would have employed the services of so slight and inconsiderable a person as yourself upon such an errand, as I certainly could expect no man of honour to act with you in the office of umpire.'

'I slight and inconsiderable!' said Craigengelt, raising his voice, and laying his hand on his cutlass; 'if it were not that the quarrel of my friend craves the precedence, and is in dependence before my own, I would give you to understand'——

'I can understand nothing upon your explanation, Captain Craigengelt. Be satisfied of that, and oblige me with your depar-ture.'

'D——n!' muttered the bully; 'and is this the answer which I am to carry back to an honourable message?'

'Tell the Laird of Bucklaw,' answered Ravenswood, 'if you are really sent by him, that when he sends me his cause of grievance by a person fitting to carry such an errand betwixt him and me, I will either explain it or maintain it.'

'Then, Master, you will at least cause to be returned to Hayston, by my hands, his property which is remaining in your possession.'

'Whatever property Bucklaw may have left behind him, sir,' replied the Master, 'shall be returned to him by my servant, as you do not show me any credentials from him which entitle you to receive it.'

'Well, Master,' said Captain Craigengelt, with malice which even his fear of the consequences could not suppress,—'you have this morning done me an egregious wrong and dishonour, but far more to yourself. A castle indeed!' he continued, looking around him; 'why, this is worse than a *coupe-gorge* house, where they receive travellers to plunder them of their property.'

'You insolent rascal,' said the Master, raising his cane, and making a grasp at the Captain's bridle, 'if you do not depart without uttering another syllable, I will batoon you to death!'

At the motion of the Master towards him, the bully turned so rapidly round, that with some difficulty he escaped throwing down his horse, whose hoofs struck fire from the rocky pavement in every direction. Recovering him, however, with the bridle, he pushed for the gate, and rode sharply back again in the direction of the village.

As Ravenswood turned round to leave the court-yard after this dialogue, he found that the Lord Keeper had descended from the hall, and witnessed, though at the distance prescribed by politeness, his interview with Craigengelt.

'I have seen,' said the Lord Keeper, 'that gentleman's face, and at no great distance of time—his name is Craig—Craig—something, is it not?'

'Craigengelt is the fellow's name,' said the Master, 'at least that by which he passes at present.'

'Craig-in-guilt,' said Caleb, punning upon the word *craig*, which in Scotch signifies throat; 'if he is Craig-in-guilt just now, he is as likely to be Craig-in-peril as ony chield I ever saw—the loon has woodie written on his very visnomy, and I wad wager twa and a plack that hemp plaits his cravat yet.'*

'You understand physiognomy, good Mr Caleb,' said the Keeper, smiling; 'I assure you the gentleman has been near such a consummation before now—for I most distinctly recollect, that, upon occasion of a journey which I made about a fortnight ago to Edinburgh, I saw Mr Craigengelt, or whatever is his name, undergo a severe examination before the Privy Council.'

'Upon what account?' said the Master of Ravenswood, with some interest.

The question led immediately to a tale which the Lord Keeper had been very anxious to introduce, when he could find a graceful and fitting opportunity. He took hold of the Master's arm, and led him back towards the hall. 'The answer to your question,' he said, 'though it is a ridiculous business, is only fit for your own ear.'

As they entered the hall, he again took the Master apart into one of the recesses of the window, where it will be easily believed that Miss Ashton did not venture again to intrude upon their conference.

CHAPTER XVII

Here is a father now,
Will truck his daughter for a foreign venture,
Make her the stop-gap to some canker'd feud,
Or fling her o'er, like Jonah, to the fishes,
To appease the sea at highest.

(*Anonymous*) *

THE Lord Keeper opened his discourse with an appearance of unconcern, marking, however, very carefully, the effect of his communication upon young Ravenswood.

'You are aware,' he said, 'my young friend, that suspicion is the natural vice of our unsettled times, and exposes the best and wisest of us to the imposition of artful rascals. If I had been disposed to listen to such the other day, or even if I had been the wily politician which you have been taught to believe me, you, Master of Ravenswood, instead of being at freedom, and with full liberty to solicit and act against me as you please, in defence of what you suppose to be your rights, would have been in the Castle of Edinburgh, or some other state prison; or, if you had escaped that destiny, it must have been by flight to a foreign country, and at the risk of a sentence of fugitation.' *

'My Lord Keeper,' said the Master, 'I think you would not jest on such a subject—yet it seems impossible you can be in earnest.'

'Innocence,' said the Lord Keeper, 'is also confident, and sometimes, though very excusably, presumptuously so.'

'I do not understand,' said Ravenswood, 'how a consciousness of innocence can be, in any case, accounted presumptuous.'

'Imprudent, at least, it may be called,' said Sir William Ashton, 'since it is apt to lead us into the mistake of supposing that sufficiently evident to others, of which, in fact, we are only conscious ourselves. I have known a rogue, for this very reason, make a better defence than an innocent man could have done in the same circumstances of suspicion. Having no consciousness of innocence to support him, such a fellow applies himself to all the advantages which the law will afford him, and sometimes (if his counsel be men of talent) succeeds in compelling his judges to receive him as innocent. I remember the celebrated case of Sir Coolie Condiddle, of Condiddle, who was tried for theft under trust, of which all the world knew him guilty, and yet was not only acquitted, but lived to sit in judgment on honester folk.'

'Allow me to beg you will return to the point,' said the Master; 'you seemed to say that I had suffered under some suspicion.'

'Suspicion, Master?—ay, truly—and I can show you the proofs of it; if I happen only to have them with me.—Here, Lockhard'—His attendant came—'Fetch me the little private mail with the padlocks, that I recommended to your particular charge—d'ye hear?'

'Yes, my lord.' Lockhard vanished; and the Keeper continued, as if half speaking to himself.

'I think the papers are with me—I think so, for as I was to be in this country, it was natural for me to bring them with me. I have them, however, at Ravenswood Castle, that I am sure of—so perhaps you might condescend'——

Here Lockhard entered, and put the leathern scrutoire, or mail-box, into his hands. The Keeper produced one or two papers, respecting the information laid before the Privy Council concerning the riot, as it was termed, at the funeral of Allan Lord Ravenswood, and the active share he had himself taken in quashing the proceedings against the Master. These documents had been selected with care, so as to irritate the natural curiosity of Ravenswood upon such a subject, without gratifying it, yet to show that Sir William Ashton had acted upon that trying occasion the part of an advocate and peacemaker betwixt him and the jealous authorities of the day. Having furnished his host with such subjects for examination, the Lord Keeper went to the breakfast-table, and entered into light conversation, addressed partly to old Caleb, whose resentment against the usurper of the Castle of Ravenswood began to be softened by his familiarity, and partly to his daughter.

After perusing these papers, the Master of Ravenswood remained for a minute or two with his hand pressed against his brow, in deep and profound meditation. He then again ran his eye hastily over the papers, as if desirous of discovering in them some deep purpose, or some mark of fabrication, which had escaped him at first perusal. Apparently the second reading confirmed the opinion which had pressed upon him at the first, for he started from the stone bench on which he was sitting, and, going to the Lord Keeper, took his hand, and, strongly pressing it, asked his pardon repeatedly for the injustice he had done him, when it appeared he was experiencing, at his hands, the benefit of protection to his person, and vindication to his character.

The statesman received these acknowledgments at first with well-feigned surprise, and then with an affectation of frank cordiality. The tears began already to start from Lucy's blue eyes at viewing this unexpected and moving scene. To see the Master, late so haughty and reserved, and whom she had always supposed the injured person, supplicating her father for forgiveness, was a change at once surprising, flattering, and affecting.

'Dry your eyes, Lucy,' said her father; 'why should you weep, because your father, though a lawyer, is discovered to be a fair and honourable man?—What have you to thank me for, my dear Master,' he continued, addressing Ravenswood, 'that you would not have done in my case? "*Suum cuique tribuito*," was the Roman justice, and I learned it when I studied Justinian.* Besides, have you not overpaid me a thousand times, in saving the life of this dear child?'

'Yes,' answered the Master, in all the remorse of self-accusation; 'but the little service I did was an act of mere brutal instinct; *your* defence of my cause, when you knew how ill I thought of you, and how much I was disposed to be your enemy, was an act of generous, manly, and considerate wisdom.'

'Pshaw!' said the Lord Keeper, 'each of us acted in his own way; you as a gallant soldier, I as an upright judge and privy-councillor. We could not, perhaps, have changed parts—at least I should have made a very sorry *Tauridor*, and you, my good Master, though your cause is so excellent, might have pleaded it perhaps worse yourself, than I who acted for you before the council.'

'My generous friend!' said Ravenswood;—and with that brief word, which the Keeper had often lavished upon him, but which he himself now pronounced for the first time, he gave to his feudal enemy the full confidence of an haughty but honourable heart. The Master had been remarked among his contemporaries for sense and acuteness, as well as for his reserved, pertinacious, and irascible character. His prepossessions accordingly, however obstinate, were of a nature to give way before love and gratitude; and the real charms of the daughter, joined to the supposed services of the father, cancelled in his memory the vows of vengeance which he had taken so deeply on the eve of his father's funeral. But they had been heard and registered in the book of fate.

Caleb was present at this extraordinary scene, and he could conceive no other reason for a proceeding so extraordinary than an alliance betwixt the houses, and Ravenswood Castle assigned for the young lady's dowry. As for Lucy, when Ravenswood uttered the most passionate excuses for his ungrateful negligence, she could but smile through her tears, and, as she abandoned her hand to him, assure him, in broken accents, of the delight with which she beheld the complete reconciliation between her father and her deliverer. Even the statesman was moved and affected by the fiery, unreserved, and generous self-abandonment with which the Master of Ravenswood renounced his feudal enmity, and threw himself without hesitation upon his forgiveness. His eyes glistened as he looked upon a couple who were obviously becoming attached, and who seemed made for each other. He thought how high the proud and chivalrous character of Ravenswood might rise under many circumstances, in which *he* found himself 'over-crowed,' to use a phrase of Spenser,* and kept under, by his brief pedigree, and timidity of disposition. Then his daughter—his favourite child—his constant playmate—seemed formed to live happy in a union with such a commanding spirit as Ravenswood; and even the fine, delicate, fragile form of Lucy Ashton seemed to require the support of the Master's muscular strength and masculine character. And it was not merely during a few minutes that Sir William Ashton looked upon their marriage as a probable and even desirable event, for a full hour intervened ere his imagination was crossed by recollection of the Master's poverty, and the sure displeasure of Lady Ashton. It is certain, that the very unusual flow of kindly feeling with which the Lord Keeper had been thus surprised, was one of the circumstances which gave much tacit encouragement to the attachment between the Master and his daughter, and led both the lovers distinctly to believe that it was a connexion which would be most agreeable to him. He himself was supposed to have admitted this in effect, when, long after the catastrophe of their love, he used to warn his hearers against permitting their feelings to obtain an ascendency over their judgment, and affirm, that the greatest misfortune of his life was owing to a very temporary predominance of sensibility over self-interest. It must be owned, if such was the case, he was long and severely punished for an offence of very brief duration.

After some pause, the Lord Keeper resumed the conversation.—'In your surprise at finding me an honester man than you expected, you have lost your curiosity about this Craigengelt, my good Master; and yet your name was brought in, in the course of that matter too.'

'The scoundrel!' said Ravenswood; 'my connexion with him was of the most temporary nature possible; and yet I was very foolish to hold any communication with him at all.—What did he say of me?'

'Enough,' said the Keeper, 'to excite the very loyal terrors of some of our sages, who are for proceeding against men on the mere grounds of suspicion or mercenary information.—Some nonsense about your proposing to enter into the service of France, or of the Pretender, I don't recollect which, but which the Marquis of A——, one of your best friends, and another person, whom some call one of your worst and most interested enemies, could not, somehow, be brought to listen to.'

'I am obliged to my honourable friend—and yet'—shaking the Lord Keeper's hand—'and yet I am still more obliged to my honourable enemy.'

'*Inimicus amicissimus*,'* said the Lord Keeper, returning the pressure; 'but this gentleman—this Mr Hayston of Bucklaw—I am afraid the poor young man—I heard the fellow mention his name—is under very bad guidance.'

'He is old enough to govern himself,' answered the Master.

'Old enough, perhaps, but scarce wise enough, if he has chosen this fellow for his *fidus Achates*.* Why, he lodged an information against him—that is, such a consequence might have ensued from his examination, had we not looked rather at the character of the witness than the tenor of his evidence.'

'Mr Hayston of Bucklaw,' said the Master, 'is, I believe, a most honourable man, and capable of nothing that is mean or disgraceful.'

'Capable of much that is unreasonable, though; that you must needs allow, Master. Death will soon put him in possession of a fair estate, if he hath it not already; old Lady Girnington—an excellent person, excepting that her inveterate ill-nature rendered her intolerable to the whole world—is probably dead by this time. Six heirs portioners have successively died to make her wealthy.* I know the estates well; they march[22] with my own—a noble property.'

'I am glad of it,' said Ravenswood, 'and should be more so, were I confident that Bucklaw would change his company and habits with his fortunes. This appearance of Craigengelt, acting in the capacity of his friend, is a most vile augury for his future respectability.'

'He is a bird of evil omen, to be sure,' said the Keeper, 'and croaks of jail and gallows-tree.*—But I see Mr Caleb grows impatient for our return to breakfast.'

CHAPTER XVIII

Sir, stay at home and take an old man's counsel;
Seek not to bask you by a stranger's hearth;
Our own blue smoke is warmer than their fire.
Domestic food is wholesome, though 'tis homely,
And foreign dainties poisonous, though tasteful.

(*The French Courtezan*)*

THE Master of Ravenswood took an opportunity to leave his guests to prepare for their departure, while he himself made the brief arrangements necessary previous to his absence from Wolf's Crag for a day or two. It was necessary to communicate with Caleb on this occasion, and he found that faithful servitor in his sooty and ruinous den, greatly delighted with the departure of their visitors, and computing how long, with good management, the provisions which had been unexpended might furnish forth the Master's table. 'He's nae belly god, that's ae blessing; and Bucklaw's gane, that could have eaten a horse behind the saddle. Cresses or water-purpie, and a bit ait-cake, can serve the Master for breakfast as weel as Caleb. Then for dinner—there's no muckle left on the spule-bane; it will brander, though—it will brander²³ very weel.'

His triumphant calculations were interrupted by the Master, who communicated to him, not without some hesitation, his purpose to ride with the Lord Keeper as far as Ravenswood Castle, and to remain there for a day or two.

'The mercy of Heaven forbid!' said the old serving-man, turning as pale as the table-cloth which he was folding up.

'And why, Caleb?' said his master, 'why should the mercy of Heaven forbid my returning the Lord Keeper's visit?'

'Oh, sir!' replied Caleb—'O Mr Edgar! I am your servant, and it ill becomes me to speak—but I am an auld servant—have served baith your father and gudesire, and mind to have seen Lord Randal, your great-grandfather—but that was when I was a bairn.'

'And what of all this, Balderstone?' said the Master; 'what can it possibly have to do with my paying some ordinary civility to a neighbour?'

'O Mr Edgar,—that is, my lord!' answered the butler, 'your ain conscience tells you it isna for your father's son to be neighbouring wi' the like o' him—it isna for the credit of the family. An he were ance come to terms, and to gie ye back your ain, e'en though ye suld honour his house wi' your alliance, I suldna say na—for the young leddy is a winsome sweet creature—But keep your ain state wi' them—I ken the race o' them weel—they will think the mair o' ye.'

'Why, now, you go farther than I do, Caleb,' said the Master, drowning a certain degree of consciousness in a forced laugh; 'you are for marrying me into a family that you will not allow me to visit—how's this?—and you look as pale as death besides.'

'O, sir,' repeated Caleb again, 'you would but laugh if I tauld it; but Thomas the Rhymer, whose tongue couldna be fause, spoke the word of your house that will e'en prove ower true if you go to Ravenswood this day—O, that it should e'er have been fulfilled in my time!'*

'And what is it, Caleb?' said Ravenswood, wishing to soothe the fears of his old servant.

Caleb replied, 'he had never repeated the lines to living mortal—they were told to him by an auld priest that had been confessor to Lord Allan's father when the family were catholic. But mony a time,' he said, 'I hae soughed thae dark words ower to mysell, and, well-a-day! little did I think of their coming round this day.'

'Truce with your nonsense, and let me hear the doggerel which has put it into your head,' said the Master, impatiently.

With a quivering voice, and a cheek pale with apprehension, Caleb faltered out the following lines:—

'When the last Laird of Ravenswood to Ravenswood shall ride,
And woo a dead maiden to be his bride,
He shall stable his steed in the Kelpie's flow,
And his name shall be lost for evermoe!'*

'I know the Kelpie's flow well enough,' said the Master; 'I suppose, at least, you mean the quick-sand betwixt this tower and Wolf's-hope; but why any man in his senses should stable a steed there'——

'O, never speer ony thing about that, sir—God forbid we should ken what the prophecy means—but just bide you at hame, and let the strangers ride to Ravenswood by themselves. We have done eneugh for them; and to do mair, would be mair against the credit of the family than in its favour.'

'Well, Caleb,' said the Master, 'I give you the best possible credit for your good advice on this occasion; but as I do not go to Ravenswood to seek a bride, dead or alive, I hope I shall choose a better stable for my horse than the Kelpie's quicksand, and especially as I have always had a particular dread of it since the patrol of dragoons were lost there ten years since. My father and I saw them from the tower struggling against the advancing tide, and they were lost long before any help could reach them.'

'And they deserved it weel, the southern loons!' said Caleb; 'what had they ado capering on our sands, and hindering a wheen honest folk frae bringing on shore a drap brandy?*I hae seen them that busy, that I wad hae fired the auld culverin, or the demisaker that's on the south bartizan at them, only I was feared they might burst in the ganging aff.'

Caleb's brain was now fully engaged with abuse of the English solidery and excisemen, so that his master found no great difficulty in escaping from him and rejoining his guests. All was now ready for their departure; and one of the Lord Keeper's grooms having saddled the Master's steed, they mounted in the court-yard.

Caleb had, with much toil, opened the double doors of the outward gate, and thereat stationed himself, endeavouring, by the reverential, and, at the same time, consequential air which he assumed, to supply, by his own gaunt, wasted, and thin person, the absence of a whole baronial establishment of porters, warders, and liveried menials.

The Keeper returned his deep reverence with a cordial farewell, stooping at the same time from his horse, and sliding into the butler's hand the remuneration, which in those days was always given by a departing guest to the domestics of the family where he had been entertained. Lucy smiled on the old man with her usual sweetness, bade him adieu, and deposited her guerdon with a grace of action, and a gentleness of accent, which could not have failed to have won the faithful retainer's heart, but for Thomas the Rhymer, and the successful lawsuit against his master. As it was, he might have adopted the language of the Duke, in *As you Like it*—

> 'Thou wouldst have better pleased me with this deed,
> If thou hadst told me of another father.'*

Ravenswood was at the lady's bridle-rein, encouraging her timidity, and guiding her horse carefully down the rocky path which led to the moor, when one of the servants announced from the rear that Caleb was calling loudly after them, desiring to speak with his master. Ravenswood felt it would look singular to neglect this summons, although inwardly cursing Caleb for his impertinent officiousness; therefore he was compelled to relinquish to Mr Lockhard the agreeable duty in which he was engaged, and to ride back to the gate of the court-yard. Here he was beginning, somewhat peevishly, to ask Caleb the cause of his clamour, when the good old man exclaimed, 'Whisht, sir! whisht, and let me speak just ae word that I couldna say afore folk—there'—(putting into his lord's hand the money he had just received)—'there's three gowd pieces—and ye'll want siller upby yonder—But stay, whisht now!'—for the Master was beginning to exclaim against this transference—'never say a word, but just see to get them changed in the first town ye ride through, for they are bran new frae the mint, and kenspeckle a wee bit.'

'You forget, Caleb,' said his master, striving to force back the money on his servant, and extricate the bridle from his hold—'You forget that I have some gold pieces left of my own. Keep these to yourself, my old friend; and, once more, good day to you. I assure you I have plenty. You know you have managed that our living should cost us little or nothing.'

'Aweel,' said Caleb, 'these will serve for you another time; but see ye hae eneugh, for, doubtless, for the credit of the family, there maun be some civility to the servants, and ye maun hae something to mak a show with when they say, Master, will you bet a broad piece? Then ye maun tak out your purse, and say, I carena if I do; and tak care no to agree on the articles of the wager, and just put up your purse again, and'——

'This is intolerable, Caleb—I really must be gone.'

'And you will go, then?' said Caleb, loosening his hold upon the Master's cloak, and changing his didactics into a pathetic and mournful tone—'And you *will* go, for a' I have told you about the prophecy, and the dead bride, and the Kelpie's quicksand?— Aweel! a wilful man maun hae his way—he that will to Cupar maun to Cupar.* But pity of your life, sir, if ye be fowling or shooting in the Park—beware of drinking at the Mermaiden's well——He's gane! he's down the path, arrow-flight after her!— The head is as clean taen aff the Ravenswood family this day, as I wad chap the head aff a sybo!'

The old butler looked long after his master, often clearing away the dew as it rose to his eyes, that he might, as long as possible, distinguish his stately form from those of the other horsemen. 'Close to her bridle-rein—ay, close to her bridle-rein!—Wisely saith the holy man, "By this also you may know that woman hath dominion over all men;"*—and without this lass would not our ruin have been a'thegither fulfilled.'

With a heart fraught with such sad auguries did Caleb return to his necessary duties at Wolf's Crag, as soon as he could no longer distinguish the object of his anxiety among the group of riders, which diminished in the distance.

In the meantime the party pursued their route joyfully. Having once taken his resolution, the Master of Ravenswood was not of a character to hesitate or pause upon it. He abandoned himself to the pleasure he felt in Miss Ashton's company, and displayed an assiduous gallantry, which approached as nearly to gaiety as the temper of his mind and state of his family permitted. The Lord Keeper was much struck with his depth of observation, and the unusual improvement which he had derived from his studies. Of these accomplishments Sir William Ashton's profession and habits of society rendered him an excellent judge; and he well knew how to appreciate a quality to which he himself was a total stranger,— the brief and decided dauntlessness of the Master of Ravenswood's disposition, who seemed equally a stranger to doubt and to fear.

In his heart the Lord Keeper rejoiced at having conciliated an adversary so formidable, while, with a mixture of pleasure and anxiety, he anticipated the great things his young companion might achieve, were the breath of court-favour to fill his sails.

'What could she desire,' he thought, his mind always conjuring up opposition in the person of Lady Ashton to his now prevailing wish—'What could a woman desire in a match, more than the sopiting of a very dangerous claim, and the alliance of a son-in-law, noble, brave, well-gifted, and highly connected—sure to float whenever the tide sets his way—strong, exactly where we are weak, in pedigree and in the temper of a swordsman?—Sure no reasonable woman would hesitate.—But, alas!'—Here his argument was stopped by the consciousness that Lady Ashton was not always reasonable, in his sense of the word. 'To prefer some clownish Merse laird to the gallant young nobleman, and to the secure possession of Ravenswood upon terms of easy compromise—it would be the act of a madwoman!'

Thus pondered the veteran politician, until they reached Bittlebrains House, where it had been previously settled they were to dine and repose themselves, and prosecute their journey in the afternoon.

They were received with an excess of hospitality; and the most marked attention was offered to the Master of Ravenswood, in particular, by their noble entertainers. The truth was, that Lord Bittlebrains had obtained his peerage by a good deal of plausibility, an art of building up a character for wisdom upon a very trite style of commonplace eloquence, a steady observation of the changes of the times, and the power of rendering certain political services to those who could best reward them. His lady and he not feeling quite easy under their new honours, to which use had not adapted their feelings, were very desirous to procure the fraternal countenance of those who were born denizens of the regions into which they had been exalted from a lower sphere. The extreme attention which they paid to the Master of Ravenswood, had its usual effect in exalting his importance in the eyes of the Lord Keeper, who, although he had a reasonable degree of contempt for Lord Bittlebrains' general parts, entertained a high opinion of the acuteness of his judgment in all matters of self-interest.

'I wish Lady Ashton had seen this,' was his internal reflection; 'no man knows so well as Bittlebrains on which side his bread is buttered; and he fawns on the Master like a beggar's messan on a cook. And my lady, too, bringing forward her beetle-browed misses to skirl and play upon the virginals, as if she said, pick and choose. They are no more comparable to Lucy than an owl is to a cygnet, and so they may carry their black brows to a farther market.'

The entertainment being ended, our travellers, who had still to measure the longest part of their journey, resumed their horses; and after the Lord Keeper, the Master, and the domestics, had drunk *doch-an-dorroch*, or the stirrup-cup,* in the liquors adapted to their various ranks, the cavalcade resumed its progress.

It was dark by the time they entered the avenue of Ravenswood Castle, a long straight line leading directly to the front of the house, flanked with huge elm-trees, which sighed to the night-wind, as if they compassionated the heir of their ancient proprietors, who now returned to their shades in the society, and almost in the retinue, of their new master. Some feelings of the same kind oppressed the mind of the Master himself. He gradually became silent, and dropped a little behind the lady, at whose bridle-rein he had hitherto waited with such devotion. He well recollected the period, when, at the same hour in the evening, he had accompanied his father, as that nobleman left, never again to return to it, the mansion from which he derived his name and title. The extensive front of the old castle, on which he remembered having often looked back, was then 'as black as mourning weed.'* The same front now glanced with many lights, some throwing far forward into the night a fixed and stationary blaze, and others hurrying from one window to another, intimating the bustle and busy preparation preceding their arrival, which had been intimated by an avant-courier. The contrast pressed so strongly upon the Master's heart, as to awaken some of the sterner feelings with which he had been accustomed to regard the new lord of his paternal domain, and to impress his countenance with an air of severe gravity, when, alighted from his horse, he stood in the hall no longer his own, surrounded by the numerous menials of its present owner.

The Lord Keeper, when about to welcome him with the cordiality which their late intercourse seemed to render proper, became aware of the change, refrained from his purpose, and only intimated the ceremony of reception by a deep reverence to his guest, seeming thus delicately to share the feelings which predominated on his brow.

Two upper domestics, bearing each a huge pair of silver candlesticks, now marshalled the company into a large saloon, or withdrawing room, where new alterations impressed upon Ravenswood the superior wealth of the present inhabitants of the castle. The mouldering tapestry, which, in his father's time, had half covered the walls of this stately apartment, and half streamed from them in tatters, had given place to a complete finishing of wainscot, the cornice of which, as well as the frames of the various compartments, were ornamented with festoons of flowers and with birds, which, though carved in oak, seemed, such was the art of the chisel, actually to swell their throats, and flutter their wings. Several old family portraits of armed heroes of the house of Ravenswood, together with a suit or two of old armour, and some military weapons, had given place to those of King William and Queen Mary, of Sir Thomas Hope and Lord Stair, two distinguished Scottish lawyers.* The pictures of the Lord Keeper's father and mother were also to be seen; the latter, sour, shrewish, and solemn, in her black hood and close pinners, with a book of devotion in her hand; the former, exhibiting beneath a black silk Geneva cowl, or skull-cap,* which sate as close to the head as if it had been shaven, a pinched, peevish, puritanical set of features, terminating in a hungry, reddish, peaked beard, forming on the whole a countenance, in the expression of which the hypocrite seemed to contend with the miser and the knave. And it is to make room for such scarecrows as these, thought Ravenswood, that my ancestors have been torn down from the walls which they erected! He looked at them again, and, as he looked, the recollection of Lucy Ashton (for she had not entered the apartment with them) seemed less lively in his imagination. There were also two or three Dutch drolleries, as the pictures of Ostade and Teniers were then termed, with one good painting of the Italian School.* There was, besides, a noble full-length of the Lord Keeper in his robes of office, placed beside his lady in silk and ermine, a haughty beauty, bearing in her looks all the pride of the House of Douglas, from which she was descended. The painter, notwithstanding his skill, overcome by the reality, or, perhaps, from a suppressed sense of humour, had not been able to give the husband on the canvass that air of awful rule and right supremacy, which indicates the full possession of domestic authority. It was obvious, at the first glance, that, despite mace and gold frogs, the Lord Keeper was somewhat henpecked. The floor of this fine saloon was laid with rich carpets, huge fires blazed in the double chimneys, and ten silver sconces, reflecting with their bright plates the lights which they supported, made the whole seem as brilliant as day.

'Would you choose any refreshment, Master?' said Sir William Ashton, not unwilling to break the awkward silence.

He received no answer, the Master being so busily engaged in marking the various changes which had taken place in the apartment, that he hardly heard the Lord Keeper address him. A repetition of the offer of refreshment, with the addition, that the family meal would be presently ready, compelled his attention, and reminded him, that he acted a weak, perhaps even a ridiculous part, in suffering himself to be overcome by the circumstances in which he found himself. He compelled himself, therefore, to enter into conversation with Sir William Ashton, with as much appearance of indifference as he could well command.

'You will not be surprised, Sir William, that I am interested in the changes you have made for the better in this apartment. In my father's time, after our misfortunes compelled him to live in retirement, it was little used, except by me as a playroom, when the weather would not permit me to go abroad. In that recess was my little workshop, where I treasured the few carpenter's tools which old Caleb procured for me, and taught me how to use—there, in yonder corner, under that handsome silver sconce, I kept my fishing-rods, and hunting poles, bows, and arrows.'

'I have a young birkie,' said the Lord Keeper, willing to change the tone of the conversation, 'of much the same turn—He is never happy, save when he is in the field—I wonder he is not here.—Here, Lockhard—send William Shaw for Mr Henry—I suppose he is, as usual, tied to Lucy's apron string—that foolish girl, Master, draws the whole family after her at her pleasure.'

Even this allusion to his daughter, though artfully thrown out, did not recall Ravenswood from his own topic.

'We were obliged to leave,' he said, 'some armour and portraits in this apartment—may I ask where they have been removed to?'

'Why,' answered the Keeper, with some hesitation, 'the room was fitted up in our absence—and *cedant arma togæ*, is the maxim of lawyers, you know—I am afraid it has been here somewhat too literally complied with.* I hope—I believe they are safe—I am sure I gave orders—may I hope that when they are recovered, and put in proper order, you will do me the honour to accept them at my hand, as an atonement for their accidental derangement?'

The Master of Ravenswood bowed stiffly, and, with folded arms, again resumed his survey of the room.

Henry, a spoilt boy of fifteen, burst into the room, and ran up to his father. 'Think of Lucy, papa; she has come home so cross and so fractious, that she will not go down to the stable to see my new pony, that Bob Wilson brought from the Mull of Galloway.'*

'I think you were very unreasonable to ask her,' said the Keeper.

'Then you are as cross as she is,' answered the boy; 'but when mamma comes home, she'll claw up both your mittens.'

'Hush your impertinence, you little forward imp!' said his father; 'where is your tutor?'

'Gone to a wedding at Dunbar—I hope he'll get a haggis to his dinner;' and he began to sing the old Scottish song,

> 'There was a haggis in Dunbar,
>> Fal de ral, &c.
> Mony better and few waur,
>> Fal de ral,' &c.*

'I am much obliged to Mr Cordery* for his attentions,' said the Lord Keeper; 'and pray who has had the charge of you while I was away, Mr Henry?'

'Norman and Bob Wilson—forby my own self.'

'A groom and a gamekeeper, and your own silly self—proper guardians for a young advocate!—Why, you will never know any statutes but those against shooting red-deer, killing salmon,* and'——

'And speaking of red-game,' said the young scape-grace, interrupting his father without scruple or hesitation, 'Norman has shot a buck, and I showed the branches to Lucy, and she says they have but eight tynes; and she says that you killed a deer with Lord Bittlebrains' hounds, when you were west away, and, do you know, she says it had ten tynes—is it true?'

'It may have had twenty, Henry, for what I know; but if you go to that gentleman, he can tell you all about it—Go speak to him, Henry—it is the Master of Ravenswood.'

While they conversed thus, the father and son were standing by the fire; and the Master having walked towards the upper end of the apartment, stood with his back towards them, apparently engaged in examining one of the paintings. The boy ran up to him, and pulled him by the skirt of the coat with the freedom of a spoilt child, saying, 'I say, sir—if you please to tell me'——but when the Master turned round, and Henry saw his face, he became suddenly and totally disconcerted—walked two or three steps backward, and still gazed on Ravenswood with an air of fear and wonder, which had totally banished from his features their usual expression of pert vivacity.

'Come to me, young gentleman,' said the Master, 'and I will tell you all I know about the hunt.'

'Go to the gentleman, Henry,' said his father; 'you are not used to be so shy.'

But neither invitation nor exhortation had any effect on the boy. On the contrary, he turned round as soon as he had completed his survey of the Master, and walking as cautiously as if he had been treading upon eggs, he glided back to his father, and pressed as close to him as possible. Ravenswood, to avoid hearing the dispute betwixt the father and the over-indulged boy, thought it most polite to turn his face once more towards the pictures, and pay no attention to what they said.

'Why do you not speak to the Master, you little fool?' said the Lord Keeper.

'I am afraid,' said Henry, in a very low tone of voice.

'Afraid, you goose!' said his father, giving him a slight shake by the collar,—'What makes you afraid?'

'What makes him so like the picture of Sir Malise Ravenswood, then?' said the boy, whispering.

'What picture, you natural?' said his father. 'I used to think you only a scape-grace, but I believe you will turn out a born idiot.'

'I tell you it is the picture of old Malise of Ravenswood, and he is as like it as if he had loupen out of the canvass;* and it is up in the old Baron's hall that the maids launder the clothes in, and it has armour, and not a coat like the gentleman—and he has not a beard and whiskers like the picture—and it has another kind of thing about the throat, and no band-strings as he has—and'——

'And why should not the gentleman be like his ancestor, you silly boy?' said the Lord Keeper.

'Ay; but if he is come to chase us all out of the castle,' said the boy, 'and has twenty men at his back in disguise—and is come to say, with a hollow voice, *I bide my time*—and is to kill you on the hearth as Malise did the other man, and whose blood is still to be seen!'

'Hush! nonsense!' said the Lord Keeper, not himself much pleased to hear these disagreeable coincidences forced on his notice.—'Master, here comes Lockhard to say supper is served.'

And, at the same instant, Lucy entered at another door, having changed her dress since her return. The exquisite feminine beauty of her countenance, now shaded only by a profusion of sunny tresses; the sylph-like form disencumbered of her heavy riding-skirt, and mantled in azure silk; the grace of her manner and of her smile, cleared, with a celerity which surprised the Master himself, all the gloomy and unfavourable thoughts which had for some time overclouded his fancy. In those features, so simply sweet, he could trace no alliance with the pinched visage of the peak-bearded, black-capped puritan, or his starched withered spouse, with the craft expressed in the Lord Keeper's countenance, or the haughtiness which predominated in that of his lady; and, while he gazed on Lucy Ashton, she seemed to be an angel descended on earth, unallied to the coarser mortals among whom she deigned to dwell for a season. Such is the power of beauty over a youthful and enthusiastic fancy.

CHAPTER XIX

——————— I do too ill in this,
And must not think but that a parent's plaint
Will move the heavens to pour forth misery
Upon the head of disobediency.
Yet reason tells us, parents are o'erseen,
When with too strict a rein they do hold in
Their child's affection, and control that love,
Which the high powers divine inspire them with.

(*The Hog hath lost his Pearl*) *

THE feast of Ravenswood Castle was as remarkable for its profusion, as that of Wolf's Crag had been for its ill-veiled penury.
The Lord Keeper might feel internal pride at the contrast, but he
had too much tact to suffer it to appear. On the contrary, he
seemed to remember with pleasure what he called Mr Balderstone's bachelor's meal, and to be rather disgusted than pleased
with the display upon his own groaning board.

'We do these things,' he said, 'because others do them——but I
was bred a plain man at my father's frugal table, and I should like
well would my wife and family permit me to return to my sowens
and my poor-man-of-mutton.'[24]

This was a little overstretched. The Master only answered, 'That
different ranks——I mean,' said he, correcting himself, 'different
degrees of wealth require a different style of housekeeping.'

This dry remark put a stop to further conversation on the
subject, nor is it necessary to record that which was substituted in
its place. The evening was spent with freedom, and even cordiality; and Henry had so far overcome his first apprehensions, that
he had settled a party for coursing a stag with the representative
and living resemblance of grim Sir Malise of Ravenswood, called
the Revenger. The next morning was the appointed time. It rose
upon active sportsmen and successful sport. The banquet came in
course; and a pressing invitation to tarry yet another day was given

and accepted. This Ravenswood had resolved should be the last of his stay; but he recollected he had not yet visited the ancient and devoted servant of his house, old Alice, and it was but kind to dedicate one morning to the gratification of so ancient an adherent.

To visit Alice, therefore, a day was devoted, and Lucy was the Master's guide upon the way. Henry, it is true, accompanied them, and took from their walk the air of a *tête-à-tête,* while, in reality, it was little else, considering the variety of circumstances which occurred to prevent the boy from giving the least attention to what passed between his companions. Now a rook settled on a branch within shot—anon a hare crossed their path, and Henry and his greyhound went astray in pursuit of it—then he had to hold a long conversation with the forester, which detained him a while behind his companions—and again he went to examine the earth of a badger, which carried him on a good way before them.

The conversation betwixt the Master and his sister, meanwhile, took an interesting, and almost a confidential turn. She could not help mentioning her sense of the pain he must feel in visiting scenes so well known to him, bearing now an aspect so different; and so gently was her sympathy expressed, that Ravenswood felt it for a moment as a full requital of all his misfortunes. Some such sentiment escaped him, which Lucy heard with more of confusion than displeasure; and she may be forgiven the imprudence of listening to such language, considering that the situation in which she was placed by her father seemed to authorize Ravenswood to use it. Yet she made an effort to turn the conversation, and she succeeded; for the Master also had advanced farther than he intended, and his conscience had instantly checked him when he found himself on the verge of speaking of love to the daughter of Sir William Ashton.

They now approached the hut of old Alice, which had of late been rendered more comfortable, and presented an appearance less picturesque, perhaps, but far neater than before. The old woman was on her accustomed seat beneath the weeping birch, basking, with the listless enjoyment of age and infirmity, in the beams of the autumn sun. At the arrival of her visitors she turned her head towards them. 'I hear your step, Miss Ashton,' she said, 'but the gentleman who attends you is not my lord, your father.'

'And why should you think so, Alice?' said Lucy; 'or how is it possible for you to judge so accurately by the sound of a step, on this firm earth, and in the open air?'

'My hearing, my child, has been sharpened by my blindness, and I can now draw conclusions from the slightest sounds, which formerly reached my ears as unheeded as they now approach yours. Necessity is a stern, but an excellent schoolmistress, and she that has lost her sight must collect her information from other sources.'

'Well, you hear a man's step, I grant it,' said Lucy; 'but why, Alice, may it not be my father's?'

'The pace of age, my love, is timid and cautious—the foot takes leave of the earth slowly, and is planted down upon it with hesitation; it is the hasty and determined step of youth that I now hear, and—could I give credit to so strange a thought—I should say it was the step of a Ravenswood.'

'This is indeed,' said Ravenswood, 'an acuteness of organ which I could not have credited had I not witnessed it.—I am indeed the Master of Ravenswood, Alice—the son of your old master.'

'You?' said the old woman, with almost a scream of surprise— 'you the Master of Ravenswood—here—in this place, and thus accompanied?—I cannot believe it—Let me pass my old hand over your face, that my touch may bear witness to my ears.'

The Master sate down beside her on the earthen bank, and permitted her to touch his features with her trembling hand.

'It is indeed!' she said, 'it is the features as well as the voice of Ravenswood—the high lines of pride, as well as the bold and haughty tone.—But what do you here, Master of Ravenswood?—what do you in your enemy's domain, and in company with his child?'

As old Alice spoke, her face kindled, as probably that of an ancient feudal vassal might have done, in whose presence his youthful liege-lord had showed some symptom of degenerating from the spirit of his ancestors.

'The Master of Ravenswood,' said Lucy, who liked not the tone of this expostulation, and was desirous to abridge it, 'is upon a visit to my father.'

'Indeed!' said the old blind woman, in an accent of surprise.

'I knew,' continued Lucy, 'I should do him a pleasure by conducting him to your cottage.'

'Where, to say the truth, Alice,' said Ravenswood, 'I expected a more cordial reception.'

'It is most wonderful!' said the old woman, muttering to herself; 'but the ways of Heaven are not like our ways, and its judgments are brought about by means far beyond our fathoming.—Hearken, young man,' she said; 'your fathers were implacable, but they were honourable foes; they sought not to ruin their enemies under the mask of hospitality. What have you to do with Lucy Ashton?—why should your steps move in the same footpath with hers?—why should your voice sound in the same chord and time with those of Sir William Ashton's daughter?—Young man, he who aims at revenge by dishonourable means'——

'Be silent, woman!' said Ravenswood, sternly; 'is it the devil that prompts your voice?—Know that this young lady has not on earth a friend, who would venture farther to save her from injury or from insult.'

'And is it even so?' said the old woman, in an altered but melancholy tone—'Then God help you both!'

'Amen! Alice,' said Lucy, who had not comprehended the import of what the blind woman had hinted, 'and send you your senses, Alice, and your good-humour. If you hold this mysterious language, instead of welcoming your friends, they will think of you as other people do.'

'And how do other people think?' said Ravenswood, for he also began to believe the old woman spoke with incoherence.

'They think,' said Henry Ashton, who came up at that moment, and whispered into Ravenswood's ear, 'that she is a witch, that should have been burned with them that suffered at Haddington.'*

'What is that you say?' said Alice, turning towards the boy, her sightless visage inflamed with passion; 'that I am a witch, and ought to have suffered with the helpless old wretches who were murdered at Haddington?'

'Hear to that now,' again whispered Henry, 'and me whispering lower than a wren cheeps!'

'If the usurer, and the oppressor, and the grinder of the poor man's face, and the remover of ancient land-marks, and the subverter of ancient houses, were at the same stake with me, I could say, light the fire, in God's name!'

'This is dreadful,' said Lucy; 'I have never seen the poor deserted woman in this state of mind; but age and poverty can ill bear reproach.—Come, Henry, we will leave her for the present—she wishes to speak with the Master alone. We will walk homeward, and rest us,' she added, looking at Ravenswood, 'by the Mermaiden's Well.'

'And Alice,' said the boy, 'if you know of any hare that comes through among the deer, and makes them drop their calves out of season, you may tell her, with my compliments to command, that if Norman has not got a silver bullet ready for her, I'll lend him one of my doublet-buttons on purpose.'*

Alice made no answer till she was aware that the sister and brother were out of hearing. She then said to Ravenswood, 'And you, too, are angry with me for my love?—it is just that strangers should be offended, but you, too, are angry!'

'I am not angry, Alice,' said the Master, 'only surprised that you, whose good sense I have heard so often praised, should give way to offensive and unfounded suspicions.'

'Offensive?' said Alice—'Ay, truth is ever offensive—but, surely, not unfounded.'

'I tell you, dame, most groundless,' replied Ravenswood.

'Then the world has changed its wont, and the Ravenswoods their hereditary temper, and the eyes of Old Alice's understanding are yet more blind than those of her countenance. When did a Ravenswood seek the house of his enemy, but with the purpose of revenge?—and hither are you come, Edgar Ravenswood, either in fatal anger, or in still more fatal love.'

'In neither,' said Ravenswood, 'I give you mine honour—I mean, I assure you.'

Alice could not see his blushing cheek, but she noticed his hesitation, and that he retracted the pledge which he seemed at first disposed to attach to his denial.

'It is so, then,' she said, 'and therefore she is to tarry by the Mermaiden's Well! Often has it been called a place fatal to the race of Ravenswood—often has it proved so—but never was it likely to verify old sayings as much as on this day.'

'You drive me to madness, Alice,' said Ravenswood; 'you are more silly and more superstitious than old Balderstone. Are you such a wretched Christian as to suppose I would in the present day levy war against the Ashton family, as was the sanguinary custom in elder times? or do you suppose me so foolish, that I cannot walk by a young lady's side without plunging headlong in love with her?'

'My thoughts,' replied Alice, 'are my own; and if my mortal sight is closed to objects present with me, it may be I can look with more steadiness into future events. Are you prepared to sit lowest at the board which was once your father's own, unwillingly, as a connexion and ally of his proud successor?—Are you ready to live on his bounty—to follow him in the bypaths of intrigue and chicane, which none can better point out to you—to gnaw the bones of his prey when he has devoured the substance?—Can you say as Sir William Ashton says—think as he thinks—vote as he votes, and call your father's murderer your worshipful father-in-law and revered patron?—Master of Ravenswood, I am the eldest servant of your house, and I would rather see you shrouded and coffined!'

The tumult in Ravenswood's mind was uncommonly great; she struck upon and awakened a chord which he had for some time successfully silenced. He strode backwards and forwards through the little garden with a hasty pace; and at length checking himself, and stopping right opposite to Alice, he exclaimed, 'Woman! on the verge of the grave, dare you urge the son of your master to blood and to revenge?'

'God forbid!' said Alice solemnly; 'and therefore I would have you depart these fatal bounds, where your love, as well as your hatred, threatens sure mischief, or at least disgrace, both to yourself and others. I would shield, were it in the power of this withered hand, the Ashtons from you, and you from them, and both from their own passions. You can have nothing—ought to have nothing, in common with them—Begone from among them; and if

God has destined vengeance on the oppressor's house, do not you be the instrument.'

'I will think on what you have said, Alice,' said Ravenswood, more composedly. 'I believe you mean truly and faithfully by me, but you urge the freedom of an ancient domestic somewhat too far. But farewell; and if Heaven afford me better means, I will not fail to contribute to your comfort.'

He attempted to put a piece of gold into her hand, which she refused to receive; and, in the slight struggle attending his wish to force it upon her, it dropped to the earth.

'Let it remain an instant on the ground,' said Alice, as the Master stooped to raise it; 'and believe me, that piece of gold is an emblem of her whom you love; she is as precious, I grant, but you must stoop even to abasement before you can win her. For me, I have as little to do with gold as with earthly passions; and the best news that the world has in store for me is, that Edgar Ravenswood is an hundred miles distant from the seat of his ancestors, with the determination never again to behold it.'

'Alice,' said the Master, who began to think this earnestness had some more secret cause than arose from any thing that the blind woman could have gathered from this casual visit, 'I have heard you praised by my mother for your sense, acuteness, and fidelity; you are no fool to start at shadows, or to dread old superstitious saws, like Caleb Balderstone; tell me distinctly where my danger lies, if you are aware of any which is tending towards me. If I know myself, I am free from all such views respecting Miss Ashton as you impute to me. I have necessary business to settle with Sir William—that arranged, I shall depart; and with as little wish, as you may easily believe, to return to a place full of melancholy subjects of reflection, as you have to see me here.'

Alice bent her sightless eyes on the ground, and was for some time plunged in deep meditation. 'I will speak the truth,' she said at length, raising up her head—'I will tell you the source of my apprehensions, whether my candour be for good or for evil.—Lucy Ashton loves you, Lord of Ravenswood!'

'It is impossible,' said the Master.

'A thousand circumstances have proved it to me,' replied the blind woman. 'Her thoughts have turned on no one else since you saved her from death, and that my experienced judgment has won from her own conversation. Having told you this—if you are indeed a gentleman and your father's son—you will make it a motive for flying from her presence. Her passion will die like a lamp, for want of that the flame should feed upon; but, if you remain here, her destruction, or yours, or that of both, will be the inevitable consequence of her misplaced attachment. I tell you this secret unwillingly, but it could not have been hid long from your own observation; and it is better you learn it from mine. Depart, Master of Ravenswood—you have my secret. If you remain an hour under Sir William Ashton's roof without the resolution to marry his daughter, you are a villain—if with the purpose of allying yourself with him, you are an infatuated and predestined fool.'

So saying, the old blind woman arose, assumed her staff, and, tottering to her hut, entered it and closed the door, leaving Ravenswood to his own reflections.

CHAPTER XX

> Lovelier in her own retired abode
> ——than Naiad by the side
> Of Grecian brook——or Lady of the Mere
> Lone sitting by the shores of old romance.
>
> (Wordsworth)*

THE meditations of Ravenswood were of a very mixed complexion. He saw himself at once in the very dilemma which he had for
some time felt apprehensive he might be placed in. The pleasure
he felt in Lucy's company had indeed approached to fascination,
yet it had never altogether surmounted his internal reluctance to
wed with the daughter of his father's foe; and even in forgiving
Sir William Ashton the injuries which his family had received, and
giving him credit for the kind intentions he professed to entertain,
he could not bring himself to contemplate as possible an alliance
betwixt their houses. Still he felt that Alice spoke truth, and that
his honour now required he should take an instant leave of
Ravenswood Castle, or become a suitor of Lucy Ashton. The
possibility of being rejected, too, should he make advances to her
wealthy and powerful father—to sue for the hand of an Ashton
and be refused—this were a consummation too disgraceful. 'I wish
her well,' he said to himself, 'and for her sake I forgive the
injuries her father has done to my house; but I will never—no,
never see her more!'

With one bitter pang he adopted this resolution, just as he came
to where two paths parted; the one to the Mermaiden's Fountain,
where he knew Lucy waited him, the other leading to the castle
by another and more circuitous road. He paused an instant when
about to take the latter path, thinking what apology he should
make for conduct which must needs seem extraordinary, and had
just muttered to himself, 'Sudden news from Edinburgh—any
pretext will serve—only let me dally no longer here,' when young
Henry came flying up to him, half out of breath—'Master, Master,

you must give Lucy your arm back to the castle, for I cannot give her mine; for Norman is waiting for me, and I am to go with him to make his ring-walk, and I would not stay away for a gold Jacobus, and Lucy is afraid to walk home alone, though all the wild nowt have been shot, and so you must come away directly.'

Betwixt two scales equally loaded, a feather's weight will turn the scale. 'It is impossible for me to leave the young lady in the wood alone,' said Ravenswood; 'to see her once more can be of little consequence, after the frequent meetings we have had—I ought, too, in courtesy, to apprise her of my intention to quit the castle.'

And having thus satisfied himself that he was taking not only a wise, but an absolutely necessary step, he took the path to the fatal fountain. Henry no sooner saw him on the way to join his sister, than he was off like lightning in another direction, to enjoy the society of the forester in their congenial pursuits. Ravenswood, not allowing himself to give a second thought to the propriety of his own conduct, walked with a quick step towards the stream, where he found Lucy seated alone by the ruin.

She sate upon one of the disjointed stones of the ancient fountain, and seemed to watch the progress of its current, as it bubbled forth to daylight, in gay and sparkling profusion, from under the shadow of the ribbed and darksome vault, with which veneration, or perhaps remorse, had canopied its source. To a superstitious eye, Lucy Ashton, folded in her plaided mantle, with her long hair, escaping partly from the snood and falling upon her silver neck, might have suggested the idea of the murdered Nymph of the Fountain. But Ravenswood only saw a female exquisitely beautiful, and rendered yet more so in his eyes—how could it be otherwise—by the consciousness that she had placed her affections on him. As he gazed on her, he felt his fixed resolution melting like wax in the sun, and hastened, therefore, from his concealment in the neighbouring thicket. She saluted him, but did not arise from the stone on which she was seated.

'My mad-cap brother,' she said, 'has left me, but I expect him back in a few minutes—for fortunately, as any thing pleases him for a minute, nothing has charms for him much longer.'

Ravenswood did not feel the power of informing Lucy that her brother meditated a distant excursion, and would not return in haste. He sate himself down on the grass, at some little distance from Miss Ashton, and both were silent for a short space.

'I like this spot,' said Lucy at length, as if she had found the silence embarrassing; 'the bubbling murmur of the clear fountain, the waving of the trees, the profusion of grass and wild-flowers, that rise among the ruins, make it like a scene in romance. I think, too, I have heard it is a spot connected with the legendary lore which I love so well.'

'It has been thought,' answered Ravenswood, 'a fatal spot to my family; and I have some reason to term it so, for it was here I first saw Miss Ashton—and it is here I must take my leave of her for ever.'

The blood, which the first part of this speech called into Lucy's cheeks, was speedily expelled by its conclusion.

'To take leave of us, Master!' she exclaimed; 'what can have happened to hurry you away?—I know Alice hates—I mean dislikes my father—and I hardly understood her humour to-day, it was so mysterious. But I am certain my father is sincerely grateful for the high service you rendered us. Let me hope that having won your friendship hardly, we shall not lose it lightly.'

'Lose it, Miss Ashton?' said the Master of Ravenswood,—'No—wherever my fortune calls me—whatever she inflicts upon me—it is your friend—your sincere friend, who acts or suffers. But there is a fate on me, and I must go, or I shall add the ruin of others to my own.'

'Yet do not go from us, Master,' said Lucy; and she laid her hand, in all simplicity and kindness, upon the skirt of his cloak, as if to detain him—'You shall not part from us. My father is powerful, he has friends that are more so than himself—do not go till you see what his gratitude will do for you. Believe me, he is already labouring in your behalf with the Council.'

'It may be so,' said the Master, proudly; 'yet it is not to your father, Miss Ashton, but to my own exertions, that I ought to owe success in the career on which I am about to enter. My preparations are already made—a sword and a cloak, and a bold heart and a determined hand.'

Lucy covered her face with her hands, and the tears, in spite of her, forced their way between her fingers. 'Forgive me,' said Ravenswood, taking her right hand, which, after slight resistance, she yielded to him, still continuing to shade her face with the left—'I am too rude—too rough—too intractable to deal with any being so soft and gentle as you are. Forget that so stern a vision has crossed your path of life—and let me pursue mine, sure that I can meet with no worse misfortune after the moment it divides me from your side.'

Lucy wept on, but her tears were less bitter. Each attempt which the Master made to explain his purpose of departure, only proved a new evidence of his desire to stay; until, at length, instead of bidding her farewell, he gave his faith to her for ever, and received her troth in return. The whole passed so suddenly, and arose so much out of the immediate impulse of the moment, that ere the Master of Ravenswood could reflect upon the consequences of the step which he had taken, their lips, as well as their hands, had pledged the sincerity of their affection.

'And now,' he said, after a moment's consideration, 'it is fit I should speak to Sir William Ashton—he must know of our engagement. Ravenswood must not seem to dwell under his roof, to solicit clandestinely the affections of his daughter.'

'You would not speak to my father on the subject?' said Lucy, doubtingly; and then added more warmly, 'O do not—do not! Let your lot in life be determined—your station and purpose ascertained, before you address my father; I am sure he loves you—I think he will consent—but then my mother!'——

She paused, ashamed to express the doubt she felt how far her father dared to form any positive resolution on this most important subject, without the consent of his lady.

'Your mother, my Lucy?' replied Ravenswood, 'she is of the house of Douglas, a house that has intermarried with mine, even when its glory and power were at the highest—what could your mother object to my alliance?'

'I did not say object,' said Lucy; 'but she is jealous of her rights, and may claim a mother's title to be consulted in the first instance.'

'Be it so,' replied Ravenswood; 'London is distant, but a letter will reach it and receive an answer within a fortnight—I will not press on the Lord Keeper for an instant reply to my proposal.'

'But,' hesitated Lucy, 'were it not better to wait—to wait a few weeks?—Were my mother to see you— to know you—I am sure she would approve; but you are unacquainted personally, and the ancient feud between the families'——

Ravenswood fixed upon her his keen dark eyes, as if he was desirous of penetrating into her very soul.

'Lucy,' he said, 'I have sacrificed to you projects of vengeance long nursed, and sworn to with ceremonies little better than heathen—I sacrificed them to your image, ere I knew the worth which it represented. In the evening which succeeded my poor father's funeral, I cut a lock from my hair, and, as it consumed in the fire, I swore that my rage and revenge should pursue his enemies, until they shrivelled before me like that scorched-up symbol of annihilation.'

'It was a deadly sin,' said Lucy, turning pale, 'to make a vow so fatal.'

'I acknowledge it,' said Ravenswood, 'and it had been a worse crime to keep it. It was for your sake that I abjured these purposes of vengeance, though I scarce knew that such was the argument by which I was conquered, until I saw you once more, and became conscious of the influence you possessed over me.'

'And why do you now,' said Lucy, 'recall sentiments so terrible—sentiments so inconsistent with those you profess for me—with those your importunity has prevailed on me to acknowledge?'

'Because,' said her lover, 'I would impress on you the price at which I have bought your love—the right I have to expect your constancy. I say not that I have bartered for it the honour of my house, its last remaining possession—but though I say it not, and think it not, I cannot conceal from myself that the world may do both.'

'If such are your sentiments,' said Lucy, 'you have played a cruel game with me. But it is not too late to give it over—take back the faith and troth which you could not plight to me without suffering abatement of honour—let what is passed be as if it had not been—forget me—I will endeavour to forget myself.'

'You do me injustice,' said the Master of Ravenswood; 'by all I hold true and honourable, you do me the extremity of injustice—if I mentioned the price at which I have bought your love, it is only to show how much I prize it, to bind our engagement by a still firmer tie, and to show, by what I have done to attain this station in your regard, how much I must suffer should you ever break your faith.'

'And why, Ravenswood,' answered Lucy, 'should you think that possible?—Why should you urge me with even the mention of infidelity?—Is it because I ask you to delay applying to my father for a little space of time? Bind me by what vows you please; if vows are unnecessary to secure constancy, they may yet prevent suspicion.'

Ravenswood pleaded, apologized, and even kneeled, to appease her displeasure; and Lucy, as placable as she was single-hearted, readily forgave the offence which his doubts had implied. The dispute thus agitated, however, ended by the lovers going through an emblematic ceremony of their troth-plight, of which the vulgar still preserve some traces. They broke betwixt them the thin broad-piece of gold which Alice had refused to receive from Ravenswood.*

'And never shall this leave my bosom,' said Lucy, as she hung the piece of gold round her neck, and concealed it with her handkerchief, 'until you, Edgar Ravenswood, ask me to resign it to you—and, while I wear it, never shall that heart acknowledge another love than yours.'

With like protestations, Ravenswood placed his portion of the coin opposite to his heart. And now, at length, it struck them, that time had hurried fast on during this interview, and their absence at the castle would be subject of remark, if not of alarm. As they arose to leave the fountain which had been witness of their mutual engagement, an arrow whistled through the air, and struck a raven perched on the sere branch of an old oak, near to where they had been seated.* The bird fluttered a few yards, and dropped at the feet of Lucy, whose dress was stained with some spots of its blood.

Miss Ashton was much alarmed, and Ravenswood, surprised and angry, looked everywhere for the marksman, who had given them a proof of his skill as little expected as desired. He was not long of discovering himself, being no other than Henry Ashton, who came running up with a crossbow in his hand.

'I knew I should startle you,' he said; 'and do you know you looked so busy that I hoped it would have fallen souse on your heads before you were aware of it.—What was the Master saying to you, Lucy?'

'I was telling your sister what an idle lad you were, keeping us waiting here for you so long,' said Ravenswood, to save Lucy's confusion.

'Waiting for me? Why, I told you to see Lucy home, and that I was to go to make the ring-walk with old Norman in the Hayberry thicket, and you may be sure that would take a good hour, and we have all the deer's marks and furnishes got,* while you were sitting here with Lucy, like a lazy loon.'

'Well, well, Mr Henry,' said Ravenswood; 'but let us see how you will answer to me for killing the raven. Do you know the ravens are all under the protection of the Lords of Ravenswood, and, to kill one in their presence, is such bad luck that it deserves the stab?'

'And that's what Norman said,' replied the boy; 'he came as far with me, as within a flight-shot of you, and he said he never saw a raven sit still so near living folk, and he wished it might be for good luck; for the raven is one of the wildest birds that flies, unless it be a tame one—and so I crept on and on, till I was within three score yards of him, and then whiz went the bolt, and there he lies, faith! Was it not well shot?—and, I daresay, I have not shot in a crossbow—not ten times, maybe.'

'Admirably shot indeed,' said Ravenswood; 'and you will be a fine marksman if you practise hard.'

'And that's what Norman says,' answered the boy; 'but I am sure it is not my fault if I do not practise enough; for, of free will, I would do little else, only my father and tutor are angry some-times, and only Miss Lucy there gives herself airs about my being busy, for all she can sit idle by a well-side the whole day, when she has a handsome young gentleman to prate with—I have known her do so twenty times, if you will believe me.'

The boy looked at his sister as he spoke, and, in the midst of his mischievous chatter, had the sense to see that he was really inflicting pain upon her, though without being able to comprehend the cause or the amount.

'Come now, Lucy,' he said, 'don't greet; and if I have said any thing beside the mark, I'll deny it again—and what does the Master of Ravenswood care if you had a hundred sweethearts?—so ne'er put finger in your eye about it.'*

The Master of Ravenswood was, for the moment, scarce satisfied with what he heard; yet his good sense naturally regarded it as the chatter of a spoilt boy, who strove to mortify his sister in the point which seemed most accessible for the time. But, although of a temper equally slow in receiving impressions, and obstinate in retaining them, the prattle of Henry served to nourish in his mind some vague suspicion, that his present engagement might only end in his being exposed like a conquered enemy in a Roman triumph, a captive attendant on the car of a victor, who meditated only the satiating his pride at the expense of the vanquished. There was, we repeat it, no real ground whatever for such an apprehension, nor could he be said seriously to entertain such for a moment. Indeed, it was impossible to look at the clear blue eye of Lucy Ashton, and entertain the slightest permanent doubt concerning the sincerity of her disposition. Still, however, conscious pride and conscious poverty combined to render a mind suspicious, which, in more fortunate circumstances, would have been a stranger to that as well as to every other meanness.

They reached the castle, where Sir William Ashton, who had been alarmed by the length of their stay, met them in the hall.

'Had Lucy,' he said, 'been in any other company than that of one who had shown he had so complete power of protecting her, he confessed he should have been very uneasy, and would have dispatched persons in quest of them. But, in the company of the Master of Ravenswood, he knew his daughter had nothing to dread.'

Lucy commenced some apology for their long delay, but, conscience struck, became confused as she proceeded; and when

Ravenswood, coming to her assistance, endeavoured to render the explanation complete and satisfactory, he only involved himself in the same disorder, like one who, endeavouring to extricate his companion from a slough, entangles himself in the same tenacious swamp. It cannot be supposed that the confusion of the two youthful lovers escaped the observation of the subtle lawyer, accustomed, by habit and profession, to trace human nature through all her windings. But it was not his present policy to take any notice of what he observed. He desired to hold the Master of Ravenswood bound, but wished that he himself should remain free; and it did not occur to him that his plan might be defeated by Lucy's returning the passion which he hoped she might inspire. If she should adopt some romantic feelings towards Ravenswood, in which circumstances, or the positive and absolute opposition of Lady Ashton, might render it unadvisable to indulge her, the Lord Keeper conceived they might be easily superseded and annulled by a journey to Edinburgh, or even to London, a new set of Brussels lace, and the soft whispers of half a dozen lovers, anxious to replace him whom it was convenient she should renounce. This was his provision for the worst view of the case. But, according to its more probable issue, any passing favour she might entertain for the Master of Ravenswood, might require encouragement rather than repression.

This seemed the more likely, as he had that very morning, since their departure from the castle, received a letter, the contents of which he hastened to communicate to Ravenswood. A foot-post had arrived with a packet to the Lord Keeper from that friend whom we have already mentioned, who was labouring hard under-hand to consolidate a band of patriots, at the head of whom stood Sir William's greatest terror, the active and ambitious Marquis of A——. The success of this convenient friend had been such, that he had obtained from Sir William, not indeed a directly favourable answer, but certainly a most patient hearing. This he had reported to his principal, who had replied, by the ancient French adage, '*Château qui parle, et femme qui écoute, l'un et l'autre va se rendre.*'* A statesman who hears you propose a change of measures without reply, was, according to the Marquis's opinion, in the situation of the fortress which parleys, and the lady who listens, and he resolved to press the siege of the Lord Keeper.

The packet, therefore, contained a letter from his friend and ally, and another from himself to the Lord Keeper, frankly offering an unceremonious visit. They were crossing the country to go to the southward—the roads were indifferent—the accommodation of the inns as execrable as possible—the Lord Keeper had been long acquainted intimately with one of his correspondents, and though more slightly known to the Marquis, had yet enough of his lordship's acquaintance to render the visit sufficiently natural, and to shut the mouths of those who might be disposed to impute it to a political intrigue. He instantly accepted the offered visit, determined, however, that he would not pledge himself an inch farther for the furtherance of their views than *reason* (by which he meant his own self-interest) should plainly point out to him as proper.

Two circumstances particularly delighted him; the presence of Ravenswood, and the absence of his own lady. By having the former under his roof, he conceived he might be able to quash all such hazardous and hostile proceedings as he might otherwise have been engaged in, under the patronage of the Marquis; and Lucy, he foresaw, would make, for his immediate purpose of delay and procrastination, a much better mistress of his family than her mother, who would, he was sure, in some shape or other, contrive to disconcert his political schemes by her proud and implacable temper.

His anxious solicitations that the Master would stay to receive his kinsman, were of course readily complied with, since the *éclaircissement* which had taken place at the Mermaiden's Fountain had removed all wish for sudden departure. Lucy and Lockhard had, therefore, orders to provide all things necessary in their different departments, for receiving the expected guests, with a pomp and display of luxury very uncommon in Scotland at that remote period.

CHAPTER XXI

MARALL. Sir, the man of honour's come,
    Newly alighted——
OVERREACH. In without reply,
    And do as I command.——
    Is the loud music I gave order for
    Ready to receive him?——

(New Way to Pay Old Debts) *

SIR WILLIAM ASHTON, although a man of sense, legal information, and great practical knowledge of the world, had yet some
points of character which corresponded better with the timidity
of his disposition and the supple arts by which he had risen in the
world, than to the degree of eminence which he had attained; as
they tended to show an original mediocrity of understanding,
however highly it had been cultivated, and a native meanness of
disposition, however carefully veiled. He loved the ostentatious
display of his wealth, less as a man to whom habit has made it
necessary, than as one to whom it is still delightful from its novelty.
The most trivial details did not escape him; and Lucy soon learned
to watch the flush of scorn which crossed Ravenswood's cheek,
when he heard her father gravely arguing with Lockhard, nay,
even with the old housekeeper, upon circumstances which, in
families of rank, are left uncared for, because it is supposed
impossible they can be neglected.

'I could pardon Sir William,' said Ravenswood, one evening
after he had left the room, 'some general anxiety upon this
occasion, for the Marquis's visit is an honour, and should be
received as such; but I am worn out by these miserable minutiæ
of the buttery, and the larder, and the very hen-coop—they drive
me beyond my patience; I would rather endure the poverty of
Wolf's Crag, than be pestered with the wealth of Ravenswood
Castle.'

'And yet,' said Lucy, 'it was by attention to these minutiæ that my father acquired the property'——

'Which my ancestors sold for lack of it,' replied Ravenswood. 'Be it so; a porter still bears but a burden, though the burden be of gold.'

Lucy sighed; she perceived too plainly that her lover held in scorn the manners and habits of a father, to whom she had long looked up as her best and most partial friend, whose fondness had often consoled her for her mother's contemptuous harshness.

The lovers soon discovered that they differed upon other and no less important topics. Religion, the mother of peace, was, in those days of discord, so much misconstrued and mistaken, that her rules and forms were the subject of the most opposite opinions, and the most hostile animosities. The Lord Keeper, being a whig, was, of course, a Presbyterian, and had found it convenient, at different periods, to express greater zeal for the kirk, than perhaps he really felt. His family, equally of course, were trained under the same institution. Ravenswood, as we know, was a High-Church man, or Episcopalian, and frequently objected to Lucy the fanaticism of some of her own communion, while she intimated, rather than expressed, horror at the latitudinarian principles which she had been taught to think connected with the prelatical form of church-government.

Thus, although their mutual affection seemed to increase rather than to be diminished, as their characters opened more fully on each other, the feelings of each were mingled with some less agreeable ingredients. Lucy felt a secret awe, amid all her affection for Ravenswood. His soul was of an higher, prouder character, than those with whom she had hitherto mixed in intercourse; his ideas were more fierce and free; and he contemned many of the opinions which had been inculcated upon her, as chiefly demanding her veneration. On the other hand, Ravenswood saw in Lucy a soft and flexible character, which, in his eyes at least, seemed too susceptible of being moulded to any form by those with whom she lived. He felt that his own temper required a partner of a more independent spirit, who could set sail with him on his course of life, resolved as himself to dare indifferently the storm and the favouring breeze. But Lucy was so beautiful, so devoutly attached to him, of a temper so exquisitely soft and kind, that, while he could have wished it were possible to inspire her with a greater degree of firmness and resolution, and while he sometimes became impatient of the extreme fear which she expressed of their attachment being prematurely discovered, he felt that the softness of a mind, amounting almost to feebleness, rendered her even dearer to him, as a being who had voluntarily clung to him for protection, and made him the arbiter of her fate for weal or woe. His feelings towards her at such moments, were those which have been since so beautifully expressed by our immortal Joanna Baillie:

> ———'Thou sweetest thing,
> That e'er did fix its lightly-fibred sprays
> To the rude rock, ah! wouldst thou cling to me?
> Rough and storm-worn I am—yet love me as
> Thou truly dost, I will love thee again
> With true and honest heart, though all unmeet
> To be the mate of such sweet gentleness.'*

Thus the very points in which they differed, seemed, in some measure, to ensure the continuance of their mutual affection. If, indeed, they had so fully appreciated each other's character before the burst of passion in which they hastily pledged their faith to each other, Lucy might have feared Ravenswood too much ever to have loved him, and he might have construed her softness and docile temper as imbecility, rendering her unworthy of his regard. But they stood pledged to each other; and Lucy only feared that her lover's pride might one day teach him to regret his attachment; Ravenswood, that a mind so ductile as Lucy's might, in absence or difficulties, be induced, by the entreaties or influence of those around her, to renounce the engagement she had formed.

'Do not fear it,' said Lucy, when upon one occasion a hint of such suspicion escaped her lover; 'the mirrors which receive the reflection of all successive objects are framed of hard materials like glass or steel—the softer substances, when they receive an impression, retain it undefaced.'

'This is poetry, Lucy,' said Ravenswood; 'and in poetry there is always fallacy, and sometimes fiction.'

'Believe me then, once more, in honest prose,' said Lucy, 'that, though I will never wed man without the consent of my parents, yet neither force nor persuasion shall dispose of my hand till you renounce the right I have given you to it.'

The lovers had ample time for such explanations. Henry was now more seldom their companion, being either a most unwilling attendant upon the lessons of his tutor, or a forward volunteer under the instructions of the foresters or grooms. As for the Keeper, his mornings were spent in his study, maintaining correspondences of all kinds, and balancing in his anxious mind the various intelligence which he collected from every quarter concerning the expected change of Scottish politics, and the probable strength of the parties who were about to struggle for power. At other times he busied himself about arranging, and countermanding, and then again arranging, the preparations which he judged necessary for the reception of the Marquis of A——, whose arrival had been twice delayed by some necessary cause of detention.

In the midst of all these various avocations, political and domestic, he seemed not to observe how much his daughter and his guest were thrown into each other's society, and was censured by many of his neighbours, according to the fashion of neighbours in all countries, for suffering such an intimate connexion to take place betwixt two young persons. The only natural explanation was, that he designed them for each other; while, in truth, his only motive was to temporize and procrastinate, until he should discover the real extent of the interest which the Marquis took in Ravenswood's affairs, and the power which he was likely to possess of advancing them. Until these points should be made both clear and manifest, the Lord Keeper resolved that he would do nothing to commit himself, either in one shape or other; and, like many cunning persons, he overreached himself deplorably.

Amongst those who had been disposed to censure, with the greatest severity, the conduct of Sir William Ashton, in permitting the prolonged residence of Ravenswood under his roof, and his constant attendance on Miss Ashton, was the new Laird of Girnington, and his faithful squire and bottle-holder, personages formerly well known to us by the names of Hayston and Bucklaw, and his companion Captain Craigengelt. The former had at length succeeded to the extensive property of his long-lived grand-aunt, and to considerable wealth besides, which he had employed in redeeming his paternal acres, (by the title appertaining to which he still chose to be designated,) notwithstanding Captain Craigengelt had proposed to him a most advantageous mode of vesting the money in Law's scheme, which was just then broached, and offered his services to travel express to Paris for the purpose. * But Bucklaw had so far derived wisdom from adversity, that he would listen to no proposal which Craigengelt could invent, which had the slightest tendency to risk his newly-acquired independence. He that had once eat pease-bannocks, drank sour wine, and slept in the secret chamber at Wolf's Crag, would, he said, prize good cheer and a soft bed as long as he lived, and take special care never to need such hospitality again.

Craigengelt, therefore, found himself disappointed in the first hopes he had entertained of making a good hand of the Laird of Bucklaw. Still, however, he reaped many advantages from his friend's good fortune. Bucklaw, who had never been at all scrupulous in choosing his companions, was accustomed to, and entertained by a fellow, whom he could either laugh with, or laugh at, as he had a mind, who would take, according to Scottish phrase, 'the bit and the buffet,' * understood all sports, whether within or without doors, and, when the laird had a mind for a bottle of wine, (no infrequent circumstance,) was always ready to save him from the scandal of getting drunk by himself. Upon these terms Craigengelt was the frequent, almost the constant, inmate of the house of Girnington.

In no time, and under no possibility of circumstances, could good have been derived from such an intimacy, however its bad consequences might be qualified by the thorough knowledge which Bucklaw possessed of his dependant's character, and the high contempt in which he held it. But as circumstances stood, this evil communication was particularly liable to corrupt what good principles nature had implanted in the patron.

Craigengelt had never forgiven the scorn with which Ravenswood had torn the mask of courage and honesty from his countenance; and to exasperate Bucklaw's resentment against him, was the safest mode of revenge which occurred to his cowardly, yet cunning and malignant disposition.

He brought up, on all occasions, the story of the challenge which Ravenswood had declined to accept, and endeavoured, by every possible insinuation, to make his patron believe that his honour was concerned in bringing that matter to an issue by a present discussion with Ravenswood. But respecting this subject, Bucklaw imposed on him, at length, a peremptory command of silence.

'I think,' he said, 'the Master has treated me unlike a gentleman, and I see no right he had to send me back a cavalier answer when I demanded the satisfaction of one—But he gave me my life once—and, in looking the matter over at present, I put myself but on equal terms with him. Should he cross me again, I shall consider the old accompt as balanced, and his Mastership will do well to look to himself.'

'That he should,' re-echoed Craigengelt; 'for when you are in practice, Bucklaw, I would bet a magnum you are through him before the third pass.'

'Then you know nothing of the matter,' said Bucklaw, 'and you never saw him fence.'

'And I know nothing of the matter?' said the dependant—'a good jest, I promise you!—and though I never saw Ravenswood fence, have I not been at Monsieur Sagoon's school, who was the first *maître d'armes* at Paris; and have I not been at Signor Poco's at Florence, and Meinheer Durchstossen's at Vienna, and have I not seen all their play?'*

'I don't know whether you have or not,' said Bucklaw; 'but what about it, though you had?'

'Only that I will be d—d if ever I saw French, Italian, or High-Dutchman ever make foot, hand, and eye, keep time half so well as you, Bucklaw.'

'I believe you lie, Craigie,' said Bucklaw; 'however, I can hold my own, both with single rapier, backsword, sword and dagger, broadsword, or case of falchions—and that's as much as any gentleman need know of the matter.'

'And the double of what ninety-nine out of a hundred know,' said Craigengelt; 'they learn to change a few thrusts with the small sword, and then, forsooth, they understand the noble art of defence! Now, when I was at Rouen in the year 1695, there was a Chevalier de Chapon and I went to the Opera, where we found three bits of English birkies'——

'Is it a long story you are going to tell?' said Bucklaw, interrupting him without ceremony.

'Just as you like,' answered the parasite, 'for we made short work of it.'

'Then I like it short,' said Bucklaw; 'is it serious, or merry?'

'Devilish serious, I assure you, and so they found it; for the Chevalier and I'——

'Then I don't like it at all,' said Bucklaw; 'so fill a brimmer of my auld auntie's claret, rest her heart! And, as the Hielandman says, *Skioch doch na skiaill.*'[25]

'That was what tough old Sir Evan Dhu used to say to me when I was out with the metall'd lads in 1689.* "Craigengelt," he used to say, "you are as pretty a fellow as ever held steel in his grip, but you have one fault."'

'If he had known you as long as I have done,' said Bucklaw, 'he would have found out some twenty more; but hang long stories, give us your toast, man.'

Craigengelt rose, went a tiptoe to the door, peeped out, shut it carefully, came back again—clapped his tarnished gold-laced hat on one side of his head, took his glass in one hand, and touching the hilt of his hanger with the other, named, 'The King over the water.'*

'I tell you what it is, Captain Craigengelt,' said Bucklaw; 'I shall keep my mind to myself on these subjects, having too much respect for the memory of my venerable aunt Girnington to put her lands and tenements in the way of committing treason against established authority. Bring me King James to Edinburgh, Captain, with thirty thousand men at his back, and I'll tell you what I think about his title; but as for running my neck into a noose, and my good broad lands into the statutory penalties, "in that case made and provided,"* rely upon it, you will find me no such fool. So, when you mean to vapour with your hanger and your dram-cup in support of treasonable toasts, you must find your liquor and company elsewhere.'

'Well, then,' said Craigengelt, 'name the toast yourself, and be it what it like, I'll pledge you, were it a mile to the bottom.'

'And I'll give you a toast that deserves it, my boy,' said Bucklaw; 'what say you to Miss Lucy Ashton?'

'Up with it,' said the Captain, as he tossed off his brimmer, 'the bonniest lass in Lothian. What a pity the old sneck-drawing whigamore, her father, is about to throw her away upon that rag of pride and beggary, the Master of Ravenswood!'

'That's not quite so clear,' said Bucklaw, in a tone, which, though it seemed indifferent, excited his companion's eager curiosity; and not that only, but also his hope of working himself into some sort of confidence, which might make him necessary to his patron, being by no means satisfied to rest on mere sufferance, if he could form by art or industry a more permanent title to his favour.

'I thought,' said he, after a moment's pause, 'that was a settled matter—they are continually together, and nothing else is spoken of betwixt Lammerlaw and Traprain.'*

'They may say what they please,' replied his patron, 'but I know better; and I'll give you Miss Lucy Ashton's health again, my boy.'

'And I would drink it on my knee,' said Craigengelt, 'if I thought the girl had the spirit to jilt that d—d son of a Spaniard.'

'I am to request you will not use the word jilt and Miss Ashton's name together,' said Bucklaw, gravely.

'Jilt, did I say?—discard, my lad of acres—by Jove, I meant to say discard,' replied Craigengelt; 'and I hope she'll discard him like a small card at piquet, and take in the King of Hearts, my boy!—But yet'——

'But what?' said his patron.

'But yet I know for certain they are hours together alone, and in the woods and the fields.'

'That's her foolish father's dotage—that will be soon put out of the lass's head, if it ever gets into it,' answered Bucklaw. 'And now fill your glass again, Captain, I am going to make you happy—I am going to let you into a secret—a plot—a noosing plot—only the noose is but typical.'

'A marrying matter?' said Craigengelt, and his jaw fell as he asked the question; for he suspected that matrimony would render his situation at Girnington much more precarious than during the jolly days of his patron's bachelorhood.

'Ay, a marriage, man,' said Bucklaw; 'but wherefore droops thy mighty spirit, and why grow the rubies on thy cheek so pale?*The board will have a corner, and the corner will have a trencher, and the trencher will have a glass beside it; and the board-end shall be filled, and the trencher and the glass shall be replenished for thee, if all the petticoats in Lothian had sworn the contrary—What, man! I am not the boy to put myself into leading strings?'

'So says many an honest fellow,' said Craigengelt, 'and some of my special friends; but, curse me if I know the reason, the women could never bear me, and always contrived to trundle me out of favour before the honeymoon was over.'

'If you could have kept your ground till that was over, you might have made a good year's pension,' said Bucklaw.

'But I never could,' answered the dejected parasite; 'there was my Lord Castle-Cuddy—we were hand and glove—I rode his horses—borrowed money, both for him and from him—trained his hawks, and taught him how to lay his bets; and when he took a fancy of marrying, I married him to Katie Glegg, whom I thought myself as sure of as man could be of woman. Egad, she had me out of the house, as if I had run on wheels, within the first fortnight!'

'Well!' replied Bucklaw, 'I think I have nothing of Castle-Cuddy about me, or Lucy of Katie Glegg. But you see the thing will go on whether you like it or no—the only question is, will you be useful?'

'Useful?' exclaimed the Captain;—'and to thee, my lad of lands, my darling boy, whom I would tramp barefooted through the world for?—name time, place, mode, and circumstances, and see if I will not be useful in all uses that can be devised.'

'Why, then, you must ride two hundred miles for me,' said the patron.

'A thousand, and call them a flea's leap,' answered the dependant; 'I'll cause saddle my horse directly.'

'Better stay till you know where you are to go, and what you are to do,' quoth Bucklaw. 'You know I have a kinswoman in Northumberland, Lady Blenkensop by name, whose old acquaintance I had the misfortune to lose in the period of my poverty, but the light of whose countenance shone forth upon me when the sun of my prosperity began to arise.'

'D——n all such double-faced jades!' exclaimed Craigengelt, heroically; 'this I will say for John Craigengelt, that he is his friend's friend through good report and bad report, poverty and riches; and you know something of that yourself, Bucklaw.'

'I have not forgot your merits,' said his patron; 'I do remember, that, in my extremities, you had a mind to *crimp* me for the service of the French king, or of the Pretender; and, moreover, that you afterwards lent me a score of pieces, when, as I firmly believe, you had heard the news that old Lady Girnington had a touch of the dead palsy. But don't be downcast, John; I believe, after all, you like me very well in your way, and it is my misfortune to have no better counsellor at present. To return to this Lady Blenkensop, you must know she is a close confederate of Duchess Sarah.'

'What! of Sall Jennings?' exclaimed Craigengelt; 'then she must be a good one.'

'Hold your tongue, and keep your Tory rants to yourself, if it be possible,' said Bucklaw; 'I tell you, that through the Duchess of Marlborough has this Northumbrian cousin of mine become a crony of Lady Ashton, the Keeper's wife, or, I may say, the Lord Keeper's Lady Keeper, and she has favoured Lady Blenkensop with a visit on her return from London, and is just now at her old mansion-house on the banks of the Wansbeck.* Now, sir, as it has been the use and wont of these ladies to consider their husbands as of no importance in the management of their own families, it has been their present pleasure, without consulting Sir William Ashton, to put on the *tapis* a matrimonial alliance, to be concluded between Lucy Ashton and my own right honourable self, Lady Ashton acting as self-constituted plenipotentiary on the part of her daughter and husband, and Mother Blenkensop, equally unaccredited, doing me the honour to be my representative. You may suppose I was a little astonished when I found that a treaty, in which I was so considerably interested, had advanced a good way before I was even consulted.'

'Capot me if I think that was according to the rules of the game,' said his confident; 'and pray, what answer did you return?'

'Why, my first thought was to send the treaty to the devil, and the negotiators along with it, for a couple of meddling old women; my next was to laugh very heartily; and my third and last was a settled opinion that the thing was reasonable, and would suit me well enough.'

'Why, I thought you had never seen the wench but once—and then she had her riding-mask on—I am sure you told me so.'

'Ay—but I liked her very well then. And Ravenswood's dirty usage of me—shutting me out of doors to dine with the lackeys, because he had the Lord Keeper, forsooth, and his daughter, to be guests in his beggarly castle of starvation—D—n me, Craigengelt, if I ever forgive him till I play him as good a trick!'

'No more you should, if you are a lad of mettle,' said Craigengelt, the matter now taking a turn in which he could sympathize; 'and if you carry this wench from him, it will break his heart.'

'That it will not,' said Bucklaw; 'his heart is all steeled over with reason and philosophy—things that you, Craigie, know nothing about more than myself, God help me—But it will break his pride, though, and that's what I'm driving at.'

'Distance me,' said Craigengelt, 'but I know the reason now of his unmannerly behaviour at his old tumble-down tower yonder—Ashamed of your company?—no, no!—Gad, he was afraid you would cut in and carry off the girl.'

'Eh! Craigengelt?' said Bucklaw— 'do you really think so?—but no, no!—he is a devilish deal prettier man than I am.'

'Who—he?' exclaimed the parasite—'he's as black as the crook; and for his size—he's a tall fellow, to be sure—but give me a light, stout, middle-sized'——

'Plague on thee!' said Bucklaw, interrupting him, 'and on me for listening to you!—you would say as much if I were hunchbacked. But as to Ravenswood—he has kept no terms with me—I'll keep none with him—if I *can* win this girl from him, I *will* win her.'

'Win her?—'sblood, you *shall* win her, point, quint, and quatorze, my king of trumps—you shall pique, repique, and capot him.'

'Prithee, stop thy gambling cant for one instant,' said Bucklaw. 'Things have come thus far, that I have entertained the proposal of my kinswoman, agreed to the terms of jointure, amount of fortune, and so forth, and that the affair is to go forward when Lady Ashton comes down, for she takes her daughter and her son in her own hand. Now they want me to send up a confidential person with some writings.'

'By this good wine, I'll ride to the end of the world—the very gates of Jericho, and the judgment-seat of Prester John,* for thee!' ejaculated the Captain.

'Why, I believe you would do something for me, and a great deal for yourself. Now, any one could carry the writings; but you will have a little more to do. You must contrive to drop out before my Lady Ashton, just as if it were a matter of little consequence, the residence of Ravenswood at her husband's house, and his close intercourse with Miss Ashton; and you may tell her, that all the country talks of a visit from the Marquis of A——, as it is supposed, to make up the match betwixt Ravenswood and her daughter. I should like to hear what she says to all this; for, rat me, if I have any idea of starting for the plate at all if Ravenswood is to win the race, and he has odds against me already.'

'Never a bit—the wench has too much sense—and in that belief I drink her health a third time; and, were time and place fitting, I would drink it on bended knees, and he that would not pledge me, I would make his guts garter his stockings.'

'Hark ye, Craigengelt; as you are going into the society of women of rank,' said Bucklaw, 'I'll thank you to forget your strange blackguard oaths and damme's—I'll write to them, though, that you are a blunt untaught fellow.'

'Ay, ay,' replied Craigengelt; 'a plain, blunt, honest, downright soldier.'*

'Not too honest, nor too much of the soldier neither; but such as thou art, it is my luck to need thee, for I must have spurs put to Lady Ashton's motions.'

'I'll dash them up to the rowel-heads,' said Craigengelt; 'she shall come here at the gallop, like a cow chased by a whole nest of hornets, and her tail twisted over her rump like a corkscrew.'

'And hear ye, Craigie,' said Bucklaw; 'your boots and doublet are good enough to drink in, as the man says in the play,* but they are somewhat too greasy for tea-table service—prithee, get thyself a little better rigged out, and here is to pay all charges.'

'Nay, Bucklaw—on my soul, man—you use me ill—However,' added Craigengelt, pocketing the money, 'if you will have me so far indebted to you, I must be conforming.'

'Well, horse and away!' said the patron, 'so soon as you have got your riding livery in trim. You may ride the black crop-ear—and, hark ye, I'll make you a present of him to boot.'

'I drink to the good luck of my mission,' answered the ambassador, 'in a half-pint bumper.'

'I thank ye, Craigie, and pledge you—I see nothing against it but the father or the girl taking a tantrum, and I am told the mother can wind them both round her little finger. Take care not to affront her with any of your jacobite jargon.'

'O ay, true—she is a whig, and a friend of old Sall of Marlborough—thank my stars, I can hoist any colours at a pinch. I have fought as hard under John Churchill as ever I did under Dundee or the Duke of Berwick.'*

' I verily believe you, Craigie,' said the lord of the mansion; 'but, Craigie, do you, pray, step down to the cellar, and fetch us up a bottle of the Burgundy, 1678—it is in the fourth bin from the right-hand turn—And I say, Craigie, you may fetch up half-a-dozen whilst you are about it.—Egad, we'll make a night on't!'

CHAPTER XXII

And soon they spied the merry-men green,
And eke the coach and four.

(Duke upon Duke) *

CRAIGENGELT set forth on his mission so soon as his equipage
was complete, prosecuted his journey with all diligence, and
accomplished his commission with all the dexterity for which
Bucklaw had given him credit. As he arrived with credentials from
Mr Hayston of Bucklaw, he was extremely welcome to both
ladies; and those who are prejudiced in favour of a new acquaintance can, for a time at least, discover excellencies in his very faults,
and perfections in his deficiencies. Although both ladies were
accustomed to good society, yet, being predetermined to find out
an agreeable and well-behaved gentleman in Mr Hayston's friend,
they succeeded wonderfully in imposing on themselves. It is true
that Craigengelt was now handsomely dressed, and that was a
point of no small consequence. But, independent of outward
show, his blackguard impudence of address was construed into
honourable bluntness, becoming his supposed military profession;
his hectoring passed for courage, and his sauciness for wit. Lest,
however, any one should think this a violation of probability, we
must add, in fairness to the two ladies, that their discernment was
greatly blinded, and their favour propitiated, by the opportune
arrival of Captain Craigengelt in the moment when they were
longing for a third hand to make a party at tredrille, in which, as
in all games, whether of chance or skill, that worthy person was
a great proficient.

When he found himself established in favour, his next point was
how best to use it for the furtherance of his patron's views. He
found Lady Ashton prepossessed strongly in favour of the motion,
which Lady Blenkensop, partly from regard to her kinsman, partly
from the spirit of match-making, had not hesitated to propose to

her; so that his task was an easy one. Bucklaw, reformed from his prodigality, was just the sort of husband which she desired to have for her Shepherdess of Lammermoor; and while the marriage gave her an easy fortune, and a respectable country gentleman for her husband, Lady Ashton was of opinion that her destinies would be fully and most favourably accomplished. It so chanced, also, that Bucklaw, among his new acquisitions, had gained the management of a little political interest in a neighbouring county, where the Douglas family originally held large possessions. It was one of the bosom-hopes of Lady Ashton, that her eldest son, Sholto, should represent this county in the British Parliament, and she saw this alliance with Bucklaw as a circumstance which might be highly favourable to her wishes. *

Craigengelt, who in his way by no means wanted sagacity, no sooner discovered in what quarter the wind of Lady Ashton's wishes sate, than he trimmed his course accordingly. 'There was little to prevent Bucklaw himself from sitting for the county—he must carry the heat—must walk the course. Two cousins-german—six more distant kinsmen, his factor and his chamberlain, were all hollow votes—and the Girnington interest had always carried, betwixt love and fear, about as many more. But Bucklaw cared no more about riding the first horse, and that sort of thing, than he, Craigengelt, did about a game at birkie—it was a pity his interest was not in good guidance.'

All this Lady Ashton drank in with willing and attentive ears, resolving internally to be herself the person who should take the management of the political influence of her destined son-in-law, for the benefit of her eldest born, Sholto, and all other parties concerned.

When he found her ladyship thus favourably disposed, the Captain proceeded, to use his employer's phrase, to set spurs to her resolution, by hinting at the situation of matters at Ravenswood Castle, the long residence which the heir of that family had made with the Lord Keeper, and the reports which (though he would be d—d ere he gave credit to any of them) had been idly circulated in the neighbourhood. It was not the Captain's cue to appear himself to be uneasy on the subject of these rumours; but he easily saw from Lady Ashton's flushed cheek, hesitating voice, and flashing eye, that she had caught the alarm which he intended to communicate. She had not heard from her husband so often or so regularly as she thought him bound in duty to have written, and of this very interesting intelligence, concerning his visit to the Tower of Wolf's Crag, and the guest whom, with such cordiality, he had received at Ravenswood Castle, he had suffered his lady to remain altogether ignorant, until she now learned it by the chance information of a stranger. Such concealment approached, in her apprehension, to a misprision, at least, of treason, if not to actual rebellion against her matrimonial authority;* and in her inward soul did she vow to take vengeance on the Lord Keeper, as on a subject detected in meditating revolt. Her indignation burned the more fiercely, as she found herself obliged to suppress it in presence of Lady Blenkensop, the kinswoman, and of Craigengelt, the confidential friend of Bucklaw, of whose alliance she now became trebly desirous, since it occurred to her alarmed imagination, that her husband might, in his policy or timidity, prefer that of Ravenswood.

The Captain was engineer enough to discover that the train was fired; and therefore heard, in the course of the same day, without the least surprise, that Lady Ashton had resolved to abridge her visit to Lady Blenkensop, and set forth with the peep of morning on her return to Scotland, using all the dispatch which the state of the roads, and the mode of travelling, would possibly permit.

Unhappy Lord Keeper!—little was he aware what a storm was travelling towards him in all the speed with which an old-fashioned coach and six could possibly achieve its journey. He, like Don Gayferos, 'forgot his lady fair and true,'* and was only anxious about the expected visit of the Marquis of A———. Sooth-fast tidings had assured him that this nobleman was at length, and without fail, to honour his castle at one in the afternoon, being a late dinner-hour; and much was the bustle in consequence of the annunciation. The Lord Keeper traversed the chambers, held consultation with the butler in the cellars, and even ventured, at the risk of a *démêlé* with a cook, of a spirit lofty enough to scorn the admonitions of Lady Ashton herself, to peep into the kitchen. Satisfied, at length, that every thing was in as active a train of preparation as was possible, he summoned Ravenswood and his daughter to walk upon the terrace, for the purpose of watching, from that commanding position, the earliest symptoms of his lordship's approach. For this purpose, with slow and idle step, he paraded the terrace, which, flanked with a heavy stone battlement, stretched in front of the castle upon a level with the first story; while visitors found access to the court by a projecting gate-way, the bartizan or flat-leaded roof of which was accessible from the terrace by an easy flight of low and broad steps. The whole bore a resemblance partly to a castle, partly to a nobleman's seat; and though calculated, in some respects, for defence, evinced that it had been constructed under a sense of the power and security of the ancient Lords of Ravenswood.

This pleasant walk commanded a beautiful and extensive view. But what was most to our present purpose, there were seen from the terrace two roads, one leading from the east, and one from the westward, which, crossing a ridge opposed to the eminence on which the castle stood, at different angles, gradually approached each other, until they joined not far from the gate of the avenue. It was to the westward approach that the Lord Keeper, from a sort of fidgeting anxiety, his daughter, from complaisance to him, and Ravenswood, though feeling some symptoms of internal impatience, out of complaisance to his daughter, directed their eyes to see the precursors of the Marquis's approach.

These were not long of presenting themselves. Two running footmen, dressed in white, with black jockey-caps, and long staffs in their hands, headed the train; and such was their agility, that they found no difficulty in keeping the necessary advance, which the etiquette of their station required, before the carriage and horsemen. Onward they came at a long swinging trot, arguing unwearied speed in their long-breathed calling. Such running footmen are often alluded to in old plays, (I would particularly instance Middleton's 'Mad World my Masters,') and perhaps may be still remembered by some old persons in Scotland, as part of the retinue of the ancient nobility when travelling in full ceremony.[26]* Behind these glancing meteors, who footed it as if the Avenger of Blood had been behind them,* came a cloud of dust, raised by riders who preceded, attended, or followed, the state-carriage of the Marquis.

The privilege of nobility, in those days, had something in it impressive on the imagination. The dresses and liveries and number of their attendants, their style of travelling, the imposing, and almost warlike air of the armed men who surrounded them, placed them far above the laird, who travelled with his brace of footmen; and as to rivalry from the mercantile part of the community, these would as soon have thought of imitating the state equipage of the Sovereign. At present it is different; and I myself, Peter Pattieson, in a late journey to Edinburgh, had the honour, in the mail-coach phrase, to 'change a leg' with a peer of the realm.* It was not so in the days of which I write; and the Marquis's approach, so long expected in vain, now took place in the full pomp of ancient aristocracy. Sir William Ashton was so much interested in what he beheld, and in considering the ceremonial of reception in case any circumstance had been omitted, that he scarce heard his son Henry exclaim, 'There is another coach and six coming down the east road, papa—can they both belong to the Marquis of A——?'

At length, when the youngster had fairly compelled his attention by pulling his sleeve,

> 'He turned his eyes, and, as he turn'd, survey'd
> An awful vision.'*

Sure enough, another coach and six, with four servants or out-riders in attendance, was descending the hill from the eastward, at such a pace as made it doubtful which of the carriages thus approaching from different quarters would first reach the gate at the extremity of the avenue. The one coach was green, the other blue; and not the green and blue chariots in the Circus of Rome or Constantinople excited more turmoil among the citizens than the double apparition occasioned in the mind of the Lord Keeper.* We all remember the terrible exclamation of the dying profligate, when a friend, to destroy what he supposed the hypochondriac idea of a spectre appearing in a certain shape at a given hour, placed before him a person dressed up in the manner he described. 'Mon Dieu!' said the expiring sinner, who, it seems, saw both the real and polygraphic apparition—'il y en a deux!'*

The surprise of the Lord Keeper was scarcely less unpleasing at the duplication of the expected arrival; his mind misgave him strangely. There was no neighbour who would have approached so unceremoniously, at a time when ceremony was held in such respect. It must be Lady Ashton, said his conscience, and followed up the hint with an anxious anticipation of the purpose of her sudden and unannounced return. He felt that he was caught 'in the manner.' * That the company in which she had so unluckily surprised him was likely to be highly distasteful to her, there was no question; and the only hope which remained for him was her high sense of dignified propriety, which, he trusted, might prevent a public explosion. But so active were his doubts and fears, as altogether to derange his purposed ceremonial for the reception of the Marquis.

These feelings of apprehension were not confined to Sir William Ashton. 'It is my mother—it is my mother!' said Lucy, turning as pale as ashes, and clasping her hands together as she looked at Ravenswood.

'And if it be Lady Ashton,' said her lover to her in a low tone, 'what can be the occasion of such alarm?—Surely the return of a lady to the family from which she has been so long absent, should excite other sensations than those of fear and dismay.'

'You do not know my mother,' said Miss Ashton, in a tone almost breathless with terror; 'what will she say when she sees you in this place!'

'My stay has been too long,' said Ravenswood, somewhat haughtily, 'if her displeasure at my presence is likely to be so formidable. My dear Lucy,' he resumed, in a tone of soothing encouragement, 'you are too childishly afraid of Lady Ashton; she is a woman of family—a lady of fashion—a person who must know the world, and what is due to her husband and her husband's guests.'

Lucy shook her head; and, as if her mother, still at the distance of half a mile, could have seen and scrutinized her deportment, she withdrew herself from beside Ravenswood, and, taking her brother Henry's arm, led him to a different part of the terrace. The Keeper also shuffled down towards the portal of the great gate, without inviting Ravenswood to accompany him, and thus he remained standing alone on the terrace, deserted and shunned, as it were, by the inhabitants of the mansion.

This suited not the mood of one who was proud in proportion to his poverty, and who thought that, in sacrificing his deep-rooted resentments so far as to become Sir William Ashton's guest, he conferred a favour and received none. 'I can forgive Lucy,' he said to himself; 'she is young, timid, and conscious of an important engagement assumed without her mother's sanction; yet she should remember with whom it has been assumed, and leave me no reason to suspect that she is ashamed of her choice. For the Keeper, sense, spirit, and expression seem to have left his face and manner since he had the first glimpse of Lady Ashton's carriage. I must watch how this is to end; and, if they give me reason to think myself an unwelcome guest, my visit is soon abridged.'

With these suspicions floating on his mind, he left the terrace, and, walking towards the stables of the castle, gave directions that his horse should be kept in readiness, in case he should have occasion to ride abroad.

In the meanwhile the drivers of the two carriages, the approach of which had occasioned so much dismay at the castle, had become aware of each other's presence, as they approached upon different lines to the head of the avenue, as a common centre. Lady Ashton's driver and postilions instantly received orders to get foremost, if possible, her ladyship being desirous of dispatching her first inter-view with her husband before the arrival of these guests, whoever they might happen to be. On the other hand, the coachman of the Marquis, conscious of his own dignity and that of his master, and observing the rival charioteer was mending his pace, resolved, like a true brother of the whip, whether ancient or modern, to vindicate his right of precedence. So that, to increase the confu-sion of the Lord Keeper's understanding, he saw the short time which remained for consideration abridged by the haste of the contending coachmen, who, fixing their eyes sternly on each other, and applying the lash smartly to their horses, began to thunder down the descent with emulous rapidity, while the horsemen who attended them were forced to put on to a hand-gallop.

Sir William's only chance now remaining was the possibility of an overturn, and that his lady or visitor might break their necks. I am not aware that he formed any distinct wish on the subject, but

I have no reason to think that his grief in either case would have been altogether inconsolable. This chance, however, also disappeared; for Lady Ashton, though insensible to fear, began to see the ridicule of running a race with a visitor of distinction, the goal being the portal of her own castle, and commanded her coachman, as they approached the avenue, to slacken his pace, and allow precedence to the stranger's equipage; a command which he gladly obeyed, as coming in time to save his honour, the horses of the Marquis's carriage being better, or, at least, fresher than his own. He restrained his pace, therefore, and suffered the green coach to enter the avenue, with all its retinue, which pass it occupied with the speed of a whirlwind. The Marquis's laced charioteer no sooner found the *pas d'avance* was granted to him, than he resumed a more deliberate pace, at which he advanced under the embowering shade of the lofty elms, surrounded by all the attendants; while the carriage of Lady Ashton followed, still more slowly, at some distance.

In the front of the castle, and beneath the portal which admitted guests into the inner court, stood Sir William Ashton, much perplexed in mind, his younger son and daughter beside him, and in their rear a train of attendants of various ranks, in and out of livery. The nobility and gentry of Scotland, at this period, were remarkable even to extravagance for the number of their servants, whose services were easily purchased in a country where men were numerous beyond proportion to the means of employing them.*

The manners of a man, trained like Sir William Ashton, are too much at his command to remain long disconcerted with the most adverse concurrence of circumstances. He received the Marquis, as he alighted from his equipage, with the usual compliments of welcome; and, as he ushered him into the great hall, expressed his hope that his journey had been pleasant. The Marquis was a tall, well-made man, with a thoughtful and intelligent countenance, and an eye, in which the fire of ambition had for some years replaced the vivacity of youth; a bold, proud, expression of countenance, yet chastened by habitual caution, and the desire which, as the head of a party, he necessarily entertained of acquiring popularity.* He answered with courtesy the courteous enquiries of the Lord Keeper, and was formally presented to Miss Ashton, in the course of which ceremony the Lord Keeper gave the first symptom of what was chiefly occupying his mind, by introducing his daughter as 'his wife, Lady Ashton.'

Lucy blushed; the Marquis looked surprised at the extremely juvenile appearance of his hostess, and the Lord Keeper with difficulty rallied himself so far as to explain. 'I should have said my daughter, my lord; but the truth is, that I saw Lady Ashton's carriage enter the avenue shortly after your lordship's, and'——

'Make no apology, my lord,' replied his noble guest; 'let me entreat you will wait on your lady, and leave me to cultivate Miss Ashton's acquaintance. I am shocked my people should have taken precedence of our hostess at her own gate; but your lordship is aware, that I supposed Lady Ashton was still in the south. Permit me to beseech you will waive ceremony, and hasten to welcome her.'

This was precisely what the Lord Keeper longed to do; and he instantly profited by his lordship's obliging permission. To see Lady Ashton, and encounter the first burst of her displeasure in private, might prepare her, in some degree, to receive her unwelcome guests with due decorum. As her carriage, therefore, stopped, the arm of the attentive husband was ready to assist Lady Ashton in dismounting. Looking as if she saw him not, she put his arm aside, and requested that of Captain Craigengelt, who stood by the coach with his laced hat under his arm, having acted as *cavalière servente*, or squire in attendance, during the journey. Taking hold of this respectable person's arm as if to support her, Lady Ashton traversed the court, uttering a word or two by way of direction to the servants, but not one to Sir William, who in vain endeavoured to attract her attention, as he rather followed than accompanied her into the hall, in which they found the Marquis in close conversation with the Master of Ravenswood: Lucy had taken the first opportunity of escaping. There was embarrassment on every countenance except that of the Marquis of A——; for even Craigengelt's impudence was hardly able to veil his fear of Ravenswood, and the rest felt the awkwardness of the position in which they were thus unexpectedly placed.

After waiting a moment to be presented by Sir William Ashton, the Marquis resolved to introduce himself. 'The Lord Keeper,' he said, bowing to Lady Ashton, 'has just introduced to me his daughter as his wife—he might very easily present Lady Ashton as his daughter, so little does she differ from what I remember her some years since.—Will she permit an old acquaintance the privilege of a guest?'

He saluted the lady with too good a grace to apprehend a repulse, and then proceeded—'This, Lady Ashton, is a peace-making visit, and therefore I presume to introduce my cousin, the young Master of Ravenswood, to your favourable notice.'

Lady Ashton could not choose but curtsy; but there was in her obeisance an air of haughtiness approaching to contemptuous repulse. Ravenswood could not choose but bow; but his manner returned the scorn with which he had been greeted.

'Allow me,' she said, 'to present to your lordship *my* friend.' Craigengelt, with the forward impudence which men of his cast mistake for ease, made a sliding bow to the Marquis, which he graced by a flourish of his gold-laced hat. The lady turned to her husband—'You and I, Sir William,' she said, and these were the first words she had addressed to him, 'have acquired new acquaintances since we parted—let me introduce the acquisition I have made to mine—Captain Craigengelt.'

Another bow, and another flourish of the gold-laced hat, which was returned by the Lord Keeper without intimation of former recognition, and with that sort of anxious readiness, which intimated his wish, that peace and amnesty should take place betwixt the contending parties, including the auxiliaries on both sides. 'Let me introduce you to the Master of Ravenswood,' said he to Captain Craigengelt, following up the same amicable system. But the Master drew up his tall form to the full extent of his height, and without so much as looking towards the person thus introduced to him, he said, in a marked tone, 'Captain Craigengelt and I are already perfectly well acquainted with each other.'

'Perfectly—perfectly,' replied the Captain, in a mumbling tone, like that of a double echo, and with a flourish of his hat, the circumference of which was greatly abridged, compared with those which had so cordially graced his introduction to the Marquis and the Lord Keeper.

Lockhard, followed by three menials, now entered with wine and refreshments, which it was the fashion to offer as a whet before dinner; and when they were placed before the guests, Lady Ashton made an apology for withdrawing her husband from them for some minutes upon business of special import. The Marquis, of course, requested her ladyship would lay herself under no restraint; and Craigengelt, bolting with speed a second glass of racy canary, hastened to leave the room, feeling no great pleasure in the prospect of being left alone with the Marquis of A—— and the Master of Ravenswood; the presence of the former holding him in awe, and that of the latter in bodily terror.

Some arrangements about his horse and baggage formed the pretext for his sudden retreat, in which he persevered, although Lady Ashton gave Lockhard orders to be careful most particularly to accommodate Captain Craigengelt with all the attendance which he could possibly require. The Marquis and the Master of Ravenswood were thus left to communicate to each other their remarks upon the reception which they had met with, while Lady Ashton led the way, and her lord followed somewhat like a condemned criminal, to her ladyship's dressing-room.

So soon as the spouses had both entered, her ladyship gave way to that fierce audacity of temper, which she had with difficulty suppressed, out of respect to appearances. She shut the door behind the alarmed Lord Keeper, took the key out of the spring-lock, and with a countenance which years had not bereft of its haughty charms, and eyes which spoke at once resolution and resentment, she addressed her astounded husband in these words:—'My lord, I am not greatly surprised at the connexions you have been pleased to form during my absence—they are entirely in conformity with your birth and breeding; and if I did expect any thing else, I heartily own my error, and that I merit, by having done so, the disappointment you had prepared for me.'

'My dear Lady Ashton—my dear Eleanor,' said the Lord Keeper, 'listen to reason for a moment, and I will convince you I have acted with all the regard due to the dignity, as well as the interest, of my family.'

'To the interest of *your* family I conceive you perfectly capable of attending,' returned the indignant lady, 'and even to the dignity of your own family also, as far as it requires any looking after—But as mine happens to be inextricably involved with it, you will excuse me if I choose to give my own attention so far as that is concerned.'

'What would you have, Lady Ashton?' said the husband—'What is it that displeases you? Why is it, that on your return after so long an absence, I am arraigned in this manner?'

'Ask your own conscience, Sir William, what has prompted you to become a renegade to your political party and opinions, and led you, for what I know, to be on the point of marrying your only daughter to a beggarly jacobite bankrupt, the inveterate enemy of your family to the boot.'

'Why, what, in the name of common sense and common civility, would you have me do, madam?' answered her husband—'Is it possible for me, with ordinary decency, to turn a young gentleman out of my house, who saved my daughter's life and my own, but the other morning as it were?'

'Saved your life! I have heard of that story,' said the lady—'the Lord Keeper was scared by a dun cow, and he takes the young fellow who killed her for Guy of Warwick—any butcher from Haddington may soon have an equal claim on your hospitality.'

'Lady Ashton,' stammered the Keeper, 'this is intolerable—and when I am desirous, too, to make you easy by any sacrifice—if you would but tell me what you would be at.'

'Go down to your guests,' said the imperious dame, 'and make your apology to Ravenswood, that the arrival of Captain Craigengelt and some other friends, renders it impossible for you to offer him lodgings at the castle—I expect young Mr Hayston of Bucklaw.'

'Good heavens, madam!' ejaculated her husband—'Ravenswood to give place to Craigengelt, a common gambler and an informer!—it was all I could do to forbear desiring the fellow to get out of my house, and I was much surprised to see him in your ladyship's train.'

'Since you saw him there, you might be well assured,' answered this meek helpmate, 'that he was proper society. As to this

Ravenswood, he only meets with the treatment which, to my certain knowledge, he gave to a much-valued friend of mine, who had the misfortune to be his guest some time since. But take your resolution; for, if Ravenswood does not quit the house, I will.'

Sir William Ashton paced up and down the apartment in the most distressing agitation; fear, and shame, and anger contending against the habitual deference he was in the use of rendering to his lady. At length it ended, as is usual with timid minds placed in such circumstances, in his adopting a *mezzo termine*, a middle measure.

'I tell you frankly, madam, I neither can nor will be guilty of the incivility you propose to the Master of Ravenswood—he has not deserved it at my hand. If you will be so unreasonable as to insult a man of quality under your own roof, I cannot prevent you; but I will not at least be the agent in such a preposterous proceeding.'

'You will not?' asked the lady.

'No, by heavens, madam!' her husband replied; 'ask me any thing congruent with common decency, as to drop his acquaintance by degrees, or the like—but to bid him leave my house is what I will not, and cannot consent to.'

'Then the task of supporting the honour of the family will fall on me, as it has often done before,' said the lady.

She sat down, and hastily wrote a few lines. The Lord Keeper made another effort to prevent her taking a step so decisive, just as she opened the door to call her female attendant from the ante-room. 'Think what you are doing, Lady Ashton—you are making a mortal enemy of a young man, who is like to have the means of harming us'——

'Did you ever know a Douglas who feared an enemy?' answered the lady contemptuously.

'Ay, but he is as proud and vindictive as an hundred Douglasses, and an hundred devils to boot. Think of it for a night only.'

'Not for another moment,' answered the lady;—'here, Mrs Patullo, give this billet to young Ravenswood.'

'To the Master, madam?' said Mrs Patullo.

'Ay, to the Master, if you call him so.'

'I wash my hands of it entirely,' said the Keeper; 'and I shall go down into the garden, and see that Jardine gathers the winter fruit for the dessert.'

'Do so,' said the lady, looking after him with glances of infinite contempt; 'and thank God that you leave one behind you as fit to protect the honour of the family, as you are to look after pippins and pears.'

The Lord Keeper remained long enough in the garden to give her ladyship's mind time to explode, and to let, as he thought, at least the first violence of Ravenswood's displeasure blow over. When he entered the hall, he found the Marquis of A—— giving orders to some of his attendants. He seemed in high displeasure, and interrupted an apology which Sir William had commenced, for having left his lordship alone.

'I presume, Sir William, you are no stranger to this singular billet with which my kinsman of Ravenswood' (an emphasis on the word *my*) 'has been favoured by your lady—and, of course, that you are prepared to receive my adieus—My kinsman is already gone, having thought it unnecessary to offer any on his part, since all former civilities had been cancelled by this singular insult.'

'I protest, my lord,' said Sir William, holding the billet in his hand, 'I am not privy to the contents of this letter. I know Lady Ashton is a warm-tempered and prejudiced woman, and I am sincerely sorry for any offence that has been given or taken; but I hope your lordship will consider that a lady'——

'Should bear herself towards persons of a certain rank with the breeding of one,' said the Marquis, completing the half-uttered sentence.

'True, my lord,' said the unfortunate Keeper; 'but Lady Ashton is still a woman'——

'And as such, methinks,' said the Marquis, again interrupting him, 'should be taught the duties which correspond to her station. But here she comes, and I will learn from her own mouth the reason of this extraordinary and unexpected affront offered to my near relation, while both he and I were her ladyship's guests.'

Lady Ashton accordingly entered the apartment at this moment. Her dispute with Sir William, and a subsequent interview with her daughter, had not prevented her from attending to the duties of her toilette. She appeared in full dress; and, from the character of her countenance and manner, well became the splendour with which ladies of quality then appeared on such occasions.

The Marquis of A—— bowed haughtily, and she returned the salute with equal pride and distance of demeanour. He then took from the passive hand of Sir William Ashton the billet he had given him the moment before he approached the lady, and was about to speak, when she interrupted him. 'I perceive, my lord, you are about to enter upon an unpleasant subject. I am sorry any such should have occurred at this time, to interrupt, in the slightest degree, the respectful reception due to your lordship—but so it is.—Mr Edgar Ravenswood, for whom I have addressed the billet in your lordship's hand, has abused the hospitality of this family, and Sir William Ashton's softness of temper, in order to seduce a young person into engagements without her parents' consent, and of which they never can approve.'

Both gentlemen answered at once,—'My kinsman is incapable,'——said the Lord Marquis.

'I am confident that my daughter Lucy is still more incapable'——said the Lord Keeper.

Lady Ashton at once interrupted, and replied to them both.— 'My Lord Marquis, your kinsman, if Mr Ravenswood has the honour to be so, has made the attempt privately to secure the affections of this young and inexperienced girl. Sir William Ashton, your daughter has been simple enough to give more encouragement than she ought to have done to so very improper a suitor.'

'And I think, madam,' said the Lord Keeper, losing his accustomed temper and patience, 'that if you had nothing better to tell us, you had better have kept this family secret to yourself also.'

'You will pardon me, Sir William,' said the lady, calmly; 'the noble Marquis has a right to know the cause of the treatment I have found it necessary to use to a gentleman whom he calls his blood-relation.'

'It is a cause,' muttered the Lord Keeper, 'which has emerged since the effect has taken place; for, if it exists at all, I am sure she knew nothing of it when her letter to Ravenswood was written.'

'It is the first time that I have heard of this,' said the Marquis; 'but since your ladyship has tabled a subject so delicate, permit me to say, that my kinsman's birth and connexions entitled him to a patient hearing, and at least a civil refusal, even in case of his being so ambitious as to raise his eyes to the daughter of Sir William Ashton.'

'You will recollect, my lord, of what blood Miss Lucy Ashton is come by the mother's side,' said the lady.

'I do remember your descent—from a younger branch of the house of Angus,' said the Marquis—'and your ladyship—forgive me, lady—ought not to forget that the Ravenswoods have thrice intermarried with the main-stem. Come, madam—I know how matters stand—old and long-fostered prejudices are difficult to get over—I make every allowance for them—I ought not, and I would not otherwise have suffered my kinsman to depart alone, expelled, in a manner, from this house—but I had hopes of being a mediator. I am still unwilling to leave you in anger—and shall not set forward till after noon, as I rejoin the Master of Ravenswood upon the road a few miles from hence. Let us talk over this matter more coolly.'

'It is what I anxiously desire, my lord,' said Sir William Ashton, eagerly. 'Lady Ashton, we will not permit my Lord of A—— to leave us in displeasure. We must compel him to tarry dinner at the castle.'

'The castle,' said the lady, 'and all that it contains, are at the command of the Marquis, so long as he chooses to honour it with his residence; but touching the farther discussion of this disagreeable topic'——

'Pardon me, good madam,' said the Marquis; 'but I cannot allow you to express any hasty resolution on a subject so important. I see that more company is arriving; and since I have the good fortune to renew my former acquaintance with Lady Ashton, I hope she will give me leave to avoid perilling what I prize so highly upon any disagreeable subject of discussion—at least, till we have talked over more pleasant topics.'

The lady smiled, curtsied, and gave her hand to the Marquis, by whom, with all the formal gallantry of the time, which did not permit the guest to tuck the lady of the house under the arm, as a rustic does his sweetheart at a wake, she was ushered to the eating-room.

Here they were joined by Bucklaw, Craigengelt, and other neighbours, whom the Lord Keeper had previously invited to meet the Marquis of A——. An apology, founded upon a slight indisposition, was alleged as an excuse for the absence of Miss Ashton, whose seat appeared unoccupied. The entertainment was splendid to profusion, and was protracted till a late hour.

CHAPTER XXIII

Such was our fallen father's fate,
    Yet better than mine own;
He shared his exile with his mate,
    I'm banish'd forth alone.

(Waller)*

I WILL not attempt to describe the mixture of indignation and regret with which Ravenswood left the seat which had belonged to his ancestors. The terms in which Lady Ashton's billet was couched rendered it impossible for him, without being deficient in that spirit of which he perhaps had too much, to remain an instant longer within its walls. The Marquis, who had his share in the affront, was, nevertheless, still willing to make some efforts at conciliation. He therefore suffered his kinsman to depart alone, making him promise, however, that he would wait for him at the small inn called the Tod's-hole, situated, as our readers may be pleased to recollect, half way betwixt Ravenswood Castle and Wolf's Crag, and about five Scottish miles distant from each.* Here the Marquis proposed to join the Master of Ravenswood, either that night or the next morning. His own feelings would have induced him to have left the castle directly, but he was loath to forfeit, without at least one effort, the advantages which he had proposed from his visit to the Lord Keeper; and the Master of Ravenswood was, even in the very heat of his resentment, unwilling to foreclose any chance of reconciliation which might arise out of the partiality which Sir William Ashton had shown towards him, as well as the intercessory arguments of his noble kinsman. He himself departed without a moment's delay, farther than was necessary to make this arrangement.

At first he spurred his horse at a quick pace through an avenue of the park, as if, by rapidity of motion, he could stupify the confusion of feelings with which he was assailed. But as the road grew wilder and more sequestered, and when the trees had hidden the turrets of the castle, he gradually slackened his pace, as if to indulge the painful reflections which he had in vain endeavoured to repress. The path in which he found himself led him to the Mermaiden's Fountain, and to the cottage of Alice; and the fatal influence which superstitious belief attached to the former spot, as well as the admonitions which had been in vain offered to him by the inhabitant of the latter, forced themselves upon his memory. 'Old saws speak truth,' he said to himself; 'and the Mermaiden's Well has indeed witnessed the last act of rashness of the heir of Ravenswood.—Alice spoke well,' he continued, 'and I am in the situation which she foretold—or rather, I am more deeply dishonoured—not the dependant and ally of the destroyer of my father's house, as the old sibyl presaged, but the degraded wretch, who has aspired to hold that subordinate character, and has been rejected with disdain.'

We are bound to tell the tale as we have received it; and, considering the distance of the time, and propensity of those through whose mouths it has passed to the marvellous, this could not be called a Scottish story, unless it manifested a tinge of Scottish superstition. As Ravenswood approached the solitary fountain, he is said to have met with the following singular adventure:—His horse, which was moving slowly forward, suddenly interrupted its steady and composed pace, snorted, reared, and, though urged by the spur, refused to proceed, as if some object of terror had suddenly presented itself. On looking to the fountain, Ravenswood discerned a female figure, dressed in a white, or rather greyish mantle, placed on the very spot on which Lucy Ashton had reclined while listening to the fatal tale of love. His immediate impression was, that she had conjectured by which path he would traverse the park on his departure, and placed herself at this well-known and sequestered place of rendezvous, to indulge her own sorrow and his in a parting interview. In this belief he jumped from his horse, and, making its bridle fast to a tree, walked hastily towards the fountain, pronouncing eagerly, yet under his breath, the words, 'Miss Ashton!—Lucy!'

The figure turned as he addressed it, and displayed to his wondering eyes the features, not of Lucy Ashton, but of old blind

Alice. The singularity of her dress, which rather resembled a shroud than the garment of a living woman—the appearance of her person, larger, as it struck him, than it usually seemed to be—above all, the strange circumstance of a blind, infirm, and decrepit person being found alone and at a distance from her habitation, (considerable, if her infirmities be taken into account,) combined to impress him with a feeling of wonder approaching to fear. As he approached, she arose slowly from her seat, held her shrivelled hand up as if to prevent his coming more near, and her withered lips moved fast, although no sound issued from them. Ravenswood stopped; and as, after a moment's pause, he again advanced towards her, Alice, or her apparition, moved or glided backwards towards the thicket, still keeping her face turned towards him. The trees soon hid the form from his sight; and, yielding to the strong and terrific impression that the being which he had seen was not of this world, the Master of Ravenswood remained rooted to the ground whereon he had stood when he caught his last view of her. At length, summoning up his courage, he advanced to the spot on which the figure had seemed to be seated; but neither was there pressure of the grass, nor any other circumstance, to induce him to believe that what he had seen was real and substantial.

Full of those strange thoughts and confused apprehensions which awake in the bosom of one who conceives he has witnessed some preternatural appearance, the Master of Ravenswood walked back towards his horse, frequently however looking behind him, not without apprehension, as if expecting that the vision would re-appear. But the apparition, whether it was real, or whether it was the creation of a heated and agitated imagination, returned not again; and he found his horse sweating and terrified, as if experiencing that agony of fear, with which the presence of a supernatural being is supposed to agitate the brute creation. The Master mounted, and rode slowly forward, soothing his steed from time to time, while the animal seemed internally to shrink and shudder, as if expecting some new object of fear at the opening of every glade. The rider, after a moment's consideration, resolved to investigate the matter further. 'Can my eyes have deceived me,' he said, 'and deceived me for such a space of time?—Or are this

woman's infirmities but feigned, in order to excite compassion?—
And even then, her motion resembled not that of a living and
existing person. Must I adopt the popular creed, and think that
the unhappy being has formed a league with the powers of
darkness?—I am determined to be resolved—I will not brook
imposition even from my own eyes.'

In this uncertainty he rode up to the little wicket of Alice's
garden. Her seat beneath the birch-tree was vacant, though the
day was pleasant, and the sun was high. He approached the hut,
and heard from within the sobs and wailing of a female. No answer
was returned when he knocked, so that, after a moment's pause,
he lifted the latch and entered. It was indeed a house of solitude
and sorrow. Stretched upon her miserable pallet lay the corpse of
the last retainer of the house of Ravenswood, who still abode on
their paternal domains! Life had but shortly departed; and the little
girl, by whom she had been attended in her last moments, was
wringing her hands and sobbing, betwixt childish fear and sorrow,
over the body of her mistress.

The Master of Ravenswood had some difficulty to compose the
terrors of the poor child, whom his unexpected appearance had
at first rather appalled than comforted; and when he succeeded,
the first expression which the girl used intimated that 'he had
come too late.' Upon enquiring the meaning of this expression,
he learned that the deceased, upon the first attack of the mortal
agony, had sent a peasant to the castle to beseech an interview of
the Master of Ravenswood, and had expressed the utmost impatience for his return. But the messengers of the poor are tardy and
negligent: the fellow had not reached the castle, as was afterwards
learned, until Ravenswood had left it, and had then found too
much amusement among the retinue of the strangers to return in
any haste to the cottage of Alice. Meantime her anxiety of mind
seemed to increase with the agony of her body; and, to use the
phrase of Babie, her only attendant, 'she prayed powerfully that
she might see her master's son once more, and renew her warning.' She died just as the clock in the distant village tolled one; and
Ravenswood remembered, with internal shuddering, that he had
heard the chime sound through the wood just before he had seen

what he was now much disposed to consider as the spectre of the deceased.

It was necessary, as well from his respect to the departed as in common humanity to her terrified attendant, that he should take some measures to relieve the girl from her distressing situation. The deceased, he understood, had expressed a desire to be buried in a solitary churchyard, near the little inn of the Tod's-hole, called the Hermitage, or more commonly Armitage, in which lay interred some of the Ravenswood family, and many of their followers. Ravenswood conceived it his duty to gratify this predilection, so commonly found to exist among the Scottish peasantry, and dispatched Babie to the neighbouring village to procure the assistance of some females, assuring her that, in the meanwhile, he would himself remain with the dead body, which, as in Thessaly of old, it is accounted highly unfit to leave without a watch.*

Thus, in the course of a quarter of an hour or little more, he found himself sitting a solitary guard over the inanimate corse of her, whose dismissed spirit, unless his eyes had strangely deceived him, had so recently manifested itself before him. Notwithstanding his natural courage, the Master was considerably affected by a concurrence of circumstances so extraordinary. 'She died expressing her eager desire to see me. Can it be, then,'—was his natural course of reflection—'can strong and earnest wishes, formed during the last agony of nature, survive its catastrophe, surmount the awful bounds of the spiritual world, and place before us its inhabitants in the hues and colouring of life?—And why was that manifested to the eye which could not unfold its tale to the ear?—and wherefore should a breach be made in the laws of nature, yet its purpose remain unknown? Vain questions, which only death, when it shall make me like the pale and withered form before me, can ever resolve.'

He laid a cloth, as he spoke, over the lifeless face, upon whose features he felt unwilling any longer to dwell. He then took his place in an old carved oaken chair, ornamented with his own armorial bearings, which Alice had contrived to appropriate to her own use in the pillage which took place among creditors, officers, domestics, and messengers of the law, when his father left Ravenswood Castle for the last time. Thus seated, he banished, as much as he could, the superstitious feelings which the late incident naturally inspired. His own were sad enough, without the exaggeration of supernatural terror, since he found himself transferred from the situation of a successful lover of Lucy Ashton, and an honoured and respected friend of her father, into the melancholy and solitary guardian of the abandoned and forsaken corse of a common pauper.

He was relieved, however, from his sad office sooner than he could reasonably have expected, considering the distance betwixt the hut of the deceased and the village, and the age and infirmities of three old women, who came from thence, in military phrase, to relieve guard upon the body of the defunct. On any other occasion the speed of these reverend sibyls would have been much more moderate, for the first was eighty years of age and upwards, the second was paralytic, and the third lame of a leg from some accident. But the burial duties rendered to the deceased, are, to the Scottish peasant of either sex, a labour of love. I know not whether it is from the temper of the people, grave and enthusiastic as it certainly is, or from the recollection of the ancient Catholic opinions, when the funeral rites were always considered as a period of festival to the living; but feasting, good cheer, and even inebriety, were, and are, the frequent accompaniments of a Scottish old-fashioned burial. * What the funeral feast, or *dirgie*, as it is called, was to the men, the gloomy preparations of the dead body for the coffin were to the women. To straight the contorted limbs upon a board used for that melancholy purpose, to array the corpse in clean linen, and over that in its woollen shroud, were operations committed always to the old matrons of the village, and in which they found a singular and gloomy delight.

The old women paid the Master their salutations with a ghastly smile, which reminded him of the meeting betwixt Macbeth and the witches on the blasted heath of Forres. * He gave them some money, and recommended to them the charge of the dead body of their contemporary, an office which they willingly undertook; intimating to him at the same time that he must leave the hut, in order that they might begin their mournful duties. Ravenswood readily agreed to depart, only tarrying to recommend to them due attention to the body, and to receive information where he was to find the sexton, or beadle, who had in charge the deserted churchyard of the Armitage, in order to prepare matters for the reception of old Alice in the place of repose which she had selected for herself.

'Ye'll no be pinched to find out Johnie Mortsheugh,'* said the elder sibyl, and still her withered cheek bore a grisly smile—'he dwells near the Tod's-hole, an house of entertainment where there has been mony a blithe birling—for death and drink-draining are near neighbours to ane anither.'

'Ay! and that's e'en true, cummer,' said the lame hag, propping herself with a crutch which supported the shortness of her left leg, 'for I mind when the father of this Master of Ravenswood that is now standing before us, sticked young Blackhall with his whinger, for a wrang word said ower their wine, or brandy, or what not—he gaed in as light as a lark, and he came out wi' his feet foremost. I was at the winding of the corpse; and when the bluid was washed off, he was a bonny bouk of man's body.'

It may be easily believed that this ill-timed anecdote hastened the Master's purpose of quitting a company so evil-omened and so odious. Yet, while walking to the tree to which his horse was tied, and busying himself with adjusting the girths of the saddle, he could not avoid hearing, through the hedge of the little garden, a conversation respecting himself, betwixt the lame woman and the octogenarian sibyl. The pair had hobbled into the garden to gather rosemary, southernwood, rue, and other plants proper to be strewed upon the body, and burned by way of fumigation in the chimney of the cottage.* The paralytic wretch, almost exhausted by the journey, was left guard upon the corpse, lest witches or fiends might play their sport with it.

The following low croaking dialogue was necessarily overheard by the Master of Ravenswood:—

'That's a fresh and full-grown hemlock, Annie Winnie—mony a cummer lang syne wad hae sought nae better horse to flee over hill and how, through mist and moonlight, and light down in the King of France's cellar.'*

'Ay, cummer! but the very deil has turned as hard-hearted now as the Lord Keeper, and the grit folk that hae breasts like whin-stane. They prick us and they pine us, and they pit us on the pinnywinkles for witches;* and, if I say my prayers backwards ten times ower, Satan will never gie me amends o' them.'

'Did ye ever see the foul thief?' asked her neighbour.

'Na!' replied the other spokeswoman; 'but I trow I hae dreamed of him mony a time, and I think the day will come they will burn me for't.—But ne'er mind, cummer! we hae this dollar of the Master's, and we'll send doun for bread and for yill, and tobacco, and a drap brandy to burn, and a wee pickle saft sugar—and be there deil, or nae deil, lass, we'll hae a merry night o't.'

Here her leathern chops uttered a sort of cackling ghastly laugh, resembling, to a certain degree, the cry of the screech-owl.

'He's a frank man, and a free-handed man, the Master,' said Annie Winnie, 'and a comely personage—broad in the shouthers, and narrow around the lungies—he wad mak a bonny corpse—I wad like to hae the streaking and winding o' him.'

'It is written on his brow, Annie Winnie,' returned the octogenarian, her companion, 'that hand of woman, or of man either, will never straught him—dead-deal will never be laid on his back—make you your market of that, for I hae it frae a sure hand.'

'Will it be his lot to die on the battle-ground then, Ailsie Gourlay?—Will he die by the sword or the ball, as his forbears hae dune before him, mony ane o' them?'

'Ask nae mair questions about it—he'll no be graced sae far,' replied the sage.

'I ken ye are wiser than ither folk, Ailsie Gourlay—But wha tell'd ye this?'

'Fashna your thumb about that, Annie Winnie,' answered the sibyl—'I hae it frae a hand sure eneugh.'

'But ye said ye never saw the foul thief,' reiterated her inquisitive companion.

'I hae it frae as sure a hand,' said Ailsie, 'and frae them that spaed his fortune before the sark gaed ower his head.'

'Hark! I hear his horse's feet riding aff,' said the other; 'they dinna sound as if good luck was wi' them.'

'Mak haste, sirs,' cried the paralytic hag from the cottage, 'and let us do what is needfu', and say what is fitting; for, if the dead corpse binna straughted, it will girn and thraw, and that will fear the best o' us.'

Ravenswood was now out of hearing. He despised most of the ordinary prejudices about witchcraft, omens, and vaticination, to which his age and country still gave such implicit credit, that to express a doubt of them, was accounted a crime equal to the unbelief of Jews or Saracens; he knew also that the prevailing belief concerning witches, operating upon the hypochondriac habits of those whom age, infirmity, and poverty rendered liable to suspicion, and enforced by the fear of death, and the pangs of the most cruel tortures, often extorted those confessions which encumber and disgrace the criminal records of Scotland during the seventeenth century.* But the vision of that morning, whether real or imaginary, had impressed his mind with a superstitious feeling which he in vain endeavoured to shake off. The nature of the business which awaited him at the little inn, called Tod's-hole, where he soon after arrived, was not of a kind to restore his spirits.

It was necessary he should see Mortsheugh, the sexton of the old burial-ground at Armitage, to arrange matters for the funeral of Alice; and as the man dwelt near the place of her late residence, the Master, after a slight refreshment, walked towards the place where the body of Alice was to be deposited. It was situated in the nook formed by the eddying sweep of a stream, which issued from the adjoining hills. A rude cavern in an adjacent rock, which, in the interior, was cut into the shape of a cross, formed the hermitage, where some Saxon saint had in ancient times done penance, and given name to the place. The rich Abbey of Coldinghame* had, in latter days, established a chapel in the neighbourhood, of which no vestige was now visible, though the churchyard which surrounded it was still, as upon the present occasion, used for the interment of particular persons. One or two shattered yew-trees still grew within the precincts of that which had once been holy ground. Warriors and barons had been buried there of old, but their names were forgotten, and their monuments demolished. The only sepulchral memorials which remained, were the upright headstones which mark the graves of persons of inferior rank. The abode of the sexton was a solitary cottage adjacent to the ruined wall of the cemetery, but so low, that, with its thatch, which nearly

reached the ground, covered with a thick crop of grass, fog, and
house-leeks, it resembled an overgrown grave. On enquiry, however, Ravenswood found that the man of the last mattock was
absent at a bridal, being fiddler as well as grave-digger to the
vicinity. He therefore retired to the little inn, leaving a message
that early next morning he would again call for the person, whose
double occupation connected him at once with the house of
mourning and the house of feasting.

An outrider of the Marquis arrived at Tod's-hole shortly after,
with a message, intimating that his master would join Ravenswood at that place on the following morning; and the Master, who
would otherwise have proceeded to his old retreat at Wolf's Crag,
remained there accordingly, to give meeting to his noble kinsman.

CHAPTER XXIV

HAMLET. Has this fellow no feeling of his business—he sings at grave making.
HORATIO. Custom hath made it in him a
property of easiness.
HAMLET. 'Tis e'en so: the hand of little employment hath the daintier sense.

*(Hamlet, Act V. Scene I)** *

THE sleep of Ravenswood was broken by ghastly and agitating
visions, and his waking intervals disturbed by melancholy reflections on the past, and painful anticipations of the future. He was
perhaps the only traveller who ever slept in that miserable kennel
without complaining of his lodgings, or feeling inconvenience
from their deficiencies. It is when 'the mind is free the body's
delicate.'* Morning, however, found the Master an early riser, in
hopes that the fresh air of the dawn might afford the refreshment
which night had refused him. He took his way toward the solitary
burial-ground, which lay about half a mile from the inn.

The thin blue smoke, which already began to curl upward, and
to distinguish the cottage of the living from the habitation of the
dead, apprized him that its inmate had returned and was stirring.
Accordingly, on entering the little churchyard, he saw the old man
labouring in a half-made grave. My destiny, thought Ravenswood, seems to lead me to scenes of fate and of death; but these
are childish thoughts, and they shall not master me. I will not again
suffer my imagination to beguile my senses.—The old man rested
on his spade as the Master approached him, as if to receive his
commands; and as he did not immediately speak, the sexton
opened the discourse in his own way.

'Ye will be a wedding customer, sir, I'se warrant?'

'What makes you think so, friend?' replied the Master.

'I live by twa trades, sir,' replied the blithe old man; 'fiddle, sir, and spade; filling the world, and emptying of it; and I suld ken baith cast of customers by head-mark in thirty years' practice.'

'You are mistaken, however, this morning,' replied Ravenswood.

'Am I?' said the old man, looking keenly at him, 'troth and it may be; since, for as brent as your brow is, there is something sitting upon it this day, that is as near akin to death as to wedlock. Weel, weel; the pick and shovel are as ready to your order as bow and fiddle.'

'I wish you,' said Ravenswood, 'to look after the decent interment of an old woman, Alice Gray, who lived at the Craig-foot in Ravenswood Park.'

'Alice Gray! blind Alice!' said the sexton; 'and is she gane at last? that's another jow of the bell to bid me be ready. I mind when Habbie Gray brought her down to this land; a likely lass she was then, and looked ower her southland nose at us a'. I trow her pride got a downcome. And is she e'en gane?'

'She died yesterday,' said Ravenswood; 'and desired to be buried here, beside her husband; you know where he lies, no doubt?'

'Ken where he lies?' answered the sexton, with national indirection of response, 'I ken whar a' body lies, that lies here. But ye were speaking o' her grave?—Lord help us—it's no an ordinar grave that will haud her in, if a's true that folk said of Alice in her auld days; and if I gae to six feet deep,—and a warlock's grave shouldna be an inch mair ebb, or her ain witch cummers would soon whirl her out of her shroud for a' their auld acquaintance—and be't six feet, or be't three, wha's to pay the making o't, I pray ye?'*

'I will pay that, my friend, and all other reasonable charges.'

'Reasonable charges?' said the sexton; 'ou, there's grundmail—and bell-siller—(though the bell's broken nae doubt)—and the kist—and my day's wark—and my bit fee—and some brandy and yill to the drigie—I am no thinking that you can inter her, to ca' decently, under saxteen pund Scots.'

'There is the money, my friend,' said Ravenswood, 'and something over. Be sure you know the grave.'

'Ye'll be ane o' her English relations, I'se warrant,' said the hoary man of skulls; 'I hae heard she married far below her station; it was very right to let her bite on the bridle when she was living, and it's very right to gie her a decent burial now she's dead, for that's a matter o' credit to yoursell rather than to her. Folk may let their kindred shift for themsells when they are alive, and can bear the burden of their ain misdoings; but it's an unnatural thing to let them be buried like dogs, when a' the discredit gangs to the kindred—what kens the dead corpse about it?'

'You would not have people neglect their relations on a bridal occasion neither?' said Ravenswood, who was amused with the professional limitation of the grave-digger's philanthropy.

The old man cast up his sharp grey eyes with a shrewd smile, as if he understood the jest, but instantly continued, with his former gravity,—'Bridals—wha wad neglect bridals, that had ony regard for plenishing the earth?* To be sure, they suld be celebrated with all manner of good cheer, and meeting of friends, and musical instruments, harp, sackbut, and psaltery; or gude fiddle and pipes, when these auld-warld instruments of melody are hard to be compassed.'

'The presence of the fiddle, I daresay,' replied Ravenswood, 'would atone for the absence of all the others.'

The sexton again looked sharply up at him, as he answered, 'Nae doubt—nae doubt—if it were weel played;—but yonder,' he said, as if to change the discourse, 'is Halbert Gray's lang hame, that ye were speering after, just the third bourock beyond the muckle through-stane that stands on sax legs yonder, abune some ane of the Ravenswoods; for there is mony of their kin and followers here, deil lift them! though it isna just their main burial-place.'

'They are no favourites, then, of yours, these Ravenswoods?' said the Master, not much pleased with the passing benediction which was thus bestowed on his family and name.

'I kenna wha should favour them,' said the grave-digger; 'when they had lands and power, they were ill guides of them baith, and now their head's down, there's few care how lang they may be of lifting it again.'

'Indeed!' said Ravenswood; 'I never heard that this unhappy family deserved ill-will at the hands of their country. I grant their poverty—if that renders them contemptible.'

'It will gang a far way till't,' said the sexton of Hermitage, 'ye may tak my word for that—at least, I ken naething else that suld mak myself contemptible, and folk are far frae respecting me as they wad do if I lived in a twa-lofted sclated house. But as for the Ravenswoods, I hae seen three generations of them, and deil ane to mend other.'

'I thought they had enjoyed a fair character in the country,' said their descendant.

'Character! Ou, ye see, sir,' said the sexton, 'as for the auld gude-sire body of a lord, I lived on his land when I was a swanking young chield, and could hae blawn the trumpet wi' ony body, for I had wind eneugh then—and touching this trumpeter Marine that I have heard play afore the Lords of the Circuit,* I wad hae made nae mair o' him than of a bairn and a bawbee whistle—I defy him to hae played "Boot and saddle," or "Horse and away," or "Gallants, come trot," with me—he hadna the tones.'*

'But what is all this to old Lord Ravenswood, my friend?' said the Master, who, with an anxiety not unnatural in his circumstances, was desirous of prosecuting the musician's first topic—'What had his memory to do with the degeneracy of the trumpet music?'

'Just this, sir,' answered the sexton, 'that I lost my wind in his service. Ye see I was trumpeter at the castle, and had allowance for blawing at break of day, and at dinner-time, and other whiles when there was company about, and it pleased my lord; and when he raised his militia to caper awa to Bothwell Brigg against the wrang-headed wastland whigs, I behoved, reason or nane, to munt a horse and caper awa wi' them.'

'And very reasonable,' said Ravenswood; 'you were his servant and vassal.'

'Servitor, say ye?' replied the sexton, 'and so I was—but it was to blaw folk to their warm dinner, or at the warst to a decent kirkyard, and no to skirl them awa to a bluidy brae side, where there was deil a bedral but the hooded craw. But bide ye—ye shall hear what cam o't, and how far I am bund to be bedesman to the

Ravenswoods.—Till't, ye see, we gaed on a braw simmer morning, twenty-fourth of June, saxteen hundred and se'enty-nine, of a' the days of the month and year,*—drums beat—guns rattled—horses kicked and trampled. Hackstoun of Rathillet keepit the brigg wi' musket and carabine and pike, sword and scythe for what I ken, and we horsemen were ordered down to cross at the ford,—I hate fords at a' times, let abe when there's thousands of armed men on the other side.* There was auld Ravenswood brandishing his Andrew Ferrara* at the head, and crying to us to come and buckle to, as if we had been gaun to a fair,—there was Caleb Balderstone, that is living yet, flourishing in the rear, and swearing Gog and Magog,* he would put steel through the guts of ony man that turned bridle,—there was young Allan Ravenswood, that was then Master, wi' a bended pistol in his hand,—it was a mercy it gaed na aff,—crying to me, that had scarce as much wind left as serve the necessary purpose of my ain lungs, "Sound, you poltroon! sound, you damned cowardly villain, or I will blow your brains out!" and, to be sure, I blew sic points of war, that the scraugh of a clockin-hen was music to them.'

'Well, sir, cut all this short,' said Ravenswood.

'Short!—I had like to hae been cut short mysell, in the flower of my youth, as Scripture says;* and that's the very thing that I compleen o'.—Weel! in to the water we behoved a' to splash, heels ower head, sit or fa'—ae horse driving on anither, as is the way of brute beasts, and riders that hae as little sense,—the very bushes on the ither side were ableeze, wi' the flashes of the whig guns; and my horse had just taen the grund, when a blackavised westland carle—I wad mind the face o' him a hundred years yet—an ee like a wild falcon's, and a beard as broad as my shovel, clapped the end o' his lang black gun within a quarter's length of my lug!—by the grace o' Mercy, the horse swarved round, and I fell aff at the tae side as the ball whistled by at the tither, and the fell auld lord took the whig such a swauk wi' his broadsword that he made twa pieces o' his head, and down fell the lurdane wi' a' his bowk abune me.'

'You were rather obliged to the old lord, I think,' said Ravenswood.

'Was I? my sartie! first for bringing me into jeopardy, would I nould I—and then for whomling a chield on the tap o' me, that dang the very wind out of my body?—I hae been short-breathed ever since, and canna gang twenty yards without peghing like a miller's aiver.'

'You lost, then, your place as trumpeter?' said Ravenswood.

'Lost it? to be sure I lost it,' replied the sexton, 'for I couldna hae played pew upon a dry humlock;—but I might hae dune weel eneugh, for I keepit the wage and the free house, and little to do but play on the fiddle to them, but for Allan, last Lord Ravenswood, that was far waur than ever his father was.'

'What,' said the Master, 'did my father—I mean, did his father's son—this last Lord Ravenswood, deprive you of what the bounty of his father allowed you?'

'Ay, troth did he,' answered the old man; 'for he loot his affairs gang to the dogs, and let in this Sir William Ashton on us, that will gie naething for naething, and just removed me and a' the puir creatures that had bite and soup at the castle, and a hole to put our heads in, when things were in the auld way.'

'If Lord Ravenswood protected his people, my friend, while he had the means of doing so, I think they might spare his memory,' replied the Master.

'Ye are welcome to your ain opinion, sir,' said the sexton; 'but ye winna persuade me that he did his duty, either to himsell or to huz puir dependent creatures, in guiding us the gate he has done—he might hae gien us liferent tacks of our bits o' houses and yards—and me, that's an auld man, living in yon miserable cabin, that's fitter for the dead than the quick, and killed wi' rheumatise, and John Smith in my dainty bit mailing, and his window glazen, and a' because Ravenswood guided his gear like a fule!'*

'It is but too true,' said Ravenswood, conscience-struck; 'the penalties of extravagance extend far beyond the prodigal's own sufferings.'

'However,' said the sexton, 'this young man Edgar is like to avenge my wrangs on the haill of his kindred.'

'Indeed?' said Ravenswood; 'why should you suppose so?'

'They say he is about to marry the daughter of Leddy Ashton; and let her leddyship get his head ance under her oxter, and see you if she winna gie his neck a thraw. Sorra a bit, if I were him—Let her alane for hauding a' thing in het water that draws near her—sae the warst wish I shall wish the lad is, that he may take his ain creditable gate o't, and ally himsell wi' his father's enemies, that have taken his broad lands and my bonny kailyard from the lawful owners thereof.'

Cervantes acutely remarks, that flattery is pleasing even from the mouth of a madman;* and censure, as well as praise, often affects us, while we despise the opinions and motives on which it is founded and expressed. Ravenswood, abruptly reiterating his command that Alice's funeral should be attended to, flung away from the sexton, under the painful impression that the great, as well as the small vulgar, would think of his engagement with Lucy like this ignorant and selfish peasant.

'And I have stooped to subject myself to these calumnies, and am rejected notwithstanding! Lucy, your faith must be true and perfect as the diamond, to compensate for the dishonour which men's opinions, and the conduct of your mother, attach to the heir of Ravenswood!'

As he raised his eyes, he beheld the Marquis of A——, who, having arrived at the Tod's-hole, had walked forth to look for his kinsman.

After mutual greetings, he made some apology to the Master for not coming forward on the preceding evening. 'It was his wish,' he said, 'to have done so, but he had come to the knowledge of some matters which induced him to delay his purpose. I find,' he proceeded, 'there has been a love affair here, kinsman; and though I might blame you for not having communicated with me, as being in some degree the chief of your family'——

'With your lordship's permission,' said Ravenswood, 'I am deeply grateful for the interest you are pleased to take in me—but I am the chief and head of my family.'

'I know it—I know it,' said the Marquis; 'in a strict heraldic and genealogical sense, you certainly are so—what I mean is, that being in some measure under my guardianship'——

'I must take the liberty to say, my lord,' answered Ravenswood—and the tone in which he interrupted the Marquis boded no long duration to the friendship of the noble relatives, when he himself was interrupted by the little sexton, who came puffing after them, to ask if their honours would choose music at the change-house to make up for short cheer.

'We want no music,' said the Master abruptly.

'Your honour disna ken what ye're refusing, then,' said the fiddler, with the impertinent freedom of his profession. 'I can play, "Wilt thou do't again," and "the Auld Man's Mear's Dead," sax times better than ever Pattie Birnie.* I'll get my fiddle in the turning of a coffin-screw.'

'Take yourself away, sir,' said the Marquis.

'And if your honour be a north-country gentleman,' said the persevering minstrel, 'whilk I wad judge from your tongue, I can play "Liggeram Cosh," and "Mullin Dhu," and "the Cummers of Athole." '*

'Take yourself away, friend; you interrupt our conversation.'

'Or if, under your honour's favour, ye should happen to be a thought honest, I can play,' (this in a low and confidential tone,) ' "Killiecrankie," and "the King shall hae his ain," and "the Auld Stewarts back again,"*—and the wife at the change-house is a decent discreet body, neither kens nor cares what toasts are drucken, and what tunes are played in her house—she's deaf to a' thing but the clink o' the siller.'

The Marquis, who was sometimes suspected of jacobitism, could not help laughing as he threw the fellow a dollar, and bid him go play to the servants if he had a mind, and leave them at peace.

'Aweel, gentlemen,' said he, 'I am wishing your honours gude day—I'll be a' the better of the dollar, and ye'll be the waur of wanting the music, I'se tell ye—But I'se gang hame, and finish the grave in the tuning o' a fiddle-string, lay by my spade, and then get my tother bread-winner, and awa to your folk, and see if they hae better lugs than their masters.'

CHAPTER XXV

True love, an thou be true,
　　Thou has ane kittle part to play;
For fortune, fashion, fancy, and thou,
　　Maun strive for many a day.

I've kend by mony a friend's tale,
　　Far better by this heart of mine,
What time and change of fancy avail
　　A true-love knot to untwine.

(Hendersoun)*

'I WISHED to tell you, my good kinsman,' said the Marquis, 'now that we are quit of that impertinent fiddler, that I had tried to discuss this love affair of yours with Sir William Ashton's daughter. I never saw the young lady but for a few minutes to-day; so, being a stranger to her personal merits, I pay a compliment to you, and offer her no offence, in saying you might do better.'

'My lord, I am much indebted for the interest you have taken in my affairs,' said Ravenswood. 'I did not intend to have troubled you in any matter concerning Miss Ashton. As my engagement with that young lady has reached your lordship, I can only say, that you must necessarily suppose that I was aware of the objections to my marrying into her father's family, and of course must have been completely satisfied with the reasons by which these objections are overbalanced, since I have proceeded so far in the matter.'

'Nay, Master, if you had heard me out,' said his noble relation, 'you might have spared that observation; for, without questioning that you had reasons which seemed to you to counterbalance every other obstacle, I set myself, by every means that it became me to use towards the Ashtons, to persuade them to meet your views.'

'I am obliged to your lordship for your unsolicited intercession,' said Ravenswood; 'especially as I am sure your lordship would never carry it beyond the bounds which it became me to use.'

'Of that,' said the Marquis, 'you may be confident; I myself felt the delicacy of the matter too much to place a gentleman nearly connected with my house in a degrading or dubious situation with these Ashtons. But I pointed out all the advantages of their marrying their daughter into a house so honourable, and so nearly related with the first in Scotland; I explained the exact degree of relationship in which the Ravenswoods stand to ourselves; and I even hinted how political matters were like to turn, and what cards would be trumps next Parliament. I said I regarded you as a son—or a nephew, or so—rather than as a more distant relation; and that I made your affair entirely my own.'

'And what was the issue of your lordship's explanation?' said Ravenswood, in some doubt whether he should resent or express gratitude for his interference.

'Why, the Lord Keeper would have listened to reason,' said the Marquis; 'he is rather unwilling to leave his place, which, in the present view of a change, must be vacated; and, to say truth, he seemed to have a liking for you, and to be sensible of the general advantages to be attained by such a match. But his lady, who is tongue of the trump, Master,'——

'What of Lady Ashton, my lord?' said Ravenswood; 'let me know the issue of this extraordinary conference—I can bear it.'

'I am glad of that, kinsman,' said the Marquis, 'for I am ashamed to tell you half what she said. It is enough—her mind is made up—and the mistress of a first-rate boarding-school could not have rejected with more haughty indifference the suit of a half-pay Irish officer, beseeching permission to wait upon the heiress of a West India planter, than Lady Ashton spurned every proposal of mediation which it could at all become me to offer in behalf of you, my good kinsman. I cannot guess what she means. A more honourable connexion she could not form, that's certain. As for money and land, that used to be her husband's business rather than hers; I really think she hates you for having the rank which her husband has not, and perhaps for not having the lands that her goodman has. But I should only vex you to say more about it—here we are at the change-house.'

The Master of Ravenswood paused as he entered the cottage, which reeked through all its crevices, and they were not few, from the exertions of the Marquis's travelling-cooks to supply good cheer, and spread, as it were, a table in the wilderness. *

'My Lord Marquis,' said Ravenswood, 'I already mentioned that accident has put your lordship in possession of a secret, which, with my consent, should have remained one even to you, my kinsman, for some time. Since the secret was to part from my own custody, and that of the only person besides who was interested in it, I am not sorry it should have reached your lordship's ears, as being fully aware that you are my noble kinsman and friend.'

'You may believe it is safely lodged with me, Master of Ravenswood,' said the Marquis; 'but I should like well to hear you say, that you renounced the idea of an alliance, which you can hardly pursue without a certain degree of degradation.'

'Of that, my lord, I shall judge,' answered Ravenswood, 'and I hope with delicacy as sensitive as any of my friends. But I have no engagement with Sir William and Lady Ashton. It is with Miss Ashton alone that I have entered upon the subject, and my conduct in the matter shall be entirely ruled by hers. If she continues to prefer me in my poverty to the wealthier suitors whom her friends recommend, I may well make some sacrifice to her sincere affection—I may well surrender to her the less tangible and less palpable advantages of birth, and the deep-rooted prejudices of family hatred. If Miss Lucy Ashton should change her mind on a subject of such delicacy, I trust my friends will be silent on my disappointment, and I shall know how to make my enemies so.'

'Spoke like a gallant young nobleman,' said the Marquis; 'for my part I have that regard for you, that I should be sorry the thing went on. This Sir William Ashton was a pretty enough pettifogging kind of a lawyer twenty years ago, and betwixt battling at the bar, and leading in committees of Parliament, he has got well on—the Darien matter lent him a lift, for he had good intelligence and sound views, and sold out in time—but the best work is had out of him. * No government will take him at his own, or rather his wife's, extravagant valuation; and betwixt his indecision and her insolence, from all I can guess, he will outsit his market, and be had cheap when no one will bid for him. I say nothing of Miss Ashton; but I assure you, a connexion with her father will be neither useful nor ornamental, beyond that part of your father's spoils which he may be prevailed upon to disgorge by way of tocher good—and take my word for it, you will get more if you have spirit to bell the cat with him in the House of Peers. *—And I will be the man, cousin,' continued his lordship, 'will course the fox for you, and make him rue the day that ever he refused a composition too honourable for him, and proposed by me on the behalf of a kinsman.'

There was something in all this that, as it were, overshot the mark. Ravenswood could not disguise from himself that his noble kinsman had more reasons for taking offence at the reception of his suit, than regarded his interest and honour, yet he could neither complain nor be surprised that it should be so. He contented himself therefore with repeating, that his attachment was to Miss Ashton personally; that he desired neither wealth nor aggrandizement from her father's means and influence; and that nothing should prevent his keeping his engagement, excepting her own express desire that it should be relinquished—and he requested as a favour that the matter might be no more mentioned betwixt them at present, assuring the Marquis of A—— that he should be his confident in its progress or its interruption.

The Marquis soon had more agreeable, as well as more interesting subjects on which to converse. A foot post, who had followed him from Edinburgh to Ravenswood Castle, and had traced his steps to the Tod's-hole, brought him a packet laden with good news. The political calculations of the Marquis had proved just, both in London and at Edinburgh, and he saw almost within his grasp, the pre-eminence for which he had panted.—The refreshments which the servants had prepared were now put on the table, and an epicure would perhaps have enjoyed them with additional zest, from the contrast which such fare afforded to the miserable cabin in which it was served up.

The turn of conversation corresponded with and added to the social feelings of the company. The Marquis expanded with pleasure on the power which probable incidents were likely to assign to him, and on the use which he hoped to make of it in serving his kinsman Ravenswood. Ravenswood could but repeat the gratitude which he really felt, even when he considered the topic as too long dwelt upon. The wine was excellent, notwithstanding its having been brought in a runlet from Edinburgh; and the habits of the Marquis, when engaged with such good cheer, were somewhat sedentary. And so it fell out that they delayed their journey two hours later than was their original purpose.

'But what of that, my good young friend?' said the Marquis; 'your Castle of Wolf's Crag is but at five or six miles distance, and will afford the same hospitality to your kinsman of A——, that it gave to this same Sir William Ashton.'

'Sir William took the castle by storm,' said Ravenswood, 'and, like many a victor, had little reason to congratulate himself on his conquest.'

'Well, well!' said Lord A——, whose dignity was something relaxed by the wine he had drunk,—'I see I must bribe you to harbour me—Come, pledge me in a bumper health to the last young lady that slept at Wolf's Crag, and liked her quarters.—My bones are not so tender as hers, and I am resolved to occupy her apartment to-night, that I may judge how hard the couch is that love can soften.'

'Your lordship may choose what penance you please,' said Ravenswood; 'but I assure you, I should expect my old servant to hang himself, or throw himself from the battlements, should your lordship visit him so unexpectedly—I do assure you, we are totally and literally unprovided.'

But his declaration only brought from his noble patron an assurance of his own total indifference as to every species of accommodation, and his determination to see the Tower of Wolf's Crag. His ancestor, he said, had been feasted there, when he went forward with the then Lord Ravenswood to the fatal battle of Flodden, in which they both fell. * Thus hard pressed, the Master offered to ride forward to get matters put in such preparation as time and circumstances admitted; but the Marquis protested his kinsman must afford him his company, and would only consent that an avant-courier should carry to the destined Seneschal, Caleb Balderstone, the unexpected news of this invasion.

The Master of Ravenswood soon after accompanied the Marquis in his carriage, as the latter had proposed; and when they became better acquainted in the progress of the journey, his noble relation explained the very liberal views which he entertained for his relation's preferment, in case of the success of his own political schemes. They related to a secret, and highly important commission beyond sea, which could only be intrusted to a person of rank, talent, and perfect confidence, and which, as it required great trust and reliance on the envoy employed, could not but prove both honourable and advantageous to him.* We need not enter into the nature and purpose of this commission, farther than to acquaint our readers that the charge was in prospect highly acceptable to the Master of Ravenswood, who hailed with pleasure the hope of emerging from his present state of indigence and inaction, into independence and honourable exertion.

While he listened thus eagerly to the details with which the Marquis now thought it necessary to intrust him, the messenger who had been dispatched to the Tower of Wolf's Crag, returned with Caleb Balderstone's humble duty, and an assurance that 'a' should be in seemly order, sic as the hurry of time permitted, to receive their lordships as it behoved.'

Ravenswood was too well accustomed to his Seneschal's mode of acting and speaking, to hope much from this confident assurance. He knew that Caleb acted upon the principle of the Spanish generals, in the campaign of ——, who, much to the perplexity of the Prince of Orange, their commander-in-chief, used to report their troops as full in number, and possessed of all necessary points of equipment, not considering it consistent with their dignity, or the honour of Spain, to confess any deficiency either in men or munition, until the want of both was unavoidably discovered in the day of battle.* Accordingly, Ravenswood thought it necessary to give the Marquis some hint, that the fair assurance which they had just received from Caleb, did not by any means insure them against a very indifferent reception.

'You do yourself injustice, Master,' said the Marquis, 'or you wish to surprise me agreeably. From this window I see a great light in the direction where, if I remember aright, Wolf's Crag lies; and, to judge from the splendour which the old Tower sheds around it, the preparations for our reception must be of no ordinary description. I remember your father putting the same deception on me, when we went to the Tower for a few days' hawking, about twenty years since, and yet we spent our time as jollily at Wolf's Crag as we could have done at my own hunting seat at B——.'

'Your lordship, I fear, will experience that the faculty of the present proprietor to entertain his friends is greatly abridged,' said Ravenswood; 'the will, I need hardly say, remains the same. But I am as much at a loss as your lordship to account for so strong and brilliant a light as is now above Wolf's Crag,—the windows of the Tower are few and narrow, and those of the lower story are hidden from us by the walls of the court. I cannot conceive that any illumination of an ordinary nature could afford such a blaze of light.'

The mystery was soon explained; for the cavalcade almost instantly halted, and the voice of Caleb Balderstone was heard at the coach window, exclaiming, in accents broken by grief and fear, 'Och, gentlemen—Och, my gude lords—Och, haud to the right!—Wolf's Crag is burning, bower and ha'—a' the rich plenishing outside and inside—a' the fine graith, pictures, tapestries, needle-wark, hangings, and other decorements—a' in a bleeze, as if they were nae mair than sae mony peats, or as muckle peas-strae! Haud to the right, gentlemen, I implore ye—there is some sma' provision making at Lucky Sma'trash's—but O, wae for this night, and wae for me that lives to see it!'

Ravenswood was at first stunned by this new and unexpected calamity; but after a moment's recollection, he sprang from the carriage, and hastily bidding his noble kinsman good-night, was about to ascend the hill towards the castle, the broad and full conflagration of which now flung forth a high column of red light, that flickered far to seaward upon the dashing waves of the ocean.

'Take a horse, Master,' exclaimed the Marquis, greatly affected by this additional misfortune, so unexpectedly heaped upon his young protegé; 'and give me my ambling palfrey;—and haste forward, you knaves, to see what can be done to save the furniture, or to extinguish the fire—ride, you knaves, for your lives!'

The attendants bustled together, and began to strike their horses with the spur, and call upon Caleb to show them the road. But the voice of that careful Seneschal was heard above the tumult, 'O stop—sirs, stop—turn bridle, for the luve of mercy—add not loss of lives to the loss of warld's gear!—Thirty barrels of powther, landed out of a Dunkirk dogger in the auld lord's time—a' in the vau'ts of the auld tower,—the fire canna be far aff it, I trow— Lord's sake, to the right, lads—to the right—let's pit the hill atween us and peril,—a wap wi' a corner-stane o' Wolf's Crag wad defy the doctor!'

It will readily be supposed that this annunciation hurried the Marquis and his attendants into the route which Caleb prescribed, dragging Ravenswood along with them, although there was much in the matter which he could not possibly comprehend. 'Gunpowder!' he exclaimed, laying hold of Caleb, who in vain endeavoured to escape from him, 'what gunpowder? How any quantity of powder could be in Wolf's Crag without my knowledge, I cannot possibly comprehend.'

'But I can,' interrupted the Marquis, whispering him, 'I can comprehend it thoroughly—for God's sake, ask him no more questions at present.'

'There it is, now,' said Caleb, extricating himself from his master, and adjusting his dress, 'your honour will believe his lordship's honourable testimony—His lordship minds weel, how, in the year that him they ca'd King Willie died'——*

'Hush! hush, my good friend!' said the Marquis; 'I shall satisfy your master upon that subject.'

'And the people at Wolf's-hope'—said Ravenswood, 'did none of them come to your assistance before the flame got so high?'

'Ay did they, mony ane of them, the rapscallions!' said Caleb; 'but truly I was in nae hurry to let them into the Tower, where there were so much plate and valuables.'

'Confound you for an impudent liar!' said Ravenswood, in uncontrollable ire, 'there was not a single ounce of——

'Forby,' said the butler, most irreverently raising his voice to a pitch which drowned his master's, 'the fire made fast on us, owing to the store of tapestry and carved timmer in the banqueting ha', and the loons ran like scauded rats sae sune as they heard of the gunpouther.'

'I do entreat,' said the Marquis to Ravenswood, 'you will ask him no more questions.'

'Only one, my lord—What has become of poor Mysie?'

'Mysie?' said Caleb, 'I had nae time to look about ony Mysie— she's in the tower, I'se warrant, biding her awful doom.'

'By heaven,' said Ravenswood, 'I do not understand all this! The life of a faithful old creature is at stake—my lord, I will be withheld no longer—I will at least ride up, and see whether the danger is as imminent as this old fool pretends.'

'Weel, then, as I live by bread,' said Caleb, 'Mysie is weel and safe. I saw her out of the castle before I left it mysell. Was I ganging to forget an auld fellow-servant?'

'What made you tell me the contrary this moment?' said his master.

'Did I tell you the contrary?' said Caleb; 'then I maun hae been dreaming surely, or this awsome night has turned my judgment— but safe she is, and ne'er a living soul in the castle, a' the better for them—they wad have gotten an unco heezy.'

The Master of Ravenswood, upon this assurance being solemnly reiterated, and notwithstanding his extreme wish to witness the last explosion, which was to ruin to the ground the mansion of his fathers, suffered himself to be dragged onward towards the village of Wolf's-hope, where not only the change-house, but that of our well-known friend the cooper, were all prepared for reception of himself and his noble guest, with a liberality of provision which requires some explanation.

We omitted to mention in its place, that Lockhard, having fished out the truth concerning the mode by which Caleb had obtained the supplies for his banquet, the Lord Keeper, amused with the incident, and desirous at the time to gratify Ravenswood, had recommended the cooper of Wolf's-hope to the official situation under government, the prospect of which had reconciled him to the loss of his wild-fowl. Mr Girder's preferment had occasioned a pleasing surprise to old Caleb; for when, some days after his master's departure, he found himself absolutely compelled, by some necessary business, to visit the fishing hamlet, and was gliding like a ghost past the door of the cooper, for fear of being summoned to give some account of the progress of the solicitation in his favour, or, more probably, that the inmates might upbraid him with the false hope he had held out upon the subject, he heard himself, not without some apprehension, summoned at once in treble, tenor, and bass,—a trio performed by the voices of Mrs Girder, old Dame Loup-the-dike, and the goodman of the dwelling—'Mr Caleb—Mr Caleb—Mr Caleb Balderstone! I hope ye arena ganging dry-lipped by our door, and we sae muckle indebted to you?'

This might be said ironically as well as in earnest. Caleb augured the worst, turned a deaf ear to the trio aforesaid, and was moving doggedly on, his ancient castor pulled over his brows, and his eyes bent on the ground, as if to count the flinty pebbles with which the rude pathway was causewayed. But on a sudden he found himself surrounded in his progress, like a stately merchantman in the Gut of Gibraltar (I hope the ladies will excuse the tarpaulin phrase) by three Algerine galleys.*

'Gude guide us, Mr Balderstone!' said Mrs Girder.

'Wha wad hae thought it of an auld and kend friend!' said the mother.

'And no sae muckle as stay to receive our thanks,' said the cooper himself, 'and frae the like o' me that seldom offers them! I am sure I hope there's nae ill seed sawn between us, Mr Balderstone—Ony man that has said to ye, I am no gratefu' for the situation of Queen's cooper, let me hae a whample at him wi' mine eatche[27]—that's a'.'

'My good friends—my dear friends,' said Caleb, still doubting how the certainty of the matter might stand, 'what needs a' this ceremony?—ane tries to serve their friends, and sometimes they may happen to prosper, and sometimes to misgie—naething I care to be fashed wi' less than thanks—I never could bide them.'

'Faith, Mr Balderstone, ye suld hae been fashed wi' few o' mine,' said the downright man of staves and hoops, 'if I had only your gude-will to thank ye for—I suld e'en hae set the guse, and the wild-deukes, and the runlet of sack, to balance that account. Gude-will, man, is a geizen'd tub, that hauds in nae liquor—but gude deed's like the cask, tight, round, and sound, that will haud liquor for the king.'

'Have ye no heard of our letter,' said the mother-in-law, 'making our John the Queen's cooper for certain?—and scarce a chield that had ever hammered gird upon tub but was applying for it?'

'Have I heard ! ! !' said Caleb, (who now found how the wind set,) with an accent of exceeding contempt at the doubt expressed—'Have I heard, quo' she ! ! !'—and as he spoke, he changed his shambling, skulking, dodging pace, into a manly and authoritative step, re-adjusted his cocked hat, and suffered his brow to emerge from under it in all the pride of aristocracy, like the sun from behind a cloud.

'To be sure, he canna but hae heard,' said the good woman.

'Ay, to be sure, it's impossible but I should,' said Caleb; 'and sae I'll be the first to kiss ye, joe, and wish you, cooper, much joy of your preferment, naething doubting but ye ken wha are your friends, and *have* helped ye, and *can* help ye. I thought it right to look a wee strange upon it at first,' added Caleb, 'just to see if ye were made of the right mettle—but ye ring true, lad, ye ring true!'

So saying, with a most lordly air he kissed the women, and abandoned his hand, with an air of serene patronage, to the hearty shake of Mr Girder's horn-hard palm. Upon this complete, and to Caleb most satisfactory, information, he did not, it may readily be believed, hesitate to accept an invitation to a solemn feast, to which were invited, not only all the *notables* of the village, but even his ancient antagonist, Mr Dingwall himself. At this festivity he was, of course, the most welcome and most honoured guest; and so well did he ply the company with stories of what he could do with his master, his master with the Lord Keeper, the Lord Keeper with the Council, and the Council with the King,* that before the company dismissed, (which was, indeed, rather at an early hour than a late one,) every man of note in the village was ascending to the top-gallant of some ideal preferment by the ladder of ropes which Caleb had presented to their imagination. Nay, the cunning butler regained in that moment, not only all the influence he possessed formerly over the villagers, when the baronial family which he served were at the proudest, but acquired even an accession of importance. The writer—the very attorney himself—such is the thirst of preferment—felt the force of the attraction, and taking an opportunity to draw Caleb into a corner, spoke, with affectionate regret, of the declining health of the sheriff-clerk of the county.*

'An excellent man—a most valuable man, Mr Caleb—but fat sall I say!*—we are peer feckless bodies—here the day, and awa by cock-screech the morn—and if he failzies, there maun be somebody in his place—and gif that ye could airt it my way, I sall be thankful, man—a gluve stuffed wi' gowd nobles—an' hark ye, man, something canny till yoursell—and the Wolf's-hope carles to settle kindly wi' the Master of Ravenswood—that is, Lord Ravenswood—God bless his lordship!'

A smile, and a hearty squeeze by the hand, was the suitable answer to this overture—and Caleb made his escape from the jovial party, in order to avoid committing himself by any special promises.

'The Lord be gude to me,' said Caleb, when he found himself in the open air, and at liberty to give vent to the self-exultation with which he was, as it were, distended; 'did ever ony man see sic a set of green-gaislings!—the very pick-maws and solan-geese outby yonder at the Bass hae ten times their sense!—God, an I had been the Lord High Commissioner to the Estates o' Parliament,* they couldna hae beflumm'd me mair—and, to speak Heaven's truth, I could hardly hae beflumm'd them better neither! But the writer—ha! ha! ha!—ah, ha! ha! ha! mercy on me, that I suld live in my auld days to gie the gang-by to the very writer!—Sheriff-clerk ! ! !—But I hae an auld account to settle wi' the carle; and to make amends for byganes, the office shall just cost him as much time-serving and tide-serving, as if he were to get it in gude earnest—of whilk there is sma' appearance, unless the Master learns mair the ways of this warld, whilk it is muckle to be doubted that he never will do.'—

CHAPTER XXVI

Why flames yon far summit—why shoot to the blast
Those embers, like stars from the firmament cast?—
'Tis the fire-shower of ruin, all dreadfully driven
From thine eyry, that beacons the darkness of Heaven.

(Campbell) *

THE circumstances announced in the conclusion of the last
chapter, will account for the ready and cheerful reception of the
Marquis of A—— and the Master of Ravenswood in the village
of Wolf's-hope. In fact, Caleb had no sooner announced the
conflagration of the tower, than the whole hamlet were upon foot
to hasten to extinguish the flames. And although that zealous
adherent diverted their zeal by intimating the formidable contents
of the subterranean apartments, yet the check only turned their
assiduity into another direction. Never had there been such
slaughtering of capons, and fat geese, and barn-door fowls,—
never such boiling of *reested* hams,—never such making of
car-cakes and sweet scones, Selkirk bannocks, cookies, and pet-
ticoat-tails,—delicacies little known to the present generation.
Never had there been such a tapping of barrels, and such uncork-
ing of greybeards, in the village of Wolf's-hope. All the inferior
houses were thrown open for the reception of the Marquis's
dependants, who came, it was thought, as precursors of the shower
of preferment, which hereafter was to leave the rest of Scotland
dry, in order to distil its rich dews on the village of Wolf's-hope
under Lammermoor. The minister put in his claim to have the
guests of distinction lodged at the Manse, having his eye, it was
thought, upon a neighbouring preferment, where the incumbent
was sickly; but Mr Balderstone destined that honour to the cooper,
his wife, and wife's mother, who danced for joy at the preference
thus assigned them.

Many a beck and many a bow welcomed these noble guests to
as good entertainment as persons of such rank could set before

such visitors; and the old dame, who had formerly lived in Ravenswood Castle, and knew, as she said, the ways of the nobility, was in no whit wanting in arranging matters, as well as circumstances permitted, according to the etiquette of the times. The cooper's house was so roomy, that each guest had his separate retiring room, to which they were ushered with all due ceremony, while the plentiful supper was in the act of being placed upon the table.

Ravenswood no sooner found himself alone, than, impelled by a thousand feelings, he left the apartment, the house, and the village, and hastily retraced his steps to the brow of the hill, which rose betwixt the village, and screened it from the tower, in order to view the final fall of the house of his fathers. Some idle boys from the hamlet had taken the same direction out of curiosity, having first witnessed the arrival of the coach-and-six and its attendants. As they ran one by one past the Master, calling to each other to 'come and see the auld tower blaw up in the lift like the peelings of an ingan,' he could not but feel himself moved with indignation. 'And these are the sons of my father's vassals,' he said—'of men bound, both by law and gratitude, to follow our steps through battle, and fire, and flood; and now the destruction of their liege-lord's house is but a holiday's sight to them!'

These exasperating reflections were partly expressed in the acrimony with which he exclaimed, on feeling himself pulled by the cloak,—'What do you want, you dog?'

'I am a dog, and an auld dog too,'* answered Caleb, for it was he who had taken the freedom, 'and I am like to get a dog's wages—but it does not signification a pinch of sneeshing, for I am ower auld a dog to learn new tricks, or to follow a new master.'

As he spoke, Ravenswood attained the ridge of the hill from which Wolf's Crag was visible; the flames had entirely sunk down, and, to his great surprise, there was only a dusky reddening upon the clouds immediately over the castle, which seemed the reflection of the embers of the sunken fire.

'The place cannot have blown up,' said the Master; 'we must have heard the report—if a quarter of the gunpowder was there you tell me of, it would have been heard twenty miles off.'

'It's very like it wad,' said Balderstone, composedly.

'Then the fire cannot have reached the vaults?'

'It's like no,' answered Caleb, with the same impenetrable gravity.

'Hark ye, Caleb,' said his master, 'this grows a little too much for my patience. I must go and examine how matters stand at Wolf's Crag myself.'

'Your honour is ganging to gang nae sic gate,' said Caleb, firmly.

'And why not?' said Ravenswood, sharply; 'who or what shall prevent me?'

'Even I mysell,' said Caleb, with the same determination.

'You, Balderstone!' replied the Master; 'you are forgetting yourself, I think.'

'But I think no,' said Balderstone; 'for I can just tell ye a' about the castle on this knowe-head as weel as if ye were at it. Only dinna pit yoursell into a kippage, and expose yoursell before the weans, or before the Marquis, when ye gang down-by.'

'Speak out, you old fool,' replied his master, 'and let me know the best and the worst at once.'

'Ou, the best and the warst is, just that the tower is standing hail and feir, as safe and as empty as when ye left it.'

'Indeed!—and the fire?' said Ravenswood.

'Not a gleed of fire, then, except the bit kindling peat, and maybe a spunk in Mysie's cutty-pipe,' replied Caleb.

'But the flame?' demanded Ravenswood; 'the broad blaze which might have been seen ten miles off—what occasioned that?'

'Hout awa! it's an auld saying and a true,—

>Little's the light
>Will be seen far in a mirk night. *

A wheen fern and horse litter that I fired in the court-yard, after sending back the loun of a footman; and, to speak heaven's truth, the next time that ye send or bring ony body here, let them be gentles allenarly, without ony fremd servants, like that chield Lockhard, to be gledging and gleeing about, and looking upon the wrang side of ane's housekeeping, to the discredit of the family, and forcing ane to damn their souls wi' telling ae lee after another faster than I can count them—I wad rather set fire to the tower in gude earnest, and burn it ower my ain head into the bargain, or I see the family dishonoured in the sort.'

'Upon my word, I am infinitely obliged by the proposal, Caleb,' said his master, scarce able to restrain his laughter, though rather angry at the same time. 'But the gunpowder?—is there such a thing in the tower?—The Marquis seemed to know of it.'

'The pouther—ha! ha! ha!—the Marquis—ha! ha! ha!' replied Caleb; 'if your honour were to brain me, I behooved to laugh—the Marquis—the pouther!—was it there? ay, it was there. Did he ken o't?—my certie! the Marquis kend o't, and it was the best o' the game; for, when I couldna pacify your honour wi' a' that I could say, I aye threw out a word mair about the gunpouther, and garr'd the Marquis tak the job in his ain hand.'

'But you have not answered my question,' said the Master, impatiently; 'how came the powder there, and where is it now?'

'Ou, it came there, an ye maun needs ken,' said Caleb, looking mysteriously, and whispering, 'when there was like to be a wee bit rising here; and the Marquis, and a' the great lords of the north, were a' in it, and mony a gudely gun and broadsword were ferried ower frae Dunkirk forby the pouther—awfu' wark we had getting them into the tower under cloud o' night, for ye maun think it wasna every body could be trusted wi' sic kittle jobs—But if ye will gae hame to your supper, I will tell you a' about it as ye gang down.'

'And these wretched boys,' said Ravenswood, 'is it your pleasure they are to sit there all night, to wait for the blowing up of a tower that is not even on fire?'

'Surely not, if it is your honour's pleasure that they suld gang hame; although,' added Caleb, 'it wadna do them a grain's damage—they wad screigh less the next day, and sleep the sounder at e'en—But just as your honour likes.'

Stepping accordingly towards the urchins who manned the knolls near which they stood, Caleb informed them, in an authoritative tone, that their Honours Lord Ravenswood and the Marquis of A—— had given orders that the tower was not to blow up till next day at noon. The boys dispersed upon this comfortable assurance. One or two, however, followed Caleb for more information, particularly the urchin whom he had cheated while

officiating as turnspit, who screamed, 'Mr Balderstone! Mr Balderstone! than the castle's gane out like an auld wife's spunk?'

'To be sure it is, callant,' said the butler; 'do ye think the castle
of as great a lord as Lord Ravenswood wad continue in a bleeze,
and him standing looking on wi' his ain very een?—It's aye right,'
continued Caleb, shaking off his ragged page, and closing in to his
master, 'to train up weans, as the wise man says, in the way they
should go, and, aboon a', to teach them respect to their superiors.'*

'But all this while, Caleb, you have never told me what became
of the arms and powder,' said Ravenswood.

'Why, as for the arms,' said Caleb, 'it was just like the bairn's
rhyme—

> "Some gaed east, and some gaed west,
> And some gaed to the craw's nest:"*

And for the pouther, I e'en changed it, as occasion served, with
the skippers o' Dutch luggers and French vessels, for gin and
brandy, and it served the house mony a year—a gude swap too,
between what cheereth the soul of man and that which dingeth it
clean out of his body; forby, I keepit a wheen pounds of it for
yoursell when ye wanted to take the pleasure o' shooting—whiles,
in these latter days, I wad hardly hae kend else whar to get pouther
for your pleasure.—And now that your anger is ower, sir, wasna
that weel managed o' me, and arena ye far better sorted doun
yonder, than ye could hae been in your ain auld ruins upby
yonder, as the case stands wi' us now?—the mair's the pity.'

'I believe you may be right, Caleb; but, before burning down
my castle, either in jest or in earnest,' said Ravenswood, 'I think
I had a right to be in the secret.'

'Fie for shame, your honour!' replied Caleb; 'it fits an auld carle
like me weel eneugh to tell lees for the credit of the family, but it
wadna beseem the like o' your honour's sell; besides, young folk
are no judicious—they cannot make the maist of a bit figment.
Now this fire—for a fire it sall be, if I suld burn the auld stable to
make it mair feasible—this fire, besides that it will be an excuse
for asking ony thing we want through the country, or doun at the
haven—this fire will settle mony things on an honourable footing
for the family's credit, that cost me telling twenty daily lees to a

wheen idle chaps and queans, and, what's waur, without gaining credence.'

'That was hard indeed, Caleb; but I do not see how this fire should help your veracity or your credit.'

'There it is now!' said Caleb; 'wasna I saying that young folk had a green judgment?—How suld it help me, quotha?—it will be a creditable apology for the honour of the family for this score of years to come, if it is weel guided. Where's the family pictures? says ae meddling body—the great fire at Wolf's Crag, answers I. Where's the family plate? says another—the great fire, says I; wha was to think of plate, when life and limb were in danger?— Where's the wardrobe and the linens?—where's the tapestries and the decorements?—beds of state, twilts, pands and testors, napery and broidered wark?—The fire—the fire—the fire. Guide the fire weel, and it will serve ye for a' that ye suld have and have not—and, in some sort, a gude excuse is better than the things themselves; for they maun crack and wear out, and be consumed by time, whereas a gude offcome, prudently and creditably handled, may serve a nobleman and his family, Lord kens how lang!'

Ravenswood was too well acquainted with his butler's pertinacity and self-opinion, to dispute the point with him any farther. Leaving Caleb, therefore, to the enjoyment of his own successful ingenuity, he returned to the hamlet, where he found the Marquis and the good women of the mansion under some anxiety—the former on account of his absence, the others for the discredit their cookery might sustain by the delay of the supper. All were now at ease, and heard with pleasure that the fire at the castle had burned out of itself without reaching the vaults, which was the only information that Ravenswood thought it proper to give in public concerning the event of his butler's stratagem.

They sat down to an excellent supper. No invitation could prevail on Mr and Mrs Girder, even in their own house, to sit down at table with guests of such high quality. They remained standing in the apartment, and acted the part of respectful and careful attendants on the company. Such were the manners of the time. The elder dame, confident through her age and connexion with the Ravenswood family, was less scrupulously ceremonious.

She played a mixed part betwixt that of the hostess of an inn, and the mistress of a private house, who receives guests above her own degree. She recommended, and even pressed, what she thought best, and was herself easily entreated to take a moderate share of the good cheer, in order to encourage her guests by her own example. Often she interrupted herself, to express her regret that 'my Lord did not eat—that the Master was pyking a bare bane—that, to be sure, there was naething there fit to set before their honours—that Lord Allan, rest his saul, used to like a pouthered guse, and said it was Latin for a tass o' brandy—that the brandy came frae France direct; for, for a' the English laws and gaugers, the Wolf's-hope brigs hadna forgotten the gate to Dunkirk.'

Here the cooper admonished his mother-in-law with his elbow, which procured him the following special notice in the progress of her speech.

'Ye needna be dunshin that gate, John,' continued the old lady; 'naebody says that *ye* ken whar the brandy comes frae; and it wadna be fitting ye should, and you the queen's cooper; and what signifies't,' continued she, addressing Lord Ravenswood, 'to king, queen, or keiser, whar an auld wife like me buys her pickle sneeshin, or her drap brandy-wine, to haud her heart up?'

Having thus extricated herself from her supposed false step, Dame Loup-the-dyke proceeded, during the rest of the evening, to supply, with great animation, and very little assistance from her guests, the funds necessary for the support of the conversation, until, declining any further circulation of their glass, her guests requested her permission to retire to their apartments.

The Marquis occupied the chamber of dais, which, in every house above the rank of a mere cottage, was kept sacred for such high occasions as the present. The modern finishing with plaster was then unknown, and tapestry was confined to the houses of the nobility and superior gentry. The cooper, therefore, who was a man of some vanity, as well as some wealth, had imitated the fashion observed by the inferior landholders and clergy, who usually ornamented their state apartments with hangings of a sort of stamped leather, manufactured in the Netherlands, garnished with trees and animals executed in copper foil, and with many a pithy sentence of morality, which, although couched in Low

Dutch, were perhaps as much attended to in practice as if written in broad Scotch. The whole had somewhat of a gloomy aspect; but the fire, composed of old pitch-barrel staves, blazed merrily up the chimney; the bed was decorated with linen of most fresh and dazzling whiteness, which had never before been used, and might, perhaps, have never been used at all, but for this high occasion. On the toilette beside, stood an old-fashioned mirror, in a fillagree frame, part of the dispersed finery of the neighbouring castle. It was flanked by a long-necked bottle of Florence wine, by which stood a glass nearly as tall, resembling in shape that which Teniers usually places in the hands of his own portrait, when he paints himself as mingling in the revels of a country village.* To counterbalance those foreign centinels, there mounted guard on the other side of the mirror two stout warders of Scottish lineage; a jug, namely, of double ale, which held a Scotch pint, and a quegh, or bicker, of ivory and ebony, hooped with silver, the work of John Girder's own hands, and the pride of his heart. Besides these preparations against thirst, there was a goodly diet-loaf, or sweet cake; so that, with such auxiliaries, the apartment seemed victualled against a siege of two or three days.

It only remains to say, that the Marquis's valet was in attendance, displaying his master's brocaded night-gown, and richly embroidered velvet cap, lined and faced with Brussels lace, upon a huge leathern easy chair, wheeled round so as to have the full advantage of the comfortable fire which we have already mentioned. We therefore commit that eminent person to his night's repose, trusting he profited by the ample preparations made for his accommodation,—preparations which we have mentioned in detail, as illustrative of ancient Scottish manners.*

It is not necessary we should be equally minute in describing the sleeping apartment of the Master of Ravenswood, which was that usually occupied by the goodman and goodwife themselves. It was comfortably hung with a sort of warm-coloured worsted, manufactured in Scotland, approaching in texture to what is now called shaloon. A staring picture of John Girder himself ornamented this dormitory, painted by a starving Frenchman, who had, God knows how or why, strolled over from Flushing or Dunkirk to Wolf's-hope in a smuggling dogger. The features were, indeed, those of the stubborn, opinionative, yet sensible artisan, but Monsieur had contrived to throw a French grace into the look and manner, so utterly inconsistent with the dogged gravity of the original, that it was impossible to look at it without laughing. John and his family, however, piqued themselves not a little upon this picture, and were proportionably censured by the neighbourhood, who pronounced that the cooper, in sitting for the same, and yet more in presuming to hang it up in his bedchamber, had exceeded his privilege as the richest man of the village; at once stept beyond the bounds of his own rank, and encroached upon those of the superior orders; and, in fine, had been guilty of a very overweening act of vanity and presumption. Respect for the memory of my deceased friend, Mr Richard Tinto, has obliged me to treat this matter at some length; but I spare the reader his prolix, though curious observations, as well upon the character of the French school, as upon the state of painting in Scotland, at the beginning of the eighteenth century.*

The other preparations of the Master's sleeping apartment, were similar to those in the chamber of dais.

At the usual early hour of that period, the Marquis of A—— and his kinsman prepared to resume their journey. This could not be done without an ample breakfast, in which cold meat and hot meat, and oatmeal flummery, wine and spirits, and milk varied by every possible mode of preparation, evinced the same desire to do honour to their guests, which had been shown by the hospitable owners of the mansion upon the evening before. All the bustle of preparation for departure now resounded through Wolf's-hope. There was paying of bills and shaking of hands, and saddling of horses, and harnessing of carriages, and distributing of drink-money. The Marquis left a broad piece for the gratification of John Girder's household, which he, the said John, was for some time disposed to convert to his own use; Dingwall the writer assuring him he was justified in so doing, seeing he was the disburser of those expenses which were the occasion of the gratification. But, notwithstanding this legal authority, John could not find in his heart to dim the splendour of his late hospitality, by pocketing any thing in the nature of a gratuity. He only assured his menials he would consider them as a damned ungrateful pack, if they bought a gill of brandy elsewhere than out of his own stores; and as the drink-money was likely to go to its legitimate use, he comforted himself that, in this manner, the Marquis's donative would, without any impeachment of credit and character, come ultimately into his own exclusive possession.

While arrangements were making for departure, Ravenswood made blithe the heart of his ancient butler, by informing him, cautiously however, (for he knew Caleb's warmth of imagination,) of the probable change which was about to take place in his fortunes. He deposited with Balderstone, at the same time, the greater part of his slender funds, with an assurance, which he was obliged to reiterate more than once, that he himself had sufficient supplies in certain prospect. He, therefore, enjoined Caleb, as he valued his favour, to desist from all farther manœuvres against the inhabitants of Wolf's-hope, their cellars, poultry-yards, and substance whatsoever. In this prohibition, the old domestic acquiesced more readily than his master expected.

'It was doubtless,' he said, 'a shame, a discredit, and a sin, to harry the puir creatures, when the family were in circumstances to live honourably on their ain means; and there might be wisdom,' he added, 'in giving them a whiles breathing time at any rate, that they might be the more readily brought forward upon his honour's future occasions.'

This matter being settled, and having taken an affectionate farewell of his old domestic, the Master rejoined his noble relative, who was now ready to enter his carriage. The two landladies, old and young, having received in all kindly greeting, a kiss from each of their noble guests, stood simpering at the door of their house, as the coach-and-six, followed by its train of clattering horsemen, thundered out of the village. John Girder also stood upon his threshold, now looking at his honoured right hand, which had been so lately shaken by a marquis and a lord, and now giving a glance into the interior of his mansion, which manifested all the disarray of the late revel, as if balancing the distinction which he had attained with the expenses of the entertainment.

At length he opened his oracular jaws. 'Let every man and woman here set about their ain business, as if there was nae sic thing as marquis or master, duke or drake, laird or lord, in this world. Let the house be redd up, the broken meat set by, and if there is ony thing totally uneatable, let it be gien to the puir folk; and, gudemother and wife, I hae just ae thing to entreat ye, that ye will never speak to me a single word, good or bad, anent a' this nonsense wark, but keep a' your cracks about it to yoursells and your kimmers, for my head is weelnigh dung donnart wi' it already.'

As John's authority was tolerably absolute, all departed to their usual occupations, leaving him to build castles in the air, if he had a mind, upon the court favour which he had acquired by the expenditure of his worldly substance.

CHAPTER XXVII

Why, now I have Dame Fortune by the forelock,
And if she escapes my grasp, the fault is mine;
He that hath buffeted with stern adversity,
Best knows to shape his course to favouring breezes.

(*Old Play*) *

OUR travellers reached Edinburgh without any farther adventure, and the Master of Ravenswood, as had been previously settled, took up his abode with his noble friend.

In the meantime, the political crisis which had been expected, took place, and the Tory party obtained, in the Scottish, as in the English councils of Queen Anne, a short-lived ascendency, of which it is not our business to trace either the cause or consequences. * Suffice it to say, that it affected the different political parties according to the nature of their principles. In England, many of the High Church party, with Harley, afterwards Earl of Oxford, at their head, affected to separate their principles from those of the Jacobites, and, on that account, obtained the denomination of Whimsicals. * The Scottish High Church party, on the contrary, or, as they termed themselves, the Cavaliers, were more consistent, if not so prudent, in their politics, and viewed all the changes now made, as preparatory to calling to the throne, upon the queen's demise, her brother, the Chevalier de St George. * Those who had suffered in his service, now entertained the most unreasonable hopes, not only of indemnification, but of vengeance upon their political adversaries; while families attached to the Whig interest, saw nothing before them but a renewal of the hardships they had undergone during the reigns of Charles the Second and his brother, and a retaliation of the confiscation which had been inflicted upon the Jacobites during that of King William.

But the most alarmed at the change of system, was that prudential set of persons, some of whom are found in all governments, but who abound in a provincial administration like that of Scotland during the period, and who are what Cromwell called waiters upon Providence,* or, in other words, uniform adherents to the party who are uppermost. Many of these hastened to read their recantation to the Marquis of A——; and, as it was easily seen that he took a deep interest in the affairs of his kinsman, the Master of Ravenswood, they were the first to suggest measures for retrieving at least a part of his property, and for restoring him in blood against his father's attainder.

Old Lord Turntippet professed to be one of the most anxious for the success of these measures; for 'it grieved him to the very saul,' he said, 'to see so brave a young gentleman, of sic auld and undoubted nobility, and, what was mair than a' that, a bluid relation of the Marquis of A——, the man whom,' he swore, 'he honoured most upon the face of the yearth, brought to so severe a pass. For his ain puir peculiar,'* as he said, 'and to contribute something to the rehabilitation of sae auld ane house,' the said Turntippet sent in three family pictures lacking the frames, and six high-backed chairs, with worked Turkey cushions, having the crest of Ravenswood broidered thereon, without charging a penny either of the principal or interest they had cost him, when he bought them, sixteen years before, at a roup of the furniture of Lord Ravenswood's lodgings in the Canongate.*

Much more to Lord Turntippet's dismay than to his surprise, although he affected to feel more of the latter than the former, the Marquis received his gift very drily, and observed, that his lordship's restitution, if he expected it to be received by the Master of Ravenswood and his friends, must comprehend a pretty large farm, which, having been mortgaged to Turntippet for a very inadequate sum, he had contrived, during the confusion of the family affairs, and by means well understood by the lawyers of that period, to acquire to himself in absolute property.*

The old time-serving lord winced excessively under this requisition, protesting to God, that he saw no occasion the lad could have for the instant possession of the land, seeing he would doubtless now recover the bulk of his estate from Sir William Ashton, to which he was ready to contribute by every means in his power, as was just and reasonable; and finally declaring, that he was willing to settle the land on the young gentleman, after his own natural demise.

But all these excuses availed nothing, and he was compelled to disgorge the property, on receiving back the sum for which it had been mortgaged. Having no other means of making peace with the higher powers, he returned home sorrowful and malecontent, complaining to his confidents, 'that every mutation or change in the state had hitherto been productive of some sma' advantage to him in his ain quiet affairs; but that the present had (pize upon it!) cost him one of the best pen-feathers o' his wing.'

Similar measures were threatened against others who had profited by the wreck of the fortune of Ravenswood; and Sir William Ashton, in particular, was menaced with an appeal to the House of Peers against the judicial sentences under which he held the Castle and Barony of Ravenswood. With him, however, the Master, as well for Lucy's sake as on account of the hospitality he had received from him, felt himself under the necessity of proceeding with great candour. He wrote to the late Lord Keeper, for he no longer held that office, stating frankly the engagement which existed between him and Miss Ashton, requesting his permission for their union, and assuring him of his willingness to put the settlement of all matters between them upon such a footing, as Sir William himself should think favourable.

The same messenger was charged with a letter to Lady Ashton, deprecating any cause of displeasure which the Master might unintentionally have given her, enlarging upon his attachment to Miss Ashton, and the length to which it had proceeded, and conjuring the lady, as a Douglas in nature as well as in name, generously to forget ancient prejudices and misunderstandings; and to believe that the family had acquired a friend, and she herself a respectful and attached humble servant, in him who subscribed himself Edgar, Master of Ravenswood.

A third letter Ravenswood addressed to Lucy, and the messenger was instructed to find some secret and secure means of delivering it into her own hands. It contained the strongest protestations of continued affection, and dwelt upon the approaching change of the writer's fortunes, as chiefly valuable by tending to remove the impediments to their union. He related the steps he had taken to overcome the prejudices of her parents, and especially of her mother, and expressed his hope they might prove effectual. If not, he still trusted that his absence from Scotland upon an important and honourable mission might give time for prejudices to die away; while he hoped and trusted Miss Ashton's constancy, on which he had the most implicit reliance, would baffle any effort that might be used to divert her attachment. Much more there was, which, however interesting to the lovers themselves, would afford the reader neither interest nor information.* To each of these three letters the Master of Ravenswood received an answer, but by different means of conveyance, and certainly couched in very different styles.

Lady Ashton answered his letter by his own messenger, who was not allowed to remain at Ravenswood a moment longer than she was engaged in penning these lines. 'For the hand of Mr Ravenswood of Wolf's Crag—These:

'SIR, UNKNOWN,
'I have received a letter, signed Edgar, Master of Ravenswood, concerning the writer whereof I am uncertain, seeing that the honours of such a family were forfeited for high treason in the person of Allan, late Lord Ravenswood. Sir, if you shall happen to be the person so subscribing yourself, you will please to know, that I claim the full interest of a parent in Miss Lucy Ashton, which I have disposed of irrevocably in behalf of a worthy person. And, sir, were this otherwise, I would not listen to a proposal from you, or any of your house, seeing their hand has been uniformly held up against the freedom of the subject, and the immunities of God's kirk.* Sir, it is not a flightering blink of prosperity which can change my constant opinion in this regard, seeing it has been my lot before now, like holy David, to see the wicked great in power, and flourishing like a green bay tree; nevertheless I passed, and they were not, and the place thereof knew them no more.* Wishing you to lay these things to your heart for your own sake, so far as they may concern you, I pray you to take no farther notice of her, who desires to remain your unknown servant,

MARGARET DOUGLAS,
'otherwise ASHTON.'

About two days after he had received this very unsatisfactory epistle, the Master of Ravenswood, while walking up the High Street of Edinburgh, was jostled by a person, in whom, as the man pulled off his hat to make an apology, he recognised Lockhard, the confidential domestic of Sir William Ashton. The man bowed, slipt a letter into his hand, and disappeared. The packet contained four close-written folios, from which, however, as is sometimes incident to the compositions of great lawyers, little could be extracted, excepting that the writer felt himself in a very puzzling predicament.

Sir William spoke at length of his high value and regard for his dear young friend, the Master of Ravenswood, and of his very extreme high value and regard for the Marquis of A——, his very dear old friend;— he trusted that any measures that they might adopt, in which he was concerned, would be carried on with due regard to the sanctity of decreets, and judgments obtained *in foro contentioso;* * protesting, before men and angels, that if the law of Scotland, as declared in her supreme courts, were to undergo a reversal in the English House of Lords, * the evils which would thence arise to the public would inflict a greater wound upon his heart, than any loss he might himself sustain by such irregular proceedings. He flourished much on generosity and forgiveness of mutual injuries, and hinted at the mutability of human affairs, always favourite topics with the weaker party in politics. He pathetically lamented, and gently censured, the haste which had been used in depriving him of his situation of Lord Keeper, which his experience had enabled him to fill with some advantage to the public, without so much as giving him an opportunity of explaining how far his own views of general politics might essentially differ from those now in power. He was convinced the Marquis of A—— had as sincere intentions towards the public, as himself or any man; and if, upon a conference, they could have agreed upon the measures by which it was to be pursued, his experience and his interest should have gone to support the present administration. Upon the engagement betwixt Ravenswood and his daughter, he spoke in a dry and confused manner. He regretted so premature a step as the engagement of the young people should have been taken, and conjured the Master to remember he had never given any encouragement thereunto; and observed, that, as a transaction *inter minores*, and without concurrence of his daughter's natural curators, the engagement was inept, and void in law.* This precipitate measure, he added, had produced a very bad effect upon Lady Ashton's mind, which it was impossible at present to remove. Her son, Colonel Douglas Ashton, had embraced her prejudices in the fullest extent, and it was impossible for Sir William to adopt a course disagreeable to them, without a fatal and irreconcilable breach in his family; which was not at present to be thought of. Time, the great physician, he hoped, would mend all.

In a postscript, Sir William said something more explicitly, which seemed to intimate, that rather than the law of Scotland should sustain a severe wound through his sides, by a reversal of the judgment of her supreme courts, in the case of the Barony of Ravenswood, through the intervention of what, with all submission, he must term a foreign court of appeal,* he himself would extrajudicially consent to considerable sacrifices.

From Lucy Ashton, by some unknown conveyance, the Master received the following lines:—'I received yours, but it was at the utmost risk; do not attempt to write again till better times. I am sore beset, but I will be true to my word, while the exercise of my reason is vouchsafed to me. That you are happy and prosperous is some consolation, and my situation requires it all.' The note was signed L.A.

This letter filled Ravenswood with the most lively alarm. He made many attempts, notwithstanding her prohibition, to convey letters to Miss Ashton, and even to obtain an interview; but his plans were frustrated, and he had only the mortification to learn, that anxious and effectual precautions had been taken to prevent the possibility of their correspondence. The Master was the more distressed by these circumstances, as it became impossible to delay his departure from Scotland, upon the important mission which had been confided to him. Before his departure, he put Sir William Ashton's letter into the hands of the Marquis of A——, who observed with a smile, that Sir William's day of grace was past, and that he had now to learn which side of the hedge the sun had got to. It was with the greatest difficulty that Ravenswood extorted from the Marquis a promise, that he would compromise the proceedings in Parliament, providing Sir William should be disposed to acquiesce in a union between him and Lucy Ashton.

'I would hardly,' said the Marquis, 'consent to your throwing away your birth-right in this manner, were I not perfectly confident that Lady Ashton, or Lady Douglas, or whatever she calls herself, will, as Scotchmen say, keep her threep; and that her husband dares not contradict her.'

'But yet,' said the Master, 'I trust your lordship will consider my engagement as sacred?'

'Believe my word of honour,' said the Marquis, 'I would be a friend even to your follies; and having thus told you *my* opinion, I will endeavour, as occasion offers, to serve you according to your own.'

The Master of Ravenswood could but thank his generous kinsman and patron, and leave him full power to act in all his affairs. He departed from Scotland upon his mission, which, it was supposed, might detain him upon the continent for some months.*

CHAPTER XXVIII

Was ever woman in this humour wooed?
Was ever woman in this humour won?
I'll have her.

(*Richard the Third*)*

TWELVE months had passed away since the Master of Ravenswood's departure for the continent, and, although his return to Scotland had been expected in a much shorter space, yet the affairs of his mission, or, according to a prevailing report, others of a nature personal to himself, still detained him abroad. In the meantime, the altered state of affairs in Sir William Ashton's family may be gathered from the following conversation which took place betwixt Bucklaw and his confidential bottle companion and dependant, the noted Captain Craigengelt.

They were seated on either side of the huge sepulchral-looking freestone chimney in the low hall at Girnington. A wood fire blazed merrily in the grate; a round oaken table, placed between them, supported a stoup of excellent claret, two rummer glasses, and other good cheer; and yet, with all these appliances and means to boot, the countenance of the patron was dubious, doubtful, and unsatisfied, while the invention of his dependant was taxed to the utmost, to parry what he most dreaded, a fit, as he called it, of the sullens, on the part of his protector. After a long pause, only interrupted by the devil's tattoo, which Bucklaw kept beating against the hearth with the toe of his boot, Craigengelt at last ventured to break silence. 'May I be double distanced,' said he, 'if ever I saw a man in my life have less the air of a bridegroom! Cut me out of feather, if you have not more the look of a man condemned to be hanged!'

'My kind thanks for the compliment,' replied Bucklaw; 'but I suppose you think upon the predicament in which you yourself are most likely to be placed;—and pray, Captain Craigengelt, if it please your worship, why should I look merry, when I'm sad, and devilish sad too?'

'And that's what vexes me,' said Craigengelt. 'Here is this match, the best in the whole country, and which you were so anxious about, is on the point of being concluded, and you are as sulky as a bear that has lost its whelps.'*

'I do not know,' answered the laird, doggedly, 'whether I should conclude it or not, if it was not that I am too far forwards to leap back.'

'Leap back!' exclaimed Craigengelt, with a well-assumed air of astonishment, 'that would be playing the back-game with a witness! Leap back! Why, is not the girl's fortune'——

'The young lady's, if you please,' said Hayston, interrupting him.

'Well, well, no disrespect meant—Will Miss Ashton's tocher not weigh against any in Lothian?'

'Granted,' answered Bucklaw; 'but I care not a penny for her tocher—I have enough of my own.'

'And the mother, that loves you like her own child?'

'Better than some of her children, I believe,' said Bucklaw, 'or there would be little love wared on the matter.'

'And Colonel Sholto Douglas Ashton, who desires the marriage above all earthly things?'

'Because,' said Bucklaw, 'he expects to carry the county of —— through my interest.'

'And the father, who is as keen to see the match concluded, as ever I have been to win a main?'

'Ay,' said Bucklaw, in the same disparaging manner, 'it lies with Sir William's policy to secure the next best match, since he cannot barter his child to save the great Ravenswood estate, which the English House of Lords are about to wrench out of his clutches.'

'What say you to the young lady herself?' said Craigengelt; 'the finest young woman in all Scotland, one that you used to be so fond of when she was cross, and now she consents to have you, and gives up her engagement with Ravenswood, you are for jibbing—I must say, the devil's in ye, when ye neither know what you would have, nor what you would want.'

'I'll tell you my meaning in a word,' answered Bucklaw, getting up and walking through the room; 'I want to know what the devil is the cause of Miss Ashton's changing her mind so suddenly?'

'And what need you care,' said Craigengelt, 'since the change is in your favour?'

'I'll tell you what it is,' returned his patron, 'I never knew much of that sort of fine ladies, and I believe they may be as capricious as the devil; but there is something in Miss Ashton's change, a devilish deal too sudden, and too serious for a mere flisk of her own. I'll be bound Lady Ashton understands every machine for breaking in the human mind, and there are as many as there are cannon-bits, martingales, and cavessons for young colts.'

'And if that were not the case,' said Craigengelt, 'how the devil should we ever get them into training at all?'

'And that's true too,' said Bucklaw, suspending his march through the dining-room, and leaning upon the back of a chair.— 'And besides, here's Ravenswood in the way still; do you think he'll give up Lucy's engagement?'

'To be sure he will,' answered Craigengelt; 'what good can it do him to refuse, since he wishes to marry another woman, and she another man?'

'And you believe seriously,' said Bucklaw, 'that he is going to marry the foreign lady we heard of?'

'You heard yourself,' answered Craigengelt, 'what Captain Westenho said about it, and the great preparation made for their blithesome bridal.'

'Captain Westenho,' replied Bucklaw, 'has rather too much of your own cast about him, Craigie, to make what Sir William would call a "famous witness."* He drinks deep, plays deep, swears deep, and I suspect can lie and cheat a little into the bargain. Useful qualities, Craigie, if kept in their proper sphere, but which have a little too much of the freebooter to make a figure in a court of evidence.'

'Well, then,' said Craigengelt, 'will you believe Colonel Douglas Ashton, who heard the Marquis of A——— say in a public circle, but not aware that he was within ear-shot, that his kinsman had made a better arrangement for himself than to give his father's land for the pale-cheeked daughter of a broken-down fanatic, and that

Bucklaw was welcome to the wearing of Ravenswood's shaughled shoes.'

'Did he say so, by heavens!' cried Bucklaw, breaking out into one of those incontrollable fits of passion to which he was constitutionally subject,—'if I had heard him, I would have torn the tongue out of his throat before all his peats and minions, and Highland bullies into the bargain. Why did not Ashton run him through the body?'

'Capote me if I know,' said the Captain. 'He deserved it sure enough; but he is an old man, and a minister of state, and there would be more risk than credit in meddling with him. You had more need to think of making up to Miss Lucy Ashton the disgrace that's like to fall upon her, than of interfering with a man too old to fight, and on too high a stool for your hand to reach him.'

'It *shall* reach him, though, one day,' said Bucklaw, 'and his kinsman Ravenswood to boot. In the meantime, I'll take care Miss Ashton receives no discredit for the slight they have put upon her. It's an awkward job, however, and I wish it were ended; I scarce know how to talk to her,—but fill a bumper, Craigie, and we'll drink her health. It grows late, and a night-cowl of good claret is worth all the considering-caps in Europe.'

CHAPTER XXIX

It was the copy of our conference.
In bed she slept not, for my urging it;
At board she fed not, for my urging it;
Alone, it was the subject of my theme;
In company I often glanced at it.

(Comedy of Errors) *

THE next morning saw Bucklaw, and his faithful Achates, Craigengelt, at Ravenswood Castle. They were most courteously received by the knight and his lady, as well as by their son and heir, Colonel Ashton. After a good deal of stammering and blushing,—for Bucklaw, notwithstanding his audacity in other matters, had all the sheepish bashfulness common to those who have lived little in respectable society,—he contrived at length to explain his wish to be admitted to a conference with Miss Ashton upon the subject of their approaching union. Sir William and his son looked at Lady Ashton, who replied with the greatest composure, 'that Lucy would wait upon Mr Hayston directly. I hope,' she added with a smile, 'that as Lucy is very young, and has been lately trepanned into an engagement, of which she is now heartily ashamed, our dear Bucklaw will excuse her wish, that I should be present at their interview?'

'In truth, my dear lady,' said Bucklaw, 'it is the very thing that I would have desired on my own account; for I have been so little accustomed to what is called gallantry, that I shall certainly fall into some cursed mistake, unless I have the advantage of your ladyship as an interpreter.'

It was thus that Bucklaw, in the perturbation of his embarrassment upon this critical occasion, forgot the just apprehensions he had entertained of Lady Ashton's overbearing ascendency over her daughter's mind, and lost an opportunity of ascertaining, by his own investigation, the real state of Lucy's feelings.

The other gentlemen left the room, and in a short time, Lady Ashton, followed by her daughter, entered the apartment. She appeared, as he had seen her on former occasions, rather composed than agitated; but a nicer judge than he could scarce have determined, whether her calmness was that of despair, or of indifference. Bucklaw was too much agitated by his own feelings minutely to scrutinize those of the lady. He stammered out an unconnected address, confounding together the two or three topics to which it related, and stopt short before he brought it to any regular conclusion. Miss Ashton listened, or looked as if she listened, but returned not a single word in answer, continuing to fix her eyes on a small piece of embroidery, on which, as if by instinct or habit, her fingers were busily employed. Lady Ashton sat at some distance, almost screened from notice by the deep embrasure of the window in which she had placed her chair. From this she whispered, in a tone of voice, which, though soft and sweet, had something in it of admonition, if not command,—— 'Lucy, my dear, remember——have you heard what Bucklaw has been saying?'

The idea of her mother's presence seemed to have slipped from the unhappy girl's recollection. She started, dropped her needle, and repeated hastily, and almost in the same breath, the contradictory answers, 'Yes, madam——no, my lady——I beg pardon, I did not hear.'

'You need not blush, my love, and still less need you look so pale and frightened,' said Lady Ashton, coming forward; 'we know that maiden's ears must be slow in receiving a gentleman's language; but you must remember Mr Hayston speaks on a subject on which you have long since agreed to give him a favourable hearing. You know how much your father and I have our hearts set upon an event so extremely desirable.'

In Lady Ashton's voice, a tone of impressive, and even stern innuendo was sedulously and skilfully concealed, under an appearance of the most affectionate maternal tenderness. The manner was for Bucklaw, who was easily enough imposed upon; the matter of the exhortation was for the terrified Lucy, who well knew how to interpret her mother's hints, however skilfully their real purport might be veiled from general observation.

Miss Ashton sat upright in her chair, cast round her a glance, in which fear was mingled with a still wilder expression, but remained perfectly silent. Bucklaw, who had in the meantime paced the room to and fro, until he had recovered his composure, now stopped within two or three yards of her chair, and broke out as follows:—'I believe I have been a d—d fool, Miss Ashton; I have tried to speak to you as people tell me young ladies like to be talked to, and I don't think you comprehend what I have been saying; and no wonder, for d—n me if I understand it myself! But, however, once for all, and in broad Scotch, your father and mother like what is proposed, and if you can take a plain young fellow for your husband, who will never cross you in any thing you have a mind to, I will place you at the head of the best establishment in the three Lothians;* you shall have Lady Girnington's lodging in the Canongate of Edinburgh, go where you please, do what you please, and see what you please, and that's fair. Only I must have a corner at the board-end for a worthless old play-fellow of mine, whose company I would rather want than have, if it were not that the d—d fellow has persuaded me that I can't do without him; and so I hope you won't except against Craigie, although it might be easy to find much better company.'

'Now, out upon you, Bucklaw,' said Lady Ashton, again interposing,—'how can you think Lucy can have any objection to that blunt, honest, good-natured creature, Captain Craigengelt?'

'Why, madam,' replied Bucklaw, 'as to Craigie's sincerity, honesty, and good-nature, they are, I believe, pretty much upon a par—but that's neither here nor there—the fellow knows my ways, and has got useful to me, and I cannot well do without him, as I said before. But all this is nothing to the purpose; for, since I have mustered up courage to make a plain proposal, I would fain hear Miss Ashton, from her own lips, give me a plain answer.'

'My dear Bucklaw,' said Lady Ashton, 'let me spare Lucy's bashfulness. I tell you, in her presence, that she has already consented to be guided by her father and me in this matter.— Lucy, my love,' she added, with that singular combination of suavity of tone and pointed energy which we have already noticed—'Lucy, my dearest love! speak for yourself, is it not as I say?'

Her victim answered in a tremulous and hollow voice—'I *have* promised to obey you,—but upon one condition.'

'She means,' said Lady Ashton, turning to Bucklaw, 'she expects an answer to the demand which she has made upon the man at Vienna, or Ratisbon, or Paris—or where is he—for restitution of the engagement in which he had the art to involve her. You will not, I am sure, my dear friend, think it is wrong that she should feel much delicacy upon this head; indeed, it concerns us all.'

'Perfectly right—quite fair,' said Bucklaw, half humming, half speaking the end of the old song—

> 'It is best to be off wi' the old love
> Before you be on wi' the new.'*

'But I thought,' said he, pausing, 'you might have had an answer six times told from Ravenswood. D—n me, if I have not a mind to go and fetch one myself, if Miss Ashton will honour me with the commission.'

'By no means,' said Lady Ashton, 'we have had the utmost difficulty of preventing Douglas, (for whom it would be more proper,) from taking so rash a step; and do you think we could permit you, my good friend, almost equally dear to us, to go to a desperate man upon an errand so desperate? In fact, all the friends of the family are of opinion, and my dear Lucy herself ought so to think, that, as this unworthy person has returned no answer to her letter, silence must on this, as in other cases, be held to give consent, and a contract must be supposed to be given up, when the party waives insisting upon it. Sir William, who should know best, is clear upon this subject; and therefore, my dear Lucy'——

'Madam,' said Lucy, with unwonted energy, 'urge me no farther—if this unhappy engagement be restored, I have already said you shall dispose of me as you will—till then I should commit a heavy sin in the sight of God and man, in doing what you require.'

'But, my love, if this man remains obstinately silent'——

'He will *not* be silent,' answered Lucy; 'it is six weeks since I sent him a double of my former letter by a sure hand.'

'You have not—you could not—you durst not,' said Lady Ashton, with violence inconsistent with the tone she had intended to assume; but instantly correcting herself, 'My dearest Lucy,' said she, in her sweetest tone of expostulation, 'how could you think of such a thing?'

'No matter,' said Bucklaw; 'I respect Miss Ashton for her sentiments, and I only wish I had been her messenger myself.'

'And pray how long, Miss Ashton,' said her mother, ironically, 'are we to wait the return of your Pacolet—your fairy mess-enger—since our humble couriers of flesh and blood could not be trusted in this matter?'*

'I have numbered weeks, days, hours, and minutes,' said Miss Ashton; 'within another week I shall have an answer, unless he is dead.—Till that time, sir,' she said, addressing Bucklaw, 'let me be thus far beholden to you, that you will beg my mother to forbear me upon this subject.'

'I will make it my particular entreaty to Lady Ashton,' said Bucklaw. 'By my honour, madam, I respect your feelings; and, although the prosecution of this affair be rendered dearer to me than ever, yet, as I am a gentleman, I would renounce it, were it so urged as to give you a moment's pain.'

'Mr Hayston, I think, cannot apprehend that,' said Lady Ashton, looking pale with anger, 'when the daughter's happiness lies in the bosom of the mother.—Let me ask you, Miss Ashton, in what terms your last letter was couched?'

'Exactly in the same, madam,' answered Lucy, 'which you dictated on a former occasion.'

'When eight days have elapsed, then,' said her mother, resum-ing her tone of tenderness, 'we shall hope, my dearest love, that you will end this suspense.'

'Miss Ashton must not be hurried, madam,' said Bucklaw, whose bluntness of feeling did not by any means arise from want of good-nature—'messengers may be stopped or delayed. I have known a day's journey broke by the casting off a fore-shoe.—Stay, let me see my calendar—the 20th day from this is St Jude's,* and, the day before, I must be at Caverton Edge to see the match between the Laird of Kittlegirth's black mare, and Johnston the meal-monger's four-year-old colt;* but I can ride all night, or Craigie can bring me word how the match goes; and I hope, in the meantime, as I shall not myself distress Miss Ashton with any further importunity, that your ladyship yourself, and Sir William, and Colonel Douglas, will have the goodness to allow her uninterrupted time for making up her mind.'

'Sir,' said Miss Ashton, 'you are generous.'

'As for that, madam,' answered Bucklaw, 'I only pretend to be a plain good-humoured young fellow, as I said before, who will willingly make you happy if you will permit him, and show him how to do so.'

Having said this, he saluted her with more emotion than was consistent with his usual train of feeling, and took his leave; Lady Ashton, as she accompanied him out of the apartment, assuring him that her daughter did full justice to the sincerity of his attachment, and requesting him to see Sir William before his departure, 'since,' as she said, with a keen glance reverting towards Lucy, 'against St Jude's day, we must all be ready to *sign and seal*.'

'To sign and seal!' echoed Lucy in a muttering tone, as the door of the apartment closed—'To sign and seal—to do and die!'* and, clasping her extenuated hands together, she sunk back on the easy-chair she occupied, in a state resembling stupor.

From this she was shortly after awakened by the boisterous entry of her brother Henry, who clamorously reminded her of a promise to give him two yards of carnation ribbon to make knots to his new garters. With the most patient composure Lucy arose, and opening a little ivory-cabinet, sought out the ribbon the lad wanted, measured it accurately, cut it off into proper lengths, and knotted into the fashion his boyish whim required.

'Dinna shut the cabinet yet,' said Henry, 'for I must have some of your silver wire to fasten the bells to my hawk's jesses,—and yet the new falcon's not worth them neither; for do you know, after all the plague we had to get her from an eyry, all the way at Posso, in Mannor Water,* she's going to prove, after all, nothing better than a rifler—she just wets her singles in the blood of the partridge, and then breaks away, and lets her fly; and what good can the poor bird do after that, you know, except pine and die in the first heather-cow or whin-bush she can crawl into?'

'Right, Henry—right, very right,' said Lucy, mournfully, holding the boy fast by the hand, after she had given him the wire he wanted; 'but there are more riflers in the world than your falcon,

and more wounded birds that seek but to die in quiet, that can
find neither brake nor whin-bush to hide their heads in.'

'Ah! that's some speech out of your romances,' said the boy;
'and Sholto says they have turned your head. But I hear Norman
whistling to the hawk—I must go fasten on the jesses.'

And he scampered away with the thoughtless gaiety of boy-
hood, leaving his sister to the bitterness of her own reflections.

'It is decreed,' she said, 'that every living creature, even those
who owe me most kindness, are to shun me, and leave me to those
by whom I am beset. It is just it should be thus. Alone and
uncounselled, I involved myself in these perils—alone and uncounselled, I must extricate myself or die.'

CHAPTER XXX

――――――What doth ensue
But moody and dull melancholy,
Kinsman to grim and comfortless despair,
And, at her heels, a huge infectious troop
Of pale distemperatures, and foes to life?

(Comedy of Errors) *

As some vindication of the ease with which Bucklaw (who otherwise, as he termed himself, was really a very good-humoured fellow) resigned his judgment to the management of Lady Ashton, while paying his addresses to her daughter, the reader must call to mind the strict domestic discipline, which, at this period, was exercised over the females of a Scottish family.

The manners of the country in this, as in many other respects, coincided with those of France before the revolution.* Young women of the higher ranks seldom mingled in society until after marriage, and, both in law and fact, were held to be under the strict tutelage of their parents, who were too apt to enforce the views for their settlement in life, without paying any regard to the inclination of the parties chiefly interested. On such occasions, the suitor expected little more from his bride than a silent acquiescence in the will of her parents; and as few opportunities of acquaintance, far less of intimacy, occurred, he made his choice by the outside, as the lovers in the Merchant of Venice select the casket, contented to trust to chance the issue of the lottery, in which he had hazarded a venture.*

It was not therefore surprising, such being the general manners of the age, that Mr Hayston of Bucklaw, whom dissipated habits had detached in some degree from the best society, should not attend particularly to those feelings in his elected bride, to which many men of more sentiment, experience, and reflection, would, in all probability, have been equally indifferent. He knew what all accounted the principal point, that her parents and friends, namely, were decidedly in his favour, and that there existed most powerful reasons for their predilection.

In truth, the conduct of the Marquis of A——, since Ravenswood's departure, had been such as almost to bar the possibility of his kinsman's union with Lucy Ashton. The Marquis was Ravenswood's sincere, but misjudging friend; or rather, like many friends and patrons, he consulted what he considered to be his relation's true interest, although he knew that in doing so he run counter to his inclinations.

The Marquis drove on, therefore, with the plenitude of ministerial authority, an appeal to the British House of Peers against those judgments of the courts of law, by which Sir William became possessed of Ravenswood's hereditary property. As this measure, enforced with all the authority of power, was new in Scottish judicial proceedings, though now so frequently resorted to, it was exclaimed against by the lawyers on the opposite side of politics, as an interference with the civil judicature of the country, equally new, arbitrary, and tyrannical. * And if it thus affected even strangers connected with them only by political party, it may be guessed what the Ashton family themselves said and thought under so gross a dispensation. Sir William, still more worldly minded than he was timid, was reduced to despair by the loss by which he was threatened. His son's haughtier spirit was exalted into rage at the idea of being deprived of his expected patrimony. But to Lady Ashton's yet more vindictive temper, the conduct of Ravenswood, or rather of his patron, appeared to be an offence challenging the deepest and most immortal revenge. Even the quiet and confiding temper of Lucy herself, swayed by the opinions expressed by all around her, could not but consider the conduct of Ravenswood as precipitate, and even unkind. 'It was my father,' she repeated with a sigh, 'who welcomed him to this place, and encouraged, or at least allowed, the intimacy between us. Should he not have remembered this, and requited it with at least some moderate degree of procrastination in the assertion of his own alleged rights? I would have forfeited for him double the value of these lands, which he pursues with an ardour that shows he has forgotten how much I am implicated in the matter.'

Lucy, however, could only murmur these things to herself, unwilling to increase the prejudices against her lover entertained by all around her, who exclaimed against the steps pursued on his account, as illegal, vexatious, and tyrannical, resembling the worst measures in the worst times of the worst Stewarts, and a degradation of Scotland, the decisions of whose learned judges were thus subjected to the review of a court, composed indeed of men of the highest rank, but who were not trained to the study of any municipal law, and might be supposed specially to hold in contempt that of Scotland.* As a natural consequence of the alleged injustice meditated towards her father, every means was resorted to, and every argument urged, to induce Miss Ashton to break off her engagement with Ravenswood, as being scandalous, shameful, and sinful, formed with the mortal enemy of her family, and calculated to add bitterness to the distress of her parents.

Lucy's spirit, however, was high; and although unaided and alone, she could have borne much—she could have endured the repinings of her father—his murmurs against what he called the tyrannical usage of the ruling party—his ceaseless charges of ingratitude against Ravenswood—his endless lectures on the various means by which contracts may be voided and annulled—his quotations from the civil, the municipal, and the canon law—and his prelections upon the *patria potestas*.*

She might have borne also in patience, or repelled with scorn, the bitter taunts and occasional violence of her brother Colonel Douglas Ashton, and the impertinent and intrusive interference of other friends and relations. But it was beyond her power effectually to withstand or elude the constant and unceasing persecution of Lady Ashton, who, laying every other wish aside, had bent the whole efforts of her powerful mind to break her daughter's contract with Ravenswood, and to place a perpetual bar between the lovers, by effecting Lucy's union with Bucklaw. Far more deeply skilled than her husband in the recesses of the human heart, she was aware, that in this way she might strike a blow of deep and decisive vengeance upon one, whom she esteemed as her mortal enemy; nor did she hesitate at raising her arm, although she knew that the wound must be dealt through the bosom of her daughter. With this stern and fixed purpose, she sounded every deep and shallow of her daughter's soul, assumed alternately every disguise of manner which could serve her object, and prepared at leisure every species of dire machinery, by which the human mind can be wrenched from its settled determination. Some of these were of an obvious description, and require only to be cursorily mentioned; others were characteristic of the time, the country, and the persons engaged in this singular drama.

It was of the last consequence, that all intercourse betwixt the lovers should be stopped, and, by dint of gold and authority, Lady Ashton contrived to possess herself of such a complete command of all who were placed around her daughter, that, in fact, no leaguered fortress was ever more completely blockaded; while, at the same time, to all outward appearance, Miss Ashton lay under no restriction. The verge of her parents' domains became, in respect to her, like the viewless and enchanted line drawn around a fairy castle, where nothing unpermitted can either enter from without, or escape from within. Thus every letter, in which Ravenswood conveyed to Lucy Ashton the indispensable reasons which detained him abroad, and more than one note which poor Lucy had addressed to him through what she thought a secure channel, fell into the hands of her mother. It could not be, but that the tenor of these intercepted letters, especially those of Ravenswood, should contain something to irritate the passions, and fortify the obstinacy, of her into whose hands they fell; but Lady Ashton's passions were too deep-rooted to require this fresh food. She burnt the papers as regularly as she perused them; and as they consumed into vapour and tinder, regarded them with a smile upon her compressed lips, and an exultation in her steady eye, which showed her confidence that the hopes of the writers should soon be rendered equally unsubstantial.

It usually happens, that fortune aids the machinations of those who are prompt to avail themselves of every chance that offers. A report was wafted from the Continent, founded, like others of the same sort, upon many plausible circumstances, but without any real basis, stating the Master of Ravenswood to be on the eve of marriage with a foreign lady of fortune and distinction. This was greedily caught up by both the political parties, who were at once struggling for power and for popular favour, and who seized, as usual, upon the most private circumstances in the lives of each other's partisans, to convert them into subjects of political discussion.

The Marquis of A——— gave his opinion aloud and publicly, not indeed in the coarse terms ascribed to him by Captain Craigengelt, but in a manner sufficiently offensive to the Ashtons:—'He thought the report,' he said, 'highly probable, and heartily wished it might be true. Such a match was fitter and far more creditable for a spirited young fellow, than a marriage with the daughter of an old whig lawyer, whose chicanery had so nearly ruined his father.'

The other party, of course, laying out of view the opposition which the Master of Ravenswood received from Miss Ashton's family, cried shame upon his fickleness and perfidy, as if he had seduced the young lady into an engagement, and wilfully and causelessly abandoned her for another.

Sufficient care was taken that this report should find its way to Ravenswood Castle through every various channel, Lady Ashton being well aware, that the very reiteration of the same rumour from so many quarters could not but give it a semblance of truth. By some it was told as a piece of ordinary news, by some communicated as serious intelligence; now it was whispered to Lucy Ashton's ear in the tone of malignant pleasantry, and now transmitted to her as a matter of grave and serious warning.

Even the boy Henry was made the instrument of adding to his sister's torments. One morning he rushed into the room with a willow branch in his hand, which he told her had arrived that instant from Germany for her special wearing.* Lucy, as we have seen, was remarkably fond of her younger brother, and at that moment his wanton and thoughtless unkindness seemed more keenly injurious than even the studied insults of her elder brother. Her grief, however, had no shade of resentment; she folded her arms about the boy's neck, and saying, faintly, 'Poor Henry! you speak but what they tell you,' she burst into a flood of unrestrained tears. The boy was moved, notwithstanding the thoughtlessness of his age and character. 'The devil take me,' said he, 'Lucy, if I fetch you any more of these tormenting messages again; for I like you better,' said he, kissing away the tears, 'than the whole pack of them; and you shall have my grey pony to ride on, and you shall canter him if you like,—ay, and ride beyond the village, too, if you have a mind.'

'Who told you,' said Lucy, 'that I am not permitted to ride where I please?'

'That's a secret,' said the boy; 'but you will find you can never ride beyond the village but your horse will cast a shoe, or fall lame, or the castle bell will ring, or something will happen to bring you back.—But if I tell you more of these things, Douglas will not get me the pair of colours they have promised me,* and so good-morrow to you.'

This dialogue plunged Lucy in still deeper dejection, as it tended to show her plainly what she had for some time suspected, that she was little better than a prisoner at large in her father's house. We have described her in the outset of our story as of a romantic disposition, delighting in tales of love and wonder, and readily identifying herself with the situation of those legendary heroines, with whose adventures, for want of better reading, her memory had become stocked. The fairy wand, with which in her solitude she had delighted to raise visions of enchantment, became now the rod of a magician, the bond slave of evil genii, serving only to invoke spectres at which the exorcist trembled. She felt herself the object of suspicion, of scorn, of dislike at least, if not of hatred, to her own family; and it seemed to her that she was abandoned by the very person on whose account she was exposed to the enmity of all around her. Indeed, the evidence of Ravenswood's infidelity began to assume every day a more determined character.

A soldier of fortune, of the name of Westenho, an old familiar of Craigengelt's, chanced to arrive from abroad about this time. The worthy Captain, though without any precise communication with Lady Ashton, always acted most regularly and sedulously in support of her plans, and easily prevailed upon his friend, by dint of exaggeration of real circumstances, and coining of others, to give explicit testimony to the truth of Ravenswood's approaching marriage.

Thus beset on all hands, and in a manner reduced to despair, Lucy's temper gave way under the pressure of constant affliction and persecution. She became gloomy and abstracted, and, contrary to her natural and ordinary habit of mind, sometimes turned with spirit, and even fierceness, on those by whom she was long and closely annoyed. Her health also began to be shaken, and her hectic cheek and wandering eye gave symptoms of what is called a fever upon the spirits. In most mothers this would have moved compassion; but Lady Ashton, compact and firm of purpose, saw these waverings of health and intellect with no greater sympathy than that with which the hostile engineer regards the towers of a beleagured city as they reel under the discharge of his artillery; or rather, she considered these starts and inequalities of temper as symptoms of Lucy's expiring resolution; as the angler, by the throes and convulsive exertions of the fish which he has hooked, becomes aware that he soon will be able to land him. To accelerate the catastrophe in the present case, Lady Ashton had recourse to an expedient very consistent with the temper and credulity of those times, but which the reader will probably pronounce truly detestable and diabolical.

CHAPTER XXXI

* * * * * * *

In which a witch did dwell, in loathly weeds,
And wilful want, all careless of her needs;
So choosing solitary to abide,
Far from all neighbours, that her devilish deeds
And hellish arts from people she might hide,
And hurt far off, unknown, whome'er she envied.

(*Fairy Queen*)*

THE health of Lucy Ashton soon required the assistance of a person more skilful in the office of a sick nurse than the female domestics of the family. Ailsie Gourlay, sometimes called the Wise Woman of Bowden,* was the person whom, for her own strong reasons, Lady Ashton selected as an attendant upon her daughter.

This woman had acquired a considerable reputation among the ignorant by the pretended cures which she performed, especially in *oncomes*, as the Scotch call them, or mysterious diseases, which baffle the regular physician. Her pharmacopeia consisted partly of herbs selected in planetary hours, partly of words, signs, and charms, which sometimes, perhaps, produced a favourable influence upon the imagination of her patients. Such was the avowed profession of Lucky Gourlay, which, as may well be supposed, was looked upon with a suspicious eye, not only by her neighbours, but even by the clergy of the district. In private, however, she traded more deeply in the occult sciences; for, notwithstanding the dreadful punishments inflicted upon the supposed crime of witchcraft, there wanted not those who, steeled by want and bitterness of spirit, were willing to adopt the hateful and dangerous character, for the sake of the influence which its terrors enabled them to exercise in the vicinity, and the wretched emolument which they could extract by the practice of their supposed art.

Ailsie Gourlay was not indeed fool enough to acknowledge a compact with the Evil One, which would have been a swift and ready road to the stake and tar-barrel.* Her fairy, she said, like Caliban's, was a harmless fairy.* Nevertheless, she 'spaed fortunes,' read dreams, composed philtres, discovered stolen goods, and made and dissolved matches as successfully as if, according to the belief of the whole neighbourhood, she had been aided in those arts by Beelzebub himself. The worst of the pretenders to these sciences was, that they were generally persons who, feeling themselves odious to humanity, were careless of what they did to deserve the public hatred. Real crimes were often committed under pretence of magical imposture; and it somewhat relieves the disgust with which we read, in the criminal records, the conviction of these wretches, to be aware that many of them merited, as poisoners, suborners, and diabolical agents in secret domestic crimes, the severe fate to which they were condemned for the imaginary guilt of witchcraft.

Such was Ailsie Gourlay, whom, in order to attain the absolute subjugation of Lucy Ashton's mind, her mother thought it fitting to place near her person. A woman of less consequence than Lady Ashton had not dared to take such a step; but her high rank and strength of character set her above the censure of the world, and she was allowed to have selected for her daughter's attendant the best and most experienced sick-nurse 'and mediciner' in the neighbourhood, where an inferior person would have fallen under the reproach of calling in the assistance of a partner and ally of the great Enemy of mankind.

The beldam caught her cue readily and by innuendo, without giving Lady Ashton the pain of distinct explanation. She was in many respects qualified for the part she played, which indeed could not be efficiently assumed without some knowledge of the human heart and passions. Dame Gourlay perceived that Lucy shuddered at her external appearance, which we have already described when we found her in the death-chamber of blind Alice; and while internally she hated the poor girl for the involuntary horror with which she saw she was regarded, she commenced her operations by endeavouring to efface or overcome those prejudices which, in her heart, she resented as mortal offences. This was easily done, for the hag's external ugliness was soon balanced by a show of kindness and interest, to which Lucy had of late been little accustomed; her attentive services and real skill gained her the ear, if not the confidence, of her patient; and under pretence of diverting the solitude of a sick room, she soon led her attention captive by the legends in which she was well skilled, and to which Lucy's habits of reading and reflection induced her to 'lend an attentive ear.'* Dame Gourlay's tales were at first of a mild and interesting character—

> Of fays that nightly dance upon the wold,
> And lovers doom'd to wander and to weep,
> And castles high, where wicked wizards keep
> Their captive thralls.*

Gradually, however, they assumed a darker and more mysterious character, and became such as, told by the midnight lamp, and enforced by the tremulous tone, the quivering and livid lip, the uplifted skinny fore-finger, and the shaking head of the blue-eyed hag, might have appalled a less credulous imagination, in an age more hard of belief.* The old Sycorax saw her advantage, and gradually narrowed her magic circle around the devoted victim on whose spirit she practised. Her legends began to relate to the fortunes of the Ravenswood family, whose ancient grandeur and portentous authority, credulity had graced with so many superstitious attributes. The story of the fatal fountain was narrated at full length, and with formidable additions, by the ancient sibyl. The prophecy, quoted by Caleb, concerning the dead bride, who was to be won by the last of the Ravenswoods, had its own mysterious commentary; and the singular circumstance of the apparition, seen by the Master of Ravenswood in the forest, having partly transpired through his hasty enquiries in the cottage of old Alice, formed a theme for many exaggerations.

Lucy might have despised these tales, if they had been related concerning another family, or if her own situation had been less despondent. But circumstanced as she was, the idea that an evil fate hung over her attachment, became predominant over her other feelings; and the gloom of superstition darkened a mind, already sufficiently weakened by sorrow, distress, uncertainty, and an oppressive sense of desertion and desolation. Stories were told by her attendant so closely resembling her own in their circumstances, that she was gradually led to converse upon such tragic and mystical subjects with the beldam, and to repose a sort of confidence in the sibyl, whom she still regarded with involuntary shuddering. Dame Gourlay knew how to avail herself of this imperfect confidence. She directed Lucy's thoughts to the means of enquiring into futurity,—the surest mode, perhaps, of shaking the understanding and destroying the spirits. Omens were expounded, dreams were interpreted, and other tricks of jugglery perhaps resorted to, by which the pretended adepts of the period deceived and fascinated their deluded followers. I find it mentioned in the articles of dittay against Ailsie Gourlay,—(for it is some comfort to know that the old hag was tried, condemned, and burned on the top of North-Berwick Law, by sentence of a commission from the Privy Council,)*—I find, I say, it was charged against her, among other offences, that she had, by the aid and delusions of Satan, shown to a young person of quality, in a mirror glass, a gentleman then abroad, to whom the said young person was betrothed, and who appeared in the vision to be in the act of bestowing his hand upon another lady.* But this and some other parts of the record appear to have been studiously left imperfect in names and dates, probably out of regard to the honour of the families concerned. If Dame Gourlay was able actually to play off such a piece of jugglery, it is clear she must have had better assistance to practise the deception, than her own skill or funds could supply. Meanwhile, this mysterious visionary traffic had its usual effect, in unsettling Miss Ashton's mind. Her temper became unequal, her health decayed daily, her manners grew moping, melancholy, and uncertain. Her father, guessing partly at the cause of these appearances, and exerting a degree of authority unusual with him, made a point of banishing Dame Gourlay from the castle; but the arrow was shot, and was rankling barb-deep in the side of the wounded deer.

It was shortly after the departure of this woman, that Lucy Ashton, urged by her parents, announced to them, with a vivacity by which they were startled, 'that she was conscious heaven and earth and hell had set themselves against her union with

Ravenswood; still her contract,' she said, 'was a binding contract, and she neither would nor could resign it without the consent of Ravenswood. Let me be assured,' she concluded, 'that he will free me from my engagement, and dispose of me as you please, I care not how. When the diamonds are gone, what signifies the casket?'

The tone of obstinacy with which this was said, her eyes flashing with unnatural light, and her hands firmly clenched, precluded the possibility of dispute; and the utmost length which Lady Ashton's art could attain, only got her the privilege of dictating the letter, by which her daughter required to know of Ravenswood whether he intended to abide by, or to surrender, what she termed, 'their unfortunate engagement.' Of this advantage Lady Ashton so far and so ingeniously availed herself, that, according to the wording of the letter, the reader would have supposed Lucy was calling upon her lover to renounce a contract which was contrary to the interests and inclinations of both. Not trusting even to this point of deception, Lady Ashton finally determined to suppress the letter altogether, in hopes that Lucy's impatience would induce her to condemn Ravenswood unheard and in absence. In this she was disappointed. The time, indeed, had long elapsed, when an answer should have been received from the Continent. The faint ray of hope which still glimmered in Lucy's mind was wellnigh extinguished. But the idea never forsook her, that her letter might not have been duly forwarded. One of her mother's new machinations unexpectedly furnished her with the means of ascertaining what she most desired to know.

The female agent of hell having been dismissed from the castle, Lady Ashton, who wrought by all variety of means, resolved to employ, for working the same end on Lucy's mind, an agent of a very different character. This was no other than the Reverend Mr Bide-the-bent, a Presbyterian clergyman, formerly mentioned, of the very strictest order, and the most rigid orthodoxy, whose aid she called in, upon the principle of the tyrant in the tragedy:—

> 'I'll have a priest shall preach her from her faith,
> And make it sin not to renounce that vow,
> Which I'd have broken.'*

But Lady Ashton was mistaken in the agent she had selected. His prejudices, indeed, were easily enlisted on her side, and it was no difficult matter to make him regard with horror the prospect of a union betwixt the daughter of a God-fearing, professing, and Presbyterian family of distinction, with the heir of a bloodthirsty prelatist and persecutor, the hands of whose fathers had been dyed to the wrists in the blood of God's saints. This resembled, in the divine's opinion, the union of a Moabitish stranger with a daughter of Zion.* But with all the more severe prejudices and principles of his sect, Bide-the-bent possessed a sound judgment, and had learnt sympathy even in that very school of persecution, where the heart is so frequently hardened. In a private interview with Miss Ashton, he was deeply moved by her distress, and could not but admit the justice of her request to be permitted a direct communication with Ravenswood, upon the subject of their solemn contract. When she urged to him the great uncertainty under which she laboured, whether her letter had been ever forwarded, the old man paced the room with long steps, shook his grey head, rested repeatedly for a space on his ivory-headed staff, and, after much hesitation, confessed that he thought her doubts so reasonable, that he would himself aid in the removal of them.

'I cannot but opine, Miss Lucy,' he said, 'that your worshipful lady mother hath in this matter an eagerness, whilk, although it ariseth doubtless from love to your best interests here and here-after,—for the man is of persecuting blood, and himself a perse-cutor, a cavalier or malignant, and a scoffer, who hath no inheritance in Jesse,*—nevertheless, we are commanded to do justice unto all, and to fulfil our bond and covenant, as well to the stranger, as to him who is in brotherhood with us.* Wherefore myself, even I myself, will be aiding unto the delivery of your letter to the man Edgar Ravenswood, trusting that the issue thereof may be your deliverance from the nets in which he hath sinfully engaged you. And that I may do in this neither more nor less than hath been warranted by your honourable parents, I pray you to transcribe, without increment or subtraction, the letter formerly expeded under the dictation of your right honourable mother; and I shall put it into such sure course of being delivered, that if, honoured young madam, you shall receive no answer, it will be necessary that you conclude that the man meaneth in silence to abandon that naughty contract, which, peradventure, he may be unwilling directly to restore.'

Lucy eagerly embraced the expedient of the worthy divine. A new letter was written in the precise terms of the former, and consigned by Mr Bide-the-bent to the charge of Saunders Moonshine, a zealous elder of the church when on shore, and, when on board his brig, as bold a smuggler as ever ran out a sliding bowsprit to the winds that blow betwixt Campvere and the east coast of Scotland.* At the recommendation of his pastor, Saunders readily undertook that the letter should be securely conveyed to the Master of Ravenswood at the court where he now resided.

This retrospect became necessary to explain the conference betwixt Miss Ashton, her mother, and Bucklaw, which we have detailed in a preceding chapter.

Lucy was now like the sailor, who, while drifting through a tempestuous ocean, clings for safety to a single plank, his powers of grasping it becoming every moment more feeble, and the deep darkness of the night only checkered by the flashes of lightning, hissing as they show the white tops of the billows, in which he is soon to be engulfed.

Week crept away after week, and day after day. St Jude's day arrived, the last and protracted term to which Lucy had limited herself, and there was neither letter nor news of Ravenswood.

CHAPTER XXXII

How fair these names, how much unlike they look
To all the blurr'd subscriptions in my book!
The bridegroom's letters stand in row above,
Tapering, yet straight, like pine-trees in his grove;
While free and fine the bride's appear below,
As light and slender as her jessamines grow.

(Crabbe)*

St jude's day came, the term assigned by Lucy herself as the furthest date of expectation, and, as we have already said, there were neither letters from, nor news of, Ravenswood. But there were news of Bucklaw, and of his trusty associate Craigengelt, who arrived early in the morning for the completion of the proposed espousals, and for signing the necessary deeds.

These had been carefully prepared under the revisal of Sir William Ashton himself, it having been resolved, on account of the state of Miss Ashton's health, as it was said, that none save the parties immediately interested should be present when the parchments were subscribed. It was further determined, that the marriage should be solemnized upon the fourth day after signing the articles, a measure adopted by Lady Ashton, in order that Lucy might have as little time as possible to recede, or relapse into intractability. There was no appearance, however, of her doing either. She heard the proposed arrangement with the calm indifference of despair, or rather with an apathy arising from the oppressed and stupified state of her feelings. To an eye so unobserving as that of Bucklaw, her demeanour had little more of reluctance than might suit the character of a bashful young lady, who, however, he could not disguise from himself, was complying with the choice of her friends, rather than exercising any personal predilection in his favour.

When the morning compliments of the bridegroom had been paid, Miss Ashton was left for some time to herself; her mother remarking, that the deeds must be signed before the hour of noon, in order that the marriage might be happy.

Lucy suffered herself to be attired for the occasion as the taste of her attendants suggested, and was of course splendidly arrayed. Her dress was composed of white satin and Brussels lace, and her hair arranged with a profusion of jewels, whose lustre made a strange contrast to the deadly paleness of her complexion, and to the trouble which dwelt in her unsettled eye.

Her toilette was hardly finished, ere Henry appeared, to conduct the passive bride to the state apartment, where all was prepared for signing the contract. 'Do you know, sister,' he said, 'I am glad you are to have Bucklaw after all, instead of Ravenswood, who looked like a Spanish grandee come to cut our throats, and trample our bodies under foot. And I am glad the broad seas are between us this day, for I shall never forget how frightened I was when I took him for the picture of old Sir Malise walked out of the canvass. Tell me true, are you not glad to be fairly shot of him?'

'Ask me no questions, dear Henry,' said his unfortunate sister; 'there is little more can happen to make me either glad or sorry in this world.'

'And that's what all young brides say,' said Henry; 'and so do not be cast down, Lucy, for you'll tell another tale a twelvemonth hence—and I am to be bride's-man, and ride before you to the kirk, and all our kith, kin, and allies, and all Bucklaw's, are to be mounted and in order—and I am to have a scarlet laced coat, and a feathered hat, and a sword-belt, double bordered with gold, and *point d'espagne*, and a dagger instead of a sword; and I should like a sword much better, but my father won't hear of it. All my things, and a hundred besides, are to come out from Edinburgh to-night with old Gilbert, and the sumpter mules—and I will bring them, and show them to you the instant they come.'

The boy's chatter was here interrupted by the arrival of Lady Ashton, somewhat alarmed at her daughter's stay. With one of her sweetest smiles, she took Lucy's arm under her own, and led her to the apartment where her presence was expected.

There were only present, Sir William Ashton, and Colonel Douglas Ashton, the last in full regimentals—Bucklaw, in bridegroom trim—Craigengelt, freshly equipt from top to toe by the bounty of his patron, and bedizened with as much lace as might have become the dress of the Copper Captain,* together with the Rev. Mr Bide-the-bent; the presence of a minister being, in strict Presbyterian families, an indispensable requisite upon all occasions of unusual solemnity.

Wines and refreshments were placed on a table, on which the writings were displayed, ready for signature.

But before proceeding either to business or refreshment, Mr Bide-the-bent, at a signal from Sir William Ashton, invited the company to join him in a short extemporary prayer, in which he implored a blessing upon the contract now to be solemnized between the honourable parties then present. With the simplicity of his times and profession, which permitted strong personal allusions, he petitioned, that the wounded mind of one of these noble parties might be healed, in reward of her compliance with the advice of her right honourable parents; and that, as she had proved herself a child after God's commandment, by honouring her father and mother, she and hers might enjoy the promised blessing—length of days in the land here, and a happy portion hereafter in a better country.* He prayed farther, that the bride-groom might be weaned from those follies which seduce youth from the path of knowledge; that he might cease to take delight in vain and unprofitable company, scoffers, rioters, and those who sit late at the wine, (here Bucklaw winked to Craigengelt,) and cease from the society that causeth to err. A suitable supplication in behalf of Sir William and Lady Ashton, and their family, concluded this religious address, which thus embraced every individual present, excepting Craigengelt, whom the worthy divine probably considered as past all hopes of grace.

The business of the day now went forward; Sir William Ashton signed the contract with legal solemnity and precision; his son, with military *nonchalance*; and Bucklaw, having subscribed as rapidly as Craigengelt could manage to turn the leaves, concluded by wiping his pen on that worthy's new laced cravat.

It was now Miss Ashton's turn to sign the writings, and she was guided by her watchful mother to the table for that purpose. At her first attempt, she began to write with a dry pen, and when the circumstance was pointed out, seemed unable, after several attempts, to dip it in the massive silver ink-standish, which stood full before her. Lady Ashton's vigilance hastened to supply the deficiency. I have myself seen the fatal deed, and in the distinct characters in which the name of Lucy Ashton is traced on each page, there is only a very slight tremulous irregularity, indicative of her state of mind at the time of the subscription.* But the last signature is incomplete, defaced and blotted; for, while her hand was employed in tracing it, the hasty tramp of a horse was heard at the gate, succeeded by a step in the outer gallery, and a voice, which, in a commanding tone, bore down the opposition of the menials. The pen dropped from Lucy's fingers, as she exclaimed with a faint shriek—'He is come—he is come!'

CHAPTER XXXIII

This by his tongue should be a Montague!
Fetch me my rapier, boy;
Now, by the faith and honour of my kin,
To strike him dead I hold it not a sin.

(Romeo and Juliet)*

HARDLY had Miss Ashton dropped the pen, when the door of the apartment flew open, and the Master of Ravenswood entered the apartment.

Lockhard and another domestic, who had in vain attempted to oppose his passage through the gallery or antechamber, were seen standing on the threshold transfixed with surprise, which was instantly communicated to the whole party in the state-room. That of Colonel Douglas Ashton was mingled with resentment; that of Bucklaw, with haughty and affected indifference; the rest, even Lady Ashton herself, showed signs of fear, and Lucy seemed stiffened to stone by this unexpected apparition. Apparition it might well be termed, for Ravenswood had more the appearance of one returned from the dead, than of a living visitor.

He planted himself full in the middle of the apartment, opposite to the table at which Lucy was seated, on whom, as if she had been alone in the chamber, he bent his eyes with a mingled expression of deep grief and deliberate indignation. His dark-coloured riding cloak, displaced from one shoulder, hung around one side of his person in the ample folds of the Spanish mantle. The rest of his rich dress was travel-soil'd, and deranged by hard riding. He had a sword by his side, and pistols in his belt. His slouched hat, which he had not removed at entrance, gave an additional gloom to his dark features, which, wasted by sorrow, and marked by the ghastly look communicated by long illness, added to a countenance naturally somewhat stern and wild, a fierce and even savage expression. The matted and dishevelled locks of hair which escaped from under his hat, together with his fixed and unmoved posture, made his head more resemble that of a marble bust than that of a living man. He said not a single word, and there was a deep silence in the company for more than two minutes.

It was broken by Lady Ashton, who in that space partly recovered her natural audacity. She demanded to know the cause of this unauthorized intrusion.

'That is a question, madam,' said her son, 'which I have the best right to ask—and I must request of the Master of Ravenswood to follow me, where he can answer it at leisure.'

Bucklaw interposed, saying, 'No man on earth should usurp his previous right in demanding an explanation from the Master.— Craigengelt,' he added, in an under tone, 'd—n ye, why do you stand staring as if you saw a ghost? fetch me my sword from the gallery.'

'I will relinquish to none,' said Colonel Ashton, 'my right of calling to account the man who has offered this unparalleled affront to my family.'

'Be patient, gentlemen,' said Ravenswood, turning sternly towards them, and waving his hand as if to impose silence on their altercation. 'If you are as weary of your lives as I am, I will find time and place to pledge mine against one or both; at present, I have no leisure for the disputes of triflers.'

'Triflers!' echoed Colonel Ashton, half unsheathing his sword, while Bucklaw laid his hand on the hilt of that which Craigengelt had just reached him.

Sir William Ashton, alarmed for his son's safety, rushed between the young men and Ravenswood, exclaiming, 'My son, I command you—Bucklaw, I entreat you—keep the peace, in the name of the Queen and of the law!'

'In the name of the law of God,' said Bide-the-bent, advancing also with uplifted hands between Bucklaw, the Colonel, and the object of their resentment—'In the name of Him who brought peace on earth, and good-will to mankind, I implore—I beseech—I command you to forbear violence towards each other! God hateth the bloodthirsty man—he who striketh with the sword, shall perish with the sword.'*

'Do you take me for a dog, sir,' said Colonel Ashton, turning fiercely upon him, 'or something more brutally stupid, to endure this insult in my father's house?—Let me go, Bucklaw! He shall account to me, or, by Heaven, I will stab him where he stands!'

'You shall not touch him here,' said Bucklaw; 'he once gave me my life, and were he the devil come to fly away with the whole house and generation, he shall have nothing but fair play.'

The passions of the two young men thus counteracting each other, gave Ravenswood leisure to exclaim, in a stern and steady voice, 'Silence!—let him who really seeks danger, take the fitting time when it is to be found; my mission here will be shortly accomplished.—Is *that* your handwriting, madam?' he added in a softer tone, extending towards Miss Ashton her last letter.

A faltering 'Yes,' seemed rather to escape from her lips, than to be uttered as a voluntary answer.

'And is *this* also your handwriting?' extending towards her the mutual engagement.

Lucy remained silent. Terror, and a yet stronger and more confused feeling, so utterly disturbed her understanding, that she probably scarcely comprehended the question that was put to her.

'If you design,' said Sir William Ashton, 'to found any legal claim on that paper, sir, do not expect to receive any answer to an extrajudicial question.'

'Sir William Ashton,' said Ravenswood, 'I pray you, and all who hear me, that you will not mistake my purpose. If this young lady, of her own free will, desires the restoration of this contract, as her letter would seem to imply—there is not a withered leaf which this autumn wind strews on the heath, that is more valueless in my eyes. But I must and will hear the truth from her own mouth—without this satisfaction I will not leave this spot. Murder me by numbers you possibly may; but I am an armed man—I am a desperate man—and I will not die without ample vengeance. This is my resolution, take it as you may. I WILL hear her determination from her own mouth; from her own mouth, alone, and without witnesses, will I hear it. Now, choose,' he said, drawing his sword with the right hand, and, with the left, by the same motion taking a pistol from his belt and cocking it, but turning the point of one weapon and the muzzle of the other to the ground,—'Choose if you will have this hall floated with blood, or if you will grant me the decisive interview with my affianced bride, which the laws of God and the country alike entitle me to demand.'

All recoiled at the sound of his voice, and the determined action by which it was accompanied; for the ecstasy of real desperation seldom fails to overpower the less energetic passions by which it may be opposed. The clergyman was the first to speak. 'In the name of God,' he said, 'receive an overture of peace from the meanest of his servants. What this honourable person demands, albeit it is urged with over violence, hath yet in it something of reason. Let him hear from Miss Lucy's own lips that she hath dutifully acceded to the will of her parents, and repenteth her of her covenant with him; and when he is assured of this, he will depart in peace unto his own dwelling, and cumber us no more. Alas! the workings of the ancient Adam are strong even in the regenerate—surely we should have long suffering with those who, being yet in the gall of bitterness and bond of iniquity, are swept forward by the uncontrollable current of worldly passion.* Let, then, the Master of Ravenswood have the interview on which he insisteth; it can but be as a passing pang to this honourable maiden, since her faith is now irrevocably pledged to the choice of her parents. Let it, I say, be thus: it belongeth to my functions to entreat your honour's compliance with this healing overture.'

'Never!' answered Lady Ashton, whose rage had now over-come her first surprise and terror—'never shall this man speak in private with my daughter, the affianced bride of another! Pass from this room who will, I remain here. I fear neither his violence nor his weapons, though some,' she said, glancing a look towards Colonel Ashton, 'who bear my name, appear more moved by them.'

'For God's sake, madam,' answered the worthy divine, 'add not fuel to firebrands. The Master of Ravenswood cannot, I am sure, object to your presence, the young lady's state of health being considered, and your maternal duty. I myself will also tarry; peradventure my grey hairs may turn away wrath.'*

'You are welcome to do so, sir,' said Ravenswood; 'and Lady Ashton is also welcome to remain, if she shall think proper; but let all others depart.'

'Ravenswood,' said Colonel Ashton, crossing him as he went out, 'you shall account for this ere long.'

'When you please,' replied Ravenswood.

'But I,' said Bucklaw, with a half smile, 'have a prior demand on your leisure, a claim of some standing.'

'Arrange it as you will,' said Ravenswood; 'leave me but this day in peace, and I will have no dearer employment on earth, to-morrow, than to give you all the satisfaction you can desire.'

The other gentlemen left the apartment; but Sir William Ashton lingered.

'Master of Ravenswood,' he said, in a conciliating tone, 'I think I have not deserved that you should make this scandal and outrage in my family. If you will sheathe your sword, and retire with me into my study, I will prove to you, by the most satisfactory arguments, the inutility of your present irregular procedure'——

'To-morrow, sir—to-morrow—to-morrow,* I will hear you at length,' reiterated Ravenswood, interrupting him; 'this day hath its own sacred and indispensable business.'

He pointed to the door, and Sir William left the apartment.

Ravenswood sheathed his sword, uncocked and returned his pistol to his belt, walked deliberately to the door of the apartment, which he bolted—returned, raised his hat from his forehead, and, gazing upon Lucy with eyes in which an expression of sorrow overcame their late fierceness, spread his dishevelled locks back from his face, and said, 'Do you know me, Miss Ashton?—I am still Edgar Ravenswood.' She was silent, and he went on with increasing vehemence—'I am still that Edgar Ravenswood, who, for your affection, renounced the dear ties by which injured honour bound him to seek vengeance. I am that Ravenswood, who, for your sake, forgave, nay, clasped hands in friendship with the oppressor and pillager of his house—the traducer and murderer of his father.'

'My daughter,' answered Lady Ashton, interrupting him, 'has no occasion to dispute the identity of your person; the venom of your present language is sufficient to remind her, that she speaks with the mortal enemy of her father.'

'I pray you to be patient, madam,' answered Ravenswood; 'my answer must come from her own lips.—Once more, Miss Lucy

Ashton, I am that Ravenswood to whom you granted the solemn engagement, which you now desire to retract and cancel.'

Lucy's bloodless lips could only falter out the words, 'It was my mother.'

'She speaks truly,' said Lady Ashton, 'it *was* I, who, authorized alike by the laws of God and man, advised her, and concurred with her, to set aside an unhappy and precipitate engagement, and to annul it by the authority of Scripture itself.'

'Scripture!' said Ravenswood, scornfully.

'Let him hear the text,' said Lady Ashton, appealing to the divine, 'on which you yourself, with cautious reluctance, declared the nullity of the pretended engagement insisted upon by this violent man.'

The clergyman took his clasped Bible from his pocket, and read the following words: '*If a woman vow a vow unto the Lord, and bind herself by a bond, being in her father's house in her youth; and her father hear her vow, and her bond wherewith she hath bound her soul, and her father shall hold his peace at her: then all her vows shall stand, and every vow wherewith she hath bound her soul shall stand.*'

'And was it not even so with us?' interrupted Ravenswood.

'Control thy impatience, young man,' answered the divine, 'and hear what follows in the sacred text:—"*But if her father disallow her in the day that he heareth; not any of her vows, or of her bonds wherewith she hath bound her soul, shall stand: and the Lord shall forgive her, because her father disallowed her.*" '*

'And was not,' said Lady Ashton, fiercely and triumphantly breaking in,—'was not ours the case stated in the holy writ?—Will this person deny, that the instant her parents heard of the vow, or bond, by which our daughter had bound her soul, we disallowed the same in the most express terms, and informed him by writing of our determination?'

'And is this all?' said Ravenswood, looking at Lucy—'Are you willing to barter sworn faith, the exercise of free will, and the feelings of mutual affection, to this wretched hypocritical sophistry?'

'Hear him!' said Lady Ashton, looking to the clergyman—'hear the blasphemer!'

'May God forgive him,' said Bide-the-bent, 'and enlighten his ignorance!'

'Hear what I have sacrificed for you,' said Ravenswood, still addressing Lucy, 'ere you sanction what has been done in your name. The honour of an ancient family, the urgent advice of my best friends, have been in vain used to sway my resolution; neither the arguments of reason, nor the portents of superstition, have shaken my fidelity. The very dead have arisen to warn me, and their warning has been despised. Are you prepared to pierce my heart for its fidelity, with the very weapon which my rash confidence intrusted to your grasp?'

'Master of Ravenswood,' said Lady Ashton, 'you have asked what questions you thought fit. You see the total incapacity of my daughter to answer you. But I will reply for her, and in a manner which you cannot dispute. You desire to know whether Lucy Ashton, of her own free will, desires to annul the engagement into which she has been trepanned. You have her letter under her own hand, demanding the surrender of it; and, in yet more full evidence of her purpose, here is the contract which she has this morning subscribed, in presence of this reverend gentleman, with Mr Hayston of Bucklaw.'

Ravenswood gazed upon the deed, as if petrified. 'And it was without fraud or compulsion,' said he, looking towards the clergyman, 'that Miss Ashton subscribed this parchment?'

'I vouch it upon my sacred character.'

'This is indeed, madam, an undeniable piece of evidence,' said Ravenswood, sternly; 'and it will be equally unnecessary and dishonourable to waste another word in useless remonstrance or reproach. There, madam,' he said, laying down before Lucy the signed paper and the broken piece of gold—'there are the evidences of your first engagement; may you be more faithful to that which you have just formed. I will trouble you to return the corresponding tokens of my ill-placed confidence—I ought rather to say, of my egregious folly.'

Lucy returned the scornful glance of her lover with a gaze, from which perception seemed to have been banished; yet she seemed partly to have understood his meaning, for she raised her hands as if to undo a blue ribbon which she wore around her neck. She was unable to accomplish her purpose, but Lady Ashton cut the ribbon asunder, and detached the broken piece of gold which Miss Ashton had till then worn concealed in her bosom; the written counterpart of the lovers' engagement she for some time had had in her own possession. With a haughty curtsy, she delivered both to Ravenswood, who was much softened when he took the piece of gold.

'And she could wear it thus,' he said—speaking to himself— 'could wear it in her very bosom—could wear it next to her heart—even when—But complaint avails not,' he said, dashing from his eye the tear which had gathered in it, and resuming the stern composure of his manner. He strode to the chimney, and threw into the fire the paper and piece of gold, stamping upon the coals with the heel of his boot, as if to insure their destruction. 'I will be no longer,' he then said, 'an intruder here—Your evil wishes, and your worse offices, Lady Ashton, I will only return, by hoping these will be your last machinations against your daughter's honour and happiness.—And to you, madam,' he said, addressing Lucy, 'I have nothing farther to say, except to pray to God that you may not become a world's wonder for this act of wilful and deliberate perjury.'—Having uttered these words, he turned on his heel, and left the apartment.

Sir William Ashton, by entreaty and authority, had detained his son and Bucklaw in a distant part of the castle, in order to prevent their again meeting with Ravenswood; but as the Master descended the great staircase, Lockhard delivered him a billet, signed Sholto Douglas Ashton, requesting to know where the Master of Ravenswood would be heard of four or five days from hence, as the writer had business of weight to settle with him, so soon as an important family event had taken place.

'Tell Colonel Ashton,' said Ravenswood, composedly, 'I shall be found at Wolf's Crag when his leisure serves him.'

As he descended the outward stair which led from the terrace, he was a second time interrupted by Craigengelt, who, on the part of his principal, the Laird of Bucklaw, expressed a hope, that Ravenswood would not leave Scotland within ten days at least, as he had both former and recent civilities for which to express his gratitude.

'Tell your master,' said Ravenswood, fiercely, 'to choose his own time. He will find me at Wolf's Crag, if his purpose is not forestalled.'

'*My* master?' replied Craigengelt, encouraged by seeing Colonel Ashton and Bucklaw at the bottom of the terrace; 'give me leave to say, I know of no such person upon earth, nor will I permit such language to be used to me!'

'Seek your master, then, in hell!' exclaimed Ravenswood, giving way to the passion he had hitherto restrained, and throwing Craigengelt from him with such violence, that he rolled down the steps, and lay senseless at the foot of them.—'I am a fool,' he instantly added, 'to vent my passion upon a caitiff so worthless.'

He then mounted his horse, which at his arrival he had secured to a balustrade in front of the castle, rode very slowly past Bucklaw and Colonel Ashton, raising his hat as he passed each, and looking in their faces steadily while he offered this mute salutation, which was returned by both with the same stern gravity. Ravenswood walked on with equal deliberation until he reached the head of the avenue, as if to show that he rather courted than avoided interruption. When he had passed the upper gate, he turned his horse, and looked at the castle with a fixed eye; then set spurs to his good steed, and departed with the speed of a demon dismissed by the exorcist.

CHAPTER XXXIV

Who comes from the bridal chamber?
It is Azrael, the angel of death.

(*Thalaba*)*

AFTER the dreadful scene that had taken place at the castle, Lucy was transported to her own chamber, where she remained for some time in a state of absolute stupor. Yet afterwards, in the course of the ensuing day, she seemed to have recovered, not merely her spirits and resolution, but a sort of flighty levity, that was foreign to her character and situation, and which was at times chequered by fits of deep silence and melancholy, and of capricious pettishness. Lady Ashton became much alarmed, and consulted the family physicians. But as her pulse indicated no change, they could only say that the disease was on the spirits, and recommended gentle exercise and amusement. Miss Ashton never alluded to what had passed in the state-room. It seemed doubtful even if she was conscious of it, for she was often observed to raise her hands to her neck, as if in search of the ribbon that had been taken from it, and mutter, in surprise and discontent, when she could not find it, 'It was the link that bound me to life.'

Notwithstanding all these remarkable symptoms, Lady Ashton was too deeply pledged, to delay her daughter's marriage even in her present state of health. It cost her much trouble to keep up the fair side of appearances towards Bucklaw. She was well aware, that if he once saw any reluctance on her daughter's part, he would break off the treaty, to her great personal shame and dishonour. She therefore resolved, that, if Lucy continued passive, the marriage should take place upon the day that had been previously fixed, trusting that a change of place, of situation, and of character, would operate a more speedy and effectual cure upon the unsettled spirits of her daughter, than could be attained by the slow measures which the medical men recommended. Sir William

Ashton's views of family aggrandisement, and his desire to strengthen himself against the measures of the Marquis of A——, readily induced him to acquiesce in what he could not have perhaps resisted if willing to do so. As for the young men, Bucklaw and Colonel Ashton, they protested, that after what had happened, it would be most dishonourable to postpone for a single hour the time appointed for the marriage, as it would be generally ascribed to their being intimidated by the intrusive visit and threats of Ravenswood.

Bucklaw would indeed have been incapable of such precipitation, had he been aware of the state of Miss Ashton's health, or rather of her mind. But custom, upon these occasions, permitted only brief and sparing intercourse between the bridegroom and the betrothed; a circumstance so well improved by Lady Ashton, that Bucklaw neither saw nor suspected the real state of the health and feelings of his unhappy bride.*

On the eve of the bridal day, Lucy appeared to have one of her fits of levity, and surveyed with a degree of girlish interest the various preparations of dress, &c. &c., which the different members of the family had prepared for the occasion.

The morning dawned bright and cheerily. The bridal guests assembled in gallant troops from distant quarters. Not only the relations of Sir William Ashton, and the still more dignified connexions of his lady, together with the numerous kinsmen and allies of the bridegroom, were present upon this joyful ceremony, gallantly mounted, arrayed, and caparisoned, but almost every presbyterian family of distinction, within fifty miles, made a point of attendance upon an occasion which was considered as giving a sort of triumph over the Marquis of A——, in the person of his kinsman. Splendid refreshments awaited the guests on their arrival, and after these were finished, the cry was to horse. The bride was led forth betwixt her brother Henry and her mother. Her gaiety of the preceding day had given rise to a deep shade of melancholy, which, however, did not misbecome an occasion so momentous. There was a light in her eyes, and a colour in her cheek, which had not been kindled for many a day, and which, joined to her great beauty, and the splendour of her dress, occasioned her entrance to be greeted with an universal murmur of applause, in which even the ladies could not refrain from joining. While the cavalcade were getting to horse, Sir William Ashton, a man of peace and of form, censured his son Henry for having begirt himself with a military sword of preposterous length, belonging to his brother, Colonel Ashton.

'If you must have a weapon,' he said, 'upon such a peaceful occasion, why did you not use the short poniard sent from Edinburgh on purpose?'

The boy vindicated himself, by saying it was lost.

'You put it out of the way yourself, I suppose,' said his father, 'out of ambition to wear that preposterous thing, which might have served Sir William Wallace—But never mind, get to horse now, and take care of your sister.'

The boy did so, and was placed in the centre of the gallant train. At the time, he was too full of his own appearance, his sword, his laced cloak, his feathered hat, and his managed horse, to pay much regard to any thing else; but he afterwards remembered to the hour of his death, that when the hand of his sister, by which she supported herself on the pillion behind him, touched his own, it felt as wet and cold as sepulchral marble.

Glancing wide over hill and dale, the fair bridal procession at last reached the parish church, which they nearly filled; for, besides domestics, above a hundred gentlemen and ladies were present upon the occasion. The marriage ceremony was performed according to the rites of the Presbyterian persuasion, to which Bucklaw of late had judged it proper to conform.

On the outside of the church, a liberal dole was distributed to the poor of the neighbouring parishes, under the direction of Johnny Mortsheugh, who had lately been promoted from his desolate quarters at the Hermitage, to fill the more eligible situation of sexton at the parish church of Ravenswood. Dame Gourlay, with two of her contemporaries, the same who assisted at Alice's late-wake, seated apart upon a flat monument, or *through-stane*, sate enviously comparing the shares which had been allotted to them in dividing the dole.

'Johnny Mortsheugh,' said Annie Winnie, 'might hae minded auld lang syne, and thought of his auld kimmers, for as braw as he is with his new black coat. I hae gotten but five herring instead o' sax, and this disna look like a gude saxpennys, and I daresay this bit morsel o' beef is an unce lighter than ony that's been dealt round; and it's a bit o' the tenony hough, mair by token, that yours, Maggie, is out o' the back sey.'

'Mine, quo' she?' mumbled the paralytic hag, 'mine is half banes, I trow. If grit folk gie poor bodies ony thing for coming to their weddings and burials, it suld be something that wad do them gude, I think.'

'Their gifts,' said Ailsie Gourlay, 'are dealt for nae love of us—nor out of respect for whether we feed or starve. They wad gie us whinstanes for loaves, if it would serve their ain vanity, and yet they expect us to be as gratefu', as they ca' it, as if they served us for true love and liking.'

'And that's truly said,' answered her companion.

'But, Ailsie Gourlay, ye're the auldest o' us three, did ye ever see a mair grand bridal?'

'I winna say that I have,' answered the hag; 'but I think soon to see as braw a burial.'

'And that wad please me as weel,' said Annie Winnie; 'for there's as large a dole, and folk are no obliged to girn and laugh, and mak murgeons, and wish joy to these hellicat quality, that lord it ower us like brute beasts. I like to pack the dead-dole in my lap, and rin ower my auld rhyme,—

> "My loaf in my lap, my penny in my purse,
> Thou art ne'er the better, and I'm ne'er the worse." '[28] *

'That's right, Annie,' said the paralytic woman; 'God send us a green Yule and a fat kirkyard!' *

'But I wad like to ken, Lucky Gourlay, for ye're the auldest and wisest amang us, whilk o' these revellers' turns it will be to be streekit first?'

'D'ye see yon dandilly maiden,' said Dame Gourlay, 'a' glistenin' wi' goud and jewels, that they are lifting up on the white horse behind that harebrained callant in scarlet, wi' the lang sword at his side?'

'But that's the bride!' said her companion, her cold heart touched with some sort of compassion; 'that's the very bride hersell! Eh, whow! sae young, sae braw, and sae bonny—and is her time sae short?'

'I tell ye,' said the sibyl, 'her winding sheet is up as high as her throat already, believe it wha list.* Her sand has but few grains to rin out, and nae wonder—they've been weel shaken. The leaves are withering fast on the trees, but she'll never see the Martinmas wind gar them dance in swirls like the fairy rings.'

'Ye waited on her for a quarter,' said the paralytic woman, 'and got twa red pieces, or I am far beguiled.'

'Ay, ay,' answered Ailsie, with a bitter grin; 'and Sir William Ashton promised me a bonny red gown to the boot o' that—a stake, and a chain, and a tar barrel, lass!—what think ye o' that for a propine?—for being up early and doun late for fourscore nights and mair wi' his dwining daughter. But he may keep it for his ain leddy, cummers.'

'I hae heard a sough,' said Annie Winnie, 'as if Leddy Ashton was nae canny body.'

'D'ye see her yonder,' said Dame Gourlay, 'as she prances on her grey gelding out at the kirkyard?—there's mair o' utter deevilry in that woman, as brave and fair-fashioned as she rides yonder, than in a' the Scotch witches that ever flew by moonlight ower North-Berwick Law.'*

'What's that ye say about witches, ye damned hags?' said Johnny Mortsheugh; 'are ye casting yer cantrips in the very kirkyard, to mischieve the bride and bridegroom? Get awa hame, for if I tak my souple t'ye, I'll gar ye find the road faster than ye wad like.'

'Hech, sirs!' answered Ailsie Gourlay; 'how bra' are we wi' our new black coat and our weel-pouthered head, as if we had never kend hunger nor thirst oursells! and we'll be screwing up our bit fiddle, doubtless, in the ha' the night, amang a' the other elbo'-jiggers for miles round. Let's see if the pins haud, Johnny—that's a', lad.'

'I take ye a' to witness, gude people,' said Mortsheugh, 'that she threatens me wi' mischief, and forespeaks me. If ony thing but gude happens to me or my fiddle this night, I'll make it the blackest night's job she ever stirred in. I'll hae her before Presbytery and Synod*—I'm half a minister mysell, now that I'm a bedral in an inhabited parish.'

Although the mutual hatred betwixt these hags and the rest of mankind had steeled their hearts against all impressions of festivity, this was by no means the case with the multitude at large. The splendour of the bridal retinue—the gay dresses—the spirited horses—the blithesome appearance of the handsome women and gallant gentlemen assembled upon the occasion, had the usual effect upon the minds of the populace. The repeated shouts, of 'Ashton and Bucklaw for ever!'—the discharge of pistols, guns, and musketoons, to give what was called the bridal-shot, evinced the interest the people took in the occasion of the cavalcade, as they accompanied it upon their return to the castle. If there was here and there an elder peasant or his wife who sneered at the pomp of the upstart family, and remembered the days of the long-descended Ravenswoods, even they, attracted by the plentiful cheer which the castle that day afforded to rich and poor, held their way thither, and acknowledged, notwithstanding their prejudices, the influence of *l'Amphitrion où l'on dîne.* *

Thus accompanied with the attendance both of rich and poor, Lucy returned to her father's house. Bucklaw used his privilege of riding next to the bride, but, new to such a situation, rather endeavoured to attract attention by the display of his person and horsemanship, than by any attempt to address her in private. They reached the castle in safety, amid a thousand joyous acclamations.

It is well known, that the weddings of ancient days were celebrated with a festive publicity rejected by the delicacy of modern times. * The marriage-guests, on the present occasion, were regaled with a banquet of unbounded profusion, the relics of which, after the domestics had feasted in their turn, were distributed among the shouting crowd, with as many barrels of ale as made the hilarity without correspond to that within the castle. The gentlemen, according to the fashion of the times, indulged, for the most part, in deep draughts of the richest wines, while the ladies, prepared for the ball which always closed a bridal entertainment, impatiently expected their arrival in the state gallery. At length the social party broke up at a late hour, and the gentlemen crowded into the saloon, where, enlivened by wine and the joyful occasion, they laid aside their swords, and handed their impatient partners to the floor. The music already rung from the gallery, along the fretted roof of the ancient state apartment. According to strict etiquette, the bride ought to have opened the ball, but Lady Ashton, making an apology on account of her daughter's health, offered her own hand to Bucklaw as substitute for her daughter's.

But as Lady Ashton raised her head gracefully, expecting the strain at which she was to begin the dance, she was so much struck by an unexpected alteration in the ornaments of the apartment, that she was surprised into an exclamation,—'Who has dared to change the pictures?'

All looked up, and those who knew the usual state of the apartment, observed, with surprise, that the picture of Sir William Ashton's father was removed from its place, and in its stead that of old Sir Malise Ravenswood seemed to frown wrath and vengeance upon the party assembled below. The exchange must have been made while the apartments were empty, but had not been observed until the torches and lights in the sconces were kindled for the ball. The haughty and heated spirits of the gentlemen led them to demand an immediate enquiry into the cause of what they deemed an affront to their host and to themselves; but Lady Ashton, recovering herself, passed it over as the freak of a crazy wench who was maintained about the castle, and whose susceptible imagination had been observed to be much affected by the stories which Dame Gourlay delighted to tell concerning 'the former family,' so Lady Ashton named the Ravenswoods. The obnoxious picture was immediately removed, and the ball was opened by Lady Ashton, with a grace and dignity which supplied the charms of youth, and almost verified the extravagant encomiums of the elder part of the company, who extolled her performance as far exceeding the dancing of the rising generation.

When Lady Ashton sat down, she was not surprised to find that her daughter had left the apartment, and she herself followed, eager to obviate any impression which might have been made upon her nerves by an incident so likely to affect them as the mysterious transposition of the portraits. Apparently she found her apprehensions groundless, for she returned in about an hour, and whispered the bridegroom, who extricated himself from the dancers, and vanished from the apartment. The instruments now played their loudest strains—the dancers pursued their exercise with all the enthusiasm inspired by youth, mirth, and high spirits, when a cry was heard so shrill and piercing, as at once to arrest the dance and the music. All stood motionless; but when the yell was again repeated, Colonel Ashton snatched a torch from the sconce, and demanding the key of the bridal-chamber from Henry, to whom, as bride's-man, it had been intrusted, rushed thither, followed by Sir William and Lady Ashton, and one or two others, near relations of the family. The bridal guests waited their return in stupified amazement.

Arrived at the door of the apartment, Colonel Ashton knocked and called, but received no answer except stifled groans. He hesitated no longer to open the door of the apartment, in which he found opposition from something which lay against it. When he had succeeded in opening it, the body of the bridegroom was found lying on the threshold of the bridal chamber, and all around was flooded with blood. A cry of surprise and horror was raised by all present; and the company, excited by this new alarm, began to rush tumultuously towards the sleeping apartment. Colonel Ashton, first whispering to his mother,—'Search for her—she has murdered him!' drew his sword, planted himself in the passage, and declared he would suffer no man to pass excepting the clergyman, and a medical person present. By their assistance, Bucklaw, who still breathed, was raised from the ground, and transported to another apartment, where his friends, full of suspicion and murmuring, assembled round him to learn the opinion of the surgeon.

In the meanwhile, Lady Ashton, her husband, and their assistants, in vain sought Lucy in the bridal bed and in the chamber. There was no private passage from the room, and they began to think that she must have thrown herself from the window, when one of the company, holding his torch lower than the rest, discovered something white in the corner of the great old-fashioned chimney of the apartment. Here they found the unfortunate girl, seated, or rather couched like a hare upon its form—her head-gear dishevelled; her night-clothes torn and dabbled with blood,—her eyes glazed, and her features convulsed into a wild paroxysm of insanity. When she saw herself discovered, she gibbered, made mouths, and pointed at them with her bloody fingers, with the frantic gestures of an exulting demoniac.

Female assistance was now hastily summoned; the unhappy bride was overpowered, not without the use of some force. As they carried her over the threshold, she looked down, and uttered the only articulate words that she had yet spoken, saying, with a sort of grinning exultation,—'So, you have ta'en up your bonny bridegroom?' She was by the shuddering assistants conveyed to another and more retired apartment, where she was secured as her situation required, and closely watched. The unutterable agony of the parents—the horror and confusion of all who were in the castle—the fury of contending passions between the friends of the different parties, passions augmented by previous intemperance, surpass description.

The surgeon was the first who obtained something like a patient hearing; he pronounced that the wound of Bucklaw, though severe and dangerous, was by no means fatal, but might readily be rendered so by disturbance and hasty removal. This silenced the numerous party of Bucklaw's friends, who had previously insisted that he should, at all rates, be transported from the castle to the nearest of their houses. They still demanded, however, that, in consideration of what had happened, four of their number should remain to watch over the sick-bed of their friend, and that a suitable number of their domestics, well armed, should also remain in the castle. This condition being acceded to on the part of Colonel Ashton and his father, the rest of the bridegroom's friends left the castle, notwithstanding the hour and the darkness of the night. The cares of the medical man were next employed in behalf of Miss Ashton, whom he pronounced to be in a very dangerous state. Farther medical assistance was immediately summoned. All night she remained delirious. On the morning, she fell into a state of absolute insensibility. The next evening, the physicians said, would be the crisis of her malady. It proved so; for although she awoke from her trance with some appearance of calmness, and suffered her night-clothes to be changed, or put in order, yet so soon as she put her hand to her neck, as if to search for the fatal blue ribbon, a tide of recollections seemed to rush upon her, which her mind and body were alike incapable of bearing. Convulsion followed convulsion, till they closed in death, without her being able to utter a word explanatory of the fatal scene.

The provincial judge of the district arrived the day after the young lady had expired, and executed, though with all possible delicacy to the afflicted family, the painful duty of enquiring into this fatal transaction. But there occurred nothing to explain the general hypothesis, that the bride, in a sudden fit of insanity, had stabbed the bridegroom at the threshold of the apartment. The fatal weapon was found in the chamber, smeared with blood. It was the same poniard which Henry should have worn on the wedding-day, and which his unhappy sister had probably contrived to secrete on the succeeding evening, when it had been shown to her among other articles of preparation for the wedding.

The friends of Bucklaw expected that on his recovery he would throw some light upon this dark story, and eagerly pressed him with enquiries, which for some time he evaded under pretext of weakness. When, however, he had been transported to his own house, and was considered as in a state of convalescence, he assembled those persons, both male and female, who had considered themselves as entitled to press him on this subject, and returned them thanks for the interest they had exhibited in his behalf, and their offers of adherence and support. 'I wish you all,' he said, 'my friends, to understand, however, that I have neither story to tell, nor injuries to avenge. If a lady shall question me henceforward upon the incidents of that unhappy night, I shall remain silent, and in future consider her as one who has shown herself desirous to break off her friendship with me; in a word, I will never speak to her again. But if a gentleman shall ask me the same question, I shall regard the incivility as equivalent to an invitation to meet him in the Duke's Walk,[29] and I expect that he will rule himself accordingly.'

A declaration so decisive admitted no commentary; and it was soon after seen that Bucklaw had arisen from the bed of sickness a sadder and a wiser man than he had hitherto shown himself. * He dismissed Craigengelt from his society, but not without such a provision as, if well employed, might secure him against indigence, and against temptation.

Bucklaw afterwards went abroad, and never returned to Scotland; nor was he known ever to hint at the circumstances attending his fatal marriage. By many readers this may be deemed overstrained, romantic, and composed by the wild imagination of an author, desirous of gratifying the popular appetite for the horrible; but those who are read in the private family history of Scotland during the period in which the scene is laid, will readily discover, through the disguise of borrowed names and added incidents, the leading particulars of AN OWER TRUE TALE.

CHAPTER XXXV

Whose mind's so marbled, and his heart so hard,
That would not, when this huge mishap was heard,
To th' utmost note of sorrow set their song,
To see a gallant, with so great a grace,
So suddenly unthought on, so o'erthrown,
And so to perish, in so poor a place,
By too rash riding in a ground unknown!

(*Poem, in Nisbet's Heraldry*, Vol. II) *

WE have anticipated the course of time to mention Bucklaw's recovery and fate, that we might not interrupt the detail of events which succeeded the funeral of the unfortunate Lucy Ashton. This melancholy ceremony was performed in the misty dawn of an autumnal morning, with such moderate attendance and ceremony as could not possibly be dispensed with. A very few of the nearest relations attended her body to the same churchyard to which she had so lately been led as a bride, with as little free will, perhaps, as could be now testified by her lifeless and passive remains. An aisle adjacent to the church had been fitted up by Sir William Ashton as a family cemetery; and here, in a coffin bearing neither name nor date, were consigned to dust the remains of what was once lovely, beautiful, and innocent, though exasperated to frenzy by a long tract of unremitting persecution. While the mourners were busy in the vault, the three village hags, who, notwithstanding the unwonted earliness of the hour, had snuffed the carrion like vultures, were seated on the 'through-stane,' and engaged in their wonted unhallowed conference.

'Did not I say,' said Dame Gourlay, 'that the braw bridal would be followed by as braw a funeral?'

'I think,' answered Dame Winnie, 'there's little bravery at it; neither meat nor drink, and just a wheen silver tippences to the poor folk; it was little worth while to come sae far road for sae sma' profit, and us sae frail.'

'Out, wretch!' replied Dame Gourlay, 'can a' the dainties they could gie us be half sae sweet as this hour's vengeance? There they are that were capering on their prancing nags four days since, and they are now ganging as dreigh and sober as oursells the day. They were a' glistening wi' gowd and silver—they're now as black as the crook. And Miss Lucy Ashton, that grudged when an honest woman came near her, a taid may sit on her coffin the day, and she can never scunner when he croaks. And Lady Ashton has hell-fire burning in her breast by this time; and Sir William, wi' his gibbets, and his faggots, and his chains, how likes he the witcheries of his ain dwelling-house?'

'And is it true, then,' mumbled the paralytic wretch, 'that the bride was trailed out of her bed and up the chimley by evil spirits, and that the bridegroom's face was wrung round ahint him?'

'Ye needna care wha did it, or how it was done,' said Ailsie Gourlay; 'but I'll uphaud it for nae stickit[30] job, and that the lairds and leddies ken weel this day.'

'And was it true,' said Annie Winnie, 'sin ye ken sae mickle about it, that the picture of Auld Sir Malise Ravenswood came down on the ha' floor, and led out the brawl before them a'?'*

'Na,' said Ailsie; 'but into the ha' came the picture—and I ken weel how it came there—to gie them a warning that pride would get a fa'. But there's as queer a ploy, cummers, as ony o' thae, that's gaun on even now in the burial vault yonder—ye saw twall mourners, wi' crape and cloke, gang down the steps pair and pair?'

'What should ail us to see them?' said the one old woman.

'I counted them,' said the other, with the eagerness of a person to whom the spectacle had afforded too much interest to be viewed with indifference.

'But ye did not see,' said Ailsie, exulting in her superior observation, 'that there's a thirteenth amang them that they ken naething about; and, if auld freets say true, there's ane o' that company that'll no be lang for this warld. But come awa, cummers; if we bide here, I'se warrant we get the wyte o' whatever ill comes of it, and that gude will come of it nane o' them need ever think to see.'

And thus, croaking like the ravens when they anticipate pestilence, the ill-boding sibyls withdrew from the churchyard.*

In fact, the mourners, when the service of interment was ended, discovered that there was among them one more than the invited number, and the remark was communicated in whispers to each other. The suspicion fell upon a figure, which, muffled in the same deep mourning with the others, was reclined, almost in a state of insensibility, against one of the pillars of the sepulchral vault. The relatives of the Ashton family were expressing in whispers their surprise and displeasure at the intrusion, when they were interrupted by Colonel Ashton, who, in his father's absence, acted as principal mourner. 'I know,' he said in a whisper, 'who this person is; he has, or shall soon have, as deep cause of mourning as ourselves—leave me to deal with him, and do not disturb the ceremony by unnecessary exposure.' So saying, he separated himself from the group of his relations, and taking the unknown mourner by the cloak, he said to him, in a tone of suppressed emotion, 'Follow me.'

The stranger, as if starting from a trance at the sound of his voice, mechanically obeyed, and they ascended the broken ruinous stair which led from the sepulchre into the churchyard. The other mourners followed, but remained grouped together at the door of the vault, watching with anxiety the motions of Colonel Ashton and the stranger, who now appeared to be in close conference beneath the shade of a yew-tree, in the most remote part of the burial-ground.

To this sequestered spot Colonel Ashton had guided the stranger, and then turning round, addressed him in a stern and composed tone.—'I cannot doubt that I speak to the Master of Ravenswood?' No answer was returned. 'I cannot doubt,' resumed the Colonel, trembling with rising passion, 'that I speak to the murderer of my sister?'

'You have named me but too truly,' said Ravenswood, in a hollow and tremulous voice.

'If you repent what you have done,' said the Colonel, 'may your penitence avail you before God; with me it shall serve you nothing. Here,' he said, giving a paper, 'is the measure of my sword, and a memorandum of the time and place of meeting. Sun-rise to-morrow morning, on the links to the east of Wolf's-hope.'

The Master of Ravenswood held the paper in his hand, and seemed irresolute. At length he spoke—'Do not,' he said, 'urge to farther desperation a wretch who is already desperate.* Enjoy your life while you can, and let me seek my death from another.'

'That you never, never shall!' said Douglas Ashton. 'You shall die by my hand, or you shall complete the ruin of my family by taking my life. If you refuse my open challenge, there is no advantage I will not take of you, no indignity with which I will not load you, until the very name of Ravenswood shall be the sign of every thing that is dishonourable, as it is already of all that is villainous.'

'That it shall never be,' said Ravenswood, fiercely; 'if I am the last who must bear it, I owe it to those who once owned it, that the name shall be extinguished without infamy. I accept your challenge, time, and place of meeting. We meet, I presume, alone?'

'Alone we meet,' said Colonel Ashton, 'and alone will the survivor of us return from that place of rendezvous.'

'Then God have mercy on the soul of him who falls!' said Ravenswood.

'So be it!' said Colonel Ashton; 'so far can my charity reach even for the man I hate most deadly, and with the deepest reason. Now, break off, for we shall be interrupted. The links by the sea-shore to the east of Wolf's-hope—the hour, sun-rise—our swords our only weapons.'

'Enough,' said the Master, 'I will not fail you.'

They separated; Colonel Ashton joining the rest of the mourners, and the Master of Ravenswood taking his horse, which was tied to a tree behind the church. Colonel Ashton returned to the castle with the funeral guests, but found a pretext for detaching himself from them in the evening, when, changing his dress to a riding habit, he rode to Wolf's-hope that night, and took up his abode in the little inn, in order that he might be ready for his rendezvous in the morning.

It is not known how the Master of Ravenswood disposed of the rest of that unhappy day. Late at night, however, he arrived at Wolf's Crag, and aroused his old domestic, Caleb Balderstone, who had ceased to expect his return. Confused and flying rumours of the late tragical death of Miss Ashton, and of its mysterious cause, had already reached the old man, who was filled with the utmost anxiety, on account of the probable effect these events might produce upon the mind of his master.

The conduct of Ravenswood did not alleviate his apprehensions. To the butler's trembling entreaties, that he would take some refreshment, he at first returned no answer, and then suddenly and fiercely demanding wine, he drank, contrary to his habits, a very large draught. Seeing that his master would eat nothing, the old man affectionately entreated that he would permit him to light him to his chamber. It was not until the request was three or four times repeated, that Ravenswood made a mute sign of compliance. But when Balderstone conducted him to an apartment which had been comfortably fitted up, and which, since his return, he had usually occupied, Ravenswood stopped short on the threshold.

'Not here,' said he, sternly; 'show me the room in which my father died; the room in which SHE slept the night they were at the castle.'

'Who, sir?' said Caleb, too terrified to preserve his presence of mind.

'*She*, Lucy Ashton!—would you kill me, old man, by forcing me to repeat her name?'

Caleb would have said something of the disrepair of the chamber, but was silenced by the irritable impatience which was expressed in his master's countenance; he lighted the way trembling and in silence, placed the lamp on the table of the deserted room, and was about to attempt some arrangement of the bed, when his master bid him begone in a tone that admitted of no delay. The old man retired, not to rest, but to prayer; and from time to time crept to the door of the apartment, in order to find out whether Ravenswood had gone to repose. His measured heavy step upon the floor was only interrupted by deep groans; and the repeated stamps of the heel of his heavy boot, intimated too clearly, that the wretched inmate was abandoning himself at such moments to paroxysms of uncontrolled agony. The old man thought that the morning, for which he longed, would never have dawned; but time, whose course rolls on with equal current, however it may seem more rapid or more slow to mortal apprehension, brought the dawn at last, and spread a ruddy light on the broad verge of the glistening ocean. It was early in November, and the weather was serene for the season of the year. But an easterly wind had prevailed during the night, and the advancing tide rolled nearer than usual to the foot of the crags on which the castle was founded.

With the first peep of light, Caleb Balderstone again resorted to the door of Ravenswood's sleeping apartment, through a chink of which he observed him engaged in measuring the length of two or three swords which lay in a closet adjoining to the apartment. He muttered to himself, as he selected one of these weapons, 'It is shorter—let him have this advantage, as he has every other.'

Caleb Balderstone knew too well, from what he witnessed, upon what enterprise his master was bound, and how vain all interference on his part must necessarily prove. He had but time to retreat from the door, so nearly was he surprised by his master suddenly coming out, and descending to the stables. The faithful domestic followed; and, from the dishevelled appearance of his master's dress, and his ghastly looks, was confirmed in his conjecture that he had passed the night without sleep or repose. He found him busily engaged in saddling his horse, a service from which Caleb, though with faltering voice and trembling hands, offered to relieve him. Ravenswood rejected his assistance by a mute sign, and having led the animal into the court, was just about to mount him, when the old domestic's fear giving way to the strong attachment which was the principal passion of his mind, he flung himself suddenly at Ravenswood's feet, and clasped his knees, while he exclaimed, 'Oh, sir! oh, master! kill me if you will, but do not go out on this dreadful errand! Oh! my dear master, wait but this day—the Marquis of A—— comes to-morrow, and a' will be remedied.'

'You have no longer a master, Caleb,' said Ravenswood, endeavouring to extricate himself; 'why, old man, would you cling to a falling tower?'

'But I *have* a master,' cried Caleb, still holding him fast, 'while the heir of Ravenswood breathes. I am but a servant; but I was born your father's—your grandfather's servant—I was born for the family—I have lived for them—I would die for them!—Stay but at home, and all will be well!'

'Well, fool! well?' said Ravenswood; 'vain old man, nothing hereafter in life will be well with me, and happiest is the hour that shall soonest close it!'

So saying, he extricated himself from the old man's hold, threw himself on his horse, and rode out at the gate; but instantly turning back, he threw towards Caleb, who hastened to meet him, a heavy purse of gold.

'Caleb!' he said, with a ghastly smile, 'I make you my executor;' and again turning his bridle, he resumed his course down the hill.

The gold fell unheeded on the pavement, for the old man ran to observe the course which was taken by his master, who turned to the left down a small and broken path, which gained the seashore through a cleft in the rock, and led to a sort of cove, where, in former times, the boats of the castle were wont to be moored. Observing him take this course, Caleb hastened to the eastern battlement, which commanded the prospect of the whole sands, very near as far as the village of Wolf's-hope. He could easily see his master riding in that direction, as fast as the horse could carry him. The prophecy at once rushed on Balderstone's mind, that the Lord of Ravenswood should perish on the Kelpie's Flow, which lay half way betwixt the tower and the links, or sand knolls, to the northward of Wolf's-hope. He saw him accordingly reach the fatal spot, but he never saw him pass further.

Colonel Ashton, frantic for revenge, was already in the field, pacing the turf with eagerness, and looking with impatience towards the tower for the arrival of his antagonist. The sun had now risen, and showed its broad disk above the eastern sea, so that he could easily discern the horseman who rode towards him with speed which argued impatience equal to his own. At once the figure became invisible, as if it had melted into the air. He rubbed his eyes, as if he had witnessed an apparition, and then hastened to the spot, near which he was met by Balderstone, who came from the opposite direction. No trace whatever of horse or rider could be discerned; it only appeared, that the late winds and high tides had greatly extended the usual bounds of the quicksand, and that the unfortunate horseman, as appeared from the hoof-tracks, in his precipitated haste, had not attended to keep on the firm sands on the foot of the rock, but had taken the shortest and most dangerous course. One only vestige of his fate appeared. A large sable feather had been detached from his hat, and the rippling waves of the rising tide wafted it to Caleb's feet. The old man took it up, dried it, and placed it in his bosom.

The inhabitants of Wolf's-hope were now alarmed, and crowded to the place, some on shore, and some in boats, but their search availed nothing. The tenacious depths of the quicksand, as is usual in such cases, retained its prey.

Our tale draws to a conclusion. The Marquis of A——, alarmed at the frightful reports that were current, and anxious for his kinsman's safety, arrived on the subsequent day to mourn his loss; and, after renewing in vain a search for the body, returned, to forget what had happened amid the bustle of politics and state affairs.

Not so Caleb Balderstone. If worldly profit could have consoled the old man, his age was better provided for than his earlier years had ever been; but life had lost to him its salt and its savour. * His whole course of ideas, his feelings, whether of pride or of apprehension, of pleasure or of pain, had all arisen from his close connexion with the family which was now extinguished. He held up his head no longer—forsook all his usual haunts and occupations, and seemed only to find pleasure in moping about those apartments in the old castle, which the Master of Ravenswood had last inhabited. He ate without refreshment, and slumbered without repose; and, with a fidelity sometimes displayed by the canine race, but seldom by human beings, he pined and died within a year after the catastrophe which we have narrated.

The family of Ashton did not long survive that of Ravenswood. * Sir William Ashton outlived his eldest son, the Colonel, who was slain in a duel in Flanders; and Henry, by whom he was succeeded, died unmarried. Lady Ashton lived to the verge of extreme old age, the only survivor of the group of unhappy persons, whose misfortunes were owing to her implacability. That she might internally feel compunction, and reconcile herself with Heaven whom she had offended, we will not, and we dare not, deny; but to those around her, she did not evince the slightest symptom either of repentance or remorse. In all external appearance, she bore the same bold, haughty, unbending character, which she had displayed before these unhappy events. A splendid marble monument records her name, titles, and virtues, while her victims remain undistinguished by tomb or epitaph.

SCOTT'S NOTES

With the exception of those marked 'Ist edn.' in parentheses, these notes were written for the Magnum Opus edition. Where necessary, further information on Scott's comments is given in the Editor's Notes.

1. See Introduction to the Chronicles of the Canongate.

2. Law's Memorialls, p. 226.

3. Memoirs of John Earl of Stair, by an Impartial Hand. London, printed for C. Cobbet, p. 7.

4. The fall from his horse, by which he was killed.

5. I have compared the satire, which occurs in the first volume of the curious little collection called a Book of Scottish Pasquils, 1827, with that which has a more full text, and more extended notes, and which is in my own possession, by gift of Thomas Thomson, Esq. Register-Depute. In the second Book of Pasquils, p. 72, is a most abusive epitaph on Sir James Hamilton of Whitelaw.

6. This elegy is reprinted in the appendix to a topographical work by the same author, entitled 'A Large Description of Galloway, by Andrew Symson, Minister of Kirkinner,' 8vo, Taits, Edinburgh, 1823. The reverend gentleman's elegies are extremely rare, nor did the author ever see a copy but his own, which is bound up with the Tripatriarchicon, a religious poem from the Biblical History, by the same author.

7. *Hauds out.* Holds out, *i.e.* presents his piece.

8. President of the Court of Session. He was pistolled in the High Street of Edinburgh, by John Chiesley of Dalry, in the year 1689. The revenge of this desperate man was stimulated by an opinion that he had sustained injustice in a decreet-arbitral pronounced by the President, assigning an alimentary provision of about L. 93 in favour of his wife and children. He is said at first to have designed to shoot the judge while attending upon divine worship, but was diverted by some feeling concerning the sanctity of the place. After the congregation was dismissed, he dogged his victim as far as the

head of the close on the south side of the Lawnmarket, in which
the President's house was situated, and shot him dead as he was
about to enter it. This act was done in the presence of numerous
spectators. The assassin made no attempt to fly, but boasted of the
deed, saying, 'I have taught the President how to do justice.' He
had at least given him fair warning, as Jack Cade says on a similar
occasion. The murderer, after undergoing the torture, by a special
act of the Estates of Parliament, was tried before the Lord Provost
of Edinburgh, as high sheriff, and condemned to be dragged on a
hurdle to the place of execution, to have his right hand struck off
while he yet lived, and, finally, to be hung on the gallows with the
pistol wherewith he shot the President tied round his neck. This
execution took place on the 3d of April 1689; and the incident was
long remembered as a dreadful instance of what the law books call
the *perfervidum ingenium Scotorum*. (1st edn.)

9. *Wind him a pirn*, proverbial for preparing a troublesome business for
    some person.

10. *i.e.* Let him pay with his person, who cannot pay with his purse.

11. Drinking cups of different sizes, made out of staves hooped together.
    The *quaigh* was used chiefly for drinking wine or brandy; it might
    hold about a gill, and was often composed of rare wood, and
    curiously ornamented with silver. (1st edn.)

12. That is, absolute rights of property for the payment of a sum
    annually, which is usually a trifle in such cases as are alluded to in
    the text.

13. Burke's Speech on Economical Reform.—Works, vol. iii. p. 250.
    (1st edn.)

14. *i.e.* To act as may be necessary and legal, a Scottish law phrase.

15. *Weid*, a feverish cold; a disorder incident to infants and to females,
    is so called.

16. Monetæ Scoticæ, scilicet. ['In Scottish money, that is to say'] (1st
    edn.)

17. Taking up his abode.

18. RAID OF CALEB BALDERSTONE. The Raid of Caleb Balderstone on
    the cooper's kitchen, has been universally considered on the south-
    ern side of the Tweed as grotesquely and absurdly extravagant. The
    author can only say, that a similar anecdote was communicated to
    him, with date and names of the parties, by a noble Earl lately

deceased, whose remembrances of former days, both in Scotland and England, while they were given with a felicity and power of humour never to be forgotten by those who had the happiness of meeting his lordship in familiar society, were especially invaluable from their extreme accuracy.

Speaking after my kind and lamented informer, with the omission of names only, the anecdote ran thus:—There was a certain bachelor gentleman in one of the midland counties of Scotland, second son of an ancient family, who lived on the fortune of a second son, videlicet, upon some miserably small annuity, which yet was so managed and stretched out by the expedients of his man John, that his master kept the front rank with all the young men of quality in the county, and hunted, dined, diced, and drank with them, upon apparently equal terms.

It is true, that as the master's society was extremely amusing, his friends contrived to reconcile his man John to accept assistance of various kinds under the rose, which they dared not to have directly offered to his master. Yet, very consistently with all this good inclination to John, and John's master, it was thought among the young fox-hunters, that it would be an excellent jest, if possible, to take John at fault.

With this intention, and, I think, in consequence of a bet, a party of four or five of these youngsters arrived at the bachelor's little mansion, which was adjacent to a considerable village. Here they alighted a short while before the dinner hour—for it was judged regular to give John's ingenuity a fair start—and, rushing past the astonished domestic, entered the little parlour; and, telling some concerted story of the cause of their invasion, the self-invited guests asked their landlord if he could let them have some dinner. Their friend gave them a hearty and unembarrassed reception, and, for the matter of dinner, referred them to John. He was summoned accordingly—received his master's orders to get dinner ready for the party who had thus unexpectedly arrived; and, without changing a muscle of his countenance, promised prompt obedience. Great was the speculation of the visitors, and probably of the landlord also, what was to be the issue of John's fair promises. Some of the more curious had taken a peep into the kitchen, and could see nothing there to realize the prospect held out by the *Major-Domo*. But punctual as the dinner hour struck on the village clock, John placed before them a stately rump of boiled beef, with a proper accompaniment of greens, amply sufficient to dine the whole party, and to decide the bet against those among the visitors who expected to take John napping. The explanation was the same as in the case of Caleb Balderstone. John had used the freedom to carry off the *kail-pot* of a rich old chuff in the village, and brought it to his master's house, leaving the proprietor and his friends to dine on bread and cheese; and, as John said, 'good enough for them.' The fear of giving offence to so many persons of distinction, kept the poor man sufficiently quiet, and he was afterwards remunerated by some indirect patronage, so that the jest was admitted a good one on all sides. In England, at any period, or in some parts of Scotland at the present day, it might not have passed off so well.

19. *Cuitle* may answer to the elegant modern phrase *diddle*.

20. ANCIENT HOSPITALITY. It was once the universal custom to place ale, wine, or some strong liquor, in the chamber of an honoured guest, to assuage his thirst should he feel any on awaking in the night, which, considering that the hospitality of that period often reached excess, was by no means unlikely. The author has met some instances of it in former days, and in old-fashioned families. It was, perhaps, no poetic fiction that records how

> 'My cummer and I lay down to sleep
> With two pint stoups at our bed-feet;
> And aye when we waken'd we drank them dry:
> What think you o' my cummer and I?'

It is a current story in Teviotdale, that in the house of an ancient family of distinction, much addicted to the Presbyterian cause, a Bible was always put into the sleeping apartment of the guests, along with a bottle of strong ale. On some occasion there was a meeting of clergymen in the vicinity of the castle, all of whom were invited to dinner by the worthy Baronet, and several abode all night. According to the fashion of the times, seven of the reverend guests were allotted to one large barrack-room, which was used on such occasions of extended hospitality. The butler took care that the divines were presented, according to custom, each with a Bible and a bottle of ale. But after a little consultation among themselves, they are said to have recalled the domestic as he was leaving the apartment. 'My friend,' said one of the venerable guests, 'you must know, when we meet together as brethren, the youngest minister reads aloud a portion of Scripture to the rest;—only one Bible, therefore, is necessary; take away the other six, and in their place bring six more bottles of ale.'

This synod would have suited the 'hermit sage' of Johnson, who answered a pupil who enquired for the real road to happiness, with the celebrated line,

'Come, my lad, and drink some beer!'

21.　APPEAL TO PARLIAMENT. The power of appeal from the Court of Session, the supreme Judges of Scotland, to the Scottish Parliament, in cases of civil right, was fiercely debated before the Union. It was a privilege highly desirable for the subject, as the examination and occasional reversal of their sentences in Parliament, might serve as a check upon the judges, which they greatly required at a time when they were much more distinguished for legal knowledge than for uprightness and integrity.

The members of the Faculty of Advocates, (so the Scottish barristers are termed,) in the year 1674, incurred the violent displeasure of the Court of Session, on account of their refusal to renounce the right of appeal to Parliament; and, by a very arbitrary procedure, the majority of the number were banished from Edinburgh, and consequently deprived of their professional practice for several sessions, or terms. But, by the articles of the Union, an appeal to the British House of Peers has been secured to the Scottish subject, and that right has, no doubt, had its influence in forming the impartial and independent character which, much contrary to the practice of their predecessors, the Judges of the Court of Session have since displayed.

It is easy to conceive, that an old lawyer like the Lord Keeper in the text, should feel alarm at the judgments given in his favour, upon grounds of strict penal law, being brought to appeal under a new and dreaded procedure in a Court eminently impartial, and peculiarly moved by considerations of equity.

In earlier editions of this Work, this legal distinction was not sufficiently explained.

22.　*i.e.* They are bounded by my own.

23.　Broil.

24.　POOR-MAN-OF-MUTTON. The blade-bone of a shoulder of mutton is called in Scotland 'a poor man,' as in some parts of England it is termed 'a poor knight of Windsor;' in contrast, it must be presumed, to the baronial Sir Loin. It is said, that in the last age an old Scottish peer, whose conditions (none of the most gentle) were marked by a strange and fierce-looking exaggeration of the Highland countenance, chanced to be indisposed while he was in London attending Parliament. The master of the hotel where he lodged, anxious to show attention to his noble guest, waited on him to enumerate the contents of his well-stocked larder, so as to endeavour to hit on something which might suit his appetite. 'I think, landlord,' said his lordship, rising up from his couch, and throwing back the tartan plaid with which he had screened his grim and ferocious visage—'I think I could eat a morsel of a *poor man*.' The landlord fled in terror, having no doubt that his guest was a cannibal, who might be in the habit of eating a slice of a tenant, as light food, when he was under regimen.

25.   'Cut a drink with a tale;' equivalent to the English adage of boon companions, 'don't preach over your liquor.' (1st edn.)

26.   Hereupon I, Jedediah Cleishbotham, crave leave to remark, *primo*, which signifies, in the first place, that, having in vain enquired at the Circulating Library in Gandercleugh, albeit it aboundeth in similar vanities, for this samyn Middleton and his Mad World, it was at length shown unto me amongst other ancient fooleries carefully compiled by one Dodsley, who, doubtless, hath his reward for neglect of precious time; and having misused so much of mine as was necessary for the purpose, I therein found that a play-man is brought in as a footman, whom a knight is made to greet facetiously with the epithet of 'linen stocking, and three-score miles a-day.'

   Secundo, (which is secondly in the vernacular,) under Mr Pattieson's favour, some men not altogether so old as he would represent them, do remember this species of menial, or forerunner. In evidence of which, I, Jedediah Cleishbotham, though mine eyes yet do me good service, remember me to have seen one of this tribe clothed in white, and bearing a staff, who ran daily before the state-coach of the umquhile John, Earl of Hopeton, father of this Earl, Charles, that now is; unto whom it may be justly said, that Renown playeth the part of a running footman, or precursor; and, as the poet singeth—

> 'Mars standing by asserts his quarrel,
> And Fame flies after with a laurel.'

J. C. (1st edn.)

27.   *Anglicé,* adze. (1st edn.)

28.   Reginald Scott tells of an old woman who performed so many cures by means of a charm, that she was suspected of witchcraft. Her mode of practice being enquired into, it was found, that the only fee which she would accept of, was a loaf of bread and a silver penny; and that

the potent charm with which she wrought so many cures, was the doggerel couplet in the text.

29. A walk in the vicinity of Holyrood-house, so called, because often frequented by the Duke of York, afterwards James II., during his residence in Scotland. It was for a long time the usual place of rendezvous for settling affairs of honour.

30. *Stickit*, imperfect.

APPENDIX

The Bride of Lammermoor and
Scottish History

1603   James VI of Scotland (1566–1625) succeeds to the English throne as James I. He leaves Scotland to set up court in London, and, despite a promise to revisit every three years, returns to Scotland only once, in 1617. He governs Scotland through his Privy Council and Commissioner to Parliament, beginning the system of 'delegated authority' criticized by the narrator of *The Bride of Lammermoor*. From 1603, Scotland and England have the same monarch but are still separate kingdoms with separate institutions of government.

1625   James is succeeded by his son, Charles I (1600–49), who marries the French princess, Henrietta Maria. At some point in Charles's reign, Edgar Ravenswood's grandmother attends the 'court balls' of the queen.

1638   The National Covenant is drawn up to protect the Presbyterian Church Establishment in Scotland, consolidating opposition to the king's interference in church affairs (such as the new Scottish Prayer Book, introduced in 1637).

1643   The Solemn League and Covenant between the Scottish Presbyterians and the English Parliament commits them to preserving the reformed religion in both countries.

1649   Charles I is executed. The Scots declare Charles II (1630–85) their king, and in 1650 he signs both Covenants to ensure Scottish support. However, Scotland is in effect conquered by the armies of Oliver Cromwell (1599–1658). During the Commonwealth and Protectorate, Scotland is governed in union with England, its affairs being managed by eight commissioners appointed by the English Parliament (after 1655, by a nine-member Council of State including two Scotsmen).

1660   Charles II is restored as king. The possibility of a formal legislative and administrative union between England and Scotland is discussed by commissioners drawn from both countries, but is taken no further.

1662   Despite the hopes of the Covenanters that Charles II will honour
       his promises to them, episcopacy is restored in Scotland. Many
       Presbyterian clergy lose their parishes, and field meetings or
       conventicles become a common form of worship, particularly in
       the south-west.

1674   Scottish judges and the Faculty of Advocates disgree over the right
       of appeal to monarch and Parliament against decisions made by
       the Court of Session. Advocates upholding the right of appeal are
       barred from residing within 12 miles of Edinburgh. The issue
       remains contentious, and an attempt is later made to resolve it, by
       the terms of the Revolution settlement (1689).

1679   A resurgence of Covenanting activity follows the murder of James
       Sharp, the Archbishop of St Andrews (3 May), culminating in the
       battles of Drumclog (1 June), won by the Covenanters, and
       Bothwell Bridge (22 June), won by the Royalist forces under the
       Duke of Monmouth. In the novel's account of Bothwell Bridge,
       Allan Ravenswood leads a group of men in the Royalist army,
       including the enthusiastic Caleb Balderstone and the reluctant
       Johnnie Mortsheugh. Mortsheugh loses his place as Ravens-
       wood's trumpeter after being injured in battle.

1681   The Test Act and Oath requires all office-holders to recognize the
       king as supreme in spriritual as well as in temporal matters. It is
       impossible for Covenanters to take such an oath, and persecution
       of them increases during the so-called 'killing time' of 1681–5. In
       the novel, their sufferings are vividly remembered by Bide-the-
       bent, the Presbyterian minister of Wolf's-hope. The convictions
       of the Ashton family (Presbyterian) and the Ravenswood family
       (Episcopalian) are sharply contrasted in the religious and civil
       troubles of these years.

1685   The 9th Earl of Argyll raises forces to oppose the accession of James
       VII and II (1633–1701), whose plans to secure toleration for his
       fellow Roman Catholics provoke deep distrust. The rebellion is
       defeated and Argyll is executed.

1688   English magnates invite William of Orange (1650–1702), the
       husband of James's Protestant daughter Mary (1662–94), to en-
       sure the powers of a free parliament in England. James flees to
       France, an action which the English interpret as abdication, and
       William and Mary accept the crown of England. James is sup-
       ported in exile by Louis XIV of France. Those working to restore
       James and his descendants to the throne are known in future as

'Jacobites' (from the Latin *Jacobus*, meaning James). *The Bride of Lammermoor* refers to the events of this year and the next as 'the revolution'.

1689   On 11 April the Scottish Convention of Estates issues the Claim of Right , which establishes certain constitutional principles and secures the right of appeal to monarch and Parliament. The Estates declare that James VII has forfeited the crown of Scotland, which it offers to William and Mary. The status of the Claim of Right as a basic contract between monarch and country is contested by those who support the monarch's absolute authority, and is never as clear as was intended. John Graham of Claverhouse, Viscount Dundee (1648–89), who commanded the Royalist forces at Drumclog in 1679 and played an active part in the suppression of the Covenanters, leads a rebellion against William and Mary, which loses momentum after the death of Dundee during his army's victory at the battle of Killiecrankie (27 July). In the novel, Allan Ravenswood takes part in Dundee's rebellion, is convicted of high treason, and loses his title. Under William and Mary, Sir William Ashton becomes a successful politician, a member of the Privy Council, and Lord Keeper of the Great Seal of Scotland.

1690   Presbyterianism is re-established in Scotland, ending the persecution of the Covenanters, and measures are taken to restrict Episcopal services. The family of Ravenswood now finds itself out of step with the dominant religious and political opinions of the times.

1692   The Glencoe massacre blackens the reputation of the Scottish administration. Discontent with the Scottish policies of William and his advisers increases, and in the following year William institutes an Assurance by which all office-holders must recognize him as king *de jure* as well as *de facto*.

1695   The Company of Scotland Trading to Africa and the Indies is formed, its key project being to establish a free port for Scotland on the Isthmus of Darien (Panama). The scheme leads to three failed expeditions and great tension between Scotland and England, as the king is seen to sacrifice Scottish to English interests. Sir William Ashton later avoids the losses made by many investors in the scheme by selling out of the Company.

1701   After the death of James VII and II, Louis XIV declares James's son (James Francis Stewart, 1688–1766) James VIII and III. The War of the Spanish Succession (1701–14) begins, bringing

England into conflict with France. The English pass the Act of Settlement which secures the throne of England to the Protestant Sophia, Electress of Hanover, in the event of William's heir, Anne (1665–1714), dying without issue.

1702 William dies. The last Stewart monarch, Anne, second daughter of James VII and II, succeeds to the throne of both countries. The Scottish Parliament is not called until ninety days after William's death, in breach of an Act of 1696, and this delay allows the Scottish Privy Council to declare war on France (30 May), in support of English interests. This provokes deep resentment in Scotland. In the novel, Allan Ravenswood and the Marquis of A—— take part in a conspiracy to reclaim the crown for James Francis Stewart.

1703 By the Act anent Peace and War, the Scots declare that no successor of Anne may declare a war involving Scotland without consulting the Scottish Parliament.

1704 The Act of Security, passed by the Scottish Parliament the year before, is given the royal assent. It states that the Scottish Parliament is to meet within twenty days of Queen Anne's death to name a successor who must be Protestant, and a descendant of the house of Stewart, but not the person named by the English Parliament unless Scottish independence is guaranteed. With the Act anent Peace and War, this represents a serious challenge to the administration of two countries by one monarch.

1705 In retaliation, the English pass the so-called 'Alien Act', which declares that Scots are to be treated as aliens in England and that certain exports from Scotland to England are to cease, unless Scotland accepts the Hanoverian succession and appoints commissioners to treat for union.

1706 Scotland and England each appoint thirty-one commissioners to consider terms of union. Although popular opposition to union is strong, particularly in Scotland, only one of the commissioners representing Scotland is known to be opposed to the scheme (this exception being George Lockhart of Carnwath). By July the commissioners agree on twenty-five Articles of Union.

1707 The Articles of Union are ratified by a vote of 110 to 67 in the Scottish Parliament on 16 January, and the Act of Union comes into effect on 1 May. The Act unites Scotland and England in a new kingdom, Great Britain, under one monarchy and flag, and declares that Great Britain is to have a joint parliament, uniform public law, standard customs and excise laws, and standard coinage, weights, and measures. It is agreed that an 'Equivalent' of £398,085 10s. is to be paid to Scotland to offset future liability for the English national debt. The Scottish legal system remains independent, and it is stated that no legal cause in Scotland is to be tried in English courts. Scottish laws respecting private right (such as the laws governing the dispute between Ashton and Ravenswood) are to remain intact and cannot be altered 'except for evident utility of the subjects within Scotland'. Although the Act of Union makes no mention of the right of appeal to the House of Lords against decisions of the Court of Session (despite Scott's comments in note 21, which suggest that it does), the right is soon established in practice. In the Magnum Opus version of the novel, the changes brought about by the Act of Union allow Ravenswood to appeal to the House of Lords, rather than to the old Scottish Parliament, against the decisions which gave his father's estate to Sir William Ashton.

1708   In breach of the terms of the Union, the Scottish Privy Council and Scottish Treasury are disbanded. A French fleet escorts James Francis Stewart to the Scottish coast, but is intercepted by British ships, and the attempted rebellion fails. Agents working for the exiled Stewart family and for the French court (such as the novel's Captain Craigengelt) are active in plots like this.

1710   The Tories win a general election, and Harley heads the new administration. In the novel, Ravenswood's kinsman, the Tory Marquis of A——, acquires new power, and presses forward with Ravenswood's appeal. Ravenswood himself is now abroad, taking part in negotiations at various European courts, presumably in connection with the War of the Spanish Succession.

1711   The House of Lords upholds the appeal of James Greenshields, a Scottish Episcopal minister punished for using the Anglican liturgy, against the decision of the Court of Session. Victories such as this, which are decided on English rather than on Scottish legal principles, highlight the problems caused by appeals to the House of Lords. There is some justification for Sir William Ashton's complaint that the House of Lords is essentially a 'foreign court'.

1712   The Toleration Act permits Episcopal worship in Scotland and requires that all clergymen take an oath of allegiance to the crown and abjure the 'Pretender', James Francis Stewart. Dissatisfaction with the Union grows in Scotland when attempts are made to apply the malt tax there.

1713 In June, a formal proposal to repeal the Act of Union is supported by representatives of all Scottish parties in the House of Lords, and is only narrowly defeated. At Utrecht, the first group of treaties bringing an end to the War of the Spanish Succession is signed.

1714 On Anne's death, George, Elector of Hanover (1660–1727), succeeds to the British throne as George I. Harley's administration collapses, and Harley himself is impeached for treason the following year.

1715 The 11th Earl of Mar (1675–1732) leads an unsuccessful rebellion in favour of James Francis Stewart. Further rebellions follow in 1719 and 1745–6.

EDITOR'S NOTES

For clarification of relevant points of Scots law, I have drawn upon the manuscript notes of the late Lord Normand (1884–1962), Lord Justice General of Scotland and President of the Court of Session, which are held by the National Library of Scotland (MSS 23070–23116). My precise debts to Lord Normand's work are recorded in individual notes. I am grateful to Frank Romany and to my colleagues at Hertford College, particularly Stephanie West and Stuart Anderson, for their help on several points of fact. For the abbreviations used, see the footnotes to my Introduction. References to Shakespeare's plays are taken from the *Riverside Shakespeare*.

> *epigraphs*: the first (p. xlvii) is the opening stanza of 'On the Late Captain Grose's Peregrinations thro' Scotland, collecting the Antiquities of that Kingdom', by Robert Burns (1759–96). The second is from *The Adventures of Don Quixote* (1605, 1615), by Miguel de Cervantes Saavedra (1547–1616), and the third from the popular translation of *Don Quixote* by Charles Jarvis (2 vols., 1742).

INTRODUCTION (1830)

1 *on a former occasion . . . the feelings of the descendants of the parties*: Scott had commented on the origin of some of his tales in his introduction to *Chronicles of the Canongate*, 1st Series (1827), the first work to be published after he had acknowledged authorship of the Waverley Novels. He had mentioned 'for example's sake, that the terrible catastrophe of the Bride of Lammermoor actually occurred in a Scottish family of rank', concluding that further details were unnecessary and might not 'be altogether agreeable to the representatives of the families concerned in the narrative. It may be proper to say, that the events alone are imitated; but I had neither the means nor intention of copying the manners, or tracing the characters, of the persons concerned in the real story.' (*Magnum*, xli, pp. xv–xvi.)

1   *the Notes to Law's Memorials, by his ingenious friend Charles Kirkpatrick Sharpe, Esq.*: Robert Law (d. ?1690) was a moderate Covenanting preacher deprived of his benefice in 1662 for refusing to conform to episcopacy, and restored to his parish of New (or Easter) Kilpatrick in Dunbartonshire after accepting the Indulgence of 1679. The Covenanters were supporters of the National Covenant of 1638 and the Solemn League and Covenant of 1643, which affirmed the Presbyterian form of church-government (in which no higher order than that of presbyter or elder is recognized) rather than the Episcopalian (in which the three distinct orders of bishops, presbyters, and deacons govern in hierarchy). Law's *Memorialls; or, The Memorable Things that Fell Out within this Island of Brittain from 1638 to 1684* was edited in 1818 by Scott's friend Charles Kirkpatrick Sharpe (*c*.1781–1851), who provided for it an important preface on the history of witchcraft in Scotland, and detailed traditional accounts of the marriage of Janet Dalrymple in a long footnote (*Memorialls*, ed. C. K. Sharpe, pp. 226–9). Sharpe was a gentleman researcher into Scottish genealogy, history, and antiquities, and had known Scott since 1802. He provided Scott with many stories and suggestions for his novels, having a love of historical gossip: 'Strange that a man should be curious after Scandal of centuries old. Not but Charles loves it fresh and fresh also for being very much a fashionable man he is always master of the reigning report', Scott reflects in his *Journal* in 1825 (p. 2). Scott had been enthusiastic about Sharpe's projected edition of the *Memorialls* (*Letters*, iv. 538–9).

his reprint of the Rev. Mr Symson's poems, appended to the Description of Galloway: Andrew Symson (1638–1712), Scottish Episcopal minister of Kirkinner, Wigtownshire, for over 20 years before the Revolution of 1688–9, came to Edinburgh to work as an author and printer, mainly of political pamphlets for Jacobite and nonjuring friends, after all but two or three of his congregation deserted him in favour of Presbyterianism. As Symson laments in the passage Scott quotes on p. 9, David Dunbar of Baldoon was his most loyal parishioner. Symson's major publication was the *Tripatriarchicon* (1705), to which Scott refers in note 6, but his most interesting work was *A Large Description of Galloway* (1684, revised 1692), prepared as part of an abortive plan for a Scottish Atlas and eventually deposited unpublished in the Advocates' Library in Edinburgh. It was first edited in 1823 by Thomas Maitland. Scott refers here to Maitland's note to Symson's elegy on Lady Baldoon, included as an appendix to *A Large Description of Galloway* (pp. 192–4), which follows Sharpe's note to Law's *Memorialls* in suggesting that the life of Janet Dalrymple inspired 'that beautiful romance, *The Bride of Lammermoor*'. Symson's elegy is the only contemporary account of the death of Baldoon's young wife, and makes no reference to any calamity other than her sudden death a month after her marriage. For some of the varying subsequent accounts see W. S. Crockett, *The Scott Originals*, 1912, ch. 15.

connexions of his own . . . closely related to the family of the Bride: his maternal great-aunt, Margaret Swinton (d. 1780), from whom he heard the story as a child, was 'nearly related to the Lord President [Stair]', as Scott writes in his note to ch. 5 of *Peveril of the Peak* (*Magnum*, xxviii. 92). His mother, Anne Rutherford Scott (1739–1819), who also told the story (*Letters*, v. 186, vi. 118–19), was a Rutherford, like the original of the Master of Ravenswood.

James Dalrymple . . . Scottish Jurisprudence, on which he has composed an admirable work: James Dalrymple, 1st Viscount Stair (1619–95), was one of the foremost Scottish lawyers and statesmen of his age. He was made a Lord of Session in 1657, and between 1657 and 1660 was one of the commissioners for the administration of Scottish justice under the Protectorate. He continued in office under Charles II, and in 1671 became President of the Court of Session (the highest court of civil law in Scotland). In 1670 he had been one of the Scottish commissioners appointed to consider the possibility of union between England and Scotland. In 1681 he retired as President, rather than take the Test Oath of that year, and published his *Institutions of the Law of Scotland* (1681, enlarged edn., 1693), the first and still regarded as the supreme institutional treatise on Scottish law. Its title echoes Justinian's *Institutes* (see note to p. 180). In the *Institutions* Dalrymple derives rules of law from their underlying principles and their sources in Roman, canon, and feudal law, drawing on his study of the work of continental jurists, especially the Dutch. This is the 'admirable work' to which Scott refers, and in which, as a lawyer, he would have been thoroughly versed. In 1682 Dalrymple fled to Holland, preparing in exile two volumes of his *Decisions of the Court of Session, 1661–81* (1684 and 1687). He returned in 1688 with William of Orange, under whom he became Lord Advocate and, in 1689, Lord President once more following the murder of Sir George Lockhart of Carnwath (see Scott's note 8). He was created a Baronet in 1664 and received the titles of Viscount Stair, Lord Glenluce and Stranraer in 1690, five years before his death. As Scott states, he was the first member of his family to rise to eminence, and many of his descendants played key roles in Scottish affairs.

1 *the historian of her grandson, the great Earl of Stair*: James Dalrymple married Margaret Ross, coheiress of Balneil in the parish of Old Luce, Wigtownshire, in 1643. She died in 1692. Their grandson John Dalrymple, 2nd Earl of Stair (1673–1747), had a highly distinguished military and diplomatic career, and was a staunch Whig and supporter of the Hanoverian succession. The quotation is from the pamphlet *Memoirs of the Life, Family, and Character of John Late Earl of Stair*, 'by an impartial hand', 1747, p. 8.

3 *the last Lord Rutherford . . . died in 1685*: Archibald, 3rd Lord Rutherford, succeeded to the title in 1670 and died unmarried in March 1685 (James Balfour Paul, *The Scots Peerage*, 9 vols., 1904–14). The identification was confirmed at Scott's request by Charles Kirkpatrick Sharpe in December 1827 (*Letters*, x. 329 n.). Little more is known of him, and *The Bride of Lammermoor* is often given as the chief source. He was not the 'last' Lord Rutherford, but was succeeded in 1685 by his brother Robert, the 4th Lord, who died in 1724. The title has remained dormant since then, although there have been rival claimants. (G. E. C., *The Complete Peerage*, new edn., 13 vols., 1910–40.)

4 *A lady, very nearly connected with the family*: this is probably another reference to Margaret Swinton, or possibly to Anne Murray Keith of Elphinstone (1736–1818), the original of Mrs Bethune Baliol in Scott's *Chronicles of the Canongate*. The families of Elphinstone and Dalrymple were closely related.

any coarse pleasantry . . . intrusted to the brideman: in older custom, the bridal revellers accompanied the bride and groom to their bedchamber and saw them put to bed together. The brideman, or bride's man, led the bride to church and carried out various ceremonial duties, including putting the groom to bed. Describing a Scottish marriage in a period just before the events of *The Bride of Lammermoor*, the 'Editor' of *The Private Memoirs and Confessions of a Justified Sinner* (1824), by Scott's friend James Hogg (1770–1835), comments: 'It was customary, in those days, for the bride's-man and maiden, and a few select friends, to visit the new married couple after they had retired to rest, and drink a cup to their healths, their happiness, and a numerous posterity.' (ed. John Carey, 1969, p. 4.)

24th of August . . . 12th of September 1669: Scott confuses the dates here, although he gives them correctly on p. 7 on the authority of

Andrew Symson. John Murray Graham confirms Symson's dates in his *Annals and Correspondence of the Viscount and the First and Second Earls of Stair*, 2 vols., 1875, i. 44.

5   *The unfortunate Baldoon . . . 1682*: in *Annals and Correspondence of the Viscount and the First and Second Earls of Stair*, Graham records of Baldoon: 'The bridegroom Dunbar, a cultivated gentleman of unimpeached honour, not at all resembling the "Bucklaw" of the novel, afterwards married a daughter of the seventh Earl of Eglintoun, and died in 1682 by a fall from his horse.' (i. 47.)

The credulous Mr Law . . . 'was possessed by an evil spirit': this, Law's only comment, is misquoted from *Memorialls*, ed. C. K. Sharpe, pp. 225–6. Popular superstition among the Covenanters, who disliked the family of Stair because of the 1st Viscount's association with the policies of Charles II's Scottish administration, held that another of his daughters was possessed by the devil, and able to fly.

My friend, Mr Sharpe . . . 'You may marry him, but soon shall you repent it': given in C. K. Sharpe's note to *Memorialls*, pp. 226–7: 'The young lady, weltering in her blood, lay extended upon the bed, and her husband, in a state of idiotcy, was seated in the chimney, glaring with his eyes, and laughing in a hideous manner.' Lady Stair's warning in fact reads 'but *sair* shall ye repent it'. Sharpe also records another version of the story, in which Janet Dalrymple attacks Baldoon after being forced to marry him, but suggests that this is less probable because it does not implicate Lady Stair. This version includes the words 'Take up your bonnie bridegroom', and the detail that Baldoon refused afterwards to talk about the events of his wedding night, both of which Scott uses in the novel.

some highly scurrilous and abusive verses, of which I have an original copy: the most accessible version of the 'Satyre on the Familie of Stairs', to which Scott refers here, is printed in *A Book of Scotish Pasquils &c.*, edited anonymously by James Maidment in 1827. Scott's own copy had fuller marginal notes than the Maidment version, including several ascribed to William Dunlop, and until the appearance of *Scotish Pasquils* he had planned to publish this 'old blackguard Scotch lampoon' himself (*Letters*, xi. 46, 69). In note 5, Scott mentions the differences between his copy and the version printed by Maidment, but gives somewhat misleading details of Maidment's publication, conflating into one publication the separate appearances of the three books of *Scotish Pasquils* (1827, 1828, 1828). In the *Third Book of Scotish Pasquils* (1828), Maidment included the lampoon 'Upon the long wished for and tymely Death of the Right Honble the Lady Stair', referring to *The Bride of Lammermoor* in a brief introductory note.

5   *Sir William Hamilton of Whitelaw. . . . Lord President Stair*: Sir William Hamilton of Whitelaw (d. 1705) became a Senator of the College of Justice in 1693 and Lord Justice Clerk in 1704. In 1698 he successfully obstructed the admission of Sir Hew Dalrymple, Lord North Berwick (third son of the 1st Viscount Stair), as President of the Court of Session, insisting that he undergo the usual probationary procedures. Whitelaw had expected to be appointed Lord President himself, through the interest of the then Secretary of State, Lord Tullibardine, who was greatly offended at the slight. Dalrymple, however, duly went through his probationary period and took up the Presidency on 7 June 1698. (See George Brunton and David Haig, *An Historical Account of the Senators of the College of Justice*, 1832, pp. 462–3, 466.) Scott is mistaken, therefore, in stating that the 1st Viscount Stair and Lord Whitelaw were rivals for the Presidency, an office which had been vacant since Stair's death in 1695. It was the 1st Viscount's son who experienced Whitelaw's undoubtedly bitter and sustained rivalry. A 'writer' is a Writer to the Signet, originally a clerk in the office of the Secretary who kept the royal seal ('signet'), and by the late sixteenth century a lawyer conducting legal proceedings before the Court of Session. Scott often glosses the term as 'attorney' (as on p. 138), but 'solicitor' is now the most convenient English equivalent. Historically, attornies handled common law work, solicitors chancery, but by Scott's time the terms were roughly interchangeable.

'*Stair's neck . . . parricide, possessed*': the opening lines of the 'Satyre on the Familie of Stairs' in *Scotish Pasquils*, 1827, p. 43. Scott's judgement of the lampoon is borne out by its editor, Maidment, who remarks in his 'Prefatory Notice' that he hesitated before including this satire, which he terms 'perhaps . . . the most singular specimen of vulgar scurrility extant, in the whole range of Scotish literature' (p. xiii).

6   '*In al Stair's offspring . . . cured but by the fall*': substantially the same as the version given in *Scotish Pasquils*, 1827, pp. 53–4.

'*What train of curses . . . old uncle's spouse*': *Scotish Pasquils*, 1827, p. 48.

ill-treated by the calumny or just satire of his contemporaries, as an unjust and partial judge: one source is the 'abusive epitaph' on Whitelaw to which Scott refers in note 5 (where he mistakenly gives his first name as James). Another is the character analysis given by George Lockhart of Carnwath (1673–1731), the son of the Lord President Lockhart whose death Scott describes in note 8. George Lockhart gives a very unfavourable account of Whitelaw in *The Lockhart Papers*, 2 vols., 1817, i. 107, describing him as proud, vain, ill-natured, capable of justice when impartial, but partial in the extreme in cases involving friends or politics.

Robert Milne . . . to blacken the family of Stair: the Writer to the Signet and antiquary Robert Mylne (?1643–1747), a zealous supporter of the Stewarts, wrote notoriously bitter political squibs against the Whigs, most of which were circulated in manuscript only. His writings, collected by his son Robert, formed the basis of James Maidment's collections of *Scotish Pasquils*. Maidment gives details of Mylne's life in his 'Prefatory Notice' to the first collection in 1827. The Jacobites (from *Jacobus*, the Latin for James), supporters of the exiled Stewart family, opposed the Stairs because of their close involvement with the administration of William and Mary. Thomas Thomson (1768–1852), referred to in Scott's note 5, was a friend of Scott's, a jurist and legal antiquary.

7 *Nupta . . . Domum Ducta . . . Obiit . . . Sepult*: 'married', 'brought home', 'died', 'buried'.

Atropos: the eldest of the three Fates of Greek mythology, and the one who cuts the thread of life. She is 'impartial' because indifferent to individual life.

8 '*Sir, 'tis truth . . . full perfection*': printed as an appendix to *A Large Description of Galloway*, ed. Thomas Maitland, 1823, pp. 192–4. Scott modernizes several spellings and names.

As the work . . . almost to be unique: in his edition of *A Large Description of Galloway*, p. xii, Maitland comments that he has seen only one copy of Symson's elegies, including the elegy on Lady Baldoon: that being Scott's copy of *Tripatriarchicon, or, the Lives of the three Patriarchs, Abraham, Isaac, and Jacob, &c. digested into English Verse. (With the Author's Elegies on Archbishop Sharp, Sir George Mackenzie, &c. bound up at the end). With MS. note by Sir Walter Scott*, 1705. This is the copy to which Scott refers in note 6.

Priscian: figuratively, to err in grammar, as Symson does in line 2 in order to pay tribute to Baldoon, is to defy Priscian, the great sixth-century grammarian.

10 *Of Isthmian, Pythian, and Olympick games . . . the Nemæan and the Lethæan too*: the Isthmian, Pythian, Olympic, and Nemaean games were the four great festivals of ancient Greece, at which there were contests in racing, wrestling, gymnastics, and music, as well as processions and sacrifices. The 'Lethaean' games probably refer to the sports of the dead in Elysium, mentioned by Virgil, *Aeneid*, VI. 642–3. Lethe is the river of forgetfulness, of which all the dead must drink. Symson means, therefore, 'all games, including those reserved for the dead'.

11 *the author has endeavoured to explain the tragic tale on this principle*: Scott's usual practice when dealing with individuals reputed to have demonic powers was to provide psychological explanations, emphasizing the delusions produced by the individual's imagination, and the credulity of the times in which she or he (it is usually she) lived. An example is his characterization of Ulla Troil ('Norna of the Fitful Head') in *The Pirate* (1822).

Lord Stair . . . lawyers of his age: Scott's ambivalence about Stair's personal morality is prompted partly by contemporary character analyses (the author of the *Memoirs of John Late Earl of Stair*, for example, describes him as dishonest and unprincipled), and partly by the controversies of his political career. In a time of fierce civil dissention, his opponents particularly condemned him for the way in which he assumed the Presidency of the Court of Session, an office which he had first held under the Protectorate, on the Restoration of the monarchy in 1660; for his close association with the dictates of the crown and the actions of Lauderdale during the Covenanting struggles; and for his involvement in the Scottish policies of William II and III. His name was further tarnished by association with his eldest son, John, Master and later 1st Earl of Stair (1648–1707), who was William's chief Scottish adviser at the time of the massacre of Glencoe on 13 February 1692 (when troops killed thirty-eight people of the MacDonald clan after their chief had delayed in taking an oath of allegiance to William). The controversy over the 1st Viscount's political and legal career was sufficiently heated for him to publish in 1690 *An Apology for Sir James Dalrymple of Stair, President of the Session, By Himself* (ed. William Blair, Bannatyne Club, 1825), which defends his political integrity and points out his efforts to remove common abuses of the legal system. After his death, the report of a parliamentary commission on legal abuses, on which he had served, formed the basis of the Act for the Regulation of the Judicatures (1695).

Fast Castle: an isolated ruined stronghold, dramatically situated on a crag dropping sheer to the sea, 4 miles north-west of Coldingham in Berwickshire. In 1823 Scott was presented with a painting of Fast Castle by his friend John Thomson of Duddingston (1778–1840), and this has often been used as an illustration of the imaginary Wolf's Crag. Writing to James Skene in 1830, however, he comments: 'I do not believe these English folks can tell what Castles I meant, since I do not know them myself.' (*Letters*, xi. 331.) In the introduction to *Chronicles of the Canongate*, 1st Series, he warns against the enthusiasm for locating the supposed originals of his scenes, adding, 'The iron-bound coast of Scotland affords upon its headlands and promontories fifty such castles as Wolf's-Hope [*sic*]' (*Magnum*, xli, pp. xxiii–xxiv).

the mountain ridge of Lammermoor: the Lammermuir hills are southeast of Edinburgh. The original Dalrymple story took place in Wigtownshire, in south-west Scotland.

THE NOVEL

12 *epigraph*: 'The Gaberlunzie Man', dating from at least the seventeenth century and once attributed to James V, was included in many eighteenth-century collections of Scottish songs. The stanza here is closest to the version given in David Herd's *Ancient and Modern Scottish Songs, Heroic Ballads, etc.*, 2nd edn., 2 vols., 1776, ii. 51. Scott chooses it for its reference to 'cauk and keel' (chalk and ruddle), drawing materials appropriate to Dick Tinto's profession.

digito monstrarier: 'to be pointed at with the finger'.

the productions of the obscure Peter Pattieson . . . attracting even the old: in the frame-narrative of *Tales of My Landlord*, Pattieson, who teaches the lower classes of the small school in Gandercleugh, has already written *The Black Dwarf*, *Old Mortality*, and *The Heart of Midlothian*.

the question when . . . a hundred circles and coteries: like many of the comments in the frame-narratives of his novels, this is a sly allusion to Scott's own situation as an anonymous author.

to 'come in place as a lion,' for a winter in the great metropolis: meaning 'to enter society as a literary celebrity', but referring to *A Midsummer Night's Dream*, v. i. 225–6 ('For, if I should, as lion, come in strife | Into this place, 'twere pity on my life'). Scott repeatedly denied being ambitious for literary fame and was known for his generosity towards other writers. He describes his own behaviour in society when reflecting on the personality of another writer, Tom Moore, in his *Journal* for 1825: 'We are both goodhumoured fellows who rather seek to enjoy what is going forward than to maintain our dignity as Lions.' (p. 6.)

13 *roar you an 'twere any nightingale*: from Bottom's pleas to be allowed to play the lion in 'Pyramus and Thisbe', *A Midsummer Night's Dream*, I. ii. 83.

like imprisoned Sampson . . . the Philistine lords and ladies: Judges 16: 21–5.

like the iron and earthen vessels in the old fable: 'Two Pots' by the Roman fabulist Avianus (fl. *c.* AD 400) in Roger L'Estrange, *Fables of Aesop and Other Eminent Mythologists; With Morals and Reflections*, 2nd edn., 1692, no. 229.

Parve, nec invideo, sine me, liber, ibis in urbem: the opening address of Ovid's *Tristia*, Book I, which was written during the early years of his exile in Tomis (AD 8–12), mostly in the form of poetic letters to his wife and friends. It continues *ei mihi, quod domino non licet ire tuo!* ('Little book, you will go without me—and I grudge it not—to the city, whither alas your master is not permitted to go!').

Dick Tinto: the name, appropriately for a painter, is from the Italian *tinto* ('tinted'). Scott often gave his characters humorous names indicative of character or occupation, as he hints in his comment on Dame Lightbody (p. 147). There are many of these in *The Bride of Lammermoor*, including Cleishbotham ('flog-bottom'), the bedridden Hirplehooly (from 'hirple', meaning 'hobble', and 'hooly', meaning 'slowly' or 'cautiously'), Lady Girnington (with connotations of 'girning', 'crabbed'), Bittlebrains ('beetle-brains'), Dame Loup-the-Dike ('leap the fence', suggesting 'wayward'), Sir Coolie Condiddle (from 'con' and 'diddle'), Lord Castle-Cuddy ('cuddie' being an ass), and Jardine (from the French *jardin*, 'garden'). I comment briefly on others in context: see further, Coleman O. Parsons, 'Character Names in the Waverley Novels', *PMLA* xlix (1934), 276–94.

14 *tailor in ordinary to the village of Langdirdum in the west*: meaning that he holds a fixed and regular, rather than *ad hoc*, post as tailor, a rather grand application of a term usually reserved for official posts (especially, for Scott, the judges 'in ordinary' of the Court of Session). The fictitious place-name 'Langdirdum' ('dirdum' being either an

uproar, altercation, or punishment, blame) is more in keeping with Pattieson's profession than with Tinto's.

sub Jove frigido: 'under a cold sky'; that is, in the open air.

16 *the Scottish Teniers, as Wilkie has been deservedly styled*: the Flemish painter David Teniers the Younger (1610–90) was known for his popular and rather repetitive genre pictures of peasant life. His work was much admired in the eighteenth century, and frequently imitated. See Jane P. Davidson, *David Teniers the Younger*, 1980. Sir David Wilkie (1785–1841) was one of Scott's favourite contemporary artists, and is often referred to in the Waverley Novels as the only artist capable of conveying the feeling of certain scenes, particularly when these involve peasant life. He is invoked, for example, during the description of the funeral of the fisherman Steenie Mucklebackit in *The Antiquary* (1816), *Magnum*, vi. 130. Before 1825, Wilkie's work was influenced in technique and subject-matter by the Dutch and Flemish genre painters of the seventeenth century, particularly Teniers and Adriaen van Ostade, but his work was more pointedly anecdotal. After 1825 he produced larger works, many on historical subjects, was appointed Painter-in-Ordinary to George IV in 1830, and was knighted in 1836.

the nursery rhymes of Pope, could these be recovered: Alexander Pope (1688–1744) tells how 'As yet a child, nor yet a fool to fame, | I lisp'd in numbers, for the numbers came', in his 'Epistle to Dr Arbuthnot', 1735, lines 127–8.

the human face divine: *Paradise Lost*, III. 44, by John Milton (1608–74).

halcyon days . . . too serene to last long: 'Halcyon days' is taken from Joan la Pucelle's speech in *1 Henry VI*, I. ii. 131.

17 *in the style of Rubens*: the Flemish artist Sir Peter Paul Rubens (1577–1640) was famous for his draughtsmanship and luminous use of colour. His portraits, of which there are many, have recently undergone critical revaluation: see Frances Huemer, *Portraits*, 1977, and Hans Vlieghe, *Portraits II*, 1987, in *Corpus Rubenianum Ludwig Burchard*. Although Rubens painted sitters from several social classes, the implication here is that Tinto's style is ludicrously inappropriate to his subject.

the whetstone of mine host's wit: Pattieson misapplies a phrase from a work in keeping with his profession, the Preface to *The Schoolmaster* (pub. 1570), by Roger Ascham (1515–68), which suggests:

'There is no such whetstone, to sharpen a good wit and encourage a will to learning, as is praise.'

17 *that he had acted like the animal called the sloth . . . dying of inanition*: Scott follows the account of the sloth given by Georges Louis LeClerc, Comte de Buffon (1707–89), in his *Histoire Naturelle* (of which Scott owned the 1749–89 edition), and in English works following Buffon (e.g. Oliver Goldsmith's *An History of the Earth, and Animated Nature*, 8 vols., 1774, iv. 345–6). See *Buffon's Natural History of the Globe, and of Man; Beasts, Birds, Fishes, Reptiles, and Insects*, corrected by John Wright, 4 vols., 1831, ii. 254.

by the soul of Sir Joshua!: Sir Joshua Reynolds (1723–92), first President of the Royal Academy of Arts, was the late eighteenth century's most influential theorist of the nature and purpose of art. His *Discourses*, a series of lectures delivered to the Royal Academy between 1769 and his retirement in 1790, set forth his belief that artistic taste was not a matter of personal feeling but was based on rules of right and wrong, and could therefore be approached by the rules of reason and philosophy. Reynolds also argued that the purpose of art was to edify by attending to mankind's noblest qualities, and that the imitation of nature, in which artistic truth lay, demanded that the artist attend not to the details of particular objects but to the ideal form of the object. Like Dick Tinto, he began his career as a local portraitist.

18 *Sir William Wallace . . . the felon Edward*: Wallace (*c*.1270–1305), the Scottish general and patriot, was the champion of Scottish independence in the wars of resistance against Edward I of England (1239–1307), and a Guardian of the Scottish throne after the abdication of John Balliol, king of Scots (*c*.1250–1313). He was captured by the English in 1305 and executed in London on 23 August.

19 *that he ought not, like the stag in the fable . . . found unavailing*: in Aesop's fable 'A Stag Drinking' (L'Estrange, *Fables*, no. 43), the stag trusts to his antlers rather than to his legs for safety, only to be killed by hounds after his antlers catch in the bushes and prevent his escape.

Hogarth . . . Domenichino . . . Moreland . . . have exercised their talents in this manner: William Hogarth (1697–1764), the English painter and engraver, popularized sequences of anecdotal pictures satirizing social abuses. A ragged, scrawny artist is shown painting an inn-sign in his engraving *Beer Street* (1751). The reference to Domenichino (Domenico Zampieri, 1581–1641, of the Bolognese school), 'or somebody else', is deliberately vague. Far from being a painter of inn-signs, he is usually associated in this period with the style of dark sublimity evoked in Gothic fiction (Ann Radcliffe, in particular, liked to cite him in support of her descriptions). See Richard E. Spear, *Domenichino*, 2 vols., 1982. George Morland (1763–1804) was an English painter of picturesque landscapes and genre pictures, particularly of small scenes of middle- and working-class life from the rural past. He had a liking for bucolic subjects and a rather coarse, broad style. His paintings certainly include many inn-signs, but this is not quite the endorsement Tinto seeks.

20   *the Institution . . . Somerset-house . . . the hanging committee*: the Royal Academy of Arts was first based in Pall Mall, but transferred in 1780 to Somerset Palace, where its annual exhibition of paintings, sculpture, and designs was open to all artists of distinguished merit.

an obscure lodging in Swallow-street . . . until death came to his relief: the old Swallow Street, a large portion of which is included in the present Regent Street, ran south from Oxford Street to the present Vigo Street. The street now called Swallow Street was formerly Little Swallow Street. 'Dunning' traditionally refers to Joe Dun, a Lincoln bailiff famed for his skills in collecting bad debts.

A corner of the Morning Post noticed his death: the newspaper and gazetteer *The Morning Post*, which began in 1772, carried notices of events in fashionable life. Here, it significantly accords more space to the requirements of the gentlemanly collector than to the life or style of the dead artist.

21   *Bothwell . . . David Deans*: contrasted characters from previous works narrated by Pattieson. Francis Stewart of Bothwell, from *Old Mortality* (1816), is a licentious but courageous Royalist, killed at the battle of Drumclog (1 June 1679). David Deans is the strict old Covenanter living by dangerously outdated rules in *The Heart of Midlothian* (1818). A 'sergeant of invalids' is a sergeant disabled by illness or injury for active service.

'*Speak, that I may know thee*': the saying, usually in the form 'Speak, that I may see thee', is proverbial (see M. P. Tilley, *A Dictionary of the Proverbs in England in the Sixteenth and Seventeenth Centuries*, 1950, S. 735). Scott may be thinking of the instance in *Timber, or, Discoveries*, by Ben Jonson (1572/3–1637), which cites many ancient authorities: see *Ben Jonson*, ed. C. H. Herford, Percy and Evelyn Simpson, 11 vols., 1925–52, viii. 625.

21   *It is a false conclusion . . . I hate it, Peter, as I hate an unfilled can*: an almost exact appropriation of Sir Toby Belch's speech, *Twelfth Night*, II. iii. 6–7.

the doctrine of that Pythagorean toper . . . spoiled conversation: I have not identified the 'toper', but he is referred to as 'Pythagorean' because the name of Pythagoras, the Greek philosopher and mathematician of the sixth century BC, became a byword for temperance and abstinence, and possibly also because Pythagoras reputedly renounced unnecessary speech. The joke lies in describing any kind of toper as 'Pythagorean', as well as in giving any toper such abstemious opinions.

22   *the serene and silent art . . . one of our first living poets*: from 'Stanzas to Painting', 1803, st. 9, by Thomas Campbell (1777–1844), who made his name as a poet with *The Pleasures of Hope* in 1799. Scott was one of the first to recognize his ability, and they were lifelong friends. In 1810 Scott placed him among the three greatest contemporary poets in an article 'Of the Living Poets of Great Britain' written for the *Edinburgh Annual Register*. Campbell's later work disappointed him, however, and in his *Journal* in 1826 he looked back on his career as a lost opportunity: 'Yet Tom Campbell ought to have done a great deal more: his youthful promise was great.' (p. 164.)

before the mind's eye: *Hamlet*, I. ii. 185.

23   *in the Vandyke dress common to the time of Charles I*: the portraits of Sir Anthony Van Dyck (1599–1641), whose name was anglicized to 'Vandyke' when he was appointed Court Painter to Charles I in 1632, captured an image of an authoritative, dignified, cultured court. Since the 1730s it had been fashionable to have portraits painted in rich and decorative 'Van Dyck' dress. Both Reynolds and Thomas Gainsborough painted portraits of their contemporaries wearing such dress (see Christopher Brown, *Van Dyck*, 1982, ch. 5), and Reynolds observed in his seventh 'Discourse' that many artists made their work seem better than it really was by copying the details of Van Dyck costume. The Van Dyck style also had nostalgic associations with a lost aristocratic ideal, appropriate to the presentation of Ravenswood.

the darkened tube of an amateur: the tube enables him to see the picture more sharply. An 'amateur' is a leisured and possibly an affected cultivator of the arts. See the criticism of a similar 'hand-

formed tube' used by an amateur of the art of landscape in 'Picturesque; A Fragment', by John Aikin (1747–1822), lines 23–6.

24   *the Ape of the renowned Gines de Passamont . . . the present*: *Don
     Quixote*, Part 2, ch. 25. Gines de Pasamonte is already the 'famous'
     when he first appears as one of the galley-slaves rescued by Don
     Quixote (Part 1, ch. 22).

25   *Mr Puff in the Critic . . . Lord Burleigh's head*: *The Critic* (1779) by
     Richard Brinsley Sheridan (1751–1816), III. i. 124–9 ('Why, by that
     shake of the head, he gave you to understand that even though they
     had more justice in their cause, and wisdom in their measures—yet,
     if there was not a greater spirit shown on the part of the people, the
     country would at last fall a sacrifice to the hostile ambition of the
     Spanish monarchy.').

26   *epigraph*: from Salisbury's speech after the battle of St Alban's, *2
     Henry VI*, v. iii. 20–2.

     the same name with the castle itself, which was Ravenswood: it is unlikely
     that Ravenswood Castle is based on any one building (see Scott's
     comments quoted in my note to p. 11), but it has been identified
     with Winton House, Cranshaws Castle, Crichton Castle, and Wed-
     derlie House, among others. The name may have been suggested
     by Castle Ravensheuch, between Kirkcaldy and Dysart, mentioned
     in the notes to *The Lay of the Last Minstrel* (1805).

     Douglasses, Humes, Swintons, Hays . . . in the same country: these are
     ancient names of the Scottish Borders. The Douglases, Swintons,
     and Humes appear in the notes of *The Lay of the Last Minstrel*, set in
     the Border country. Scott resists adding his own family name to the
     list.

     towards the period of the Revolution: this refers to the 'Glorious
     Revolution' by which James VII and II (1633–1701) was declared
     to have forfeited the crown, which was then offered to his eldest
     daughter Mary (by his first marriage to Anne Hyde) and her husband
     William of Orange, bypassing his male issue by his second wife,
     Mary of Modena. The English crown was offered to William and
     Mary in 1688, the Scottish a year later in 1689. The decline of the
     Ravenswood fortunes coincides with the decline of absolute mon-
     archy.

     Saint Abb's Head and the village of Eyemouth . . . German Ocean: both
     are on the eastern Scottish coast between Berwick-upon-Tweed
     and Dunbar. St Abb's Head, a sheer headland with cliffs approx. 91

metres high, is now a National Nature Reserve famous for its seabirds. Eyemouth is a small fishing town.

27   *In the civil war of 1689 . . . his title abolished*:   Ravenswood has taken part in the rising in support of James VII and II in 1689, led by John Graham of Claverhouse (1648–89, created Viscount Dundee in 1688). Troops commanded by Major-General Hugh Mackay tracked Dundee's army across the Highlands, and engaged with it on 27 July at Killiecrankie, where the rebels were victorious but Dundee himself was killed. The rebels were later defeated at Dunkeld on 21 August, and finally routed at Cromdale on 1 May 1690. For Dundee's earlier career, see note to p. 100. For taking part in this rising, Lord Ravenswood has been charged with treason under the Act of July 1690. Conviction could lead to attainder (the loss of civil rights), loss of property and inheritance, and execution. Ravenswood has escaped the last two penalties, enabling his son to inherit his remaining property, but no title, after his death.

a family much less ancient . . . the great civil wars: the rise of the Ashtons complements that of the family on which they are based. The family of James Dalrymple, later 1st Viscount Stair, were Lairds of Stair, a small estate in Kyle, Ayrshire (a minor landowning family, therefore, rather than the pinched lawyers and religious fanatics of Ashton's family who are glimpsed through Ravenswood's eyes on p. 191). The anonymous author of *Memoirs of John Late Earl of Stair* states that the Dalrymples were merely lairds of a small grass farm and that their name 'was scarce known in *Scotland* till *Charles* the Second's Time; before that Period it was never borne by any Gentleman, and was looked upon even by the lowest Kind of People as a Sirname of Reproach' (p. 3).

a state divided by factions, and governed by delegated authority: factions based on the personal followings of a number of influential individuals as well as on the basic division between supporters and opponents of William's administration. Authority was 'delegated' because monarchs entrusted power to their Scottish ministers, especially their Commissioners to Parliament.

the Lord Keeper (for to this height Sir William Ashton had ascended):   the Lord Keeper of the Great Seal of Scotland, and a member of the Scottish Privy Council (a body of private advisers to, and selected by, the sovereign). The reference suggests that Sir William held this office before the Act of Union in 1707, which provided that there should be one Great Seal for Great Britain. After the Union, a new

Scottish seal was made for use in matters relating to private rights, grants, and commissions within Scotland, and this is kept by the Secretary of State for Scotland.

28 '*In those days there was no king in Israel*': Judges 17: 6, 18: 1.

Since the departure of James VI. . . . the delegated powers of sovereignty were alternately swayed: after his accession to the English throne in 1603, James VI and I held court at the Palace of St James in London, governing Scotland through his chosen representative, the Duke of Lennox, and his Privy Council. Scott considered the problems of Scottish subjects slighted in the English court of James in his novel *The Fortunes of Nigel* (1822). The problem of access to the king was exacerbated in the reign of his son Charles I, who, unlike his father, had no first-hand knowledge of Scottish affairs. After the execution of Charles I, the Scots, who had crowned Charles II as their king at Scone in 1651, were conquered by Cromwell and were governed in union with England (effective from 1652, though not made law until 1657) during the Commonwealth and Protectorate. The 'delegated powers of sovereignty' were at their most marked and most absolute after the Restoration of the monarchy in 1660. Despite earlier promises, Charles II did not visit Scotland after 1660, entrusting Scottish affairs to his Privy Council and deputing much of his personal authority to John Maitland, 2nd Earl and 1st Duke of Lauderdale (1616–82). Lauderdale's corrupt administration was appreciably more powerful than had been known before, and was much resented. John, 1st Earl of Middleton (*c.* 1608–74), and John Leslie, 7th Earl and 1st Duke of Rothes (1630–81), were also powerful in the reign of Charles II, and Charles's brother, the Duke of York and Albany (later James VII and II), was virtually viceroy of Scotland when he took over as Commissioner in 1681–2. The problems of governing Scotland in this way were an argument in favour of union with England, but William and Mary inherited a system which they did little to change. The most powerful of William's Scottish nobles were James Douglas, 4th Duke of Hamilton (1658–1712), John Murray, Marquis of Atholl (1659–1724), James Douglas, 2nd Duke of Queensberry (1662–1711), and John Hay, 1st Marquis of Tweeddale (1625–97). Those dominating during the reign of Anne were the 2nd Duke of Queensberry, James Ogilvy, 1st Earl of Seafield (1664–1730), John Hay, 2nd Marquis of Tweeddale (1645–1713), John Erskine, 11th Earl of Mar (1675–1732), John Campbell, 2nd Duke of Argyll (1678–1743), and James Douglas, 4th Duke of Hamilton (1658–1712). Many contemporary commentators thought that the Scottish administration was too much influenced by the interests of England and her continental allies. In 1703 Andrew Fletcher of Saltoun (1653–1716) complained in a speech to the Scottish Parliament: 'All our affairs since the union of the crowns have been managed by the advice of English ministers, and the principal offices of the kingdom filled with such men, as the court of England knew would be subservient to their designs: by which means they have had so visible an influence upon our whole administration, that we have from that time appeared to the rest of the world more like a conquered province, than a free independent people.' (*The Political Works of Andrew Fletcher*, 1732, p. 271.)

28   *the tenants of an Irish estate, the property of an absentee*: this is a highly charged comparison, using the widely condemned practice of absenteeism among Irish landlords to draw attention to Scottish problems under an 'absentee' monarch. The complaint was that landlords who owned properties in both England and Ireland frequently chose to spend their time in England, leaving their Irish tenants under the control of agents and managers, who could be unscrupulous and extortionate. Absenteeism sparked angry pamphlets and ineffective attempts at legislation in the eighteenth century: an attempt to institute an absentee tax was defeated in 1774, for example. The problem had recently been highlighted by Maria Edgeworth (1768–1849) in her novel *The Absentee* (*Tales of Fashionable Life*, 1812).

Abou Hassan . . . his own household: in 'The Story of the Sleeper Awakened', from the *Arabian Nights*, the merchant Abou Hassan is transferred while asleep to the palace of the Caliph and treated as Caliph for one day. See *Tales of the East*, collected by Scott's friend Henry Weber, 3 vols., 1812, i. 315–40.

29   *the adage, 'Show me the man, and I will show you the law'*: also used on p. 166, the saying is cited in several books of Scottish proverbs, including David Ferguson's *Scottish Proverbs* (*c*.1595), Allan Ramsay's *Collection of Scots Proverbs* (1737), and James Kelly's *Complete Collection of Scotish Proverbs Explained and Made Intelligible to the English Reader* (1721), where it is glossed: 'The Sentences of Judges may vary, according to the Measure of their Fear, Favour, or Affection.' (p. 289.)

poured forth . . . without even the decency of concealment: precise reference unidentified. It was a common enough charge. On bribery in legal cases during the reigns of James VI and I and Charles I, see Sir Edward Peyton's *The Divine Catastrophe of the Kingly Family of the House of Stuarts*, in Scott's *Secret History of the Court of James the First*, 2 vols., 1811, ii. 383–4; and in the period before 1689, *The History of the Sufferings of the Church of Scotland, from the Restauration to the Revolution*, 2 vols., 1721, 1722, by the antiquarian and church historian Robert Wodrow (1679–1734), i. 4.

the daring aim of Macbeth in the days of yore: in Shakespeare's version: see *Macbeth*, I. v, vii; II. ii.

She was a severe and strict observer . . . of devotion: in the early 1680s proceedings were brought against Lady Ashton's original, Lady Stair, for attending conventicles (unauthorized meetings for worship, restricted by Acts of 1662 and 1670), and she was known to be a strong supporter of Presbyterian preachers. In his notes to Law's *Memorialls* (p. 227), C. K. Sharpe comments: 'What, perhaps, created Lady Stair more enemies than even the exaltation of her family, was her own violent turn towards conventicles, and the fostering of silenced preachers in her house.' Scott was always suspicious of extreme professions of religious feeling, and, according to James Hogg, had a particular horror of religiously inclined women: 'There is nothing in this world to which I have a greater aversion than a very religious woman.' (*Anecdotes of Sir W. Scott*, ed. Douglas S. Mack, 1983, p. 38.)

31 *to which the Lord Keeper had made large additions in the style of the seventeenth century*: the description of the architecture of Ravenswood Castle carries political overtones. Scott uses similar accounts of an ancient mansion partially restored to provide modern comforts as images of the British constitution in Vision I of his political pamphlet of 1819, *The Visionary* (ed. Peter Garside, 1984, p. 20), and of Scots law in the 'Ashestiel' autobiography (*Scott on Himself*, ed. David Hewitt, 1981, p. 42).

a cause, founded, perhaps, rather in equity than in law: Normand comments that this is a surprising distinction for a Scottish lawyer to make (although Scott may have had his English readers in mind), for, due in part to the 1st Viscount Stair's careful work in establishing legal principles in his *Institutions*, Scottish law, unlike English, makes no formal distinction between common law and the principles of equity. Scottish courts have long worked with an undifferentiated body of common law incorporating equitable principles. The distinction is certainly less natural to a Scottish than to an English lawyer, but it is not wholly alien. Stair himself explicitly attributed a corrective equity function to the Court of Session (*nobile officium*), and Scott would certainly have been aware of Lord Kames's *Principles of Equity* (1760).

32   *Contrary to the custom . . . the funeral service of the church*: the reference places the action between the establishment of Presbyterianism in 1690, when the General Assembly banned private communion and baptism and appointed commissions to take action against recalcitrant members of the clergy, and the Toleration Act of 1712, which entitled all those of the Episcopal communion in Scotland to use the Anglican liturgy and to officiate at baptisms and marriages, providing that they took an oath of allegiance to the monarch and abjured the Stewart succession. As Normand points out, the Act of 1712 made no reference to Anglican burial services because they had never been expressly prohibited, although the restriction had probably been carried beyond the letter of the law. The priest who officiates at Ravenswood's funeral is of the 'English' communion in the first edition, of the 'Episcopal' in the 1823 *Novels and Tales*, and of the 'Scottish Episcopal' in the Magnum Opus. Scott himself was a Scottish Episcopalian.

the tory gentlemen, or cavaliers . . . most of his kinsmen were enrolled: 'Tory' was first used to describe the upholders of traditional monarchy in the reign of Charles II, then more generally applied to conservative factions throughout the eighteenth and early nineteenth centuries (including the Jacobites, adherents of the Stewart succession). The term 'cavalier' is a remnant of the terminology of the civil wars. A group of politicians in the reign of Anne so styled themselves. The close link between political and religious allegiances, on which this passage depends, was an accepted fact in the early eighteenth century. In his introduction to George Lockhart of Carnwath's *Memoirs Concerning the Affairs of Scotland, from Queen Anne's Accession to the Throne, to the Commencement of the Union of the Two Kingdoms of Scotland and England, in May, 1707* (1714), the advocate Sir David Dalrymple comments: 'No Man would make himself such a Novice in *Scotch* Affairs, as not to be Sensible, that an *Episcopalian* in *Scotland* is a Profess'd *Jacobite*.' (p. xvi.)

The presbyterian church-judicatory of the bounds . . . a warrant to prevent its being carried into effect: Presbyterian churches have a hierarchy of courts or councils. The lowest is the 'kirk-session', composed of the minister and elders of the parish or congregation. Next comes the 'presbytery' referred to here, which is a body of presbyters or elders, made up of every minister and one ruling elder from each parish or congregation within a particular local area. Above the presbytery is the 'synod', which consists of delegates from the presbyteries within its bounds, and above the synod the General Assembly, the governing body of the Church of Scotland. At this stage of the novel the action is firmly pre-Union, for Sir William Ashton is referred to as 'the nearest privy-councillor'; that is, a member of the Privy Council, which was abolished soon after the Union, in 1708.

the Master of Ravenswood: 'Master' refers to the eldest son of a lord, a title which Edgar's father has forfeited.

an hundred swords at once glittered in the air . . . 'You'll rue the day that clogs me with this answer': misquoted from *Macbeth*, III. vi. 42–3. Appropriately to the social and political contrasts conveyed in the funeral scene, the detail of the swords chivalrously raised recalls the famous description of Marie Antoinette at Versailles in *Reflections on the Revolution in France* (1790) by Edmund Burke (1729–97): 'I thought ten thousand swords must have leaped from their scabbards to avenge even a look that threatened her with insult.—But the age of chivalry is gone' (ed. Conor Cruise O'Brien, 1968, p. 170).

their countenances more in anger than in sorrow: reversing Horatio's description of the countenance of the ghost, *Hamlet*, I. ii. 231–2.

34 *a custom but recently abolished in Scotland . . . whose funeral they thus strangely honoured*: references in John Sinclair's *Statistical Account of Scotland 1791–1799* confirm that funeral revels, which could be ruinous to the families forced to bear the expense, still prevailed at the end of the eighteenth century, and were proving difficult to stop. See the comments of the ministers of Carmunnock in Lanarkshire (1796) and Gargunnock in Stirlingshire (1793), in the reissued *Statistical Account*, ed. Donald J. Withrington and Ian R. Grant, 20 vols., 1973–83, vii. 173–4, ix. 375.

a title which he still retained, though forfeiture had attached to that of his father: strictly, this is inconsistent with the loss of his father's title, but it could be retained through courtesy or custom.

36 *epigraph*: from 'Adam Bell, Clym of the Clough, and William of Cloudesly', III. 259–60, a ballad about three noted archers included in *Reliques of Ancient English Poetry*, 3 vols., 1765, by Thomas Percy, Bishop of Dromore (1729–1811), i. 159.

36   *legal commentators and monkish historians . . . a Scottish historian of the*
     period: the last part of the sentence is problematic. Andrew Lang
     suggests that Scott intends to refer to a Scottish 'library' rather than
     to a Scottish 'historian' (Border edition, xiv. 298). The manuscript
     reading is 'historian', and neither Scott nor his publishers ever
     changed it. Sir William Ashton's collection of legal commentaries
     would have included the *Jus Feudale* (*c.*1603, pub. 1655) by the
     Scottish feudalist Sir Thomas Craig (1538–1608); *The Lawes and
     Actes of Parliament* (1597) and the *Regiam Majestatem* (1609) by the
     first great Scottish legal antiquarian, Sir John Skene, Lord Curriehill
     (?1543–1617); *Laws and Customs of Scotland in Matters Criminal* (1674)
     and *Institution of the Law of Scotland* (1684) by Sir George Mackenzie
     of Rosehaugh (1636–91); and Stair's *Institutions*. Of the works of
     monkish historians, Scott's own library at Abbotsford included the
     Historia Ecclesiastica Gentis Anglorum (731/2) by Bede (672/3–735);
     the *Gesta Regum Anglorum* (1125) by William of Malmesbury (fl.
     1095–1143); the *Oryginale Cronykil of Scotland* by Andrew of Wyn-
     toun, Prior of Lochleven (*c.*1355–1422); the *Scotichronicon* of John
     of Fordun (*c.*1320– *c.*1384), continued to 1437 by Walter Bower,
     Abbot of Inchcolm (*c.*1385–1449); and the *History and Chronicles of
     Scotland* (1527) by Hector Boece (*c.*1465–1536), trans. John Bellen-
     den, 1531.

37   *an aggravated riot . . . stand committed*: in law, 'aggravation' increases
     the seriousness of any crime, through either the circumstances, the
     manner, or the intent in which it is committed. Here, Ashton
     wonders whether the supposed riot can be considered as 'aggra-
     vated' because of the intention of the rioters to challenge the
     political and religious establishment.

     Blackness Castle . . . prosecute the matter to that extent: Blackness Castle
     was a state prison situated on the Firth of Forth, in Linlithgowshire.
     Ashton's hopes for construing Ravenswood's actions as treason, for
     which he would have been executed, rest on the provisions of
     Scottish law before the new Treason Act of 1709. Normand notes
     that before 1709, threatening words to officers of the crown might,
     in the right circumstances and for the right people, have supported
     a charge of treason. Ashton's seemingly charitable reluctance to
     press the matter so far is no doubt compounded by the difficulty of
     supporting such a charge.

     Athole . . . by his own contemptible influence: John Murray, 2nd Earl
     and 1st Marquis of Atholl (1631–1703), succeeded to the earldom

of Atholl (the usual modern spelling) in 1642, to the earldom of Tullibardine in 1670, and was created Marquis of Atholl in 1676. He was a Royalist who became a member of the Privy Council on the Restoration of Charles II, and also served as Justice-General and Keeper of the Privy Seal. His behaviour at the time of the Revolution greatly disappointed the Jacobites, who had expected his active support, but was sufficiently ambiguous to lose him the trust of the ruling party also. He was one of the most powerful of Scottish magnates, controlling large territories in the central Highlands. His son John, 2nd Marquis and 1st Duke of Atholl (1660–1724), on whom the character of the novel's Marquis of A—— is based, was known as the Earl of Tullibardine from 1696 until he succeeded his father in 1703 (when the dukedom was created). Here, Sir William Ashton remembers one 'Athole' suspected of supporting James VII and II in 1688–9, and another of marked Tory leanings whose faction is gathering strength.

38 *in terrorem*: 'as a warning'.

'*I bide my time*': a motto of several Scottish families: see L. G. Pine, *A Dictionary of Mottoes* (1983).

39 *a bull's head . . . was placed upon the table*: at the infamous 'Black Dinner' of 1440, the young 6th Earl of Douglas and his brother were murdered in Edinburgh Castle during a dinner treacherously organized by Chancellor Crichton. The head of a black bull was brought to the table in token of the violent death awaiting them. The story is told in the *Historie and Cronicles of Scotland* by Robert Lindsay of Pitscottie (*c.* 1532–80). See also Scott's note to 'The Cout of Keeldar', *Minstrelsy of the Scottish Border*, rev. and ed. T. F. Henderson, 4 vols., 1932, iv. 275–6.

40 *Una, under escort of the generous lion . . . Miranda, in the isle of wonder and enchantment*: in Book I of *The Faerie Queene* (1590) by Edmund Spenser (*c.* 1552–99), the 'royall virgin' Una is separated from her champion the Redcrosse Knight by the enchanter Archimago, but is protected by a lion. Miranda, heroine of *The Tempest*, lives on an island with her father, the enchanter Prospero.

41 *he had been named after the head of the house*: ch. 1 of *The History of the Houses of Douglas and Angus* (1644) by David Hume of Godscroft (*c.* 1560–1630), tells 'Of Sholto Douglas the first that bare the name of Douglas, and of whom all that beare that name are descended'. According to Hume's story, a nameless man, who supported the cause of King Solvathius against the usurper Donald Bane, was

pointed out to the king after battle with the Irish words 'Sholto Du glasse'—which Hume translates as 'Behold yonder black, gray man'—and was subsequently given this name.

42   *like the gourd of the prophet*: Jonah 4: 6–10.

43   *there hasna been a better hunter since Tristrem's time . . . down goes the deer, faith*: in Scott's 1804 edition of the thirteenth-century romance *Sir Tristrem*, which he believed to be the work of Thomas of Erceldoune, Tristrem's hunting skills are the subject of Fytte 1, st. 27, 42–8. See note to p. 111, where Scott makes more extensive use of the comparison with Tristrem.

44   *the bad paymaster . . . who pays before it is done*: 'Pay beforehand was never well served' is recorded as a sixteenth-century proverb (*Oxford Dictionary of English Proverbs*, 3rd edn., 1970).

condictio indebiti: a Scots law phrase, referring to the action by which money paid in the belief that a debt is due may be recovered when it is shown that no such debt exists.

but sue a beggar, and—your honour knows what follows: 'Sue a beggar and get a louse', in *Paroemiologia Anglo-Latina* (1639), by John Clarke (d. 1658): a version with 'marrying' a beggar is recorded in Ramsay's *Scots Proverbs*, p. 46. Norman's hesitation suggests not just that he thinks the expression too coarse but also that he is slyly aware of how appropriate it is in the context of Ashton's legal dealings with the Ravenswoods.

Tyninghame: near Dunbar in East Lothian, but probably chosen to play on the word 'tyne', an antler.

45   *The monk must arise . . . worth them a'*: this adapts on old verse referring to places in Liddesdale famous for game, which Scott quotes in note 49 to *The Lay of the Last Minstrel*. The ambiguous reference to the pet doe is the first of several hints linking Lucy Ashton to the hunter's prey.

47   *epigraph*: from Florimell's approach to the cottage of the witch, *Faerie Queene*, III. vii. 5.

'And every bosky bourne from side to side': from Milton's *Comus*, 1634, line 312.

48   *that 'woman old'*: Scott is probably thinking of the same witch from *Faerie Queene*, Book III, but Spenser usually writes 'old woman'.

as Judah is represented sitting under her palm-tree: Deborah, not Judah, sits under a palm-tree giving advice to the Israelites (Judges 4: 4).

Scott makes the same mistake in describing a comparable scene in 'The Highland Widow' (*Chronicles of the Canongate*, 1st Series), when Elspat MacTavish is seen sitting beneath an oak 'exactly as Judah is represented in the Syrian medals as seated under her palm-tree' (*Magnum*, xli. 135). The role of the old, outcast woman with masculine features is common in Scott: Alice shares the role and many of the qualities of Meg Merrilies in *Guy Mannering* (1815), Magdalen Graeme in *The Abbot* (1820), and Ulla Troil in *The Pirate* (1822).

50 *the cup of joy and of sorrow which Heaven destined for me*: no precise biblical source, but the phrasing is reminiscent of Isaiah 51: 17.

51 *the downfall of the tree which overshadowed my dwelling*: in a letter of early 1819 Scott compared Charles Scott, 4th Duke of Buccleuch (1772–1819), who died while *The Bride of Lammermoor* was in progress, to 'the huge oak that grew on the brow of the hill and sheltered such an extent of ground' (*Letters*, v. 286). For Scott's use of the Tory symbol of the sheltering oak, see Caroline Franklin, 'Feud and Faction in *The Bride of Lammermoor*', *Scottish Literary Journal*, xiv (1987), 18–31.

52 *the fate of Sir George Lockhart*: Scott's note 8 requires a few additional comments. Sir George Lockhart of Carnwath (*c.*1630–89), who was Scotland's chief law-officer under the Cromwellian administration and was associated with the opposition to Lauderdale in 1674 and 1679, became President of the Court of Session in 1685. The circumstances of his murder were as Scott describes them. The Lord Provost of Edinburgh was granted a warrant by a specially convened meeting of the Estates of Parliament to torture Lockhart's murderer, Chiesley, in an attempt to discover possible accomplices. The Estates declared that the use of torture in this case was not to be used as a precedent for future cases, hence Scott's description of the warrant as a 'special act of the Estates of Parliament'. A 'decreet arbitral' is an award made by arbiters. The Lawnmarket, once a centre for linen merchants, runs eastward from Castle Hill in Edinburgh to the High Street, with closes on both north and south sides. The reference to *2 Henry VI*, IV. vi. 9–10 ('If this fellow be wise, he'll never call ye Jack Cade more. I think he hath a very fair warning') is to a speech made not by Cade himself but by his follower Smith the weaver, in response to a soldier's being killed for failing to address Cade as 'Lord Mortimer' moments after Cade has declared this to be his title. Scott makes the same mistaken

attribution twice in his *Letters*. Scott seems to have regarded the phrase *perfervidum ingenium Scotorum* ('the very fiery temper of the Scots') as a term used by lawyers (see *Letters*, i. 19, *The Heart of Midlothian*, ch. 1). The phrase *Scotorum praefervida ingenia* appears in the *Rerum Scoticarum Historia* (1582) by George Buchanan (1506–82): see *Georgii Buchanani: Opera Omnia*, ed. Thomas Ruddiman, 2 vols., 1715, i. 321.

54   *epigraph*: *Romeo and Juliet*, I. v. 117–18, with ominous implications.

the savage herds which anciently roamed free in the Caledonian forests . . . Cumbernauld: the wild white cattle which Scott describes are mentioned as still surviving in the Scottish forests, where they were thought to have originated, in *The History and Chronicles of Scotland* (1527) by Hector Boece (one of the 'old chronicles' mentioned in Scott's next sentence). In the estate of what was previously Hamilton Palace (pulled down in the 1920s), were the 'High Parks' around the ruins of Cadzow Castle. The whole area was known as Cadzow, as in Scott's imitation ballad 'Cadyow Castle', until 1445. The oaks in the High Parks are said to have been planted by David I to replace trees which had been part of the ancient Caledonian forest. Here, as recently as 1960, the Dukes of Hamilton kept a herd of wild white cattle. A herd was also kept at Drumlanrig Castle in Dumfriesshire (the ancient seat of the Queensberry family, now owned by the Duke of Buccleuch and Queensberry), and was still there in 1769, when it was described by Thomas Pennant in *A Tour in Scotland in 1769*. The estate and castle of Cumbernauld in Dunbartonshire were owned by the Fleming family until 1875.

The bull had lost the shaggy honours of his mane . . . black horns and hoofs: Scott's introduction to 'Cadyow Castle', in *Minstrelsy of the Scottish Border*, (ed. Henderson, iv. 178–9) similarly laments the decline in their appearance. There is a woodcut illustration of the bull in Thomas Bewick's *British Quadrupeds* (1789), with a description by John Bailey, steward of the Earl of Tankerville.

55   *Chillingham Castle, in Northumberland, the seat of the Earl of Tankerville*: the herd can still be seen today in the Park of Chillingham Castle near Wooler, the seat of the Bennets, Earls of Tankerville, from the early eighteenth century to 1931. It is first mentioned soon after the enclosure of Chillingham Park in 1629–34. There are eighteenth-century accounts in *The Gentleman's Magazine* in 1756 (xxvi. 75); in *The Natural History and Antiquities of Northumberland* (1769), by John Wallis (1714–93), which mentions that the cattle

were thought to have come originally from Scotland; and in William Hutchinson's *View of Northumberland in 1776*.

paternal tenderness, 'love strong as death,' sustained him: quoted, rather
incongruously, from Song of Solomon 8: 6.

57   *a second Egeria . . . the feudal Numa*: Numa Pompilius, king of Rome
     (traditionally 715–673 BC), was said in some later legends to have
     received advice from the water-nymph Egeria. Her role as coun-
     sellor is clearly irrelevant here: Scott is simply thinking of the
     relationship between a mortal and a water-spirit.

58   *Malleus Malificarum, Sprengerus, Remigius . . . a flash of sulphurous
     lightning*: the important collection of signs of witchcraft and the
     black arts, *Malleus Maleficarum* (1486), was intended and used as a
     guide for witch-hunters, and was the work of two Dominicans,
     Jakob Sprenger, Dean of Cologne University (1436–95), and Prior
     Heinrich Kramer (*c.*1430–1505). 'Remigius' is the French demon-
     ologist Nicholas Remy (*c.*1530–1612), whose *Demonolatraiae* (1595)
     to some extent replaced the *Malleus Maleficarum* as the leading
     authority on witch-hunting. Scott mentions the *Malleus Malificarum*
     and 'the learned inquisitor, Remigius' in his *Letters on Demonology
     and Witchcraft*, 1830, p. 207. Sulphur and flame were associated with
     the torments of the classical underworld and subsequently with
     those of the Christian Hell.

     the battle of Flodden not many months after: at the battle of Flodden
     (9 September 1513), the Scots under James IV were defeated by the
     English forces under the Earl of Surrey. The battle, a focus of strong
     national feeling in Scotland, is the subject of Canto VI of Scott's long
     narrative poem *Marmion* (1808).

59   *as for a Grahame to wear green . . . to cross the Ord on a Monday*: these
     are traditional taboos of the families mentioned. In his *Letters on
     Demonology and Witchcraft*, Scott remarks on the tradition that green
     is unlucky for the clan of Graham (usual modern spelling), 'inso-
     much, that we have heard that in battle a Grahame is generally shot
     through the green check of his plaid', and cites the authority of his
     late friend James Grahame as proof that the superstition has not died
     (p. 167). The Bruce taboo originates in the tradition that Robert
     the Bruce (Robert I of Scotland, 1274–1329), resolved at a low
     point in his fortunes to determine his future policy by the success
     or failure of a spider struggling to build a web near him. Scott tells
     the story in his *Tales of a Grandfather*, 1st Series, 3 vols., 1828 (i.
     115–18), adding that after this no Bruce would kill a spider 'because

it was such an insect which had shown the example of perseverance, and given a signal of good luck, to their great namesake'. The Earl of Orkney, chief of the St Clairs or Sinclairs, led forty of his men over the Ord of Caithness one Monday in 1513, on their way to join the army of James IV. All were killed at the battle of Flodden.

60   *A Montero cap and a black feather . . . somewhat sullen expression*: Ravenswood's appearance is in keeping with the convention of the dark brooding hero popularized by George Gordon, 6th Baron Byron (1788–1824), in such works as *The Giaour* (1813) and *Manfred* (1816); by Charles Robert Maturin (1782–1824) in *Bertram* (1816); and by Scott himself, especially in *Marmion* and *Rokeby* (1813).

62   *her eloquent blood*: from John Donne's *The Second Anniversary*, 'Of the Progress of the Soul', line 244.

66   *the auld Scotch saying, 'as soon comes the lamb's skin to market as the auld tup's'*: Lord Turntippet substitutes 'tup' ('ram') for 'sheep', the usual form of the proverb listed in Ramsay's *Scots Proverbs* and Kelly's *Scotish Proverbs*. The concentration of proverbs and old sayings in the following scene humorously suggests the canny old councillors' preference for indirect expression.

67   *'A wilful man maun hae his way'*: see note to p. 188.

'If he hasna gear to fine' . . . And that was our way before the Revolution: Kelly's version is 'He that has no Geer to tine ['lose'], may have shines to pine' (*Scotish Proverbs*, p. 149). Kelly's comment clarifies Turntippet's claim: 'He that has done a Misdemeanour, if he be not able to pay a Fine, may be put to corporal Punishment. I have heard it apply'd by covetous Creditors, to their insolvent Debtors; but, if put in Execution, it is vile, cruel, and ungodly.' Turntippet's name recalls the saying 'to turn one's tippet', meaning to change course, to be a turncoat.

Luitur cum persona . . . gude law Latin: 'law Latin' is the debased Latin used in legal documents. This particular phrase is Turntippet's invention, not included in John Trayner's *Latin Phrases and Maxims* (1861). Scott translates it in note 10: it ought to begin with 'luito', not 'luitur'.

my Lord Treasurer: the Scottish Treasury was abolished in 1708 and replaced by an Exchequer based on the Westminster model.

Shame be in my meal-poke, then . . . and your hand aye in the nook of it!: Kelly includes this in the form 'Poor be your Meal Poke, and ay your nieve in the Nook o't', which he explains as 'A jocose

Imprecation to them who call us Poor; as poor Boy! poor *Jack*! pretending to pity us.' (*Scotish Proverbs*, p. 278.)

you are like the miller's dog . . . the man is not fined yet: Ramsay's *Scots Proverbs* records the saying 'Ye're like the Miller's Dog, ye lick your Lips ere the Pock be opened' (p. 81). Kelly includes a similar version, explained as 'Spoken to covetous People, who are eagerly expecting a thing, and ready to receive it, before it be proffered.' (*Scotish Proverbs*, p. 361.)

I, wha hae complied wi' a' compliances . . . for these thirty years bypast: Turntippet multiplies terms describing the various tests enjoined upon those holding public office in the second half of the seventeenth century and the early years of the eighteenth. Law had commented in his *Memorialls* that 'for a long time during the changes of government in this ileand, there was nothing but oaths taken this year, and contradictorie oaths the next, a practice hateful to the very heathen' (ed. C. K. Sharpe, p. 7). From 1662 all office-holders had to declare against the Covenants. The Test Act and Oath of 1681 then demanded of them unconditional acceptance of the sovereign's supremacy in spiritual and temporal matters. This was impossible for Covenanters, for whom the spiritual head of the Church could only be Christ, and it caused widespread problems in Scotland. The 1st Viscount Stair fled to Holland in an effort to escape the severity shown to Archibald Campbell, 9th Earl of Argyll, whose 'Explication' that he took the oath 'in as far as it is consistent with itself, and the Protestant Religion' led to his conviction, attainder, and eventual execution for high treason (Wodrow, *History of the Sufferings of the Church of Scotland*, ii. 205–17). In 1693 William demanded that all civil, military, and church office-bearers swear an 'Assurance' recognizing him as king *de jure* as well as *de facto*. 'Abjuration' recalls both the demanded abjuration of the 'Apologetical Declaration' in 1684 (see note to p. 144), and the troublesome Abjuration Oath demanded of all ministers by the Toleration Act of 1712. This second Abjuration Oath, originally imposed in England in 1701, was intended to hinder those sympathetic to the claims of the Stewarts, which the oath required them to deny, but many Presbyterians would not take it because it required them to recognize the claims of the Church of England. Lord Turntippet has clearly been untroubled by the scruples which made the various tests and oaths of the period so contentious.

69 *epigraph*: anglicized from st. 28 of 'Duncan: A Fragment from an Old Scots Manuscript' (1762), by Henry Mackenzie (1745–1831) (*The Works of Henry Mackenzie*, 8 vols., 1808, viii: Scott owned this edition). The speaker has come to challenge the young husband of his niece, who has married without his consent, and his words reject her pleas for peace. In the ensuing fight she is killed by an arrow deflected from her husband's shield. The lines have limited relevance to the chapter, warriors and idle tales being loosely linked to Scott's depiction of the debased Jacobitism of Craigengelt, but they add to the anticipations of doomed love and family opposition gathering around Ravenswood and Lucy.

notwithstanding its light grey colour: in the writing of Scott and his contemporaries, 'fire' and 'expression' are qualities usually reserved for those with dark eyes. Scott's own eyes were light grey. 'I am sorry I can find no other expression in his face save good nature', wrote Lady Charlotte Bury, an enthusiastic admirer of his work, in her *Diary Illustrative of the Times of George the Fourth*, 4 vols., 1838, 1839, iii. 154.

70 *but that I hold a hasty man no better than a fool*: Craigengelt's source is unusual for him: Proverbs 29: 20 ('Seest thou a man that is hasty in his words? there is more hope of a fool than of him.')

what have I to do with the Irish brigade?: a body of troops in the pay of the French king. See next note.

secret intelligence from Saint Germains . . . should perish from the way: Craigengelt is supposedly an agent of the exiled Stewart family, who had held court under the protection of Louis XIV of France at the château of Saint-Germain-en-Laye near Paris since 1688. When James VII and II died in 1701 his 13-year-old son James Francis (1688–1766) was declared King James VIII and III. Significantly, Bucklaw refers to him here not as 'King James' but, more neutrally, as the 'Chevalier' (de St George), a title conferred on him by Louis XIV. The stronghold of Jacobite support was in the Scottish Highlands, and Bucklaw makes fun of the kind of sentimental enthusiasm on which the Stewarts could always depend from those unable to be of much practical help. Scott portrays two such Jacobite ladies in the Misses Arthuret of *Redgauntlet* (1824).

71 *the French brig L'Espoir*: the name of the ship means 'The Hope'. Although James Francis was later required to leave France by the treaty of Utrecht in 1713, all the attempts to win back Britain for the Stewarts (the most important being in 1708, 1715, 1719, and

1745–6) were built on the hope of French military support (hence Craigengelt's references to the French palace of Versailles), and greatly weakened by the lack of it. Craigengelt here emphasizes the close involvement of the French king in all Jacobite plans. See Bruce Lenman, *The Jacobite Risings in Britain 1689–1746* (1980).

72   *no time for grass to grow beneath their heels*: adapted from the proverbial expression 'He'll no let Grass grow at his Heels' (Ramsay, *Scots Proverbs*, p. 24).

art and part: in Scots law 'art and part' are the words used when making a charge of accession to a crime. Normand notes that in Scots law, unlike English, only accession before the fact involves the accessory in the same guilt as the principal, except in the charge of treason.

'The dial spoke not . . . the stroke of murder': from Bertran's self-justifying speech in the tragi-comedy *The Spanish Fryar or the Double Discovery* (1681) by John Dryden (1631–1700), IV. ii. 90–1. Scott, who had edited Dryden's works in 1808, may have had in mind the play's plot, which centres upon a usurpation and the denial of a lawful inheritance.

the Fatal Conspiracy: this is not the title of an actual play (although there are many like it, such as 'The Fatal Contract', 'The Fatal Discovery'), but a humorous reference to the treasonable plots of the Jacobites.

73   *'Thus from the grave . . . and glory leads the way'*: misquoted from Alexander's speech concluding Act IV of the tragedy *The Rival Queens; or, Alexander the Great* (1677) by Nathaniel Lee (?1649–92). Pattieson calls him 'poor Lee' because of his declining literary abilities, his period of insanity (he was confined to Bedlam for five years), and his ignominious death, hastened by alcohol.

Jacobuses: gold coins worth 25 shillings, first issued by James VI and I.

75   *he had gallows written on his brow in the hour of his birth*: meaning that he looks as if he were born to be hanged, like the Boatswain in *The Tempest*, I. i. 28–33, and the hero of *The History of Tom Jones* (1749) by Henry Fielding (1707–54), a novel which Scott greatly admired.

the expense of freight and demurrage!: the charges made for hiring a vessel to transport goods, and the compensation to be paid if the vessel is detained beyond the agreed time.

76   *it's good sleeping in a haill skin*: the saying is included in Ramsay's
      Scots Proverbs and Kelly's *Scotish Proverbs*, where it is explained as
      'An Apology of, or a Reflection upon, him that shuns Dangers'
      (p. 220).

      'Little kens the auld wife . . . hurle-burle swire': also included in
      Ramsay's *Scots Proverbs* and Kelly's *Scotish Proverbs*. Kelly suggests
      that the 'Hurle-Burle-Swire' refers to a particularly windy passage
      through a ridge of mountains separating Nithsdale from Tweeddale
      and Clydesdale, adding: 'The Meaning is, that they, who are at Ease,
      know little of the Trouble that others are expos'd to.' (p. 230.)

77   *epigraph*: st. 27 of 'Graeme and Bewick' in Scott's *Minstrelsy of the
      Scottish Border*, where the first line reads 'O hald thy tongue, now,
      billie Bewick' (ed. Henderson, iii. 83).

78   *have more reason in your wrath to-morrow*: this resembles the expres-
      sion 'Take Wit in your Anger', in Ramsay's *Scots Proverbs*, p. 59.

79   *sending, like one of Ossian's heroes, his voice before him*: James Mac-
      pherson (1736–96) created a literary sensation in the 1760s with a
      series of works which he presented as translations from the legend-
      ary Gaelic bard Ossian. Sceptics, the most influential of whom was
      Samuel Johnson, always doubted the authenticity of his work, but
      the supposed discovery of primitive heroic fragments had a genuine
      impact on the subject-matter and style of literature and on eight-
      eenth-century literary theory. A committee chaired by Henry
      Mackenzie decided in 1805 that Macpherson had liberally edited
      Gaelic poems and inserted passages of his own, a view supported by
      modern critics. The heroes of such works as *Fragments of Ancient
      Poetry, Collected in the Highlands of Scotland, and Translated from the
      Galic or Erse Language* (1760), *Fingal, an Ancient Epic Poem* (1762),
      and *Temora* (1763) included Fingal, Cuthullin, and Oscar. As ap-
      plied to the boy on the ass, this is a mock-heroic touch which does
      not follow a specific formula found in Ossian, although there are
      many passages in which heroes call aloud before battle and in which
      their voices carry far.

81   *you have indeed nourished in your bosom the snakes that are now stinging
      you*: this recalls Richard II's anger at the favourites who he thinks
      have deserted him for Bolingbroke: 'Snakes, in my heart-blood
      warm'd, that sting my heart!', *Richard II*, III. ii. 131.

      an affectionate father murdered!: echoing the comparable situation of
      Hamlet, 'the son of a dear father murthered', *Hamlet*, II. ii. 583.

82   *the expression of the English divine . . . 'Hell is paved with good intentions'*:
see the saying 'Hell is full of good meanings and wishings', no. 170
in *Jacula Prudentum* (1651: the enlarged version of *Outlandish
Proverbs*, 1640) by George Herbert (1593–1633), who entered the
priesthood towards the end of his life.

83   *A wilder, or more disconsolate dwelling, it was perhaps difficult to conceive*:
the description of Wolf's Crag strongly recalls that of the ruined
watchtower on the edge of a cliff in *The Milesian Chief* (4 vols., 1812)
by the Irish novelist and dramatist Charles Robert Maturin (1782–
1824), i. 53–6. This is the last property of a ruined aristocratic family
whose castle in Connaught has been bought by a wealthy newcomer. The love which develops between the heir, Connal O'Mor-
ven, and the daughter of his displacer, Armida Fitzalban, has
sometimes been cited as a source for Scott's story.

84   *the seven sleepers*: according to legend, seven Christian youths slept
in a cave in Mount Celion from the reign of the Emperor Decius
to the reign of Theodosius II, a period of 196 years.

my master's ghaist, or even his wraith: the difference is that a
'ghost' represents a dead person, a 'wraith' (originally and chiefly a
Scottish term) a living person whose death it frequently
portends. Scott comments in his *Minstrelsy of the Scottish Border*:
'The *wraith*, or spectral appearance, of a person shortly to die, is a
firm article in the creed of Scottish superstition.' (ed. Henderson,
i. 198.)

men of mould: meaning 'men of bodily substance', and quoting
Henry V, III. ii. 22.

85   *and never asked a whig's leave*: 'whig', used to describe adherents of
the Presbyterian cause in the second half of the seventeenth century,
was probably first used following the 'Whiggamore Raid' made by
Covenanters from the West of Scotland on Edinburgh in 1648.
From about 1679 it was used to describe those who opposed the
succession of the Roman Catholic James VII and II; from 1688–9,
to describe the supporters of the Revolution establishment under
William and Mary; and later, from 1714, to describe the supporters
of the Hanoverian succession.

let them care that come ahint: see Ramsay, *Scots Proverbs*, p. 44.

86   *the Bass and North-Berwick Law*: the Bass Rock, about 1½ miles out
to sea from North Berwick, is a small precipitous island once used
as a prison. North Berwick Law is a conical hill, approx. 187 metres

high, rising behind the town. They are feasible sights from the imagined situation of Wolf's Crag.

87   *the beams . . . combined like those of Westminster-Hall*: now the only surviving part of the original Palace of Westminster, and for centuries the chief lawcourt of England, Westminster Hall was built by William Rufus in 1097 and altered by Richard II between 1397 and 1399, when its magnificent oak hammer-beam roof was added.

88   *the bogle*: Scott distinguishes this class of spirit in his introduction to *Minstrelsy of the Scottish Border* as 'a freakish spirit, who delights rather to perplex and frighten mankind, than either to serve, or seriously to hurt, them' (ed. Henderson, i. 150).

91   *the Gowrie Conspiracy*: this refers to a mysterious affair of 5 August 1600, when James VI was invited to Gowrie House in Perth by Alexander, Master of Ruthven, and claimed to have been threatened with death there. James's followers killed the Master and Earl of Ruthven, and there has always been a suspicion that the whole affair was planned by the king to rid himself of the Ruthvens. On the whole, modern historians accept that there was some kind of treasonable conspiracy.

92   *epigraph*: Scott's own version, drawing on two stanzas (2 and 4) from Part II of 'The Heir of Linne', a ballad included in Percy's *Reliques*, ii. 313–14. The lines refer to the dilapidated 'lonesome lodge' which is all that remains of the estate of a dissolute young Scottish lord, the Heir of Linne. The Heir sells his lands to John o' the Scales before remembering a behest of his father, which leads him to three chests containing enough money to buy them back. The references in the first paragraph of this chapter are to the same ballad.

Favourable to calm reflection . . . agitated on the preceding day: Scott quotes the Latin proverb *Aurora Musis amica* ('Dawn a friend to the Muses') in his *Journal* in 1826, commenting that he strongly believes in its truth: 'If I forget a thing over night I am sure to recollect it as my eyes open in the morning—the same if I want an idea or am encumberd by some difficulty—the moment of waking always supplies the deficiency, or gives me courage to endure the alternative.' (p. 151.)

93   *the important task of self-examination*: Ravenswood is the only lay character to be seen at his religious devotions. He is implicitly contrasted to Lady Ashton, a strict observer of the 'external forms'.

the exiled Earl of Angus . . . a king's resentment: Archibald Douglas, 6th Earl of Angus (?1489–1557), married Margaret Tudor, widow of James IV, and held her young son James V in strict tutelage. He lost control over James when Albany was made regent in 1516, seized him in 1525, and in 1528 was declared guilty of treason. He lived in England as a pensioner of the court of Henry VIII from 1529 to 1542, taking part in several Border raids, and returned after the deaths of Margaret (1541) and James V (1542). His stronghold, Tantallon Castle, in which he resisted two sieges by James's forces, lies between Dunbar and North Berwick, not far from the area in which *The Bride of Lammermoor* is set. Scott tells a romanticized version of the story of the exiled Earl of Angus and James V in his long narrative poem *The Lady of the Lake* (1810).

the sleeper awakened: echoing the tale of the same name from *The Arabian Nights*, already referred to on p. 28.

does the deer that is to make the pasty run yet on foot, as the ballad has it?: 'The meate, that we must supp withall, | It runneth yet fast on fote', are lines 27–8 in Part III of 'Adam Bell, Clym of the Clough, and William of Cloudesly' (Percy's *Reliques*, i. 149).

94   *the green purse and the wee pickle gowd, as the old song says*: 'I have a green purse, and a wee pickle gowd' is the opening line of a song in Allan Ramsay's *Tea-Table Miscellany*, 4 vols., 1724–40, and in Herd's *Ancient and Modern Scottish Songs*, ii. 94.

an end of an auld sang, and an auld serving man to boot: George Lockhart of Carnwath describes how the Earl of Seafield, the last Lord Chancellor of Scotland, signed the Act of Union and 'returned it to the clerk, in the face of Parliament, with this despising and contemning remark, "Now there's ane end of ane old song" ' (*Lockhart Papers*, i. 223). Caleb's allusion to this celebrated remark is therefore apposite to the political milieu of the novel. Scott always gives Seafield's 'despising and contemning remark' an elegiac air, as in the speech of the Baron of Bradwardine, lamenting the death of Jacobite hopes at the end of *Waverley* (*Magnum*, ii. 340), and in his personal reflection on the dangers posed to the Scottish legal system by the appellate jurisdiction of the House of Lords (*Journal*, pp. 156–7).

97   *the Marquis of A——*: the Marquis of Atholl (the usual modern spelling), mentioned by name on p. 37.

The Marquis . . . a probable subversion of their power: in broad terms, Sir William Ashton is envisaged as belonging to the Court party, which adhered to the present administration, and the Marquis to the Country, or opposition, party. Scott improvises upon the character of the 2nd Marquis and 1st Duke of Atholl (see note to p. 37), who was opposed to the Union of 1707, not to the Revolution. He had served King William as Secretary of State and Commissioner to Parliament, 1696–8, resigning over his failure to secure Sir William Hamilton of Whitelaw the Presidency of the Court of Session. He was a member of Queen Anne's Privy Council, and was made Keeper of the Privy Seal in 1703. Atholl's support for the Act of Security (see Appendix, 1704) brought him into conflict with the Court party headed by the 2nd Duke of Queensberry, and he joined with the Duke of Hamilton and the Country party to oppose the proposed Union. After Hamilton's participation waned in 1706, he became the leading aristocratic opponent of the Union. In 1708 he was suspected of plotting with the Jacobites, and was cited to appear before the Privy Council, but pleaded illness. After the Tory election victory of 1710, he was chosen to sit in the House of Lords as one of Scotland's representative peers. Although he supported the Hanoverian succession in 1714, three of his sons declared for the Stewarts, and the loyalties of the Atholl family were divided during the Jacobite troubles of the eighteenth century.

97   *a probable change of ministers and measures in the Scottish administration*: in the post-Union dating of the Magnum Opus, the party currently in power would be the Court faction headed by the 2nd Duke of Queensberry, a Whig. Due in part to the unpopularity of the war with France, the British administration led by Godolphin faced increasingly strong opposition from the Tory and High Church factions, who won a decisive election victory in 1710.

98   *the stories they tell of the sloth . . . and break our necks*: see note to p. 17.

We have had one revolution too much already, I think: Bucklaw refers to the Revolution of 1688–9, which, as a professed Jacobite, he would have aimed to reverse.

by the aid of our friend Ballantyne's types: Scott first met his friend and publisher James Ballantyne (1772–1833) at school in Kelso in 1783. Ballantyne undertook publication of Scott's *Minstrelsy of the Scottish Border* in 1802 and 1803, and in 1805 Scott became a partner in his firm, which was renowned for its high standards of typography. James and his younger brother John (1774–1821), who had a publishing and bookselling business, were important figures in Scott's life, and it was to James that Scott entrusted much of the editorial work on the texts of his novels. The firm of Ballantyne and Co. printed *The Bride of Lammermoor* in 1819, but the reference here is a slip: Peter Pattieson, the novel's narrator, is supposed to have died while his works were still in manuscript.

99   *the proverb, verbum sapienti . . . a sermon to a fool*: *Dictum sapienta sat est* ('a word to the wise is enough'), in Plautus, *Persa* and Terence, *Phormio*; hence *verbum sapienti*.

sliddery ways crave wary walking: this sounds proverbial, although there is no mention of it in books of Scottish proverbs. It may be a reminiscence of a discussion of temptation in *A Practical Treatise Concerning Humility* (1707) by the English divine John Norris (1657–1711), 'the more slippery the ground is, the more circumspectly should we walk' (p. 396).

come to this our barren Highland country to kill a stag . . . inditing to you anent: the seemingly innocuous invitation has a concealed political implication. In preparation for the Jacobite rebellion of 1715, the Earl of Mar held a *tinchal*, or deer-hunt, in the Forest of Braemar, at which plans for the rebellion were made. In Scott's first novel, *Waverley*, ch. 24, the hero becomes entangled in Jacobite plots by innocently attending a similar hunt in the company of his friend Fergus MacIvor.

100   *our poor house of B——*: Blair Castle, near Blair Atholl in Perthshire, the seat of the Earls and Dukes of Atholl, was at this time the most important military post in the area. It was garrisoned in 1689 by Viscount Dundee, immediately before the battle of Killiecrankie, and partly dismantled in 1690 to prevent its farther occupation by the supporters of James VII and II. It was remodelled into a modern mansion in the eighteenth century by the 2nd Duke.

These, with haste, haste, post haste—ride and run until these be delivered: very similar to the command used as epigraph to ch. 15 of *The Antiquary* (1816), described as an 'Ancient Indorsation of Letters of Importance' (*Magnum*, v. 200).

Wit's Interpreter, or the Complete Letter-Writer: *Wit's Interpreter: the English Parnassus. Or, a Sure Guide to those Admirable Accomplishments that Compleat our English Gentry in the Most Acceptable Qualifications of Discourse or Writing, &c.* (1655), was the work of John Cotgrave. Scott owned a copy of the 3rd edition (1671). *The Complete*

Letter-Writer, a comparable manual, went through numerous editions in the second half of the eighteenth century, too late for Bucklaw.

100 *of the first and second Charles, and of the last James . . . their descendants*: the reigns of the Stewart kings Charles I (reigned 1625–49), Charles II (reigned 1660–85), and James VII and II (reigned 1685–88 in England, –89 in Scotland) were dogged by civil and religious troubles, during which the concerns of Scotland were widely seen to take second place to those of England. All three kings showed a liking for personal authority and control, culminating in the determination of James VII and II to win toleration for his fellow Roman Catholics in spite of strong popular opposition. Their Stewart descendants were expected to share this predilection.

the crop-eared dogs, whom honest Claver'se treated as they deserved: 'crop-eared' is a favourite term of abuse for Presbyterians, Covenanters, and Puritans among Scott's conservative characters. Francis Grose's *Dictionary of the Vulgar Tongue* (1785) describes it as a nickname for a Presbyterian, 'one with very short hair', but it was probably also intended to recall those whose ears had literally been cropped as punishment for obduracy in religious and political matters. Cutting in the ear was one of the persecutions suffered by the Covenanters during the 'killing time' of 1681–5. John Graham of Claverhouse commanded troops against the Covenanters at Drumclog, was present at the battle of Bothwell Bridge (both 1679), and was an active persecutor of the Covenanters in south-west Scotland between 1682 and 1685. A hero of Jacobites and Episcopalians like Bucklaw, and a figure who held considerable fascination for Scott, he is a major character in *Old Mortality* (1816), which is centred on the events of 1679. He died opposing the accession of William and Mary in 1689. See Andrew Murray Scott, *Bonnie Dundee* (1989).

101 *They first gave the dogs an ill name, and then hanged them*: based on the saying 'Give a dog an ill name and he'll soon be hanged', included in Ramsay's *Scots Proverbs* and Kelly's *Scotish Proverbs*. Ravenswood's enlightened tolerance of the Covenanters' principles distinguishes him from the novel's older Tories (the Marquis and Balderstone).

Whig and Tory . . . cant terms of idle spite and rancour: Ravenswood's views are close to Scott's own, as expressed in his *Journal* in 1826: 'So the Tories and Whigs may go be damnd together as names that have distracted Old Scotland and torn asunder the most kindly feelings since the first day they were invented.' (p. 63.) Scott had

Tory sympathies, but condemned rigid adherence to narrow partisan ideology, declaring in his political writings of 1819 that both Whig and Tory interests were necessary to balance the political system (*The Visionary*, ed. Garside, p. 5). In fact, the party division between Whig and Tory which was a feature of English politics at the time in which the novel is set was not nearly so strongly marked in Scotland. The factions and loyalties of the Scottish politicians caused considerable confusion among the English (see P. W. J. Riley, 'The Structure of Scottish Politics and the Union of 1707', in *The Union of 1707: Its Impact on Scotland*, ed. T. I. Rae, 1974, pp. 1–29). Ravenswood's words, of course, refer to party enmity on all levels, not just the parliamentary.

the iron . . . our sides and our souls: Bucklaw revises the Prayer Book's words, 'the iron entered into his soul', to emphasize the physical reality of civil struggle in seventeenth-century Scotland.

'To see good corn . . . the thing that would wanton me': Burns records lines very like these ('To see gude corn upon the rigs, | And banishment amang the Whigs, | And right restor'd where right sud be, | I think it wad do meikle for to wanton me') in the second of two 'old stanzas' which he associates with the Scottish air 'To daunton me', in notes made in his copy of *The Scots Musical Museum* by James Johnson (6 vols., 1787–1803). See *Notes on Scottish Song by Robert Burns, Written in an Interleaved Copy of the Scots Musical Museum with Additions by Robert Riddell and Others*, ed. J. C. Dick, 1908, pp. 35–6. The lines refer to the Revolution of 1688–9. Bucklaw's reference here suggests that they were acknowledged variants of the usual lines printed in collections of Scottish song.

cantabit vacuus: this is part of the line *Cantabit vacuus coram latrone viator* ('the empty-handed traveller will whistle in the robber's face'), line 22 in the Tenth Satire of Juvenal.

102   *not a pair of clean spurs . . . Border fashion of old times?*: 'We are told, that when the last bullock which Auld Wat [Scott's ancestor] had provided from the English pastures was consumed, the Flower of Yarrow [his wife] placed on her table a dish containing a pair of clean spurs; a hint to the company that they must bestir themselves for their next dinner.' (Lockhart, *Life of Scott*, i. 93.) Scott tells the tale in the introduction to *Minstrelsy of the Scottish Border*, and includes in his collection John Marriott's modern ballad 'The Feast of Spurs' (ed. Henderson, i. 154, iv. 379–84). Caleb's reference to

'an honourable and thriving family' in his reply is characteristic of
Scott's oblique celebrations of his family's past.

102   *Saint Magdalen's Eve, who was a worthy queen of Scotland in her day*:
Margaret (1046–93), daughter of Edward 'the Exile' and grand-
daughter of King Edmund Ironside, married Malcolm III of Scotland in 1069, and became renowned for her piety and good works.
She is the only Scottish saint to enjoy a universal cult in the Roman
calendar. Her feast-day is 16 November, her translation 19 June,
which makes the novel's chronology accurate at this point. Ravenswood's father is buried on 'a November morning', Bucklaw takes
refuge in Wolf's Crag on the evening of the next day, and this scene
takes place after he has spent three or four days there.

104   *epigraph*: *Ethwald*, I. i. 31–5, in vol. ii (1802) of *A Series of Plays in
which it is Attempted to Delineate the Stronger Passions of the Mind*, by
Scott's friend and favourite living dramatist, Joanna Baillie (1762–
1851).

Light meals procure light slumbers: this recalls the proverbial saying,
'Light Suppers make lang Life Days', included in Ramsay, *Scots
Proverbs*, p. 44.

105   *your lordship's right of free forestry*: rights granted by Crown charter,
encroachments on which could be severely punished under Acts of
1534, 1592, 1594, and 1627. (Normand)

108   *Take the goods . . . as the great John Dryden says*: slightly misquoted
from 'Alexander's Feast; or the Power of Musique. An Ode, in
Honour of St. Cecilia's Day' (1697), line 106.

'Hyke a Talbot!' . . . unremitting chorus: a common form of the cries
to arms associated with individual families was the name of the
family itself. Scott had made a list of these family slogans, later used
by Robert Chambers (1802–71) in *Popular Rhymes, Fireside Stories,
and Amusements, of Scotland*, 1842, p. 31. Many of Scott's hunting
details come from his knowledge of *The Book Containing the Treatises
of Hawking; Hunting; Coat-Armour; Fishing; and Blasing of Arms*
(1486), by Dame Juliana Berners (b. ?1388), and *The Noble Art of
Venerie or Hunting* (1611), both of which he had used for his edition
of *Sir Tristrem* in 1804.

109   *With his stately head bent down . . . an object of intimidation to his pursuers*:
the moment when the hunted animal turns prefigures both
Ravenswood's challenge in ch. 33 and the crisis of Lucy's wedding
night.

110   *the Cabrach*: the Buck of Cabrach is a mountain near the western
       boundary of Aberdeenshire.

       'If thou be hurt . . . thereof have lesser fear':   these lines are a standard
       element of Scott's hunting lore, introduced in note 3 of *The Lady
       of the Lake* and in the note to ch. 24 of *Waverley* (*Magnum*, i. 254).

111   *to break up the stag*: 'to break' ('dissect') is the term used in *Sir
       Tristrem* (Scott's edition, Fytte 1, st. 42) and by Dame Juliana
       Berners. Jerome Mitchell has suggested that Scott means to indicate
       a flaw in Bucklaw's gentility by having him use the expression
       incorrectly (*Scott, Chaucer, and Medieval Romance*, 1987, p. 122).
       However, Scott seems to have accepted 'to break up' as the most
       natural modern alternative, for he uses this in his own summary of
       the argument of *Sir Tristrem*, p. 4.

       to care about man or woman either: echoing *Hamlet*, II. ii. 309.

       with the precision of Sir Tristrem himself . . . now probably antiquated: in
       Sir Tristrem, Fytte 1, st. 41–8 (Scott's edition), Tristrem encounters
       a group of hunters and offers them detailed advice on the correct
       way to 'break' a stag. Of the terms referred to as 'now probably
       antiquated', 'nombles', 'flankards', and 'raven-bones' certainly
       were. 'Nombles' or 'numbles' (last recorded use before publication
       of *The Bride of Lammermoor*, 1688) is an obsolete term for the innards
       of a deer, particularly parts of the back and loins. 'Brisket' is the part
       of the animal immediately covering the breast-bone. 'Flankards' is
       an obsolete hunting term for knots in the flanks of the deer, last
       recorded in 1616 (*OED 2* makes no mention of Scott's usage).
       'Raven-bones' (last recorded use before publication of *The Bride of
       Lammermoor*, 1637) is an obsolete term for the gristle on the brisket-
       bone, so called because it was left for the ravens.

113   *ad re-œdificandum antiquam domum*: 'to rebuild the ancient house'.

114   *'Frequented by few . . . the hills that encircle the sea'*: slightly misquoted
       from st. 1 of 'Lines Written on Visiting a Scene in Argyleshire'
       (1800), which describes the ruined home of his forefathers, by
       Thomas Campbell, author of *The Pleasures of Hope* (1799).

117   *the nakedness of the land*: Genesis 42: 9, 12.

       as mad as the seven wise masters!: *The Seven Sages of Rome* or *The
       Proces of the Seuen Sages* is a metrical romance of the early fourteenth
       century, included in two collections of romances by friends of Scott
       (George Ellis's *Specimens of Early English Metrical Romances*, 1805,
       and Henry Weber's *Metrical Romances*, 1810). Scott also owned

a chapbook version. In his review of Ellis's *Specimens* and Ritson's *Ancient English Metrical Romances* for the *Edinburgh Review* in 1806, he referred to it as a romance 'long known among the school-boys of this country' (*The Miscellaneous Works of Sir Walter Scott, Bart.*, 30 vols., 1869–71, xvii. 50).

117   *this new invasion of Philistines*: the Philistines, a warlike people of ancient Palestine, contested its possession with the Israelites. There are several references to hostilities throughout the Old Testament: 2 Chronicles 28: 18 refers to an invasion.

118   *epigraph*: slightly altered from Part III, st. 5 of 'The Rime of the Ancient Mariner' (first published in *Lyrical Ballads*, 1798), by Samuel Taylor Coleridge (1772–1834).

119   *the gate of the castle was never on any account opened during meal-times*: Caleb's ruse is ludicrous, but the practice was serious enough in periods of civil strife. Scott comments on it in his note to ch. 8 of *Old Mortality* (*Magnum*, ix. 374).

like Louis XIV. . . . without directly lying: Louis XIV (1638–1715), nicknamed the 'Sun King', had reigned in France since 1643. He was known for his cultivation of absolute personal power, through which he attempted to control all aspects of the country's politics and administration, and for the manipulation and hypocrisy which this sometimes entailed. His support for the exiled Stewarts, which he never carried quite as far as they needed or expected, is a pertinent example of his policies of promise and prevarication. The chief contemporary account of his life and times was *Le Siècle de Louis XIV* (1751) by Voltaire (1694–1778). See further, John B. Wolf, *Louis XIV*, 1968.

If the king on the throne were at the gate: Anne's husband, George, Prince of Denmark (1653–1708), was never granted the title of king. Although many compensating posts and titles were conferred on him, Parliament explicitly denied him the crown matrimonial in 1701 and 1702. Caleb's reference here to the 'king' is probably a mistaken reference to King William.

121   *free as the wind at Martinmas, that pays neither land-rent nor annual*: in Scotland, Martinmas (11 November) was one of the four days in the year on which rents like land-rent and annual were due.

122   *thy very Achates, man . . . thine to life and death!*: in Virgil's *Aeneid*, Achates is the friend and squire of Aeneas, frequently referred to as 'fidus [faithful] Achates'. Craigengelt's speech has changed consid-

erably since his first appearance. He speaks here and afterwards in a pastiche of the *braggadocio* manner common in seventeenth-century drama, and in the 'gambling cant' (as Bucklaw later describes it) of such plays as Dryden's *The Wild Gallant* (printed 1669) and *The Squire of Alsatia* (1688) by Thomas Shadwell (?1642–92).

L'un n'empeche pas l'autre: 'The one does not prevent the other'.

123   *fooling him up to the top of his bent*: echoing *Hamlet*, III. ii. 384.

126   *as if the ancient founder of the castle . . . the enemy of his house*: the detail significantly recalls both the ending of *The Castle of Otranto* (1764) by Horace Walpole (1717–97), when the gigantic form of Alfonso, the ancestor and wronged spirit of Manfred's family, appears amid a 'clap of thunder' which 'shook the castle to its foundations' to announce Theodore as his true heir (ed. and introd. W. S. Lewis with notes by Joseph W. Reed, jun., 1964, p. 108); and Act III, scene iv of Scott's play *The Doom of Devorgoil*, in some ways the prototype for *The Bride of Lammermoor*, which features portentous thunder, the spectral appearance of the ancient founder of the house, and the fulfilment of an old prophecy. Scott admires the scene of Alfonso's appearance in his 'Life' of Walpole, *Misc. Works*, iii. 320–1.

128   *epigraph*: from the comedy *Love's Pilgrimage* (printed 1647) by John Fletcher (1597–1625) and another dramatist, possibly Francis Beaumont (1584–1616), II. iv. 1–4. Scott substitutes 'savour' for the original 'stink'.

130   *petty cover, as they say at the Louvre*: for *petit couvert*, or 'small place-setting', meaning an unceremonious meal. The reference is to French court life at the great palace of the Louvre, in Paris, which started to fulfil its present function when the revolutionary government opened the Musée Central des Arts in the Grande Galerie in 1793.

131   *the best jeest in a' George Buchanan*: this refers to *The Witty and Entertaining Exploits of George Buchanan, who was commonly called the King's Fool* (1781). Andrew Lang comments in 1893: 'George Buchanan's jests were, and perhaps still are, very popular in a chap-book adorned with a most unseemly frontispiece. It is now probably missing from the little shop-windows which it used to decorate thirty years ago. This George Buchanan the jester has no real connection with the celebrated scholar.' (Border edition, xiv. 298–9.)

132 *the high-spirited elephant . . . a brother in commission*: Goldsmith tells
this story in *An History of the Earth, and Animated Nature*, iv. 279: 'In
India, where they were at one time employed in launching ships, a
particular elephant was directed to force a very large vessel into the
water: the work proved superior to its strength, but not to its
endeavours; which, however, the keeper affected to despise. "Take
away," says he, "that lazy beast, and bring another better fitted for
service." The poor animal instantly upon this redoubled its efforts,
fractured its scull, and died upon the spot.'

ill advised . . . I winna deny that: such payments in kind were
originally made by a tenant to his feudal lord, and were later made
annually in part-payment of rent by tenants to the owners of the
land they farmed.

133 *the court-balls of Henrietta Maria*: the daughter of Henri IV of France,
Henrietta Maria (1609–69) was the Queen consort of Charles I, and
the focus of the pleasure-loving groups in his court. She was
regarded as an important and dangerous link with the Catholic
courts of Europe.

134 *to 'weary for his dinner'*: the expression is placed in inverted commas
as a Scottish colloquialism (which the narrator, unlike his characters,
rarely permits himself). To 'weary for' is to wait wearily or to
languish for something.

135 *epigraph*: adapted from 'The Summoner's Tale' from Chaucer's
Canterbury Tales, lines 1838–43. The greedy friar, who hypocriti-
cally claims to be 'a man of litel sustenaunce', requests food from
the wife of a dying man to whom he is to administer the last rites.

136 *the chains of feudal dependence . . . tenants at will*: land law continued
to be known as 'the feudal law' throughout the eighteenth century.
By this, the feuar paid to the lord or landowner a stipulated annual
'duty', either in money or in kind (as in 'the duty-eggs and butter'
mentioned above), and in theory this 'feu' could last indefinitely if
the conditions under which it was granted were observed. Rent
was usually a composite payment, made up of some money, some
food provision, and 'cain', which was a stipulated payment of
livestock or farm products. In addition, the tenant was often required to provide certain services, such as working for some part of
the year on the lord's home farm. 'Feu rights', which Scott explains
in note 12, established conditions of tenure, giving a security which
could not be enjoyed by the 'tenants at will'. 'Rights of commonty'
were rights of pasture on common land.

'the royal purveyors . . . an hundred caverns':   Scott quotes the greater part of a sentence from Burke's discussion of changes in the econ-omic organization of the royal household, in his 'Speech on Presen-ting to the House of Commons (On the 11th February, 1780), a Plan for the Better Security of the Independence of Parliament, and the Economical Reformation of the Civil and Other Estab-lishments', in *The Works of the Right Honourable Edmund Burke*, 6 vols., 1906–7, ii. 337. Scott owned the 14-volume edition of *Burke's Works*, 1801–22, which he cites in note 13.

the awful rule and right supremacy: quoting (as also on p. 192) the 'aweful rule, and right supremacy' of *The Taming of the Shrew*, v. ii. 109.

137   *Conscript Fathers of the village*: a translation of the term for the Roman senate, *patres conscripti*.

138   *as far as Dunse for Davie Dingwall the writer*:   the market town of Duns is in Berwickshire. For 'writer', see note to p. 5.

feu-charters of the hamlet: the deeds securing the tenancy.

139   *'twas not in the bond*: the phrase criticizes Dingwall's literal-mindedness by echoing Shylock's words denying the need to have surgeons near lest Antonio bleed to death ('I cannot find it, 'tis not in the bond'), *The Merchant of Venice*, IV. i. 262.

threats of stouthrief oppression . . . as the law termed it: in Scots law, 'stouthrief' is 'masterful' robbery, usually of dwelling houses. *Via facti*, an act of force which is unlawful if used offensively, is an awkward addition to 'by rule of thumb', which means 'by methods based entirely on practice or experience, rather than on theory'. In the manuscript, Scott added 'rule of thumb or via facti as the law phrased it' to the sentence as an afterthought, on the verso of the previous page. Probably he never quite incorporated the addition correctly. The Highlands, which Dingwall goes on to mention, had a reputation for lawlessness.

by the strong hand: 'by physical force', echoing *Hamlet*, I. i. 102.

whistling Maggy Lauder six hours without intermission: the Fife folk-song 'Maggy Lauder' is one of the best and most popular of all Scottish songs. It was first printed in Herd's *Ancient and Modern Scottish Songs*, ii. 72–3.

the El Dorado, or Peru: El Dorado is a fictitious country or city abounding in gold, which Spanish settlers in South America be-lieved to lie on the Amazon. Peru, conquered by Spain in 1531–3 and under Spanish rule for nearly 300 years, was the goal of fortune-hunters lured by reports of gold and treasure.

140   *though it was gall and wormwood to him*:   Lamentations 3: 19.

but necessity was equally imperious and lawless: a variation of the proverbial expression 'Necessity has nae Law' (Ramsay, *Scots Proverbs*, p. 50).

"Cauld Kail in Aberdeen":   several versions of this popular song exist. It was cited in Ramsay's *Tea-Table Miscellany*, but the music was first printed in Johnson's *Scots Musical Museum* in 1788 with verses written by Alexander, 4th Duke of Gordon.

141   *Jacobuses and Georgiuses baith*: for 'Jacobus', see note to p. 73. A 'Georgius' was a gold coin worth 6s. 8d., so called because of the device of St George on the obverse.

142   *'a canty carline'*:   Burns, 'The Author's Earnest Cry and Prayer', line 62.

143   *we are just killed up yonder wi' eating frae morning to night*:   Caleb's speeches at this and other points in his encounter with the Girders comically recall the description of ease and plenty in the last stanza of 'The Blythsome Bridal', included in Ramsay's *Tea-Table Miscellany*: 'Scrap'd Haddocks, Wilks, Dulse and Tangle, | And a Mill of good Snishing to prie; | When weary with eating and drinking, | We'll rise up and dance till we die.'

144   *and does she wear a habit or a railly?*:   the choice is between a riding habit, a full and rather bulky brocaded suit in the style of a man's coat, and a 'railly' (a diminutive of 'rail'), an overbodice made of fine linen and sometimes edged with lace. As well as being an indicator of fashion, the choice would reveal much about the social implications of the meeting. Ravenswood himself is struck by Lucy's much more feminine appearance when she changes into formal dress on her return to Ravenswood Castle.

lying in the hills in the persecution: Covenanters were known as 'hill-folk' because many of them sought refuge in the hills to worship secretly during the times of persecution, which began with the re-establishment of episcopacy in 1662. After 1679 those Covenanters who still resisted the Indulgence granted after the battle of Bothwell Bridge were led by Donald Cargill and Richard Cameron, and were known as 'Cameronians', or 'Society People'. They endured great sufferings as they wandered, hunted by soldiers, in the hills: if captured and convicted they could be fined, imprisoned, or transported. During the so-called 'killing time' of 1681–5 (especially 1684–5), people who refused to take the Test Oath could be executed with minimal legal procedure. In defiance of persecution, the Cameronians produced late in 1684 the 'Apologetical Declaration and Admonitory Vindication of the True Presbyterians of the Church of Scotland'. An oath abjuring this was promptly instituted, and failure to take it could lead to summary execution. See Ian B. Cowan, *The Scottish Covenanters 1660–1688*, 1976, chs. 7 and 8. Presbyterianism replaced episcopacy as the established religion in Scotland in 1690.

worthy Mr Cuffcushion . . . in like circumstances: the Anglican liturgy contained in the Book of Common Prayer (the 'service book') was opposed by Presbyterians. Charles I provoked great resentment, including a riot in St Giles Kirk in Edinburgh, by introducing the new Scottish Prayer Book in 1637. As Andrew Lang notes: 'The arguments by which Dr. McCrie [an outspoken critic of Scott's presentation of the Covenanters in *Old Mortality*] showed that the Service Book was not used in Scotland during the Restoration seem to have produced no effect on Scott.' (Border edition, xiv. 299.) Although no liturgy was made obligatory in the reign of Charles II, some Scottish ministers undoubtedly used the Book of Common Prayer, making Balderstone's comment perfectly acceptable.

ilka land has its ain lauch: the expression is included in Ramsay, *Scots Proverbs*, p. 17, and is also a line from 'Tak your Auld Cloak about you', in Herd's *Ancient and Modern Scottish Songs*, ii. 103.

145 *cooper to the Queen's stores at the Timmer Burse at Leith*: cooper by appointment to Queen Anne at the exchange of the timber merchants at Leith, the port of Edinburgh.

146 *course the old fox . . . and toss him in a blanket*: Scott may have been thinking of the fate of Sancho Panza in *Don Quixote* (one of his favourite works), Part 1, ch. 17. Don Quixote refuses to pay his bill at an inn, claiming that there is no precedent for such a payment in romances of chivalry. In punishment, his squire is tossed in a blanket, an ignominy which he recalls throughout the narrative. The parallel momentarily places Caleb in the role of Sancho Panza and Ravenswood in the role of the outdated knight.

147 *epigraph*: from Fletcher's comedy *Wit Without Money* (printed 1639), I. i. 168–70.

147 *in the name of council and kirk-session*: the courts or councils of Presbyterian church-government work in a hierarchy, the lowest being the kirk-session: see note to p. 32.

148 *it's come to muckle, but it's no come to that neither*: the expression is included in Ramsay, *Scots Proverbs*, p. 38.

149 *my substance disponed upon*: Girder's language has a legal flavour. 'Dispone' is a term in Scots law and was always used in a deed making a 'disposition' of lands by gift, sale, or by way of settlement on the granter's death. (Normand)

150 *ony suffering sant . . . I wad the less hae minded it*: the Covenanters, like Puritans of nearly all sects, were commonly known as 'saints' because they claimed to be the elect of God. After defeating Claverhouse at Drumclog, the Covenanting army, under Hackston of Rathillet and Hall of Haughhead, entered Glasgow, but was defeated on 22 June 1679 at Bothwell Bridge, on the Clyde, by the Royalist forces under the Duke of Monmouth (the illegitimate son of Charles II). Scott tells the story in *Old Mortality* and in his introduction to 'The Battle of Bothwell Bridge' in *Minstrelsy of the Scottish Border* (ed. Henderson, ii. 268–78). At this point in editions before the Magnum Opus, Girder referred to troops sent out 'against Argyle' instead of 'against the sants at Bothwell Brigg', meaning troops sent to quell the rebellion of Archibald Cameron, 9th Earl of Argyll (1629–85) against the accession of the Roman Catholic James VII and II in 1685. Argyll's rebellion was supported by some Covenanters, although Argyll himself was not even a Presbyterian. For Scott's purposes here, Argyll's rebellion lacked the resonance of a reference to Bothwell Bridge; and, as Mortsheugh later recalls, Allan Ravenswood and Caleb Balderstone were present at Bothwell Bridge.

152 *might with its burden seem both spear and shield*: Scott had a literary echo in mind here, probably of *Paradise Lost* IV. 990, for the manuscript and printed states before the Magnum Opus read ' "might seem both spear and shield" '.

153 *I have heard somewhere . . . shuffle a saraband*: I have found no precise source for the story, but it may have been suggested by Buffon's observation that a hunted bear will stop at the sound of a whistle and stand on its hind feet, allowing the hunter to shoot it with ease (*Buffon's Natural History*, corrected by John Wright, i. 417).

all great men from Louis XIV. downwards, namely, 'we will see about it':
see note to p. 119.

his share of the christening festivity: in the first edition, vol. i ended
here. The 'noble Earl lately deceased', mentioned in Scott's note
18, is Charles, 8th Earl of Haddington (1753–1828). Lockhart
describes the story as 'one of the many ludicrous delineations which
he owed to the late Lord Haddington, a man of rare pleasantry, and
one of the best tellers of old Scotch stories that I ever heard' (*Life of
Scott*, vi. 88). Scott had commented a few years earlier on his
'extreme accuracy', remarking that his anecdotes were 'as correct
as a parish register' (*Life of Scott*, vii. 258). 'Under the rose' (*sub rosa*)
means 'secretly'.

154 *epigraph*: in the introduction to *Chronicles of the Canongate*, 1st
Series, Scott confesses that the quotations used as epigraphs to his
chapters 'in the general case, are pure invention', and that 'in some
cases, where actual names are affixed to the supposed quotations, it
would be to little purpose to seek them in the works of the authors
referred to' (*Magnum*, xli. pp. xxiv–xxv). Those marked 'Old Play'
or 'Anonymous' are particularly suspicious. Most of the epigraphs
of *The Bride of Lammermoor* are traceable, but this, like the epigraphs
to chs. 17 and 27, appears to have been written by Scott himself,
albeit in a style which imitates other works and authors. Scott's use
of epigraphs to anticipate the action and to provide tangential
comments on characters and situations was more systematic than
had been known before, and widely influential.

157 *He then disappeared . . . the other with brandy*: Scott's note (20) on this
scene requires some comment. The rhyme 'My cummer and I lay
down to sleep' is st. 3 of 'Todlen Hame', in Herd's *Ancient and
Modern Scottish Songs*, ii. 106–7. The story of the clergymen and beer
comes from the Riddell family. Lockhart recalls a ride through the
ancient woods of the Riddell estate during which Scott 'told us a
world of stories, some tragical, some comical, about the old lairds
of this time-honoured lineage; and among others, that of the seven
Bibles and the seven bottles of ale, which he afterwards inserted in
a note to *The Bride of Lammermoor*' (*Life of Scott*, vi. 76). 'Come, my
lad, and drink some beer' is from Johnson's comic reply to the
question 'What is bliss?' in his parody of Thomas Warton, recorded
by James Boswell under 18 September 1777 in his *Life of Johnson*,
ed. George Birkbeck Hill, rev. L. F. Powell, 6 vols., 1934–64, iii.
159.

157   *auld Micklestob*: the spelling of this name is an interesting example
      of Scott's efforts to improve a detail which entered the text only
      through a misreading between manuscript and first edition. The
      manuscript read 'Mickletale', which the first edition printed as
      'Mickletob', and which Scott, his original intention long forgotten,
      then revised to the more plausible-sounding 'Micklestob' for the
      Magnum Opus.

158   *to suffer the sun to set upon your anger*: Ashton refers to one of Paul's
      instructions in his Epistle to the Ephesians 4: 26 ('let not the sun go
      down upon your wrath').

161   *epigraph*: from the speech of the extortioner Sir Giles Overreach in
      the comedy *A New Way to Pay Old Debts* (printed 1633), by Philip
      Massinger (1583–1640), III. iii. 50–6. Scott is probably thinking of
      its relevance to the Marquis of A——, but it also anticipates
      Ashton's actions towards Ravenswood.

      the versatile old Earl of Northampton . . . not of the oak: William Parr
      (1513–71), later Marquis of Northampton and Earl of Essex, was
      the brother of Catherine Parr, the last wife of Henry VIII. He was
      a member of the Privy Council in the reigns of Henry (from 1543)
      and Edward VI, undertaking several important state commissions.
      After Edward's death he supported the claim of Lady Jane Grey,
      and was condemned to death by Mary I, but later pardoned. His
      fortunes revived on the accession of Elizabeth, and in 1558 he was
      again made a member of the Privy Council.

162   *a change in the Scottish cabinet . . . proving ultimately successful*: the
      reference to the 'Scottish cabinet' can only mean the Scottish Privy
      Council, abolished in May 1708. Scott probably intends to indicate
      a shift in the balance of power within the Scottish administration,
      culminating in the Tory victory in the election of 1710.

      liable, under the Treaty of Union . . . 'a protestation for remeid in law':
      until the Magnum Opus, this read 'liable to be reviewed by the
      Estates of the Kingdom, *i.e.* by the Scottish Parliament, under an
      appeal by the party injured, or, as it was technically termed, "a
      protestation for remeid in law" '. My Appendix describes the
      background to the Act of Union (1707), and gives details of its main
      provisions. In fact, the Act of Union made no mention of any right
      of appeal from the Scottish courts to the House of Lords. It was a
      vexed issue which had hampered previous attempts at union. In
      1670, when the 1st Viscount Stair was one of the Scottish commis-
      sioners appointed to consider union, the English commissioners had

refused to accept the Scottish demand that no case should be tried in England even by appeal, and later rejected the proposal that a Supreme Court of Appeal for Scotland should be established in Edinburgh. Unable to agree on the problem of appeals, both Scottish and English commissioners probably thought it best to pass over it in silence in the Articles of 1706–7. See note to p. 166 for discussion of the legal situation.

163 *Scott of Scotstarvet . . . outstaggered in our time*: the Scottish lawyer, statesman, and benefactor of learning, Sir John Scot of Scotstarvet (1585–1670), was a Privy Councillor and a Lord of Session in the reign of James VI and I, but lost both place and influence during the civil wars. His exposure of the wiles and misfortunes of state-craft, *The Staggering State of the Scots Statesmen for One Hundred Years, viz. from 1550 to 1650*, was circulated in manuscript (hence the somewhat conspicuous reference to Sir William's copy) until its publication in 1754. Scott owned a copy of this edition and refers to it for information in his *Letters*.

'Neque dives . . . durabit in terra': 'neither a rich man nor a strong, but not even a wise Scot, shall long endure upon earth when envy prevails.' The *Scotichronicon* of the fourteenth-century Scottish chronicler John of Fordun was edited by William F. Skene in 1871–2.

a party in the British Parliament: until the Magnum Opus, this read 'a parliament according to his will'.

fifth in descent from the Knight of Tillibardine: the earldom of Tulli-bardine passed to the 2nd Earl and 1st Marquis of Atholl in 1670, and was held by his descendants, including his son, the original of the novel's Marquis of A——. As a title associated with the family of Atholl, its specific use here is difficult to ascertain, but it is probably just Sir William's way of avoiding repeating Atholl's name. The most celebrated holder of the title was the active Jacobite William Murray, Marquis of Tullibardine (1689–1746), the second and eldest surviving son of the 2nd Marquis and 1st Duke of Atholl.

those unarmed and unable Mephibosheths: Dryden refers to 'lame Mephibosheth the Wisard's Son' (based on 2 Samuel 4: 4), in his contribution to Nahum Tate's *The Second Part of Absalom and Achitophel* (1682), line 405.

called over the coals in the House of Peers: until the Magnum Opus, this read 'called over the coals in parliament'. Similar references to the House of Lords were added on pp. 265, 287, 289, 293, and 304.

164 *his king and country*: another slip, indicative of Scott's conception of Ashton as a Williamite politician.

165 *Sarah, Duchess of Marlborough . . . considerable resemblance*: Sarah Churchill (1660–1744), wife of the 1st Duke of Marlborough, was the imperious and powerful favourite of Queen Anne, whom she served as a lady of the bedchamber from 1683, and under whom she held several prestigious appointments. She dominated Anne throughout their friendship, when they were 'Mrs Morley' and 'Mrs Freeman' to each other, but her high temper and unceasing demands led to many disagreements, and her Whig sympathies frequently clashed with Anne's Tory inclinations. Her influence eventually declined with the rise in favour of Abigail Hill (later Masham) and Robert Harley.

166 *Since the Claim of Right . . . 'for remeid in law'*: until the Magnum Opus, the section reading 'if the English House of Lords . . . "for remeid in law" ' read 'if the Scottish parliament should be disposed to act upon the protestation of the Master of Ravenswood "for remeid in law" '. Scott's brief summary of Ravenswood's legal situation requires clarification under two headings: (*a*) the Claim of Right and the status of appeals to the Scottish Parliament before 1707; and (*b*) appeals to the House of Lords after 1707:

(*a*) By the Claim of Right (11 April 1689), the Scottish Convention of Estates laid down several constitutional principles by which it wished William and Mary to govern. These included declarations that no Roman Catholic could reign or bear office in Scotland, that the royal prerogative could not override law, and that Parliament should meet frequently and debate freely. In addition, the Claim of Right stated that it was the right of every subject 'to protest for Remeed of law to the King and Parliament', thus attempting to resolve an issue which had seriously divided the Scottish legal profession (see Appendix, 1674). The legal status of the Claim of Right was unclear, however, partly because of uncertainty as to whether William had accepted it before taking the coronation oath. The legal authorities which Scott might have consulted, especially the *Institutes of the Law of Scotland* (1773) by John Erskine (1695–1768) suggest that the appellate jurisdiction was still in dispute between 1689 and 1707, although instances of appeals are given in the *Acts of the Parliament of Scotland* which Scott's friend Thomas Thomson had started to edit: see Peter Garside, 'Union and *The Bride of Lammermoor* ', *Studies in Scottish Literature*, xix (1984), 72–93.

(*b*) Although it was not included in the Articles of Union, the right of appeal to the House of Lords against decisions of the Court of Session was first tested in 1708 and has been assumed to exist ever since. In principle, it need not have influenced Scots law, since the Lords were bound to judge Scottish appeals according to the principles of Scots, not English, law. In practice, confusions between the two systems were difficult to avoid. Until the Appellate Jurisdiction Act of 1876, there was no statutory provision for the presence of Scottish judges when the Lords heard Scottish appeals. (See Robert Stevens, *Law and Politics: The House of Lords as Judicial Body, 1800–1976*, 1978, pp. 47–67). Appeals were heard by a house with a heavy majority of English peers, who were unlikely to have any knowledge of Scots law, and it was a real danger that a decision made by the Court of Session might be overturned by the House of Lords on principles which contradicted those of the original trial. The resulting influence of English over Scots law has been regarded with mixed feelings by legal commentators. John Bruce's *Report on the Events and Circumstances, which Produced the Union* (2 vols., 1799) argues, like the narrator of *The Bride of Lammermoor*, that the system of appeal to the House of Lords was an indirect way of improving the operation of Scots law, and strongly approves it; but see E. J. MacGillivray, 'The Influence of English Law', in *An Introductory Survey of the Sources and Literature of Scots Law*, ed. Hector McKechnie, Stair Society, 1936, pp. 207–25. Scott's own opinion was more variable than might be suggested by comments in *The Bride of Lammermoor*. In 1826 he reflected: 'The consequence will in time be that the Scottish Supreme court will be in effect situated in London. Then down fall—as national objects of respect and veneration—the Scottish bench—the Scottish Bar—the Scottish Law herself—And—And—there is an end of an auld Sang.' (*Journal*, pp. 156–7.)

Besides, judging, though most inaccurately . . . anticipated the loss of his lawsuit: this passage, added for the Magnum Opus, is the longest interpolation made to place the novel's action firmly in the post-Union period. Although *The Bride of Lammermoor* consistently represents the House of Lords as a more disinterested body than the Court of Session, less likely to be swayed by political considerations in a distant part of the country, there is evidence that early appeals were decided on party lines. See Athol L. Murray, 'Administration and Law', in *The Union of 1707*, ed. Rae, pp. 30–57.

167   *the Master might be reponed against the attainder*: restoring the rights
lost when his father was attainted of treason, which could be done,
but only by an Act of Parliament.

170   *epigraph*: the words of a gentleman bringing a challenge to Bessus
in *A King and No King* (printed 1619) by Beaumont and Fletcher,
III. ii. 43–6.

actions of compt and reckoning . . . declarations of the expiry of the legal:
by an 'action of compt and reckoning' (the process now called
'count and reckoning'), the creditor can force the debtor to give an
account of transactions between them and pay any balance due. A
'multiplepoinding' is an action initiated by a debtor to settle the
competing claims of several creditors to his money and property.
Its rough English equivalent is 'interpleading'. An 'adjudication' is
an action by which the heritable estate of a debtor is transferred to
the creditor as security for and satisfaction of the debt, the debtor
being able to redeem it by paying the debt within a certain time. A
'wadset' corresponds roughly to an English mortgage, by which
land is transferred as security for a loan, to be redeemed on repay-
ment. Wadsets may be either 'proper', in which the creditor (or
'wadsetter') holds the land as a proprietor, entitled to the rents and
profits from the land until the loan is repaid; or 'improper', in which
the wadsetter may take the rents but must account to the borrower
for an excess of rents over agreed interest. By 'poinding of the
ground', also called a real poinding, moveables belonging to tenants
occupying the land can be taken by the creditor, but only to the
extent of their rent. The 'legal' is the period (usually 10 years) within
which the debtor has a right to redeem lands taken by the creditor,
by paying off the debt. If the debt is not paid, the creditor can claim
an absolute right over the property by obtaining a decree declaring
the expiry of the legal. Ravenswood's own analysis on p. 171 shows
that he has a clear lay insight into the principles obscured by
Ashton's volley of specialized legal terms.

171   *debitum fundi*: a Scots law term, referring to those types of debt
which are attached to land and which remain as a burden on it
irrespective of who owns it.

advised in the only courts competent: the 'advising' of a case is the giving
of judgment by the court. (Normand)

172   *in the House of British Peers . . . the hour of redemption has passed away*:
until the Magnum Opus, it was in 'the Estates of the nation, in the
supreme Court of Parliament, that we must parley together. The

belted lords and knights of Scotland, her ancient peers and baronage, must decide . . .'. The belt is the distinctive cincture of an earl or knight. In theory, the whole body of peers, not the specially appointed body of experienced judges used today, constituted the tribunal of appeal. On the information given in Scott's note 21, which takes this opportunity to explain the matter of appeals to Parliament, see my notes to pp. 162 and 166. Scott is mistaken in stating that the appellate jurisdiction of the Lords was secured by the Articles of Union, and his statement that previous editions had not made the distinction between pre- and post-Union appeals sufficiently clear disguises the important revisions made to legal references in the text of the Magnum Opus.

173 *the relics of the supper . . . the morning meal*: echoing *Hamlet*, I. ii. 180–1.

174 *the very moral of one who would say, Stand, to a true man*: meaning that Craigengelt looks like a highwayman. Scott had used the formula in *Rob Roy* (1818), when Justice Inglewood tells Frank Osbaldistone that he is not 'the first bully-boy that has said stand to a true man' (*Magnum*, vii. 123). 'Moral' means 'counterpart' or 'likeness' in this context.

176 *woodie written on his very visnomy . . . plaits his cravat yet*: see note to p. 75. Caleb refers to the hempen rope used to hang criminals.

178 *epigraph*: probably written by Scott himself.

a sentence of fugitation: better known as 'outlawry', by which, in Scots law, an individual forfeited all moveable property to the Crown, was barred from holding public office and also barred from defending, or giving testimony in, any legal action.

180 *'Suum cuique tribuito' . . . Justinian*: 'give to each his own' was one of the three fundamental legal maxims laid down by the Emperor Justinian (483–565), who supervised a revision of the law, codified in his *Codex*, *Digest*, and *Institutes*. The *Corpus Juris Civilis*, as these and other works were known collectively, introduced new material as well as retaining much older Roman law, and profoundly influenced legal thinking throughout Europe.

181 *'over-crowed,' to use a phrase of Spenser*: although Spenser used it only twice in this sense, the term clearly made an impression on Scott. In *Rob Roy* Frank Osbaldistone, an enthusiast for tales of romance, describes himself as 'fairly *overcrowed*, as Spenser would have termed it' (*Magnum*, vii. 259).

182 *Inimicus amicissimus*: 'a very friendly enemy'.

183 *fidus Achates*: see note to p. 122.

Six heirs portioners have successively died to make her wealthy: this is an extreme version of a situation in the Scots law of succession, by which the heritable property left by an individual who dies without male heirs is divided equally either between the individual's daughters or between other female relatives of the same degree of relationship to the deceased. The wealth eventually inherited by Lady Girnington has increased as the number of co-heirs sharing it has diminished.

He is a bird of evil omen . . . and croaks of jail and gallows-tree: the 'bird of evil omen' dominating the novel is the raven, by tradition the harbinger of pestilence and death, whose ill-boding cry is usually described as 'croaking' (literary examples abound: see e.g. *Hamlet*, III. ii. 254, *Macbeth*, I. v. 38–40, *Troilus and Cressida*, V. ii. 190–1). A raven croaking near a house foretells the death of one of the inmates. A useful collection of raven-lore contemporary with Scott's writing may be found in *Observations on Popular Antiquities*, by John Brand, rev. Henry Ellis, 2 vols., 1813, ii. 526–8.

184 *epigraph*: there are no records of a play called *The French Courtezan*: it is probably Scott's invention. The title echoes *The Dutch Courtezan* (printed 1605) by John Marston (?1575–1634), and the substance of the lines recalls a speech in Dryden's *The Spanish Fryar*, II. i. 7–11 ('What learn our youth abroad, but to refine | The homely vices of their native land? | Give me an honest home-spun country clown | Of our own growth; his dulness is but plain, | But theirs embroidered').

185 *Thomas the Rhymer . . . fulfilled in my time!*: The thirteenth-century Scottish poet and prophet Thomas of Erceldoune, also known as 'the Rhymer' and 'True Thomas', is reputed to have predicted the death of Alexander III (d. 1286) and to have produced a series of prophecies about major events in Scottish history. The earliest of the many compositions claimed as his or deriving authority from him is the tale of his meeting with the 'lady gaye' and his stay in fairyland, to which many of the prophecies are traditionally traced. See *The Romance and Prophecies of Thomas of Erceldoune*, ed. James A. H. Murray, Early English Text Society, 1875. Scott discusses him in the introduction to *Sir Tristrem*, the introductions to the three parts of 'Thomas the Rhymer' in *Minstrelsy of the Scottish Border*, and in *Letters on Demonology and Witchcraft*, pp. 132–40. He also

published a fragment of a romance about Thomas the Rhymer as Appendix 1 to the General Preface of the Waverley Novels (*Magnum*, i. pp. xli–liv). As this list suggests, Thomas the Rhymer held a special interest for Scott, partly because he is associated with the Eildon Hills near Scott's home at Abbotsford. In addition to the oral traditions associated with him, of which Caleb's prophecy is typical, his 'Whole Prophecies' were popular in chapbook form throughout the eighteenth century.

'*When the last Laird . . . lost for evermoe*': commenting on the prophecies of Thomas of Erceldoune in his *Popular Rhymes, Fireside Stories, and Amusements, of Scotland*, p. 7, Robert Chambers argues: 'Those rhymes of True Thomas which bear most appearance of being genuine (that is, really uttered by him), are generally of a melancholy and desponding cast, such as might well be expected to proceed from a man of a fine turn of mind, who felt himself and his country on the verge of great calamities.'

186 *hindering a wheen honest folk frae bringing on shore a drap brandy*: this is another emphatically post-Union reference. Article 18 of the Act of Union provided that the laws regulating trade, customs, and excise should be standardized on the English model. The administration of the new system met with considerable difficulty, and there was resentment at what was seen as excessive English interference and patronage. The nominally independent Scottish Boards for Customs and Excise, set up in 1707, were dependent on England for trained personnel and guidance, and were subject to Treasury control and patronage. The Scots believed, probably mistakenly, that most customs and excise officers were sent from England. See P. W. J. Riley, *The English Ministers and Scotland 1707–1727* (1964). In a note to *Rob Roy* Scott contends: 'The introduction of gaugers, supervisors, and examiners, was one of the great complaints of the Scottish nation, though a natural consequence of the Union.' (*Magnum*, vii. 49.)

187 '*Thou wouldst . . . told me of another father*': this conflates three lines from the speech of the usurper Duke Frederick to Orlando, *As You Like It*, I. ii. 227, 228, 230.

188 *a wilful man maun hae his way—he that will to Cupar maun to Cupar*: the first sentence seems not to have been inextricably bound to the second, which is listed as proverbial in Ramsay's *Scots Proverbs* (p. 31), but they are frequently found together, and 'a wilful man

maun hae his way' is now regarded as proverbial in its own right.
The old burgh of Cupar is in Fife.

188   *'By this also . . . dominion over all men'*: Caleb's remark may be
a comic misrepresentation of Paul's words on the subjection of
women to men (see e.g. 1 Corinthians 11: 8–12). As in Augustine's
De Continentia, IX. 23, women are usually said to have dominion
over all living creatures except men.

190   *doch-an-dorroch, or the stirrup-cup*: Scott's customary spelling of
'Deoch an dorais', which Donald Macintosh glosses in his *Collection
of Gaelic Proverbs and Familiar Phrases* (1785) as 'Drink at the door;
or the parting cup'.

'as black as mourning weed': I have found no precise source for
this consciously literary phrase, which possibly recalls the
'mourning weeds' of *3 Henry VI*, III. iii. 229 and *Titus Andronicus*,
I. i. 70.

191   *King William . . . two distinguished Scottish lawyers*: the portraits
indicate Sir William's political sympathies and legal training. Mary
II (1662–94), the eldest child of James VII and II by his first wife
Anne Hyde, ruled jointly with her husband, William II (of Scotland) and III (of England) (1650–1702). Sir Thomas Hope of
Craighall (?1580–1646), Lord Advocate from 1626, was the author
of the *Minor Practicks*, the *Major Practicks*, and reports of decisions of
the Court of Session. He was thought to approve privately of the
aims of the Covenanters, declared the National Covenant legal, and
refused to defend episcopacy.

a black silk Geneva cowl, or skull-cap: the black gowns and white
neckbands worn by the Calvinist ministers of Geneva were later
introduced into other Protestant churches. The unusual term
'Geneva cowl' is not included in *OED 2*, but Scott means the
garment mentioned in *The Abbot* ('Geneva gowns, and black silk
skull-caps', *Magnum*, xx. 88). Presbyterian ministers wore black
skull-caps over slightly larger white ones, with the white edges
turned back.

Dutch drolleries . . . painting of the Italian school: paintings of low life,
rich in comic incidents and types (drinking scenes, brothel scenes,
peasant dances), of the kind now known as 'genre', were characteristic of seventeenth-century Dutch and Flemish art. They were
sometimes known as 'drolleries' to English visitors, and were often
assumed to be second-rate art. (Reynolds, for example, admired the

abilities of the leading genre artist, Jan Steen, but disapproved of his subject-matter.) Adriaen van Ostade (1610–85) was a master of the mature phase of Haarlem genre, producing grotesque, sometimes cruel, but morally directive portrayals of squalid life. For David Teniers the Younger, see note to p. 16. In contrast, Ashton's 'one good painting of the Italian school' would present an unequivocally dignified beauty, its subject perhaps religious or taken from classical literature and myth. Even in the details of the paintings he owns, therefore, Ashton's low origins and high aspirations are contrasted.

193   *cedant arma togæ . . . too literally complied with*: Ashton refers to part of a verse quoted by Cicero, *De Officiis*, I. xxii. 77: *Cedant arma togae, concedat laurea laudi* ('Yield, ye arms, to the toga; to civil praises, ye laurels').

   the Mull of Galloway: Galloway was once the name for a large region in south-west Scotland, including the present counties of Wigtown and Kirkcudbright. The Mull of Galloway is the promontory south of Kirkmaiden, the southernmost point of Scotland. A Galloway is a small, strong, horse, originally bred there.

   'There was a haggis . . . Fal de ral' , *&c.*: Henry quotes part of a brief comic rhyme, which was one of Charles Kirkpatrick Sharpe's favourites and included in his *Ballad Book*, 1818, no. 26.

   Mr Cordery: the tutor's name recalls the Belgian theologian Balthasar Corderius (1592–1650), who wrote a series of biblical paraphrases and commentaries used in schools.

194   *statutes . . . against shooting red-deer, killing salmon*: there were many late sixteenth-century statutes against shooting red deer and killing salmon. See *Acts of Parliament of Scotland*, ed. Thomas Thomson and Cosmo Innes, 12 vols., 1834–95. (Normand)

195   *the picture of old Malise . . . loupen out of the canvass*: the detail again recalls Walpole's *The Castle of Otranto*, in which the young hero Theodore strikingly resembles the portrait of the ancestor he is to avenge (ed. Lewis and Reed, pp. 38–9, 52). Ravenswood's resemblance to Malise similarly marks his role as the figure of the past come to life.

196   *epigraph*: from Carracus's speech in Robert Tailor's comedy *The Hog hath Lost his Pearl* (1613), I. i. Carracus muses on the rights and wrongs of marrying his betrothed, Maria, against her father's wishes, not knowing that his treacherous friend Albert has just seduced her in disguise. The situation of the lover and father in opposition is all

Scott means to recall here, but the quotation carries ominous associations of love stolen by a friend.

199   *a witch . . . them that suffered at Haddington*: the ancient burgh of Haddington in East Lothian, about 17 miles east of Edinburgh, saw many trials and executions of local witches, among them a group of 6 (5 of whom were women) in 1661, a group of 15 (12 of whom were women) convicted by the High Court of Justiciary in 1662, and 2 convicted by the Privy Council in 1677. See Christina Larner, Christopher Hyde Lee, and Hugh V. McLachlan, *A Source-Book of Scottish Witchcraft* (1977).

200   *any hare that comes through among the deer . . . doublet-buttons on purpose*: witches were believed to metamorphose at will into animal shape, the shape of the hare being a particular favourite in Scotland. Charges of metamorphosis were common in Scottish witchcraft trials. During her trial in 1662, Isobel Gowdie revealed the various charms which witches used to transform themselves into animals, including hares. Scott comments on her case, and on the case of Julian Coxe (1663), who was also accused of assuming the shape of a hare, in his *Letters on Demonology and Witchcraft*, esp. pp. 161–2, 288. The silver bullet was thought to be the only way of killing someone protected by the devil. The most famous instance of this superstition concerns John Graham of Claverhouse, Viscount Dundee, who was believed by his enemies to have the devil's protection against lead shot, and so was rumoured to have been killed at the battle of Killiecrankie in 1689 by a silver button used as a bullet. Scott recounts the superstition in his note to ch. 16 of *Old Mortality* and in *Tales of a Grandfather*, 2nd series, 1829, iii. 157–9.

204   *epigraph*: Scott adapts the description of the tall fern 'Queen Osmunda' ('Plant lovelier, in its own retired abode | On Grasmere's beach, than Naiad . . .'), in 'Poems on the Naming of Places', iv (1800), by William Wordsworth (1770–1850).

209   *emblematic ceremony . . . refused to receive from Ravenswood*: it was an ancient custom, particularly among working people, to break a piece of gold or silver as a token of a verbal contract of marriage. T. S. Knowlson comments: 'Prior to the exchange of rings, it was accounted sufficient if the contracting parties broke a piece of gold or silver (each keeping a half), and drank a glass of wine.' (*The Origins of Popular Superstitions and Customs*, 1910, p. 95.) Several literary examples are given in Brand, *Observations on Popular Antiquities*, rev. Ellis, 1813, ii. 21–5.

struck a raven . . . near to where they had been seated: the incident, as Norman realizes, is heavily ominous, particularly since the family of Ravenswood closely associates itself with the ill-boding raven of its name.

210 *make the ring-walk . . . we have all the deer's marks and furnishes got*: Scott follows the preparations for the hunt described in his books of old hunting craft. The terms used show his close reading of the passage from *The Noble Art of Venerie, or Hunting*, quoted in note 33 to *Rokeby* (1813): 'let him harbour him if he can, still marking all his tokens, as well by the slot as by the entries, foyles, or such-like. That done, let him plash or bruse down small twigges, some aloft and some below, as the art requireth, and therewithall, whilest his hound is hote, let him beat the outsides, and make his ring-walkes, twice or thrice about the wood.'

211 *so ne'er put finger in your eye about it*: colloquial, meaning 'so don't cry about it'.

212 *the ancient French adage, 'Château qui parle . . . va se rendre'*: 'The castle which parleys, and the woman who listens, both the one and the other are about to surrender', included in *A New Dictionary of Foreign Phrases and Classical Quotations*, ed. Hugh Percy Jones, 1902, p. 212.

214 *epigraph*: from Sir Giles Overreach's commands to his daughter in Massinger's comedy *A New Way to Pay Old Debts*, III. ii. 153–8, serving both to introduce the visit of the Marquis and to provide a parallel to Ashton's exploitation of Lucy.

216 *'Thou sweetest thing . . . such sweet gentleness'*: Joanna Baillie's *Constantine Paleologus; or, the Last of the Caesars: a Tragedy* (in *Miscellaneous Plays*, 1804), II. ii. 54–60.

218 *Law's scheme . . . express to Paris for the purpose*: John Law (1671–1729) of Lauriston, near Edinburgh, who founded the successful Banque Générale in Paris in 1716, set up a company in 1717 to develop the resources of Louisiana and the Mississippi valley, at that time under French control. He hoped to rival the success of the East India Company, but in 1720 confidence in the 'Mississippi Scheme' faltered, and speculators began to realize their gains. Law eventually settled in Italy where he died in comparative poverty.

'the bit and the buffet': 'Take the Bit and the Buffet wi't' is included in Ramsay's *Scots Proverbs* and Kelly's *Scotish Proverbs*, where it is glossed 'Bear some ill Usage of them by whom you get

Advantage.' (p. 311.) 'The bit and the buffet' means 'food and a blow'.

219 *Monsieur Sagoon's school . . . Meinheer Durchstossen*: these names appear to be comic inventions, playing on the connection with fencing. 'Durchstossen', for example, means 'through-thrust'.

220 *Sir Evan Dhu . . . out with the metall'd lads in 1689*: another reference to Dundee's rising, in which Ravenswood's father had taken part. Sir Ewen or Evan Cameron of Lochiel (1629–1719), chief of the Camerons and nicknamed 'the Black' ('Dhu'), led his clan in support of Dundee in 1689, and fought at Killiecrankie.

'The King over the water': a reference to the exiled Stewart claimant, James Francis, across the Channel in France.

the statutory penalties, 'in that case made and provided': legal phraseology, also used by the legal pedant Clerk Jobson in *Rob Roy* (*Magnum*, vii. 138).

221 *betwixt Lammerlaw and Traprain*: the Lammer Law is one of the Lammermuir hills, about 8 miles south of Haddington. Traprain Law is a distinctive whale-backed hill, a fortified site in ancient times, about 4 miles east of Haddington.

222 *but wherefore droops . . . thy cheek so pale?*: this is typical of Scott's pastiche of other writers. The question recalls *Samson Agonistes*, line 594 ('So much I feel my genial spirits droop') and *A Midsummer Night's Dream*, I. i. 128–9 ('why is your cheek so pale? | How chance the roses there do fade so fast?').

223 *the banks of the Wansbeck*: the River Wansbeck, in Northumberland, joins the North Sea at North Seaton.

225 *the very gates of Jericho, and the judgment-seat of Prester John*: Jericho is used in various slang phrases to refer to some far distant place, possibly in allusion to 2 Samuel 10: 5. In medieval legend, Prester John was a Christian emperor of Asia, Lord of the Tartars, or (from the fourteenth century) Emperor of Ethiopia or Abyssinia.

a plain, blunt, honest, downright soldier: the role Craigengelt invents for himself strongly recalls 'honest Iago' in *Othello*, who conceals intrigue and evil beneath a show of soldierly plainness and bluntness.

as the man says in the play: Bucklaw means Sir Toby Belch's remark to Maria, *Twelfth Night*, I. iii. 11–12.

226 *John Churchill . . . Dundee or the Duke of Berwick*: Craigengelt means that he has served under Whig as well as Jacobite generals. John

Churchill, 1st Duke of Marlborough (1650–1722), won a series of battles against the French in the War of the Spanish Succession (1701–14), the most celebrated being the battle of Blenheim (1704). His politics were sharply opposed to those of the next two generals named by Craigengelt. Dundee was a royalist and later a Jacobite. James Fitz-James, Duke of Berwick (1670–1734), the illegitimate son of James VII and II by Marlborough's sister Arabella Churchill, was for a short time Commander-in-Chief of his father's forces in Ireland. In 1693 he was appointed a lieutenant-general in the French army, and in 1706 was made a Marshal of France, serving in campaigns against British and Alliance forces in Flanders and Spain.

227 *epigraph*: misquoted from lines 115–16 of 'Duke upon Duke', a ballad of which a 'good part' was ascribed to Pope by Joseph Spence on Pope's authority (see *Alexander Pope: Minor Poems*, ed. Norman Ault and John Butt, pp. 217–24). Scott included it in his 'Miscellanies in Verse, by Mr Pope, Dr Arbuthnot, Mr Gay, &c.' in his edition of *The Works of Jonathan Swift* (1814).

228 *It was one of the bosom-hopes . . . highly favourable to her wishes*: by the Act of Union, Scotland sent elected representatives of 30 counties and 15 burghs to the Parliament at Westminster, instead of the 159 constituencies formerly represented in its own Parliament. The new arrangement was more disruptive in the burghs than in the counties, where the basis of the electoral system continued to be the Act of 1681 which had given the franchise to freeholders of land valued at £400 Scots. Corruption was commonplace, the Act of Union having failed to allow the Court of Session powers to review the conduct of elections. Immediately after the Union, for example, the Duke of Queensberry was blatantly controlling elections within his territories by conferring estates by 'trust conveyances' on individuals in return for their votes. In addition to securing 'safe' votes for Sholto (as Craigengelt goes on to suggest), Bucklaw's influence might well have been necessary to secure Sholto's right to contest an election, since only freeholders included in a county's roll of electors were eligible to represent it.

229 *a misprision . . . against her matrimonial authority*: the English law of misprision of treason, by which it was an offence to conceal knowledge of a treasonable plot from the authorities, became applicable to Scotland in 1709. Sir William is suspected of concealing a plot if not of being the principal in it.

229 *He, like Don Gayferos, 'forgot his lady fair and true'*: in Spanish romance, Gayferos is the kinsman of Charlemagne's most celebrated paladin Roland, and the husband of Charlemagne's daughter Melisenda, whom he rescues from the Moors. Gines de Pasamonte gives a puppet show version of the story in *Don Quixote*, Part 2, ch. 26, which quotes two lines of a song, 'Jugando está a las tablas don Gaiferos, que ya de Melisendra está olvidado' ('Gaiferos is playing at the tables, and now his Melisendra is forgotten').

230 *Middleton's 'Mad World my Masters' . . . travelling in full ceremony*: the reference is to the comedy *A Mad World, My Masters* (printed 1608) by Thomas Middleton (1580–1627). The pedantic note (26) signed 'J. C.' (Jedediah Cleishbotham, his only appearance in this novel), cites the play as included in vol. v of the *Select Collection of Old Plays* (12 vols., 1744) by Robert Dodsley (1703–64), which reprints plays written before the death of Charles I, and provides a preface on the history of English drama. The facetious greeting is quoted from the speech of Sir Bounteous Progress (*A Mad World, My Masters*, II. i. 7–8). Cleishbotham's reference to the two earls of Hopetoun is puzzling. The 'present' earl was John (not Charles) Hope, 4th Earl and 2nd Baron of Hopetoun (1765–1823), who had succeeded to the title in 1816. He had served in the West Indies and Egypt, and had taken command at the battle of Corunna (1809) on the death of Sir John Moore (hence Cleishbotham's reference to Mars and fame). He was the son of John, 2nd Earl of Hopetoun (1704–81), by his second wife, and he had a half-brother called Charles (1768–1828), who may be the cause of Scott's mistake. I have not identified the couplet quoted at the end of Cleishbotham's note.

as if the Avenger of Blood had been behind them: in Jewish polity, the Avenger of Blood was the man who had the right to avenge the murder of a kinsman. See Joshua 20: 3, 5, Deuteronomy 19: 6, 12.

231 *to 'change a leg' with a peer of the realm*: before changing the position of their legs, passengers travelling inside mail coaches would request the consent of the person sitting opposite.

'He turned his eyes . . . An awful vision': unidentified.

the green and blue chariots . . . the Lord Keeper: during the reign of Justinian, the rivalry between men of the blue and green chariots in the circus at Byzantium developed into disruptive political factionalism. Here, the two coaches represent the competing factions in the Scottish administration.

'Mon Dieu! . . . il y en a deux!': ('My God! there are two of them!')
Among the many ghost-stories Scott narrates in the course of his
Letters on Demonology and Witchcraft, the nearest to this is the story
of the dying man and the skeleton-apparition, pp. 26–33.

232 *caught 'in the manner':* caught in the act of committing a crime.

234 *whose services were easily purchased . . . to the means of employing them:*
it has been calculated that at the time of the Union the total
population of Scotland was just over one million, and that four-
fifths of this number derived their livelihood from the land, which
made little return beyond basic sustenance. Only about a quarter of
the land was fit for cultivation, the system of land-holding did not
encourage agricultural improvement, and the methods of farming
used were undeveloped. In Scott's *Visionary* (1819), Somnambulus
comments on the scantiness of productive land relative to
population (ed. Garside, p. 34). Industry and trade were growing
in importance, but were still limited. See William Ferguson, *Scotland 1689 to the Present,* Edinburgh History of Scotland, iv, 1968,
ch. 3.

The Marquis . . . acquiring popularity: George Lockhart of Carnwath,
whose account of Atholl tallies in many respects with Scott's,
describes him as selfish, vain, and ambitious, a Jacobite who tem-
porized to retain power (*Lockhart Papers,* i. 72–4). Lockhart comments: 'He was endow'd with good natural parts, tho' by reason of
his proud, imperious, haughty, passionate temper, he was no ways
capable to be the leading man of a party, which he aim'd at.'

238 *scared by a dun cow . . . Guy of Warwick:* the encounter with the Dun
Cow of Dunsmore is one of the many exploits narrated in the
popular verse romance *Guy of Warwick,* in which Guy, son of the
steward of the Earl of Warwick, fights to win the hand of the Earl's
daughter. Three romances dealing with Guy of Warwick are to be
found in the Auchinleck Manuscript, with which Scott was familiar, and a shorter version is included in Ellis's *Specimens.* Scott also
owned two chapbook versions and a 1729 prose version.

244 *epigraph:* not found in Waller. See note to p. 154.

about five Scottish miles distant from each: the Scottish mile was 1.8
kilometres, nearly one-eighth longer than the English mile.

248 *as in Thessaly of old . . . to leave without a watch:* Thessalian women
were reputed to be especially powerful witches. To leave a body
unattended would be to leave it open to demonic attack.

249 *the frequent accompaniments of a Scottish old-fashioned burial*: Andrew
Lang comments in 1893: 'These are still customary in parts of
Scotland. There is a story of a man who, after drinking well at the
funeral feast, arose and proposed "the health of the Bride and
Bridegroom." Some one pulled him down. "Man, do ye no ken
where ye are?" "Weel, be it bridal or be it burial, *it's grand!*" Another
worthy, in the spirit of Ailsie Gourlay, remarked that a bridal was
all very well, "but gie me a gude solid burial." ' (Border edition,
xv. 165.)

the meeting betwixt Macbeth and the witches on the blasted heath of Forres:
Macbeth, I. iii. Macbeth calls Forres a 'blasted heath' in line 77.

250 *Mortsheugh*: the name means a 'heugh' ('dell') of death.

rosemary, southernwood, rue . . . fumigation in the chimney of the cottage:
all these herbs have strongly scented leaves and were cultivated for
medicinal purposes. Rosemary and rue were common strewing
herbs, used to ward off contagion and vermin. During funeral
preparations they were strewn on the shroud, burned in the death-
chamber, and woven into wreaths. The mention of rue carries
additional overtones of witchcraft, for rue was an essential ingre-
dient in nearly all charms and spells, and was also used in exorcizing
evil spirits.

mony a cummer lang syne . . . in the King of France's cellar: in John
Aubrey's *Miscellanies* a letter dated 1695 tells the story of a member
of the aristocratic Duffus family: 'That upon a time, when he was
walking abroad in the Fields near to his own House, he was
suddenly carried away, and found the next Day at *Paris* in the *French*
King's Cellar with a Silver Cup in his Hand' (2nd edn., 1721,
p. 158: Scott owned this edition). Scott relates the tradition in his
introduction to 'The Young Tamlane', *Minstrelsy of the Scottish
Border*, ed. Henderson, ii. 366–8. The allusion also recalls an anecdote associated with the North Berwick witches (see note to p. 334),
for the black-letter pamphlet, *Newes from Scotland, Declaring the
Damnable Life of Doctor Fian* (one of the main figures accused and
executed), tells of a pedlar from Tranent, who was 'in a moment
convayed at midnight from Scotland to Burdeux, in France, (being
places of no small distance) into a merchante's sellar there'. See
Law's *Memorialls*, ed. C. K. Sharpe, p. xxx.

251 *They prick us and they pine us, and they pit us on the pinnywinkles for
witches*: it was the practice of professional 'prickers' to run long
needles into marks on the bodies of those suspected of witchcraft,

to test for the devil's mark, which was thought to be immune to pain. The 'pinnywinkles' or 'pilniewinks' were vices used to crush the fingers. Other tortures regularly used to exact confessions included crushing the limbs in stocks, pulling out the fingernails, keeping without sleep, and whipping. Scott further condemns these practices in a note to 'Christie's Will' in his *Minstrelsy of the Scottish Border* (ed. Henderson, iv, 77–8) and in *Letters on Demonology and Witchcraft*, pp. 292, 297–8, 311–2, 327–8. The costs of trial, torture, and execution in cases of witchcraft were met by the accused.

252 *those confessions . . . during the seventeenth century*: an estimated 4,400 witches were executed in Scotland before the formal repeal of the 'Acts anentis witchcraft' in 1736. The persecution intensified during the reign of James VI and was at its worst in the periods 1590–7, 1640–4, and 1660–3. Although no confession was needed to secure the trial and execution of a witch (a general charge of 'habit and repute' sufficed as evidence), many of those accused produced under torture long and fantastic confessions, often implicating others. Scott describes the injustices of the system of prosecution in witchcraft cases in *Letters on Demonology and Witchcraft*, pp. 298–303, and expresses his personal disgust at the Scottish trials, p. 315.

The rich Abbey of Coldinghame: the Abbey of Coldingham, a few miles from Eyemouth on the Berwickshire coast, was founded by Edgar, king of Scots (1072–1107), in the last years of the eleventh century.

254 *epigraph*: *Hamlet*, v. i. 65–70. The home truths of the meeting between Ravenswood and Mortsheugh are clearly inspired by the gravediggers scene.

It is when 'the mind is free the body's delicate': the 'miserable kennel' turns Scott's mind to the hovel in which Kent tries to persuade Lear to shelter. He quotes from Lear's contrast between physical and mental tempest, *King Lear*, iii. iv. 11–12.

255 *it's no an ordinar grave that will haud her in . . . I pray ye?*: the superstition that witches rose from their graves to join in Satan's revels is best illustrated by Burns's 'Tam O'Shanter' (1791), in which the coffins of Alloway kirkyard lie open as the witches dance.

256 *ony regard for plenishing the earth*: echoing the biblical 'replenish the earth', Genesis 1: 28, 9: 1.

257 *this trumpeter Marine that I have heard play afore the Lords of the Circuit*: as Laing points out, the name of Francis Marine is included in the

list of Queen Anne's Trumpeters for Scotland (whose duty it was to announce royal proclamations and attend the Circuit Courts of Justiciary) in 1710, and this is probably the 'Trumpet Marine' mentioned in a variant of a popular song about the battle of Sheriffmuir (1715), included in Joseph Ritson's *Scotish Songs*, 2 vols., 1794, ii. 56–67, 67 n. (The reference once again pushes the historical framework of the novel forward, this time to the Jacobite rebellion organized by the Earl of Mar in 1715.) The fate of 'Trumpet Marine' at Sheriffmuir may have suggested some of Mortsheugh's experiences at Bothwell Bridge: the song tells how he fell, broke his trumpet, and 'Came off without musick at a', man'.

257 *'Boot and saddle,' or 'Horse and away,' or 'Gallants, come trot' . . . he hadna the tones*: these are orders to prepare for battle given to the cavalry by trumpet signals. Trumpeters were attached to the households of the nobility, as well as to the royal household, and traditionally gave signals and fanfares in battle and on ceremonial occasions. In 1641 the Articles of War specifically stated that signals for the cavalry in the Scottish army were to be made by trumpet and drum. See Sir John Graham Dalyell, *Musical Memoirs of Scotland*, 1849, p. 175.

258 *twenty-fourth of June . . . the month and year*: a slip for 22 June, when the battle of Bothwell Bridge was fought.

Hackstoun of Rathillet . . . armed men on the other side: David Hackston of Rathillet in Fife (d. 1680), one of the Covenanters' most trusted leaders, was one of the party who murdered Archbishop Sharp on 3 May 1679, although he declined to take an active part because of a personal quarrel with Sharp which would have sullied the group's motives. A leader at the battles of Drumclog and Bothwell Bridge, he was surprised at the skirmish of Aird's Moss on 22 July 1680 and executed with particular cruelty in Edinburgh eight days later. The battle at Bothwell centred on the defence of the narrow bridge, which was held by a group of 300 men under Hackston and Hall of Haughhead. Mortsheugh, as a trumpeter to the Royalist cavalry, is ordered to attempt an alternative crossing at the ford.

Andrew Ferrara: Scott comments in a note to ch. 50 of *Waverley* that the name of this North Italian swordsmith of the late sixteenth century was 'inscribed on all the Scottish broadswords which are accounted of peculiar excellence' (*Magnum*, ii. 201). It is now thought that the inscriptions of his name on Scottish swords were forged, a common practice.

swearing Gog and Magog: a reference to Revelation 20: 8, where the nations are to be gathered into the last great struggle of good and evil at the Battle of Armageddon.

in the flower of my youth, as Scripture says: properly, 'shall die in the flower of their age' (1 Samuel 2: 33): the 'cutting off' recalls Psalms 103: 15–16 ('as a flower of the field').

259 *he might hae gien us liferent tacks . . . guided his gear like a fule!*: Ravenswood might have protected his tenants by giving them written rights to hold their tenancies for life. William Ferguson comments that Scots law 'meticulously safeguarded the rights of proprietors but it did little to protect tenants, particularly those— and they were numerous—who had no tacks or written agreements' (*Scotland 1689 to the Present*, p. 73). The 'dainty bit mailing', which Mortsheugh laments, is a rented farm or piece of land.

260 *Cervantes acutely remarks, that flattery is pleasing even from the mouth of a madman*: referring to the narrator's comments on Don Quixote's praise of Don Lorenzo's verses, *Don Quixote*, Part 2, ch. 18.

261 *I can play, 'Wilt thou do't again,' . . . better than ever Pattie Birnie*: Patrick or 'Patie' Birnie (b. *c*.1635) was a noted fiddler from Kinghorn in Fife. 'O wiltu, wiltu do't again' was a tune he played often, and is said to have written. The words and air of 'The Auld Man's Mear's Dead' are also attributed to him, although the words were improved by Burns in the eighteenth century. There is a story that, like Mortsheugh, he went to Bothwell Bridge but ran away, all the way home to Kinghorn. Allan Ramsay's 'The Life and Acts of, or An Elegy on Patie Birnie' (1721) celebrates his skills, mentions the two songs, and refers (like Mortsheugh) to his fiddle as 'his Breadwinner' (st. 3).

'Liggeram Cosh,' . . . 'the Cummers of Athole': 'Liggeram Cosh' appears to be Scott's spelling of a Gaelic air, but the title is not recognizable. 'Mullin Dhu' is Scott's spelling of the reel 'Muileann Dubh' ('The Black Mill'). With 'Athole Cummers', a strathspey, it is included in *The Athole Collection of the Dance Music of Scotland*, compiled and arranged by James Stewart-Robertson, 1961.

'Killiecrankie,' . . . 'the Auld Stewarts back again': Jacobite songs included in *The Jacobite Relics of Scotland*, 2 vols., 1819, collected by James Hogg.

262 *epigraph*: 'Hendersoun' is an alternative form of the name of the Scottish poet Robert Henryson (?1430–?1506), but the lines are not

his. A form of complicated ornamental knot was used as a pledge of true love and betrothal.

264   *spread, as it were, a table in the wilderness*: Psalms 78: 19.

the Darien matter . . . but the best work is had out of him: William Paterson's scheme to establish a Scottish trading colony on the Isthmus of Darien (or Panama) became the major project of the 'Company of Scotland Trading to Africa and the Indies', set up in 1695 as a Scottish rival to the East India Company and financed rapidly and enthusiastically by a wide variety of Scottish investors. It was planned to overcome the trading problems caused by England's closed system of trade with the colonies, which greatly disadvantaged Scottish goods. The Darien settlement was a focus of national pride and a source of increasingly bitter feeling against England, for the three expeditions failed not only because of lack of provision, fever, and repeated attack from the surrounding Spanish territories, but also because the English colonies in North America and the West Indies were forbidden to offer assistance. The Darien scheme threatened English foreign policy and it was strongly resented in Scotland that William, who was Scotland's king as well as England's, had sacrificed Scottish to English interests in the affair. The cost of the venture has been estimated at £200,000 and nearly 2,000 lives (P. W. J. Riley, *English Ministers and Scotland*). In this context there is a bitter pointedness and even a sense of national betrayal in Ashton's having 'got a lift' from his financial and political acumen in selling out of the Company before its collapse.

265   *to bell the cat with him in the House of Peers*: by allusion to the fable of the mice and the cat, Archibald Douglas, 5th Earl of Angus (*c.*1449–1513), was nicknamed 'Bell the Cat' for leading the conspiracy by which the favourites of James III were hanged at Lauder in 1482. The story is told in note 69 to *Marmion*.

266   *the fatal battle of Flodden, in which they both fell*: see note to p. 58. The Ravenswood ancestor is presumably Raymond, who is said to have died there after the loss of his 'Naiad' lover.

267   *highly important commission beyond sea . . . advantageous to him*: from the later references to Ratisbon, Vienna, and Paris, it seems likely that Ravenswood is imagined as playing a part in negotiations between the two sides in the War of the Spanish Succession, in which France supported the claim of Louis XIV's grandson, Philip of Anjou, to the Spanish throne, and was opposed by the Grand Alliance of England, Austria, and Holland. Scott's allusion is vague,

but secret negotiations for peace began in·1710 under Harley's leadership, had Jacobite overtones, and caused political turmoil when they were denounced by the Whigs in 1711.

the Spanish generals . . . unavoidably discovered in the day of battle: Prince William of Orange, in alliance with Mary I of England, commanded 20,000 Spanish soldiers in the campaign of 1554–7 against France.

269　*His lordship minds weel, how, in the year that him they ca'd King Willie died*: there was no Jacobite rising following William's death on 8 March 1702, although intriguing of the kind Scott envisages for the Marquis was common. Atholl's name, however, was prominent in the tension and suspicion which beset Scotland in the first years of Anne's reign (see Appendix on the main causes and manifestations of this). Simon Fraser of Beaufort, self-styled Lord Lovat, produced forged letters which implicated Atholl and several other leading statesmen in a plot to restore the Stewarts. Although there was no serious evidence against Atholl, he lost his place as Lord Privy Seal. The accusations made in the 'Scots' Plot' (as it was known in England) seriously discredited the Commissioner, Queensberry, and were later investigated by a committee set up by the House of Lords.

271　*like a stately merchantman in the Gut of Gibraltar . . . by three Algerine galleys*: merchant vessels using the Mediterranean Sea and the vital shipping route through the Strait of Gibraltar were plagued by the Barbary pirates, who operated from Algeria on the North African coast. The pirates were at their most powerful during the seventeenth century but were still active in the early years of the nineteenth, when Britain made several attempts to suppress them. 'Tarpaulin', a cloth covered with tar to make it waterproof, and much used by sailors, came to be used, figuratively, to mean 'belonging to a sailor'.

272　*and the Council with the King*: another slip suggesting that William is still king. The 'Council' is the Privy Council.

273　*the sheriff-clerk of the county*: a clerk of the sheriff's court. The sheriff, the highest legal officer of a county, had a wide civil and criminal jurisdiction in Scotland.

but fat sall I say!: the presentation of Dingwall's speech indicates that he uses the Aberdeenshire or North-Eastern Scottish dialect, in which the Standard Scots 'wh' becomes 'f' and 'oo' becomes 'ee'. See Graham Tulloch, *The Language of Walter Scott: A Study of his Scottish and Period Language*, 1980, p. 254.

273   *the Lord High Commissioner to the Estates o' Parliament*: before the Union, the Commissioner was the sovereign's representative at both the Scottish Parliament (with its four Estates) and the General Assembly. After the Union, he represented the sovereign at the General Assembly only.

274   *epigraph*: from the Wizard's premonition of the consequences of the Jacobite rebellion of 1745–6 in Campbell's 'Lochiel's Warning' (1802).

275   *I am a dog, and an auld dog too*: the exchange recalls that between Oliver and Adam, *As You Like It*, I. i. 81–4.

276   *Little's the light . . . far in a mirk night*: it may well be old, but the present instance is the only entry in the *Oxford Dictionary of English Proverbs*, 3rd edn.

278   *to train up weans, as the wise man says . . . respect to their superiors*: a very general remark, not traceable to any particular wise man.

      'Some gaed east . . . gaed to the craw's nest': the last lines of a rhyme chanted in an old Scottish game for children, after the person who is to be 'in' or 'it' has been chosen (a process known as 'chappin out' in Scotland during Scott's time). Robert Chambers includes the rhyme in full in *Popular Rhymes, Fireside Stories, and Amusements, of Scotland*, p. 62.

281   *resembling in shape . . . the revels of a country village*: for Teniers, see note to p. 16. Large earthenware tankards are common in the work of Teniers and in other genre paintings of the period featuring carousing, fighting, peasants (particularly those by Adriaen van Ostade and Adriaen Brouwer). See the tankard in Teniers' *The Smoker* (1643), the sitter for which is thought to have been one of his brothers, but who bears a distinct resemblance to Teniers himself. *Village Festival* (1649) is an example of the pictures of revelry Scott has in mind. I suspect, however, that Scott is thinking of the general style and subject-matter of genre here rather than of the work of Teniers alone.

      illustrative of ancient Scottish manners: in the 'Postscript, which should have been a Preface' to his first novel, *Waverley*, Scott had declared that he hoped to preserve in his novels the characteristic manners and habits of the Scottish people of earlier times, emulating the portrayal of Irish life in the works of Maria Edgeworth. This scheme became more pronounced in the narratives written for *Tales of My Landlord*. Cleishbotham's Dedication to the 1st Series in 1816 specifically describes them as 'Illustrative of Ancient Scottish Manners, and of the Traditions of their Respective Districts'.

282 *the character of the French school . . . at the beginning of the eighteenth century*: French art of the period was dominated by the dictates of the Académie Royale de Peinture et de Sculpture, the state institution of the arts founded in 1648, which produced a large number of talented artists. It is characterized by the emergence of the rococo manner, and best known through the works of Jean-Antoine Watteau (1684–1721). See Philip Conisbee, *Painting in Eighteenth-Century France* (1981). With the important exception of the work of William Aikman (1682–1731), Scottish painting did not flourish in this period. Many Scottish painters of the late seventeenth century worked in London, the most notable being Michael Wright (*c.*1625–1700). Aikman himself moved there after eleven years of unprofitable business as a portrait-painter in Edinburgh. A few portraitists, including the Scougalls (father and son), worked in Scotland. See J. L. Caw, *Scottish Painting, Past and Present, 1620–1908* (1908); S. Cursiter, *Scottish Art to the Nineteenth Century* (1948).

285 *epigraph*: Fortune or 'Occasion' had to be grasped by the long hair which obscured her face because the back of her head was bald (as described in the Latin proverb *Fronte capillata, post est occasion calva*). See *Faerie Queene*, II. iv. 12; *Paradise Regained*, III, 173.

the political crisis . . . either the cause or consequences: in the historical scheme imposed by the Magnum Opus, this must refer to the Tory victory in the election of 1710, after which Robert Harley (1661–1724: Earl of Oxford from 1711) headed the administration. He had built up a strong interest with Queen Anne while in opposition, assisted by the influence of his cousin, Abigail Hill (later Masham). He was a moderate, but allied with the High Tories. His government was defeated in the House of Lords in 1711 after revelations of secret negotiations for peace with France, but Harley re-established control by persuading the queen to dismiss the Duke of Marlborough and to create twelve new peerages. After increasing internal dissention which weakened his ministry, Harley lost power in 1714, and was impeached for treason in 1715. Although the Tories gained control in 1710, the Scottish administration formed under Harley did not work on strict party lines, and Atholl certainly did not have the supreme political power implied in the novel. (For possibilities within the novel's original pre-Union dating, see Jane Millgate, 'Text and Context: Dating the

Events of *The Bride of Lammermoor* ', *The Bibliotheck*, ix, 1979, 200–213.)

285 *Harley . . . the denomination of Whimsicals*: the reference to 'Whim-sicals' suggests a period a little later than the election of 1710, and the term is probably used loosely. In a note to Swift's 'Some Free Thoughts upon the Present State of Affairs' (1714), Scott explains the group known as Whimsicals as 'Tories, who deserted their party after peace was concluded' (a reference to the Treaty of Utrecht, 1713): *The Works of Jonathan Swift*, ed. Scott, 19 vols., 1814, v .396 n. A looser description is given in 'My Aunt Margaret's Mirror', in which Aunt Margaret thinks herself one of 'the party, which, in Queen Anne's time, were called *Whimsicals*; because they were sometimes operated upon by feelings, sometimes by principle' (*Magnum*, xli. 304).

The Scottish High Church party . . . the Chevalier de St George: the election of 1710 gave political power to some Cavaliers for the first time since 1707. Robert Wodrow commented on the aftermath of the election: 'The Jacobites are mighty uppish, and plainly say that this 1710 is just another 1660; and they talk of nothing but Resig-nation, Restauration, and Recission, their three R.s; and they talk their King will be over, either by act of Parliament or invasion, by Agust nixt. They boast mighty, which I hope shall ruin their cause.' (*Scottish Diaries and Memoirs 1550–1746*, ed. J. G. Fyfe, 1927, p. 380.) The Chevalier was properly Anne's half-brother, the child of her father's second wife.

286 *what Cromwell called waiters upon Providence*: the remark is similar to several phrases in Cromwell's speeches: no precise source identified.

his ain puir peculiar: 'his own small contribution'. Normand com-ments that Scott's choice of words is again influenced by his legal training, 'peculiar' being the term given to the small personal property allowed to the son of a Roman slave.

Lord Ravenswood's lodgings in the Canongate: the Canongate, former-ly the eastern entrance to Edinburgh, is the road and surrounding district stretching westward from the Palace of Holyrood to the Netherbow. It was a separate burgh until 1856. Because of its proximity to the Palace, many of the Scottish nobility had town residences there. In contrast to Ravenswood, Bucklaw can later offer Lucy his 'aunt's lodgings there (p. 298).

to acquire to himself in absolute property: see the explanation of adjudication and declarations of the expiry of the legal in my note to p. 170.

288 *Much more there was . . . neither interest nor information*: Scott's settled prejudice against giving the details of courtship and lovers' language had been in evidence since his early days as a poet. In letters written after the publication of *The Lady of the Lake* (1810), he wrote: 'As for my lover I find with deep regret that however interesting lovers are to each other it is no easy matter to render them generally interesting', and 'you ladies can hardly comprehend how very stupid lovers are to every body but mistresses' (*Letters*, ii. 354, 464). He felt the same way about the letters of courtship between his daughter Sophia and John Gibson Lockhart before their marriage in 1820.

against the freedom of the subject, and the immunities of God's kirk: by this general slur, Lady Ashton means that the Ravenswoods, as Royalists and Episcopalians, have obstructed the powers of Parliament secured by the Revolution settlement, and the establishment of Presbyterian church-government. By 'immunities', she means the Church's freedom from the control of the monarch and the political establishment. In 1703 the General Assembly formally repeated its belief that Presbyterianism was agreeable to the Word of God and was the only government of Christ's Church in Scotland, and successfully remonstrated against the introduction of a parliamentary bill which would have allowed for the toleration of all non-Roman Catholic dissenters from the established Presbyterian Church.

like holy David . . . and the place thereof knew them no more: Lady Ashton combines phrases from one Psalm of David ('I have seen the wicked in great power, and spreading himself like a green bay tree', Psalms 36: 35; the version with 'flourishing' occurs in the Book of Common Prayer), with phrases from another ('For the wind passeth over it, and it is gone; and the place thereof shall know it no more', Psalms 103: 16).

289 *in foro contentioso*: in an action contested in the law courts, where the parties have been fully heard and a decree granted.

if the law of Scotland . . . House of Lords: until the Magnum Opus, this read 'if the law of Scotland, as declared in her established courts, were to undergo a reversal in any popular assembly'.

290   *inter minores . . . the engagement was inept, and void in law*: in Scots
      law, any contract made by a minor without the consent of parents
      or guardians ('natural curators') could be declared null. Lucy is 17.

      through the intervention of . . . a foreign court of appeal: this clause was
      missing in editions before the Magnum Opus.

291   *detain him upon the continent for some months*: in the first edition, vol.
      ii ended here.

292   *epigraph*: Richard's speech on his successful wooing of Lady Anne,
      Richard III, I. ii. 227–9, is clearly inappropriate to Bucklaw's char-
      acter and situation, except for the hint in the half-line Scott sup-
      presses ('but I will not keep her long').

293   *as sulky as a bear that has lost its whelps*: this alludes to the saying 'As
      savage as a she-bear when she is robbed of her whelps' (Tilley,
      Dictionary of Proverbs, S. 292).

294   *what Sir William would call a 'famous witness'*: a legalistic term for a
      reliable witness, one of good repute.

296   *epigraph*: Scott changes the pronouns in Adriana's account of how
      she reprehended her husband's supposed infidelity, in *Comedy of
      Errors*, v. i. 62–6.

298   *the best establishment in the three Lothians*: East, West, and Mid
      Lothian form the bulk of the central part of Scotland south of
      Edinburgh. For the Canongate, see note to p. 286.

299   *'It is best to be off wi' the old love . . . the new'*: from the opening stanza
      of 'It's gude to be merry and wise', in *Songs of England and Scotland*,
      compiled by Peter Cunningham, 2 vols., 1835, ii. 73.

300   *your Pacolet . . . trusted in this matter*: Pacolet is the dwarf messenger
      of the giant Ferragus in the early French romance *Valentine and
      Orson*, which Scott knew in French and English forms and of which
      he possessed several chapbook versions. Pacolet has a magic wooden
      horse which conveys him instantly wherever he wishes.

      the 20th day from this is St Jude's: the feast day of St Jude is 28
      October, so the present scene takes place on the 8th, placing it either
      eleven or twenty-three months after the funeral of Ravenswood's
      father. Neither quite fits the references elsewhere in the novel. The
      date may have been chosen because St Jude, the first-century apostle
      and martyr, is known as the patron of hopeless causes.

      Caverton Edge . . . four-year-old colt: annual horse races took place at
      Caverton Edge in the parish of Eckford, Roxburghshire.

301   *To sign and seal—to do and die!*: sealing had long ceased to be a
necessary formality for the execution of all important documents.
An Act of 1584 made sealing unnecessary when the deed was to be
recorded, and in practice sealing was only used in Crown grants.
(Normand) 'To do or die' is a familiar phrase, used in Burns's
'Sketch: inscribed to C. J. Fox' and Campbell's 'Gertrude of
Wyoming', III. 37.

Posso, in Mannor Water: about 5 miles south-west of Peebles.

303   *epigraph*: from the Abbess's reply to Adriana's speech (used as the
epigraph of the previous chapter), *Comedy of Errors*, v. i. 78–82.

The manners of the country . . . France before the revolution: among
aristocratic families, marriages between partners chosen by parents
were common in the early part of the eighteenth century. French
commentators thought the situation more pronounced in France
than in England: see Lawrence Stone, *The Family, Sex and Marriage
in England 1500–1800*, 1977, pp. 318, 322. The 'revolution' is the
first French Revolution, of 1789. Stone notes that parental control
over marriages in the higher ranks of the Scottish aristocracy
survived until the mid-eighteenth century, when it had disappeared
in other social groups, and cites the example of Caroline, daughter
of the 2nd Duke of Argyll, who fell in love with Lord Quarendon
but was forced to marry Lord Dalkeith (p. 186).

*as the lovers in the Merchant of Venice select the casket . . . hazarded a
venture*: the romantic plot of *The Merchant of Venice*, in which
Portia's suitors must choose between three caskets of gold, silver,
and lead to decide who may marry her, is intended to demonstrate
the folly of choosing by external appearance alone. For the moral,
made explicit on Bassanio's correct choice, see III. ii. 131–2. 'Hazard' may have been suggested by Portia's use of the word before
Bassanio makes his choice.

304   *As this measure . . . equally new, arbitrary, and tyrannical*: until the
Magnum Opus, this read simply: 'As this measure was enforced with
all the authority of power, it was exclaimed against by the members
on the opposite side of politics, as an interference with the civil
judicature of the country, equally new, arbitrary, and tyrannical.'

305   *in the worst times of the worst Stewarts, and a degradation of Scotland . . .
specially to hold in contempt that of Scotland*: until the Magnum Opus,
the sentence ended at 'the worst times of the worst Stuarts'. Municipal law is the law of a particular state. See note to p. 166 on
appeals procedure.

305 *patria potestas*: the term given to the power which, under civil law, the *paterfamilias* had the right to exercise over all members of his family: see Trayner, *Latin Maxims*. Although this power was never as extensive in Scots law as in Roman law, fathers had considerable rights over the custody, education, and property of their children during minority.

307 *a willow branch in his hand . . . for her special wearing*: to wear willow was to mourn a lost lover, as in the song of 'Willow' remembered by Desdemona in *Othello*, IV. iii. 26–58. Lucy is expected to believe that Ravenswood has callously sent her this token from his travels.

308 *the pair of colours they have promised me*: a pair of silken flags carried in ceremonial processions; hence the commission of an ensign, the lowest commissioned military officer.

310 *epigraph*: *Faerie Queene*, III. vii. 6.

   the Wise Woman of Bowden: the reference to Bowden, which is in Roxburghshire, about 4 miles south-east of Scott's home at Abbotsford, is out of keeping with the novel's imagined setting.

311 *the stake and tar-barrel*: barrels of tar were used in building fires for executions at the stake.

   like Caliban's, was a harmless fairy: Caliban is the offspring of the witch Sycorax in *The Tempest*: for the 'harmless fairy', see Stephano's speech, IV. i. 196–7.

312 *to 'lend an attentive ear'*: the inverted commas indicate a variation on a clichéd phrase rather than a quotation.

   Of fays that nightly dance . . . captive thralls: unidentified. Scott also uses 'The fays, which nightly dance upon the wold' as a quotation in *Minstrelsy of the Scottish Border*, ed. Henderson, ii. 349.

   told by the midnight lamp . . . in an age more hard of belief: see Scott's account of the ideal conditions for telling tales of terror in 'My Aunt Margaret's Mirror' (*Magnum*, xli. 306–7). The lip and finger once again recall the three witches of *Macbeth*, I. iii. 44–5 ('By each at once her choppy finger laying | Upon her skinny lips'). The 'blue-eyed hag' refers to Caliban's mother, the witch Sycorax (to whom Ailsie is explicitly likened in the next sentence), *The Tempest*, I. ii. 269.

313 *the articles of dittay against Ailsie Gourlay . . . sentence of a commission from the Privy Council*: the usual procedure for the trial of a suspected witch was that the Privy Council would appoint a commission of

local gentlemen, 3 or 5 of whom could act to investigate alleged witchcraft, and who in turn authorized the sheriff to summon an assize of no more than 45 local men, from whom 15 were selected to act as a jury. After an indictment ('dittay') had been drawn up, the accused was not permitted to dispute its accuracy. The reference to the Privy Council in the case of Ailsie Gourlay is an anachronism in the novel's post-Union setting, and executions for witchcraft were in any case becoming rarer in the early eighteenth century. Her execution on specific charges of witchcraft is feasible, however. Two of the Pittenweem witches were executed in 1704; in 1709 Elspeth Ross was the last person to be tried on the general charge of being a notorious witch and making threats, but was branded and banished rather than executed; and in 1727 Janet Horne was burned on the specific charge of using her daughter as a flying horse. Two Scottish witches bore the name 'Gourlay': Agnes (condemned in 1649) and Margaret (1659).

shown to a young person of quality . . . in the act of bestowing his hand upon another lady: the original of this story is also linked to the Dalrymple family. It happened to Eleanor, Viscountess Primrose (d. 1759), who married John, 2nd Earl of Stair, the son of Janet Dalrymple's brother. She is reported to have seen her faithless first husband, who was then abroad, in a magic mirror. See Robert Chambers, *Traditions of Edinburgh*, 1825, pp. 63–9. Scott tells the story at length in 'My Aunt Margaret's Mirror', in which he states that his aunt vouched for it 'with particular confidence, alleging indeed that one of her own family had been an eye-witness of the incidents recorded in it' (*Magnum*, xli. 294).

314 *'I'll have a priest . . . Which I'd have broken'*: unidentified.

315 *the union of a Moabitish stranger with a daughter of Zion*: see Ezra 9: 1, where the Israelites are forbidden to mingle with other races, including the Moabites, whose 'abominations' are condemned. The peoples of Zion and Moab are in conflict at various points in the Old Testament. With characteristic caution, Scott added the qualification 'in the divine's opinion' in proof.

a cavalier or malignant, and a scoffer, who hath no inheritance in Jesse: a 'malignant' is one who departs from the true religion, a 'scoffer' one who scoffs at it. The terms are used here by a Presbyterian to describe Episcopalians. To have 'inheritance in *the son of* Jesse', the father of David, is to be part of the true stem of Israel (2 Samuel 20: 1, 1 Kings 12: 16, 2 Chronicles 10: 16).

315 *we are commanded to do justice unto all . . . in brotherhood with us*:
     Bide-the-bent does not quote specific commands on justice and
     enemies, but his interpretation is in keeping with New Testament
     dicta (e.g. Matthew 5: 44, 7: 1–2). To 'keep covenant' is a common
     biblical phrase.

316 *betwixt Campvere and the east coast of Scotland*: until 1795 the Scots
     had a privileged trading post at Campvere (now Veere), on the
     island of Walcheron in Holland. It handled Scottish imports and
     exports, particularly exports of linen and woollen cloth. An ap-
     pointed Conservator looked after the interests of Scottish mer-
     chants.

317 *epigraph*: slightly altered from *The Parish Register* (1807), II. 284–9,
     by George Crabbe (1754–1832). 'Jessamine' is an obsolete form of
     'jasmine'.

319 *the Copper Captain*: a sham captain, especially Michaell Perez, from
     Fletcher's play *Rule a Wife and Have a Wife* (performed 1624).

     the promised blessing—length of days . . . a better country: Exodus 20:
     12 ('Honour thy father and thy mother: that thy days may be long
     upon the land which the LORD thy God giveth thee'): also cited in
     Deuteronomy 5: 16, Matthew 15: 4, and several other times in
     the New Testament. 'Length of days' is the phrase used in the
     promise of Proverbs 3: 1–2. 'A better country' recalls Hebrews
     11: 16.

320 *I have myself seen the fatal deed . . . the time of the subscription*: the
     speaker is Peter Pattieson, not Scott, who is most unlikely to have
     seen Janet Dalrymple's marriage contract. W. S. Crockett includes
     a copy of it in *The Scott Originals* (1912).

321 *epigraph*: misquoted from Tybalt's speech, *Romeo and Juliet*, I. v.
     54–5, 58–9. The missing lines refer to Romeo's 'antic face', which
     would hardly be appropriate for Ravenswood.

322 *he who striketh with the sword, shall perish with the sword*: Matthew 26:
     52, Revelation 13: 10.

324 *he will depart in peace unto his own dwelling . . . worldly passion*:
     characteristic of the biblical assimilations of Bide-the-bent's lan-
     guage. For 'depart in peace' see Luke 2: 29, James 2: 16; 'the gall of
     bitterness and bond of iniquity', Acts 8: 23.

     peradventure my grey hairs may turn away wrath: Bide-the-bent sub-
     stitutes 'grey hairs' for the 'wise men' of Proverbs 29: 8, and the 'soft
     answer' of Proverbs 15: 1.

325 *To-morrow, sir—to-morrow—to-morrow, I will hear you at length*: Ravenswood's words echo Macbeth's reaction to his wife's death, *Macbeth*, V. v. 19.

326 *'If a woman vow a vow . . . because her father disallowed her'*: Numbers 30: 3–5, quoted more accurately for the Magnum Opus.

330 *epigraph*: these are the closing lines of Book VII of the Eastern romance *Thalaba the Destroyer* (1801), by Scott's friend and correspondent Robert Southey (1774–1843), who shared many of Scott's interests in legend, history, and the marvellous. They presage the death of Thalaba's bride Oneiza on her wedding night. Azrael is the Islamic angel of death, mentioned in the Koran.

331 *that Bucklaw neither saw nor suspected . . . his unhappy bride*: because Scott bypassed revisions made for the 1823 *Novels and Tales* when he made corrections for the Magnum Opus, the 1823 edition contains an alternative ending to this sentence, which had been left unfinished in other versions. In 1823 it ends 'that Bucklaw neither saw nor suspected what would otherwise have been obvious to him'.

333 *'My loaf in my lap . . . I'm ne'er the worse'*: the rhyme and the story of the old woman appear in the enlightened attack on popular beliefs in witchcraft and the black arts, *The Discoverie of Witchcraft* (1584), by Reginald Scot (?1538–99), p. 245. Scot surveyed a wide range of contemporary beliefs about witchcraft, alchemy, magic, and the existence of spirits, and argued that belief in the black arts contradicted both reason and religion. His important work attracted widespread attention (including that of James VI and I, whose *Demonologie* of 1597 is often thought to have been written in response to Scot's arguments). Scott refers to *The Discoverie of Witchcraft* many times in his *Letters on Demonology and Witchcraft*, with particular approval on p. 188.

God send us a green Yule and a fat kirkyard!: alluding to the proverbial saying 'A green Yule makes a fat Kirk-yard', meaning that warm winters are unhealthy, included in Ramsay (*Scots Proverbs*, p. 4) and Kelly, who denounces it as superstitious (*Scotish Proverbs*, p. 30).

334 *her winding sheet is up as high as her throat already, believe it wha list*: in *A Description of the Western Islands of Scotland* (1716), Martin Martin records the superstition that 'When a Shroud is perceiv'd about one, it is a sure Prognostick of Death: The time is judged according to the height of it about the Person' (p. 302). It is also one of the omens seen by Theoclymenus in Homer's *Odyssey*, XX. 351–2.

334   *a' the Scotch witches that ever flew by moonlight ower North-Berwick Law*:
      the trials of the North Berwick witches (1590–2) were the first of
      the major witchcraft trials in Scotland, and produced some of the
      most memorable confessions and allegations. They began with the
      confession under torture of a young domestic servant, and event-
      ually implicated some seventy people, including the Earl of Both-
      well. The confessions centred on the demonic rites performed in
      the kirkyard of North Berwick on All Hallow's Eve by a gathering
      of nearly 100 witches who, it was claimed, had sailed there in sieves;
      and on various conspiracies entered into by the witches against the
      life of the king, James VI. James himself took an eager interest in
      the trials, personally questioning one of the accused, Agnes Sam-
      pson, who convinced him of the truth of her powers by repeating
      to him the words he had spoken to his new queen, Anne of
      Denmark, on their wedding night. The trials owed much of their
      intensity to his obsessive involvement, and marked a new phase in
      the history of Scottish witchcraft. The main figures were strangled
      and burned after torture. Scott discusses the trials in *Letters on
      Demonology and Witchcraft*, pp. 309–15. See further, Helen Stafford,
      'Notes on Scottish Witchcraft Cases, 1590–91', in *Essays in Honor
      of Conyers Read*, ed. Norton Downs, 1953, pp. 96–118.

      I'll hae her before Presbytery and Synod: courts of the Presbyterian
      Church. See note to p. 32.

335   *l'Amphitrion où l'on dîne*:   a reference to Sosie's speech in the come-
      dy *Amphitryon* (1668) by Molière (1622–73), III. v: 'Le véritable
      Amphitryon|Est l'Amphitryon où l'on dîne', meaning that the
      person who provides the feast is the real host. The comedy is based
      on the mythological story in which Zeus assumes the form of
      Amphitryon to seduce his wife Alcmene.

      It is well known, that the weddings of ancient days . . . modern times: a
      useful insight into the conduct of weddings in families of the
      Ashtons' rank at this time is given in 'Some Observations of the
      Change of Manners in My Own Time, 1700–1790' by Elizabeth
      Mure (1714–95), in *Scottish Diaries and Memoirs 1746–1843*, ed. J. G.
      Fyfe, 1942, p. 68. Mure's account of the wedding of Sir James
      Stewart (Solicitor-General 1714–17), and the daughter of Sir Hew
      Dalrymple, Lord North Berwick (President of the Court of Session)
      describes the festivities, which lasted several days so that all the
      relatives and friends of both families could join in, and the boisterous
      ceremony to tear off the bride's 'favours' (ribbons) and garter.

339 *a sadder and a wiser man than he had hitherto shown himself:* 'A sadder
and a wiser man' is the penultimate line of Coleridge's 'Rime of the
Ancient Mariner'.

341 *epigraph:* quoted, with two lines missing, from a poem written by
Alexander Garden on the death of Sir James Lawson of Humbie in
1612, included in *A System of Heraldry Speculative and Practical* by
Alexander Nisbet (1657–1725), 2 vols., 1722 (ii, Appendix). Scott
owned the 2nd (1804) edition.

342 *that the picture of Auld Sir Malise Ravenswood . . . led out the brawl before
them a':* the figure which steps out of a portrait is one of the
supernatural effects introduced in Walpole's *The Castle of Otranto*,
ch. 1. Scott comments approvingly on the scene in his 'Life' of
Walpole: 'The descent of the picture of Manfred's ancestor, although it borders on extravagance, is finely introduced, and inter-
rupts an interesting dialogue with striking effect.' (*Misc. Works*, iii.
319–20.)

croaking like the ravens . . . withdrew from the churchyard: this final
reference to a persistent theme was deliberately introduced. Scott
changed the reference from 'vultures' to 'ravens' in proof.

344 *Do not . . . urge to farther desperation a wretch who is already desperate:*
recalling Romeo's warning to Paris beside Juliet's tomb, 'tempt not
a desp'rate man', *Romeo and Juliet*, v. iii. 59.

348 *life had lost to him its salt and its savour:* echoing the biblical phrase,
'but if the salt have lost his savour', Matthew 5: 13, Luke 14: 34.

The family of Ashton did not long survive that of Ravenswood: for
obvious reasons of poetic justice, Scott alters the fates of the members of the Dalrymple family who were the originals of the central
characters in the novel. Lady Stair did not outlive her husband, who
was himself survived by four sons and three daughters. In spite of
prophecies dooming the whole family, several of their descendants
were distinguished in the law and historical scholarship, and in
Scott's time the Stairs were still one of Scotland's great legal families.

GLOSSARY

THE glossary lists words in Scots (omitting those easily surmised or explained in context), unfamiliar words in English, and some legal and foreign-language phrases, except where these are explained in the Editor's Notes. The sources used include the glossary to the Magnum Opus edition (vol. xlviii, 1833), the glossary to the Dryburgh edition of *The Bride of Lammermoor* (1893), *OED 2*, and the *Scottish National Dictionary*.

a-bleeze: ablaze

aboon, abune: above

adjudication: the legal seizure of a debtor's estate on behalf of a creditor

ae: one

agé: to act for another as a law agent

ahint: behind

ail: to interfere with, prevent

airt: to direct

aits: oats

aiver: a horse used for heavy work; hence, pejoratively, an old work-horse

allenarly: solely, exclusively

aneath: beneath

anent: about, concerning

an it like: if it pleases

anker: a liquid measure and the barrel containing it

annual: annual payment from land or property

aroint: avaunt, begone

ass: ashes

a'thegither: altogether

attainder: a loss of civil rights through conviction for high treason

attaint: to deprive of civil rights by conviction for high treason

Auld Reekie: 'Old Smoky', a nickname for Edinburgh

avant-courier: a messenger sent on in advance

awa: away

awe: to owe

aweel: used like 'well' in introducing a remark, often expressing agreement, resignation, or submission

awfu': terrible

aye: always

back sey: a part of the loin, usually the sirloin

backsword: a sword with only one cutting edge

bailie: a Scottish municipal officer, next in rank to the Provost

bairn: child

baith: both

band-strings: strings or cords used as an ornamental fastening for a garment *bannock*: a flat round cake of oatmeal, barley, pease, or flour, baked on a girdle

bartizan: 'bratticing', a battlemented parapet on a castle

batoon: to strike with a batoon or cudgel, to thrash

bawbee: a coin originally worth 6 Scots pennies, a halfpenny

beck: a curtsy, bow

bedesman: usually one who prays for another, here a dependant

bedral: a church officer with duties akin to those of an English beadle, but often combining those of clerk, sexton, and bell-ringer

beetle-browed: having prominent, heavy, or bushy eyebrows

beflum: to befool with flattering or cajoling language

behint: behind

beldam: an old woman

bell-siller: the money paid to the bell-ringer at a funeral

belly-god: one who makes a god of his belly, a glutton

ben: the inner apartment, or further into the inside of a house

bend-leather: thick leather for boot soles

bicker: a wooden drinking cup or bowl with staves

bickering: sparkling, brightly burning

bide: to stay, wait; *bide a wee*—wait a moment

biggonets: linen caps or coifs in the style worn by the Beguine sisterhood

bink: a wooden frame for holding crockery, a shelf or plate-rack

birkie: a lively young fellow; also the simple card game of beggar-my-neighbour

birling: a carousal

bit: used as a diminutive, as in *bit wean*—a little child

bit and the buffet: food and a blow

blackavised: black-visaged, dark-complexioned

black-cock: the male of the black grouse

black jack: a large waxed pitcher for holding ale

blade-bone: the shoulder bone

blate: bashful, diffident

blown: winded, exhausted

bluid: blood

bogle: a goblin

bosky: full of thickets, bushy

bouk, bowk: a body, bulk

boul: a handle; *boul o' a pint stoup*—the handle of a two-quart pot

bourock: a mound

brach: a hunting hound

brae: a hillside

brander: a gridiron; also to cook on the gridiron, to grill or broil

bravery: finery

braw, bra': brave, fine, splendid; *brawly*—bravely, finely

brawl: a French dance resembling a cotillion

brent: straight, steep; *brent brow*—
a smooth, unwrinkled
forehead

brewis: a broth, liquid in which
beef and vegetables have been
boiled

bride in: taken to the bridal
chamber

brideman, bride's man: a young
man who performs various
ceremonial duties at a
wedding

brig: a type of ship

brigg: a bridge

brimmer: a brimming cup or
goblet

broche: a roasting-spit

bumper: a cup or glass of wine,
filled to the brim, especially
when drunk as a toast

busk: to dress up, arrange, adorn

but: an outer apartment, or
towards the outer part of a
house

butter crabs: buttered crabs

by: besides; also yonder, not far
off

by bit: an extra bit or a snack
between meals

cabage: to cut off the head of a
deer close behind the horns

cadgy: sportive, cheerful

caikling: cackling

callant: a youth

cam ower: overcame, fooled

can: a vessel, made of wood or
earthenware as well as of metal

canary: a light sweet wine from
the Canary Islands

cannon-bit: a smooth round bit
for horses

canny: shrewd, cautious,
prudent; also favourable, of
good omen

cantrips: spells, charms,
malicious incantations

canty: cheerful, merry

caparisoned: harnessed, dressed

capot, capote: to win all the tricks
in piquet, hence *capote me!*, an
imprecation

carbonaded: made into a
carbonade, broiled, grilled

car-cake: a small cake, baked
with eggs, usually eaten on
Fastern's Een (Shrove
Tuesday)

carle: a common man, of low
birth and rude manners, a
churl

carline: an old woman

cast: lot, fate, as in *cauld be my
cast*

cast o': kind of

castor: a hat, originally of
beaver's fur or intended to be
taken as such

cattle: beasts

cauk: chalk

causeway: a paved area,
roadway, pavement

cavalière servente: a man who
devotes himself wholly to
attendance on a lady

cavesson: a band of iron, leather,
or wood fixed to the nostrils
of a horse to control it

chamber of dais: the best bedroom

change-house: a small inn,
alehouse

chap: to chop

chappin: a liquid measure, a Scots half-pint

chappit: struck, rung

chaumer: a chamber

chaunce: to happen, chance

cheek of the chimney-nook: the side of the chimney-corner

chicane: chicanery, trickery

chiel, chield: a fellow

clavering: chattering, gossiping

clavers: idle, foolish talk

claw up both your mittens: to finish you off, do for you

clean: completely

cleckit: hatched

cleugh: a narrow gorge or chasm with high rocky sides

clockin-hen: a brood-hen

cloke-bag: a bag in which to carry clothes, a portmanteau

cockernony: a woman's cap with a starched crown

cogging: cheating

coign of vantage: a position, properly a projecting corner, giving a good view

comfits: sweetmeats made of fruit, root, etc., preserved with sugar

commonty: right of pasture on the commons

conform till your rank: in accordance with, conformably to, your rank

contrair: contrary

corbeilles: pieces of carved work, often in the shape of baskets filled with flowers or fruit, used as decoration

coupe-gorge house: a den of cut-throats

cousins-german: first cousins

couteau: a hunting-knife

crack: a chat, particularly boastful chat, brag

craig: a neck, throat; also a rock or cliff, as in *Craig-foot*

crimp: to procure servicemen by decoying or trapping them

crook: a hook for suspending a pot in a fireplace

crowdy: a mixture of oatmeal and cold water, eaten raw, and sometimes used to describe porridge or food in general

cuitle: to coax, wheedle

cullion: a base, despicable fellow

culs de lampe: ornaments used to fill blank spaces on a printed page

culverin: a kind of cannon

cummer, kimmer: a gossip, used as a familiar or contemptuous address to a woman; also a witch

currycomb: a comb or metal instrument used for rubbing down and dressing horses

cutty-pipe: a stumpy tobacco-pipe

cutty spoon: a short-handled spoon, generally of horn

daffing: foolery, frolic

daft: crazy, mad

dais: a raised platform at one end of a hall, used for seats of honour (see also *chamber of dais*)

dandilly: petted, pampered, spoilt by too much admiration

dang: drove, knocked

dead-deal: the board on which a dead body is stretched

dead-dole: the dole distributed to the poor at a funeral

dead-foundered: utterly broken down with lameness

dead-thraw: the death throe, last agonies

decore: to decorate

decorement: a decoration

deil: the devil

démêlé: a quarrel, tussle

demisaker: a light field-piece

dentier: more dainty, more delicate

depone: to testify, declare upon oath

desuetude: a state of disuse

diet-loaf: a kind of sweet sponge cake

dight: to put on apparel or armour

ding: to knock, strike, beat; *dung*—knocked

dink: neat, trim

dirge, dirgie: a funeral feast

dirk: a short Highland dagger

discard: to reject a card from the hand

dispone: to bestow upon

dittay: an indictment

dogger: a two-masted fishing vessel, ketch

doited: confused in mind, enfeebled, generally through age or drink

dollar: a slang term for a 5s. piece

donjon: the great tower or keep of a castle

donnart: stupid, dazed, especially through age

doo: dove; *doocot*—dove-cot

double distanced: doubly 'distanced', beaten by a distance in a horse-race

douceur: a conciliatory present, bribe

doun: down

dour: severe, hard

downcome: downfall

drap-de-berry: fine woollen cloth made in Berri, France

dreigh: dreary, gloomy, doleful

drigie: a variant of *dirgie*, a funeral feast

driving: whiling away the time

drouthy: dry, thirsty

drucken: drunk

drum-head: the skin or membrane stretched over a drum

duds: clothes, used humorously, 'rags'

dun: to importune, pester, especially for debt

dunshin: nudging

dwining: pining, wasting away

eatche: an adze

ebb: shallow

éclaircissement: a revelation, explanation

ee, een: the eye, eyes

eh! sirs: an exclamation of surprise or dismay, an abbreviation of 'God preserve us'

elbo-jigger: a belittling term for a violin-player

eneugh, enow: enough

exies: hysterics

extrajudicial: lying outside court proceedings, informal

eyess: an eyas, a young hawk taken from the nest to be trained

factor: a steward, agent

failzie: in legal phraseology, to default

falchion: a broad curved sword with the blade on the convex side

fash: to vex, trouble, as in *fashna your thumb*, *fashna your beard*—don't trouble yourself

fause: false

fear: to frighten; *feared*—frightened

feckless: feeble, useless, ineffective

feir: entire

fell: fierce, cruel; also a skin or hide, as in *flesh and fell*—flesh and skin, the whole body; hence 'entirely'

feuar: a Scottish lease-holder

flam: a kind of custard

flankard: the side of the lower part of the abdomen

flightering: transient

flisk: a caper, whim

flummery: a sweet dish made with milk, flour, and eggs

flunky: a contemptuous term for a manservant, lackey

flyting: angry scolding

fog: moss

forby: besides

forespeak: to bewitch, curse with the evil tongue

forgather: to come together, fall in together

fortalice: a small fort

fou: full, replete; also, as a dry measure, approx. 1½ bushels of barley or oats

foy: a feast given for a departing friend

freebooter: a plunderer

freit, freet: an omen

fremd: unrelated, not belonging to one's own family; in this case, applied to a servant of another household

frogs: ornamental fastenings of a military coat or cloak

fugitation: a sentence of outlawry

furnishes: an animal's droppings, hence tracks

gaberlunzie: a professional beggar

gae, gang: to go; *gaen, gane*—gone; *gaed*—went

gaisling: gosling

galloway: a small, strong horse, originally bred in Galloway in south-west Scotland

gar: to make, compel

gate: way, manner

gauger: an exciseman

gaunch: a bite, snatch

gawsie: plump, jolly, comely

gear: property, goods

geizen'd: leaky

gentles: gentlefolk

gett: an urchin

gie: to give; *gien*—given

gif: if

gin: suppose, if

gird: a hoop

girn: to grin, grimace

girth: a band of leather or cloth placed round a horse's body to secure the saddle

glaik: a trick, prank, deception

gledging: looking askance or slyly

gleed: a spark, flame

gleeing: squinting

glent: to whisk, flash

goud, gowd: gold

gowk: a cuckoo, fool

graith: furnishings, trappings

gravaminous: serious, important

gree: to agree

greet: to weep

greybeard: a stone jug for holding ale or liquor

grogram: a coarse fabric of silk, mohair, and wool, often stiffened with gum

grund-mail: a duty paid for the right to have a corpse interred in a churchyard

gudeman: the master of the household, husband

gudemother: a mother-in-law

gudesire: a grandfather

gudewife: the mistress of the household

guide: to take care of, treat

gusting their gabs: tickling their palates

habit: a costume

hackney: a horse of middle size and quality, used for everyday riding

hae: to have

hail, haill: whole, entire

hallan: a wall inside a cottage, extending from the front wall backward, to shelter the inner part of the house

hamstrung: having the hamstrings cut, disabled

hanger: a short broadsword

harle: to drag, trail

harry: to plunder

hatted kitt: a preparation of milk with a creamy top, made from buttermilk, milk, sugar, and spices

haud: to hold, maintain; *haud out*—to present a firearm

haver: *to talk foolishly*

havings: behaviour, manners

head-mark: the distinguishing peculiarity of an animal's face and head

heather-cow: a stalk or tuft of heath

hebdomadal: lasting seven days

hech, sirs: an exclamation of sorrow or surprise

heezy: a drubbing, used humorously for anything upsetting

hellicat: giddy, irresponsible, crazy (Scott's remoulding of an earlier word, 'hallockit')

hempie: someone destined for a hempen rope, to be hanged; therefore used jocularly of a mischievous or unruly person

hopeful lad: a promising lad

hough: a thigh, ham

hough'd: disabled by a cut to the sinew or tendons of the thigh

house-leek: the plant *sempervivum tectorum*, a succulent herb commonly found growing on the walls and roofs of houses

housewifeskep: housewifery

hout, hout tout: tut, an
exclamation
hout awa: nonsense, get away
with you
hout na: a strong negative
how: a hollow
humlock: hemlock
hurdies: buttocks
huz: his
hyke: to move with a jerk

ilk: as in *of that ilk*, of the place
of the same name
ilka: each, every
ill-cleckit: ill-hatched
ill-deedy: mischievous
ill-faured: ugly, evil-looking
ingan: an onion
ingle: a fire
inlake: a breach, deficiency,
shortage

jeest: a jest, joke
jessamine: an antiquated form of
'jasmine'
jesses: leather straps tied round a
hawk's legs
jib: to stop short, balk
joe: a sweetheart
Johnny Newcome: a newcomer,
upstart
jow: a toll

kail: cabbage or broth made
from cabbage
kailyard: a cabbage garden
kain: a payment in kind made
by a tenant as part of rent
kebbuck: a cheese
keekit: peeped
keel: ruddle, red chalk

keep her threep: keep her
resolution
ken: to know
kenspeckle: conspicuous
kimmer: see *cummer*
kippage: a rage, turmoil
kirk: a church, especially the
Presbyterian Church of
Scotland
kist: a coffin
kith: acquaintance
kittle: ticklish in the sense of
'difficult', 'tricky'
knowe: a knoll, hillock
kye: cattle

laird: the lord of a manor
lammer: amber
Lammerlaw: one of the
Lammermuir hills
landward: country, rural
lang-headed: sagacious
lang syne: long ago
late-wake: the watch over a dead
body
lauch: a law, custom
law: a hill
lawing: a bill, a tavern reckoning
leal: loyal
let abe: leave alone
limmer: a loose woman
links: sand dunes
lippening word: a thoughtless
word
list: to wish
lith: a joint
loon, loun: a young rascal
loot: allowed
loupen: leaped
lowe: a flame, fire
luckie, lucky: goody, gammer

lug: an ear
lugger: a small ship
lumm: a chimney
lungies: loins
lurdane: a blockhead

mailing: a smallholding, rented farm
main: a hand at dice
maist: most, almost
maître d'armes: a swordsman, fencing master
Major Domo: the head servant of a wealthy foreign household, playfully used of a butler or steward
malignant: a supporter of Charles I, a royalist; also used by Covenanters of their opponents
malison: a curse
manse: a parsonage
martingale: a strap fastened to the bit or reins and also to the girth to prevent a horse from rearing or throwing back its head
maun: must
maut: malt
meal-monger: a dealer in oatmeal
meal-poke: a bag for oatmeal
mear: a mare
melter: the male fish when full of spawn
menage: the members of a household
merk: a coin worth two-thirds of a Scots pound, about 13½d. sterling
messan: a cur
metall'd: spirited

mill: a snuff-box
mind: to remember, pay attention to
minister: the usual name for a Presbyterian clergyman
mirk: dark
misca': to malign, abuse
mischieve: to do a mischief to
misgie: to go wrong, fail
mittens: worsted gloves
Montero cap: a Spanish hunter's cap with flaps to draw over the ears
moping and mowing: grimacing
mort: a death-note
moss: a morass, marsh
muckle: much, great
murgeons: mouths, grimaces
musketoon: a short musket, hand-gun
my sartie, my certie: an expression of surprise or emphasis

Naiad: in classical mythology, a water-nymph
napery: table-linen
nar: never
natheless: nevertheless
natural: an idiot
naughty: worthless
near: niggardly
needfu': necessary
ne'er a bit: not a whit
ne'er-do-well: a scapegrace
neest, neist: next
nevoy: a nephew
no: not
nook, neuk: a corner
nould: would not
nouriceship: the office of nurse
nowt: black cattle

od guide us: God help us, *od* being a minced form of 'God'

offcome: an excuse, subterfuge

oncomes: mysterious diseases

ordinar: ordinary, common

ou: oh

out by, outby: away from home, a little way out

ower: over, too

owercrow: to triumph over

owerlook: to ignore

oxter : the armpit

pands: bed-curtains

park-pale: a park fence

parochine: a parish

pas d'avance: the lead, precedence

pattens: clogs worn to raise shoes above mud

patter: to talk

pearlings: lace trimmings

pease-bannock: a bannock made with cheap pease flour

peas-strae: the withered stalks of the pea plant, used as cheap fodder or bedding for animals

peats: unsophisticated, naïve people

peculiar: a small contribution

pegh: to puff and pant

petit: little

petticoat-tail: part of a woman's dress; also a triangular short-cake biscuit with scalloped edges

pettifogging: acting as a pettifogger, a rascally, shifty lawyer

pickle: a small quantity, grain

pick-maw: a small sea-gull

pig: a stoneware vessel, pitcher

pine: to hurt, punish

pinners: a cap with lappets, formerly worn by women of rank

pinnywinkles: an instrument of torture, consisting of a board with holes into which the fingers were thrust and pressed with screw-pegs

pint, Scottish: formerly equivalent to approx. 3 imperial pints

pique: winning 30 points in a game of piquet

piquet: a card game, played by two persons, in which points are scored on various groups or combinations of cards

pirn: a reel, bobbin

pistole: a gold coin, worth approx. 17*s*. sterling

pit-mirk: as dark as pitch

pize upon it: an imprecatory expression

placebo: a sop

plack: a small copper coin, worth 4*d*. Scots, 1/3*d*. sterling

plenishing: furnishing

pliskie: a prank, trick

ploy: a merrymaking

plumdamas: a Damson plum, prune

pock-pudding: a pudding steamed in a bag; a contemptuous term for the English

poind: to distrain

point: in piquet, the number of cards of the most numerous suit in one's hand after discarding

point d'appui: the point of support

point d'espagne: Spanish lace

poke: a bag, pouch

poor-man-of-mutton: a Scottish colloquial name for the remains of a shoulder of mutton, broiled

pouther, powther: gunpowder

pouthered: salted, cured (meat)

prelatist: a hostile term for a supporter of episcopacy

prent: to print

press money: payment to a soldier of sailor on enlistment

pretermit: to omit

pretty: gallant, fine, good-looking

process: proceedings in an action of law

propine: a gift

pu': pluck

pudding: a type of sausage

pund Scots: one-twelfth of a pound sterling

pyking: picking

quatorze: in piquet, a set of four similar cards held by one player, which count as 14 points

quean: a wench

quegh, quaigh: a small drinking cup of hooped staves, ornamented with silver, chiefly used for wine or brandy

quick: living

quint: in piquet, a sequence of five cards of the same suit, which count as 15 points

rae: a roe deer

reaving: open violent thieving

redd up: to tidy, put in order

rede: to advise

red wud: stark mad

reek: to smoke

reested ham: a smoke-dried ham

remeid: in law, redress for one's grievances, especially through appeal to a higher court

repique: in piquet, winning 30 points on cards alone before beginning play

reponed: reinstated

rifler: a hawk which does not return to the lure

ring-walk: the track of a stag

rokelay: a short cloak

round: to whisper

roup: an auction

rowel-heads: the sharp points of the small wheel at the end of a spur

rudas: a scolding old woman, hag

rummer: a large drinking glass

runlet, rundlet: a barrel, holding approx. 84 litres

sack: dry white wine

sackbut: a musical instrument, a bass trumpet

sad-coloured: dark or sober in colour

sall: shall

samyn: same

sant: a saint

saraband: a slow stately Spanish dance

sark: a shirt

saul: soul

saut: salt, salted

saumon: a salmon

sax, saxteen: six, sixteen

scattergood: good for nothing

scauded: scalded, also disgusted

sclater: a slater

scraugh: a screech

screigh: a shriek

scunner: to shudder with disgust

scurvy-grass: a plant with medicinal properties against scurvy

sea-maw, sea-mew: a sea-gull

sell: self

sere: dry, withered

sets: becomes, suits

sewer: an attendant at a meal, who superintends the arrangement of the table, serving, etc.

shaloon: a closely woven woollen material

shaughled: worn down

shouthers: shoulders

shovel-board: a game in which players try to drive coins or counters to certain marks or lines on the table

sib: related to by blood

sic, siccan: such

siller: silver, money

sin': since

singles: the talons of a hawk

skart: a scratch

skirl: to cry out, squeal, wail

sliddery: slippery

sloken: quench, quenched

sneck-drawer: a latch-lifter, hence a crafty, deceitful person

sneck-drawing: crafty

snishing, sneeshing: snuff

snood: a band or fillet for holding back the hair, worn by unmarried women

soi-disant: self-styled

solan-geese: gannets

soopit: swept

sopite: in Scots law, to settle, pacify

sort: to arrange, supply, organize; also to give a drubbing

sough: a whisper, hence rumour

soughed: whispered

soup: a sup

souple: a cudgel

souse: 'thump', the sound of a heavy fall

sowens: a kind of gruel made from the husks of oats

spae: to foretell

speer: to ask, enquire, invite

spikenard: an aromatic substance obtained from an Eastern plant

spule-bane: a shoulder bone

spunk: a spark of fire

stanchelled: provided with stanchions, upright bars

stead: instead

steading: a farm, farmyard

steer: to disturb, stir, molest

stickit: imperfect, bungled

stoup: a wooden drinking vessel

strae: straw

straught, straughted, streekit: stretched, laid out

streak: to stretch, lay out a corpse

suld: should; *suldna*—should not

sumph: a blockhead, dunce

sumpter: a pack or baggage horse; *sumpter mules*—baggage mules; *sumpter cloth*—covering for a pack animal

surbated: foot-sore

swanking: active, agile

swarve: to swerve

swauk: a thwack, blow

swire: a pass or hollow between two hills

sybo: an onion that does not form a bulb at the root

synd: to rinse

syne: since, ago

tack: a lease

tae: the one

taen, tane: taken

taid: a toad

tait: a bunch, handful

tap of tow: the quantity of unworked flax which is made up, in a conical figure, to be put on the distaff

tapis: a table-cloth, as in *to put on the* tapis—to bring under discussion or consideration

tass: a cup

taupie: a slow awkward girl

Tauridor: an obsolete form of 'toreador', a bull-fighter

tause: a strap

tenony: stringy, sinewy

tent: to attend to

testor: a canopy over a bed; more generally, a hanging or covering

teugh: tough

thae: those

thegither: together

the night: tonight

thickset: a stout twilled cotton cloth, a kind of fustian

thowless: lacking energy or spirit, ineffectual, lethargic

thraw: to twist, distort

through-stane: a flat gravestone

thunner: thunder

tiend: a tithe

till: to, for

timmer: timber

Timmer Burse: the exchange of the timber-merchants

tippence: twopence

tither: the other

tocher-good, tocher: a dowry, marriage-portion

tod: a fox

tokay: a fiery Hungarian wine

tolbooth: a prison

tongue of the trump: the vibrating fork in the Jew's harp; hence, figuratively, the essential or principal person

toom: empty

tother: the other

tout: a fit of ill temper, a huff

tow: the unworked stem or fibre of flax

tredrille: a card game played by three persons

trow: to believe, think, reckon

truck: trade

tup: a ram

twa: two

twal: twelve

twa-lofted: two-storied

twalpennies: a Scottish shilling, 1 d. sterling

twilt: a quilted bed-cover

tyne: an antler

Uds daggers and scabbard: *Ud* is a minced form of 'God'

umquhile: deceased, late

unco: strange, uncommon

until: to

up by: up the way, a little way farther on

uphaud: maintain

vaik: to fall vacant

vaticination: the utterance of predictions or prophecies

videlicet: that is to say

visie: inspection, a look

visnomy: physiognomy

vivers: victuals, food

wad: would

wadset: in Scots law, an agreement by which land is held as security for a loan

wae: woe, woeful

wake: keeping vigil over a corpse

walking sword: a sword worn by a non-military gentleman

walth: plenty

wame: a belly

wanton: to overjoy

wap: a smart stroke

ware: to bestow

warlock: one in league with the Devil, a sorcerer, wizard

warrand: to warrant

wastland: west country

water-purpie: brook lime or horsewell grass

waur: worse

waured: worsted, vanquished

wean: an infant, child

weary on him: used imprecatively, to express exasperation, as in 'plague on him'

wee: small; *bide a wee*—wait a moment

weel-favoured: good-looking

weid: a feverish cold

wether: a ram, especially a castrated ram

wha: who

whample: a blow, stroke

whar: where

wheen: a few, a little

whigamore: a Presbyterian or Covenanter, in reference to the Whiggamore Raid of 1648

whigmaleeries: trinkets

whiles: now and again

whilk: which

whim-whams: fancy pastry

whin-bush: a furze bush, gorse

whinger: a kind of sword used as a knife at meals and in fights

whin-stane: a kind of hard dark rock or stone

whisht: hush

white-hass: a meat pudding, stuffed with oatmeal and suet

whomling: overturning, set upside down

win: to make way, get; *won into*—made way into

withie: a halter

wonne: to dwell

wood-fee: a grant of money to a forester

woodie: the gallows

wot: to know

wraith: an apparition of a person still living

wrang: wrong

wud: mad

wull: will

wull a wins!: a fanciful form of 'walawa'; alas

wuss: to wish

wyte: blame, responsibility

ye's: you will

yestreen: yesterday evening

yill: ale

THE WORLD'S CLASSICS

A Select List

IZAAK WALTON and CHARLES COTTON:
The Compleat Angler
Edited by John Buxton
Introduction by John Buchan

MRS HUMPHREY WARD: Robert Elsmere
Edited by Rosemary Ashton

OSCAR WILDE: Complete Shorter Fiction
Edited by Isobel Murray

The Picture of Dorian Gray
Edited by Isobel Murray

MARY WOLLSTONECRAFT:
Mary *and* The Wrongs of Woman
Edited by Gary Kelly

ÉMILE ZOLA:
The Attack on the Mill and other stories
Translated by Douglas Parmeé

A complete list of Oxford Paperbacks, including The World's Classics, OPUS, Past Masters, Oxford Authors, Oxford Shakespeare, and Oxford Paperback Reference, is available in the UK from the Arts and Reference Publicity Department (RS), Oxford University Press, Walton Street, Oxford OX2 6DP.

In the USA, complete lists are available from the Paperbacks Marketing Manager, Oxford University Press, 200 Madison Avenue, New York, NY 10016.

Oxford Paperbacks are available from all good bookshops. In case of difficulty, customers in the UK can order direct from Oxford University Press Bookshop, Freepost, 116 High Street, Oxford, OX1 4BR, enclosing full payment. Please add 10 per cent of published price for postage and packing.